of love & life

ISBN 0-276-44110-9

www.readersdigest.co.uk

The Reader's Digest Association Limited, 11 Westferry Circus, Canary Wharf, London E14 4HE

For information as to ownership of copyright in the material of this book, and acknowledgments, see last page.

# of love & life

Three novels selected and condensed
by Reader's Digest

The Reader's Digest Association Limited, London

CONTENTS

MAKING YOUR
MIND
UP
by
Jill
Mansell
annie B.

Walking barefoot through a Cotswold village, soaking wet, wearing only a tiny turquoise bikini and a man's suit jacket, with a most handsome stranger at her side, would be enough to get tongues wagging about the average mother of two. But the villagers of Hestacombe have grown used to the antics of Lottie Carlyle . . .

Chapter 1

'YOU MAAAAAKE ME FEEEEEL,' Lottie Carlyle warbled soulfully at the top of her voice, 'like a natural womaaaaan.'

Oh yes, the great thing about singing when your ears were underwater was that it made you sound *so* much better than in real life. Not super-fantastic like Joss Stone or Barbra Streisand, obviously, but not so alarmingly bad that small children burst into tears whenever you opened your mouth to sing. Which had been known to happen on dry land.

Which was why she was enjoying herself so much now, in Hestacombe Lake. It was a blisteringly hot day in August, her afternoon off, and she was floating on her back in the water gazing up at a cloudless, cobalt-blue sky.

Well, nearly cloudless. When it was four o'clock in the afternoon and you were the mother of two children, there was always that one small bothersome cloud hovering on the horizon:

What to cook for dinner.

Something, preferably, that didn't take ages to make but sounded like a proper meal. Something that contained the odd vitamin. Something, furthermore, that both Nat and Ruby would deign to eat. Pasta, perhaps?

But Nat, who was seven, would only consent to eat pasta with olives and mint sauce, and Lottie knew there were no olives left in the fridge.

Vegetable stir-fry? Now she really was wandering into the realms of fantasy. In her nine years Ruby had never knowingly eaten a vegetable.

Lottie sighed and closed her eyes. As the cool water of the lake lapped around her temples she lazily twitched away an insect. Cooking for such an unappreciative clientele really was the pits. Maybe if she stayed out here long enough someone would eventually call Social Services and

Ruby and Nat would be whisked away to some echoing Dickensian children's home, forced to eat liver and turnip soup. And after a couple of weeks of that, *then* they might appreciate what a thankless task she had, endlessly having to think what to give her finicky children for dinner.

Freddie Masterson stood at the drawing-room window of Hestacombe House and experienced that familiar lift to his spirits as he surveyed the most glorious view in the whole of the Cotswolds. Across the valley the hills rose up dotted with trees, houses, sheep and cows. Below, the reed-fringed lake glittered in the afternoon sunlight. And closer to hand, his own garden was in full bloom, the freshly mown emerald lawn sloping down towards the lake, the fuchsia bushes bobbing as bumble bees swooped greedily from one fragile flower to the next. A pair of woodpeckers, energetically digging in the grass for worms, flew off in disgust as a human made its way down the narrow path towards them.

This could be it, then. Watching as Tyler Klein paused to admire the view himself, Freddie knew the American was equally impressed. Their meeting had gone well; Tyler undoubtedly had a fine brain and had the money to buy the business. And, so far, he appeared to like what he saw.

Well, how could he not?

Tyler Klein was now heading for the side gate that led out into the lane. With his dark blue suit jacket slung casually over one shoulder and his lilac shirt loosened at the neck, he moved more like an athlete than a businessman. Clark Gable hair, thought Freddie, that was what Tyler Klein had, with most of it slicked back but that one dark lock falling uncontrollably into his eyes. His beloved wife Mary had always had a bit of a thing for Clark Gable. Ruefully, Freddie ran a hand over his own sparsely covered head. And to think the poor darling had ended up with him instead.

Glimpsing a flash of brilliant turquoise out of the corner of his eye, he thought for a split second that a kingfisher was darting across the surface of the lake. Then he smiled, because once his vision had had time to adjust he saw that it was Lottie, wearing a turquoise bikini, rolling over in the water. If he were to tell her that he'd mistaken her for a kingfisher, Lottie would say teasingly, 'Freddie, time to get your eyes tested.'

He hadn't told her that he already had.

And the rest.

The lane that ran alongside the garden of Hestacombe House was narrow and banked high on both sides with poppies, cow parsley and blackberry bushes. Turning left, Tyler Klein worked out, would lead you back up to the village of Hestacombe. Turning right took you down to the lake. As he took the right turn, Tyler heard the sound of running feet and giggling.

Rounding the first bend in the lane, he saw two small children, twenty or thirty yards away, clambering over a stile. Dressed in shorts, T-shirts and baseball caps, the one in front was carrying a rolled-up yellow-and-white striped towel, whilst his companion clutched a haphazard bundle of clothes. Glancing up the lane and spotting Tyler, they leapt down from the stile into the cornfield beyond. By the time he reached the stile they'd scurried out of sight, no doubt having taken some short cut back to the village following their dip in the lake.

The lane opened out into a sandy clearing that sloped down to meet a small artificial beach. Freddie Masterson had had this constructed several years ago, chiefly for the benefit of visitors to his lakeside holiday cottages, but also—as Tyler had just witnessed—to be enjoyed by the inhabitants of Hestacombe. Shielding his eyes from the glare of the afternoon sun as it bounced off the lake, Tyler saw a girl in a bright turquoise bikini floating lazily on her back in the water. As Tyler watched, the girl turned onto her front and began to swim slowly back to shore.

It could almost be that scene from *Dr No*, where Sean Connery observes Ursula Andress emerging goddess-like from a tropical sea. Except he wasn't hiding in the bushes and this girl didn't have a large knife strapped to her thigh. She wasn't blonde either. Her long dark hair was a riot of snaky curls plastered to her shoulders, her body curvy and deeply tanned. Impressed, because an encounter like this was the last thing he'd been expecting, Tyler nodded in a friendly fashion as she paused to wring water from her dripping hair and said, 'Good swim?'

The girl surveyed him steadily, then looked around the tiny beach. Finally she said, 'Where's my stuff?'

Stuff. Taken aback, Tyler gazed around too, even though he had no idea what he was meant to be looking for. For one bizarre moment he wondered if she had arranged to meet a drug dealer here. That was what people said, wasn't it, when they met up with their dealer?

'What stuff?'

'The usual stuff you leave out of the water when you go for a swim. Clothes. Towel. Diamond earrings.'

Tyler said, 'Where did you put them?'

'Right there where you're standing.' She narrowed her eyes at him. 'Is this a joke?'

'I guess it is. But I'm not the one playing it.' Half turning, Tyler indicated the narrow lane behind him. 'I passed a couple of kids back there, carrying off stuff.'

She had her hands on her hips now, and was surveying him with growing disbelief. 'And it didn't occur to you to stop them?'

'I thought it was their stuff.' This was ridiculous, he'd never said the word *stuff* so many times before in his life.

'You thought the size twelve pink halter-necked dress and size five silver sandals belonged to them.' The sarcasm—that particularly British form of sarcasm—was evident in her voice.

'I didn't actually get a close look. I was thirty yards away.'

'But you thought they'd been swimming.' Gazing at him intently, the girl said, 'Tell me something. Were they . . . *wet*?'

Shit. The kids hadn't been wet. Unwilling to concede defeat, Tyler said, 'Did you really leave diamond earrings with your clothes?'

'Do I look completely stupid? No, of course I didn't. Diamonds don't dissolve in water.' Impatiently she shook back her hair to show him the studs glittering in her earlobes. 'Right, what did these kids look like?'

'Like kids. I don't know.' Tyler shrugged. 'They were wearing T-shirts, I guess. And, um, shorts . . .'

The girl raised her eyebrows. 'That's incredible. Your powers of observation are dazzling. OK, was it a boy and a girl?'

'Maybe.' He'd assumed they were boys, but one had had longer hair than the other. 'Like I said, I only saw them from a distance.'

'Dark hair? Thin and wiry?' the girl persisted. 'Did they look like a couple of Gypsies?'

'Yes.' Tyler was instantly on the alert; when Freddie Masterson had been singing the praises of Hestacombe he hadn't mentioned any Gypsies. 'Are they a problem around here?'

'Damn right they're a problem around here. They're my children.' Intercepting the look of horror on his face, the girl broke into a smile. 'Relax, they're not really Gypsies. You haven't just mortally offended me.'

'Well,' said Tyler, 'I'm glad about that.'

'I didn't see a thing. They must have crawled through the bushes and sneaked off with my stuff when I wasn't looking. That's what happens when you have kids who are hellbent on joining the SAS. But this isn't funny.' No longer amused, the girl said impatiently, 'They don't *think*, do they? Because now I'm stuck here with *no* clothes—'

'You're welcome to borrow my jacket.'

'And *no* shoes.'

'I'm not lending you my shoes,' Tyler drawled.

'Wuss.' Thinking hard, the girl said, 'OK, look, can you do me a favour? Go back up to the village, past the pub, and my house is three doors down on the right. Piper's Cottage. The doorbell's broken so you'll have to bang on the door. Tell Ruby and Nat to give you my clothes.

Then you can bring them back down to me. How does that sound?'

Tyler frowned. 'What if the kids aren't there?'

'Right, now I know this isn't ideal, but you have an honest face so I'm going to have to trust you. If they aren't there, you'll just have to take the front-door key out from under the tub of geraniums by the porch and let yourself into the house. My bedroom's on the left at the top of the stairs. Just grab something from the wardrobe.'

'I can't do this.' Tyler shook his head. 'You don't even know me.'

'Hi.' Seizing his hand, she enthusiastically shook it. 'I'm Lottie Carlyle. There, now I've introduced myself. And you are?'

'Tyler. Tyler Klein. By the way, leaving your key under a tub by the porch is an open invitation to burglars. And I'm still not doing it.'

'Well, you're a big help. I'm going to look a right wally walking through the village like this.'

'I told you, you can borrow my jacket.' Seeing as she was dripping wet and his suit jacket was silk-lined and seriously expensive, he felt this was a generous offer. Lottie Carlyle, however, seemed unimpressed.

'You could lend me your shirt,' she wheedled. 'That'd be better.'

Tyler was here on business. He had no intention of removing his shirt. Firmly he said, 'I don't think so. It's the jacket or nothing.'

Realising when she was beaten, Lottie Carlyle took the jacket from him and put it on. 'You drive a hard bargain. There, do I look completely ridiculous?'

'Yes.'

'You're too kind.' She looked sadly down at her bare feet. 'Any chance of a piggy back?'

Tyler looked amused. 'Don't push your luck.'

'Are you saying I'm fat?'

'I'm thinking of my street cred.'

Interested, Lottie said, 'What are you doing here, anyway? In your smart city suit and shiny shoes?'

Tyler glanced back at the lake. Casually he said, 'Just visiting.'

Gingerly picking her way along the stony, uneven lane, Lottie winced and said meaningfully, 'Ouch, my feet.'

Lottie Carlyle attracted a fair amount of attention as they made their way through Hestacombe. Something told Tyler that irrespective of what she was wearing, she always would. Passing motorists tooted their horns, villagers out in their gardens waved and made teasing comments, and, in turn, Lottie in turn told them exactly what she was going to do with Ruby and Nat when she got her hands on them.

As they approached Piper's Cottage they spotted the children playing with a watering can in the front garden, taking it in turns to spin round holding the watering can at arm's length and spray each other with water.

'Viewers of a nervous disposition may wish to look away now,' said Lottie. 'This is where I go into scary mother mode.' Raising her voice, she called out, 'Hey, you two. Put that watering can *down*.'

The children looked at their mother, promptly abandoned the watering can and, giggling wildly, shot up into the branches of the apple tree overhanging the front wall.

'I know what you did.' Reaching the garden, Lottie peered up into the tree. 'And trust me, you're in *big* trouble.'

From the depths of the leafy branches, an innocent voice said, 'We were just watering the flowers. Otherwise they'd die.'

'I'm talking about my clothes. That wasn't funny, Nat. Running off with someone's clothes is no joke.'

'We didn't do it,' Nat said immediately.

Ruby chimed in, 'It wasn't us.'

Tyler looked over at Lottie Carlyle. Maybe he'd made a mistake. Catching his concerned expression, she rolled her eyes. 'Please don't believe them. The more guilty they are, the more they deny it.'

'Mum, we really didn't take your clothes,' said Ruby.

'No? Well, this man here says you did. Because he saw you,' Lottie explained, 'and unlike you two, he doesn't tell lies. So you can climb down from there and go and get my clothes this minute.'

'We don't know where they are!' Ruby let out a wail of outrage.

Without a word, Lottie disappeared inside the cottage. Through the open windows they heard the banging and crashing of cupboards and wardrobes being opened and shut. Finally, triumphantly, she re-emerged carrying a scrunched-up pink dress, a pair of flat silver sandals and a yellow-and-white striped towel.

'It wasn't us,' Nat blurted out.

'Really. Funny how they happened to be in the back garden then, isn't it?' As she spoke, Lottie was shrugging off the miles-too-big suit jacket, handing it back to Tyler and wriggling into her crumpled sundress. 'Now, listen, taking my clothes was bad enough. Telling lies and denying it is even worse.'

'But it was somebody else,' squealed Ruby.

'This man says it was you. And out of the three of you, funnily enough, I believe him. So get down out of that tree, get into the house and start tidying your bedrooms.'

First Ruby, then Nat dropped down from the branches. Dark eyes glared at Tyler. As Ruby stalked past him she muttered, '*You're* the big liar.'

'Ruby. Stop that.'

Nat, with bits of twig caught in his hair, looked up at Tyler and said with a scowl, 'I'm going to tell my dad on you.'

'Ooh, he's so scared.' Lottie deftly swept him past Tyler. 'Inside. Now.'

Nat and Ruby disappeared into the house. By this time feeling terrible, Tyler said, 'Listen, maybe I did make a mistake.'

'They're children, it's their job to get up to mischief.' Knowingly, Lottie said, 'I'm guessing you don't have any of your own.'

Tyler shook his head. 'No.'

'Look, they hate you for grassing them up.' Lottie's eyes sparkled. 'They're doing their best to make you feel bad. But you never have to see them again, do you, so what does it matter? Thanks for the jacket. I hope it isn't too damp.' She paused, raking her fingers through her wet hair, then broke into a dazzling smile. 'It was kind of nice to meet you.'

'Kind of nice to meet you, too.'

Changed into a lime-green vest top and white jeans, Lottie made her way out onto the broad terrace behind Hestacombe House, where Freddie was sitting at the table levering open a bottle of wine.

'There you are. Have a seat,' said Freddie, thrusting a glass into her hand, 'and get some of this down you. You're going to need it.'

'Why?' Lottie had been wondering why he'd asked her to come over to the house this evening. Not normally reticent, Freddie had been out and about a lot recently without letting on what he was up to. Tonight, in his white polo shirt and pressed khaki trousers, he was looking tanned and fit. Don't say he'd found himself a lady friend at last.

'Cheers.' Freddie clinked his glass against hers. There was definitely a secret in there, waiting to burst out.

'Cheers. Don't tell me.' Delighted for her employer, Lottie held up her free hand to stop him in his tracks. 'I think I've already guessed!'

'Actually, you probably haven't.' Freddie was leaning back, smiling at her as he lit a cigar. 'But fire away. Tell me what you think.'

'I *thiiiiiink*,' Lottie drew out the word, 'that love could be in the air.'

'Lottie, I'm too old for you.'

She pulled a face at him. 'I meant with someone your own age. Am I wrong then?'

'Just a bit.' Freddie was puffing away on his cigar.

'You should, you know. Find someone lovely.' Since Mary's death, Freddie hadn't so much as looked at another woman, yet if the right one were to come along Lottie knew he could be happy again.

'Well, that's not going to happen. Are you drinking that or just letting it evaporate?'

Lottie obediently took a couple of giant gulps.

'Like it?' Freddie surveyed her with amusement.

'It's red, it's warm, it's not corked. Of course I like it.'

'Good, seeing as it's a Chateau Margaux 1988.'

Lottie, who was to fine wines what Johnny Vegas was to tightrope walking, nodded knowledgeably and said, 'Ah, yes, thought so.'

His eyes sparkling, Freddie said, 'Two fifty a bottle.'

'Excellent. Is that one of those half-price offers in the supermarket?'

'Two hundred and fifty pounds a bottle, you philistine.'

Spluttering and almost spilling the rest of the wine on her jeans, Lottie clunked the glass onto the table. 'What are you doing, giving me stuff like that to drink? You *know* I'm a philistine, so it's just a complete *waste*.'

'You said you liked it,' Freddie pointed out.

'But I didn't *appreciate* it, did I? I just guzzled it down like Tizer, because you told me to! Well, you can finish my glass.' Lottie pushed it across the table towards him. 'Because I'm not touching another drop.'

'Sweetheart, I bought this wine ten years ago,' said Freddie. 'It's been in the cellar all this time, waiting for a special occasion.'

Lottie rolled her eyes in despair. 'It's certainly a special occasion now. The day your assistant spattered Chateau Margaux-whatever-it-is all over your terrace. You'd have been better leaving it in the cellar for another ten years.'

'Yes, well. Maybe I don't want to. Anyway, you haven't asked me yet why this is a special occasion.'

'Go on, then, tell me.'

Freddie sat back. 'I'm selling the business.'

Startled, Lottie said, 'But why?'

'I'm sixty-four. People retire at my age, don't they? It's time to hand over and do things I want to do. Plus, the right buyer happened to come along. Don't worry, your job's safe.' His eyes twinkling, Freddie said, 'In fact, I think the two of you might get on extremely well.'

Since this was Hestacombe and not some bustling city metropolis, it didn't take a genius to work it out.

'The American guy,' said Lottie, exhaling slowly. 'The one in the suit.'

'The very same.' Nodding, Freddie said slyly, 'Don't try to pretend you can't remember his name.'

'Tyler Klein.' Freddie was right; when strangers were so good-looking, their names simply didn't slip your mind. 'We met down at the lake.'

'He did happen to mention it.' Entertained, Freddie took a puff of his cigar. 'Interesting encounter, by the sound of things.'

'You could say that. Is he buying everything? Are you moving away? Oh, Freddie, I can't imagine this place without you.'

Lottie meant it. Freddie and Mary Masterson had moved to Hestacombe House, all of twenty-two years ago. Freddie was part of the village and they would all miss him if he was no longer around.

Plus, he was a great boss.

'I'm not selling this house. Just the business.'

Relieved, Lottie said, 'Oh well, that's not so bad then. So you'll still be here. It won't really be that different after all.'

Hestacombe Holiday Cottages had been built up by Freddie and Mary into a successful concern over the years; eight original properties, painstakingly renovated, were either dotted around the lakeside or, for greater seclusion, tucked away in the woods. Guests, many of them devoted regulars, rented the ravishingly pretty homes for anything between a couple of nights and a month at a time, safe in the knowledge that their every whim would be catered for while they enjoyed their break away from it all in the heart of the Cotswolds.

'Here, drink your drink.' Freddie pushed the glass back across the table towards her. 'Tyler Klein's a good man. Everything'll be fine.' With a twinkle in his eye he added, 'You'll be in safe hands.'

Now there was a mental image to conjure with.

This time, taking a girlie sip, Lottie did her utmost to appreciate the expensiveness of the Chateau Margaux. It was nice, of course it was, but she'd still never have known. 'So where will he be living?'

'Fox Cottage. We only have to rejig a few bookings. As long as the guests are moved into something better they won't mind.'

Fox Cottage, their most recent acquisition, had spent the last three months being extensively redesigned. It was one of their smaller properties, the first floor now knocked through to make one huge bedroom with floor-to-ceiling windows affording a stupendous view over the lake.

'Not very big.' Innocently, Lottie said, 'Won't his wife find it cramped?'

Freddie grinned. 'I think what you're trying to ask is, is he married?'

So much for being subtle. Kicking off her sandals and tucking her feet under her on the padded chair, she said, 'And?'

'He's single.'

Excellent, Lottie thought happily. Although the experience of meeting Nat and Ruby had probably put him off her for life.

But something else was still puzzling her. 'Where did you find him, then? You didn't even tell me you were thinking of selling the business.'

'Fate.' Freddie shrugged. 'Remember Marcia and Walter?'

Of course. Marcia and Walter Klein, from New York. For the past five years the Kleins had been coming to Hestacombe every year without fail.

'They're his parents.' Lottie realised that the son Marcia had been boasting about all these years was in fact Tyler. 'But he's some kind of hotshot Wall Street banker type, isn't he? Why ever would he want to give that up and move over here?'

'Tyler wants a change. I'm sure he'll tell you his reasons for doing it. Anyway, Marcia rang a couple of weeks ago to arrange their booking for next Easter and we got chatting about retirement,' said Freddie. 'I happened to mention that I was thinking of selling up. Two days later she rang back and said she'd mentioned it to her son, who was interested. Tyler rang me and I told him what I was asking for the business and put him in touch with my accountant so he could go through the figures. Last night he flew into Heathrow and came to see the place for himself. And two hours ago he made me a fair offer.'

'Which you accepted,' said Lottie.

'Which I accepted.'

'Are you sure this is the right thing to do?'

'Absolutely sure.' Freddie nodded.

Oh well, then. He was entitled to a bit of fun. 'In that case, congratulations. Here's to a long and happy retirement.' Raising her glass and clinking it against his, Lottie said encouragingly, 'Think of all the things you'll be able to do.' Teasingly, because Freddie loathed the game with a passion, she added, 'Who knows, you might even take up golf.'

This time Freddie's smile didn't quite reach his eyes. 'There's something else.'

'Oh God. Not Morris dancing.'

'Actually, it's worse than Morris dancing.' His fingers tightening round the stem of his glass, Freddie said simply, 'I have a brain tumour.'

Lottie looked at him, unable to speak. Then she said, 'Oh, Freddie.'

'I know, bit of a conversation-stopper. Sorry about that.' Evidently relieved to have it out in the open, Freddie added, 'Although I must say, I never thought I'd see you at a loss for words.'

Lottie gathered her wits. 'Well, it's a *shock*. But the doctors can do so much now, it'll be fine, they just whip them out these days, don't they? You wait, you'll be as good as new in no time.'

It was what she wanted to believe, but even as the words were tumbling out, Lottie knew the situation was far worse than that. This wasn't like cradling a child with a grazed knee, sticking a Disney plaster on and reassuring them that it would stop hurting in a minute.

This wasn't something she could kiss better.

'Right, I'm telling you this but I'd appreciate it if you don't pass it on to anyone else,' said Freddie. 'The tumour is inoperable so the surgeons can't whip it out. Chemo and radiotherapy won't cure me, but they might buy me a little more time. Well, funnily enough I wasn't tempted by that so I said thanks but no thanks.'

'But—'

'I'd also appreciate it if you didn't interrupt,' Freddie said calmly. 'Now that I've started I'd quite like to finish. So, anyway, I decided pretty much straight away that if I don't have long to live, I'd rather live it on my own terms. We both know what Mary went through.' He looked at Lottie. 'Two years of surgery, endless nightmare treatments. All that pain and what good did it do? At the end of it all, she died anyway. So I'm going to give that a miss. According to my consultant, I have six good months, maybe a year. Well, that's fine. I'll make the most of it.'

It was all too much to take in. Lottie, her hands trembling, reached for her glass and knocked it onto its side. Five minutes ago she would have thrown herself across the table and licked up the spilt wine rather than waste it. Now she simply poured herself some more.

'Am I allowed to ask questions yet?'

Freddie nodded graciously. 'Fire away.'

'How long have you known?'

'A fortnight.' His smile was crooked. 'Of course it was a shock at first. But it's surprising how fast you get used to it.'

'I didn't even know you were ill.'

'That's just it, I don't *feel* ill.' Freddie spread his hands. 'Headaches, that was all it was. I thought I probably needed new reading glasses, so I saw my optician . . . and when she looked into my eyes with that light instrument of hers, she was able to see that I had a problem. Next thing I knew, I was being referred to a neurologist, having scans and all manner of tests. Then, boom, that was it. Diagnosis. Lottie, if you're crying I'll throw my drink over you. Stop it at once.'

Hastily Lottie blinked the tears back into her eyes, sniffed loudly and ordered herself to get a grip.

'Right. Done.' She sniffed again, took a gulp of wine and said defensively, 'Sorry, but it's just not fair. You don't deserve this.'

'I know, I'm marvellous.' Stubbing out his cigar, Freddie said, 'Practically a saint.'

'Especially not after what happened to Mary.' Lottie's throat tightened; she couldn't bear it.

'Sweetheart, don't get angry on my behalf. Mary isn't here any more.' Reaching across the table, Freddie took her hand between both of his.

'Don't you see? That makes it *easier*. Finding out about this thing in my head isn't the most terrible thing that's ever happened to me. Not even close. Losing Mary and having to carry on without her beats this tumour of mine hands down.'

Now Lottie really was in danger of bursting into tears.

'I've made it to sixty-four and that's not so bad,' said Freddie. 'When I was sixteen I was knocked off my pushbike by a lorry and cracked a few ribs. But I could have been killed. And there's the time Mary and I were on holiday in Geneva. We got so plastered on our last night that we missed our flight home. And what happened? The plane crashed.'

Lottie had heard this story before. 'It didn't crash,' she corrected him. 'One of the wheels came off on the runway. Nobody was killed.'

'But we could have been. People were injured.'

'Bumps and bruises don't count.' Lottie wasn't to be swayed.

Freddie eyed her with amusement. 'Are we bickering?'

'No.' Ashamed of herself, Lottie instantly backed down. Bickering with a dying man; how could she stoop so low?

Evidently reading her mind, Freddie said, 'Yes, we are, and don't you start giving in. If you won't bicker with me any more, I'll find someone else who will. I don't want the kid-glove treatment, OK?'

'You don't want any treatment at all,' Lottie retaliated heatedly. 'The thing is, maybe radiotherapy and chemo *would* work.'

'You're allowed to bicker,' Freddie said firmly, 'but you definitely aren't allowed to nag. Or I shall have to sack you.'

'You're selling the business.'

'Ah, but I could sack you now. Sweetheart, I'm a grown-up. I've made my decision. If I've got six good months left on this earth, then I want to make the most of them. That's where you come in. There's something I'm going to need a hand with, Lottie. And I'd like you to help me out.'

For an appalling moment Lottie thought he meant help with doing away with himself when the time came. Jolted, she said, 'In what way?'

'Good grief, not that kind of help.' Yet again reading her mind—or more likely the look of absolute horror on her face—Freddie gave a shout of laughter. 'I've seen you clay-pigeon shooting. The only thing you managed to hit was a tree. If I need putting down when the time comes, I'll ask a damn sight better shot than you.'

'Don't joke about it.' Lottie glared at him. 'It's not funny.'

'Sorry,' Freddie said, his tone consoling. 'We all have to go some time, don't we? I could have a heart attack and drop dead tomorrow. Compared with that, being given six months' notice is a luxury. And that's why I'm not going to waste it.'

Lottie braced herself. 'So what will you do?'

'Well, I've given this a lot of thought. And it's actually not as easy as you'd imagine.' Freddie pulled a face. 'I mean, what would you do? If money was no object?'

This was surreal. But if Freddie could do it, so could she. Lottie said, 'OK, it's a cliché, but I suppose I'd take the kids to Disneyland.'

'Exactly.' Looking pleased, Freddie nodded vigorously. 'Because you know it's what *they'd* love more than anything.'

Defensively, Lottie said, 'I'd love it too!'

'Of course you would. But if the kids couldn't make it, would you go along by yourself?'

The penny dropped. Feeling terrible all over again, Lottie longed to hug him. Instead she said, 'No, I suppose not.'

'You see? My point exactly.' Freddie sat forward, his elbows on the table. 'Years ago, before she became ill, Mary and I used to dream of retiring one day and travelling the world. She wanted to walk the Great Wall of China, visit the Victoria Falls and explore the lost city of Peru. Top of my list was a fortnight at the Gritti Palace in Venice, followed by trips to New Zealand and Polynesia.' He paused, gazing at the almost empty bottle of Chateau Margaux. 'But that's the thing, isn't it? The plan was that we'd be old *together*. Now I can afford to go anywhere I want in the world, but I only wanted to see those places with Mary.'

Lottie pictured him in front of some spectacular view with no one he cared about to share it with. It was how she would feel, sitting all alone in a carriage on one of the roller-coaster rides in Disneyland. Without Nat and Ruby there at her side, how could she possibly enjoy it?

'Travelling's out, then.'

Freddie nodded. 'And I've decided to give the dangerous sports a miss. Doing a parachute jump, abseiling, white-water rafting.' His mouth twitched. 'Not really my scene.'

How *could* he be this cheerful? Mystified Lottie said, 'So what *are* you going to do?'

'Well, that's why I'm asking you to help me.' Freddie looked pleased with himself. 'You see, I have a plan.'

Nat and Ruby had been despatched to their father's house for the evening. When Lottie arrived at nine o'clock to pick them up, she was greeted at the door by Nat, who threw himself into her arms and said, 'We've been having *fun*.'

'Hooray.' After the last couple of traumatic hours digesting Freddie's news, Lottie gave him an extra-fierce hug.

'Ow, Mum, let go. Dad's told us all about VD.'

'Has he?' She blinked. Had Mario gone completely mad?

Nat dragged Lottie through to the kitchen, exclaiming, 'VD's my favourite thing.'

'Not veedee, you plank.' Ruby rolled her eyes with nine-year-old superiority. 'It's voodoo.'

'I'm not a plank. You're the plank.'

'Why's Daddy been telling you about voodoo?' Lottie interjected.

'We told him about the horrible man. Didn't we, Daddy?' As Mario entered the kitchen, Nat turned to him eagerly. 'The one who told the lies about us this afternoon. And Dad said what we needed was to get our own back and we should try VD.'

From the doorway, Mario grinned. 'I find it generally does the trick.'

'*Voodoo*,' Lottie emphasised.

'Voodoo. So Dad told us how you make models of people you don't like and stick pins in them. So that's what we've been doing!' Triumphantly, Nat rushed over to the kitchen table and brandished a plasticine figure bristling with cocktail sticks. 'This is the man, see? And every time you stick a stick in him, he gets a real pain in the place where you've stuck it. Like *this*,' he continued with relish, jabbing another cocktail stick into the plasticine figure's left leg. 'In real life he's hopping around now, going OW!'

Lottie looked at her ex-husband. 'Remind me again, how old are you?'

Mario was grinning broadly. 'It's just a bit of fun.'

Exasperated, she said, 'It's irresponsible.'

'No it isn't, it's great.' Ruby was happily prodding her own voodoo doll with cocktail sticks. 'Anyway, we didn't take your clothes so that horrible man deserves it.'

'That horrible man is going to be my new boss,' Lottie sighed. 'So you're just going to have to get used to him.'

'See? Even you think he's horrible.' Interestedly, Nat studied her face. 'Is that why you've been crying?'

'I haven't been crying. It's just hay fever.' Pulling herself together, Lottie realised how hard keeping the news of Freddie's illness to herself was going to be. 'Come on, you two, time to take you home.'

'No need to rush off. Give them ten minutes in the garden.' Mario, shooing them out through the back door, steered Lottie gently onto a kitchen chair and said, 'You look as if you could do with a drink. I'll get us both a lager.'

Chateau Margaux one minute, a can of Heineken the next. Oh well, why not? Kicking off her sandals and leaning back in the chair, Lottie watched him fetch the cans from the fridge. She loved being divorced from Mario, but it was still possible to admire his good looks and toned body. In fact it was probably easier now, without the associated emotional ties and that perpetual sense of anxiety in the pit of her stomach that he might be sharing his body with someone else on the quiet.

Which, in the end, was exactly what had happened.

'There you go. Cheers.' Having poured the Heineken into two glass tumblers, Mario handed one over and surveyed her over the rim of the other. 'So are you going to tell me why you've been crying?'

Lottie shook her head. 'It's nothing. Freddie and I were just talking about Mary. It got a bit emotional, that's all.'

'And there was me thinking you were upset because today's our wedding anniversary,' Mario teased.

Heavens, was it? August the 6th. Crikey, it was too. How weird not to have remembered. Weirder still that Mario had.

'It isn't our wedding anniversary. It would have been,' Lottie corrected him, 'if we'd stayed married.'

'Ah, but you left me. You broke my heart.' Mario looked convincingly bereft.

'Excuse me, I left you because you were a cheating weasel.'

'Ten years ago today.' His expression softened at the memory. 'That was such a great day, wasn't it?'

Actually, it had been. Lottie smiled. She had been twenty years old—far too young really—and Mario had been twenty-three. Mario's Italian mother had invited hordes of her excitable relations over from Sicily for the occasion and Lottie's girlfriends had been entranced by the male cousins' smouldering dark looks. The weather had been glorious and the dancing had carried on until dawn. Lottie, all in white and only slightly pregnant, had wondered if it was possible to be happier than this. She had Mario and a baby on the way; her life was officially perfect.

And to be fair, it had been pretty perfect for the first few years. Mario was charming, irresistible, and a fantastic father who adored his children. But Mario's legendary capacity to charm was coupled with flirtatiousness, and after a while Lottie had begun to experience the downside of being married to a man who enjoyed being the centre of attention. Other girls made their interest in him only too blindingly obvious. Lottie, no shrinking violet herself, told Mario the flirting had to stop. But it simply wasn't in his nature. That was when the arguments had begun. It was crushing to realise that you'd married a man who, essentially, wasn't the marrying kind. Staying with someone you were unable to trust wasn't something Lottie could countenance;

sooner or later she knew they would begin to hate each other.

For the sake of Nat and Ruby, and before the bitterness could take hold, Lottie announced to Mario that their marriage was over. Mario was devastated and did his best to persuade her to change her mind, but Lottie stood firm. It was the only way, if they were to remain friends.

'But I love you,' Mario protested.

He did; she knew that.

'I love you too. But you're having an affair with your receptionist.'

Shocked, Mario insisted, 'It's not an *affair*. She means nothing to me!'

That last bit was probably true as well.

'Maybe, but you mean everything to her. She phoned me in tears last night to tell me just how much. For an *hour*.' Lottie sighed. 'And don't tell me you'll change, because we both know that would be a big lie. It's better this way, trust me. Now, why don't we sit down and decide who's going to live where?'

Mercifully money wasn't an issue. Mario was the manager of a glossy car dealership in Cheltenham and, it went without saying, a superlative salesman with an income to match. They agreed that Lottie and the children should stay at Piper's Cottage, while Mario would buy one of the new houses on the other side of the village. It hadn't occurred to either of them that they wouldn't both stay in Hestacombe. Nat and Ruby would still be able to see Mario whenever they wanted, and he would be able to continue to be a proper father to them.

It had all worked out incredibly well. Mario Carlyle may have been a less than ideal husband but you couldn't ask for a better ex.

Apart from when he thoughtlessly taught his children to stick pins in plasticine effigies of Lottie's new boss.

'**H**ello? You're miles away.' Mario was waving his hand in front of her face.

'Sorry.' Brought back to the present with a bump, Lottie said, 'I was just thinking how much nicer it is, not being married to you any more.'

'Not being married to anyone, you mean.' Mario enjoyed mickey-taking about her lack of love life. 'Since we split up you've been out on *one date*.' He held up one finger in case she was unable to comprehend the shameful *singleness* of the number.

'I blame being married to you. It's scarred me for life,' Lottie said.

'You're too picky, that's your problem.'

'Unlike you. You're the opposite of picky.'

'Thanks a lot. I'll tell Amber you said that. In fact,' Mario turned his head at the sound of a car pulling into the drive, 'I'll tell her right now.'

'Apart from Amber,' said Lottie. In the three years since she and Mario had separated, a constant stream of girlfriends had passed through Mario's life. Which would have been fine as far as Lottie was concerned, but for the fact that there was Nat and Ruby to consider. Most of these girlfriends had been wildly unsuitable and invariably pretended to adore Ruby and Nat because they were so keen to impress Mario. In order to court popularity and win their friendship they were always buying them sweets and ice creams. Last year, without thinking to consult Lottie or Mario first, a chirpy brunette called Babs had promised Ruby *faithfully* that on her ninth birthday she would take her into Cheltenham to have her belly button pierced.

After that it had been bye-bye Babs. God knows what she might have had planned as an encore. Sneaking Nat off to a tattoo parlour, possibly.

But Amber was the longest-lasting girlfriend to date, and Amber was different. She genuinely liked Mario's children and Lottie in turn liked her. If she could organise everyone's lives—God, wouldn't that be *great*?—she would choose Amber to settle down with Mario, tame him, marry him and become stepmother to Ruby and Nat.

The front door opened and banged shut, and Amber appeared in the kitchen. Blonde and petite, with a perky smile and a penchant for short skirts and vertiginously high heels, she wouldn't immediately strike anyone as ideal stepmother material, but beneath the low-cut tops beat a heart of gold. Amber was feisty, hard-working and addicted to sparkly jewellery. She and Mario had been seeing each other for seven months now and she wasn't the type to put up with any nonsense. So far, he'd managed to keep himself in check.

'Hi, there. Monsters in the garden?'

'Don't worry, I'm taking them home now.' Lottie offered her the lager she'd barely touched. 'We'll leave you in peace. Good day?'

Amber ran her own busy hairdressing salon in Tetbury, employed four part-time stylists and had earned herself a devoted clientele.

'Interesting day. I've been offered a free holiday in the South of France.'

Mario said, 'That's nothing. When I opened my post this morning I was offered twenty-five grand and a trip to Australia. Sweetheart, it's called junk mail. They don't really give you all this stuff for free.'

'You're hilarious. This is a genuine offer.' Her many bracelets jangling as she delved into her pink diamanté-studded rucksack, Amber produced a travel brochure and pulled up a chair next to Lottie. 'Come on, I'll show you. One of my clients booked a fortnight in St Tropez for herself and her boyfriend, but they broke up last week. She asked me if I'd be interested instead. Here we go, page thirty-seven. It looks fantastic, there's a private pool and everything, and it's only five minutes from the harbour where all the billionaires moor their yachts.'

'Wow. Flash apartment too.' Lottie was poring over the photographs in the brochure. 'And how about that view over the bay?'

Interested now, Mario leaned across to take a look. 'I've never been to St Tropez. When's it booked for?'

'The beginning of September.'

'I could manage a fortnight then. I've still got three weeks to take before Christmas. Could be just what we need.' Mario looked at Amber. 'I'll have to brush up on my French before we get there. *Voulez vous coucher avec moi, mon ange, ma petite . . .*'

'Actually,' Amber broke in, 'she invited just me, not you.'

Mario looked confused. 'But you said—'

'Mandy broke up with her boyfriend, but she's still taking the holiday. She asked me if I'd like to go with her in his place.'

'Oh. Right.' Crestfallen, Mario shrugged. 'So you've already said yes.'

'I have.' Amber nodded, her long silver earrings dancing around her shoulders. 'Well, I'd be mad to turn down a free holiday, wouldn't I? Patsy and Liz are going to work extra hours in the salon. There's no reason not to go. God, I'm excited already!'

Lottie was pleased for Amber, who worked her socks off and deserved a break, but she could think of a reason why she shouldn't go. If Mario was left to his own devices for an entire fortnight, who knew what he might get up to? Without realising it, Amber could be putting their whole relationship at risk. But much as Lottie didn't want that to happen, it wasn't her place to interfere.

'Eeeurgh, yuk, *monsters*!' Feigning horror and disgust, Amber shielded herself with the holiday brochure as Nat and Ruby exploded into the kitchen. 'Urrgh, don't let them near me, they're so *ugly*.'

'You like us really.' Nat beamed and leaned against her chair. 'Did you bring us any sweets?'

'No, I did not. Sweets make all your teeth go rotten and fall out. You're scary enough as it is.' Amber began to tickle him in the ribs, expertly reducing Nat to a shrieking, giggling heap, as Ruby helped.

Watching Amber interacting so effortlessly with them, Lottie felt her heart expand with love. All she wanted in the world was for her children to be happy. If she were to die and Ruby and Nat were living full-time with Mario, she couldn't ask for a better potential stepmother than Amber.

God, please don't let Mario mess everything up. Maybe she should consider breaking both his legs, forcing him to spend the fortnight flat on his back in traction while Amber was away.

Chapter 2

HOW TO LOSE FRIENDS and really annoy people, thought Cressida, her skin prickling with embarrassment at what she could be about to do. On the other hand, she'd clearly be doing this man a favour.

Hastily running her hands over her flyaway light brown hair—yes, even here in Hestacombe village shop it was making a valiant attempt to fly away—Cressida mentally rehearsed what she would say.

Ted, who ran the shop, was busy serving someone at the counter. At the back of the shop, the man Cressida was currently stalking sifted dispiritedly, yet again, through the collection of greetings cards on sale and murmured to his son, 'It's no good, there's nothing here. We'll have to drive into Stroud, find something decent.'

The boy looked distraught. For the second time he whined, 'But, Dad, we're supposed to be fishing. You *promised*.'

'I know, but we just have to do this first. It's Gran's birthday tomorrow and you know what she's like when it comes to cards.'

The boy, who was about twelve, said frustratedly, 'Well, get her that one then,' and whipped a card from the rickety carousel.

From the corner of her eye, Cressida saw that the card he'd chosen featured a cuddly, overweight bunny clutching a bunch of flowers. The boy's father said flatly, 'Gran would hate it. She'd think I couldn't be bothered to choose her something decent. Look, if we drive into Stroud now, we can be back by midday.'

The boy rolled his eyes in disbelief. 'Then you'll say it's not worth going fishing because it's too late now—'

'Ahem.' Clearing her throat and double-checking that Ted was still otherwise occupied at the far end of the shop, Cressida said in a low voice, 'I might be able to help you out.'

This was it, then. The point of no return. She'd just approached a complete stranger in a public place and shamelessly solicited her wares.

The man and his son both turned, clearly startled. The man said, 'Excuse me?'

Pulling a keep-your-voice-down face, Cressida said, 'Sorry, I shouldn't be doing this, bit of a cheek. But if you like I could make you a card.'

The boy said, '*What?*'

'Making greetings cards is what I do.' Faintly annoyed by the boy's manner, Cressida said, 'I live just up the road. I'll be out of here in two minutes, if you're interested. Otherwise, no problem.'

Aware that her cheeks were burning, Cressida grabbed a bottle of washing-up liquid from the shelf and slipped away from them. Reaching the chill cabinet she helped herself to milk and butter then moved towards the counter.

'Bloody holidaymakers,' grumbled Ted as the door jangled shut behind the man and his son. To come into the shop and leave without buying anything he regarded as a personal affront.

Cressida reminded herself that there was really no need to feel racked with guilt; the man hadn't been about to buy one of the sad little collection of cards on the carousel anyway.

But her conscience wasn't about to let her off that easily.

'I know, they're a pain, aren't they? I'll have a packet of fruit gums as well, Ted.'

'And a walnut cake? Fresh in this morning.' Nodding encouragingly, Ted was already reaching for a patisserie box.

'Go on, then.' Cressida caved in.

Outside in the sunshine the man and his son were loitering some twenty yards away from the shop. Joining them, Cressida said, 'Sorry, I know you must have thought I was a bit strange, but I promise you I'm not. That's my house just up there, overlooking the village green.'

'This is all very MI5.' The man made a feeble stab at humour as Cressida glanced both ways before unlocking her green front door.

'Ted can be a bit touchy. I'd hate to be banned for life from the only shop in the village. Come on through, my workroom's at the end of the hall.' Cressida showed them into the large, sunny ex-dining room, painted yellow and white and cluttered with piled-up boxes. Against one wall was a desk containing her computer; thanks to the internet, this was how she attracted most of her business. Next to it, the work she was currently making a start on was spread out over a ten-foot long table.

'Right, I won't keep you long, I know you're in a hurry to go fishing.' Cressida glanced at the boy, who was shuffling his feet, evidently counting every second under his breath. 'But if you tell me what your mother would like, I can do you a card right away. I make them to order.'

The man moved towards the table, the vibration from his footsteps on the wooden floor causing the computer screen to shimmer into life. Having taken in the sheets of heavy card, the reels of silk and ribbons, the bowls of dried petals, feathers and coloured glass beads, he looked again at the VDU and read, 'Cressida Forbes Cards. Is that your name?'

'That's me,' Cressida said. 'Perfect cards for every occasion!'

The boy, who she was fast beginning to dislike, gave the kind of under-his-breath snort that clearly translated as: you are *such* a dork.

'*Anyway*.' Grasping the mouse, she clicked from her website's home page onto a sample of greetings cards and rapidly scrolled through them. 'I can make any one of these and personalise it for you.'

The boy looked dismayed. 'How long's *that* going to take?'

'Not long. Less than half an hour,' said Cressida to wind him up.

'Half an *hour*!'

'I like this one.' The man was pointing to a lilac card with an impressionistic garden design composed of pale green iridescent gauze, rose quartz beads, silver ribbon and drawn-in metallic green trees. Turning to Cressida he said, 'And could you put "Mum, have a wonderful 70th birthday" on the front?'

'Of course I can. Anything you want.'

'Half an *hour*!'

'Here.' Reaching past the grumpy boy, Cressida took a ready-folded A5 sheet of lilac card and matching envelope from one of the trays on her desk. Opening out the card, she handed his father a black fountain pen and said, 'Write inside it and address the envelope. Go off and do your fishing. I'll have the card finished and in the post by lunchtime.'

'Yeah, but how do we know you'll send it?'

This was a boy sorely in need of a slap. With a sweet smile Cressida said, 'When you ring your grandmother tomorrow to wish her a happy birthday, you could ask her if she likes her card.'

'Donny, behave yourself. I do apologise.' Having finished writing inside the card and addressing the envelope, the man pulled out his wallet. 'This is very kind. And my mother will love it. How much do I owe you?'

Cressida watched from the window as the two of them made their way down the High Street, climbed into their dark blue Volvo and drove off. The card Donny's father had chosen sold for four pounds but, embarrassed at having practically hijacked him and frogmarched him into her house, she had asked for two pounds. And on top of that she had to supply the first class stamp and walk down to the postbox herself.

Let's face it, she was never going to have to worry about becoming a tycoon and being forced to go and live in tax exile.

Still, he'd seemed like a nice man. Even if she hadn't even found out his name. All she knew was that his mother was Mrs E. Turner, that she lived in Sussex and that tomorrow she would be seventy.

Oh, and that her grandson was a sulky spoilt brat.

The doorbell went at seven o'clock that evening. Halfway through a chicken Madras on a tray in front of the television, Cressida guessed it was Lottie popping in for a drink and a chat.

'Oh!' Horribly conscious that her breath must reek of curry, she took a surprised step back when she saw that it wasn't Lottie at all.

'You undercharged me this morning. And I didn't get the chance to introduce myself.' The son of Mrs E. Turner was back on her doorstep, sunburnt and smiling and wearing a clean blue shirt. He was also holding a wrapped bunch of freesias. 'Tom Turner.'

Flustered, she said, 'Tom, how nice to see you again. Um . . . I posted your mother's card.'

'I knew you would. You have an honest face. Here.' He held out the flowers. 'My way of saying thank you for helping me out this morning.'

Cressida took the freesias. 'They're beautiful. Thank you so much. You really didn't have to do this.'

'As I said, you undercharged me. I saw the prices on your website.' Tom smiled. 'I also wanted to apologise for Donny's behaviour. He wasn't at his most charming, I'm afraid.'

You could say that again. Peering over Tom's shoulder, Cressida said, 'Well, he's at that age. Is he waiting in the car?'

'No. I've left him at the cottage, hunched over his GameBoy.'

There was a pause. Tom was still standing there, making no move to leave. Conscious that she might have curry breath but keen to cover the awkward silence, Cressida said brightly, 'So, did you catch anything?'

Tom looked startled. 'Excuse me?'

Oh marvellous, now he probably thought she was quizzing him about sexually transmitted diseases. 'You were going fishing,' Cressida said hurriedly. 'I meant did you catch any fish?'

'Oh, right, sorry. Yes, yes, we managed to—'

'Come in for a drink!' Out of the corner of her eye, Cressida had glimpsed Ted from the village shop ambling down the High Street towards them on his way to the Flying Pheasant.

Cressida was startled to realise that without even thinking about it she had reached out, unceremoniously yanked Tom Turner into her hallway and slammed the front door shut behind him.

Amused, he said, 'I thought you'd never ask.'

'Sorry. Ted, from the shop. Come on through.' Flinging open windows in the kitchen and chucking away the plastic container her microwaveable Madras had come in, Cressida said, 'Sorry about the smell of curry. Now, let me just put these in something. Tea, coffee or a glass of wine?'

Tom looked at the freesias she was busy unwrapping. 'I think they'd probably prefer water.'

'OK.' Cressida nodded, realising she'd been gabbling again. 'Water for the flowers. And we'll have the wine. It's only cheap, I'm afraid.'

Tom smiled. 'Stop apologising.'

They sat outside on the patio and Cressida learned that Tom and his son were from Newcastle, staying in one of Freddie's holiday cottages. They were three days into a fortnight's holiday and plenty more fishing was planned. This afternoon they had caught six trout and five perch.

'Which cheered Donny up no end,' said Tom. 'That was another reason I wanted to see you again, I suppose. To let you know that Donny isn't always as stroppy as he was this morning. He's a good lad really. The last couple of years have been tough for him.'

'You got divorced?' It was an educated guess; father and son holidaying alone together. No wedding ring in sight.

Tom nodded. 'My wife ran off with another man.'

'Oh God. I'm so sorry.'

He acknowledged this with a shrug. 'It hit Donny hard. We hadn't any idea. She just walked out one morning and that was that. Left a note, didn't even say goodbye. She's living in Norfolk now with her new chap. Poor Donny, it's just the two of us now. I do my best and we muddle through. But it's not the same, is it?'

'It's not the same.' Cressida nodded sympathetically, feeling terrible for having decided earlier that Donny would benefit from a slap. Her heart went out to the man sitting opposite her. 'But it must have been awful for you too.'

'What can I say?' Tom shook his head. 'You just have to carry on, pick up the pieces. I'm forty-two years old and a single parent. Never imagined that happening, but it has. God, listen to me.' He grimaced, then broke into a smile. 'Now it's my turn to apologise. Talk about cheerful! Let's turn this conversation around, shall we? Tell me about you instead.'

'Well, I'm thirty-nine. And divorced.' Oh Lord, she sounded like a lonely hearts advert. Dismissing the last bit with a wave of her hand, Cressida said, 'But that was years ago. And I love living here in Hestacombe, running my own little business. I'll never be rich, but I make a living and the hours are flexible. If I want to take a day off to go bungee jumping, I can. Other times, I'll be up all night making fifty wedding invitations or birth announcements. You never know what you'll be asked to do next and I love it.'

There, that was cheerful and positive, wasn't it? She sounded wild and free, spontaneous and impulsive . . .

'Bungee jumping?'

'OK, maybe not bungee jumping. But if I feel like it, I can take a day off and go shopping.'

'Nothing wrong with that.' Tom nodded in agreement. 'As far as my ex-wife was concerned, a week without new shoes was a week wasted.'

'Was she incredibly glamorous?' She'd always longed to be glamorous herself but Cressida knew glamour was beyond her. No matter how many times she set out determined to buy something tailored and chic, she always seemed to end up being inexorably drawn to long Gypsyish skirts, billowing cotton shirts, and embroidered jackets.

'Glamorous? Not especially.' Tom considered this. 'Angie was always smart, though. Well,' he added, 'I daresay she still is.'

Something else I'll never be, thought Cressida. Smart implied being acquainted with a steam iron and she wasn't. Could a man who'd been married to a well-turned-out woman ever be interested in someone who didn't own an ironing board?

Oh dear, now she was definitely getting too carried away. The poor fellow had only come round to thank her for helping him out.

'Not that Donny appreciated it,' Tom continued easily. 'Angie was always trying to get him to dress smartly too, and all he ever wanted to wear was holey sweatshirts and camouflage combats. These days I just let him wear anything he likes. Kids have their own ideas of how they want to look, don't they? You must find the same.'

'Well, um—'

'Sorry.' Seeing that she was taken aback, Tom said, 'I couldn't help noticing the photos in the kitchen of you and your daughter. That's how I knew you'd understand about Donny, being a single parent yourself.'

All she had to do was laugh it off. Ridiculously, though, Cressida felt a surge of pride mixed with sadness because the pain might be hidden but it never really went away.

'What's her name?' said Tom.

'Jojo.'

'Jojo.' He nodded. 'And she's what, roughly the same age as Donny?'

It was no big deal. She didn't have to tell him the whole story. Crikey, she might never set eyes on him again after tonight.

'Jojo's twelve. And I love her to bits.' Forcing herself to smile, Cressida said, 'But she isn't my daughter. I just look after her a lot.'

Tyler Klein saw them as he was driving into Hestacombe the next morning. Two children, emerging from a modern house on the outskirts of the village, wearing shorts, T-shirts and baseball caps. He couldn't swear they were the ones but he could soon find out. Tyler braked and pulled up alongside them.

The heat hit him as he stepped out of the air-conditioned hire car. The flash of recognition in their eyes told Tyler all he needed to know.

'Hi there.' Tyler smiled easily. 'Was it you two I saw a couple of days ago, down by the lake? Running off with someone else's clothes?'

They regarded him warily. Finally the taller boy said, 'That wasn't us.'

'Look. You're not in trouble. I just really need to know the truth.'

The younger boy said earnestly, 'We didn't take any clothes.'

'Fine. Well, there are tests that can be done to find out who did. DNA,' said Tyler. 'Fingerprints.'

Behind the boys, their mother had appeared in the doorway of the house, young and plump and carrying an even plumper baby on her hip. She watched impassively as her youngest son blurted out, 'But she got them back. We threw them over the wall into her garden.'

'I know.' Tyler nodded. 'But thanks for confirming it.'

'*Ow*,' cried the boy as his brother elbowed him painfully in the ribs.

'You big *stupid*, you *told* him.'

'That hurt!'

Catching their mother's eye, Tyler said, 'Sorry about this.'

'Don't be sorry. Little buggers, I'll give them something to be sorry about. Harry, Ben, get inside the house.' As the boys slid past their mother and the fat baby placidly watched, she clipped each of them smartly around the ear. The older of the two, clutching the side of his head, turned and glared at Tyler before disappearing into the hallway.

As far as the under-eleven population of Hestacombe was concerned, Tyler realised, he was undoubtedly Public Enemy Number One.

Lottie was hard at work on the computer in the office when she heard the crunch of tyres on gravel outside heralding Tyler Klein's arrival. Glad of the break from processing bookings, she picked up her bottle of Orangina and went outside to greet him.

'Giving the suit a miss today then.' Leaning against the open door of the annexe, just across the drive from Hestacombe House, she watched him emerge from the car. He was wearing a pink-striped shirt and faded jeans, and there was no denying that as new bosses went, he was pretty damn gorgeous.

'I hate suits. I've had to wear them for the last twelve years.' Tyler Klein's dark eyes glittered as he shook Lottie's hand. 'From now on, if you catch me in a suit you'll know I'm either on my way to a wedding or a funeral.'

Lottie winced at the mention of the word funeral. It wasn't his fault; he didn't know Freddie was ill.

'Freddie's spending the day in Cheltenham, but he said you wanted to see how things are run around here.' She checked her watch. 'Teacher's Cottage is being cleaned before the next guests arrive. Shall I show you what we do to get it ready?'

Tyler shrugged and nodded. 'You're the boss. Fire away.'

'Actually, you're the boss.' Lottie closed the door of the office behind her. 'And I just hope you don't fire me.'

Teacher's Cottage was a four-bedded Grade II listed property in its own magical gardens. Lottie introduced Tyler to Liz, the cleaner, as she was leaving, then showed him over the cottage.

'We leave fresh food in the fridge. And a homemade cake on the kitchen table to welcome the new arrivals. Fresh flowers in the living room and bedrooms. Magazines and books are always going walkabout so we replace them regularly.'

'Speaking of going walkabout, I guess I owe your two kids an apology.' Tyler pulled a face. 'I found out who made off with your clothes.'

'Don't worry about it. I finally believed them.' As she spoke Lottie was busily straightening pictures on the walls, plumping up cushions and re-angling the coffee table. The pictures were already straight and the cushions plumped but there was no harm in letting your new boss know how efficient and hardworking you were. 'Who did it?'

'Two young boys.' Tyler wasn't about to tell her their names. 'They won't be doing it again.'

'Ben and Harry Jenkins then.' Entertained by the expression on his face, Lottie said, 'This isn't New York. Everyone knows everyone. Can I ask you a question?'

Tyler spread his hands. 'Anything you like.'

'Are you actually going to be living here, running the business yourself? Or will you be popping down here every couple of weeks to keep an eye on your investment?'

'Living right here running the business.' Amused by the unfamiliar expression, Tyler said, 'Where would I be *popping* down here from?'

'I don't know. London, I suppose. Or New York. You work in banking.' Lottie hadn't been able to figure it out for the life of her. 'It's a bit of a switch, isn't it? I thought maybe you'd carry on doing that and just kind of dabble in this on your days off.'

'Because you don't think I could cope with it full time?'

'Because it's not going to be as lucrative as being a financial high-flier, wheeler-dealing on the stock exchange, trading zillions of shares and buying companies and stuff.' Aware that her grasp of the financial markets was tenuous to say the least, Lottie hurriedly bent down to straighten the magazines, yet again, on the coffee table. 'And if you're rich enough to be able to afford to buy all these holiday homes, isn't it going to be a bit weird, living in Fox Cottage? I mean, you must be used to so much better, a penthouse apartment overlooking Central Park or something. And working here isn't going to be at all what you're used to.' Lottie felt obliged to warn him. 'What will you do when a guest rings you up at three o'clock in the morning to tell you that a pipe's burst and water's pouring through the ceiling? Or that one of the drains is blocked? How are you going to deal with stuff like that?'

'OK, OK.' Tyler held up both hands. 'The thing about asking a million questions is you have to stop occasionally to let other people answer.'

'Sorry. I'm just nosy. And I talk too much.'

'And you think I'm some clueless wanker-banker type who wouldn't know a monkey wrench from a plunger. Look, leave those magazines alone, Freddie's already told me you're indispensable.' Leading the way through to the kitchen, Tyler began briskly inspecting the cupboards. 'But I'm not actually that hopeless. I'm not afraid of hard physical work either. But if there are any emergencies I really can't handle myself, I'll do what any normal person would do and call in an expert.'

Had she offended him by suggesting that he wasn't up to the job?

'I didn't think you were a namby-pamby wanker-banker,' Lottie protested. 'I just wondered why you don't want to *be* a banker any more.'

Having thoroughly investigated the kitchen, Tyler leaned back against the granite worktop, hands thrust casually into his jeans pockets.

'OK. Let me tell you what it's like. We're talking high-pressure lifestyle here. Up at five every morning, off to the gym before work, then twelve hours in the office. Nonstop meetings, having to make decisions that could make or break people's businesses—even their lives. Then wondering if you've made the right decision, dealing with the fallout when it all goes wrong. I'm telling you, it takes over your world. Nothing matters except making the next deal, the next million. You turn into a machine.' He paused, then said flatly, 'And it can end up killing you.'

The look in his dark eyes was bleak. Oh Jesus, thought Lottie, not you too.

'It killed my best friend.'

Oh. That was OK then. Well, not *OK*, obviously . . .

'His name was Curtis Segal,' Tyler went on. 'We grew up in the same street. We were closer than brothers. During college vacations we worked together on a ranch in Wyoming. After college we ended up going into the same business. Curtis was on a roll, getting promotion after promotion at his company, raking the money in and never getting enough sleep. But he was a fit guy. You never think anything bad's going to happen, do you, when you're in your thirties? Until Curtis had a major presentation one day—not the biggest he'd ever handled, but still pretty important—and he told his secretary he had a pain in his left arm five minutes before the presentation was due to begin. She wanted to call the company doctor in to see him but Curtis wouldn't let her do it, because everyone was up there in the boardroom waiting for him to make that presentation.'

Silence. Tyler was still leaning against the worktop, lost in thought. Finally he continued. 'So he went up there and made it. Well, half of it. Then he collapsed and died, right there on the floor of the boardroom. And guess what happened after that?'

'What?' said Lottie.

'His company lost the account. The other guys decided they didn't want to do business with the kind of bank where their top executives keel over and drop dead on you.'

His eyes were narrowed with disgust. Lottie's heart went out to Tyler. But since she could hardly fling her arms round him she said, 'When did this happen?'

'Five months ago. That's when I realised it could have been me. More to the point, it could be me *next*. And I made my decision just like that.' Tyler clicked his fingers. 'The day after Curtis's funeral I handed in my notice. Everyone told me I was mad. But I knew I was doing the right thing. I went to visit my parents and they were showing me all their holiday photos. They're so in love with this place, you have no idea.' He relaxed visibly. 'My mother happened to mention that Freddie was thinking of selling the business. Two minutes later she said wouldn't it be great if I bought it, because then she and my father could come and stay for free.'

As he shook his head with good-natured amusement, Lottie sensed his genuine fondness for his mother.

'That evening I took a look at your website, purely out of curiosity, and all of a sudden it occurred to me that I could do it, that it might be just the change I needed. It's a fantastic place—my parents had already vouched for that. And if the price was fair, there'd be no risk. With properties like these . . . well, you can't go wrong. That's when I picked up the phone and called Freddie.' He paused. 'That was less than two weeks ago. And now here I am. Beats Wall Street hands down.'

Lottie marvelled at Tyler's ability to make such a life-changing decision and to act upon it. He'd bought eight holiday homes, just like that. She'd spent longer choosing a new winter coat.

Aloud she said, 'You make it all sound so easy. Didn't you have to be interrogated by immigration?'

Tyler said drily, 'The British Consulate couldn't wait to grant me the visa, once they heard how much money I was planning to invest.'

Crikey, he must be loaded. Curious, Lottie said, 'Are you sure Fox Cottage is going to be OK for you?'

'Hey, I'm no namby-pamby.' Tyler clearly found the unfamiliar expression hilarious. 'Besides, it's only for a few months. I can handle that.'

A few months. Disappointment settled over Lottie like a sheet over a parrot's cage. She gave herself a mental shake. 'And after that?'

'Didn't Freddie tell you? He's planning to move out of Hestacombe House after Christmas. If I'm interested, I can buy it from him then.'

This time Lottie's heart turned over. She still hadn't been able to come to terms with the thought that Freddie was dying. *Planning to move out.*

'You don't look exactly thrilled,' Tyler observed.

'No, it's not that.' He didn't know, he didn't know, and she couldn't tell him. 'I just hadn't—'

Lottie was saved by the sound of a car pulling up outside. Relieved, she checked her watch. 'Oh, that'll be the Harrisons.'

Tyler sauntered after her out of the cottage. The doors of a maroon people carrier were flung open and Glynis and Duncan Harrison and their five boisterous children spilled out.

'Here she is, waiting to welcome us,' Glynis exclaimed with delight. The Harrisons had been coming to Teacher's Cottage for the last ten years. 'Hello, Lottie love, you're looking well!' She enveloped Lottie in a rib-crushing, violet-scented hug. 'Ooh, it's so lovely to be back.'

'It's lovely to have you back.' Lottie meant it, she'd grown fond of so many of her clients. 'Good journey?'

'Roadworks on the M5 and the kids trying to murder each other in the back seats, but we're used to that by now. And who's this then?' Releasing Lottie in order to give Tyler an appreciative once-over, Glynis said, 'Got yourself a new fellow at last, love? I say, well *done*.' Eager to be introduced, she stuck out her hand and beamed up at Tyler. 'I was only saying to Duncan on the way down—wasn't I, Duncan?—it's about time Lottie found herself a nice young man.'

Lottie opened her mouth to explain but Tyler beat her to it. Greeting Glynis with a warm handshake and a wicked smile, he drawled, 'Tyler Klein. Good to meet you. And I couldn't agree with you more about Lottie. It's definitely time she found herself the right man.'

Cressida was running a bath when her mobile phone launched into its jaunty tune. Locating it under the pile of clothes she'd just discarded on the bed, she made her way back through to the bathroom to choose which bubble bath to add to the gushing water.

'Cressida? Hi, it's Sacha.'

'Hi, Sacha. How are you?'

'Oh, busy busy as usual. What's that noise in the background?'

'I'm running a bath.' Cressida selected the bottle of Marks & Spencer's Florentyna and shook a generous dollop under the taps.

'Lucky you! Having a lovely relaxing bath at five in the afternoon,' Sacha exclaimed. 'I wish I could do that. Now listen, Robert's stuck in a meeting in Bristol and I'm up to my ears with clients. We don't know when we're going to be able to get away. OK if Jojo comes over to you?'

'No problem.' Cressida swirled the bathwater with her free hand, generating foam. 'What time will you be over to pick her up?'

'Well, the thing is, I'm being pressured to take the new clients out to dinner so I don't know how late it might be. And Robert thinks he may not be back before midnight, so . . .'

'How about if Jojo stays the night with me? Would that be easier?' Cressida wondered what Sacha would do if she told her she wasn't able to take Jojo. One day she must try it, see what happened.

'Cress, you're a star!' Having got what she needed, Sacha put on her I'm-in-*such*-a-hurry voice. 'That's great, I'll give Jojo a ring and let her know. Well, it's chaos here so—'

'You'd better get back to them,' Cressida said helpfully.

'I really must. And you can get back to your bath! *Ciao!*'

Cressida switched off the phone. Was it just her, or was everyone else driven nuts by the annoying way Sacha trilled *Ciao!* at the end of every phone conversation? Whatever possessed a woman who'd been born and bred in Bootle to say *Ciao*? Maybe it was something that was drummed into you on training courses when you were learning to become a hotshot, high-flying photocopier saleswoman.

Lying back in the bath, Cressida ran her hand lightly over the familiar silver scar traversing her stomach. How different might her life have been had that scar never needed to be made? She closed her eyes and imagined herself, twenty-three again and still happily married to Robert. Both of them had been so excited by the prospect of the baby and although they knew it was far too soon, they had been unable to resist rushing out and buying all kinds of baby paraphernalia. It had been the most joyful shopping spree of Cressida's life. To be a mother was all she'd ever wanted.

Back at home that evening, surrounded by babygros, tiny knitted hats, a satin-lined Moses basket and a musical mobile that played nursery rhymes, Cressida had begun to experience the first excruciating knife-like pains in her stomach. She had crawled on all fours to the phone, petrified and plunged into icy panic, and tried to contact Robert who was out playing cricket for his company team. Unable to reach him, she had been on the verge of dialling 999 when the pain had intensified and everything had turned black. When Robert arrived home at ten o'clock that night, he found her unconscious and barely breathing. An ambulance rushed Cressida to hospital where emergency surgery was carried out to save her life. The pregnancy had been ectopic and her fallopian tube had ruptured. A total hysterectomy had been the only option.

When Cressida woke up to find Robert weeping silently at her bedside she knew her life was over. Their longed-for child was gone and, along with it, any chance of motherhood.

Awash with grief, Cressida sank into a depression so deep it was as if all the happiness had been sucked out of the world. Nobody could help her to feel better because there was nothing that could *make* her feel better. Everywhere she went, she saw pregnant women proudly displaying their bumps, mothers holding newborn babies and fathers playing rumbustious games of football with their sons.

But at least, as everyone was forever telling her, she and Robert still had each other. Their marriage was rock-solid. Together they would gain strength and get through this.

In fact their marriage was so rock-solid that eleven months after the night their lives had changed forever, Robert moved out of the house overlooking Hestacombe village green. He told Cressida he wanted a divorce and Cressida said fine. Compared with the loss of their baby, losing Robert paled into insignificance.

That's not to say she wasn't hurt by Robert's next action. But then again, men were thoughtless. Having by this time moved into a rented flat in Cheltenham, he embarked on a whirlwind romance with a fiercely ambitious young sales rep called Sacha, who had just moved down from Liverpool to join the company. Cressida and Robert's divorce went through and four months later Robert and Sacha were married. Six months after that, Robert arrived on Cressida's doorstep one day to tell her that he and Sacha had just put in an offer to buy one of the houses on the new estate on the edge of the village. Taken aback, Cressida said, 'What, you mean *this* village? But *why*?'

'Cress, my flat's too small. We need somewhere with more space. I like Hestacombe and this new house is perfect. OK, so we're divorced.'

Robert shrugged and said reasonably, 'But we can still be civilised towards each other, can't we?'

Her heart heavy, Cressida said, 'I suppose so. Sorry.'

Robert looked relieved. Then he said, 'Oh, and I suppose I should tell you that Sacha's pregnant. That's another reason for the move.'

Cressida felt as if she'd been plunged into a vat of dry ice. Her tongue was sticking to the roof of her mouth but she managed to stammer, 'G-gosh. C-congratulations.'

'Well, it wasn't exactly planned.' Robert's tone was rueful. 'Sacha really wanted to concentrate on her career for the next few years, but these things happen. I'm sure she'll cope.'

It was as if he was stabbing her with a long gleaming blade, over and over again. Stab stab.

As if realising he might not have been too subtle, Robert shoved his hands into his pockets and said defensively, 'I'm sorry, but you can't expect me to go through life not having children, just because of what happened to you. Don't make me feel guilty, Cress. You know how much I wanted a proper family.'

Cressida nodded, wanting him to leave. 'I do. It's OK, I'm f-fine.'

Relieved, Robert said, 'Good. That's that, then. Life goes on.'

Now, lying in the bath, Cressida studied her orangey-pink painted toenails. Life had indeed gone on. She had thrown herself into her work as a legal secretary and in her spare time had redecorated the house. Five months later she heard that Sacha had given birth to a seven-pound baby, a girl. That had been a hard day. Robert and Sacha named their daughter Jojo and Cressida sent them a card she had made herself, to congratulate them.

Another milestone survived.

When Jojo was two months old, a nanny was hired and Sacha went back to work. Astrid, who was from Sweden and far more of a fresh-air fiend than Sacha, could be seen every day pushing Jojo in her Silver Cross pram around the village. Keen to practise her English, Astrid stopped to chat with everyone she saw, which was how Cressida, unloading a supermarket carrier bag from the boot of her car, met her outside the house.

'I am Astrid,' the girl said. 'I am working as a nanny for Robert and Sacha Forbes.'

Cressida, who already knew this, tactfully didn't say, 'Hi, Astrid, I'm Cressida Forbes, Robert's first wife.' Instead she said, 'And I'm Cressida. It's very nice to meet you.'

Astrid beamed at her, then turned the pram round and said brightly,

'But I must not be forgetting my manners! I have also to introduce you to Jojo.'

Cressida held her breath and looked down at the baby lying in the pram. Jojo gazed inscrutably back at her. Waiting for the familiar stabbing pain in her stomach, Cressida was relieved when it didn't come.

'She is so beautiful, don't you think?' Astrid spoke with pride, leaning forward to tickle Jojo's chin.

'Yes, she is.' Cressida's heart expanded as, in response to the tickling, Jojo broke into a gummy smile.

'Such a good baby, too. I am enjoying very much looking after her. And are you having children as well?'

There was the stabbing pain. She knew Astrid meant 'do you have children', but this time Cressida didn't correct her. Clutching the supermarket bag containing her lonely meal-for-one, a packet of biscuits and a single pint of milk she said, 'No, I'm not having children.'

For eight months Astrid had been the perfect nanny. Cressida often thought afterwards that she owed practically her entire relationship with Jojo to a moment's carelessness on the part of Astrid's mother.

Cressida had been coming out of Ted's shop one morning, with her newspaper and a naughty packet of Revels, when she saw Sacha's company car heading down the High Street towards her. Screeching to a halt, Sacha stuck her head out of the driver's window and said, 'Cressida, can you save my life?'

She was looking decidedly harassed. On the brief occasions they had met before, Cressida had been struck by Sacha's air of calm and superefficiency. Her clothes were efficient. Even her hair—neat and short and expertly highlighted—was efficient. Today, by way of startling contrast, there were milk stains on Sacha's sweatshirt and her hair was uncombed. Strapped into her baby seat in the back of the car, Jojo was wearing a T-shirt and a bulging nappy and was screaming her head off.

'What's wrong?' Cressida was alarmed. 'Is Jojo ill?'

'Astrid's mother's in hospital with multiple fractures. Crashed her car into a bridge last night. Astrid's gone to Sweden to see her and doesn't know when she'll be back.' As the words came tumbling out, the volume of Jojo's wailing increased. Sacha's knuckles whitened as she gripped the steering wheel. 'And Robert's away on a bloody management training course in Edinburgh, and in two hours' time I'm due in Reading to pitch for the biggest account of my entire career. If I don't get there on time I don't know *what* I'll do—'

'Where are you going now?' Cressida cut in, because Sacha's voice was on an hysterical upward spiral.

'The health centre! I thought maybe one of the nurses would keep an eye on Jojo for me if I paid them enough. Unless you know anyone who could help? That's why I stopped,' Sacha gabbled on wildly, 'because you know more people in the village than I do. Can you think of anyone around here who'd look after a baby for the day?'

As if Jojo was the school hamster. Lost for words, Cressida gaped at Sacha. 'Um . . . well, no.'

'Oh, for crying out *loud*.' Sacha looked as if she might actually burst into tears. '*Bloody* Astrid. What have I done to deserve this?'

'Unless . . . I suppose I could take her,' Cressida offered hesitantly. 'If it would help.'

'*You?*' Sacha's eyes widened in disbelief.

Cressida, who'd seen the film *The Hand that Rocks the Cradle*, understood completely. 'It was just a thought. Of course you wouldn't want—'

'Oh my God. I can't believe it! Don't you have to work?'

Taken aback, Cressida said, 'It's my day off.'

'But this is brilliant! Why didn't you say so before?' Reaching over and flinging open the passenger door, Sacha yelled, 'Quick, jump in.'

And that had been it. Back at Sacha and Robert's house, Cressida learned that Jojo was only bellowing at the top of her voice because she hadn't been fed or changed this morning. Normally, Sacha explained, she was a placid, cheerful baby. Sacha, having showered and dressed at warp speed, left Cressida with the keys to the house and a shouted promise over her shoulder that she'd be back by six.

Cressida looked at Jojo, who was sitting on the living-room floor solemnly chewing a Farley's rusk. After several seconds, Jojo dropped the rusk and broke into a delighted grin, revealing two pearly white bottom teeth. Seemingly unconcerned at finding herself alone in the house with a virtual stranger, she held out her arms to Cressida.

'What is it, sweetheart?' Her heart melting, Cressida crouched down in front of her.

Still grinning, Jojo laboriously manoeuvred herself into a crawling position before clutching at Cressida's trouser leg in order to haul herself to her knees. Then she imperiously raised her arms again, like the Pope.

And Cressida picked her up.

'**A**unt Cress? It's me!'

The back door opened and banged shut, heralding Jojo's arrival. Cressida, now in the kitchen putting together a mushroom risotto, called out, 'In here, sweetheart,' then turned and opened her arms wide as Jojo bounced into the kitchen and gave her a kiss.

'Good day?' Cressida asked.

'Brilliant. Swimming, tennis and making fairy cakes. I was going to bring you some but we ate them.' As they both worked full time, Sacha and Robert paid for Jojo to attend a summer holiday scheme run by one of the private schools in Cheltenham. Luckily Jojo enjoyed it. Watching her at the sink as she ran the cold tap and glugged down a glass of water, Cressida experienced a rush of love for the girl who had brought more happiness into her life than any other person. Jojo was twelve now, with fine straggly dark hair, her mother's neat features and Robert's long legs.

'Are those from the garden?' Jojo had noticed the freesias in a vase on the kitchen table.

'No. Someone gave them to me.'

'Oo-er.' Jojo raised her eyebrows. 'Man or woman?'

'As it happens, a man.' Cressida tipped chopped onions into the frying pan and turned up the heat to maximum.

'Aunt Cress! Is he your new boyfriend?'

'I made a card for his mother. He wanted to thank me, that's all.'

'But he brought you flowers. Proper ones, from a shop,' Jojo emphasised, 'and he didn't have to do that, did he? So does that mean he'd *like* to be your new boyfriend?'

Time to change the subject. Vigorously stirring the onions in the pan Cressida said, 'I shouldn't think so for one minute. Now are you going to give me a hand with these mushrooms?'

'That's what I call changing the subject.'

'OK then, no, he definitely doesn't want to be my new boyfriend. And it's just as well because he lives two hundred miles away. And these mushrooms still need to be chopped.'

'But—'

'You know, I had such a lovely time this afternoon,' said Cressida. 'I was thinking back to the very first time I looked after you. You were ten months old and you couldn't talk at all.'

'Ten months.' This time Jojo was diverted; she loved hearing about the antics she'd got up to as a baby. 'Could I walk then?'

'No, but you were an Olympic crawler.'

After that first successful day, Cressida carried on baby-sitting whenever she was asked and helped out during emergencies. It was a situation everyone was happy with.

'What's the worst thing I ever did when I was little?' Jojo was at last slicing the mushrooms.

'The most embarrassing, you mean? Probably the time you took your nappy off in the middle of the supermarket and left it in the rice and pasta aisle.' Cressida paused, then said, 'It wasn't a clean nappy.'

'Euww!' Shaking her head and laughing, Jojo said, 'Tell me the best thing I ever did.'

Cressida pulled a face. 'Can't think of any.'

'That's not true! Tell me!'

'Oh, sweetheart. The best thing?' Abandoning the sizzling onions, Cressida enveloped Jojo in a hug. 'There are too many to count.'

Chapter 3

'I WANT YOU TO FIND these people.' Freddie drew a sheet of paper from his jacket pocket and unfolded it.

There were four names written in Freddie's distinctive scrawl.

'Who are they?' Lottie asked.

'People who were important to me. People I liked.' Freddie half smiled. 'People who one way or another shaped my life. God, does that sound completely nauseating?'

'A bit. It's kind of like those schmaltzy soft-focus films you get on daytime TV.' Lottie secretly loved those kind of films.

'Well, if it's any consolation, I'm the one who wants to see them again,' said Freddie. 'There's no guarantee they're going to want to see me.'

'And do I get the back story? Are you going to tell me why they were so important?'

'Not yet.' Freddie looked amused. 'I thought I'd wait until you found them. That way, I know you'll be giving it your best shot.'

Lottie pulled a face; she was incurably nosy and he knew it. 'I'll need more details. How old they are, where they've lived in the past, what kind of work they did.'

'I'll give you as much information as I can.'

The first mystery person on the list was ridiculously easy to trace. It took less than five minutes. His name was Jeff Barrowcliffe and he owned and ran a motorcycle repair shop in Exmouth.

'That'll be him,' Freddie said confidently, peering over Lottie's shoulder at the computer screen. 'Jeff was always obsessed with motorbikes.'

In order to make sure, Lottie sent an email:

Dear Mr Barrowcliffe,
On behalf of a friend of mine who is trying to trace someone with your name, may I ask if your date of birth is December 26, 1940, and if, many years ago, you lived in Oxford?
Yours, L. Carlyle

Like magic, his reply popped into her inbox ninety seconds later:

Yes, that's me. Why?

Lottie flexed her fingers like a pianist over the keys. 'Want me to tell him?'

'No. I'll give him a ring.' Freddie had already scribbled down the repair shop's phone number featured on the website. Walking out of the office, he added, 'In private.'

'Is he going to be pleased to hear from you?'

Freddie waggled his phone. 'That's what I'm about to find out.'

He was back ten minutes later, his expression infuriatingly enigmatic.

Fixing Freddie with a get-on-with-it look, Lottie said, '*So?*'

'So what?'

'Jeff Barrowcliffe. You have to tell me, remember? Are you going to meet him?'

Freddie nodded. 'I'm driving down to Exmouth this weekend.'

'You see?' Delighted, Lottie clapped her hands. 'So he was glad to hear from you! Why did you think he wouldn't be?'

'Because I took his motorbike,' said Freddie. 'His pride and joy.'

'Big deal.'

'And crashed it. Completely wrote it off. His girlfriend was on the back at the time. The one he was going to marry.'

'Freddie! Oh God, she didn't—?'

'No, Giselle didn't die. Cuts and bruises, that's all. Bloody lucky.'

Relieved, Lottie said, 'Well, that's all right then.'

'That's what Jeff thought. Until I stole her from him.' His smile crooked, Freddie looked at the stunned expression on Lottie's face. 'So there you go. And you always thought I was a nice person. Just goes to show, doesn't it? You never can tell.'

It was Saturday lunchtime and Jojo was sunbathing in her Aunt Cress's back garden, reading the latest edition of *Phew!* magazine and listening to Avril Lavigne on her CD Walkman. Her parents were hosting a barbecue this afternoon and their house and garden were overrun with caterers, because it wasn't the kind of bash where you just invited all your friends and neighbours and had a jolly time. As usual, her mum and dad's party was an opportunity to network and make important new business connections. Impressing potential clients would be the order of the day; actually enjoying yourself—heaven forbid!—didn't feature on the agenda. When Jojo had suggested coming over to Aunt Cress's house instead, her mother had heaved a visible sigh of relief and said, 'That's a wonderful idea, darling. It wouldn't be much fun for you here.'

Jojo had been glad to leave and Aunt Cress had been delighted to see her. The sun was out and once Jojo was settled on the sun lounger in her blue cropped top and mauve striped shorts, Cressida had shot off to the supermarket for a speedy stock-up.

Jojo finished the article she was reading, about a girl who had a crush on her physics teacher. Avril Lavigne was getting repetitive and the rest of her CDs were in her bag in the kitchen. Chucking down the magazine and making her way into the house, it wasn't until Jojo unplugged herself from the Walkman that she heard the doorbell ringing.

By the time she opened the front door the callers had given up and were making their way down the street. Jojo, watching them from the doorstep, wondered if she should call out to them. Then, as if sensing she was there behind him, the man turned and saw her. He said something to the boy with him and came hurrying back.

'Hi there.' The man's manner was friendly. 'We thought there was no one home. I was ringing the bell for ages.'

'Sorry, I was out in the garden.' Jojo pointed helpfully at her ears. 'Walkman.'

'Ah yes, my son's got one of those.' The man indicated the boy behind him, loitering by the gate. 'You must be Jojo. Is your . . . um, Cressida in?'

'She's gone shopping.' Since Aunt Cress didn't exactly have hordes of strange men hammering at her door, Jojo had a shrewd idea who this one might be. With renewed interest she said, 'Are you the flower man?'

It was his turn to look confused. 'Flower man?'

'The one who bought a card and gave Aunt Cress flowers the other day, to say thank you.'

'Oh right, of course.' His face cleared.

Eager to be helpful, Jojo said, 'Did you want to buy another card?'

'Well, not exactly.'

'What is it then? If you give me a message I'll make sure she gets it.'

'Um . . . just tell her I'll ring later.'

The man went a bit red and Jojo realised he was embarrassed. As he shuffled his feet and made a move to leave, it suddenly struck her that he'd come here to invite Aunt Cress out on a date. Crikey, she'd teased her about it after the incident with the flowers but she'd actually been right! Galvanised by this discovery—and by the problems page she'd just read in *Phew!* where a girl had written in miserably wanting to know why boys always said they'd ring you but never did—Jojo knew that whatever happened she mustn't let this one slip away.

'Or I could write down your number and Aunt Cress can ring you,' she said briskly, grabbing a notebook and pen from the hall table.

'Um . . .'

'Or we could fix a time for a meeting now. I know for a fact that Aunt Cress is free this evening.'

'Well . . .'

Desperate not to let him escape—even now, he was looking as if he might bottle out and make a dash for the gate—Jojo thrust the notebook and pen at his chest and blurted out, 'Here, just write down your name and phone number, then she'll—'

'Excuse me.' The man's son, still leaning against the gate with his baseball cap pulled low over his eyes, drawled, 'Are you always this bossy?'

Jojo bristled.

His father turned and said, 'Donny, there's no need to be rude.'

'I'm not rude.' Donny shrugged sulkily. 'I just asked a question.'

'And I'm not bossy.' Jojo's jaw tightened.

He raised his eyebrows. 'Have you been listening to yourself?'

'Donny!'

Ignoring his father, Donny said, 'My dad came here to ask your aunt out on a date.'

'I know that,' Jojo retorted. 'I was just being helpful.'

'Helpful? You've scared the living daylights out of him. As if he wasn't finding it hard enough already.'

Bewildered, the boy's father looked at Jojo. 'You knew? *How* did you know?'

'Look.' Jojo heatedly addressed the boy at the gate. 'It's not my fault Aunt Cress isn't here. But what if your dad said he'd call back later and he didn't? All I was trying to do was get something organised, something he couldn't back out of.'

'My dad doesn't back out of anything, OK?'

'Now, now.' Recovering himself, the boy's father clapped his hands. 'Stop it, you two.'

'She started it,' Donny muttered under his breath.

'Donny, please. Now, let's start again.' Fixing Jojo with a look that was determined rather than panic-stricken he said, 'Yes, I came round here to ask your Aunt Cress if she'd like to come out to dinner with me, but—'

'Tonight?'

'Whenever suits her best. But as she's not here, I'll call her later. And that's a promise.'

'Tonight would be fine.' Still determined to close the deal, Jojo said, 'They do brilliant food at the Red Lion in Gresham. It's only a couple of miles from here. Wicked sticky toffee pudding. Shall I say you'll pick Aunt Cress up at seven o'clock?'

Stunned, the man said, 'But I haven't even asked her yet. She might not want to have dinner with me.'

'Oh, she will.' Jojo was confident on this score. 'Aunt Cress hasn't been out with anyone for ages. She doesn't have much luck with men.'

A flicker of a smile crossed his face. 'I'm sure she'd be thrilled to hear you saying that.'

'It's the truth.' Jojo decided he seemed nice. 'She always goes for the wrong kind. So, seven o'clock then. I'll make sure she's ready on time.'

He was definitely looking amused now. 'And what about you?'

'Me? Oh, I don't go for any kind at all. I'm only twelve.' Jojo's tone was matter-of-fact. 'Basically, all boys are dorks.'

At the gate, Donny snorted.

'I meant do you have anything planned for this evening, or would you like to join us?' The man briefly indicated Donny. 'Make up the numbers. I'm sure Donny would enjoy having someone of his own age to chat to.'

Donny looked as though he'd enjoy it about as much as performing the Birdy Dance on stage during school assembly. Jojo couldn't imagine the dinner being much fun either. On the other hand, what if Aunt Cress refused to go out with Donny's dad because she didn't want to leave Jojo on her own? The alternative would be going home and having to endure the barbeque from hell.

Really, there was no contest.

'OK, that'll be great. Thanks.' As Jojo beamed at him she heard another snort of derision emanating from Donny.

'That's settled then.' Looking a lot happier now, Donny's father said, 'I'll book the table for seven thirty.' Jovially he added, 'Sticky toffee puddings all round!'

'You what?' Cressida dumped the supermarket carriers on the kitchen table and stared open-mouthed at Jojo.

'I've got you a date.' Jojo was looking pleased with herself.

Aaarrgh. 'Who with?'

'The man who brought you flowers.'

'What?'

'*Duh*, like they're queuing up.' Grinning, Jojo said, 'You know who I mean. And you're having dinner with him this evening at the Red Lion in Gresham.'

'*This* evening?' Cressida slumped onto a kitchen chair. 'But . . . what about you? I can't just leave you here.'

'No need. I'm coming along too.' Jojo began unpacking the carriers.

Faintly, Cressida said, 'You are?'

'Me and Donny. The sulky brat, remember? We're coming along to keep an eye on you, make sure you two behave yourselves. Isn't it great? I told you he fancied you. Can I have some of this ice cream?'

Cressida nodded, her mind a whirl. It was only a dinner date, for heaven's sake, and a foursome at that. But her foolish old heart was nevertheless skipping around like Bambi in her chest. Tom Turner had been in her thoughts far more than he should have been these past few days.

'Oh God, what shall I wear?' Cressida blurted out, realising that the more ancient and out of practice you were, the longer you needed to get ready for a date. 'My eyebrows need plucking and my hair's all horrible.'

Jojo had abandoned the unpacking and was leaning against the fridge eating lemon meringue ice cream straight from the tub with a teaspoon. 'Aunt Cress, he's not exactly Johnny Depp. You'll be fine.'

'I know.' Cressida ran her fingers through her hair, which was badly in need of a cut. 'But I still don't want him to run away screaming.'

'He's not expecting a supermodel,' Jojo reasoned. 'Just do your best.'

So young, so cruel. So right.

'OK,' said Cressida.

'**W**hat did you do that for?' Donny frowned. 'It's boring out here.'

Jojo rolled her eyes and wondered how he could be so thick. As soon as their drinks order had arrived she had insisted on dragging Donny out into the Red Lion's garden. 'I was being subtle. I just thought we could give your dad and my aunt a bit of time alone together, that's all.'

'Yeah yeah.' Donny exhaled noisily. 'But what's the point? We're down here on holiday. Next week we'll be back in Newcastle.'

'So? They like each other. What's wrong with that? I know nothing's going to come of it because you live so far away, but there's no reason why they can't see each other a couple of times and leave it at that. Think of it as a practice run. Aunt Cress has had really bad luck with men, so it makes a change to see her with someone decent. And your dad's probably out of practice too.' She paused, then said, 'Or is that the problem? You don't want him to see anyone at all?'

Donny looked down at his trainers. Finally he said, 'It's not that. It just feels funny, that's all. My mum walked out on us two years ago.'

'I know. Aunt Cress told me.'

'And I know he'll probably get married again one day, but what if he chooses someone I hate? I mean, it's not like I'll have any say in the matter, is it? My friend Greg's parents got divorced and they both remarried, and Greg can't stand his stepmother *or* his stepfather.'

Feeling sorry for him Jojo said, 'But your dad might marry someone you do like. It doesn't have to be bad. I know it's the wrong way round, but my dad used to be married to Aunt Cress and I love her to bits.'

'Your dad used to be married to her? What, before you were born?' Donny frowned, working it out. 'That's weird.'

'It isn't weird. She's brilliant. I'm lucky,' Jojo insisted.

Donny picked at the loose threads around a rip in his baggy jeans. 'I bet I wouldn't be lucky, I'm never—'

'Smile!'

'What?' Looking up, he saw that Jojo was beaming at him like a lunatic. 'Look happy,' Jojo instructed, her beam unwavering. 'Aunt Cress is looking out of the window. Just make out we're fine.'

'Why?'

'Honestly, you're so thick. Because then they can relax and enjoy themselves without having to worry about us.'

'Jesus, I wish I'd brought my GameBoy,' Donny grumbled, although he did attempt something that from a distance would pass as a grin. 'You are seriously weird.'

'They're fine. Laughing and chatting away together like old friends,' Cressida announced cheerfully. 'They're probably far happier being out in the garden than stuck in here with the old fogeys. Not that you're an old fogey,' Cressida said hastily as Tom's eyebrows rose.

He smiled. 'Neither are you.'

'Although I'm sure Donny and Jojo think we are.'

'Oh well, goes without saying.'

Cressida didn't think of herself as an old fogey, not *quite*, but it was still much nicer being inside the pub, sitting at a table in the restaurant section with candles casting a romantic glow. As she settled herself back down she felt a matching warm glow in her stomach from the wine. Tom looked nicely unwrinkly too. In fact he looked nice full stop. And the cooking smells wafting through from the kitchen were mouth-watering.

'Well, I'm glad we came here. You made a good choice,' Cressida said happily.

'Don't thank me, thank Jojo. It was her idea.' Tom grinned. 'She told me what time to pick you up and where to bring you. I just did as I was told.'

'Then I'm glad about that too. Unless you're hating every minute.'

'Now why would I be doing that? I'm enjoying this holiday more than I ever imagined.' Leaning closer he confided, 'Just think, if it hadn't been my mother's birthday this week we'd never have met.'

Feeling deliciously reckless and the teeniest bit light-headed, Cressida raised her glass. 'In that case, here's to your mother.'

'My mother.' Clinking his glass against hers, Tom said, 'And to you.'

'To me.' Cressida clinked again. 'And to *you*.' As she gazed into his eyes she wished with all her heart he didn't have to live so far away. Then she told herself that she really mustn't drink any more wine on an empty stomach. 'Do you think we should order some food? I'll go and find out what Jojo and Donny want to eat and then you can tell me all about Newcastle.'

Tom looked amused. 'It's not that exotic.'

It's got you, Cressida thought as she got up from the table with the kind of squirly excitement she hadn't felt since she was a teenager, and that's exotic enough for me.

Freddie set off down the M5 after breakfast on Sunday morning. If the traffic ran smoothly he'd reach Exmouth in a couple of hours. Buzzing down the car window, he lit a cigar and determinedly ignored the persistent headache that these days settled over him like a lead helmet each morning. He was looking forward to seeing Jeff again, but apprehensive as well. Jeff had been taciturn on the phone, clearly taken aback at hearing a voice from the past—and a not particularly welcome voice at that.

Well, that was understandable. But Freddie hoped they could overcome the awkwardness, put the bad bits behind them, and recapture at least some semblance of their childhood friendship. Then, the bond between them had seemed unbreakable. But one fateful night was all it had taken to slash that bond, and after that their lives had changed for ever. Jeff had suffered then, without a doubt. But had he continued to suffer for the last forty years? Freddie didn't know the answer and deliberately hadn't asked the all-important question during their brief conversation on the phone the other day, but he was about to find out.

Of course, Jeff had always had a hot temper. He might be about to find out the hard way.

Then again, Freddie thought, maybe I deserve it.

'**H**e's drunk.' Giselle had gestured in disgust. 'Drunk as a skunk. He can't even walk, let alone ride that bike home tonight. But he needs it for work tomorrow, and if Derek gives Jeff a lift, that leaves the bike here and me with no way of getting home. It's eight *miles*,' she concluded desperately. 'I can't walk all that way on my own.'

Tonight they had all come out to a party in Abingdon, held at a pub with a reputation for lock-ins. Freddie had got a lift with Derek, five of them having crammed into Derek's black Morris Minor. Jeff and Giselle had arrived on Jeff's motorbike, his prized Norton 350.

And now Jeff was incapable of riding it home.

Freddie gazed at Giselle in her cherry-red top and full red-and-white spotted skirt, her dark hair tied back in a high ponytail.

'Jeff can go back with Derek and the others. I'll take his bike home and drop you off on the way. How about that?'

'Would you?' Giselle's eyes lit up with relief. 'Oh, Freddie, that's great.'

Jeff was duly carried out of the pub and poured into the passenger seat of Derek's Morris Minor.

'Why does he do it?' Giselle said helplessly as the car's rear lights disappeared from view. 'He's so lovely the rest of the time. Then every couple of months he just goes off on a complete bender. It's so pointless.'

It was, but Freddie couldn't bring himself to admit it. Jeff was Jeff and he wasn't going to be disloyal towards his best friend. Instead he said with forced cheerfulness, 'He'll be fine in the morning. Everyone has a few too many every now and again. Come on, let's get you home.'

They were heading back to Oxford along the deserted A34 when a fox darted into the road ahead of them. Braking violently and swerving to avoid the animal, Freddie felt the back wheel of the powerful Norton begin to slide sideways beneath him. After that it all seemed to happen in slow motion. He heard Giselle scream as he lost control of the bike and the next thing he knew they were careering towards a wall.

Impact was sudden, noisy and brutal. Giselle, catapulted off the back of the bike, landed with a sickening thud on the other side of the wall. By some miracle Freddie found himself flung sideways onto the grass verge. Pain shot through every inch of his body but he told himself that at least he could still feel pain. Stumbling to his feet, he made his way dazedly over to the drystone wall and croaked, 'Giselle? Are you all right?'

Nothing. Just an eerie silence punctuated by the hiss of steam escaping from the engine of the Norton. Somehow in the pitch darkness Freddie managed to clamber over the wall into the field where she lay. Finally he heard her gasp, as she struggled to sit up.

'Giselle! Oh God . . .'

'I'm OK. I think. I landed on some rocks. My leg hurts,' Giselle whispered, her breath catching in her throat. 'And my back.'

When Freddie touched her arm he found it sticky with blood and his heart turned over. He had almost killed the girl he loved, the girl who was engaged to be married to his closest friend. 'Oh God, what have I done?'

'Written off Jeff's bike by the sound of things.' Giselle murmured the words with difficulty as the ominous hissing noise intensified.

Shortly afterwards Freddie flagged down a passing motorist who took them both to the casualty department at the Radcliffe Infirmary. While they were waiting to be seen by the doctor, Giselle told Freddie over and over again that it wasn't his fault. With tears in his eyes Freddie shook his head and said, 'I couldn't bear it if anything happened to you.'

The next thing he knew, right there in the middle of the casualty department, with blood trickling down her arms and her cherry-red top muddy and torn, Giselle was kissing him. When the kiss finally ended she held his face gently between her hands, saw the long-hidden truth in his eyes and whispered, 'Oh, Freddie, don't you see? It already has.'

Glancing down at the blood-spattered cluster of diamond chips on her left hand, Giselle announced, 'The engagement's off.'

That was how it had happened. Overnight Freddie's life had changed. Having done such an excellent job of concealing his true feelings for Giselle during the course of the last eight months, he now found himself faced with the prospect of announcing them to the world in general and Jeff in particular. As they were leaving the casualty department at three thirty that morning, stitched up and bandaged like a couple of mummies, Giselle said, 'I'll tell Jeff today, OK? That it's all over between us and from now on I'm with you.'

'Right.' Freddie nodded and swallowed hard. Tomorrow Jeff would find out that his fiancée had chucked him and that his beloved 1959 Norton Model 50 350 was a write-off.

He would also discover who Giselle had left him *for*.

Freddie didn't sleep terribly well that night.

Jeff Barrowcliffe lived in a 1930s bungalow painted sky blue and adorned with bright hanging baskets and window boxes. As Freddie clicked open the front gate he saw Jeff on the driveway at the side of the bungalow, tinkering with the engine of a motorbike. It was ridiculous to say he hadn't changed a bit, but he was still instantly recognisable—albeit bald, wirier and more wrinkled.

Straightening up, Jeff wiped his hands on an oily rag and waited for Freddie to reach him. They'd never hugged each other in their lives and Freddie wasn't sure he had the courage to now. Thankfully, by clutching the oily rag in front of him, Jeff ensured this wasn't an option.

'Jeff. It's good to see you again.'

'You too. Took me back the other day, hearing from you out of the blue like that.' Rubbing a grimy hand over his tanned head, Jeff said, 'Still don't know why you called.'

'Curiosity, I suppose. We're all getting on a bit now,' Freddie shrugged, 'and none of us is going to live for ever. I just wanted to find out what happened to my old friends.'

Jeff said drily, 'Lost touch with a fair few of them then, have you?'

Since he deserved the jibe, Freddie simply nodded. 'Yes.' Then he said, 'The other reason I'm here is to apologise.'

'The last time I saw you, you were flat on your back and I had bruised knuckles.' There was a glimmer of a smile on Jeff's face as he recalled the occasion. 'Do I have to apologise as well?'

'No. I deserved it.' The memory of that day was etched indelibly in Freddie's mind. Giselle had told Jeff about the incident the night before, then had gone on to announce that their engagement was off and she and Freddie were now an item. Jeff had come round and hammered on his front door demanding to see him and Freddie had gone down to face him. Under the circumstances, it had seemed the least he could do.

That was the last any of them had seen of Jeff. He had packed a rucksack, left Oxford that same night and joined the army.

'Coming in for a cup of tea?' Jeff said now.

'I'd love that.' Freddie nodded. There was so much to catch up on, he barely knew where to start. Prompted by the abundance of hanging baskets he said, 'Are you married?'

'Oh, yes. Thirty-three years, two daughters, four grandkids. The wife's not here today.' As he led the way into the bungalow Jeff said over his shoulder, 'Thought it best to keep her out of the way while you're around. Wouldn't want you running off with her.'

Freddie saw that he was joking and relaxed. 'Those days are long gone.'

'How about you then?' In the tidy kitchen Jeff set about making a proper, old-fashioned pot of tea. 'Did you end up getting married too?'

'Yes.' Freddie nodded, then said drily, 'But not to Giselle.'

'So you got your nose broken for nothing.'

'We just weren't right for each other. Well, we were only kids. Twenty years old—everyone makes mistakes. Thanks.' Freddie took the cup of tea Jeff was offering him and reached for the sugar bowl.

'They do that right enough.' Nodding in agreement, Jeff lit a cigarette. 'And now we've got our kids making mistakes of their own.'

'We didn't have children. It never happened. But I married the most wonderful girl. We were so very happy.' A lump materialised in his throat. 'Almost forty years of marriage before she died four years ago.'

'I'm very sorry your wife died,' said Jeff. 'But you've still got your own hair and teeth. Might meet someone else.'

'That won't happen.' Freddie had no intention of telling Jeff about his illness; the last thing he was here for was sympathy. But talking about Mary had affected him more than he'd expected.

Evidently having noticed that he was struggling to control his emotions, Jeff said, 'How about a drop of brandy in that tea?'

Freddie nodded. 'Sorry. Sometimes it catches you off guard. Ridiculous.' Breathing out slowly, he watched as Jeff fetched a bottle of cognac from one of the kitchen cupboards and sloshed a generous measure into his cup. 'Aren't you having one?'

Jeff returned the bottle to the cupboard and sat back down.

'Not for me. I gave up the drink about two years after I last saw you. Mind you, I drank twenty years' worth in that time.'

'In the army?'

'Bloody hell, especially in the army. Then I got myself another girlfriend and she ended up leaving me too. Said I was a drunken waste of space. Funnily enough, so did the next one and the one after that.' Pausing to drink his tea, Jeff said, 'In the end, I suppose it just hit me one morning that they might be right.'

'So you stopped? Just like that?'

'There and then. I'm not saying it was easy, but I did it. And life's been good to me. Can't ask for more than that, can you?'

'And there was me, wondering if I'd ruined it.' For Freddie, the relief was tremendous.

'You weren't my favourite person for a while. But that's all in the past.'

'Good. You don't know how glad I am to hear it.' Closure, Freddie realised. This was what he'd so badly needed. Feeling better than he had in weeks, he smiled across the table at the friend he hadn't seen for so many years. 'Now, I hope you'll let me take you out to lunch.'

'It's been a great day.' Tired but happy, Freddie hadn't been able to resist calling into Piper's Cottage on his way home that evening. Lottie, who had just finished putting Nat and Ruby to bed, gave him a hug and opened a bottle of wine.

Freddie then launched into how he and Jeff had gone to lunch and caught up with each other's lives. All in all, the reunion had been a stupendous success and the difference in Freddie was heart-warming.

When the wine was finished, Lottie said, 'So who are we going to look for next? Giselle?'

Freddie's eyes twinkled. 'Giselle.'

Consumed with curiosity, there was something else Lottie was desperate to know. 'You were in love with her. But you broke up. Why?'

'Ah, well. Something happened,' said Freddie. He rose to his feet, collected his car keys and bent to kiss Lottie's cheek. 'I'm afraid I was a bad boy. Again.'

'If you don't tell me,' said Lottie, 'I won't find her for you.'

He smiled. 'I broke Giselle's heart. She thought I was about to propose and I finished with her instead.'

'Why?'

Freddie turned in the doorway. 'Because I'd fallen head over heels in love with someone else.'

Chapter 4

IT WAS SEPTEMBER THE FIRST and Lottie was in the office dealing with a mountain of post when Tyler, just back from a short trip to New York, came through the door.

God, it was fantastic to see him again. In a white polo shirt and Levi's he was looking tanned, handsome and not remotely jet-lagged. There was no doubt about it, a boss who made her mouth go dry and her heart go *twaanng* was a definite bonus.

'Hi there.' Tyler nodded at the pile of post. 'You look busy.'

'You're my new employer,' said Lottie. 'It's my job to make you think I'm busy.'

He grinned. 'You know what? I've missed you.'

Heavens, how was she supposed to respond to *that*? If he thought she was going to tell him she'd missed him too, he could think again.

'And now you're back,' Lottie said brightly, wondering what was in the glossy dark blue carrier bag at his feet.

'Oh, right.' Following her gaze, Tyler reached down and began to delve into it. 'I called into FAO Schwarz while I was in New York. Picked up something for Nat and Ruby to make up for what happened the other week.' Tyler pulled out two lavishly gift-wrapped parcels.

Deeply touched, Lottie said, 'Oh, you didn't have to do that.'

'Call it bribery.' He looked amused. 'If this is what it takes to get into their good books, that's fine by me. And, actually, I wondered if you were free this evening. Maybe we could go out for dinner. Then when I call round to pick you up, I could give Nat and Ruby their presents.'

Lottie thought for a second, then nodded. 'That'd be great.' In fact it was doubly great, because if Mario was looking after the kids he couldn't be out getting up to mischief while Amber was away in St Tropez.

'We'll do that then.' Tyler looked pleased. 'Say, seven thirty?'

'**M**um, I hate that man. Don't go out with him,' begged Nat when he discovered who Lottie was seeing that evening.

'Sweetheart, I told you, he's really very nice.' Lottie concentrated on making up her face in the bathroom mirror.

'He isn't nice, he tells *lies*.'

'OK.' Lottie sighed. 'I wasn't going to tell you this, but Tyler's bought you a present. Does that make you like him a bit more?'

Mercenary? Her son?

Nat's whole face lit up. 'What kind of present?'

'I don't know, he's bringing it over tonight. But if you hate him, maybe you shouldn't—'

Outraged by the unfairness of this revelation, Ruby said indignantly, 'Why is Nat getting a present and not me?'

'He's bought something for you too.'

Mercenary? Her daughter?

'*Has* he? What's he got me?'

'No idea. He just told me he'd been to this place in New York called Schwarz and—'

'Schwarz? Ruby leapt up from the edge of the bath, her eyes wide with delight. 'FAO Schwarz on *Fifth Avenue*?'

Bemused, Lottie said, 'How do you know that?'

'Mum! It's like the best toy shop in the whole world *ever*,' Nat gabbled. 'We saw a programme about it on CBBC, it's *amazing*.'

'Better than Disneyland,' Ruby chimed in.

Aware that they were envisaging Tyler pulling up outside the cottage in some kind of ribbon-strewn articulated truck loaded to the roof with extravagant gifts, Lottie said hastily, 'Listen, you're getting one present each. Although, like I said before, if you think Tyler's so horrible, I wonder if you deserve them.'

'If he's brought them all the way from New York, I think we should let him give them to us,' said Ruby. 'Otherwise his feelings might be hurt.'

'And if he bought them at FAO Schwarz,' Nat added seriously, 'they'll be really brilliant presents that cost loads of money.'

Mercenary? Her children?

'So I'm allowed to go out to dinner with him?' said Lottie.

'I think you should.' Ruby nodded and Nat joined in.

'Well, hooray for that. And remember,' Lottie warned them, 'manners. Whatever he's bought you, make sure that you look really pleased and—'

Rolling their eyes, Nat and Ruby chorused, 'Say thank you.'

The mercenaries were hanging out of Nat's bedroom window when Tyler pulled up outside the cottage. At the front door he murmured to Lottie, 'Nat and Ruby just waved to me. Didn't throw stones or anything.'

Lottie so wanted her children to overcome their antipathy towards Tyler. They had got off to an unfortunate start, but with luck—and presents— that was behind them now.

'Hey, you two,' Tyler greeted them easily as Nat and Ruby, looking suitably angelic, appeared at the top of the stairs. 'How are you doing?'

'OK.' Nat was wide-eyed, making a huge effort not to gaze at the gift-wrapped presents Tyler was holding.

'Very well, thank you.' Ruby was being ultra-polite. 'Did you have a nice time in America?'

'I had a great time. And guess what? I brought you each a little something. This one's for you,' Tyler held the parcel in his right hand towards Ruby. 'And this one's for you,' he extended the other towards Nat.

Together they came clattering down the stairs, took their parcels and said courteously, 'Thank you, Mr Klein.'

'My pleasure.' Tyler looked as delighted as if he'd just won an Oscar. 'And please, call me Tyler.'

Lottie led them all into the living room and crossed her fingers behind her back as Ruby and Nat began tearing into the wrappings.

Oh no. Oh God.

'Of course I had no idea what to get you,' Tyler was telling Ruby, 'but there was a really helpful saleswoman who said this would be perfect.'

Act, Lottie silently begged, *act like you've never acted before*. She willed her thoughts to be transmitted to Ruby as her daughter gazed at the Perspex case containing a rosy-cheeked china doll in Victorian clothes.

Some nine-year-old girls adored dolls, maybe some even liked the kind you kept in a Perspex case and couldn't play with. The only dolls Ruby had ever shown the remotest interest in were the voodoo kind.

'It's lovely,' Ruby said bravely, her chin wobbling with the effort of concealing her disappointment. 'Thank you, Mr Klein.'

'Tyler,' said Tyler, blithely unaware that he couldn't have chosen a worse present if he'd tried. 'I'm glad you like it.'

'She's beautiful,' Lottie blurted out before an awkward silence had a chance to develop. 'Ruby, aren't you lucky? Now, how's Nat getting along?' Turning to her son, she said brightly, 'What have you got there?'

The last layer of paper tore open at last and Lottie's heart plummeted.

'Warhammer,' said Nat, his tone expressionless. 'Thank you, Mr Klein.'

Warhammer, oh God. Requiring super-honed concentration skills, nimble fingers and endless patience—qualities Nat simply didn't possess.

'The saleswoman told me all the kids are just wild about it,' Tyler announced with pride. 'They spend hours glueing the little models together and painting them.'

Nat really looked as if he might cry. Hurriedly Lottie said, 'Isn't that fantastic? You'll *love* making all those little models, won't you?'

Nat nodded, stroking the lid of the box to demonstrate how much he loved it. In a small, wavering voice he said, 'Yes.'

'Hi, I'm here.' The front door swung open and Mario announced his arrival. 'Sorry I'm a bit late—Amber just rang. She's having a great time and sends her love. Hi, you must be Tyler.' A tall male shook Tyler's hand. 'Mario. Crikey, what's going on here?' He looked at Nat and Ruby miserably clutching their presents. 'I didn't know it was Christmas.'

'It's not.' Abandoning her present, Ruby ran into his arms. 'Daddy, can we climb trees tonight?'

'And hunt for snakes?' begged Nat.

'Right, we'll be off.' Eager to get away while the going was good, Lottie grabbed and kissed each of them in turn. 'Have a great time.'

'You too,' said Mario with a wink. 'Don't be late.'

It was a great evening. The smart restaurant in Painswick had been an inspired choice. Over dinner, Lottie got to know Tyler better and was liking him more and more. By eleven o'clock they were heading back into Hestacombe. Nat and Ruby would be fast asleep, Mario could leave and she could invite Tyler in for coffee. Just coffee, nothing else. Well, maybe a kiss wouldn't hurt, but definitely no more than that.

Then the front door burst open, spilling light and children into the garden, and that was the end of that idea.

She glanced apologetically at Tyler. 'They're supposed to be asleep.'

'No problem. They're looking pretty pleased with themselves,' he observed indulgently. 'Maybe they've been painting the Warhammer models and want to show me what they've done.'

Hmm, and maybe their new favourite food was mustard and sprouts.

Jumping out of the car, Lottie said, 'Why aren't you two in bed?'

'Dad said we didn't have to because we don't go back to school until next week. We had the best time tonight,' Nat gabbled, throwing his arms round her waist and kangarooing up and down in his excitement. 'Mum, guess what happened? You'll never guess!'

Lottie loved it so much when he was overcome with enthusiasm that she couldn't be cross with Mario for letting them stay up. 'You brushed your teeth without being asked?'

Nat looked incredulous. 'No!'

'OK, I give up.' As Nat attempted to drag her into the cottage—it was like being hauled along by a small determined tractor—Lottie called over her shoulder to Tyler, 'Coming in for a bit?' Oops, that didn't sound quite right. 'I mean, for a coffee?'

'Just try to stop me.' He locked the car and followed them up the path and into the cottage. 'I want to know what's happened.'

'It's in the kitchen,' Ruby gabbled, jumping up and down excitedly,

'I can't stand the suspense,' exclaimed Lottie, crossing the living room. 'Are you going to show me, or—'

'Jesus!' shouted Tyler, his leg kicking out. Startled, Lottie blinked and saw something dark whip past her field of vision. Before anyone could move, the object hit the opposite wall with a noise between a slap and a thud. Faster than the speed of light, Tyler reached out and grabbed Ruby and Nat. 'OK, kids, get out of here and run upstairs.'

'What *is* it?' shouted Lottie, because whatever it was had slid down the living-room wall and disappeared behind the bookcase.

'Oh hell,' Mario sighed, heading towards the bookcase.

'Daddy, Daddy, was that Bernard?' Ducking back under Tyler's arm, Ruby's voice reverberated with fear. Having rushed over to join Mario she began furiously hurling books willy-nilly from the shelves. 'Bernard, where are you? It's all right, you can come out now.'

Bewildered, but with an ominous sense of foreboding, Lottie said, 'Who's Bernard?'

'Our surprise.' Ruby was too busy burrowing through the bookcase to look up. 'We found him in the woods tonight and Dad said we could keep him . . . oh, Bernard, where are you? It's OK, don't be scared.'

'Will somebody please tell me who Bernard *is*?' Lottie demanded.

'A snake.' Tyler shook his head. 'I felt something on my foot and when I looked down I saw a snake. Kicking out like that was a reflex, When I was growing up we spent a lot of time in Wyoming—if you get bitten by a rattler you can die.'

'We don't have rattlers here,' Mario said evenly. 'Bernard's a slow-worm. Slow-worms are harmless,' he went on. 'They don't bite. In fact they're not even snakes, they're legless lizards that live in—*ah*.'

Lottie didn't need to ask what that *ah* meant. She knew. In disbelief she clutched Nat to her side as Mario reached behind the lowest shelf of the bookcase and slowly withdrew Bernard. The slow-worm was clearly dead. Kneeling on the floor next to her father, tears sprang into Ruby's dark eyes and a cry of anguish escaped her lips. She reached for Bernard and cradled his limp body in her lap.

'Oh shit,' murmured Tyler, ashen now.

Lottie couldn't bear it. Just when she'd thought everything was going to be all right, something else had to happen.

'Look, I'm sorry.' Tyler heaved a sigh. 'But when I looked down I wasn't expecting to see a snake on my foot.'

'He shouldn't have been on your foot,' Lottie declared. 'He was supposed to be in the kitchen. Why wasn't the kitchen door shut?'

'We put him in a cardboard box with straw in it.' Nat's bottom lip trembled. 'He wasn't supposed to climb out. I just opened the lid a tiny bit so he could breathe.'

'I'm sorry.' Tyler tried again. 'I didn't mean to kill him.' In desperation he said, 'Listen, I'll buy you another snake. Any kind you like.'

Tears were dripping from the end of Ruby's nose onto the dead slow-worm in her lap. With a huge sniff she turned to look at Tyler. 'I don't want you to buy me another snake. You'd probably buy a really horrible one with a china face and a lace bonnet on its head and old-fashioned clothes. And even if you bought me a real python I wouldn't want it because I hate you, and I hate that stupid doll you gave me *and* you killed Bernard. I don't want you to come to our house ever, *ever* again.'

Tyler thought about this. Finally he nodded. Turning, he murmured to Lottie, 'I'll see you at work tomorrow.'

Numbly, Lottie nodded.

'And I don't want you going out with my mum,' Nat flung at him.

Tyler didn't reply.

'And I hated my Warhammer models too,' he bellowed after Tyler as he headed for the door.

Lottie didn't bother following Tyler. Tonight probably wasn't the night for that all-important first kiss.

Cressida was reading Tom's email for the fourth time and it had only arrived in her inbox a few minutes ago.

Hi Cressida,

Just a quick note to let you know how much my mother appreciated the card. So thanks again for coming to the rescue.

It was great to meet you last week. I really enjoyed the time we spent together. I'm sure Donny did too, but he would of course rather amputate his own feet than admit it.

Well, I'm now back at work and wishing I wasn't. That's the trouble with holidays, isn't it? To add insult to injury, it's raining here in Newcastle. Maybe I should contact Freddie at Hestacombe House and see if the cottage is free for the next fortnight! [Reading this bit had caused Cressida's heart to give a foolish leap of hope.] Seriously, I hope we'll be able to book it for a week next Easter. [Cressida's heart plunged; next Easter was almost eight months away.] If we do, I very much hope we'll be able to meet up again then.

All the best,

Tom Turner.

It was so lovely to hear from Tom; the last week had dragged horribly now that he was no longer around. And he'd started off by saying 'Just a quick note', but it hadn't ended up being quick, had it? As quick emails went, it was actually quite lengthy . . .

'Aunt Cress, someone wants to order some wedding cards.'

Cressida jumped a mile as the door flew open and Jojo came in waving the cordless phone. Heavens, she'd been so enthralled by Tom's email that she hadn't even heard the phone ringing in the kitchen. Hurriedly, guiltily, she clicked on the BACK button to remove his words from the screen, took the phone from Jojo and forced herself to concentrate on the wedding plans of an overexcited bride in Bournemouth.

When the call ended—and with Jojo safely back in the kitchen—Cressida returned Tom's email to the screen and read it again. The thought of losing it was so alarming that she switched on her printer and printed a copy out. There, that was better, it was a proper letter now. She'd write back, of course, but not yet. Replying to a casual friendly email within minutes of receiving it would be far too keen.

When Merry Watkins had taken over the Flying Pheasant in Hestacombe two years ago she had been determined to make a roaring success of the venture. With a clear vision of how a country inn should be, she had set about transforming it with vigour. And to the relief of the locals Merry had achieved it, thanks largely to her charm and can-do personality. Every visitor to the pub was welcomed like a long-lost friend. The refurbished, but still traditional, bars were a comforting haven from the world, the draught beers were sublime and the back garden was family-friendly.

Picking up his drink and his change, Mario made his way outside, greeting and briefly chatting to people he knew before settling himself on a chair at the last empty table and pulling out his mobile. He rang Amber's number, reached voicemail and hung up. It was eight thirty: she and Mandy were probably in a restaurant with a no-phone rule. He'd try again later.

One week down, one to go. Putting his phone away, Mario realised how much he was missing Amber. He'd been good, though. On his best behaviour. When Jerry and the lads from work had announced they were off into Cheltenham for a night of beer and clubbing, Mario had said no. He wasn't entirely sure he wouldn't succumb to temptation should it happen to come along. It was safer to say no.

A voice to his left said hesitantly, 'Excuse me, are these seats taken?'

Looking up, Mario saw a fragile brunette in a sea-green summer dress, accompanied by a chic older woman who had to be her mother. Couldn't get safer than that.

Taking off his sunglasses and gesturing towards the empty chairs, Mario flashed them both an easy smile. 'Help yourself.'

'Just the two drinks this time?' Merry beadily enquired.

It was ten thirty and the third time Mario had come inside to order another round of drinks.

'Just the two,' Mario agreed. 'They're staying at one of the cottages. The mother's tired so she's gone back for an early night. Is that OK with you, Merry?'

She gave him a look. 'Fine by me, darling. Money in the till. Is it fine by Amber, that's what I'm wondering.'

Village life, didn't you just love it? 'I don't know. I'll give her a ring and ask her permission, shall I?' Pocketing his change and picking up the drinks, Mario said, 'Anyway, I'm not doing anything wrong. We're out there in full view of everyone. Her name's Karen, she broke up with her fiancé and she's been a bit down lately. Her mother, Marilyn, had booked one of the cottages for a week to take her mind off the ex.'

'Hmm.' It was a *hmm* loaded with meaning.

'I'm just being sociable!'

'Off with you, then, don't want her wondering where you've got to. You said that really well, by the way,' Merry called after him. Amused, she added, 'Almost as if you meant it.'

Marilyn and Karen Crane were staying at Pound Cottage, down on the lakeside. Lottie, arriving at the cottage at ten o'clock in the morning with a fresh supply of towels, found mother and daughter sitting out on the deck enjoying breakfast in their expensive silk dressing gowns. Karen was throwing bits of croissant to the ducks and sipping freshly squeezed orange juice. Marilyn was flipping through the latest edition of *Cotswold Life*. The sun was blazing down and classical music drifted elegantly through the open windows. The scene could have come straight from a Ralph Lauren ad.

Feeling hot and busy and not very Ralph Laurenish at all, Lottie hoisted the fresh towels out of the car and climbed the wooden steps leading up to the deck.

Brightly she said, 'I've brought your towels.'

'Oh, lovely. Just pop them inside, would you?' Marilyn greeted her with a warm smile and patted the empty chair beside her. 'Then come and sit down. We're planning a trip to Stratford today and we want to know what's worth seeing. Apart from the shops, obviously!'

Having deposited the towels in the bathroom, Lottie joined them.

'Coffee?' Marilyn reached for a spare cup.

'Thanks.' Real coffee; it smelt heavenly.

Marilyn combed her manicured fingernails through her dark brown fabulously cut hair. 'We'd also like somewhere special to eat.'

Lottie racked her brains. 'Well, I can really recommend a place in Painswick. I had dinner there last week and—'

'Somewhere in Stratford. For lunch, not dinner.' Karen, speaking for the first time, interrupted. 'I'm already going out this evening.'

'OK. What I can do is look up some restaurant review sites, draw—'

'Hello?' Cutting Lottie off in mid-flow again, Karen had snatched up her ringing phone. 'Oh, hi, Bea. Yeah, great, I'm just feeding the ducks. No, it's not as bad as I thought, the cottage is really sweet.'

Lottie whispered to Marilyn, '—draw up a shortlist. Then if you pop into the office before you set off, I can give you a printed-out copy.'

'. . . and you'll never guess what, I've got a date tonight!' Karen was still chattering away on the phone. 'I know, can you believe it? Mummy and I got talking to him outside the local pub, then Mummy got tired and came back here and we stayed on. I mean, I know I'm heartbroken over Jonty—the bastard—but this guy was just so much fun.'

Finishing her coffee, Lottie half rose from her seat and said, 'Well, I suppose I'd better—'

'And get this, his name's Mario,' Karen trilled into the phone.

Lottie abruptly sat back down. Feeling as if she'd been punched, she picked up her cup and swallowed a mouthful of lukewarm coffee.

'He manages a car showroom. And he isn't an oily oik either,' giggled Karen. 'Look, I'll ring you tomorrow and tell you everything then. If you see Jonty, let him know I'm not missing him a bit. Speak to you soon, bye.'

Lottie wanted to punch Mario. Why was she even surprised that he was up to his old tricks? And what could she do to stop him?

Aware that it was now or never—having finished her coffee she no longer had any reason to be sitting out here on their deck—Lottie cleared her throat. Casually she said, 'So . . . you're seeing Mario tonight.'

Karen perked up at once. 'Oh, do you know him?'

Lottie nodded. 'Very well.'

'Of course. He lives here in the village. You probably do too.' When Lottie nodded again, Marilyn said jokily, 'Don't tell me he's a complete psychopath!'

'Well, nooo . . .' Lottie drew out the word long enough to indicate that *that* wasn't the problem.

Not slow on the uptake, Marilyn raised an eyebrow. 'Is he married?'

Now wasn't the time to mention her own connection with Mario; it wasn't relevant. 'He's not married,' Lottie said hesitantly, 'but he does have a girlfriend.'

'Live-in?' demanded Karen.

'Well, no, they don't actually *live* together . . .'

'That's all right then.' Karen relaxed. 'If it was serious, he'd be living with her. I'm not going to feel guilty just because he's seeing someone. Anyway, we'd better start getting ready if we're going to Stratford.' Chucking the last shreds of croissant at the quacking, squabbling ducks, she rose to her feet and headed inside.

Lottie watched her go. Marilyn, patting her hand, said consolingly, 'Don't worry, it's just a harmless night out. Karen will be fine.'

She might be, thought Lottie. But what about Amber if she found out? How could Mario be so stupid?

Back at the office she rang him. 'It's me. What are you doing tonight?'

'Don't ask. Some boring business meeting.' Damn, he was good. The words tripped so easily off Mario's tongue it was scary.

'Liar. You're seeing Karen Crane.'

'Like I said, a boring business meeting.' Blithely Mario continued, 'She's interested in the new Audi Quattro.'

'And I'm Trevor McDonald. We both know what Karen's interested in.' At her desk, Lottie doodled a spiky, furious hedgehog on her notepad. 'And you must be out of your mind. For crying out loud, do you *want* Amber to dump you?'

Mario sighed. 'Look, we got chatting last night. I was just being friendly. And no, I didn't kiss her. Nor am I planning to.'

'You asked her out tonight.'

'I didn't. She asked me. She just wants a bit of company,' Mario protested. 'Someone to talk to. So I said yes. Is that so terrible?'

Lottie's eyes narrowed. 'Where are you taking her?'

'We're meeting at the Pheasant. Maybe we'll go for a pizza afterwards in Cheltenham. Maybe not. Hey, Lottie, will you trust me? This isn't any big deal,' said Mario. 'If it was a bloke, you wouldn't be giving me this grief.'

'I suppose not. But you lied about who you were seeing tonight.'

'That's because I knew you'd nag. Look, I promise to behave myself.'

Hmm. Doodling a harpoon about to land on the hedgehog, Lottie said, 'Just make sure you do.'

Tyler, now settled into Fox Cottage, was busy on the phone when Lottie arrived with the file of booking figures for next year. Signalling for her to stay, he carried on talking to his accountant, leaving Lottie free to explore the living room. She checked out his collections of CDs and DVDs, relieved to see that he wasn't an avid fan of country-and-western music and science-fiction movies.

Since the living room didn't take long to investigate—Tyler evidently wasn't one for clutter—Lottie moved outside into the garden. Butterflies darted around like It-girls at a party and the scent of honeysuckle hung heavy in the air. Burying her nose in a tall spear of hollyhock, Lottie almost inhaled a wasp and leapt back. Batting away the insect, she whacked the hollyhock at the same time. The wasp flew off and the hollyhock promptly bounced back like a punchball, spraying the front of her pale pink shirt with bright yellow pollen.

'Problem?' Phone call over, Tyler materialised behind her.

'Just doing battle with a vicious plant.'

Tyler said gravely, 'Looks like you lost.'

'Wait until I get my hands on a machete, then I'll get my own back.' Vigorously Lottie brushed herself down, squashing the pollen more indelibly into the thin cotton. 'I'll have to go home and change. The booking file's on your coffee table.'

'Thanks. Don't go yet.' Putting out a hand to stop her, Tyler said, 'Look, I know we haven't done very well so far, but what are you doing this evening? I thought maybe we could drive into Bath, go and see a—'

'I can't,' Lottie stopped him. 'There's something I have to do tonight.'

'OK.' Tyler paused. 'Is that a polite way of telling me to get lost?'

'No, *no*. I really do have something else to sort out.'

'Because I realise it isn't easy for you, what with your kids hating me so much, but I thought maybe if I steered clear of them it might help.' Tyler's smile was crooked. 'Then with a bit of luck they might get used to the situation and in time we can try again. How does that sound?'

Like banning certain types of food from your diet, thought Lottie, then reintroducing them to find out if you're allergic to them. The trouble was, the human body was unlikely to take pity on you and decide to change its mind about being allergic to red wine and chocolate just because it knew how much you liked them.

And neither were Nat and Ruby.

But she didn't have the heart to tell him this. Instead Lottie nodded and said, 'That sounds . . . fine.'

'So how about tomorrow night?'

God, she'd love that, she *really* would. 'Um . . . could we leave it for a few days?' Dry-mouthed and willing herself to stay strong, Lottie said, 'It's just that I'm pretty tied up for the rest of this week.'

There, talk about noble.

'If this is you playing hard to get,' Tyler said, 'you're doing it very well.'

'I'm not.' Lottie almost blurted out that where he was concerned she would in fact be ridiculously, shamelessly easy to get. With a surge of longing she said, 'Next week would be great.'

'OK. So long as you aren't messing me around.' His smile held a hint of challenge. 'Next Monday, then?'

Relief flooded through her. Lottie nodded vigorously. 'Next Monday.'

'Come here, you've got pollen on your nose.'

Moving obediently closer, she allowed him to brush it off.

'And here.' Tyler gently rubbed her left eyebrow, causing her stomach to contract with pleasure. 'And a bit more here,' he went on, stroking her right cheekbone. This time her toes began to tingle. Wherever next?

'All gone now?' Lottie murmured.

'Not quite. Just one last . . .' He touched her mouth, lightly tracing the outline of her lips. Then, closing the small distance between them, he moved his fingers aside and kissed her. Lightly and thrillingly. Phew. Eyes closed, Lottie felt his hands move to the back of her head. Her own arms found their way round his neck. It had been years, *years* since she'd been kissed like this. She'd forgotten how glorious it could be.

'There, that's better.' Tyler pulled away in order to study her face. His mouth twitched at the corners. 'Well, it's a start anyway.'

Nodding, Lottie struggled to regain control of her breathing. It was a hell of a start. Behind her she heard branches swaying as squirrels leapt playfully from tree to tree. Birds sang overhead and a pair of tortoise-shell butterflies pirouetted in tandem across the grass. All of a sudden she was in the middle of a Disney movie; at any moment she half expected a family of rabbits to burst into a rousing chorus of—

'I've been wanting to do that for a long time,' said Tyler.

'Me too.' Lottie's heart was banging against her ribcage.

'And I can't think of anything nicer than carrying on doing it.' His grey eyes flashed. 'But I suppose we should try to be faintly professional about this.'

Lottie nodded vigorously, shaking herself out of the daze that had enveloped her like a goosedown duvet. 'Absolutely. Professional.'

'I'll have to behave myself. Until next Monday,' said Tyler.

'Next Monday.' Lottie couldn't wait for him to misbehave.

'No Ruby, no Nat. Just me and you.'

'Yes.' Oops, now there was a bright yellow pollen stain on the front of his shirt from where she'd been pressed against him. Rubbing at it ineffectually, Lottie said, 'Look what I've done to you.'

Tyler's eyebrows lifted with amusement. 'That's the least of what you've done to me. But I suppose I'd better go and change my shirt. Bit of a giveaway otherwise.'

Inside the cottage, Tyler's phone began to ring. 'I'd better get that.'

He gave her hand a brief squeeze, then headed into the house. Smiling to herself, Lottie made her way back along the path. They'd just shared their first kiss.

Roll on Monday night.

When she was out of sight, the branches of the sycamore tree quivered again as the Jenkins boys, Ben and Harry, nudged each other and sniggered quietly. Sometimes when they hid in trees nothing much exciting happened but this was great. Actually watching grown-ups kissing was tons better than dropping beetles on unsuspecting heads. And not just any old grown-ups either. This was the new bloke from America, ha, and Nat and Ruby Carlyle's mother, ha *ha*.

'This is fantastic.' Harry, whose mission in life was to get one over on their rivals, punched the air triumphantly. 'Wait until Nat and Ruby hear about this.'

'**H**i there!' Spotting Mario and Karen at a corner table, Lottie waved at them and threaded her way towards them.

Mario, instantly suspicious, said, 'What are you doing here?'

'Now there's a welcome. Just as well I've already bought myself a drink!' Waggling her fingers cheerily at Karen, Lottie pulled out the third chair and sat down. 'Don't mind if I join you, do you? How was Stratford, by the way? Buy anything nice?'

'Uh, well . . . yeah.' Clearly mystified by this intrusion into their privacy, Karen looked at Mario.

'Where are the kids?' asked Mario.

'Locked up in a police cell.' Lottie pulled a face at him, then beamed. 'Cressida's baby-sitting. I just really fancied a night out.'

Mario gave her a measured look. 'I'll bet you did.'

'Hang on. Excuse me.' Her shoulders very straight, Karen demanded, 'Are you Mario's girlfriend?'

'Girlfriend? Gosh no. I'm his wife.'

Karen's eyes bulged.

'Ex-wife,' Mario corrected wearily.

'Ex-wife and mother to his children. But we still get on well, don't we?' Lottie gave Mario a friendly nudge. 'Like I get on well with Amber, his girlfriend. She's away on holiday at the moment.'

'OK.' Mario held up his hands. 'You've made your point, said what you came here to say. But there's really no need. I already told you, I'm not doing anything wrong. Karen and I are just *friends*.'

Lottie, wondering just how much he hated her right now, nodded vigorously. 'I know! And I think it's great! That's why I thought I'd join you, so we can have a fun evening and all be friends together!'

He'd been outmanoeuvred. Recognising that there was no way out, Mario shrugged good-naturedly and said, 'Fine. We'll do that.'

'Good.' Lottie's smile was dazzling. 'Karen? You don't mind, do you?'

From the look on her face, Karen was about as thrilled as if Lottie had suggested tattooing a dear little moustache on her upper lip. But since Mario had already acquiesced, she was forced to shake her head and say, 'No, of course I don't mind.'

Lying through her gritted teeth, naturally, but Lottie didn't let that bother her. Warmly she said, 'That's *great*.'

Honestly, for a girl who'd just been looking for companionship and good conversation, Karen had made precious little effort in that department. She seemed relieved when Mario dropped her back at the cottage.

'Well done,' said Mario, now pulling up outside Piper's Cottage.

Lottie's smile was serene. 'Don't mention it.'

'Pleased with yourself?'

'Delighted, thanks.'

'It wasn't necessary, you know. I didn't need a chaperone.'

'Of course you didn't.' Patting his arm, Lottie said, 'Turn off the ignition. You're staying here tonight. With us.'

''Why?' Mario rolled his eyes 'Are you after my body?'

Lottie said, 'No, but I know a girl who is.'

'She's gone.'

'Ah, but she might ring you, persuade you against your better judgment to meet up with her again. As your chaperone, it's my duty to protect you from wicked wanton women. In fact, I think you should stay with us for the rest of the week. The kids would love it.'

'And?'

'And when Amber asks me if you've been behaving yourself, I'll be able to tell her you have.'

Mario shook his head, half smiling at the look on her face. 'It really means that much to you?'

'I want my children to be happy. That means more than anything to me. And they love Amber to bits.'

'OK, OK. If it's that important, I'll stay here for the rest of the week.'

Mario was at work when an appreciative wolf whistle echoed through the air-conditioned showroom. Looking up he saw the cause of it; Amber was stepping through the automatic doors.

'You're a lucky sod.' Jerry, the perpetrator of the wolf whistle, stroked his designer-stubbled chin. 'If you ever decide you don't want her, I'll take her off your hands.'

Mario had no intention of offloading Amber onto anyone. Watching her make her way across the showroom, he was struck by how fantastic she was looking in a sunflower-yellow silk top and flippy white skirt. Her hair was blonder and her tan deeper than ever. She glowed with vitality.

'You're back.' It had been annoying at the time, but now he was glad Lottie had appointed herself his guardian. His conscience was clear; he hadn't done anything wrong and it felt great. Hugging Amber, breathing in the gorgeous smell of her skin, he gave her a kiss. 'I've missed you.'

'Really?' Turning to Mario's co-workers, Amber said playfully, 'Has he?'

'Not at all.' Jerry, ever-helpful, said, 'I'd dump him if I were you. Fancy going out with me instead?'

'Does she look desperate?' Reaching for her hand, Mario said, 'Let's go somewhere more private.'

Out in the car park behind the showroom, he kissed her again. 'What time did you get back? I wasn't expecting to see you until tonight.'

'The plane landed at one o'clock, we were home by two thirty. But I can't see you this evening. One of my regulars got desperate and tried to do her own highlights while I was away. Apparently she is refusing to leave her house until I've sorted out the mess.'

'But . . . you were coming over to *us*.' Mario couldn't believe it, he'd spent the last week practically counting down the hours. 'We've got all the food for a barbeque. The kids have been dying to see you.'

Amber searched his face. 'How about you?'

'Me too.' How could she even ask him that?

'Well, good. But Maisie's highlights are going to take hours to sort out, and I know I'm going to be shattered tonight. So I'll see you tomorrow instead.' Amber unlocked the boot of her turquoise Fiat and lifted out a box. 'And you can give these to Nat and Ruby, that'll cheer them up.'

Unlike Tyler Klein, Amber was an inspired present-chooser, always managing to find just the right gifts. As the box was plonked into his arms Mario said, 'They'd rather have you there.'

'And they will. Tomorrow.' Checking her watch, Amber leaned across and gave him a brief peck on the cheek. 'Bye, darling. Don't forget to give the monsters a big squidgy hug from me.'

Mario stood and watched the Fiat shoot out of the car park and bomb off down the road. If he didn't know better, he'd wonder if maybe she hadn't met someone else on holiday.

No. That was ridiculous. Amber would never do that.

But there was something unnervingly different about her. Swallowing disappointment—and grimly ignoring the sense of unease in his chest—he headed back into the showroom.

'Tonight's the night . . . da da, de-da da.' Lottie sang the song quietly so no one else could hear as she surveyed her reflection in the dressing-table mirror. Her dress was dark red and shimmery and so was her mouth. Her hair, hanging loose tonight, was a mass of glossy black ringlets and her eyes were bright. Beneath the dress, her black silk bra and knickers were the kind you wore when you very much hoped they'd be seen. Also beneath the dress, her heart was racing like a hamster on a wheel as she reached for the mascara and finished her eyes. In ten minutes Mario and Amber would be arriving to pick up the kids. Nat and Ruby were spending the night at Mario's . . . oh yes, this was definitely going to be an evening to remember. Turning sideways in the mirror, Lottie critically surveyed her figure. Hearing the gentle slap-slap of flip-flops on the stairs she called out, 'Ruby? Come and tell me what you think. Does my bum look big in this dress?'

Ruby appeared in the bedroom doorway. 'Yes.'

'Excellent.' Lottie patted her shapely backside with satisfaction. If she said so herself, it was one of her finest assets. Then she saw the expression on Ruby's face. 'Rubes? What's wrong?'

'Nat's got a stomach ache. He's been sick and now he's crying.'

'Sick?' Alarmed, Lottie rushed to the door. 'Where?'

'Not on the carpet. In the loo. He says his stomach really hurts.'

Together they raced downstairs. Nat was lying on the sofa clutching his abdomen and whimpering with pain. Lottie knelt beside him and stroked his face. 'Oh, sweetheart. When did this start?'

'Not long. I felt ill at teatime but it's just got bad now.' Nat screwed up his face and gritted his teeth. 'Mummy, it hurts so much.'

Lottie was stroking his forehead. Perplexed, she said, 'Why are you all wet?'

'I washed my face after I was sick. And I pulled the flush to make it go.'

'You washed your face? *And* remembered to pull the flush?' To see if she could make him smile Lottie said, 'It's like a double miracle!'

But Nat buried his face in her neck and wailed, 'Hug me, Mummy. Make me better. *Ow*, I feel sick again . . .'

Lottie experienced a horrid feeling of trepidation. Tonight was *the* night, *her* night, and she didn't want this to be happening now. She was all dressed up, her hair done, her legs freshly shaved. Tyler was expecting her at Fox Cottage in less than thirty minutes.

'I've brought the washing-up bowl,' Ruby announced, 'for him to be sick in again if it comes up really fast.'

'Thanks.' As Nat clung to her like a limpet, Lottie sensed that this was how it would feel if your lottery numbers came up the one week you hadn't bought a ticket.

'Where's Amber?' Ruby demanded when Mario arrived minutes later.

'Busy. She can't come over tonight.' Mario eyed Nat and the washing-up bowl with trepidation. 'What's going on?'

Nat gave him a piteous look. 'I'm really ill.'

Mario visibly recoiled as if Nat might suddenly launch into projectile-vomit mode.

In desperation Lottie stroked Nat's face and said, 'Maybe you just need to go to sleep, sweetheart.'

'Noooo.' Nat shook his head and tightened his grip on her.

'Poor Mummy.' Ruby looked sympathetic. 'She's going to miss her important business meeting in Bath.'

'Business meeting?' Mario raised a sceptical eyebrow at the tight-fitting red shimmery dress.

'It's a Tourist Board do. Meeting first, dinner afterwards.' Lottie, who had been rehearsing the lie all day, said defensively, 'Everyone dresses up.'

Not that it mattered. They all knew she wasn't going anywhere.

You're going out "again" tonight?' Ruby looked horrified.

'What do you mean, "again"?' Busy clearing the breakfast table, Lottie raised her eyebrows in retaliation. 'I haven't *been* anywhere yet.'

It was the morning after, and Nat had made a suspiciously swift recovery from his stomach upset. *Alleged* stomach upset. Having already polished off a mountain of Coco Pops at record speed, he had raced upstairs to get ready for school and could now be heard clumping down again, bellowing out the new Avril Lavigne single at the top of his voice.

Ruby, sitting at the table still ploughing through her own bowl of Crunchy Nut cornflakes looked at Nat as he burst into the kitchen and said meaningfully, 'She's going out again.'

Nat abruptly stopped singing. 'Why?'

'Because you're going over to your dad's house for a barbeque tonight and I've decided to join an evening class in Cheltenham.' Pouring herself a strong coffee, Lottie said, 'That's allowed, isn't it?'

'What evening class?'

What indeed? Russian for beginners? Knit-your-own chastity belt?

'Line dancing,' Lottie said firmly.

'Where they wear cowboy hats and pointy boots? And all dance in a line?' Nat giggled. 'That's *saaaad*.'

'You don't have to wear a hat and boots.'

'It's still sad. Mega-sad. Only nerdy durr-brains do stuff like that.'

Feeling defensive on behalf of line dancers everywhere Lottie said, 'But I'll be doing it and I'm not a nerdy durr-brain.'

Ruby was scornful. 'She isn't going to any evening class. She's just saying it so she can meet that man again.'

Nat stared at Lottie. 'Is that true?'

Lottie's heart sank. Why did life have to be so difficult?

'OK, I *was* going to join the line-dancing class.' She spoke swiftly because lying was one thing; being caught lying was quite another. 'But I'm meeting Tyler afterwards.'

Ruby pushed aside her bowl of Crunchy Nut cornflakes. 'See?'

'No.' Nat shook his head. 'Mummy, don't.'

'Nat, it doesn't make any difference to you. You don't have to see him. He's a nice man,' Lottie said helplessly.

His lower lip stuck out. 'You mean *you* like him.'

'Yes, I do.' Lottie put down her coffee. 'Sweetheart, it's just one night out. With a friend.'

'And then another night out, and another,' Ruby chanted, 'and he isn't a friend, he's a *boyfriend*.' She spat out the last word as if it was botulism. 'Mum, please don't go out with that man. He hates us.'

'He doesn't hate you! How can *you* even think that? *OK*.' Lottie held up her hands as they both opened their mouths. 'We don't have time for this now. It's half past eight. We'll talk about it properly after school.'

'Fine.' Ruby pushed back her chair as Lottie began searching for the car keys. 'That means you're still going to see him tonight.'

Was there seriously any reason why she shouldn't? Picking up the half-empty cereal bowl and feeling unfairly got at, Lottie said, 'Yes, I am. And I'm looking forward to it. Now go and brush your teeth.'

The run of spectacular weather came to an abrupt end that afternoon. Charcoal-grey storm clouds rolled in from the west and the first fat drops of rain, as big as pennies, thudded onto the windscreen of Lottie's car as she drove to Oaklea School to pick up Ruby and Nat. Typically, by the time she'd found somewhere to park, the spattering of raindrops had accelerated to a downpour. Even more typically, Lottie hadn't brought a jacket. Bracing herself for a sprint up the road, she leapt from the car. Why did it always have to rain just as school ended? Glancing down, Lottie sucked in her breath. Her white shirt was wet and sticking to her like clingfilm. Proudly revealing her lacy red bra.

Feeling like a dirty old man—although if she were a dirty old man she'd surely have the luxury of a mac—Lottie lurked furtively among the trees at the back of the playground and waved to Nat and Ruby when they came spilling out of their classrooms.

'Come on, let's go.' Hustling them ahead of her, she used Ruby as a kind of human shield. 'Nat? Hurry up, sweetheart, it's raining.'

'We can't go. Miss Batson wants to see you.'

Lottie stopped dead. Were any words designed to strike a greater sense of impending doom into the heart of any mother? She was no wimp, but Nat's teacher was truly terrifying. Miss Batson—*nobody* knew her first name, possibly not even her own mother—was in her late fifties. Her iron-grey hair matched her clothes and her manner.

Lottie's insides churned. 'Why? What have you done?'

'Nothing.' His head dropping, Nat kicked at a stone.

Pointing across the playground, Ruby said, 'She's there. Waiting.'

Oh God, so she was. Clutching Nat's hand, Lottie made her way towards his teacher. 'Hello, Miss Batson. You wanted to see me?'

'Ms Carlyle. Good afternoon. Indeed I did.'

'Mrs,' said Lottie. She hated being addressed as *Mzz*, it sounded like a wasp being squashed.

Ignoring this, Miss Batson ushered Nat and Ruby into the classroom and through the maze of desks. 'You two can wait for us outside the secretary's office. *Ms* Carlyle?' With a sharp inclination of her Brillo head she directed Lottie towards one of the chairs in front of her own desk. 'Make yourself comfortable.'

Which had to be a joke, surely? The moulded plastic grey chair was designed for infant-sized pupils. Lottie's knees were higher than her bottom, her bottom was wider than the chair's seat. Plus she was dripping rain onto the floor and the cups of her red bra were glowing through her wet shirt like twin traffic lights.

'I have to tell you, Ms Carlyle, that I'm extremely concerned about Nat,' Miss Batson began.

Her mouth dry, Lottie said, 'What's he done?'

'He borrowed a ruler from Charlotte West this morning. And refused to give it back.'

'Oh right. A ruler.' Relief flooded through Lottie like alcohol. 'Well, that's not so terrible, is it?' Catching the look in Miss Batson's beady eye she added hastily, 'Well, of course it *is* terrible. I'll speak—'

'When I eventually retrieved the ruler, Nat refused to apologise. And when I sent him to the naughty corner he used a crayon in his pocket to write on the wall.'

'Oh. What did he write?'

'He wrote I HATE,' Miss Batson reported icily, 'before I took the crayon from him. Then, when I told him off for defacing school property, he burst into tears. I then spent the lunch break speaking privately to Nat to find out why he was being so disruptive. He's a very unhappy little boy, Ms Carlyle. He told me everything, the whole story. And I have to say, I find it very troubling indeed.'

Numb and incredulous, Lottie said, 'What whole story?'

'Your son is a victim of divorce, Ms Carlyle. That's a traumatic enough experience for any small child to have to deal with. But now you, a single parent, have embarked upon a relationship with another man. A man, furthermore, whom Nat does not like. He feels powerless. He's made his feelings abundantly clear to you, yet evidently you have chosen to ignore his pain.'

'But I—'

'Any mother who chooses her own happiness at the expense of her children's is displaying a lack of concern that I find breathtakingly selfish. You have to seriously consider your priorities here, Ms Carlyle. Who is more important to you? This man or your own son?' Miss Batson paused, driving the message home. 'Who do you love more?'

Lottie had never felt so small in her life. Shame welled up and a single tear slid down one cheek.

'Well?' Miss Batson was tapping her fingers, demanding an answer.

'I love my son more.' It came out as a whisper.

'Good. So do I take it we won't be needing this?'

'What is it?' Lottie looked at the card Miss Batson was holding up.

'The contact number for Social Services.'

'*What?*'

'Nat told me everything,' Miss Batson repeated coolly. 'About the mental cruelty inflicted upon him and his sister by this so-called boyfriend of yours. If you're looking for a potential stepfather for your children, you have to consider their feelings, Ms Carlyle. Well, we'll put this away. For now.' She slid the card into her desk drawer.

'Now wait a minute.' All the blood rushed to Lottie's cheeks as she realised what Miss Batson was implying. 'There hasn't been any mental cruelty! Tyler isn't a monster! He's never meant to upset my children! If they'd just give him another chance they'd realise how—'

'Maybe we'll be needing this number after all.' Miss Batson's bony fingers swooped back down to the desk drawer.

'No, we won't!' Now Lottie wanted to stab her with a sharp pencil. 'We *won't*, OK? But I'm just trying to explain to you that this has been blown out of all proportion!'

'And I'm trying to explain to you,' Miss Batson said evenly, 'that I gave up my lunch hour to listen to a seven-year-old boy pouring his heart out about how devastated he is by the unwanted arrival of this man in his life.'

'But—'

'That will be all, Ms Carlyle.' Rising to her feet, Miss Batson checked her watch. 'Thank you for your time.'

Hi Tom,

If I make lots of mistakes it's because I'm typing this with gluey fingers—for the last four hours I've been sticking tiny white marabou feathers onto christening cards and only realised when I'd finished that I've run out of acetone so can't clean it off!

Is Donny settling back at school OK? Jojo's started learning Russian this term and was over here earlier asking me to help her with her homework, which is way too much for my poor frazzled brain to cope with. Did you watch that murder mystery on ITV last night? I was so sure the vicar was the baddie. Spent ages trying to remember what else the actress who played his wife has been in. Still can't remember and it's—

The doorbell rang, making Cressida jump. Since Tom's first stilted message they had both relaxed and were now corresponding on a daily basis. Every time she clicked onto her email she experienced a thrill of anticipation, wondering if there would be something from him.

'Hi!' Opening the front door, she was delighted to find a drowned rat on the doorstep clutching two bottles of wine. Taking them from her, Cressida said, 'For me? Thank you so much! Goodbye!'

'Not so fast.' Lottie already had her foot in the door.

Cressida grinned. 'Come on in. You look terrible.'

'Thanks. So would you if you'd had a day like mine. Corkscrew,' Lottie demanded, making straight for the kitchen. 'Glasses. Your individual attention and lots and lots of sympathy, that's all I ask.'

'Oh, poor you. I'll be with you in two seconds.' Veering off to the office, Cressida rushed over to the computer and typed at lightning speed: Got to go now—my friend Lottie's just turned up and she's having a crisis. Red wine being opened as I speak. Love and hugs, Cress xxxx.

Then she pressed SEND and raced back to the kitchen.

'So what else could I do?' Half an hour had passed and the first bottle was well on its way to being emptied. Lottie had related the entire cringe-making lecture from Miss Batson practically verbatim. 'We got home and I had a long talk with Ruby and Nat. It turns out that Ben and Harry Jenkins saw me and Tyler together the other day. We were having a bit of a moment outside his cottage. Not *that* kind of moment,' she added defensively as Cressida's eyebrows shot up. 'Just a kiss. But bloody Ben and Harry were hiding up a tree and it all blew up from there. Anyway, I packed the kids off to Mario's at seven and phoned Tyler to tell him we couldn't see each other again. Well, apart from at work. Obviously. So that's it. All done.'

'What did Tyler say when you told him?'

'He just said it was a shame and he was sorry things had turned out this way, but he agreed that I had to put my kids first.'

'I suppose it's all you *can* do.' Cressida was sympathetic. 'It just seems so unfair. When you're fifteen and you go out with an eighteen-year-old bad boy, you expect your parents to stop you seeing him. But it never occurs to you that in years to come your own children might do the same thing.'

'It never occurred to me that I'd have children like Ruby and Nat.' Lottie's eyes filled with tears. 'Oh God, I love them so much. They're my whole life. I didn't realise what I was doing to them. Peanuts.'

'Sorry?'

'Peanuts. And chocolate. They'll make us feel better, cheer us up. Not that you look as if you need cheering up,' Lottie called as Cressida headed into the kitchen to mount a raid on the snack cupboard. 'In fact you're looking quite perky and sparkly.'

'I'm not.'

'Oh, yes, you *are*.' Lottie wiggled an accusing finger at her. 'All perky and sparkly and *zingy*, as if you're hiding some brilliant secret. And I need to know what it is, for the good of my health.'

Cressida, always hopeless at keeping secrets, went pink and felt her eyes flicker in the direction of the office where even now a new email from Tom could be waiting, tantalisingly unread, in her inbox.

'You've got a man,' Lottie crowed, spotting the flicker and almost knocking over her drink with excitement. 'A man, hiding in your office!'

'It's Tom Turner,' Cressida blurted out, 'and he isn't hiding in my office. We're just emailing each other.' Pausing, she added, 'Every day.'

'Tom Turner! That's fantastic!' Lottie clapped her hands. 'So it could *become* love?'

Love. A squiggle of apprehension wormed its way through Cressida's stomach. Oh God. *Love*.

Had she? Or hadn't she?

It was eleven o'clock, Lottie had just left and Cressida was in front of the computer, unable to ignore the niggling fear a minute longer. She had the toe-curling suspicion she had miswritten something.

Following Tom's lead she carefully signed off her replies to him with 'All the best'. But when she was replying to the jokey, affectionate emails Jojo sent her on an almost daily basis she invariably wrote Love and hugs, Cress xxxx.

And now she had the most horrible feeling that in those few moments following Lottie's arrival, when she had dashed off the end of her message to Tom, she had unthinkingly put 'Love and hugs, Cress xxxx'.

Not having saved a copy of her email, she couldn't check.

Cheeks aflame, Cressida feverishly logged in and drummed her fingers on the table, waiting to see if Tom had replied.

He hadn't. She took a gulp of wine. She had no way of knowing whether his failure to respond meant he hadn't yet read it or that he had and was too startled by her brazen signal to know what to do next.

Oh hell, what to do to redeem the situation?

Obviously she had to write back.

Dear Tom,

Not sure if I should be writing this (bit pissed) but I'm really sorry if I wrote Love and hugs at the end of my last email. Meant to put All the best but got confused—what's new?—and thought you were Jojo. Well, what I mean is I thought I was finishing an email to Jojo, not you, because obviously I wouldn't send you hugs and a row of kisses.

Not that I don't like you, of course. You're a very nice man and I really really look forward to your emails, which is why I hope my last one didn't scare you off. Anyway, just wanted to explain. Sorry again. Please write back soon and let me know you don't think I'm barking mad. Unless you do, in which case I'd rather not know.

All the best,

Cress.

See? No kisses.

Was that OK? Friendly and casual. Explanatory but light-hearted. Oh yes, it'd be fine. Completely fine.

Feeling a lot happier, Cressida pressed SEND.

There, done. Time for bed.

Chapter 5

WAS SOMETHING THE MATTER with Amber?

It was Lottie's morning off and she was in the salon having deep red lowlights in addition to a trim, in an effort to cheer herself up. Normally she loved coming to the salon with its buzzy, gossipy atmosphere and comforting hairdressery smells, but the other girls were off today which meant she and Amber were alone. And for the first time since Lottie could remember the conversation wasn't flowing naturally.

'Amber? Is anything wrong?' Lottie asked.

Behind her, in the mirror, Amber shrugged. 'You tell me.'

There was definitely something wrong. Lottie shook her head and the foil wedges around her temples flapped like spaniel's ears. 'Tell you what?'

Amber put down the flat brush she'd been using to paint dye on the separate sections of hair. 'About Mario.'

'Mario? He's fine.'

'I know he's fine.' Amber's gaze was steady in the mirror. 'I just want to know if he's been seeing someone else.'

Lottie shifted, her fingers twisting together beneath the cape draped over her shoulders. As convincingly as she could, she said, 'No, he hasn't.'

'I think he has.'

'Like who?'

Another pause. Then Amber said, 'Like you.'

Lottie was so relieved she burst out laughing. 'Is that what this is all about?' she said finally. 'You think there's something going on between me and Mario? Amber, I'd tell you if there was. But there isn't. I *wouldn't*, not in a million years! And that's a promise.'

Amber exhaled slowly. 'OK. Sorry. I believe you. It's just . . . I called into the shop yesterday and Ted was really surprised to see me.'

'Well, that's because you've been away for a couple of weeks.'

'That's what I thought. Then he said he'd thought you and Mario were back together. Then some old dear chimed in with, "That's what I reckoned too, what with him spending every night at Piper's Cottage."'

Village gossips. Couldn't you just throw them in the lake?

'He slept on the sofa,' said Lottie. Then she shifted again, guessing what was coming next.

Amber nodded. 'That's fine. But what I'd really like to know is whose idea it was that Mario should stay over in the first place.'

'Well, the kids *loved* having him there,' Lottie began brightly, but Amber quelled her with a look.

'It was your idea, wasn't it? It was your way of making sure he didn't get up to anything while I was away.'

Amber was nobody's fool. Lottie shrugged, signalling defeat. 'OK. Mario wouldn't deliberately set out to do anything wrong, but I just thought he'd be safer with us than going out with the lads and—'

'Forgetting he has a girlfriend,' Amber said bluntly. She parcelled up the last of the foil packages and wiped her hands on a cloth.

'I'm sorry. Men, eh? Why can't they appreciate how lucky they are?'

Amber was busy spooning coffee into mugs. 'Some do.'

'I suppose. But it's more likely to be the man who plays away, isn't it? I mean, if I had a gorgeous man I'd never be tempted to lie or cheat. Neither would you. So why do—?'

'I have.'

'*Have* you?' Fascinated, Lottie said, 'What, you've actually cheated on a boyfriend? Who was that?'

Amber carefully poured boiling water into the mugs, added milk and stirred. 'Mario. Sugar?'

Lottie was stunned; this wasn't what she'd been expecting at all. 'Two. My God, when did this happen?'

Amber said, 'On holiday.'

'I don't believe it! You met someone in France! Oh my *God*!'

'Actually I didn't.' Amber handed over Lottie's mug and sat down on a stool, nursing her own. 'We went to France together.'

Lottie's brain was in a whirl; she felt as if she were at a fairground trapped on the Waltzers. 'But . . . you said . . .'

'I know. I told you I was going on holiday with my friend Mandy.' Cheerfully Amber said, 'I didn't. That was a lie.'

Blimey. Lottie put her coffee down before she spilt it. 'Who then?'

'His name's Quentin.'

Yikes. *Quentin?*

'OK, I know what you're thinking,' Amber said, drily. 'As names go, men called Quentin don't generally have movie star looks and rippling biceps, do they? And this one doesn't either. He's just ordinary. We went out together a couple of years ago. It was one of those easy relationships, you know? Quentin phoned when he said he'd phone. He turned up whenever he said he'd turn up. Bought me flowers. He even queued up all night once to buy tickets to see Elton John in concert for my birthday.'

'Wow. Can't argue with that.' Lottie was openly envious. 'But you broke up. So what happened?'

Amber shrugged. 'I got a bit . . . bored. I thought I wanted more excitement, someone who'd make my heart race and my knees go weak. So I told Quentin I didn't think we had a future, that he was too good for me.' Her expression wry, she went on, 'And being the gentleman he is, Quentin didn't put pressure on me to change my mind. He said he hoped I would find what I was looking for, and that I deserved to be happy. And the next thing I knew, he'd jacked in his job and moved to London.'

'And now he's back.' Lottie was simultaneously shocked and enthralled. She knew she shouldn't be riveted but she couldn't help it.

'He is.' Amber nodded. 'He dropped in here six weeks ago to say hi, but I was rushed off my feet so I arranged to meet him for a coffee after work. Just to chat and catch up. It was nice to see him again, that was all. Quentin told me about his work and what he'd been up to. I told him about Mario. He asked me if Mario was the one I'd been looking for. I said I didn't know but I was enjoying myself. And that was it.' Pausing to fiddle with her earrings, Amber went on, 'Then that night Mario and I went to a party and this girl spent the whole evening chatting him up. We were there as a couple but she completely ignored me. And Mario was chatting away to her as if nothing was wrong. He really didn't seem to notice what she was doing. Which made me furious. So when Quentin rang my doorbell the next evening, I invited him in for a drink.'

'Just a drink?' Lottie's tone was mischievous.

'Yes. He'd brought me a little bunch of freesias. Then he told me he still loved me. And I suddenly realised that there were worse things than being loved by a genuinely nice man.'

The back of Lottie's neck began to prickle with alarm. 'So just how serious is this thing between you?'

'I haven't slept with him, if that's what you mean.' Her eyes bright, Amber said, 'Not this time, anyway.'

'But you've just been on holiday together! For a whole fortnight!'

'Separate bedrooms. The holiday was Quentin's idea. He knew how torn I was. I needed some time away from Mario before I could make up my mind.'

Wild with impatience, Lottie said, 'And h*ave* you made up your mind?'

'Nearly,' said Amber.

'*Nearly?* Tell me!' Lottie squealed.

'No. That wouldn't be fair. I have to tell them first.' Amber inspected Lottie's magenta lowlights. 'You're ready. Come over to the basin.'

As the basin filled with discarded foils and warm water cascaded over her tilted-back head, Lottie said, 'I still can't believe you did it. You're worried that Mario might cheat on you so you go away for a fortnight with some other guy. Isn't that a bit . . . unfair?'

'Probably.' Energetically Amber began to massage almond-scented shampoo into Lottie's hair. 'But if Mario cheated on me he'd be doing it because he was flattered or bored or just fancied a bit of how's your father. I went away with Quentin because I need to make a decision that's going to change the rest of my life.'

It was eleven o'clock in the morning. Cressida winced and clutched her aching head when she saw there was a new email from Tom waiting in her inbox. This was all Lottie's fault, coming over here last night with bottles of wine and getting her drunk.

Cressida mentally braced herself. OK. *Click.*

Hi Cress.
It's only nine o'clock in the morning but you've already brightened my day. Your email was wonderful. You say you look forward to mine but I look forward to yours more, I promise you. No need at all to apologise for sending Love and hugs (which you did, by the way. Followed by several kisses). I'm flattered. And definitely no need to be embarrassed.

Oh, thank heavens for that. Cressida exhaled slowly, giddy with relief. And there was more . . .

Now, a suggestion. Donny mentioned Jojo last night. Despite feigning indifference, when I asked if he'd like to see her again he grunted and said "Dunno", which for a thirteen-year-old boy is pretty positive. So I was wondering if you and Jojo would like to come up to Newcastle one weekend. There's plenty going on here to keep the kids happy. Anyway, just a suggestion. I know it's a long way to travel but if you and Jojo would like to visit, we'd love to see you again. Let me know what you think.

Love and hugs, Tom xxxxxx

Let him know what she thought? Let him know what she *thought*? It was all Cressida could do not to launch into a jig before throwing open the windows and bellowing *Yesssssssss!* This must be how footballers felt when they scored a winning goal in the Cup Final.

The rest of her life might not be going according to plan but Lottie was enjoying being a private detective. She hadn't been able to trace the second name on Freddie's list, Giselle Johnston, but since Johnston was her maiden name and she was now sixty-two, this was hardly a surprise. She had had more luck with the next name on the list. Fenella McEvoy.

'I've got her,' Lottie told Freddie, bursting into the living room of Hestacombe House and waving a sheet of paper in triumph. 'Now you have to tell me who she is.'

Fenella. Freddie lit a cigar and smiled to himself. This was going to be interesting. 'First you have to tell me how you found her.'

'Well, I wrote to the address you gave me and the man who lives there now called me back. He and his wife bought the house from the McEvoys twenty years ago. The McEvoys moved abroad, to Spain. But he heard on the grapevine a couple of years ago that Fenella was back in Oxford. Then last summer she walked past his house while he was out in the garden and they got chatting. She told him she was living in Hutton Court, an apartment block overlooking the river. *So*,' Lottie gaily announced, 'I Googled Hutton Court and found a web designer who lives there and works from home. I rang and asked him if he knew a Fenella and he said, "Oh, you mean Fenella Britton, she lives on the top floor." You know, I am brilliant.' Lottie looked suitably modest. 'If I say so myself, I'd make a fantastic international spy.'

'And now she's written back.' Freddie's eyes were on the letter Lottie was keeping tantalisingly out of reach.

'She has. Your turn,' Lottie prompted.

'Some people have a moment of madness.' Puffing on his cigar and picturing Fenella as she had looked all those years ago, Freddie settled back in his leather armchair. 'I had a month. I was with Giselle. Fenella was married. I couldn't help myself,' he went on. 'She was like a drug I couldn't resist. We had an affair.'

'And I thought young people had morals in those days.' Lottie tut-tutted as she handed over the letter. 'Who dumped who?'

'She dumped me. As you young people so charmingly put it.' Remembering how devastated he had been, Freddie smiled and tapped the ash from his cigar. 'Fenella was a high-maintenance woman. She already had a successful husband. Basically I just wasn't rich enough.'

Unlike Jeff Barrowcliffe, who had been initially cautious, Fenella was overjoyed to hear from Freddie.

'A voice from the past!' she exclaimed with delight when he called her. 'Freddie, how wonderful, of *course* I'd love to see you again! Where are you living now? Near Cheltenham? Why, that's no distance at all! Do you want to pop up here or shall I come down to you?'

As easy as that.

Putting the phone down several minutes later, Freddie wondered why it couldn't have been that simple thirty-eight years ago.

The first time he had seen Fenella McEvoy she had been in a leather shop in the centre of Oxford, choosing a pair of gloves. Freddie, dropping in to pick up a repaired watch strap, observed her trying on one supple dove-grey kid glove and one satin-lined pale pink one. Aware that she was being watched, Fenella turned and waggled her fingers at him. 'Which do you think? To go with a white suit.'

She was stunning, as dark and elegant as Audrey Hepburn. Confidence emanated from her like French perfume.

'The pink ones,' Freddie replied at once, and she had flashed him a mesmerising smile before turning back to the assistant.

'A gentleman of taste. I'll take them.'

Freddie was already captivated.

Somehow they had left the shop together. As it started to rain outside, Fenella said, 'Of course what I should have bought was an umbrella. I'm never going to find a taxi now.'

'My car's just over there.' Freddie pointed across the road. 'Where are you heading?'

'Not only a gentleman of taste.' Cheerfully, Fenella moved towards the car. 'A knight in shining armour too. And what a beautiful car.'

'Not that one.' Slightly shamefacedly, Freddie steered her away from the gleaming Bentley and unlocked the doors of his own less than gleaming Austin 7, parked behind it. 'Still want a lift?'

Fenella laughed at the dig. 'It's better than a bicycle made for two.'

He dropped her outside her house, an imposing Edwardian villa on leafy, upmarket Carlton Avenue. By this time he'd already learned that she was married to Cyril who was fifteen years older than her. Cyril, it transpired, was something big in textiles.

'What are you doing on Wednesday evening?' Fenella asked him.

'Seeing my girlfriend, Giselle.'

'Make an excuse. Come and see me instead. Cyril's going to be away.'

Freddie began to perspire. 'I can't do that.'

'Of course you can. Eight o'clock.' Fenella regarded him with amusement. 'Don't look so shocked. You know you want to.'

And, hating himself but unable to help himself, Freddie discovered that he did.

Having thought that Giselle was the love of his life, the explosion of Fenella into his world came as a shock to Freddie. On Wednesday night she seduced Freddie expertly and repeatedly. The sex was mind-blowing. Luckily Cyril was often away on business trips.

'You're working too hard,' Giselle complained four weeks later when he told her, yet again, that he wouldn't be able to see her that night.

'I know, but the boss needs me to close the deal. It won't be for ever,' Freddie promised. And he knew it wouldn't. He and Fenella were meant to be together. Life without her was unimaginable. Hours later, in bed, he told her so and asked her to leave Cyril.

'Darling, how sweet.' Fenella ran her toes playfully along his bare leg. 'But why on earth would I want to do that?'

'Because I love you!' Utterly bewitched, Freddie was taken aback by her failure to understand what was happening here. 'We can't just carry on like this. I'll finish with Giselle. You can divorce Cyril.'

Fenella giggled. 'Heavens, he'll be furious!'

'This isn't about him,' Freddie said urgently. 'It's about us. I want to marry you.'

'And keep me in the manner to which I'm accustomed?' Gesturing around the vast and tastefully furnished master bedroom, encompassing the wardrobes bursting with expensive clothes and shoes, Fenella said, 'Freddie, be serious. Exactly how much *do* you earn?'

Being plunged into a barrel of ice couldn't have shocked him more. Feeling his jaw muscles tighten, Freddie said, 'I thought you loved me.'

'Oh, Freddie. I like you.' Fenella stroked his face. 'We've had fun together, haven't we? But it was never meant to be serious.'

Freddie noted her use of the past tense. He also realised that Fenella had done this before, and that while she didn't love Cyril she had absolutely no intention of leaving him.

'I'll be off then.' Feeling crushed, foolish and miserable, Freddie slid out of bed and began hunting for his hurriedly discarded clothes.

Fenella nodded sympathetically. 'Probably best. Sorry, darling.'

Freddie was sorry too. He'd betrayed Giselle, who truly loved him. And now he'd made a complete idiot of himself.

It was over. Because he couldn't afford her. *He wasn't rich enough.*

Fenella gave a little cry of delight and held out her arms to Freddie. 'My darling, just look at you—all silver-haired and distinguished and more handsome than ever! Oh, it's so good to see you again!'

Freddie's head was aching badly, but if anything was capable of making him forget the pain it was the sight of Fenella in a pink and yellow summer dress and floaty matching scarf. Her dark eyes glowed, she still wore her hair in a gamine Audrey Hepburn crop, and her legs were as slender and spectacular as ever. If he hadn't known she was sixty-three, he'd have put her at mid-fifties.

'And it's wonderful to see you.' Bending his head and breathing in the fresh, flowery scent of her perfume, Freddie gave Fenella a kiss on each powdered cheek. 'Thank you so much for coming. Please, let me take care of that,' he added as she unfastened the clasp on her handbag.

Freddie paid the taxi driver, tipped him a tenner and said, 'If I'd known you were catching the train I'd have met you at the station.'

'Maybe I was worried you might pick me up in that terrible old Austin 7 of yours.' Fenella's gaze, alight with mischief, slid across to the gleaming burgundy Daimler parked on the driveway. 'Looks like you've done pretty well for yourself, darling. I'm so happy for you.'

Forty years ago his lack of money had meant Fenella hadn't taken him seriously. Since then he *had* done well for himself but the slight had always rankled like an itch beneath the skin. Seeing her again and showing her what she'd missed out on completed a kind of circle.

They had lunch in the conservatory and caught up with each other's lives. Fenella was full of admiration for the house and Freddie told her how he had built up his property business. In turn he learned that she and Cyril had divorced after twenty-three years of marriage.

'He took early retirement and we moved to Puerto Banus. Being married to someone who's working nonstop at least gives you time on your own,' Fenella confided. 'Once Cyril gave up work there was no escape from him. It drove me mad. *He* drove me mad. Well, I couldn't stand it. So we broke up and I got involved with Jerry Britton, who played plenty of golf and kept the bars of Puerto Banus in business,' she continued wryly. 'But he was great fun and he made me feel young and desirable again. After twenty-three years of being married to Cyril that meant a lot, I can tell you.'

'And you married him.' Freddie couldn't resist asking the question. 'Was he wealthy?'

Fenella smiled sadly and said, 'Oh, yes. All my life I've needed the comfort of financial security. I was a silly, shallow woman, I can see that now. Jerry turned out to be a complete bastard. I'd never been so miserable. He was sleeping around . . .' Putting down her knife and fork, she said sadly, 'And the thing was, I knew deep down that I deserved it. This was my punishment for being so shallow and mercenary all my life. I'd deserved my comeuppance and now here it was. When I divorced Jerry I could have fought for a fabulous settlement, but I didn't. I came back to England and resolved to be a better person.'

'Don't be too hard on yourself. At least you were honest about it.'

'Oh, darling, and look where it got me.' Fenella shook her head. 'And the really ironic thing is . . . no, nothing, forget it.'

Freddie watched her wave the words away.

'What's the really ironic thing?' he prompted.

'OK, but I warn you it makes me sound completely pathetic.' She took a sip of wine and gazed steadily at him. 'I missed you, Freddie. I loved you. I know I never told you this, but that was because I couldn't. I'd made my bed and I had to lie in it. But I never forgot you. I never stopped comparing other men with you, wishing they could *be* more like you.'

'Like me if I'd been a lot richer.' Freddie's tone was dry.

'No, like *you*,' Fenella insisted. 'Look, I know this must sound ridiculous but can you understand how excited I was when I opened that letter from your friend Lottie? Discovering that you were looking for me and wanted to see me again? I felt like a teenager! This was my chance to make up for the terrible way I'd treated you before . . . and, less unselfishly, I thought it could be my chance to be happy again with my first love. Because that's what you were, Freddie. I may not have been able to admit it at the time, but it's true.' She gave a brittle laugh. 'And now I'm here, and it's all gone wrong again. I think I must be jinxed.'

Bemused, Freddie said, 'Why are you jinxed?'

'Because the whole point of seeing you again and . . . whatever . . .' another wave of her hand, 'was to prove to you that I really have changed! But now I can't, because you aren't poor any more. You have all this! When you told me your address I assumed Hestacombe House was a block of flats, so when the taxi driver pulled up outside this place I almost fainted. But it means I can't flirt with you, because if I did you'd think I was only doing it because you're rich.'

'I don't know what to say.' Freddie paused, then decided he may as well come clean. 'OK. If I'm honest, that's one of the reasons I wanted to see you again. To prove to you that I'd made something of myself, against the odds and despite the fact that you broke my heart.'

Fenella's hand flew to her mouth. 'Did I break your heart? Really?'

'Oh, yes.'

'I thought you'd just go back to that sweet girl of yours . . . what was her name?'

'Giselle.' Freddie's heart contracted. 'I messed up. After you and I broke up, I was hard to live with. We struggled on but we were both unhappy,' said Freddie. 'Then I met someone else. And that was it, I finished with Giselle. Started seeing the other girl.'

'Whose name was?'

'Mary. Within six months we were married. She died four years ago.'

'Oh, Freddie. And you were happy together? Of course you were,' Fenella exclaimed. 'I can tell by the look in your eyes. That's wonderful. I'm so glad you found the right one in the end.'

Unable to speak for a moment, Freddie nodded and leaned forward to top up her wineglass.

'Poor darling.' Fenella reached over and touched his hand. 'You must miss her terribly. It's the loneliness, isn't it? I just can't bear to think of you on your own. You're still a very attractive man, you know.' Breaking into a smile, Fenella said, 'If it wasn't for all this wretched money of yours, who knows . . . Oh heavens, just ignore me, I'm a silly old woman . . .'

As her voice trailed away, Freddie realised he had to explain to Fenella that any kind of future together simply wasn't on.

'Of course you aren't silly. Or old,' he added hastily. 'But I'm really not looking for a relationship. That isn't why I wanted to see you again.'

Startled, Fenella said, 'Oh.'

'Sorry if I misled you.' Freddie felt guilty, since he clearly had. 'I just thought it would be nice to find out how life had treated you.'

'Oh, well.' Summoning a brave smile, Fenella said, 'And now you know. Would you like me to leave now that you're all up-to-date?'

'No, no, *no*.' Freddie shook his head vehemently, which did his headache no good at all. 'Fenella, I'm just being honest, letting you know how things are. We can still have a nice day together, surely?'

'Handsome and persuasive. How can I refuse?' Fenella's gaze softened. 'Now, tell me all about your wonderful wife.'

There was no torture, Lottie was discovering, like the torture of working for someone you lusted after but couldn't actually get lusty with. Being allowed to look but not touch was starting to get to her in a major way.

Tyler was already there in the office when she arrived at nine o'clock, looking breathtaking as usual in a navy polo shirt and faded jeans and prompting her stomach to do a quick loop-the-loop. He really was causing havoc with her hormones. As ever, the question buzzing around Lottie's brain, bursting to be let out, was *What are you like in bed?*

'Hi. How are the kids?'

He always asked. It was the only reference Tyler made to their over-before-it-had-begun relationship.

Lottie threw her sunglasses and car keys onto the desk and reached for the mail. 'Fine. Getting on well at school.'

'That's good.'

She nodded; it certainly was. It would kill her to think she'd made all that sacrifice for nothing.

'We've got a request for Walnut Lodge.' He tapped the screen. 'For the second week in December. They want it for their honeymoon.'

'No problem. Ooh, it's Zach and Jenny!' Leaning forward to read the email on the screen, Lottie exclaimed, 'They're a lovely couple, but Jenny despaired of ever getting Zach down the aisle because he'd always vowed never to marry.' A lump sprang into her throat. 'And now they are. Isn't that brilliant? Happy endings still exist.'

'Unless he doesn't know he's getting married and she's arranging it all in secret,' Tyler drawled.

'Only a man could think that.' Lottie swiped him on the shoulder with her handful of letters. 'You're so cynical.'

'Trust me, when it happens to you, it's no fun at all.'

Her mouth dropped open. '*Did* it happen to you?'

Tyler winked. 'And you're so gullible.'

'At least I'm not unromantic.' Lottie took another swipe at him with the sheaf of letters. 'All bitter and twisted and—'

'Now you're being unfair.' Deftly catching her wrist Tyler said, 'I can be romantic when I want to be. It all depends on the girl.'

Uh-oh, dangerous. As the adrenaline skipped joyfully through her body, Lottie realised she'd gone too far. Time to pull herself together and backtrack fast. Oh, but she didn't *want* to . . .

Drop the flirting and step away from the man, ordered a stern voice scarily reminiscent of Miss Batson. Step *away* from the *man*.

Lottie stepped away. 'Right, well, Freddie loves a happy ending. I'm going to tell him about Zach and Jenny. He'll be thrilled.'

Lottie let herself in through the kitchen as she did most mornings. As a rule Freddie was ensconced at the table reading the paper and enjoying a leisurely breakfast, but today the kitchen was empty.

Lottie wandered through to the panelled hallway, then saw that the door to the study was ajar. Hearing the faint sound of a drawer being opened she realised that Freddie must be in there.

Afterwards she wondered why she hadn't called out his name as she usually did. Instead, making her way over to the study, she saw the back of a slender, dark-haired woman wrapped in an oversized dressing gown, standing in front of Freddie's desk.

As Lottie watched through the crack in the door, the woman finished examining the papers in her hand and returned them to the right-hand drawer of the desk. Closing it, she then stealthily opened the left-hand drawer and surveyed the contents, pulling out a couple of letters and rapidly scanning them.

Lottie had no intention of interrupting proceedings, but the next moment a floorboard creaked beneath her foot and the woman spun round. So this was Fenella Britton.

'I'd ask what you were doing,' Lottie said evenly, 'but that would be a silly question.'

'You almost gave me a heart attack!' Clapping her hand to her chest, Fenella shook her head. 'I'm sorry, I know how this must look. But it's Freddie. I'm just so worried about him.'

Lottie had been worried about Freddie for weeks. With a jolt of fear she wondered if he had been taken ill during the night. 'Why? Where is he? What's happened?'

'Nothing's happened.' Fenella fiddled with the lapels of the olive-green towelling dressing gown. 'But something is wrong with Freddie, isn't it? I saw all the painkillers in the bathroom cabinet. Some are prescription only.' Indicating the letter that now lay uppermost on the desk she said, 'And this is from a neurologist. He's talking about the results of the latest scan and the prognosis being poor . . . oh God, I can't bear it! I've just found him again after all these years and now I'm going to lose him!'

Tears were pouring down Fenella Britton's cheeks. She looked as if she might pass out.

'You'd better sit down,' said Lottie. 'Where's Freddie?'

'Upstairs. Having a b-bath. I'm sorry. Fenella Britton.' Fenella held out a trembling hand. 'You must be Lottie. Freddie's told me all about you.'

Lottie didn't say that she'd heard all about her too. This was the woman who had discarded Freddie because he hadn't been rich enough. And here she was, having discovered that he was now very wealthy indeed, snooping through his private papers. Despite the copious tears Lottie couldn't bring herself to warm to Fenella Britton.

'Typical Freddie,' said Fenella, wiping her eyes. 'He didn't mention it.

He wouldn't want to upset me. He's always been so considerate.'

'Well, you can talk about it when he comes downstairs. Are you leaving this morning?' Lottie checked her watch. 'Because I can give you a lift to the station if—'

'Leaving? How can I leave, now that I know the truth?' Vehemently Fenella shook her head. 'Oh, no, I let Freddie down once before. I'm not going to do it again. He *needs* me.'

'You only met him again yesterday,' said Lottie. Incredulity mingled with suspicion; was Fenella planning to move into Hestacombe House?

'I've loved him for forty years,' Fenella said simply. 'Freddie has no family. He can't be on his own at a time like this.'

Lottie wondered if the no family bit was significant in other ways.

Aloud she said, 'He won't be on his own.'

And then she saw the glint in the older woman's eye and knew she was right.

'You don't want me here, do you? You'd rather deny Freddie the comfort of having someone he cares about take care of him. Why *is* that exactly?' Fenella's voice was as smooth as cream but the underlying challenge was unmistakable.

'I don't know. Were there any bank statements floating around in that desk drawer?'

'No, there weren't.' Fenella tilted her head to one side. 'But that's what you're worried about, isn't it? Freddie doesn't have anyone to leave his money to. And you were hoping to keep it all for yourself.'

'Stop this.' Freddie's voice rang out behind them. 'What's going on?'

'I caught her snooping in your desk drawer,' said Lottie. 'She was reading the letters from your doctor, and God knows what else.'

'Because I was so worried about you!' Fenella, rushing past Lottie and throwing her arms round Freddie, burst into a fresh torrent of tears. 'And now I know the truth. Oh, my darling, how can life be so cruel?'

Freddie actually looked relieved. Lottie watched the tension go out of him as he cupped Fenella's heart-shaped face between his hands. 'It's OK. Sshh, don't cry, I'm sorry.'

Don't *comfort* her, Lottie longed to yell. *Shoot her!*

'Oh, Freddie, my Freddie,' Fenella sobbed into his white shirt.

Hang on, I'll get the gun!

'Now you know why I said I wasn't looking for another relationship.' Freddie's voice cracked with emotion.

'Oh, darling, don't you see? It's already happened,' Fenella whispered. 'Whether we want it to or not. And it may not be the easy option and it might not be sensible but we're in this together.' Lovingly she stroked

Freddie's face. 'Because I'm going to look after you. Right to the end.'

There's always the lake, Lottie thought longingly. We could just tie her up and tip her in.

Visibly pulling herself together, Fenella said, 'Darling, OK if I have my bath now?'

'Go ahead.' Freddie smoothed her hair. 'Take as long as you want.'

Fenella disappeared upstairs to take her bath. In the kitchen Lottie made coffee and listened to Freddie's account of yesterday's events. She especially enjoyed the bit about how Fenella had evidently seen the error of her mercenary ways and had been horrified to discover that he was a multimillionaire.

And no, they hadn't slept together last night. They had simply been talking for so long that Fenella had missed the last train home.

After hearing far more than she wanted to hear, Lottie said, 'I know this is none of my business, Freddie, but I still don't trust her. She was going through your private things.'

'But she's explained why.' He looked defensive. 'And I did tell her to make herself at home.'

This wasn't going to be easy. 'She accused me of feeling threatened by her because I want you to leave everything in your will to me. Which *isn't* true, by the way,' Lottie added hastily.

Freddie shrugged. 'So you say.'

'Freddie! I'm not!'

'I know that.' He looked amused. 'But Fenella doesn't, does she? Because she doesn't know you. Just like you don't know her.'

Bursting to retort, 'but *I* know I'm *right*', Lottie forced herself not to. She gazed steadily at Freddie.

'Touché. Look, I want you to be happy. It's what you deserve. Just . . . don't do anything hasty, OK?'

'Like rush off to the nearest register office?' One eyebrow went up. 'Or change my will and leave everything to Fenella?'

Exactly. *Exactly*.

Lottie said, 'Something like that.'

'Darling, it's sweet of you to worry about me.' Freddie's tone was consoling. 'But I think I can trust myself not to get carried away.'

Lottie, who knew better, said nothing. Of course he couldn't trust himself; he was a man.

The temperature had soared back into the eighties and Lottie was by the lake, topping up her tan, when she felt a shadow fall across her face.

Her stomach tensed. Tyler?

She opened her eyes and saw that it wasn't. Mario was standing over her looking so grim that Lottie knew at once what had happened.

Pushing herself up on her elbows, she shielded her eyes from the sun. 'What's wrong?'

Mario glanced over at Nat and Ruby, who were splashing around in the shallows. When he was satisfied they were out of earshot he said, 'Amber's chucked me.'

'Oh, no.' Lottie looked suitably shocked. 'I can't believe it! Why?'

'Turns out she's been seeing someone else.'

'Really?'

Mario nodded. 'Really. Why are women such liars?'

'How long's it been going on?' Perspiration trickled down Lottie's cleavage as she adjusted her bikini straps.

'And that includes you,' Mario continued evenly. 'Because you're lying now, pretending to be surprised. Amber told me she told you last week.'

Cheers, Amber.

'Oh, well.' Lottie wasn't going to feel guilty. 'That's just sisterly solidarity. I was being discreet. Could you move out of my sun?'

Mario sighed and sat down on the beach towel next to her. 'Is that all the sympathy I get?'

'How much do you think you deserve? I'm your ex-wife, remember. You messed around with other girls and we ended up getting divorced because of it. Now Amber's decided she can't stay with you because she can't trust you, so she's found someone she *can* trust.' Reaching for her bottle of Soltan and uncapping it, Lottie squeezed a dollop of the cream onto her stomach. 'If I were the type to gloat I'd call it poetic justice.'

Mario's eyes glittered. 'Thanks a lot. Even though I haven't been unfaithful to Amber, not once.'

'Of course you haven't. Not even when Amber was away in France,' Lottie pointedly reminded him. '*Thanks to me*.'

'And that's another thing. It wasn't until she found out you'd spent the whole time acting like a human chastity belt that she realised she couldn't carry on seeing me.' Mario gestured in disbelief. 'If it wasn't for you, we'd still be together.'

'Oh, no, don't start trying to shift the blame onto me! Amber was in France with another man while I was being your damn chastity belt!'

'So you're glad this has happened.' Mario's voice rose.

'Of course I'm not glad it happened. You know I didn't want you and Amber to break up.'

He nodded, watching Ruby and Nat as they skimmed stones across the shimmering surface of the lake.

'I know. I just can't believe it. I thought we were so happy.'

Lottie's heart went out to him. He was clearly more upset than he was letting on. Mario had always led something of a charmed life.

'Oh God, and I'm going to have to tell Ruby and Nat.' His jaw tightened. 'They're not going to like it.'

This was an understatement. Lottie knew they'd be devastated. They loved Amber as much as they hated Tyler, the difference being that this time they couldn't influence the outcome.

'I'm really sorry,' Lottie said quietly.

'Me too.' Mario hesitated, swallowing hard. 'I love her. I can't stop thinking about her being with someone else.'

Now you know how I felt when you did it to me. The words ran through Lottie's mind but she didn't voice them. Instead she put her arms round him and held him tightly. Mario might no longer be her husband but she still cared for him and right now he was in need of comfort. It hurt to see him like this.

Having spotted them Nat crowed, 'Oooh, *sexxxxy*.'

Ruby skidded up to them, excitedly clutching a coin in her hand. 'Look, I found fifty pee in the water!'

Mario said, 'That'll be the fifty fish.'

'Daddy! That's gross.'

Nat, who adored toilet humour, snorted with laughter and threw himself down on the sand next to Mario. 'I'm going to find fifty poos! Why was Mummy hugging you? Is it because you're so *sexxxxy*?'

Mario hesitated. Lottie decided to get it over with. 'Dad's fine, he's a bit sad, that's all. He and Amber aren't seeing each other any more.'

Ruby and Nat stared at her, then at Mario.

'Why?'

'These things happen.' Mario shrugged, but his jaw was set.

Ruby's hand crept into his. 'Don't you like her any more?'

'Oh, I do.'

'But she doesn't like you.' Nat's lower lip was beginning to wobble.

'Or us,' Ruby whispered.

'That's not true,' Lottie exclaimed. 'Amber loves both of you! She just found someone else.'

Nat looked outraged. 'Someone she likes better than Dad?'

Mario pulled Nat onto his lap. 'How can anyone be better than me? Amber just has weird taste in men.'

'Like Mummy,' Ruby chimed in, 'with that horrible Tyler.'

'What's her new boyfriend's name?' said Ruby.

'Quentin,' said Lottie.

'*Quentin?* That's a *dumb* name!'

Nat's eyes sparkled. 'Almost as dumb as Tyler.' Perking up, he said, 'I know, we can make another VD doll of Quentin and stick pins in it.'

Ruby was scornful. 'Voodoo, durr-brain. Honestly, you're so thick.'

'I'm so hungry,' Nat replied.

Lottie, mentally scanning the contents of her fridge, was wondering what she could possibly do that was inventive with half a packet of bacon, a jar of mint sauce and two giant bags of parsnips.

Parsnips. Buy One Get One Free had a lot to answer for.

Mario, familiar with that desperate look in her eyes, came to the rescue as she had hoped he would. 'Come on.' Shifting Nat from his lap he stood up and held out a hand to Lottie. 'Let's take them to Pizza Hut.'

The web designer's name was Phil Micklewhite.

'Hi,' said Lottie when he answered the phone on the fourth ring, 'I don't know if you remember me, but we spoke—'

'Never forget a voice,' Phil Micklewhite said cheerfully. 'You're the one who rang last week asking about Fenella Britton.'

'That's me. OK, the thing is, you sounded like a really nice person, kind and honest and completely trustworthy—'

'And you haven't been able to stop thinking about me,' said Phil. 'You want to meet me in person so we can start our mad passionate love affair. I know, I know, this happens to me all the time, but before you turn up on my doorstep I feel it's only fair to warn you that I'm fifty years old, *very* overweight and so ugly I even scare my goldfish.'

Lottie relaxed, liking him even more. 'Actually I wanted to ask you a bit more about Fenella. Is that OK?'

'Fine by me. Not sure I can help you, though. I don't know much about her.' He paused. 'Am I allowed to ask why?'

Lottie said, 'Can I trust you to be discreet?'

'Discretion is my middle name.'

Lottie briefly filled him in on the situation. 'So basically I just wondered if you knew anything that might prove me right. Or wrong.'

'I'm afraid we're a pretty quiet bunch here at Hutton Court. There are eight flats and most of the other residents are retired. We say hello and pass the time of day, but that's about it. Pretty much the only time they knock on my door is when they want to use the internet.'

'Does Fenella use your internet?'

'Hardly at all. Although she did last week. She asked me how to go about finding out something. I connected her to Google, showed her what to do and left her to it.'

Not daring to get her hopes up, Lottie said, 'When last week?'

Phil said slowly, 'Possibly the day after you phoned me.'

Lottie got her hopes up. 'Can you find out what she was looking for?'

'Give me a few seconds.'

She heard the clatter of computer keys as Phil delved expertly into files. He was back on the phone moments later.

'She got through to a website called Hestacombe Holiday Cottages.'

Bingo.

'And it was the day after you rang me. Is that helpful?'

'It's just what I needed.' Lottie nodded happily. 'It's perfect.'

Fenella went very still and looked at Freddie. 'You want me to leave, because I looked you up on the internet.'

'Because you weren't honest with me,' said Freddie.

She shook her head in disbelief. 'It's that bloody girl, isn't it? Sticking her nose in where it isn't wanted. And you're just going to let her win! I love you, Freddie. You love me. We can make each other happy!'

Three days ago Fenella had erupted into his life. Two days ago they had driven up to Oxford and returned with three suitcases of her clothes. Yesterday Lottie had taken him aside and relayed to him the details of her conversation with Phil Micklewhite.

And now he was doing what needed to be done.

'I thought I could trust you,' said Freddie.

'You *can*,' Fenella pleaded.

'Why would you want to stay with someone who's dying?'

'Because I can't bear the thought of not being with you!'

'Fine, then.' Freddie smiled. 'You can stay.'

Fenella's dark eyes widened with delight. Jumping up from the table she threw her arms round him. 'Darling! Really? Oh, you won't regret it!'

'I hope you won't.'

'Oh, *Freddie* . . .'

'Listen to what I have to say.' Freddie prepared himself. 'You should know that my will has been made and I won't be changing it. Whatever happens, you won't get anything when I'm gone. No property, no money, nothing.' He paused, allowing time for this information to sink in. 'So that's it. I'll understand if you decide to change your mind.'

He knew what Fenella's answer would be before he'd even finished the first sentence. By the time he'd reached *no property, no money, nothing*, her fingers had slipped from his shoulders.

Finally Fenella spoke. 'So who gets it all? Don't tell me you're leaving everything to some miserable animal sanctuary.'

He shook his head. 'It's all been taken care of.'

'Well, I think you're making a mistake. We could have been happy.'

'I don't think we could,' said Freddie. 'Sorry.'

Fenella took a step away from him, turned to gaze at the wondrous view of Hestacombe Lake, then visibly collected herself. 'I'm sorry too. I'll go and pack my things.'

Chapter 6

IT WAS THE OPENING night of Jumee, a glamorous new restaurant in the upmarket Montpellier district of Cheltenham. Deeply impressed by the invitation—a silver 3-D hologram printed on Mediterranean-blue Perspex—Lottie had been delighted to come along and check out the glamour first-hand on behalf of future visitors to Hestacombe. And the food of course. She had even celebrated by going out and treating herself to a slinky new black and gold dress.

So far so good.

The bad news was, she hadn't counted on having to listen to an earnest grey-haired woman doctor in a bristly-looking tweed skirt and a fawn cardigan, droning on and on and *on* about the horrors of eczema.

Half an hour ago Lottie's stomach had been rumbling away in joyful anticipation of the evening ahead, but now her stomach had undergone an abrupt change of heart. Instead of rumbling away happily, it had squashed itself into a tight, hard little knot, sullenly daring her—in true teenage fashion—to try to make it accept any food at all.

Clearly, it wasn't an ideal scenario. Lottie felt sorry for the young couple who had plunged their life savings into this new venture. Having spoken to Robbie and Michelle earlier, she'd learned that it had always been their dream to run their own restaurant. Duly selling their house and emptying their savings accounts, they had been dismayed to discover that they still didn't have enough money to make the business viable. Step forward Michelle's Uncle Bill, a hugely wealthy man, who had generously offered to back them.

When Uncle Bill had suggested using the opportunity of the opening night to raise money for his favourite charity, it would have been churlish to refuse. Even though they already knew his favourite charity was Clearaway UK. Uncle Bill's beloved son Marcus suffered dreadfully from chronic eczema.

'. . . when the skin is cracked and red, when a person's entire body is one mass of swollen weeping wounds, when members of the public turn away in revulsion from the sight of a face so hideously disfigured it is barely recognisable, life becomes *intolerable* for the sufferer,' Dr Murray pronounced.

'HIIIICCCC!'

It was one of those gulping, barking-in-reverse hiccups, possibly the loudest Lottie had ever heard. Everyone in the room turned to look at the perpetrator, who was standing just in front and to the left of her. Tall, male and rangily built, he was wearing a baggy pink shirt, faded jeans and a baseball cap.

Clearly infuriated by the interruption, Dr Murray stared at him.

'HIIICCCCCC!' gulped the man, his shoulders jerking in time with the ear-splitting noise. *'HIIIIICCCCCC!'*

Dr Murray was by this time quivering with outrage and people were starting to laugh and giggle. Acting on sheer instinct, Lottie squeezed past the fat woman to her left and managed to move up behind the world's loudest hiccupper.

'HIIII—*what the hell!*' The man let out a bellow and leapt into the air as if he'd been electrocuted. Having finally managed to escape the confines of his shirt, the ice cubes Lottie had tipped down the back of his collar dropped out and skittered like kittens across the wooden floor.

'HIIIICCCCC!'

'*Get out!*' Dr Murray roared across the restaurant, cowing the now sniggering audience into silence.

The man seized Lottie by the hand and dragged her with him. All eyes were upon them—most of them openly envious—as they made their hasty escape.

So deliriously happy to be out of the restaurant Lottie said, 'Sorry about the ice. I was just trying to stop your hiccups.'

'And you did.' He spread his hands in amazement. 'See? It's a miracle.'

'What can I say?' Lottie shrugged modestly. 'I'm good at what I do.'

'We must celebrate.' His blue eyes crinkling at the corners, he pulled off his baseball cap and ran his fingers through his unruly blond hair. 'Are you hungry?'

Eczema. Weeping wounds.

'Funnily enough, no.'

'Great. Me neither. Let's go grab a drink.'

'There's something I have to tell you,' Lottie announced as the taxi pulled up outside Piper's Cottage.

'Oh, yes, and what's that?'

'You're a bad man.' She nudged Sebastian Gill, next to her on the back seat, and peered at her watch. 'It's one o'clock in the morning and you have spent the last five hours being a very bad influence on a mother of two. And if you think you're coming in for a nightcap you're seriously mistaken.'

'You're a cruel woman.' Seb shook his head in mournful fashion. 'Am I allowed out of the car to give you a gentlemanly good-night kiss, or would that be overstepping the mark?'

'You may do that.' Fumbling for the door handle, Lottie marvelled that he was still able to enunciate such big words. She'd drunk more tonight than she'd drunk in the last month and her head was spinning like a plate on a stick.

Oh, but what a night it had been. Her sides were aching from laughing so much. She and Seb had had the best time and the more she learned about him the more perfect he became. His full name was Sebastian Aloysius Gill (which was weird, granted, but you couldn't hold someone's middle name against them). He was thirty-two and living in Kingston Ash, midway between Cheltenham and Tetbury, and like herself had been divorced for a couple of years. Best of all, he had an eight-year-old daughter, Maya, which meant he was comfortable around children and less likely to do or say the wrong thing in their company than some people Lottie could mention.

'Need a hand, love?' The taxi driver lit a cigarette as Lottie clambered out of the back seat and hesitated at the front gate.

'I'm fine, fine, absolutely fine.' She was fumbling inside her handbag. 'Just looking for my—*oops*.'

'Elephant? Lipstick? Shotgun?' Seb suggested helpfully. 'Jaffa cakes? Come on, give us a clue, how many syllables?'

'Bloody front-door key,' Lottie wailed, dropping to her knees and groping blindly around in the darkness.

'God, five syllables. They're the hardest ones to get.' Seb followed her out of the car and joined her on the ground. 'Where did you drop it?'

'If I knew where I'd dropped it, I'd be able to find it, wouldn't I?' Giggling as his hand brushed her ankle, Lottie said, 'OK, concentrate. This is serious. It could be in the road or on the pavement or in the garden or . . . or . . . *anywhere*.'

'If you ring the bell,' Seb suggested, 'wouldn't the butler let you in?'

'Sadly it's the butler's night off. A torch would be useful.'

'Bloody butlers, never around when you need them.' Kneeling up and addressing the taxi driver, Seb said, 'You wouldn't happen to have one with you, I suppose?'

'What, a butler? Nah, mate.' The taxi driver grinned broadly and took a drag of his cigarette. 'More trouble than they're worth.'

'Bleeeurrgh, *slug*.' Lottie uttered a muffled shriek.

'Ah, but does it know how to open front doors? Could it maybe *slide* under the door and unlock it from the inside? You look very cute like that, by the way. On your hands and knees.' His teeth gleaming white in the pitch darkness, Seb said cheerfully, 'Like a playful dog.'

'Look, this is all very amusing,' the taxi driver yawned, 'but you're not actually any nearer to finding the damn key, are you?'

'That's because it's the middle of the night.' Lottie regarded him loftily from her playful-dog position at the edge of the kerb. 'And we have no way of finding the damn key because none of us has a torch.'

The taxi driver heaved a sigh and knocked his gearstick into reverse. 'Right. I'll back up and shine my headlights onto the pavement.'

'That's an excellent idea.' Lottie nodded with approval. 'Truly wonderful. Now why didn't I think of that?'

'Because you're pissed as parrots, the pair of you.'

It was sod's law of course that within seconds of the taxi reversing across the road to light up Lottie's front garden, another car would appear and be unable to get past. Lottie, scurrying around on all fours heard the second car slow to a halt and their taxi driver yell across, 'Sorry, mate, couple of punters lost their marbles. Give us a minute, will you?'

Then a familiar voice reached Lottie's ears and she looked up too suddenly, causing her head to start spinning again.

'They've lost *what*?'

Lottie froze like a rabbit caught in . . . well, headlights, then said defiantly, 'Our taxi driver thinks he's being funny. All I did was drop my key. The situation'—gosh, difficult word to say when you were tired—'shichashun is *completely* under control.'

'Glad to hear it,' Tyler drawled.

Dazzled by the lights, she shielded her eyes and said impatiently, 'You could always help. Seeing as it's all your fault I can't get into my house.'

One eyebrow went up. 'And that would be . . . why?'

'Because I managed perfectly well for years keeping my spare key under the geranium pot next to the front door. Until *you* came along'—Lottie pointed an accusing finger—'and told me that I was just asking to be burgled. So I moved it, and now my spare key is sitting in the cutlery drawer in my kitchen, which is what *I* call ridiculous—'

'Found it!' cried Seb.

'Really?' Still on her knees, Lottie swivelled round in relief.

Seb flashed a grin. 'No. Only joking.'

'Oh God!'

'But just for a split second there you felt better, didn't you?'

'And now I feel *worse*,' Lottie wailed, 'and I want to go to bed, but I can't because nobody's helping me to look for my stupid sodding key!'

'Hey, you're beautiful when you're angry.' There was a *thunk* as a car door opened and closed and Seb turned to address Tyler. 'Don't you think she looks beautiful, with her hair falling all over her face and her eyes flashing? Like a stroppy springer spaniel.'

Tyler gave him an odd look. Lottie decided she'd had enough of being told she resembled a dog. Careful not to lose her balance she pushed herself upright and . . . whoops, lost her balance. Just for a moment. OK, lean against the wall and look casual. What was Tyler doing out at this time of night anyway? It was *late*.

'Right.' Tyler was standing on the pavement now, hands on hips. 'If you don't know where you dropped the key, which you clearly *don't*,' he added pointedly, 'then you're better off waiting for the morning. Let your friend go home in his taxi. You can stay at my place tonight and we'll find the key tomorrow. How does that sound?'

Lottie stifled a snigger. How did it sound? Like he didn't want Seb hanging around Piper's Cottage a minute longer than necessary.

Seb, who was evidently thinking likewise, surveyed Tyler with amusement. 'Are you her husband?'

'He's my boss.' Lottie wondered if Tyler's suggestion that she should stay the night meant he had more than a working relationship in mind.

'The grumpy one who complains about your work all the time? The one you can't stand?'

'He's joking,' Lottie said hastily. 'I didn't say any of that.'

In the end her bursting bladder made the decision for her. Lottie waved Seb off in the taxi, safe in the knowledge that they had each other's numbers keyed into their phones.

'You're going to have one hell of a hangover tomorrow,' Tyler remarked as he helped her into the passenger seat of his car.

'Thank you for pointing that out. I'd never have thought of it otherwise. We had fun. I'm allowed to have fun, aren't I?'

'As much as you like. I'm not trying to stop you.'

In the darkness, Lottie smiled. 'Sure about that?'

'Well. I'd rather you didn't hook up with a complete idiot.' Tyler's tone of voice indicated that this was his opinion of Seb.

'I like him. Don't spoil it for me.' Her head began to spin again as he rounded a sharp bend. 'Where have you been tonight anyway? Who says you haven't been sneaking off to see some dippy girl?'

'The Anderssons checked out of Walnut Lodge at eight o'clock this evening to fly back to Sweden. At ten o'clock I got a frantic phone call from them at Heathrow,' said Tyler. 'They'd left their passports in the biscuit tin in the kitchen.'

Lottie realised she was glad he hadn't been seeing some dippy girl. Aloud she said, 'So you drove all the way up there. Very noble.'

'Customer relations.' Tyler paused. 'Where are Nat and Ruby tonight?'

'With Mario.' Lottie was bursting for the loo. 'They mustn't find out I stayed with you. They'd give me no end of grief.'

'Luckily we aren't on speaking terms,' Tyler said lightly, 'so they won't be hearing it from me.'

Almost there now. Scrunching up her bladder for all she was worth, Lottie said, 'We could sleep together and they wouldn't know. That's ironic, isn't it? But I don't think we should. It wouldn't be right. Not fair on us, not fair on them.'

Heavens, where had that come from?

'Well, quite.' Tyler nodded. 'Plus I do try to make it a rule not to sleep with women who have had a lot to drink.'

Defensively Lottie said, 'No? Are you worried they might wake up the next morning and sue you?'

'Not at all.' As he pulled up outside Fox Cottage Tyler said equably, 'I'm usually worried they might snore.'

The cheek of it. As if she'd dream of doing anything so unladylike. Bursting for a wee, Lottie launched herself out of the car and hopped from one foot to the other as he struggled to open the door of the cottage.

'Are you being extra-slow on purpose?'

Tyler grinned. 'Yes.'

'I hate you.' Snatching the key from him, Lottie jabbed it manically at the lock, finally flinging the door open and racing upstairs to the loo.

Oh the relief, the blessed *blessed* relief . . . Now she could concentrate again on something other than keeping her pelvic floor clenched tight.

It was two o'clock in the morning and here she was in Tyler's cottage. Slightly miffed, Lottie studied her face in the mirror above the basin as she washed her hands. Why didn't Tyler want to sleep with her? She was looking fantastic! Surely any red-blooded male would jump at the chance? Even if she had said it wouldn't be a good idea.

Oooh, what was that heavenly smell?

Bacon!

'I don't snore,' Lottie announced from the kitchen doorway.

Tyler had his back to her. When he turned round she tossed back her hair and dazzled him with her most seductive Lauren Bacall smile.

'Excuse me?'

'I don't snore. *Yoww.*' The seductive moment was spoilt somewhat by the kitchen door swinging shut behind her and trapping her fingers.

'Well, I'm glad to hear that.' Tyler expertly flipped the sizzling rashers of bacon in the frying pan; God, he had forearms to die for.

'And I've changed my mind about tonight.' Unobtrusively sucking her pinched fingers—God, that had hurt a *lot*—Lottie said, 'This could be our only chance. I think we should go for it.'

'You do?'

'Well, it seems a shame not to. We both know we want to, don't we?'

'Er, hang on . . .'

'Oh, please! Don't pretend you don't.' Lottie spread her arms and shrugged. 'So why shouldn't we? I like mine really crispy, by the way.'

That caught his attention. Pausing with the spatula in mid-air, Tyler said, '*What?*'

'My bacon.' Lottie nodded at the pan, crammed with five rashers. 'I like it crispy. Is that two rashers for you and three for me?'

'It's five rashers for me,' Tyler said slowly. 'You went to review a restaurant tonight, remember?'

'But we didn't eat. We . . . kind of left in a hurry. You see, Seb had these *massive* hiccups and I tried to stop them, and they asked us to leave. So you see, that's why I'm so hungry. Ravenous, in fact.' Slinking across the kitchen and sliding her arms sexily round Tyler's waist she murmured, 'And we need to keep our energy levels up, don't we? Hmm? Don't want to be too weak and racked with hunger pangs to—'

'Lottie.' Tyler turned round as she pressed kisses against his shoulder blades. Disentangling himself from her grasp he gazed deep into her eyes. 'I can't cook if you're going to keep distracting me like this. You're absolutely right, we both need to eat a proper meal. So why don't you go through to the living room and make yourself at home, and as soon as the food's ready I'll bring it through. Does that sound like a good idea?'

'It sounds like a great idea.' Lottie grinned. 'Can we have fried bread and mushrooms and tomatoes too?'

'All that,' Tyler promised, and the way his mouth curved up at the corners proved too much for Lottie to resist. Teetering up on tip toe, she kissed him. Entirely his fault for having such a delectable mouth.

'You're gorgeous.' Lottie stroked his lightly stubbled jaw. 'We're going to have such a great time. We'll never forget tonight.'

'We certainly won't,' Tyler agreed, still smiling as he shooed her away. 'Now off you go. The sooner you stop molesting me the sooner I'll have this meal cooked.'

And the sooner I can ravish your glorious body, Lottie thought happily as she managed to locate the kitchen door and simultaneously wiggle her pinched fingers in a flirtatious fashion at Tyler. He grinned and wiggled his own unpinched fingers back at her.

OK, living room.

Sofa.

Slipping out of her shoes, she arranged herself alluringly against the velvet cushions. There, now when Tyler opened the living room door he would see her looking elegant, relaxed and completely irresistible . . .

'Lottie. Lottie, wake up.'

Someone was shaking her. Possibly the same person who'd glued her eyes shut. As the shaking intensified, Lottie rolled over onto her side, wincing as something heavy rolled in tandem and went clunk inside her head. Yuk, her brain. Slowly she peeled open her eyelids. Oof, sunlight.

And Tyler. Looking highly amused.

'So you wouldn't call yourself a morning person then.'

Oh God. The events of last night came crashing back, unwanted.

'What time is it?'

'Eight o'clock. Time to get up.'

He clearly wasn't planning on being remotely sympathetic. Well, she could hardly blame him for that. Lottie pictured him slaving over a hot stove before finally, triumphantly, bursting into the living room with two plates piled high with bacon, sausages, fried bread and mushrooms, only to find her asleep on the sofa.

Not to mention the other promise she'd made him.

Hmm, definitely best not to mention that one. No wonder he was a bit short on sympathy this bright morning.

'I've got a bit of a . . . a headache.' Shielding her eyes, Lottie peered hopefully up at him. 'Would you have any aspirin going spare?'

'Sorry, I don't.' He didn't *sound* sorry.

'OK,' Lottie said. 'I'm getting up. And I'm sorry I fell asleep while you were cooking my food. If you didn't throw it away, I'll eat it now.'

'Are you serious?' His dark grey eyes glittered, registering disbelief.

'Of course I am! I'm starving!'

'I meant do you seriously believe I cooked you a meal last night?'

'Oh. Didn't you?'

'When I knew for a fact you'd be snoring like a buffalo within thirty seconds of hitting that sofa?' Evidently enjoying the look on her face, Tyler drawled, 'I made myself a bacon sandwich. It was great. Five rashers of bacon all to myself. And guess what? They were really crispy.'

'So you weren't upset that I fell asleep before . . .' Lottie couldn't quite bring herself to utter the rest.

'Upset? Are you kidding, the state you were in? Let me tell you, I was counting on it. One-night stands aren't my style,' said Tyler. 'Especially when we have to work together. We'll forget it happened, shall we?'

'Oh. Of course, Sorry.' Oh yes, that was so likely.

'OK. No need to apologise. I'll make you a quick cup of tea.' He made a move towards the door. 'Feel free to use the bathroom. And there's a spare toothbrush on the shelf next to the basin.'

Hauling herself off the sofa, Lottie said, 'Did I really snore like a buffalo?'

Tyler regarded her gravely for several seconds. Finally he said, 'That's something only me and my bacon sandwich will ever know.'

'Tell me again where you were when you dropped it.'

Lottie sighed. 'I didn't drop it. The keyring got hooked on the zip of my make-up bag and when I pulled out my make-up bag the keyring just flew off the end. Kind of like a catapult.'

'OK.' Tyler managed to make it sound like: typical-stupid-bloody-woman. 'I guess we just keep looking until we find it.'

Feeling utterly ridiculous in her glitzy black and gold dress and black satin stilettos, Lottie did her best to ignore her raging hangover and get on with the task in hand.

A car slowed and Nat's voice called out, 'Mummy! What are you doing?'

'Mummy, why are you still wearing the dress you had on last night?' That question came from Ruby.

Mario grinned. 'Good question. I was wondering that myself.'

It was eight thirty and the children, smart in their blue and grey uniforms, were on their way to school.

'I just dropped my keys, that's all,' said Lottie. 'I'll see you two later, OK? You don't want to be late for school.'

'I do,' Nat said eagerly.

But Ruby's eyes had already narrowed in Tyler's direction. 'What's *he* doing here? Then, like a mini Mother Superior she demanded icily, 'Where did you sleep last night?'

Oh heavens. Flustered, Lottie blurted out, 'Here, of course!'

'So why are you still wearing that dress?'

'Because . . . well, because I like it! And so many people last night said how nice it was, I thought I'd wear it again today.'

Ruby's mouth was pursed like a cat's bottom. 'And where's your car?'

She'd make a terrifying barrister one day.

'Um . . . um . . .' Lottie was floundering badly, too hungover to keep track of what she was saying. 'Well . . .'

'Lottie, we don't have all day,' Tyler broke in. Turning to address Nat and Ruby he said, 'Your mother had a few drinks last night and left her car in Cheltenham. She rang me this morning and asked me for a lift to go and pick it up. So I turned up here ten minutes ago and as she was coming through the front gate she managed to drop her keys.'

As Tyler told them this, Nat and Ruby acted as though he didn't exist. Their eyes were roaming everywhere but in his direction.

'Is that them over there?' Nat was leaning precariously out of the passenger window, pointing at a rosebush adjacent to the front wall.

Lottie followed the direction of his finger and saw that he was right. There, glinting in the sunlight and jauntily swinging from one of the lower branches, were her keys.

And to think she'd never won anything on a hoop-la stall in her life.

'Thank God for that.' Hastening over to the rosebush, Lottie retrieved the dangling keyring.

Nat said hopefully, 'Do I get a reward?'

'Maybe later. Off you go to school now. I need to pick up my car.' She gave each of them a kiss then tapped her watch and said to Mario, 'Miss Batson'll have your guts for garters if they're late for registration.'

'Miss Batson loves me.' Mario was cheerful bordering on smug. 'She thinks I'm great. Anyway, I'll just tell her we would have been on time but you were so hung over you couldn't find your car keys.'

'You're all heart. In fact, if you do that, you'll end up with sole custody,' said Lottie. 'And it'll jolly well serve you right.'

Still laughing, Mario drove Nat and Ruby off to school. Lottie let herself into Piper's Cottage, changed into white trousers and a plain grey top and helped herself to a bottle of water from the fridge.

'Can you remember where you left your car?' said Tyler as they drove into Cheltenham.

'Of course I can remember!' Lottie was offended. She might not be able to recall *exactly* where she'd left her car but she knew which car park it was in.

'Fine. Just checking. There's a garage up ahead,' Tyler nodded, 'if you want to pick up some painkillers.'

Lottie, who had already swilled down three paracetamols and a pint of water at home, said heroically, 'No, thanks. I'm OK.'

Which was, frankly, ridiculous. She'd announced her intention to give her boss the night of his life, been politely turned down *without even realising it* and had fallen asleep in a sozzled heap on his sofa.

I mean, let's face it, what could be less OK than that?

'Your phone,' Tyler prompted as a muffled sound emanated from the handbag at Lottie's feet.

'Morning, gorgeous!' It was Seb, sounding disgustingly chirpy.

'Morning.' Lottie smiled, not feeling overly gorgeous but delighted to hear from him anyway.

'Did you spend the night with that scary boss of yours?'

'I didn't have a lot of choice.'

'I hope he behaved himself. Didn't attempt to take advantage of the situation, force his attentions upon you . . .'

'No, no, nothing like that.' Lottie hastily pressed the phone hard against her ear to stop his words spilling out.

'But does he have designs on you? After all, he is your boss,' said Seb. 'It can't be easy for him, having to work with—'

'Actually, he's here,' Lottie blurted out. 'Right next to me.'

Seb laughed. 'Lucky him. Anyhow, the reason I'm calling. I want to see you tonight.'

Tonight! Crikey. Flattered but not at all sure she could persuade Mario to take Nat and Ruby for a second night, Lottie grimaced and said, 'The thing is, I'd need to find a baby sitter.'

'Or you could bring the kids with you.' Seb was unfazed. 'There's a fair on Ambleside Common. Would they be up for that, d'you think?'

'They'd love it. If you're sure you wouldn't mind.' Flustered, Lottie realised that Tyler had stopped at a junction and was waiting for directions. 'Sorry. Left, then second right by that blue van. Um, look, I'll ring you back in a bit. We're just picking up the car.'

Seb paused. 'This boss of yours. Have you slept with him?'

'No!'

'Did he hear that?'

'Yes,' Tyler replied. 'He did.'

'Speak to you later.' Lottie hurriedly ended the call before Seb could cause any more mischief.

'Sounds like you've got yourself a date for tonight.'

Did he care? Really care? A wave of regret swept through her, because if she had the choice she wouldn't choose Seb. But, then, she was a mother whose children had taken that decision for her . . . A squiggle of excitement mingled with fear in Lottie's stomach at the prospect of introducing Seb to Nat and Ruby. What if they hated him as much as they hated Tyler? Aloud she said casually, 'Sounds like I have.'

'No. No way. I can't do it,' Seb declared flatly. 'Anything but that.'

'You have to.' Giggling helplessly, Ruby dragged him past the hoop-la stall. 'I'm going to make you go on it.'

Seb dug his heels in like a dog. '*Won't* do it. I'll be sick.'

Nat was busy tugging on his other arm. 'You won't. You have to come on it with us. Mum, tell him.'

'You have to,' Lottie told Seb, 'because someone has to look after the soft toys, and looking after soft toys really isn't a job for a grown man.'

Seb allowed himself to be hauled off to the Ghost Train and Lottie settled down on the grass to wait for them. As the lights and colours of the fairground flashed and swirled around her she breathed in the evocative smells of hot dogs, frying onions, toffee apples and diesel. It was hard to believe that in less than two hours Seb had won over both her children so effortlessly and completely. Although in truth he had achieved it within two minutes. Somehow there had been that magical spark when she had first introduced him to Ruby and Nat. Being a father himself undoubtedly helped.

A lurid lime-green stuffed dinosaur toppled against her knee. Lottie sat it firmly back upright next to the fluorescent orange fluffy spider and the giant purple pig they'd won at the shooting gallery.

'Oh God, never again,' Seb groaned, reappearing with Nat and Ruby in tow. 'That was scary. There were real ghosts in there.'

'He was frightened.' Nat was proud. 'I wasn't.'

'OK, back to the rides. That one.' Seb pointed to the contraption Lottie had been dreading, the warp-speed upside-down spinny thing.

'I'd love to,' she patted the stuffed toys, 'but these need looking after. You lot go. I'll stay here and watch.'

He pulled a face at Ruby and Nat. 'It's the children I feel sorry for. What must it be like to have a mother who's a wimp?'

'Someone has to look after everything we've won,' Lottie protested.

'Exactly. *Someone* does.' Seb gathered up the fluffy spider, the lurid dinosaur and the purple pig. Marching over to the warp-speed upside-down spinny thing he flashed a disarming smile at a couple of young teenage girls, exchanged a few words with them and handed over the toys. Returning, he said, 'But it doesn't have to be you.'

After the upside-down spinny thing came the Waltzers, the Octopus and the Dodgems. By ten o'clock they'd been on every ride at the fair, won many more stuffed toys and eaten far too many toffee apples, sticks of candyfloss and chips with curry sauce.

'That was brilliant.' Ruby heaved an ecstatic sigh as they made their way back across the field to where they'd left the car. 'Thanks, Seb.'

'Thank *you*,' Seb said gravely, 'for looking after me on the Ghost Train.'

'Can we go out again soon?' Nat gazed eagerly up at Seb.

Lottie winced in the darkness; seven-year-olds could be alarmingly direct. Even if it was a question she was interested in hearing the answer to herself.

'The thing is, I don't know if your mother would like that,' said Seb.

'Why not? She would!'

'She might have decided she doesn't like me.'

Nat was incredulous. 'She *does* like you, don't you, Mum?'

'*See?*' demanded Seb when Lottie hesitated, floundering around for a reply. 'She's trying to be polite because she doesn't want to hurt my feelings, but I think she's secretly in love with another man.'

'*Who?*' Ruby's eyes were like saucers.

Seb lowered his voice to a whisper. 'Tyson, is that his name? Her boss.'

'Noooo!' Nat let out a howl of disdain. 'She doesn't like him. We won't let her.'

'His name's Tyler,' Ruby chimed in with relish. 'And we hate him.'

'Ruby,' Lottie protested.

'Well, we *do*.'

'Your mum might not like me,' said Seb. 'We don't know yet, do we?'

'Mum,' Nat ordered, 'tell Seb you love him.'

'Nat, *no*!' Thank goodness it was dark.

'Why not?'

'Because . . . because it just isn't the kind of thing grown-ups *do*.'

'But we can all go out with Seb again. We can, can't we?'

Lottie's skin was prickling with mortification. 'If it's OK with him, it's OK with me.'

'Result,' Seb crowed, clenching his fists and punching the air.

'Give me a piggyback!' Nat leapt up and Seb expertly caught him on his back, racing off across the field while Nat let out whoops of delight.

'He's fun,' said Ruby, watching them turn in a wide circle before cantering back. 'I really like him.'

'Mm, I can tell.' Lottie's nod was non-committal but inside she was experiencing a warm Ready Brek glow.

'My turn,' Ruby shrieked as Nat was tipped to the ground. Seb expertly scooped her up and carted her off.

'I like Seb,' Nat confided, sliding a warm grubby hand into Lottie's. 'He's nice. Almost as good as Dad.'

'Yes.' A lump sprang into Lottie's throat. Maybe this time they'd all found the man of their dreams.

Chapter 7

IT WAS A WARM sunny Friday afternoon in late September, but as far as Cressida was concerned it felt like Christmas morning. Her stomach was jumping with excitement. Robert and Sacha had been only too delighted to let Jojo come away with her for a weekend and in an hour Jojo would be back from school and they'd be rattling up the M5 together.

With rising anticipation she consulted her watch for the fifteenth time in ten minutes, checked her reflection in the dressing-table mirror and fiddled with the lacy sleeves of her white shirt. Favourite shirt, new creamy-pink lipstick, new pink velvet waistcoat. It was naughty but she hadn't been able to help herself.

Zipping up her weekend case and lugging it downstairs, Cressida parked it in the narrow hallway and consulted her list. She still had to parcel up a consignment of cards and take them to the post office. The windscreen washer needed filling up. And she and Jojo would need a selection of CDs to play on the journey, as well as a couple of packets of fruit gums to keep them going.

In the kitchen, Cressida filled a plastic jug from the tap and carefully snipped the corner off the sachet of concentrated windscreen wash. Even more carefully she poured the bright turquoise liquid into the jug of water and stirred it in with a spoon. This was the kind of thing that had driven Robert crazy when they were married—if he were here now he'd be rolling his eyes in disbelief at the thought that anyone could be so stupid as to change into their best clothes *before* tackling a messy task.

But he wasn't here now—ha!—so it didn't matter. Cressida picked up the jug with both hands and made her way over to the door.

The noise was as sudden as gunshot and almost as loud. Something hit the kitchen window with an almighty thud and Cressida let out a reflexive shriek of alarm. Her arms jerked and her brain leapt into action, yelling, 'Not on the clothes, *not on the clothes*' so forcefully that the jug instantly toppled away from her body.

Turquoise water sloshed out of the somersaulting jug and cascaded over the kitchen table. Throwing out her hands in a desperate attempt to somehow catch it, Cressida screamed, '*Noooo*,' and saw it all happen in nightmarish slow motion in front of her. The white box containing the cards took the full force of the onslaught. The lid of the box was off because she hadn't yet printed out the invoice to be sent with the order. The order that had—absolutely *had*—to go out *this afternoon without fail*.

The implications were so horrible that Cressida couldn't fully take them in. Gazing down at herself in a state of deep shock, she saw that not a single drop of turquoise water had landed on her clothes.

But the cards . . . oh, *the cards* . . . were ruined. Every last one of them. Her hands now trembling violently, Cressida pushed up her sleeves and picked out the first neatly stacked pile. Each one bore the words '*Emily-Jane is here!*' in silver script. Pale pink marabou feathers, silver beads, iridescent sequins and glitter-strewn netting had been painstakingly glued into place. She had drawn a baby in a cot on the front of each card and every edge was bordered with pink velvet ribbon.

Needless to say, they were the most intricate cards she had ever been commissioned to make. Each one had taken thirty minutes to complete and there were eighty of them.

Still in a daze, knowing what this meant but still not able to face up to it, Cressida left the water drip-drip-dripping off the table and headed outside into the back garden to see what had caused the almighty crash. A starling lay on the stone path, quite dead. Flying along happily, it had crashed into the kitchen window and been killed in an instant.

Cressida bent down and picked up the limp, still warm body. Hot tears squeezed out of Cressida's eyes as she cradled it in her hands.

Bang went her weekend.

Tom said at once, 'Well, how about if we come to you instead?'

'There's no point. It's going to take me all weekend to re-do the cards. I'll be working nonstop.'

'Couldn't we help you make the cards?' Tom sounded hopeful.

'Tom, that's kind of you, but it wouldn't work. We're just going to have to forget it. I'm really sorry.'

'Don't worry.' Tom sounded distant and cool, but that was probably because she'd called him at work. 'No problem. Maybe some other time.'

'We were looking forward to seeing you.' Cressida hoped he knew she meant it.

'Yes, well.' He cleared his throat and said, 'We were too.'

There was that offhand tone again. Was he cross with her for spoiling his plans? Feeling more miserable than ever, Cressida realised that for all her foolish fantasies, she didn't actually know Tom Turner well enough to be able to tell.

'Aunt Cress? It's me. Sorry to interrupt when you're busy.'

Cressida sat back and eased her aching spine. It was nine thirty on Friday evening and so far she had completed eight cards. Only seventy-two to go.

'That's all right, darling. Where are you?'

'Up in my bedroom. Mum and Dad have got friends round for dinner.'

Poor Jojo, relegated to her room while the grown-ups sat downstairs earnestly discussing sales targets. Robert had sounded distinctly put out when Cressida had rung to let him know that she and Jojo wouldn't, after all, be away for the weekend.

'Have you eaten?'

'There wasn't enough dinner party food so I had a pizza up here,' Jojo said cheerfully.

'Anyway, I wanted to tell you that Tom was a bit worried in case you'd made up the story about the cards being ruined, but it's OK now.'

Cressida was stunned. *'What?'*

'He thought you might be making an excuse, like, sorry I can't see you tonight, I'm washing my hair, that kind of thing. Because you couldn't be bothered to drive up to Newcastle or you'd had a better offer or something. Men can be funny like that, can't they?'

'Hang on,' Cressida blurted out. 'How do you know all this?'

'It says so in my new copy of *Phew!* There's a piece in it about how boys get nervous about—'

'No, no. I meant how do you know that's what Tom was thinking?'

'Oh, Donny told me.'

Bemused, Cressida said, 'He called you?'

'Texted me. In his own grumpy way.' Jojo sounded amused. 'Said was it true about the cards being wrecked. So I texted back and said of course it was true, was he calling you a liar, and he said no, it was just that his dad was gutted and wondering what was really going on. So I said you were pretty fed up too and when I came over to your place after school you'd been crying—'

'Oh, Jojo, you didn't!' Every muscle in Cressida's body contracted in horror like a slug doused in lemon juice.

'Why not? It's the truth, isn't it? You *had* been crying.'

'I was crying because the starling was dead,' Cressida floundered.

'Aunt Cress, you know that's not true. And you don't have to worry, because Donny's dad was really pleased when Donny told him. So that's all straightened out,' Jojo said briskly, 'and we talked about fixing another date. Donny's got a boring school trip to Belgium next weekend but the weekend after that should be OK.'

'Er . . . fine,' Cressida said faintly.

'Well, I'll leave you to get on with your cards. Oh, by the way,' Jojo remembered as an afterthought, 'we thought maybe they should come down to us this time. I said you had plenty of room to put them up.'

It was the beginning of October. Autumn had arrived. The air was distinctly cooler now, there was a blustery breeze and conkers, falling from the chestnut trees, were scattered like boules across the broad terrace.

Freddie, standing at the drawing-room window of Hestacombe House, gazed out at the garden where Nat and Ruby were racing up and down the leaf-strewn lawn competing to collect the most conkers. He smiled at their endless enthusiasm, tangled hair and rosy cheeks.

'What are you thinking?' Lottie came into the drawing room behind him carrying a tea tray.

'Me? How lucky I am.' Freddie turned and made his way over to the leather sofa. 'I've just seen my last summer. You know, I'd hate to have dropped dead without any warning. I like knowing I'm seeing things for the last time. Gives me the chance to appreciate them.'

'It might not be your last time. Tumours can stop growing.'

'Maybe, but mine hasn't. I had another scan yesterday.' Taking the cup of tea she'd poured for him, Freddie said, 'My doctor told me I must start to expect things to go wrong. In fact he said I was bloody lucky to have got this far without more signs and symptoms.'

Shaking her head, Lottie blurted out frustratedly, 'Why didn't you tell me you had another scan? I could have come with you.'

'I'd still have a tumour though, wouldn't I?' Freddie's voice softened. 'You couldn't go abracadabra and make it disappear. Anyway, there's something else I want you to do for me.'

'Anything,' Lottie replied at once.

'I'd like you to find Amy Painter.'

'Not another old girlfriend. Honestly, who d'you think you are?' Lottie was busy scribbling down the name. 'Jack Nicholson?'

'She's about your age.'

'Freddie! You *do* think you're Jack Nicholson!'

'Amy isn't an old girlfriend.' As Lottie's eyes widened he added hastily, 'She isn't my daughter either.'

'Oh. Thank goodness for that. You had me going there for a minute.'

'You'll like Amy. Everyone does. In fact you may even recognise her,' said Freddie. 'I'm pretty sure the two of you have met before.'

As Lottie was leaving the house ten minutes later, Freddie said, 'I haven't even asked. How's it going with this new chap of yours?'

'It's going great.' Lottie blushed, because last night, for the first time, Seb had stayed at Piper's Cottage. They had spent the night together and made love twice. 'We really have fun. Nat and Ruby love him.'

'I'll have to meet him myself. See if he deserves you.'

'Oh, he does. I'm just not sure I deserve him.' Touched by the genuine concern in his eyes, Lottie could hardly bear to think that Freddie might not be with them for much longer. 'He's away for three weeks from tomorrow, organising a polo tournament in Dubai. But as soon as he's back I'll bring him over here, I promise.'

Lottie was downloading the addresses of potential clients who had requested brochures via the website when the door opened and Kate Moss walked into the office.

Not really Kate Moss, but similar enough to bring the name instantly to mind. This girl had long, wavy, light brown hair, a delicate heart-shaped face and incredible cheekbones. She was wearing an olive-green dress, high-heeled boots and a cream wool coat with a burnt-orange silk lining.

'Hi there, can I help you?' said Lottie.

'I sure hope so. I'm looking for Tyler?' The girl was American.

'He's not here. He's gone into Cheltenham. Can I take a message?'

The girl shook her head prettily. 'No, that's OK. Do you have any idea when Tyler might be back?'

'I couldn't give an exact time. Give me your name,' Lottie said efficiently, 'and I'll tell him you were here.'

OK, not efficiently. Nosily.

'My name's Liana.' A slender hand was held out for Lottie to shake, the fingers delicate and Barbie-like. 'I'm a good friend of Tyler's.'

That was what Lottie had been afraid of.

Lottie said, 'Is he expecting you?'

'No, I wanted it to be a surprise. Although he has invited me over lots of times,' Liana hastened to explain, 'so hopefully it'll be a nice one!'

Liana's eyes lit up at the sound of approaching footsteps. 'Oh wow, I'm so excited! Is it him? Oh my God, Tyler!'

Lottie watched as she raced over to Tyler. His response was all-important here; if he looked appalled that would indicate that she wasn't in fact as welcome as she imagined. Whereas if he—

'You're here! This is *incredible*.' Tyler, his arms outstretched, enveloped Liana in a hug and swung her round. 'Why didn't you tell me you were coming? My God, let me look at you. More beautiful than ever.'

'Sshh, you're making me blush,' Liana said, laughingly. 'And we're not alone. You mustn't embarrass other people.'

'Trust me, nothing embarrasses Lottie.'

Feeling foolish because Tyler had never so much as mentioned Liana when clearly he should have done, Lottie said, 'Well, I'll leave you to it.'

Hardly noticing, Tyler gazed down at Liana. 'How long are you staying?'

'As long as you like. I'm easy.' Liana gave his hand a squeeze. 'My cases are in the trunk of the car.'

'I don't know how to tell you this.'

'Tell me what?' As always the sound of Tom's voice on the telephone caused Cressida's heart to miss a beat. She smiled, convinced that he was teasing her. It was Friday morning and she was in the kitchen making a shepherd's pie for when Tom and Donny arrived tonight.

'My mother's had a fall and broken her hip,' said Tom.

This time Cressida's heart skipped a couple of beats, and not in a happy way. 'Is this a joke?'

'I wish it was. She's been taken to hospital and they're going to operate tomorrow.'

Tears of disappointment and frustration slid down Cressida's cheeks. Appalled by her utter selfishness she dashed them away. 'Poor thing, she must be so upset. Don't worry about us, you go to your mum. I'll make her a special Get Well Soon card.'

'I'm sorry,' said Tom.

Poor man, he sounded wretched. 'So am I. But it doesn't matter a bit.' Consolingly Cressida said, 'By the time we're in our nineties we're bound to meet up.'

When she came off the phone she vented her rage on the bag of Maris Pipers on the table, hurling potato after potato at the kitchen wall.

'Why me?' Cressida bellowed, ducking as a potato ricocheted off the ceiling and missed her face by inches. 'Why *meee?*'

Lottie had been at her desk for almost two hours when Tyler arrived in the office the next morning. She glanced at the clock on the wall—ten to eleven—and heroically resisted the urge to say good afternoon.

Because that would be childish.

'Everything OK?' Tyler took off his jacket.

I don't know. Is it? Did you spend last night having sex with Liana?

Lottie didn't say this either. Instead she said easily, 'Everything's fine. That was a nice surprise for you yesterday, Liana turning up like that.'

The look Tyler gave her told Lottie that she wasn't fooling anyone.

'It's kind of a tricky situation. Liana's a friend.'

'Quite a good friend by the look of things.'

Tyler came and sat on the edge of her desk. He looked thoughtful.

'Remember I told you why I quit my job in New York and came here?'

'Your friend died.' Lottie was super-aware of his proximity, his denim-clad thigh.

'Curtis.' Tyler nodded in agreement. 'My best friend since we were kids.' Another pause. 'He and Liana were engaged.'

Engaged. Relief rolled over Lottie like a wave on a beach. Liana had been Curtis's fiancée, nothing more than that. So she and Tyler really were just good friends. Except . . . there *was* more to it than just that.

'So if things had worked out between you and me,' Lottie said slowly, 'would she still have turned up?'

'No.' Shaking his head, Tyler picked up a pencil and began tapping it against the desk. 'This is why I have to explain what's going on. We've kept in touch since I came over here. Liana asked me if I was seeing anyone and I said no. Because I wasn't.'

'Right.' Lottie nodded. Thanks to Nat and Ruby, it was true.

'Curtis was her whole life. She was in a desperate state when he died.' The pencil between Tyler's fingers was tapping faster now. 'We spent a lot of time together. I did what I could to help her through those first months. But we were just friends. It was purely platonic.'

Lottie looked at his left foot jiggling away. 'Until . . .'

'Until one night four months later. Out of the blue, Liana asked me if I thought she'd ever meet anyone and be happy again. I told her of course she would, she was a beautiful girl with everything going for her. Then she started crying and I wiped her eyes,' said Tyler. 'That was when she started kissing me.'

Lottie knew she shouldn't ask but keeping quiet had never been her forte. 'You slept with her.'

Tyler nodded, his jaw taut. 'I did. We didn't stop to ask whether or not it was a good idea. Of course, by the next morning I'd realised it wasn't. Liana was still grieving for Curtis. The last thing she needed was to jump into a new relationship. We were friends and we didn't want to risk spoiling that.'

The pencil flicking between his fingers abruptly flew across the desk, hitting Lottie just below her left nipple. *Ouch*.

Tyler smiled briefly and said, 'Sorry. Anyway, we talked it through and Liana agreed with me. So that was it, we put it behind us and carried on as if that one night had never happened. And we did the right thing.' He shrugged. 'Because it worked. We're still friends.'

And she still looks like Kate Moss, Lottie wanted to shout at him. It was no good, this was all way too romantic for her liking. Liana had arrived for an indefinite period and was sharing Fox Cottage with Tyler which, let's face it, had only one bedroom.

Moreover, eight months on from the loss of her fiancé, Liana wasn't looking exactly prostrate with grief.

Jojo was down by the lake taking photographs of the swans when she heard footsteps behind her.

'Don't mind me,' said Freddie as she turned round. 'Snap away.'

Jojo liked Freddie. 'It's for my school geography project. I've got to map their path of migration from the Russian Arctic tundra to here. Dad lent me his digital camera. It's great, you can take as many pictures as you want and you never run out of film.'

Her bag of bread crusts lay on the ground next to her feet. The swans, eyeing the bag greedily, swam back and forth like celebs impatient to be snapped by the paparazzi.

'Why don't I take a photo of you feeding them?' said Freddie.

Jojo reached for the camera when he'd finished. 'OK, my turn now. You sit on that rock and I'll get a picture of you with the lake in the background. No, sit on the rock,' she repeated as Freddie took a couple of steps in the wrong direction and gazed blankly past her. 'OK, if you'd rather stay standing I'll—oh!'

Without uttering a sound Freddie had slumped to the ground. Jojo let out a whimper of fear and raced over to him. His eyes were half open and his breathing laboured. Terrified he was about to die, Jojo dropped to her knees and shouted, 'Help!' before grabbing handfuls of tweed jacket and hauling Freddie onto his side into the recovery position.

'Mr Masterson,' Jojo croaked, cradling his head. 'Can you hear me? Oh, no . . . please, somebody *help* . . .'

A dribble of saliva slid from the corner of Freddie's mouth. Oh God, should she stay with him or get help? She didn't have her phone with her. What if he died while she was gone? What if he died because she hadn't?

Never had the sound of running footsteps been more welcome. From being gripped with panic, Jojo felt weak with relief when Tyler Klein skidded to a halt at her side and said, 'I heard you shouting for help. What happened here?'

'He just . . . went a bit funny,' stammered Jojo. 'Then he fell over. I put him on his side . . .'

'Good girl, well done.' Tyler was taking Freddie's pulse, checking that his airway was clear. 'Looks like he's starting to come round now.'

Oh, thank God. 'Shall I go and phone for an ambulance?'

'Hang on, I've got my mobile in my pocket.'

'Don't call the ambulance,' Freddie mumbled, rolling onto his back and opening his eyes. Focusing with difficulty on Tyler, he said weakly, 'It's OK, it's happened before. No need to go to hospital. I'll be fine now.'

'You can't just crash out and expect us to carry on as if nothing's happened,' Tyler retorted.

'Help me up, then. I suppose I'd better come clean.' Ruefully Freddie said, 'It was bound to happen sooner or later.' Then he turned to Jojo. 'Sorry about that, sweetheart. I must have frightened the life out of you.'

Jojo smiled and realised she'd been trembling. 'I'm so glad you're all right. I thought you were going to die.'

Freddie patted her arm, then turned back to Tyler. 'You could give me a hand if you like, help me back to the house.'

Lottie was in the office on Monday morning opening the post when Tyler came in.

Without preamble, he said, 'I know about Freddie's illness.'

'Oh, yes?' Lottie carried on slitting open envelopes. If Tyler was bluffing, she wasn't going to be the one to give the game away.

Game. If only it was that.

'He collapsed down by the lake yesterday afternoon. I took him back to the house afterwards. He told me about the brain tumour.'

'Oh.' Lottie looked up, a lump forming in her throat. Somehow the fact that Freddie had told someone else made it all the more real. 'What kind of a collapse?' she said worriedly.

'Some kind of minor epileptic attack. It was the third one, apparently. He's going to take some tablets prescribed by his doctor to try to stop it happening again.' After a pause Tyler went on, 'So now I know why he told me I could buy Hestacombe House after Christmas. You can imagine how that made me feel.'

'Out with the old, in with the new.' Lottie shrugged and opened the next letter. 'If Liana's still around I'm sure she'll be pleased. At least then the two of you won't be so cramped.'

'Thanks for that.' The look Tyler gave her indicated that he wasn't fooled by her flippancy for a second. 'But I'm worried about Freddie being on his own. What if he has more blackouts? How's he going to manage if anything else goes wrong?'

'We're sorting that out. Freddie knows what he wants to happen. It's under control,' said Lottie, her gaze skimming over the address at the top of the letter she'd just unfolded. 'In fact . . .'

'What is it?' Tyler looked concerned as she scanned the contents of the letter. 'What's wrong?'

Upset on Freddie's behalf, Lottie clumsily pushed back the swivel chair and rose to her feet.

'Sorry, looks like everything isn't under control after all. If it's OK I'll go over and see Freddie now. There's something he needs to know.'

Freddie couldn't fault any of the nurses who had cared for his beloved wife Mary during her time in the hospital. They had all been cheerful and efficient. But Amy Painter had been special.

When she came on shift Amy's dazzling smile lit up the ward. She was always ready with a sympathetic ear or a naughty joke, whichever was appropriate at the time. Her bleached blonde hair was cropped short, her blue eyes were by turns sparkling and compassionate and she never failed to brighten Freddie's day.

Freddie still had the letter she'd written to him after Mary's death. She had attended the funeral too, and wept. And when he had received the news of his own condition from his consultant, Dr Willis, Freddie had known who he wanted to take care of him in his last days.

Now, looking at the expression on Lottie's face, Freddie sensed that all wasn't going according to plan.

'I spoke to someone at the hospice who used to work with Amy,' Lottie said. 'Officially they're not supposed to pass on personal details, but I explained about you wanting to see her again and she gave me Amy's mother's address. Her name's Barbara and she lives in London. So I wrote to her.' Pausing, Lottie held out the letter she'd opened in the office. 'And now she's written back.' Reluctantly she said, 'I'm so sorry, Freddie. Amy's dead.'

Dead? How could someone like Amy be *dead*? Feeling winded, Freddie reached across the kitchen table for the letter.

Dear Lottie,

Thanks ever so for your nice letter about my daughter. I'm very sorry to have to tell you that Amy was killed in a car accident three years ago. She had volunteered to work in a children's hospital in Uganda and was loving her time there. Sadly a Jeep overturned and Amy was thrown out. I'm told her death was instantaneous, which has been a comfort to me—although I'm sure you can understand that the last three years have been hard to bear. Amy was my whole world.

I hope this news won't upset your friend too much. You say his name is Freddie Masterson and his wife's name was Mary. Well, I remember Amy telling me about them. She was so very fond of them both.

Sorry to have been the bearer of bad news. Thanks again for your letter—it's lovely to know that Amy hasn't been forgotten and is so fondly remembered. That means so much.

Yours,

Barbara Painter

The flat was on the tenth floor of a council block in Hounslow. Now that he was no longer allowed to drive, Freddie had hired a car and driver for the day. Climbing out of the car, he told the driver to return in two hours. Then he entered the building and took the lift to the tenth floor.

'This is so strange,' said Barbara Painter, 'but so nice at the same time. I can't believe you're here. I feel as if I know you.'

'Me too.' Freddie smiled and watched her fill their teacups. The living room was bright with cushions and paintings, and there were framed photographs of Amy on every surface.

Barbara saw him looking at them. 'People have told me I'm turning the place into a shrine but they've always been there. Her father took off before Amy was born so it was only ever the two of us. Why shouldn't I have photographs everywhere of the person I loved most in the world?'

'Exactly.' Freddie didn't know how Barbara Painter could bear to carry on. She was a plump, motherly woman in her fifties with dark blonde hair, bright eyes and a subversive sense of humour. Since his arrival over an hour ago they had exchanged reminiscences about Mary and Amy, talked about his brain tumour and struck up quite a rapport.

'Oh. look, you've finished your tea. Can you manage another cup?'

'Thanks.' Checking his watch, Freddie saw that it was time for his afternoon dose of medication. Taking the bottle out of his inside pocket he struggled for a few moments with the childproof cap before shaking a carbemazepine tablet into the palm of his hand. Then, because his head was pounding, he added a couple of painkillers.

'How long did the doctors say you probably had?' Barbara asked.

'A year. Ish.' Freddie appreciated the straightforward approach. 'Well, that was back in the summer, so more like eight or nine months now.'

'Amy would have been so flattered to think you'd wanted her to take care of you. So what will you do now?'

Freddie shrugged and swallowed the pills, one after the other. 'Advertise, I suppose. Try to find someone I can bear to have around. Something tells me I'm not going to be the most patient of patients.'

'You mean you're a stroppy bugger. I've dealt with plenty of those in my time, let me tell you.' Barbara looked amused. 'Take a look at that photo over there on the board.'

Freddie rose obediently from his seat and went over to the corkboard, where several photos were pinned amidst the cab company cards, scribbled reminders and phone numbers. One of the photographs was of Barbara and Amy laughing together, listening to each other's chests through stethoscopes and wearing matching uniforms.

'You're a nurse?'

'I am.' Barbara nodded.

'Where are you working?'

'Nowhere. I retired in March.' She paused then said, 'And been going mad with boredom ever since.'

Freddie was almost afraid to ask the question. 'Would you consider taking care of a stroppy bugger until he kicks the bucket?'

'If you shout at me, would I be allowed to shout back?'

'I'd be offended if you didn't,' said Freddie.

'In that case, let's give it a whirl.' Barbara Painter's eyes glistened as she smiled proudly at the snap on the corkboard of Amy and herself. 'You know what? I think she'd be tickled pink about that.'

Chapter 8

'MUM, I'M TRYING really hard to be nice to Ruby but she won't stop *singing*,' Nat complained, 'and it's getting on my *nerves*.'

'I know, sweetheart. She's just excited.' Lottie gave him a cuddle as the kitchen door flew open and Ruby came dancing in.

'I'm ten, I'm ten, I'm ten ten ten.'

Nat rolled his eyes in disgust. '*See?*'

It was Thursday. Far more important, it was Ruby's tenth birthday and nobody was being allowed to forget it. Since the party to which all her schoolfriends were invited was being held on Saturday, this evening Mario was coming round straight from work and the four of them were going out to Pizza Hut.

In fact—phew, relief—wasn't that his car pulling up outside now?

'Sounds like Dad's here,' said Lottie, prompting both Nat and Ruby to race down the hallway to the front door. Lottie checked her watch; it was twenty to six. Mario must have left work early and—

'Yaaaaay!' A scream of delight echoed down the hallway, prompting

Lottie to follow Nat and Ruby out of the kitchen. Kneeling there with a child clamped to each hip and a slew of wrapped presents on the floor was Amber.

'You're here,' Ruby cried ecstatically. 'I thought we weren't ever going to see you again, but you didn't forget.'

'Oh, Monster Munch, how could I forget your birthday?' Kissing each of them in turn, Amber said, 'And I told you I'd be here when I phoned.'

Ruby instantly looked sheepish and said quickly, 'I forgot.'

Lottie knew at once that she hadn't. 'It's fine by me.' She looked at Amber. 'It's just that Mario's coming over. We're going to Pizza Hut.'

'Well, I can't stay long. I'll probably be gone before he gets here.'

'Or you could come with us.' Ruby turned hopefully to Lottie. 'She could, Mum, couldn't she? That'd be great.'

Lottie and Amber exchanged glances, both acknowledging that this had been Ruby's Big Plan.

'Sweetie, I can't. It's really kind of you to think of it,' Amber said carefully, 'but my boyfriend's waiting outside for me.'

Ruby's face fell.

'Is he nice?' said Nat.

'Oh, yes, very nice.'

'Dad doesn't have a girlfriend.'

'Doesn't he? I'm sure he'll find one soon. *Anyway*,' Amber went on brightly, 'it's somebody's birthday and I'm here for the next hour. My friend has his laptop with him and plenty of work to keep him busy, so are we going to make the most of it and have fun?'

'Yay.' Ruby rested her head on Amber's shoulder. 'Will you do my hair in a French plait?'

'Of course I will. Can your mum still not do them properly?'

'No, she's rubbish.'

'Thanks very much,' said Lottie, picking up the scattered birthday presents. 'I think I'll open these myself.'

When Mario arrived at Piper's Cottage he had to park behind a very clean imperial blue Ford Focus. As he climbed out of his car he saw a man sitting in the driver's seat. Briefly glancing up, the man acknowledged Mario with a polite nod before returning his attention to the laptop he was using.

A guest from the holiday cottages, Mario thought.

'Daddy, you're here! Guess who's in the living room?' Nat dragged Mario down the hallway.

'Keira Knightley, I hope.'

'*Loads* better than that!'

Ruby was sitting cross-legged on a chair in the middle of the room, beaming all over her face and having her dark hair expertly fashioned into a French plait by Amber. Mario, his mouth dry, realised at once who the owner of the Ford Focus was. Bloody hell, what was Amber doing with someone who looked like a geography teacher?

'Daddy! It's my birthday!' Keeping her head still, Ruby waved both hands at him. 'And look what Amber bought me! Isn't it brilliant?'

It took some effort for Mario to nod and admire the green sparkly top Ruby was wearing, and to act as if Amber wasn't in the room. How many weeks had it been now since he'd last seen her? She was looking fantastic in an apricot angora cropped cardigan, pinstriped orange and cream jeans and cream, rhinestone-studded cowboy boots. He had always loved her idiosyncratic style of dressing. Oh God, he had missed her *so much*.

'And she bought me an electric spider,' Nat chimed in, 'to make up for it not being my birthday.'

'I've shown her my room.' Ruby was intensely proud of her redecorated bedroom. 'She wishes she had pink glittery wallpaper like mine.'

'Just say the word,' Mario attempted humour, 'and I'll be round with my pasting table.'

Amber smiled, fastened the ends of Ruby's plait with a pink hairband and said, 'There, all done. You look like a princess.'

How do *I* look? Mario longed to ask. As bloody awful as I feel? The last weeks have been the most wretched of my life.

Amber, checking her watch, pulled a face. 'I didn't realise I'd been here so long. Poor Quentin, he'll be wondering if I'm ever going to leave.'

Mario glanced out of the living-room window and said, 'He's gone. Must have got fed up with waiting and driven off.'

Annoyingly Amber didn't jump up and peer out of the window to check he was still there. Instead, gathering together her things, she replied easily, 'Quentin wouldn't do that. He's not the type.'

'Neither am I. I'd never drive off and leave you.'

'No, I don't suppose you would.' Amber smiled briefly at him. 'But the chances are you'd spend your time out there chatting up any pretty girl who happened to walk past.'

'I would not.' The accusation was like a slap in the face. 'I *wouldn't*.'

Ruby, her expression pitying, said, 'Daddy, you probably would.'

'**T**his is worse than the ghost train.' Seb stood back to survey his handiwork. 'I'm scared to look at any of you.'

'Raaaarrrggh,' roared Nat, unrecognisable in green-and-red face paint.

'My teeth are making me dribble.' Giggling, Ruby slurped up saliva and pushed her vampire fangs more securely into place.

'Daddy, you have to dress up too,' Maya ordered, her own face a startling shade of purple with heavy black shadows beneath her eyes. 'You and Lottie have to be scary as well. Come on, let's get them ready.'

Lottie sat back as together Ruby and Maya worked on her face. Next to her on the sofa, Seb was having his done by Nat. Smiling at the expressions of earnest concentration on their faces, Lottie realised that she was experiencing a moment of undiluted happiness, the kind of memory you captured in a box and treasured for ever.

It was Halloween and they were going out trick or treating, all five of them together because Maya was down from London for the weekend visiting Seb. Mildly apprehensive that Nat and Ruby might not hit it off with Seb's eight-year-old daughter, Lottie's fears had been allayed within minutes of them meeting each other for the first time. In no time at all they had bonded, become a trio.

'There, done,' Ruby pronounced with pride, stepping back at last and allowing Maya to hold up the mirror. Lottie surveyed her reflection. She had black lips, fluorescent orange eye shadow, green mascara and big brown moles all over her face. She looked at Seb, wearing a mad professor wig, warty false nose, charcoal-grey face and rotten teeth.

'Why, Mith Carlyle, you're tho beautiful.' Struggling with the teeth, Seb kissed her hand with a ghastly slobbering noise.

'Mr Gill.' Lottie fluttered green lashes back at him. 'At last I've met the man of my dreams.'

Last Halloween it had rained but tonight the weather couldn't have been more perfect. The air was thick with swirling fog through which lights gleamed eerily and sounds seemed distorted. It was eight o'clock and, having finished with the High Street, they were now making their way towards the holiday cottages, the children zigzagging excitedly ahead down the lane. In the darkness Seb took out his teeth and kissed Lottie.

'We'll have to leave at nine,' he murmured between kisses. 'I'm going to drive Maya back to London tonight.'

'It's been fun.'

'It'll be even more fun when we trick or treat your boss.'

'Oh, no, we're not doing that.'

'Why not? He lives down here, doesn't he? We can't miss him out.'

'Nat and Ruby won't want to do it,' Lottie protested.

'Hey, the guy's a Yank. They're big on Halloween, right? Besides, the kids can play a trick on him. They'll love that.'

Encouraged by Seb, they probably would. Lottie breathed a sigh of relief when they reached Fox Cottage and saw that all the lights were off.

'They're out.'

Phew, thought Lottie.

Maya said longingly, 'Shall I put a plastic spider through their letter-box?'

'*Yes.*' Nat spoke with relish.

'Sshh.' Ruby raised a hand. 'Someone's coming down the lane.'

They listened, heard the fog-muffled sound of voices.

'I bet it's Ben and Harry Jenkins.' Nat's eyes gleamed at the thought of meeting their greatest rivals. 'We can scare them!'

'OK, everyone hide,' Seb instructed.

Everyone hid, melting into the darkness behind trees and bushes. Lottie and Ruby tucked themselves out of sight behind the wall bordering the garden of Fox Cottage.

They heard a burst of laughter and approaching footsteps. Lottie whispered, 'Doesn't sound like the Jenkins boys.'

'Mum, *ssshhhh*.'

Lottie did as she was told. Seconds later she heard a voice that definitely didn't belong to either Ben or Harry Jenkins, but she knew who it did belong to.

'RaaaAAARRGGHHH!' roared Seb, Maya, Ruby and Nat, leaping from their hiding places and waving their arms. 'Trick or treat?'

'Jesus, you scared the life out of me,' Liana said testily, 'and I don't have anything *on* me.'

'Trick then!' Maya gleefully took aim and fired her water pistol.

Liana let out a high-pitched shriek as something dark sprayed the front of her cream coat. 'Are you completely mad? You can't *do* that!'

'It's *okaaay*.' Maya rolled her eyes at the over-reaction. 'It's disappearing ink. In two minutes it'll be gone.'

Behind the garden wall, Lottie let out a low groan. She hadn't even known that Maya was carrying a pistol of disappearing ink. There was a good chance that a still-discernible mark would be left.

'This coat cost thousands of dollars.' Liana was still shaking her head in horrified disbelief.

'Hey, it's Halloween,' Seb protested. 'We're just having a bit of fun.'

Belatedly realising who it was beneath the make-up, Tyler surveyed Nat and Ruby in silence before addressing Seb. 'Does Lottie *know* what you've got her children doing?'

Ruby and Nat were eyeing Tyler with dislike. Seb, placing a protective arm round each of their shoulders, said, 'I don't know, why don't we ask her?' Raising his voice he turned towards the wall and mimicked, 'Lottie? Do you *know* what I've got your children doing?'

Slowly Lottie rose to her feet, hideously aware of her black lips, drawn-on wrinkles and the big witchy moles all over her face.

'OK, now look.' Tyler sounded resigned. 'I'm not trying to be a killjoy here, but this is beyond a joke. You could give someone a heart attack jumping out of the fog like that. You could kill one of our guests.'

'They're kids.' His eyebrows raised, Seb indicated Maya, Ruby and Nat. 'At the risk of repeating myself, it's Halloween. And we heard your voice,' he added casually, 'so we knew who was coming down the lane.'

So he *had* known. Lottie didn't know whether to laugh or cry.

Liana, clearly upset, demanded, 'And if my coat's ruined?'

'Then we'll pay for a new one. Come along, kids.' Seb ushered them protectively past Tyler and Liana. 'Have to start saving your pocket money.'

'**L**ook, it was an idiotic trick to play,' Tyler repeated. 'You have to admit that.' It was Monday morning and he and Lottie were in the office.

It *had* been an idiotic trick to play, but Lottie was damned if she'd admit it. Instead she said heatedly, 'Maybe when you have children of your own, you'll lighten up a bit. The kids were having fun. They'd been looking forward to Halloween for weeks.'

'That's all well and good.' Tyler raised his hands. 'But they shouldn't—'

'Enjoy themselves? Be a bit mischievous? You know what, we went all round the village last night and everyone else got into the spirit of the occasion. Not one other person threatened to see us in court.'

'We didn't say that. I'm just pointing out that an apology might be in order. Not to me,' Tyler went on coolly, 'but to Liana.'

'Maya lives in London. Nat and Ruby didn't even know she had a water pistol, let alone one with ink in it. Neither of them pulled the trigger. I don't see why they should have to apologise.'

Tyler said, 'In that case, maybe your boyfriend could do the honours.'

Oh, yes, that was highly likely to happen. Struggling to regain control over her breathing, Lottie heard a car pull up outside. 'Fine, I'll tell him. In fact we'll both apologise. Would on bended knee be good enough, do you think, or would prostrate on the ground be required?'

They glared at each other across the office as the door opened. Any paying guest walking in would instantly have been aware of the hostile atmosphere. Luckily it wasn't a paying guest, it was Liana.

'Oh, no, you two haven't been arguing, have you? I feel terrible! Lottie, I'm *so* sorry about last night. Can you forgive me for being such a grump?'

Terrific, what was she supposed to do now? Feeling her face redden,

Lottie summed up her apologetic voice and said, 'You weren't. We're the ones who are sorry. We shouldn't have . . . messed up your coat.'

Why did Tyler have to be here, listening to every word and with something dangerously close to a smirk twitching at the corners of his mouth?

'No, no, you mustn't apologise, it was all my fault for being so miserable. I can't bear to think I might have upset your children.' Liana, enchanting in baby-pink cashmere and Earl jeans, went on, 'Here, I got them some candy. Call it a belated Halloween treat. Will you give it to them and say Liana's sorry?'

Worse and worse. Miserably, Lottie took the expensive bags of sweets. 'Thanks. Of course I will. You didn't need to do that.'

'Oh, but I *did*. And the lady in the dry-cleaners has promised me my coat will be fine. She's dealt with disappearing ink stains before.'

'Good. Well, I'd like to pay the dry-clean—'

'Don't say that, I wouldn't *hear* of it!' Liana waved her pretty hands in protest then glanced at her watch. 'Right, I must shoot, my aromatherapist awaits.' Blowing a kiss at Tyler she said, 'See you later, honey. I've booked that table for dinner at Le Petit Blanc.'

Lottie watched her leave and wondered what it must be like to have an aromatherapist waiting to . . . aromatherapise you. She also wondered what it might be like to blow kisses at Tyler and call him honey.

Freddie took a turn for the worse. His doctor was called and made grim predictions about his illness. He didn't have long to go now; had the time perhaps come for him to move into a hospice?

'No.' Propped up in bed, Freddie shook his head wearily. 'I'm not going to change my mind. I want to stay here.'

'Very well.' The doctor accepted his decision. 'I'll speak to Barbara about the pain management.' Nodding approvingly he added, 'You chose a good one there.'

'Hands off. You've already got a wife at home,' said Freddie.

The doctor smiled and scribbled out a couple of prescriptions. 'Just take things easy. Get plenty of rest.'

Ha. 'Give up the rugby, you mean? All I do is lie here and rest.'

'And admire the best view in England.' Turning, the doctor indicated the lake, the hills rising up beyond it and the sun hovering just above the treeline turning the clouds pomegranate pink.

'God, I'm so *tired*.' As he yawned, Freddie realised that his words had begun to slur again. And it had been a week since his last drink.

'I'll leave you to it,' murmured the doctor.

Freddie was asleep before he'd even closed the bedroom door.

The phone was ringing as Lottie let herself in to the kitchen of Hestacombe House. Barbara, watering the pots of basil and coriander on the window ledge, picked it up and said, 'Yes?'

Lottie waited for Barbara to finish dealing with the call.

'The thing is, Freddie's not able to come to the phone just now. Why don't I take your name and pass on a message?' Miming to Lottie that Freddie was sleeping, Barbara grabbed a pen from the dresser. Lottie helpfully supplied her with the back of an envelope. Having listened carefully, Barbara scribbled down a name then paused, looked over at Lottie and said, 'Mr Barrowcliffe, can I ask you to hold on for just a few seconds? I need to speak to someone else.'

'Jeff Barrowcliffe?' Lottie's eyebrows went up, betraying her surprise.

Nodding, Barbara covered the receiver. 'That's the one. He's ringing to invite Freddie to a party in December.'

A lump swam into Lottie's throat. Reaching for the phone she said, 'I'll do it.'

Freddie had taken to delegating the task of informing others of his illness to Lottie and Barbara. Introducing herself to Jeff Barrowcliffe, Lottie explained to him that Freddie was unwell and wouldn't be able to attend the party.

Jeff sounded distinctly put out. 'But it isn't for another five weeks. He might be better by then.'

Gently Lottie said, 'I'm sorry, but he won't be. Freddie has a brain tumour.' Lottie hated having to say it.

'Oh God. That's awful.' Jeff was clearly shocked. 'He seemed so well when he came down to Exmouth.'

'Actually, he was diagnosed just before that. Being told he didn't have long to live was what prompted him to get in touch with you.'

'He didn't tell me that.' Lottie heard the distress in Jeff Barrowcliffe's voice. 'I had no idea.'

'He preferred it that way. But it's not something we can hide now. Look, I'll tell him you rang,' said Lottie. 'If he's feeling up to it he might call you back tomorrow, but I have to warn you that his voice is a bit slurred now. He's not always easy to understand on the phone.'

'OK, OK . . . yes, just tell him I called,' Jeff went on hurriedly. 'And tell him I'm sorry,'

The next morning Freddie watched as Barbara bustled around his bedroom, rearranging a glass bowl of scented white winter roses on the window ledge and dusting the silver photo frames.

'Do you know, I'm feeling better today.' Freddie tilted his head from side to side to see how bad the pain was. It was definitely less severe.

'Could be something to do with your morphine dosage being increased.'

'Oh. Right.' He was probably high as a kite without even realising it. 'Am I slurring?'

She smiled. 'A bit.'

'Join me in a glass of champagne?' Freddie looked hopeful.

'It's eleven o'clock in the morning. I'll make you a cup of tea, how does that sound?'

'Like a desperately poor substitute. Who's that?' They both heard the sound of a car pulling up outside.

Barbara peered out of the bedroom window. 'No idea. New guests arriving, I imagine. Lottie's dealing with them. Now how about a chicken sandwich?'

'I'm not hungry.' Indicating the chair beside his bed, Freddie said, 'Stop faffing around, woman, and help me with the crossword.'

'Let me just sort out your pillows.' Barbara helped him forwards and with her free hand expertly plumped up the goosedown pillows. 'There, isn't that better? Now where did you put the pen?'

'Dropped it,' said Freddie.

The door burst open while Barbara was on her hands and knees searching under the bed for the pen. Lottie, looking as if she'd just seen Father Christmas, said in an odd voice, 'Freddie? You have a visitor.'

Typical. Just as he and Barbara were about to tackle the crossword. Freddie frowned. 'Who is it?'

Lottie was breathing rapidly. She waited for Barbara to retrieve the pen and crawl out from under the bed. Finally she said, 'It's Giselle.'

It seemed to Freddie that the clock in the room had stopped ticking. How could Giselle be here, when Lottie hadn't been able to track her down?

For a moment, as Giselle stepped into the bedroom, he wondered if the increased dose of medication was causing him to hallucinate.

Lottie discreetly closed the door behind herself and Barbara, leaving them to it.

'It's really you.' It was a ridiculous thing to say, but he couldn't help himself. Giselle's wavy hair was the same warm brown shade he remembered. Her eyes were unchanged, her smile hesitant. She was wearing cream trousers and a light brown angora sweater over an ivory shirt.

'Oh, Freddie, it's so good to see you again.' He read the conflicting emotions on her face—genuine pleasure mixed with pity for his plight. Carefully, Giselle rested her arms on his shoulders and kissed him on each cheek. She smelt of gardenias. Freddie gestured towards the chair. He wanted to look at her, to apologise to her properly and discover how her life had turned out.

'I don't understand how you're here,' he said carefully as Giselle sat down. 'We've been looking for you.'

'So I hear. Well, I mean I did kind of know.' She clasped his hand.

Bursting with questions he needed to ask her, Freddie said, 'Tell me how you're here today. I still don't understand.'

'You mean that for once in my life I have the upper hand?' Giselle said teasingly, 'I think I should make the most of it, don't you?'

'I suppose I deserve that much.' Freddie was just happy to have her here. 'Can I say sorry? I know how much I hurt you, and you didn't deserve it. I behaved appallingly. I've always felt bad about that.'

'Clearly.' Stroking the back of his hand, Giselle said, 'Otherwise you wouldn't have tried to find me.'

'Guilty conscience.' Freddie shook his head. 'It's a terrible thing.'

'Don't be so hard on yourself. You fell out of love with me and in love with somebody else. We broke up. It happens all the time.' Her eyes sparkled. 'And if it helps, I ended up making the right choice, too.'

That was a tremendous weight off Freddie's mind. Hearing it, he felt almost physically lighter. 'So you're married.'

'Yes.' Giselle nodded. 'After we split up I took a job as a nanny. Then one day on my weekend off I decided to visit an old schoolfriend in Oxford. I caught the train up. Got off at the station. And that was when I saw him, just standing there on the platform waiting for *his* train to come in. I couldn't believe it. He spotted me and came over. We started talking and that was it. I never did go and visit my old schoolfriend.'

'Who was it?'

'The man who's made me happy for the last thirty-six years,' Giselle said simply. 'The father of my children. The man I'll love until the day I die, even if he does have his faults.'

'Love at first sight.' He gave Giselle's hand a squeeze. Just like it had been for Mary and himself. 'What's his name?'

'Hardly love at first sight,' Giselle retorted with amusement. 'And his name's Jeff Barrowcliffe.'

Downstairs in the kitchen Jeff was stirring his tea, trying to explain his reasons for hiding the truth from Freddie.

'I was jealous, pure and simple. Freddie was supposed to be my friend and he took my girl away from me. That's not to say I didn't deserve it, but I wasn't about to let him do it again.'

'I can understand that,' said Lottie.

Barbara nodded. 'Me too.'

'We hadn't seen Freddie for forty years,' Jeff continued defensively. 'Then all of a sudden I get the email from you. I was curious to see him again but I didn't know what he wanted. I didn't trust him. So I took down the family photographs and sent Giselle off to spend the day with our eldest daughter. When Freddie arrived he told me he was looking for Giselle, but he didn't say why. All I saw was an old rival, good-looking and still with all the old charm. He didn't tell me he was ill.'

Lottie was puzzling something out. 'But yesterday you rang to invite Freddie to a party.'

'I know.' Looking shamefaced, Jeff said, 'It took a while, but Giselle finally made me see sense. The thing is, meeting Freddie again was . . . great. Catching up on old times, hearing about the life he'd led. It got us thinking, after he'd left. We decided to track down a few old friends of our own and throw a big reunion party before Christmas. And Giselle told me I had to invite Freddie. And of course I knew she was right. We couldn't have a party without Freddie.' He paused, took a sip of tea and carefully placed the cup back in the saucer. 'Although now it looks as though we'll have to. I felt terrible after I spoke to you yesterday. As soon as I told Giselle she said we must come up to see him.'

Wiping her eyes, Giselle came into the kitchen and said, 'He's getting tired now. Jeff, he wants to see you before he goes to sleep.'

Jeff was on his feet in a flash. 'How's he looking?'

'Just like himself. Only dreadfully ill.' Giselle fumbled in her pocket for a fresh tissue. 'Oh dear, I wish we could have seen him sooner.'

'Never mind,' said Lottie. 'You're here now.'

So that was that. He'd found Giselle at last. Well, he hadn't, but one way or another they had managed to find each other.

Freddie opened his eyes. It was dark outside now, which meant he'd been asleep for some time. The inky-dark sky was bright with stars and an almost full moon was out, reflected in the glassy surface of the lake. Had the doctor called in again earlier? Freddie had a vague memory of him murmuring to Barbara while he had been dozing. His head wasn't hurting, but he suspected that if he tried to move it, it would.

'Freddie? Are you awake?' It was Barbara's voice, low and gentle; he wasn't alone after all. She was sitting in the chair pulled up next to the bed. Now her warm hand was resting on his arm. 'Is there anything you need? Anything I can get you?'

Sensing that if he attempted to speak it would come out all wrong,

Freddie imperceptibly moved his head from side to side. There was nothing he needed. Giselle and Jeff had forgiven him. He was sleepy again now. Sleeping was so much easier than trying to stay awake. And when he slept he was able to dream about Mary. While he waited to doze off, Freddie returned to one of his favourite memories—the one that made him shudder to think it could so easily not have happened. But that was fate, wasn't it? That was serendipity. The tiniest decisions were capable of changing your whole life . . .

It had been a gloriously sunny June morning and Freddie was on his way to a meeting with his bank manager. Early for his appointment and finding himself with thirty minutes to spare, he debated whether to stop off at the coffee bar or to wander down to the car showroom at the other end of Britton Road to harmlessly ogle the cars he couldn't afford.

Harmless ogling won the day and Freddie turned right instead of left. Moments later he encountered a girl rattling a collecting tin. Feeling in his trouser pocket, he found only a couple of coppers. Aware of the girl's eyes upon him, Freddie approached her and did his best to disguise the fact that he was sliding such a paltry sum into her tin.

Sadly his sleight of hand wasn't up to Magic Circle standards. The girl looked him straight in the eye and said bluntly, 'Is that all?'

Freddie was nettled. 'It's all the change I have.'

And that was when it happened. The girl's mouth curved up at the corners and what felt like a hand in a velvet glove simultaneously closed round Freddie's heart. Her tone playful, she said, 'I'm sure you could do much better if you tried.'

Feeling oddly breathless, Freddie turned out both trouser pockets to show her how empty they were. Then he turned and made his way down Britton Street, tinglingly aware of her presence behind him.

The cars in the showroom weren't able to hold his attention. He went into the newsagent opposite and bought a box of matches.

'That's an improvement.' The girl's dimples flashed as he dropped a series of silver coins into her collecting tin. She had bright blue eyes and long straight hair the colour of corn, and was wearing an above-the-knee purple shift dress that showed off a glorious pair of legs.

'Good,' said Freddie. 'Tell me your name.'

She smiled playfully and jangled her tin at him. This time he took a pound note from his wallet, rolled it up and fed it into the slot.

'Mary.'

'Mary. You're costing me a fortune.'

'Ah, but it's in a good cause.'

If he'd gone to the coffee bar in the first place, their paths wouldn't have crossed. Freddie double-checked that she wasn't wearing a wedding ring. 'I've got to go and see my bank manager now. Will you still be here when I come out?'

Mary raised one eyebrow. 'Might be, might not.'

Another pound note into the tin. 'Will you?'

Her eyes danced. 'Oh, all right then.'

'And when I get back, may I take you for a coffee?'

'Sorry, no.'

Freddie panicked. 'Why not?'

'I don't drink coffee. I only like tea.'

His skin prickled with relief. 'May I take you for a cup of tea then?'

Mary, breaking into a huge smile, said, 'I thought you'd never ask.'

Freddie's eyes were closed again now. Every moment of that summer's morning was engraved on his heart. He and Mary had met for tea—it was a wonder he'd been able to afford it after dropping so much money into her blasted collecting tin—and that had been it. From then on there was no going back. They had both known they were meant to be together for the rest of their lives.

And they had been, for the next thirty-four years. The last four and a half years without Mary had been an ordeal but she seemed so close now. Freddie felt as if all he had to do was to allow his thoughts to drift away and there she'd be, waiting for him . . . and yes, here she was, smiling that dear familiar smile and reaching out towards him . . .

Filled with indescribable joy, Freddie relaxed and went to her.

Chapter 9

PULLING INTO THE driveway of Hestacombe House the next morning, Lottie saw Tyler outside the office waiting for her, and she knew.

'Freddie's gone. He died in the night,' Tyler said gently when she climbed out of the car.

It was expected. It was inevitable. But it still wasn't the news you wanted to hear. Lottie covered her mouth.

'Barbara says it was very peaceful. He just slipped away.'

Freddie hadn't been in pain. He'd made his peace with Giselle and he had stayed *compos mentis* until the end. As deaths went, who could ask for more?

'Oh, Freddie.' It came out as a whisper.

'Come here.' Tyler put his arms round her and Lottie realised tears were sliding down her cheeks. Taking shameful comfort from the feel of his hands on her shoulders and her face against the soft cotton of his denim shirt, she mumbled, 'I'm just going to miss him so much.'

'Sshh, it's OK.' Tyler's voice, soothing and in control, broke through Lottie's defences. Silent tears gave way to noisy, uncontrolled sobs.

Finally, when she was feeling like a wrung-out floorcloth and doubtless looking like one too, Lottie's outburst subsided.

'Sorry.'

'Don't be.'

Of course he was used to comforting bereft women, he'd had months of practice with Liana. Except Liana wouldn't end up in a mess like this, Lottie thought, with her face streaked with mascara.

'Barbara's with him,' said Tyler, 'and the doctor's on his way over.'

'Poor Barbara. She'll be upset too.'

'She says you can go on up and see him if you want to.' Tyler indicated Freddie's bedroom window, glinting in the morning sunlight.

Lottie wiped her face with a shredded tissue and hoped Freddie wouldn't mind her looking a fright.

Nodding, she took a deep breath. 'I'd like that.'

'**H**ow are you doing? Need a hand with anything?'

Flustered and emotional, Lottie saw that Tyler was in the kitchen doorway looking concerned.

'Um, well, the drinks are waiting to be poured and someone has to fill the ice buckets and I'm worried we won't have enough glasses—'

'Whoa! OK, don't panic, let me handle it. And you only answered one half of my question.' Tyler began uncorking bottles of wine. 'I asked how you were doing.'

'Not very well,' Lottie admitted. 'I thought organising outside caterers would take the pressure off, but two of the waitresses haven't turned up and the ones that have are rubbish, so I'm just panicking instead.'

'Well don't, because you aren't.' Tyler shoved a glass of icy white wine into her hand. 'Just shut up and drink this. *Slowly*,' he added.

Lottie nodded and obediently took a sip. She felt as if she had just run a marathon. The service at Cheltenham Crematorium had been emotionally draining and now Hestacombe House was crammed with mourners she didn't feel equipped to deal with. Practically everyone from the village was here, ready to give Freddie the kind of memorable send-off he deserved, and all she wanted to do was go to bed.

'Seb not turned up?' said Tyler. 'I thought he might have been here.'

'No. He didn't know Freddie.'

'All the same, he could have come along to support you. Wouldn't you have preferred to have him here?'

Lottie took another sip of wine. Yes, she would have preferred it, but Seb had told her he was busy today meeting potential sponsors for the next polo tournament. But she wasn't going to tell Tyler that.

'I don't need my hand holding. I'm old enough to come to a funeral on my own. Anyway, I'm not on my own, am I?' Indicating the rest of the house, Lottie said, 'I know practically everyone here.' Lottie leapt to her feet. 'Oh God, the bruschettas need to go into the oven.'

'Give me thirty seconds,' said Tyler. 'I'll be back.'

He was, with a dozen or so villagers in tow, Cressida among them.

'You daft thing, getting into a flap and trying to do it all yourself.' Cressida whisked the tea towel out of Lottie's hands and gave her a hug. 'We're here, aren't we? Between us we'll have everyone fed and watered in no time.'

'Not that many of us are planning on drinking water,' publican Merry Watkins put in. 'Freddie would have something to say about that.'

Tyler steered Lottie out of the kitchen. 'Come on, I think you can leave them to it.'

Relieved, Lottie murmured, 'Thanks.'

'Don't mention it.'

'Oh, look at you with your hair all falling down!' Liana, rushing up to Lottie, exclaimed, 'And your eye shadow's gone all creased at the corners . . . You look *exhausted*.'

She meant *awful*. Which was undoubtedly true, but not what Lottie needed to be told.

'Sorry, that was tactless of me.' Liana was instantly contrite. 'I was a complete wreck after Curtis's funeral. If I hadn't had Tyler there to look after me, I don't know how I'd have got through it.' Glancing around, she said, 'Is Seb not with you?'

Were they in league with each other? Was this some kind of have-a-dig-at-Seb conspiracy? Lottie jumped as a voice behind her said, 'No, he isn't, but I'm here. And I'm great at cheering girls up.'

Turning and flashing Mario a warm smile of gratitude, Lottie gave his arm a squeeze.

'Eeurrgh! Worse than I thought!' Catching sight of her creased eye shadow and red-rimmed eyes, Mario recoiled in mock horror.

'OK, I get the message.' Lottie altered the friendly squeeze to a painful pinch. 'I'll go and do my face.'

Upstairs in the enormous blue-and-white bathroom she washed away the old make-up and applied a fresh layer and readied herself to head back downstairs and rejoin the throng.

'Oh!'

'Sorry, didn't mean to startle you.' Fenella, who had evidently been waiting for her to emerge from the bathroom, took in the reapplied make-up and refastened hair combs and gave a nod of approval. 'That's better. You looked a bit of a fright before.'

'So everyone keeps telling me.' Startled because she'd had no idea Fenella was even here, Lottie took in the familiar chic haircut and immaculately tailored black suit. 'How did you know Freddie had . . . ?'

'I saw the announcement in the *Telegraph*.' Fenella paused, gently cleared her throat. 'Well, I'd kind of been looking out for it. Hoping *not* to see it, obviously, but knowing that sooner or later it would appear.'

Lottie nodded, feeling awkward. Why *was* Fenella here? Was she perhaps still hankering after a mention in Freddie's will?

'No,' Fenella read her mind with ease. 'I'm not expecting him to have left me anything. I just wanted to pay my respects. Freddie may not have been the love of my life, but I was still very fond of him.'

'We all were.'

'So who gets his money?' Fenella's eyes were bright. 'You?'

'No.' Lottie shook her head. 'Not me.'

'Bad luck. Anyway, I just wanted to say hello before I left. It's never easy going to a funeral when the only person you know is the one in the box.' Pausing, Fenella added, 'Unless there are any eligible men you think I might like to meet?'

Ted, from the village shop? Envisaging the two of them together, Lottie said, 'No one springs to mind.'

'Not even that handsome American? Tyler?'

'I think you'd have to be thirty years younger.'

'I imagine so.' Fenella acknowledged the dig with amusement. 'But you wouldn't. Who's the very pretty girl with him?'

She was doing it deliberately. Witch. 'A friend,' said Lottie.

'Disappointing for you.'

'Not at all. I'm seeing someone far nicer.' Feeling like a fifteen-year-old, Lottie boasted, 'He organises polo tournaments. He's gorgeous looking *and* loads of fun.'

Luckily it seemed she wasn't the only one capable of juvenility. Fenella, arching her pencil-slim eyebrows, said, 'Really? What's he doing with you, then?'

They looked at each other for a long moment. Lottie smiled first. 'Thanks. You've actually made me feel better.'

'My pleasure.' Fenella returned the smile, then glanced out of the landing window at the sound of an approaching car. 'Ah, here's my taxi.'

'Come on, we'll walk down together.' Lottie held out an arm. 'Freddie was glad he'd seen you again, by the way. He didn't regret doing it.'

Side by side they descended the staircase. Fenella said, 'Did he ever manage to track down Giselle?'

'Yes.'

'Really?' Fenella's gaze darted with interest over the thronged guests in the hall below. 'I say, how fascinating. Is she here now?'

Lottie hesitated fractionally. 'No.'

Laughing, Fenella said, 'That means she is. Perhaps I should say hello?"

Lottie steered her swiftly down the last couple of stairs and in the direction of the front door. 'Your taxi's waiting outside, remember. Thank you for coming. Bye.'

Fenella laughed, her expression softening as she leaned forward and kissed Lottie on each cheek. 'Darling, I may be a gold digger but I'm not that much of a bitch.'

The taxi roared off up the drive in a swirl of late-autumn leaves and Lottie made her way back into the house. The noise level had cranked up another couple of notches by now as people reminisced happily about Freddie and relaxed into their second and third drinks.

She found Giselle and Jeff in the drawing room, chatting to Barbara.

'Here she is.' Giselle looked up as Lottie approached and handed her a photograph from the selection she'd been showing Barbara. 'Jeff and I were going through the old albums last night. Have a look at this one. That's Freddie on the left there next to Jeff.'

Smiling, Lottie gazed at the snap of Freddie and Jeff with more hair than they'd possessed for years, larking about outside someone's house. They were spraying each other with shaken-up bottles of beer while a gaggle of girls looked on and giggled, arms raised to protect their hair.

'That's you!' Lottie pointed to a sweet-faced brunette in a bright orange mini-dress and white PVC boots.

'I had a twenty-two-inch waist back then.' Giselle gazed up at Lottie. 'Who was that woman we saw you saying goodbye to just now? The one who left in a taxi?'

Forty years ago, Lottie thought but didn't say. Freddie had a torrid affair with her behind your back, but he wasn't rich enough for her so she dumped him and he came back to you.

Lottie shook her head. 'God, I'm terrible with names. I can't even remember now. I think she's just an old friend of the family.'

Later, as Lottie mingled and chatted with those who had known and loved Freddie, she overheard Merry Watkins saying bracingly to Tyler, 'Now you know what the antidote to a funeral is, don't you? A lovely romantic wedding! How about you and that pretty girlfriend of yours making an announcement, hmm? That'd cheer us all up!'

Two weeks after the funeral, Lottie and Barbara took the small rowing boat out into the middle of the lake. Gazing at the frost-covered hills rising up all around them, the swans floating serenely on the water and the rooftops of Hestacombe among the trees, Barbara said, 'I suppose there are worse places to end up.'

'If we don't get a move on, Freddie's going to end up in a swan's stomach.' Having eased the airtight lid off the pot with a soft *pfhut*, Lottie saw that the swans had metaphorically pricked up their ears and abruptly altered course. Greedily imagining that it was feeding time they were now heading in a stately convoy towards the boat.

'Did I ever tell you I was scared of swans?' said Barbara.

'You big Jessy. They won't hurt you.'

'Well, no, but remind me again why I'm out here?'

'Because this is where Freddie wanted his ashes to be scattered.'

Barbara pulled a face. 'Couldn't we have just done it from the edge of the lake?'

'In the middle's better. Then they can spread out in all directions. Right, shall we do this?' Carefully lifting the pot and tilting it with the reverence it was due, Lottie allowed the first ashes to spill out. Oh . . . *phh, tppph* . . .

'Stop!' cried Barbara. 'They're going in your hair!'

'They're going in my *mouth*.' Spluttering and coughing, Lottie almost dropped the pot into her lap. A gust of wind had sent grey dusty ash flying into her eyes, up her nose and down her throat.

'Oh God, the swans are coming . . . GO AWAY,' Barbara shrieked, leaping to her feet and causing the boat to rock wildly. One of the male swans, startled, rose up and began beating his wings. Barbara panicked and stumbled against an oarlock, knocking the oar free.

'Don't let it slip, *don't let it slip*.' Still tasting ashes and blindly rubbing her eyes, Lottie felt the pot wobble in her lap and made a grab for it.

The boat overturned as neatly as a toy, tipping Barbara and Lottie, equally neatly, into the lake. The all-over blast of iciness took Lottie's breath away and caused every muscle in her body to contract in horror.

Relieved, at least, to have had the ashes washed out of her hair and eyes, Lottie bobbed up to the surface and came face to face with Barbara. Barbara might be terrified of swans but at least she could swim. And the swans had taken off, disgusted by the flurry of activity.

Treading water, Barbara blinked and said, 'Sorry. I panicked. Poor Freddie, it wasn't supposed to happen like that.'

'He wanted the lake. He g-got the lake.' Lottie's teeth were chattering. 'C-come on, race you to the beach.'

Tyler was standing there waiting for them, shaking his head. 'I saw the boat tip over. I *was* going to dive in and rescue you.' Leaning forward, he reached out a warm hand and helped first Lottie then Barbara out of the water, 'But basically the water was just too damn cold.'

'Wimp,' Barbara said cheerfully.

'Maybe. But you're wet and I'm dry.' His dark eyes glittered with amusement. 'Oh, and here's another tip. Always best to check the direction of the wind before you start scattering ashes.'

'It's done now.' Maybe not in quite the way they'd planned, but done nevertheless. The pot containing Freddie's ashes lay at the bottom of the lake and the contents had been well and truly scattered. Lottie, shivering, said, 'You know, a gentleman would give up his sweater.'

'You're joking, it's cashmere. Come on,' Tyler said good-naturedly as Lottie shook her head, attempting to shower him with water, 'let's get you two up to the house.'

Hestacombe House, not Fox Cottage. Lottie was still getting used to the idea that it was Tyler's home now. So much had changed in the space of a fortnight. A week after the funeral when he had announced that he would be moving into Hestacombe House the following day, she had retorted indignantly, 'Shouldn't you wait until it's actually yours?'

That was when Tyler had explained that it was in fact already his, that he had bought the house from Freddie three months ago.

Showered and changed into an oversized white towelling robe of Tyler's, Lottie made her way back downstairs. Tyler was in the kitchen making mugs of tea and eating a toasted cheese sandwich.

'Barbara's train leaves at two thirty. That means we have to leave here in,' he checked his watch, 'five minutes. If you go home and change now, you might not make it back in time to say goodbye.'

'I know.' Lottie seized her mug of steaming tea and glugged it down. 'I'll wait here until you've gone. If that's all right.'

'Of course it's all right.' Tyler offered her the other half of his toasted cheese sandwich. 'You don't want to miss waving her off.'

Barbara was going back to London. Lottie shook her head, knowing she would miss her terribly. When the contents of Freddie's will had been relayed to them, nobody had been more touched and amazed than Barbara to learn that Freddie had bequeathed almost half his fortune to the children's hospital in Uganda where her daughter Amy had worked. Barbara was now planning to travel to Uganda to visit the hospital and advise how the money might best be spent in Amy's memory.

The other half of Freddie's fortune had gone to the hospice on the outskirts of Cheltenham where Amy had helped to nurse Mary through her last months of life.

The remainder of the estate had comprised an assortment of personal bequests that had brought a lump to Lottie's throat.

For Jeff Barrowcliffe, £10,000 to be spent on the motorbike of his choice, to make up for the Norton 350 Freddie had once written off.

For Giselle, £10,000 to make up for everything else.

For the villagers of Hestacombe, £5,000 to be splurged on a rip-roaring party in the Flying Pheasant.

And for Lottie Carlyle, £5,000 to be spent on an even more rip-roaring family holiday to Disneyland.

Lottie's eyes filled with tears now at the thought of their conversation way back in the summer, when Freddie had asked her where she would go if she could travel anywhere in the world. That had been on the day he'd told her about his brain tumour, yet still he had remembered.

'Here.' Tyler handed her a tissue, something he'd grown accustomed to doing over the last couple of weeks.

'Sorry.' Wiping her eyes and noisily blowing her nose, Lottie forced herself to stop. 'It's thinking about Disneyland, gets me every time.'

'Hey, you'll have a great time. Will Seb be going with you?'

'Maybe. I haven't even thought about dates yet.' In truth Lottie was torn. Seb would be brilliant, would love every minute, and Ruby and Nat would adore having him there. But a part of her sensed that this hadn't been Freddie's intention. Nothing had ever been said, but in a weird way she felt he would be disappointed if she went with Seb.

'Don't move. You've got something in your hair.'

Lottie stayed still while Tyler teased apart the wet ringlets in order to reach whatever she hadn't managed to wash out of her hair.

'What is it?' It was certainly taking him long enough. 'Dead leaf?'

Tyler gazed down into her eyes. 'Dead beetle, actually.' He held up the offending creature, a glossy dark brown corpse missing a couple of legs.

'Oh well, could have been worse.' Lottie patted her hair. Then her stomach lurched into washing-machine mode because Tyler wasn't smiling at her, he was looking as if he wanted to kiss her.

A lot.

Oo-er. Lottie gazed helplessly back, heart racing, all sensible thought wiped from her mind. Was he going to do it? Was he waiting for *her* to do it? Should she—

'Hell*oooo*? Tyler, could you be an angel and give me a hand getting these cases downstairs?' It was Barbara's voice, echoing from the landing. 'Then I'm all set to go. Don't want to miss my train!'

That was it, they'd said their goodbyes and Barbara was gone. Waving until the car had disappeared from view, Lottie closed the heavy front door and made her way through to the drawing room. She needed to get home and change into dry clothes, but not just yet.

The sage-green velvet sofa was piled with cushions and facing the window. Curling up on one end of it, Lottie bent her head and sniffed the towelling lapel of Tyler's dressing gown to see if it smelt of him. Yes, it did, faintly . . . oh God, had he really been about to kiss her just now or had she imagined it? Had it been a case of wishful thinking on her part? And what about Seb? Surely he deserved better than this?

Dammit, why did life have to be so *complicated*?

'Now what is it that this reminds me of?'

Jerking awake with a start, Lottie saw who had spoken.

'Oh, yes.' Liana clicked her fingers. '*Goldilocks and the Three Bears*.'

Lottie prayed she hadn't been dribbling in her sleep. It was bad enough that the front of the towelling dressing gown had worked loose, making it apparent that she wasn't wearing anything underneath.

'Feel free, just make yourself at home.' Liana was smiling her usual angelic smile but there was a faint edge to her voice. 'And excuse me if this is impertinent, but am I allowed to ask what you're doing here, all alone in the house, wearing Tyler's robe?'

Liana had been to the hairdresser's; her rippling hair was artfully highlighted in expensive shades of amber, nutmeg and honey. She was wearing a dove-grey polo-neck sweater, size eight—if that—grey wool trousers and a chunky silver belt draped round her teeny tiny hips. God only knew what she must be thinking. And, frankly, who could blame her? As Tyler's girlfriend she had a right to be miffed. Tugging the hem of the robe over her bare legs and feeling horribly ashamed—not to mention *big*—Lottie levered herself into a sitting position.

'Sorry, I didn't mean to fall asleep. Barbara's gone. Tyler's taken her to the station to catch her train.'

Liana frowned. 'And you're waiting for him to come back?'

'No, *no*, nothing like that! Barbara and I went out in the boat to scatter Freddie's ashes,' Lottie heard herself gabbling. 'But the swans started to chase us and Barbara panicked and, well, you can guess the rest. The boat went over and we fell in. Tyler insisted we came back here . . . well, obviously Barbara had to, because she's been living here . . . and we needed to shower and change into something dry. All my wet clothes are in a black bin bag in the kitchen. I'm taking them home now.' Rising hastily to her feet—her *big, bare* feet—Lottie discovered that her wet hair had left a huge damp patch on the green silk cushion she'd been resting against. 'I really didn't mean to fall asleep, it's just that so much has happened in the last couple of weeks. I think everything just all of a sudden caught up with me.'

'Oh, you poor thing.' Liana's expression had changed to one of sympathy. 'I'm so sorry. I knew I shouldn't have doubted you. I know how it feels—I was exactly the same after Curtis died. You spend days not being able to sleep a wink then all of a sudden it comes over you without warning and you're just completely out for the count.'

Lottie nodded, hideously aware that in the moments before she'd dozed off, she'd been fantasising about being kissed by—

'Tyler,' said Liana. 'He was the one who got me through it. He made me realise my life wasn't over.' She smiled warmly at Lottie. 'And you've got Seb to help you. We're so lucky, aren't we? Look, if you want to go upstairs and sleep a bit longer, that's fine by me. I'll tell Tyler when he gets back. He'll understand.'

'No, I'm fine, I'll just shoot home and change then get back to work. After all, that's what I'm being paid for.' Lottie, hastening towards the door in Tyler's dressing gown, felt more ashamed of herself than ever. Was there anyone on the planet more forgiving and beautiful, more generous and guilt-inducing than Liana?

Cressida was busy putting the finishing touches to an order for wedding invitations when she happened to glance out of the window and saw her ex-husband's car pulling up outside the house.

Unusual, seeing as it was ten o'clock on a Wednesday morning. Even more unusually, Robert had Sacha with him. Sensing that something was up—oh, how marvellous if they'd booked a skiing holiday and had come to ask her if she'd have Jojo for a week before Christmas—Cressida put down her hot glue gun and hurried to the front door.

Five minutes later and the happy squiggle of anticipation in her stomach had been replaced by the dull weight of dread.

'You mean . . . you're all moving to *Singapore*?' Cressida wondered if she had somehow misunderstood them.

'It's the most marvellous opportunity!' Sacha, her eyes bright with triumph, said. 'Being head-hunted is such a cloak-and-dagger business, you have no *idea*. Well, of course you don't have any idea, because I don't suppose much head-hunting goes on in the world of handmade greetings cards!'

Cressida, her heart going like a punchbag in her chest, said, 'But . . . what about Jojo?'

'She's coming with us, of course. Oh, she'll settle down in no time. Singapore's a wonderful place to live.'

But what about me? What about what *I* want? Unable to speak, Cressida listened to the buzzing in her ears and wondered if she was about to faint . . . oh, please, this couldn't be happening.

'Well, we just thought we'd drop by and let you know the news.' Robert beamed, pleased with himself. 'It's all jolly exciting stuff, isn't it? And the amount of money they'll be paying us . . . well, you wouldn't believe the package we've negotiated.'

Sacha smoothed back her hair and said smugly, 'Just goes to show how much they wanted us.'

Cressida wept unashamedly after they'd gone. Her heart felt as if it had been wrenched from her chest and stamped on. She was going to lose Jojo and it hurt so much she didn't know how she was going to bear it. This was like losing her own baby all over again.

The doorbell rang at four o'clock. Thinking it might be Jojo, Cressida took a deep breath and checked her face in the mirror before answering it.

Jojo wasn't on the doorstep. It was Robert and Sacha back again. The sense of anticlimax caused Cressida's shoulders to sag. What did they want now?

'Right, we'll come straight to the point,' Robert announced. 'One question. If Jojo wanted to stay in this country instead of coming with us to Singapore, would you be willing to become her legal guardian?'

What? *What?* 'I . . . er . . . I . . .' stammered Cressida.

'Yes or no,' Sacha said bluntly. 'That's all we need to hear. And no pressure either. It's entirely up to you.'

Yes or no? They were actually giving her the choice? Hastily, before they could change their minds and withdraw the offer, Cressida blurted out, 'Yes . . . yes . . . definitely YES!'

Sacha smiled and gave a brisk nod of satisfaction. 'Sure?'

'Yes . . . my *God* . . .' Beginning to tremble, Cressida was so overwhelmed she could have hugged them. OK, maybe not. 'I still can't believe it. Thank you *so much* . . .'

'That's excellent then. All sorted.' Robert rubbed his hands, just as he always did when concluding a successful deal. 'Now as you can imagine, we're pretty much rushed off our feet right now, lots to get organised. It would help us out if you could have Jojo for the next few days.'

Less than twenty minutes later Sacha returned with Jojo in the car.

'Aunt Cress!' Jojo scrambled out of the passenger seat as Cressida rushed down the front path in her slippers. 'You said yes!'

Cressida, her heart bursting with love, threw her arms round Jojo. 'Oh, sweetheart, of course I said yes! I'm so happy I don't know what to do with myself!'

'Right, well, I'll leave you to it.' Sacha's tone indicated that while some people might have nothing more important to do than dance around outside in their slippers, others had vital business to be getting on with.

'Bye, Mum. Thanks again.'

'Bye, darling.'

Inside the house Cressida discovered that, unbelievably, Sacha and Robert had broken the news of their move to Singapore to Jojo last night.

'I went berserk.' Jojo related what had happened. 'Well, not berserk—I'm not really the berserk type, am I?—but I told them I didn't want to go. I mean, can you really see me in Singapore? While Mum and Dad are working all hours heading up this new company? I don't mind flying out to see them during the school holidays, but I love living in England. All my friends are here. You're here. I begged them to ask if I could stay with you, but they weren't sure you'd say yes. I wanted to phone you last night but they wouldn't let me.'

From this, Cressida deduced that this morning's visit from Sacha and Robert had been designed to deliberately upset her, giving her the rest of the day in which to realise how much she would miss Jojo. That way, when they turned up again in the evening and made their take-it-or-leave-it offer, she would be that much more likely to say yes.

Except they hadn't needed to do that because she would have agreed anyway. Cressida wondered if it was possible to feel happier than this. Stroking Jojo's thin face, she said joyfully, 'Oh, sweetheart, I'm glad you went berserk.'

Jojo disappeared upstairs to shower off the mud from hockey earlier, and to text all her friends to let them know her big news. Cressida, congratulating herself on having caught up with her backlog of work, efficiently finished the last of the wedding invitations and parcelled them up for posting. In the kitchen, having checked the contents of the vegetable basket, she then set about making Jojo's favourite, cottage pie.

Jojo came flying downstairs as she was peeling and slicing the carrots.

'Put that carrot down. We're not eating here. I've decided,' Jojo pronounced with an air of importance and a flourish, 'to take you out to dinner to celebrate you becoming my legal guardian. My treat.'

Cressida was touched by the thought. 'That sounds wonderful. Where shall we go to celebrate?'

'Burger King.'

Ah.

'Lovely.' Cressida said it with good grace. As long as she and Jojo were together, what did it matter where they ate?

'Go and get changed then. No point hanging around.' Bossily Jojo whisked the carrot from her grasp. 'I'm starving, aren't you?'

Cressida did as she was told and headed upstairs to change into her ballgown and tiara. OK, a clean blue fleece and jeans. She ran a brush through her hair, dabbed on some eye shadow and lipstick and belatedly remembered to reapply her deodorant by manoeuvring the roll-on stick up under her white T-shirt.

'Ready?' Jojo called up the stairs. 'Come on, let's go.'

Cressida looked at her watch. It was ten past five and they were heading out to dinner. At this rate they'd be home again by six.

'No, not this turning,' Jojo instructed as they headed into Cheltenham and Cressida indicated left. 'There's a new Burger King just opened. Carry straight on.'

'A new one?' Cressida obediently cancelled the indicator and stayed on the main road.

'This is my surprise. It's bigger,' Jojo proudly announced, 'and better. Everyone says it's brilliant.'

Cressida smiled at her enthusiasm. 'Can't wait.'

Several miles further on, Cressida said, 'We're coming up to the big roundabout. Which way now?'

'Hang on, wait till we get closer.' Jojo squinted through the windscreen as the enormous road sign loomed up at them out of the darkness. 'You have to turn right.'

'Sweetheart, that's for the motorway. Do you mean straight on?'

'No, definitely right. We just get on the motorway and off again at the next exit. Sorry.' Jojo was apologetic. 'Didn't I mention that?'

Just as well there was petrol in the car.

Once they were installed on the motorway and doing a steady (if wimpish) sixty miles an hour, Jojo took a tube of fruit gums out of her bag and offered one to Cressida. 'By the way, I lied about turning off at the next junction.'

'What? Cressida was bewildered. 'We're not going to Burger King?'

'Oh, yes. The thing is, we're going to the one in Chesterfield.'

'*What?* But that's—'

'Halfway between Newcastle and here,' Jojo said cheerfully. 'Exactly halfway, in fact. That's where we're meeting Tom and Donny.'

By some miracle Cressida didn't jam her foot on the brake. Dazedly she said, 'No, we aren't.'

Jojo beamed. 'Oh, yes, we are, as they say in all the best pantomimes. It's all arranged.'

Cressida really wished Jojo hadn't chosen to break this news to her as they were driving along the M5. 'But it *can't* be arranged. You've got school tomorrow. You can't miss school!'

'Oh, Aunt Cress, of course I can. It's called skiving off. Pulling a sickie. All you have to do is phone in tomorrow morning and tell them I've gone down with flu. It's Thursday. We break up for Christmas on Friday so nobody will be doing any work anyway. And after that it's the holidays, so really it couldn't work out better.'

Feeling winded and utterly stunned by this glib explanation, Cressida said, 'When did you decide this?'

'Ooh, about an hour ago. As soon as Mum and Dad left your place. It's a surprise,' Jojo said eagerly, 'to celebrate everything that's happened today. I thought you'd love it, after all the times we've made plans to meet Tom and Donny and it's all fallen through.'

'Does Tom know about this?'

'Of course he knows! Otherwise we'd get to Chesterfield and there wouldn't be anyone there to meet us, would there?'

Cressida's heart broke into a gallop at the prospect of actually . . . finally . . . *unbelievably* seeing Tom again. In Chesterfield, wherever that might be. 'But how . . . how did you . . . ?'

'I rang Donny. We text and email each other all the time. I told him the plan and we decided to go for it,' Jojo said easily. 'He told his dad that we were already on our way, so he had to set off straight away to meet up with us. Donny's going to have tonsillitis tomorrow, we decided. I don't know what Tom's going to have. Maybe food poisoning.'

This was too much to take in. 'They're taking the day off as well?'

'Duh, they kind of have to.'

'So where are we staying?' said Cressida.

'Oh, we'll find a hotel in Chesterfield for tonight. Then tomorrow we'll go up to Newcastle.' Jojo was confident. 'I thought we could stay for a week.'

'I have no clothes.' As she pointed this out, Cressida experienced the first stirrings of panic. 'No spare underwear, no toothbrush, *nothing*. And nor do you.'

'That's why it's going to be an adventure!'

'And I have a business to run . . .'

'You're up-to-date with your orders. Anyway, you deserve a rest.'

Oh Lord. 'But I haven't even sent off the invites I finished this afternoon. I was going to take them to the post office first thing tomorrow.'

'Lottie's got a spare key. Ask her to do it for you.' Jojo paused. 'Or we can go home now if that's what you want. I thought you'd be pleased that I'd done this, but if you don't want to see Tom and Donny again—'

'Oh, sweetheart, it's not that!' Realising she was hurting Jojo's feelings—tonight of all nights—Cressida cried, 'I *am* pleased! If I'm honest, I'm panicking because I *do* want to see them again.' She reached for Jojo's hand and gave it a grateful squeeze. 'I'm just making silly excuses because I'm nervous. And I bet if we stop at the next service station they'll sell toothbrushes and . . . stuff.'

After three and a half hours of driving and one short break at a service station they had arrived in Chesterfield. Jojo had the road atlas open across her knees and was on the phone now to Donny as they negotiated their separate ways towards the Taplow Road branch of Burger King. So far Cressida had had to stop the car three times to ask directions.

And now, finally, they had found it. There was the familiar logo as the brightly lit restaurant loomed ahead of them out of the darkness. Breathlessly turning into the busy car park, Cressida felt gloriously intrepid, like Indiana Jones finally discovering the Holy Grail. If only she had an Indiana Jones hat to cover her frazzled hair.

Oh Lord. A fresh wave of butterflies broke free in her chest. Why couldn't she be wearing something flattering? Was the stray lipstick she'd found in the bottom of her bag too bright? At this rate the moment Tom clapped eyes on her he was going to run screaming out of the car park.

'Don't worry,' said Jojo when Cressida had nervously parked between a filthy green van and a gleaming Audi. 'You're fine.'

'I'm not, I look a sight!' Peering frantically in the rear-view mirror, Cressida ruthlessly pinched colour—*ooch*—into her pale cheeks.

'OK, now listen to me. Donny and I have been texting each other for weeks. And if anyone knows, he does. Aunt Cress, Donny's dad wants to see you again every bit as much as you want to see him. He doesn't care whether or not you're wearing posh shoes and make-up. He'd be just as happy if you were wearing a gnome suit.'

Cressida wasn't so sure about that. She definitely wouldn't be overjoyed if Tom were to turn up wearing a gnome suit.

Beep-beep, went Jojo's mobile. Having read the text, she opened the passenger door. 'Right, me and Donny are going in for a burger. You two can join us when you're ready.'

Numbly Cressida nodded; it was nine o'clock on a hitherto normal Wednesday evening and she was here in *Chesterfield*. 'Thanks.'

Jojo paused halfway out of the car. 'Is that a sarcastic thanks?'

'No, sweetheart.' Oh, how she loved Jojo. 'It's a real thanks. You arranged a fantastic surprise.'

'Well, Donny helped too. We did it between us.'

Cressida was struck by a thought. 'Are you and Donny . . . ?'

'Urrgh, no way!' Jojo's eyes widened in disbelief. 'I wouldn't fancy Donny in a million *years*. He's a friend, that's all. Like in *Phew!* it's always saying how important it is to have boys who are friends because then you can chat to them and find out how the opposite sex ticks. Well, that's how it is with Donny and me.'

'That's great.' Smiling at Jojo, Cressida thought that sometimes *Phew!* did actually make sense.

Jojo headed into the restaurant to meet up with Donny. Cressida watched her run inside, then took a deep breath and climbed out of the car herself. Brrr, it was cold. On top of everything else she was going to be greeting Tom with watering eyes and a pink nose, which would—

'Hi, Cress.'

Turning, Cressida saw him standing twenty feet away, a green wool scarf wrapped twice round his neck and the collar of his overcoat pulled up round his ears.

Cressida said, 'Fancy meeting you here.'

'Damn.' Tom moved towards her. 'I was going to ask you if you came here often.'

'Sorry.'

'Don't be. You're here.' He greeted her with a kiss on each cheek. It was so wonderful to see him again. She'd forgotten quite how much she loved the little lines fanning out from the corners of his eyes.

'What have our kids done to us, eh?' He shook his head.

Cressida nodded. 'I know. I suppose it was the last thing you needed to hear this afternoon.'

'The last thing?' Tom's laughter lines deepened. 'It was the *best* thing I could have heard. I've already rung my boss and told him I'm taking a few days off work. The only problem is . . .'

'What?' Cressida's imagination instantly careered into overdrive: he had a girlfriend, he was gay. Fearfully she said, 'Tell me.'

'OK. Well, Donny kind of sprang this on me.' Rubbing the back of his head, clearly embarrassed, Tom said, 'Tomorrow you're coming back to stay at our house. So the thing is, I have to warn you that it's not going to be what you'd call tidy. In fact it's a bit of a mess.'

Cressida blinked. 'That's the problem?'

'It's embarrassing,' said Tom. 'You're going to think I'm a slob. When we get home you'll see last night's dishes still waiting to be washed up.'

'I have dishes in my sink,' said Cressida.

'And the living-room carpet needs vacuuming.'

'Mine does too.'

'My ironing pile is spilling out of its basket.'

'Snap.'

'Come here.' Visibly relieved, Tom drew her towards him until their misty breath mingled and melted together. 'I suppose we ought to join Jojo and Donny. But before we do, can I just say how much I'm looking forward to the next week?'

He kissed her. Cressida stopped worrying about her messy hair and lack of make-up. As customers left the restaurant and headed past them back to their cars, she kissed him back and whispered joyfully, 'Me too.'

Chapter 10

MARIO WASN'T LOOKING forward to next week. Or to the one after that. He'd quietly planned to carry on at work without drawing attention to it but Jerry had put the kibosh on that. Studying the office holiday planner up on the wall yesterday, he'd said over his shoulder, 'Blimey, you've still got twelve days to use up before the end of the year. Better get on and take them, mate. They won't let you carry them over.'

Mario, studying his computer screen, had said casually, 'I'm not going to bother. Jerry, have you seen last month's sales figures for—'

'Whoa! Hold your horses just one cotton-pickin' minute there, boy.'

Jerry had a new girlfriend who was a huge line-dancing fan and had been dragging him along to classes.

'Jerry, I'm really not bothered about taking time off work.'

'Now *that* is the saddest thing I ever heard.' Jerry was incredulous. 'You and Amber broke up months ago. I can't believe you haven't got over it yet and found yourself a replacement. I mean, look at me and Pam! She's changed my life!'

She'd certainly made him an annoyingly cheerful person.

'You need to get yourself a new bird,' Jerry went on confidently. Bird, *ugh*. 'That'll sort you out. And what kind of loser comes into work when he doesn't even have to?'

'So I stay at home and do what exactly?' Mario gestured out of the window at the grey sky and bundled-up passers-by hurrying past in hats and scarves.

'Get a grip, man. You don't have to stay at home! You can buy a plane ticket and fly off somewhere with a bit of life to it and cast your eye over a few babes in bikinis. Treat yourself to a fortnight of mindless sex, man. Tenerife, that'll do the trick.'

'No, thanks.' Mario suddenly felt incredibly tired. He didn't want a holiday and a fortnight of mindless sex. He just wanted Amber.

Amber was wearing a calf-length dark blue velvet dress, neat shoes and discreet pearl studs in her ears. She looked as if she might be on her way to church. She was also looking pretty startled.

'Sorry,' said Mario. 'Maybe I should have rung first, but I needed to see you. Can I come in?'

It was seven o'clock in the evening and Jerry's holiday suggestion had been dancing through his brain all afternoon. Finally he had made up his mind and driven over to Tetbury.

From the expression on Amber's face, he guessed she'd have preferred it if he hadn't. 'Mario . . . Actually, I'm on my way out.'

'Just five minutes. It's important.' God, she had no idea how important.

'Quentin's going to be here in five minutes.'

'Where's he taking you? To the Tory Party conference?' As soon as he said it Mario knew he'd made a huge mistake.

Amber's eyes flashed. 'To meet his parents if you must know. They're quite elderly. I wanted to make a good impression.'

Mario hated it that making a good impression on Quentin's parents was important to her. 'You don't need to. Listen, you know how I feel about you. I *love* you. Come away with me.' Reaching for Amber's hand he said, 'I've got two weeks' holiday to use up, starting from now. Let me take you somewhere amazing. We'll have the best time ever, I promise.'

'Mario, are you mad? I'm not coming on holiday with you.'

'Please.'

'I mean, apart from anything else, it's *December*. And I have a busy salon to run.'

'The other girls can cover for you. I'll pay them to do it.' He'd already thought this through. 'I'll pay double.'

Amber raised an eyebrow. 'And what would I tell Quentin?'

Recklessly Mario said, 'Oh, I don't know. How about telling him you're going on holiday with your friend Mandy. That's what you usually do, isn't it?'

Bong. If the jibe about her outfit had been wrong, this was worse. Amber's jaw tightened and in that moment he knew he'd lost her.

'You shouldn't have come, Mario. Quentin will be here any minute now. He's taking me to meet his parents and—'

'That's why you're dressed as Margaret Thatcher?'

'What I choose to wear is none of your business,' Amber retorted.

'You don't even look like you.' He indicated the understated make-up, the neatly tied-back hair. 'Did you ever see *The Stepford Wives*?'

'I'm not going to argue. You live your life the way you want to live it,' said Amber, 'and I'll stick to mine, OK? Now please go.'

'Wait. I'm sorry.' Mario began to panic. 'I'm only saying it because I love you.'

'You love everyone. That's your trouble.' Amber was closing the door on him. 'Never mind, I'm sure you'll find someone else to take on holiday. Have a nice time now. Bye.'

'**S**o that's it, I'm flying out to Tenerife tonight.' Mario concluded as Lottie juggled baked potatoes out of the oven and onto a row of plates. 'Everything's booked. I should have asked you if that's OK. Sorry, I didn't think. Seeing Amber again last night just kind of knocked me for six. Am I messing up any plans?'

'Stop making out you're indispensable. We're fine. The kids'll understand. You need this break. Who knows,' she added brightly, 'you might meet the girl of your dreams!'

Mario's answering smile was bleak. Taking a folded sheet of paper out of his jacket pocket along with his phone, he said, 'Right, I've written down all the details of where I'm staying. If you need to get hold of me, this is the number of the—'

'Can't I just ring you?'

'I'm leaving my phone here.' Mario pushed it across the kitchen table towards her. 'You can look after it for me. That way it won't be so easy to make a dick of myself if I have a few drinks and decide to phone Amber.'

'OK.' Lottie nodded as she piled tuna and sweetcorn into one bowl and chilli with sour cream into another. Then she put down the chilli pan, made her way round the kitchen table and gave Mario a hug, because she hated seeing him so down.

'I've just realised,' Mario said as they all ate dinner, 'I'm going to miss your Christmas concerts.'

'I'm not bothered.' Nat shrugged. 'I'm only a sheep. I get to look in the manger and say, "Look, it's the Baby Jesus, *baaaa*."'

'You'll miss my show too.' Past the age of Nativity plays, Ruby's Christmas concerts were rather jollier affairs. 'I'm singing and dancing and everything.'

'Oh, Rubes, I'm sorry.' Stricken, Mario reached for her hand.

'But we'll be there cheering you on,' Lottie jumped in quickly. 'Me and Nat. And we'll take loads of photos, won't we?'

Her dark eyes huge, Ruby said, 'Will Seb come too?'

'We'll ask him. If he doesn't have to work I'm sure he'll want to come.'

Ruby gave Mario's hand a consoling squeeze. 'That's all right, then. Don't worry, Daddy, we'll have Seb instead.'

Mario had got away in the nick of time. Overnight, temperatures plummeted and the first snow of winter fell, sending Nat and Ruby into paroxysms of delight.

Particularly when Seb arrived on Saturday lunchtime in his new four-by-four with two toboggans in the boot. Ruby, lovingly stroking the sleek red toboggan, said, 'All we've ever had before was tea trays.'

'Poor deprived children. Come on, get your coats on,' ordered Seb. 'We're going to test these babies out on Beggarbush Hill.'

Now, screaming like banshees, Nat and Ruby were racing down the hill on their toboggans along with a cluster of other children bundled up against the cold.

'They won't have any teeth left,' Lottie marvelled as Nat, using his wellington-booted feet as brakes, threw himself off the toboggan seconds before it collided with a bigger boy already spread-eagled in the snow.

'Kids are tough. They bounce. Now, are you going to be a lily-livered woolly-wimp or will you be giving it a go yourself?' asked Seb.

Beggarbush Hill was notoriously steep and Nat and Ruby had shot down it like lightning. Hesitating, Lottie said, 'I've never been on a toboggan like this before. They're quite . . . aerodynamic, aren't they?'

'Chicken.' Seb seized on the hesitation with glee. 'Wimp.'

Lottie hated being called a wimp. She prided herself on giving anything a try. 'I didn't say I *wouldn't* do it. I'm just pointing out—'

'You're probably too old anyway,' said Seb. 'Too weak and feeble and downright past it. Maybe you should stick to knitting.'

'Mum, these toboggans are *wicked*.' Ruby had arrived, pink-cheeked and panting, back at the top of the hill. 'Did you see how *fast* we went?'

'Uh-uh.' Seb wagged a finger. 'Don't mention the f-word. Your mother doesn't do fast.'

'Oh, give me that.' Having been goaded enough, Lottie seized the toboggan from Ruby. How hard could it be anyway?

'Yay!' Ruby clapped her mittened hands. 'Mum's having a go!'

'But she's only a weak and wussy female,' Seb pointed out. 'So don't expect her to do more than two miles an hour.'

Right, that was it. Lottie threw down the toboggan with a flourish and positioned herself on it, feet either side of the runners. Fearlessly she beckoned Seb over and said, 'Give me a push.'

Ruby, unfastening her cycle helmet, said, 'Mum, do you want to borrow—'

'No!' Ha, safety helmets were for cissies. 'Come on, big push, as hard as you can . . . *wheeeeeeeeeee*! . . .'

It was nothing like sitting on an old-fashioned wooden toboggan. This one was made of sleek moulded plastic with go-faster stainless-steel runners. And it *was* going faster, Lottie discovered. Clinging onto the steering rope for grim life, she juddered over a patch of bumpy ground, zipping past people so fast, they were little more than a blur . . . OK, it was only Beggarbush Hill, any second now she'd reach the bit where the ground began to level out and you gradually reduced speed before coasting to a halt at the bot—

THUNNKKK, the toboggan hit a rock sticking out of the snow. Lottie, catapulted into the air, discovered how it felt to be fired from a cannon. Arms and legs flailing wildly, she let out a scream that echoed all the way across the valley before coming to an abrupt halt as she landed and all the air was knocked—*whooosh*—from her lungs.

But only the scream came to an abrupt halt; Lottie continued to tumble over and over, the world cartwheeling dizzily past her eyes until with a final *flummpp* she landed—and stayed—face down in the snow.

'Oh, pphuck.' Lottie let out a groan, spitting snow and blood from her mouth and feeling sick with the pain. Everything hurt so much she didn't know where to start.

'Mummy! Are you all right?' Nat was the first to reach her. Kneeling at her side he said, 'Are you hurt?'

'Just a tiny bit.' The pain in Lottie's lower back was excruciating. Smiling weakly at Nat, she said, 'Is Seb on his way down?'

'Yes, he's coming now with Ruby.' Nat reached out and stroked a strand of wet hair away from Lottie's eye, a gesture that brought a lump to her throat. 'Poor Mummy, you should have worn a crash helmet.'

Lottie nodded. Ironically the one part of her body that wasn't screaming in agony was her head.

'Mummy!' This time it was Ruby, skidding to a halt with her hand in Seb's. 'You were *flying*!'

'I know.' Lottie winced. 'I was there.'

'Talk about attention-seeking.' Crouching beside her, Seb said cheerfully, 'I think your mum's hoping someone's caught it on video so she can sell it to one of those TV programmes.' He gave Lottie a hearty pat on the back. 'OK now? Need a hand getting up?'

Getting *up*?

'I hate to sound like a feeble female,' said Lottie, 'but I think you're going to have to call an ambulance.'

By the time Lottie was finally settled in her hospital bed and the doctor had left to write up his notes, it was six in the evening. Seb and the children, allowed back onto the ward at last, clumped in together in their snow clothes and wellies. Nat and Ruby, eyeing the intravenous drip and the plaster cast, treated Lottie with new respect.

The pain radiating from Lottie's back was still intense, but hospital-strength painkillers were doing their bit to take the edge off it. She kissed Ruby and Nat then looked at Seb. 'The doctor's just told me I'm probably going to be in here for a week. The tests showed a haematoma on one of my kidneys. It's a kind of bruise or bleed or something. Anyway, I have to stay in bed until it clears up.'

Seb looked surprised. 'A week. Bloody hell.'

Bloody hell indeed. One short toboggan ride and here she was, parked up in Cheltenham General with a broken left foot, a badly sprained right wrist, several bruised ribs and one damaged kidney.

And a partridge in a pear tree.

'The problem is, the kids.' Lottie had been unable to think of anything else since discovering she was being admitted. 'Mario's in Tenerife. Cressida's up in Newcastle, so she isn't able to look after them. If you could go back to the cottage and find the phone number Mario left, I can call and tell him to come home, but I don't know what's going to happen tonight . . . oh God, what a time for Mario to be away.'

'Hey, don't panic,' said Seb. 'I'll take them.'

'What?' Lottie's heart leapt—Seb had already told her he had an important business dinner tonight, which was why she hadn't dared ask him before. 'But what about . . . ?'

'I'll just have to cancel it, won't I? These two can come and stay with me.' He ruffled Nat's hair and broke into a grin. 'How about it, then, kids? Fancy that? Or would you rather spend the night in a bus shelter?'

'We'll stay with you,' Nat said happily. 'Can we play Monopoly?'

'Maybe. Ruby, how about you?'

Ruby looked hopeful. 'Scrabble?'

Oh, the relief. Feeling the weight of responsibility fall away, Lottie smiled up at Seb and whispered, 'Thank you.' Then, turning her attention to Nat and Ruby she added, 'And you two have to promise to behave yourselves.'

Nat was offended. 'We always do.'

'OK. Now you'll need the key to the cottage.' She indicated the bedside locker where her bag was stowed. 'And could you drop by Hestacombe House and let Tyler know what's happened? And Mario's phone number is on a piece of paper in the kitchen somewhere. I think it's on the dresser.'

'I'll give him a call,' said Seb. 'You get some rest now. We'll be in to see you in the morning.'

'What would I do without you?' Lottie tried not to flinch as he leaned over to kiss her, his hand brushing her badly bruised shoulder.

Seb winked. 'I know. I'm a saint.'

This was above and beyond the call of duty. As he drove back to Kingston Ash, Seb mulled over the problem; basically, the timing couldn't have been worse. Lottie was great and he was extremely fond of her kids, but to have this happen today of all days was just a complete pain. Karina—heavenly Karina—had flown in from Dubai for the weekend and he'd already made his excuses to Lottie, explaining that he had a meeting tonight to secure sponsorship for the next polo tournament.

And now he'd told her he'd cancel the meeting in order to look after Nat and Ruby instead. Well, what else could he have done under the circumstances? Called Social Services and asked them to take the kids for the weekend?

At that moment a plan began to unfold in his mind. Seb tapped his fingers against the steering wheel and smiled to himself; the night might not turn out to be a complete wash-out after all.

Seb pulled into the snowy driveway. 'OK, here we are. Don't forget your bags, kids.'

'Seb?' Nat exchanged a hopeful look with Ruby. 'Do we have to brush our teeth at your house?'

Seb grinned, because Maya was just the same. 'Are you serious? Of course you don't have to brush your teeth.'

Nat and Ruby were in the living room setting up the Monopoly board and painstakingly sorting out the money. Making sure the kitchen door was shut, Seb rang Karina's number. She answered on the third ring.

'Change of plan,' Seb announced before briefly explaining what had happened.

'Oh, for God's sake!' Karina wailed. 'I don't believe it! I've come all this way—'

'What choice did I have? There wasn't anyone else to look after them. They're terrific kids. We're just about to play a game of Monopoly.'

'Whoop-dee-doo.'

'And then I'll be putting them to bed.' Seb paused then added meaningfully, 'Up in the spare bedroom, right at the top of the house. They'll be going to bed at . . . ooh, around nine o'clock, at a guess.'

Karina perked up. 'And then you'll come over to the hotel?'

Seb shook his head in amusement. 'Bloody hell, darling, you can tell you don't have kids. Abandon them like that and you tend to get arrested. But like I said, they'll be fast asleep by nine thirty. And there's nothing to stop you hopping in a taxi and coming over here.'

Karina sounded as if she was smiling. 'You drive a hard bargain, babe.'

'It'll be worth it.'

'Got any stuff?'

Seb grinned; he'd paid a visit to his dealer only yesterday. 'What did I just tell you, sweetie? I said it'd be worth it.'

Ruby couldn't sleep. Playing Monopoly with Nat and Seb had been brilliant, especially beating Seb, but as soon as nine o'clock had come around he had put them to bed in the attic bedroom and now she was feeling a bit funny. It was sheets and blankets for a start, not a duvet like she was used to. And Seb had said he was going to bed, but he wasn't; earlier a car had pulled up outside and now she could hear noises and voices downstairs that didn't sound like the television.

It was ten fifteen. In the twin bed next to hers Nat was fast asleep. Propelled partly by thirst and partly by curiosity, Ruby slipped out of bed, silently opened the bedroom door and went downstairs.

The hall floor was cold beneath her bare feet. The living-room door was firmly shut but there was definitely someone in there with Seb.

Tiptoeing over to the door in her blue pyjamas, Ruby crouched down and peeped through the keyhole.

Oh no, no, that couldn't be right. Jerking away in horror, then needing to double-check to prove to herself that she hadn't imagined it, Ruby looked again. Seb was on the sofa with a woman, and the woman was wearing her underwear and Seb, who didn't have his shirt on, was leaning forward over the coffee table with something that looked like a straw up his nose.

This was drugs, Ruby was almost sure. She'd seen people doing that sniffing thing on television. Then she froze in horror as she stepped back and one of the floorboards creaked.

Inside the room, the woman said, 'What was that noise?'

Ruby, her heart thumping, melted into the dark space beneath the stairs. Moments later she heard the living-room door open. Finally Seb said, 'It's OK, there's no one out here.'

The woman giggled. 'If it's those kids, just lock them in the cellar.'

'Don't worry. They're asleep. Unlike me . . .' Seb purred before closing the door again.

From where she was hiding, Ruby saw Seb's mobile phone on the spindly-legged table diagonally across the hall from her. Darting out, she grabbed it and raced up the staircase.

'Mummy . . . Mummy . . .' Back in the safety of the attic bedroom, rocking on her knees, Ruby managed to find Lottie's name on the list of favourites and rang her mother's number. 'Answer the phone, oh *please* answer the phone . . .'

But the message service kicked in and Ruby felt her eyes fill with hot tears. Clutching the mobile tightly she waited for the Beep then whispered, 'Mummy? Are you there? I wanted to . . . it's just . . .' She broke off, wiped her wet cheeks with the back of her hand and said in a wobbly voice, 'I want to go home.'

Lottie couldn't work out if she was dreaming when she heard a female voice saying, 'He won't go away until he's seen you.'

Lottie opened her eyes and saw the nurse beside her bed. 'Excuse me?'

'Your boss. Tyler, is that his name? I told him visiting hours were over but he's quite insistent. I said he could pop in for five minutes if it's all right with you.'

'Do I look terrible?' said Lottie.

'Honestly? Yes.'

'Oh, well. Fine, send him in.'

When Tyler made his way up the ward, Lottie guessed how he'd been able to persuade the staff nurse to bend the rules. He was wearing a dinner jacket and a dazzling white dress shirt, and a bow tie was dangling from his jacket pocket.

'Hey, you look awful,' Tyler announced.

The silver-tongued charmer.

'Thanks. You too. Still working as a nightclub bouncer, I see.'

'We only got home thirty minutes ago.' Keeping his voice low so as not to disturb the other sleeping patients, he pulled up a chair. 'Found a note pushed through the letterbox, but all it said was that you'd had an accident and were in hospital, and that you'd be off work for a few weeks. I was going frantic, not knowing which hospital you were in or what was wrong with you.' He paused. 'What *is* wrong with you?'

Lottie told him, moved by his concern and the efforts he'd made to track her down. It was a comfort to see him. Well, considerably more than a comfort, but some things were better left unsaid.

'So where are Ruby and Nat?' Tyler asked when she'd finished.

'Staying at Seb's place in Kingston Ash. He's been brilliant. In fact he may have left a message for me, letting me know if he got through to Mario.' Pointing with her drip-free hand, Lottie said, 'My phone's in the locker but we're not allowed to have them switched on in here. Could you take it outside and see if there's any word from Seb or Mario?'

More relieved than he'd been letting on that Lottie was OK, Tyler left the ward. Outside in the freezing night air, he saw that there was one message from Seb.

Except it wasn't.

He listened in silence to Ruby's tear-choked words. And knew that there was no way in the world he could pass this message on to Lottie.

Without hesitation he rang Seb's mobile. On the fifth ring it was answered. Evidently having seen whose phone the call was coming from, Ruby whispered with a heartbreaking tremor in her voice: 'Mummy?'

'Hey, Ruby, your mom's not allowed to make calls from the ward. This is Tyler.' He said it as gently as he could, as if she wouldn't already have guessed the moment he opened his mouth. 'Now are you OK? You sounded pretty upset when you left your message. Because if there's any kind of problem I can come straight over and pick you and Nat up.'

The silence hung between them. He was the Enemy. He knew that only too well and Ruby knew it too. Finally she said in a stiff little voice, 'No, it's all right,' and hung up.

Tyler stayed where he was under the outside light, trying to figure out what he should do now. Not tell Lottie, that was for sure; she'd go out of her mind with worry. But Ruby's voice had betrayed more than just simple homesickness. And why wasn't Seb answering his own phone? Should he be calling the police or—

The phone rang again. His heart in his mouth, Tyler answered it.

'Yes,' whispered Ruby, her voice quavering.

A few flakes of snow drifted down. Tyler said, 'You want me to come and fetch you?'

'Yes. Will you be here soon?'

Tyler exhaled with relief. 'Don't you worry, sweetheart, I'm on my way. Now listen, I know you're in Kingston Ash but I don't know which house. Are you on the main road through the village?'

'Yes, we're in the attic bedroom. I can see the road from the window.'

'OK, give me ten minutes then as soon as you see a car, start switching the bedroom light off and on so I'll know where you are. Got that?'

'Yes.'

'Good girl. Is Nat with you?'

'Yes.'

'And Seb? Is he there in the house?'

'Yes.' Ruby's voice was wobbling again. 'He's downstairs with . . . someone else.'

Tyler's jaw tightened. 'OK, now you two just hang on in there. I'm on my way. Don't worry about a thing.'

''Kay. Bye.'

Back on the ward he found Lottie dozing again, her dark hair spread out over the pillow, her cut lip swollen, the bruises on her bare arms already spectacular. The temporary plaster cast on her left leg was sticking out from under the bedclothes and her right arm, swathed in bandages, rested across her stomach. As ever, the sight of her caused something inside him to quicken.

'No messages,' Tyler said quietly, causing her eyes to flicker open. 'Mario'll probably call in the morning. Right, I'm off. I may as well take your phone with me.'

'Fine.' Sleepily Lottie smiled at him. 'Thanks for coming over. Sorry about work.'

He'd never wanted to kiss anyone so badly in his life, and was ashamed of himself for even letting the thought cross his mind. Right now he had a more important task on his hands.

'Don't worry about work. You take care of yourself. Everything's going to be fine,' said Tyler.

He hoped.

It was starting to snow again as Tyler approached the village of Kingston Ash. Carefully he manoeuvred the car along the slippery road, keeping an eye out all the time for an upstairs light being switched on and off.

Moments later he rounded the bend past the church gates and saw what he was looking for. The house, one of the biggest in the village, had a gleaming four-by-four parked on the driveway. More importantly, the light in one of the attic bedrooms was switching on and off, illuminating two small figures framed in the window.

Tyler made his way to the front door and rang the bell.

Nothing.

He rang it again.

Finally he heard footsteps and the rattle of keys. The door opened a couple of inches and there was Seb, barefoot and tousle-haired, wearing nothing but a pair of jeans.

'Hi. Lottie asked me to come and pick up the kids.'

Seb laughed. '*What?*'

'You don't need to keep them any more.' Tyler could tell at once that Seb was sky-high on something. 'I'm here to take them off your hands.'

'They're asleep. And . . . how can I put this? . . . they hate your guts. Goodbye.' Seb, still laughing wildly, attempted to slam the door shut but Tyler already had his foot in the way and it ricocheted back on him. Caught off guard, Seb staggered sideways. The doors to the kitchen and dining room were open. Pushing past him, Tyler made for the only one that was closed.

'Jesus Christ, who are you?' shrieked a blonde girl, naked but for the man's shirt she was clutching in front of her. 'I'm calling the police!'

'Excellent.' Taking in at a glance the white powder scattered across the glass-topped table and the matching white rings around her nostrils, Tyler said pleasantly, 'Tell them to bring the sniffer dogs—they'll think it's Christmas.' Closing the door, leaving the girl gaping, he turned and saw Ruby and Nat huddled together at the top of the stairs. Gesturing for them to join him he said, 'OK, you two, let's get out of here.'

'You bastard,' hissed Seb, 'coming over here and fucking up my life. I know why you've done this, it's because you're—'

'Don't try it,' Tyler warned.

Ignoring the warning, Seb launched himself with fists flying. Catching first one wrist then the other and twisting them up behind his back until he was yelping like a dog, Tyler bundled Seb out through the front door and into the garden. One clean punch to the jaw sent him flying into a snow-covered flowerbed, where he lay groaning as Tyler ushered Nat and Ruby past him and into the car.

Then Tyler went back and stood over Seb, still boiling with fury but willing himself not to beat him to a bloody pulp.

'You're not going to see Lottie again. And if she ever claps eyes on you,' said Tyler, 'I'd advise you to run for your life. She *trusted* you to look after her children.'

When Kingston Ash was behind them, Tyler stopped the car and turned round to look at Nat and Ruby on the back seat. It was at this moment he realised that if he'd been expecting an iota of gratitude he was going to be disappointed.

Luckily he hadn't.

'OK, I'm going to take you back to my place. Hestacombe House,' Tyler added, in case they thought he meant Fox Cottage.

'I want to see Mum,' said Ruby.

'I know, I know you do, but she's asleep now. And they wouldn't let you onto the ward. So we can't—'

'I'm not staying at your house.' Nat, his tone final, was gazing fixedly out of the window.

'Well, you don't have a lot of choice,' Tyler pointed out. 'What with being seven. Ruby, tell him.'

Ruby's dark eyes were expressionless. 'I don't want to stay at your house either. Just leave us at the hospital and we'll sit in the waiting room till Mum wakes up.'

Oh, for crying out loud.

'Now, listen to me. I didn't just *kidnap* you,' said Tyler. 'You were the one who phoned me, remember? You asked me to come and fetch you.'

'I didn't,' Nat retorted. 'I didn't want anyone to come and get me. I was asleep until *she* woke me up.'

'So what do you want me to do? Take you back?'

Silence.

Finally, in a low voice, Ruby muttered, 'No.'

'But we don't want to go to your house either,' Nat repeated stubbornly.

'OK, but I have to warn you, your options are pretty limited. Your dad's in Tenerife. And Lottie tells me her friend Cressida's not around. So do you want me to ask Ben and Harry Jenkins's mother if you can share their bunk beds? Or, let me see, would you rather stay with Ted from the shop? Or, hang on, what's the name of that teacher your mom's so scared of? Miss Bat-something,' said Tyler. 'Would she take you in, d'you think?'

More silence.

Tyler sighed as the snow began to fall more heavily, clogging up the windscreen. 'Right, this is my final offer. Tomorrow we'll sort out a better solution but just for tonight you stay at my place.'

Ruby, fiddling in the pocket of her trousers, produced a key. Triumphantly she said, 'We'll stay at *our* house.'

'Not on your own you don't.'

'You wouldn't call the police.'

'I bet I would.' With a glimmer of a smile Tyler said, 'And they'd throw you in jail for a week.'

Ruby glared at him. Finally she shrugged. 'Well, you're not having my mum's bed. You can sleep downstairs on the settee.'

Honestly, talk about surreal. Lottie was beginning to wonder if she'd landed on her head after all. One minute there she was thinking she felt better, the next minute she knew she must be hallucinating because Nat and Ruby were heading up the ward towards her with—ooh, *weird*—Tyler following in their wake.

'What's going on?' Lottie attempted to see past them. 'Where's Seb?'

'Hello, Mummy. We're fine.' Having planted a kiss on each cheek, Nat and Ruby moved away from the bed.

'They'll be back in ten minutes,' said Tyler as they ran out of the ward. 'And you can see they're OK. I just need to—'

'What happened?' Lottie instantly conjured up mental pictures of an accident, Seb losing control of the car in the snow, the ambulance crew managing to get Nat and Ruby out unscathed but unable to reach Seb before being flung back by a violent explosion. Sick with fear she blurted out, 'Oh God, tell me he's all right!'

Ten minutes later Tyler had told her everything. Rigid with horror and disbelief, Lottie listened in silence. By the time he reached the end she was ready to rip the intravenous drip from her arm and launch herself like Frankenstein's monster out of bed—except she couldn't even *walk*.

'I'm sorry. Here.' It wasn't until Tyler passed her a handful of tissues that she realised tears were rolling down her face. 'Hey, don't cry. I know it's a shock, but you can do better than him.'

Lottie clumsily wiped her eyes with her unbandaged left hand. 'Do you seriously think that's why I'm upset? Because that dirtbag was cheating on me? My God, what kind of a person do you think I am!'

Tyler paused. 'But you're crying.'

'Because I'm so relieved my kids are OK!' Incandescent with rage—*how* could he be so dense?—Lottie hurled a sodden tissue at him. 'Because I can't believe I was so *stupid*.' She hurled another. 'Because I trusted another person to look after my children and I *shouldn't have*!

Because I got it wrong and I'm a lousy judge of character and . . . oh God, *anything* could have happened to them.'

'But it didn't. They're fine.' Tyler's tone was soothing. 'Besides, how could you have known?'

'I just should have done.' Noisily Lottie blew her nose.

'Did you know he used cocaine?'

'No!' Although now, of course, everything made more sense. Seb's over-enthusiasm, his episodes of almost over-the-top hyperactivity, the way he sometimes laughed a bit too much at something that wasn't *that* funny. His over-the-topness was one of the reasons Nat and Ruby had enjoyed being with him. Feeling stupider than ever, Lottie said, 'Did you?'

'It crossed my mind. Hey,' Tyler handed her a clean tissue, 'I worked on Wall Street, remember? There was a bit more of that kind of thing going on in New York than you're used to in Hestacombe.'

This didn't make Lottie feel any better at all. She still wanted to tear Sebastian Gill apart with her bare hands. While he'd been high on coke and cavorting in his living room with some tart, Ruby had been upstairs so desperate to escape that she had been forced to accept help from, of all people, *Tyler*.

'I'm sorry I threw those tissues at you.'

'That's OK.' He sounded amused. 'I can handle soggy tissues.'

'And thanks for rescuing Nat and Ruby.' There was still so much she had to say. 'So does this mean they don't hate you any more?'

'Wouldn't that be nice?' Tyler gave her an ironic look. 'Sadly, there's no danger of that happening. Your children still hate me every bit as much as before.'

'Oh.' Disappointed, Lottie said, 'Is Mario on his way home yet?'

'No. We can't find the piece of paper with his details on. We've turned the kitchen upside-down, looked everywhere.' Tyler shrugged. 'It's gone. Can you remember the name of the hotel?'

Lottie looked blank. 'No.'

'We're back,' Nat announced.

'Oh, sweetheart.' Ready to burst into tears all over again, Lottie held out her good arm. 'Come here.'

Nat, dodging smartly out of the way, said, 'Yuk, get off, not if you're going to cry.'

'Poor Mummy, be nice to her.' Ruby stroked Lottie's shoulder.

Making an effort to retain control, Lottie whispered, 'I'm so sorry about last night, sweetheart. Are you sure you're all right?'

Ruby nodded before jerking her head in Tyler's direction. 'Except for having *him* looking after us.'

Lottie was mortified. 'Oh, Ruby, don't say that. Look what he *did* for you . . .'

'I still don't like him.' Ruby spoke matter-of-factly. 'Anyway, Dad'll be home soon.'

'He won't be if we can't contact him. Now think,' Lottie cajoled. 'The hotel and phone number were written on a sheet of yellow paper. It was on the dresser on Friday. It can't have just disappeared.' As she said this, she saw Nat's dark lashes flicker. 'Nat? Any ideas at all?'

'No!' He sounded outraged.

'Because if there was some kind of an accident, then that's fine,' Tyler joined in casually. 'But if it *is* still there, we'll just have to keep on looking until we find it.'

Nat glanced furtively around the ward before saying hurriedly, 'I spilled Ribena on it and the ink went all blurred. I didn't want anyone to find out, so I threw it down the toilet and pulled the flush.'

Lottie and Tyler looked at each other. Now they had no way of contacting Mario.

'I've got an idea,' Ruby said suddenly. 'Amber!'

'Yay, Amber! She could look after us.' Nat's face lit up as he clutched Lottie's arm. 'She can, can't she, Mum? We *like* Amber.'

'Give her a ring,' Lottie told Tyler. 'Her number's on my phone. Fingers crossed she can do it.'

Tyler was gone from the ward for a good fifteen minutes. When he returned he wasn't looking giddy with relief.

'She can't.'

'Oh, no.' Lottie had been pinning all her hopes on Amber riding to the rescue.

'She's too busy. Everyone wants their hair done before Christmas,' said Tyler. 'And she's doing house visits in the evenings as well.'

So that was that. Amber had been their last hope.

'It's no use glaring at me,' Tyler told Nat. 'I didn't want this either. But it looks like we're stuck with each other for the next few days. So we may as well make the best of it.'

'There isn't any best. We don't *want* you looking after us,' said Nat.

'And this is my worst nightmare,' replied Tyler. 'So that makes us even.'

Oh God. The three of them were as bad as each other.

One of the nurses came bustling over. 'Lottie, the porters are here to wheel you down for your pyelogram.'

Tyler said, 'We'll leave you to it.'

Ruby shot him a suspicious look. 'What're you going to do with us?'

'Lock you in the garage.'

When they'd left the ward, the nurse said with a smile, 'Mum goes into hospital and Dad doesn't know what's hit him. Most of them don't have the first idea when it comes to taking care of their kids, do they?'

'He's not their dad,' said Lottie. 'He's my boss.'

'Really? Heavens, lucky old you!' The nurse softened. 'And how lovely of him to be looking after your children!'

The porters had arrived to wheel her bed out of the ward. Bracing herself for knocks and judders, Lottie said wearily, 'Believe me, he didn't have a lot of choice.'

Chapter 11

'WHAT'S IN HERE? It weighs a ton.' Tyler picked up Nat's school bag, unzipped it and found it packed with—what else?—stones.

'It's *stones*. Aren't I allowed to collect stones?' Nat was ostentatiously picking crispy shards of black from his Marks & Spencer lasagne.

'Absolutely. Am I allowed to ask why?'

'It's what soldiers do. To make them strong. This is really burnt.'

Tyler rose above this slur on his culinary skills. 'I call it char-grilled.'

'I call it burnt.'

'That's how soldiers eat it.' Burrowing among the muddy stones, Tyler pulled out a mangled sheet of turquoise paper. 'What's this?'

Nat mumbled, 'Letter from school.'

'How long has it been in here?'

'I don't know. This is *so* burnt.'

Tyler began to read the photocopied letter, issued to all pupils by the school headmistress and so jollily worded that at first he found himself lulled into a false sense of security. It took a few seconds to realise what it was actually instructing him to do.

'It's half past eight on Monday night,' Tyler said slowly, 'and it says here that all children must bring cakes into school on Tuesday morning for the cake stall.' He looked first at Ruby, then at Nat. 'But we don't have any in the house and all the shops are shut.'

'You aren't allowed to buy them from the shop,' said Ruby. 'You have to make them.'

'So what happens if you go to school tomorrow without homemade cakes?'

They looked scandalised. 'We have to. Or we'll get in trouble.'

Tyler carried on reading. Everyone, the letter chirpily announced, was expected to attend the Christmas Tree and Cakes Fair on Tuesday evening and enjoy the carols being sung by Year 5 pupils in their festive Victorian attire.

He turned to Ruby. 'What year are you in?'

She gave him a *duh* look. 'Five.'

This was a learning curve and no mistake. 'You're singing carols tomorrow night? In festive Victorian attire? Where does that come from?'

'You have to ask your mum and she makes it. But she's in hospital,' said Ruby, 'so we won't be going to the Tree and Cakes Fair anyway. So don't worry about it.'

Tyler looked at her. This was a *vertical* learning curve.

'Don't try and make any cakes either,' Nat added. 'Because if you did they'd only end up burnt.'

'You made *what* last night?'

'Twenty-four fairy cakes.'

'But why . . . ? Oh my God! The Tree and Cakes Fair, I forgot all about it!' Lottie couldn't believe it had slipped her mind. 'And Ruby's supposed to be . . . oh well, they'll manage without her.'

'No, it's OK, we're going. I know about the festive Victorian attire,' Tyler said drily. 'And I've tracked down a shop in Cheltenham that hires out fancy dress.'

'You don't have to do that,' Lottie protested. 'This is Oaklea Junior School, not the London Palladium. She can go as a street urchin. Old pair of trousers cut off below the knee to look raggedy. Some shirt buttoned up all wrong, hair messed up, streaks of dirt on her face.'

Relieved, Tyler said, 'OK.'

'Don't forget to take a camera.'

'Right.'

'Oh, and I volunteered to help with selling the Christmas trees.'

'I'll do that then.'

'You'll need gardener's gloves.'

'Why, to stop Nat biting me?'

'They don't still hate you, do they?'

'More than ever. But that's OK, I can handle it.'

'What about Liana?'

'She doesn't hate me.'

'She must be getting fed up.' Lottie did her best to sound concerned.

'Can't be helped.' Abruptly changing the subject, Tyler pulled the crumpled school letter from his jacket pocket. 'Now, it's Nat's Christmas play tomorrow night.'

'The Nativity play. He's playing one of the sheep. That's easy too,' said Lottie. 'Just wrap the sheepskin rug round him and tie it on with a couple of belts.'

'He's been upgraded. Charlie Johnson's off with flu so Nat's been promoted to chief shepherd. I already checked with one of the other mothers this morning when I dropped them off at school.' Tyler was looking pleased with himself. 'Tea towel on head. Big shirt, bare feet, walking stick. No problem.'

Lottie's eyes prickled with tears. She was going to miss it.

'Don't worry, the head's videoing it,' said Tyler. 'I'm not allowed to go either.'

'You won't be there?' Lottie couldn't bear it.

'I've been banned by Nat. I have to wait outside the school hall.' Tyler waited. 'Of course I'm going to be there. He just won't know about it, that's all.'

When they arrived back at Piper's Cottage the post had been delivered. Ruby, scooping the postcard up off the mat, said, 'We did a project at school on Australia. This is Sydney Harbour Bridge.'

Tyler looked over her shoulder. 'It isn't.'

'Yes, it is.'

'No, it's not.'

'Yes, it is.'

'Turn it over then. See what it says.'

Ruby turned the card over.

'See?' Tyler pointed to the printed lettering at the bottom. 'The Tyne Bridge, Newcastle-upon-Tyne.'

Annoyed, Ruby said, 'How did you *know*?'

'Because I'm very clever.' He smiled. 'Yours was a pretty good guess though. They're very similar.'

'It's not fair.' Ruby heaved an irritated sigh. 'I wish I knew everything. I can't wait to be a grown-up and always get everything right.'

Tyler thought of Lottie and Liana and the events of the past few months. 'Trust me,' he told Ruby with feeling, 'being a grown-up doesn't mean you get everything right.'

'Do you make mistakes?' Nat looked delighted.

'Oh, yes, I've made some big mistakes. Like the time I thought you'd stolen your mom's clothes while she was swimming in the lake.'

'It wasn't us,' said Nat.

'Of course it wasn't you. I know that now. But at the time it was an honest mistake.'

'You killed Bernard,' Ruby said.

'I know. But I really didn't mean to kill him. It was an accident.' Tyler shook his head. 'I told you, grown-ups make mistakes.'

'Anyway.' Firmly changing the subject, Ruby held up the postcard. 'This is for Mum, from Cressida. Should I read it?'

'You shouldn't really read other people's mail,' Tyler pointed out.

'It's only a postcard. Everyone reads *them*.'

This was true. 'Go on, then.'

Ruby cleared her throat importantly and read aloud, '"Newcastle is perfect. So is Tom. I've never been happier in my life. The view from up here on Cloud 9 is spectacular—may not want to come down again! Love Cress. Pssss, hope all's well with you and Seb." Ha, wait until she hears about *him*.'

'So this man Tom is going to be Cress's new boyfriend. They'll be all lovey-dovey.' Nat rolled his eyes.

Lucky them, thought Tyler.

'If Cress hadn't gone up to see him,' Nat continued, 'she'd be looking after us now, instead of you.'

With difficulty Tyler managed to keep a straight face. 'I guess she's had a lucky escape. Now, anyone want to give me a hand with dinner?'

Nat looked appalled. 'My favourite programme's about to start.'

'The more help I get, the less likely it is to be burnt.'

It was Ruby's turn to heave a sigh. 'I suppose I'll have to help you then. But only for a bit.'

'Thank you.' It was a minor victory but it felt . . . God, it felt *great*. When Nat had raced off to watch TV, Tyler nodded at the postcard in Ruby's hand and said easily, 'By the way, that bit at the end. It's P.S., not Pssss.'

Ruby bristled. 'I knew that.'

'Hey, of course you did.' She looked so much like Lottie when she was defending herself. 'In fact I prefer *Psss*,' said Tyler. 'It sounds like a secret you're whispering to someone. Much better than boring old P.S.'

Ruby almost, *almost* smiled. She nodded confidently. 'Me too.'

Having skipped down the steps and raced across the playground to where the Christmas trees were being sold, Ruby hovered to one side for a few seconds before blurting out, 'Did you see me?'

Her breath hung in misty clouds in the freezing night air and she was wearing her street urchin outfit.

'I saw you. And heard you. We all did.' Tyler indicated the other helpers before untying the blue sweater from round his waist. 'You did great. Now why don't you put this on before you catch pneumonia?'

'It's *yours*.' Ruby eyed the sweater with alarm, as if he'd offered her one decorated with live cockroaches.

'But you left your coat at home, remember? And now you're cold. No, don't want it? OK, just put it over there on the wall.'

Three minutes later Ruby said, 'Did you hear me doing my solo verse in "O Come, All Ye Faithful"?'

'Are you kidding? Of course I heard it. I was the one clapping and whistling the loudest.' Tyler paused. 'Actually, better not tell Lottie I was doing that. She might think sticking your fingers in your mouth and whistling is the kind of crass thing only a dumb American would do.'

Ruby looked envious. 'I've never been able to whistle like that. With my fingers.'

'Oh well, I can teach you how to do that. Learned all about whistling when I worked on a cattle ranch in Wyoming.' Someone came up at that point to choose one of the Christmas trees. By the time Tyler had finished dealing with them Ruby had wandered over to chat to her friends around the hot chocolate stand, but she was wearing his sweater.

A small concession, but maybe . . . *maybe* . . . a start.

'**I** can't get my stupid tea towel on straight! It keeps going sideways and falling over my eye!'

'OK, OK, don't panic, I'll sort it out.'

'I'm going to be *late*.' Nat's voice rose. 'It's starting *now*.'

'Better keep still then.' Crouching in front of him in the car park, Tyler whipped off the tea towel and headband and started all over again, while Nat hopped impatiently from foot to foot.

'Quick, quick!'

'There, all done. You look terrific.' Tyler patted him on the shoulder. 'Go on in, it's showtime.'

Nat gazed up at him. 'Where will you be?'

'Don't worry, I'll wait in the car.'

After a moment's hesitation Nat said, 'Is it true that you worked on a cattle ranch, like a real cowboy?'

'Of course it's true.' So Ruby had told him about that. 'I even learned how to use a lasso.'

'And whistle really loudly with your fingers in your mouth.' Nat paused, blinked. 'You can come in and watch if you want.'

Tyler was careful not to react. But inside he was marvelling that being invited to watch a Nativity play could feel like winning the lottery. Aloud he said, 'Really? You're sure you don't mind?'

Clearly itching to get inside, Nat shrugged. 'You can if you like.'

'Thanks.' As Nat turned to leave, Tyler called after him, 'If it's a good show, am I allowed to whistle at the end?'

It was too dark to be able to tell for sure, but he was fairly certain Nat was smiling as he yelled back, 'You can if you like.'

Lottie almost had a relapse there and then when her visitors made their way onto the ward on Friday afternoon and she saw that Nat was holding Tyler's hand.

When Nat grinned and waved at her she nearly had another one. 'Oh my God, I didn't even know your tooth was loose!'

'It wathn't. I fell over in the playground during morning break and my tooth broke in half.' Intensely proud of his gap, Nat wiggled the end of his tongue through it. 'And it hurt like anything. Mith Batson phoned your mobile and Tyler anthwered and came and picked me up and took me to the dentitht. And the dentitht gave me a huge injection and that *really* hurt but I wath brave and then he pulled out the tooth and there wath loadth of blood *everywhere*.'

'Oh, Nat!' Lottie hugged him before anxiously searching his face for signs of emotional trauma. 'And I wasn't there!'

'Mum, you're choking me. My mouth wath all numb and flubbery afterwardth. It wath cool! And then I went back to thcool even though there wath blood on my shirt.' This had evidently been a badge of honour. 'And Tyler gave me a pound for being brave at the dentitht. *And* he'th taking uth ithe-thkating tomorrow.'

'Good grief.' Lottie was busy kissing Ruby and stroking her hair.

'And I heard Miss Batson talking to Tyler when we went to pick up Nat this afternoon,' Ruby chimed in. 'She was laughing and telling him what a good job he was doing, looking after us.'

Good *grief*.

Nat grinned at Tyler. 'I thaw that too. She looked ath if she wanted to kith you.'

Lottie blinked; this was truly mind-boggling stuff.

'If Miss Batson even tried to come *near* me,' Tyler warned, 'I'd stick my fingers in my mouth and whistle so hard her eardrums would burst.'

'That'th what I'm going to do when the girlth try to kith me,' said Nat.

'Tell Mum the other thing,' Ruby prompted Tyler.

'What other thing?' Lottie was beginning to feel quite light-headed.

Tyler's dark eyes glittered with amusement. 'OK, Miss Batson told me how nice it was to see your kids so happy now, because you'd got yourself involved with a man not so long ago who'd caused all kinds of problems.' Modestly he added, 'She said thank goodness you'd come to your senses and that I was clearly a much better choice. With which sentiment I naturally agreed.'

'And that'th when I told her,' Nat lisped exultantly. 'I thaid Tyler wath the one we'd hated because he'd been tho horrible to uth!'

For the first time Lottie was glad she was confined to her hospital bed. Picturing Miss Batson's formidable face she murmured faintly, 'Then what?'

Tyler said, 'Miss Batson leaned over and whispered in my ear, "Do you know, if I weren't a teacher I'd suggest boiling them in oil."'

The world was becoming more surreal by the minute. It was mad enough that Nat and Ruby were on speaking terms with Tyler, but getting to grips with the idea that Miss Batson might actually be human . . .

'Oh, yeah, and Dad phoned latht night.' Nat belatedly produced the other snippet of information they had to pass on—far less important than his bashed-out front tooth.

'At *last*.' Lottie heaved a sigh of relief. 'Is he flying straight back?'

Ruby shook her head. 'He offered. We said there was no need. We're OK without him now, aren't we?'

OK without Mario. OK with Tyler. Lottie silently digested this. A few months ago it would have been more than she could have hoped for, a turnaround on Nat and Ruby's part beyond her wildest dreams.

But that was before Liana had arrived on the scene and installed herself back in Tyler's life.

'Sweetheart, I'll be discharged from here soon. The hospital are lending me a wheelchair but I'm going to be pretty useless at home. I'll need help with everything.'

'But we've told Dad he doethn't have to come home.' Nat, chomping his way through her grapes as efficiently as a plague of locusts, said, 'Anyway, we've broken up now. We can help you.'

'Thanks, darling. I know you will.' Lottie stroked his tangled curls and wondered how she was really going to manage in a wheelchair. Piper's Cottage had narrow doorways and the bathroom was so small it—

'You *pig*,' wailed Ruby, shoving the brown paper bag at Nat's chest. 'There's only stalks left. You've eaten all the grapes!'

'Don't throw it at *me*. I'm allowed to eat them becauthe I've been to the *dentitht*.'

Separating them with an outstretched arm, Tyler said calmly, 'Ice skating. Yes or no?'

Nat and Ruby looked at each other and subsided onto the bed.

'You know, I'm starting to get the hang of this,' said Tyler.

Touched, Lottie said, 'Handled like a pro.'

Nat, giving Ruby a nudge, said, 'But he burnth everything he cookth.'

'**H**ere she is,' sang the nurse. 'Lottie, you've got another visitor.'

It was Friday evening and Lottie was engrossed in an article in a magazine about a woman giving birth to twins in her bathroom when she hadn't even realised she was pregnant.

Looking up and seeing Liana standing there at the foot of the bed gave her much the same feeling.

'You look awful.' Liana was taking in the bruises, the hair in need of a wash, the bandaged wrist and the plastered foot. 'How are you feeling?'

'Oh, um . . . better thanks.' Lottie put down the magazine.

'And smug, I should think.' Liana was smiling but in a way that didn't quite reach her eyes.

'Sorry?'

'Oh, yes, that too. Sorry, but not sorry enough to put a stop to it.'

'Put a stop to what?' But Lottie had already guessed what this was about; it was pretty self-evident that Liana was fed up with the fact that for the last six days she'd hardly seen Tyler. And who could blame her?

'You *know* what,' said Liana.

'OK, but there wasn't much else I could do, was there?' Lottie did her best to sound reasonable. 'Somebody had to look after Ruby and Nat.'

'And guess who that someone turned out to be? *My* boyfriend.'

Yikes. 'Well, I'm sorry. But the doctors think I might be able to go home on Monday, so then we'll be out of your hair.'

'And where will you be staying? In that poky little cottage of yours?'

The cheek of it! Lottie, who loved her home with a passion, retorted, 'Plenty of people manage to live in poky cottages and—'

'Tyler hasn't told you he wants you to move into Hestacombe House?'

'*What?* No!'

Liana's knuckles were white as she gripped the metal rail at the foot of the bed. 'We had the most massive row about it last night. He was most insistent, going on about the doorways being wide enough for your wheelchair and how he could turn the drawing room into a bedroom—any excuse he could think of, basically. So long as he's got you under his roof. Anyhow, I told him I'd had enough. I said if you moved in, I'd be gone. And guess what? I'm gone.'

Lottie was numb, too shocked to move or speak.

'So that's it. Looks like you won.' Tilting her head to one side she said, 'I bet you can't believe your luck, huh? Because I'm telling you now, I sure as hell can't figure it out. I'm the one who deserves him, you see. I'm beautiful, everyone says so. I'm a perfect size six. I'm intelligent and I'm always real nice to people. And my fiancé died, which means I've suffered enough. God knows, if anyone deserves to be happy, it's me.'

Her words sounded brittle, like dry twigs being snapped. Liana couldn't comprehend her rejection, let alone the possibility that she may have lost out to someone who weighed three stone more than she did.

Unless—the unedifying thought crossed Lottie's mind—maybe she hadn't. Maybe Tyler, eager to get rid of Liana, was simply using her as a handy excuse. Lottie shuddered. God, how awful if *that* hadn't occurred to her before she'd hurled herself into his arms.

'I mean, look at you.' As if to illustrate the point Liana indicated Lottie in her red dressing gown, sporting the glitter-strewn 'Get Well' badge Ruby had presented her with last night. 'May I ask you a personal question? Have you ever had a professional pedicure in your life?'

Lottie looked at her toes, the Day-Glo pink nails varnished yesterday by Ruby with a lot of love and care but maybe not that much accuracy.

'No, I haven't.'

'And as for your wardrobe. You wear the most extraordinary outfits sometimes. You *never* co-ordinate your accessories . . .'

'I'm sorry.' Lottie kept a straight face.

'But nobody seems to mind! That's what gets me! You're a single parent with two young children . . . I mean, that should be a major turn-off in anybody's book. *And* your last boyfriend was a drug addict, which doesn't say much for your powers of judgment.'

Stung, Lottie said, 'Now hang on a minute, that's not fair. I didn't *know* about—'

'Hey, no offence.' Liana held up her hands. 'Don't you see? There's no need for you to defend yourself because it doesn't seem to matter what you get wrong. Everyone forgives you anyway.' She paused. 'Whereas *I* never do anything wrong *and* I take care of myself and I spend more money on one pair of shoes than you spend on clothes in a *year*, but when it comes right down to it, for some reason they still prefer you.'

It was fantastic to see Amber again, and even more fantastic to discover she'd brought along her hairdressing scissors. Since coming out of hospital three days ago, Lottie had been getting used to manoeuvring her wheelchair around the ground floor of Hestacombe House.

'I can't believe so much has happened in the last ten days.' said Amber, fastening the towel round Lottie's shoulders and taking out her comb and scissors. 'You in hospital, Nat and Ruby being looked after by Tyler. Do you know, when they met me at the bottom of the drive they were speaking with just a *smidgen* of an American accent.' Smiling as she began Lottie's long-overdue cut, she went on, 'He's definitely won them over.'

'He has. And Liana's gone back to America.' Lottie gazed at the Christmas tree and listened to the comforting snip-snip of the scissors.

'So it's all systems go, you and Tyler together at last!'

Lottie said hastily. 'Tyler and I aren't together like that.'

'Oh. Sorry. Doctor's orders, I suppose—'

'I mean Tyler and I aren't together in *any* way. He's my boss. I'm his employee. And that's as far as it goes.'

Amber stopped cutting. 'But . . . why?'

'I don't know!'

'Has he said anything?'

'No!' wailed Lottie.

'Have you asked him?'

'Nooo!'

Amber frowned. 'But I thought he was crazy about you.'

'So did I!'

'And the only thing stopping you being together was Nat and Ruby hating him, except they don't hate him any more. And Liana and Seb are out of the picture now, so everything should be . . . well, all systems go.'

'Exactly.'

'So why isn't it?'

'Truthfully?' Lottie hated having to say the words. 'I think he's changed his mind. I think he was crazy about me, but that was months ago and now those feelings have worn off.'

Amber said robustly, 'I can't believe you haven't tackled him about it.'

Lottie couldn't either. It wasn't like her at all. But there was so much at stake she was terrified to make any kind of move in case it all went horribly wrong. 'I just can't. Anyway, look at me.' She indicated the cast on her foot, the still spectacularly bruised wrist and the wheelchair. 'It's not as if I can wrestle him to the ground and force him to change his mind. And at least if I don't say anything I'll still have some pride left.'

'So how long will you stay on here?' Amber asked.

'Only a few more days. As soon as the wrist's better I'll be able to get around on crutches. Then we can go home.' Keen to change the subject, Lottie waved her hand. 'Anyway, enough about me. How's it going with you and Quentin?'

'Oh, fine! I've been rushed off my feet at work but he never complains.' Amber said fondly, 'I got home at ten o'clock last night and he'd cooked the most amazing roast dinner, can you believe it?'

'Mario would never have done that,' said Lottie.

'I *know*. That's the difference between them.' Amber's turquoise and silver earrings swung from side to side as she shook her head. 'Quentin's so thoughtful. And trustworthy. All he wants to do is make me happy.'

Lottie said, 'Yes, but does he make you laugh?'

'If you start on me,' Amber pointed the business end of the scissors at her, 'I shall run down to the office and ask Tyler why he hasn't made a pass at you. I'll tell him you *luuuurve* him and that you want to—'

'I'm not starting!' Lottie hurriedly raised both hands in surrender.

'Good.'

'There's just one tiny thing I want to mention, if that's allowed.'

Already suspicious, Amber narrowed her eyes. 'What?'

'Mario rang me yesterday. He hasn't slept with anyone while he's been on holiday. He just hasn't wanted to,' said Lottie.

'That's what he says.'

'But it's the truth, because he doesn't need to lie to me, does he? You know, I really think you—'

'Don't say it!' Amber tapped her on the head, quite painfully, with her metal comb. 'I don't care what you think. I've got Quentin and he makes me happy, thank you very much.'

Rubbing her head, Lottie belatedly remembered the golden rule: never annoy your hairdresser halfway through your own haircut.

Maybe Amber didn't mind that Quentin didn't make her laugh.

As each new delay had been announced, every other passenger had become increasingly bad-tempered. Now that they were home at last their collective mood improved. The plane had landed nine hours late but they were finally back in Bristol and thank God for that.

The exception was Mario, who basically wasn't bothered either way. As far as he was concerned the airport was as good a place as any to pass a bit of time. Apart from seeing Nat and Ruby again, what else did he have to look forward to? Nothing at all.

Oh well. Hauling his case off the luggage carousel, he wheeled it through the milling crowds and made his way towards Customs. The glass doors slid open and Mario found himself in the arrivals hall, decorated for Christmas and still busy despite the fact that it was gone midnight. A couple of nuns were sitting at a café table drinking tea from a flask, groups of returning travellers were being greeted with cries of delight by friends and relatives and there was a girl sleeping on a bench with a woolly hat on. At first glance Mario experienced a cattle-prod jolt of recognition because beneath the woolly hat she had blonde hair like Amber's, but he was becoming accustomed to these jolts now. Several times a day on holiday he'd glimpse someone in the distance and think for a heart-stopping moment that it was Amber.

This one was wearing Amber-type clothes, which was what had captured his attention: a short ruffled purple skirt, pink glittery sweater and rainbow-coloured hat and scarf. She was wearing pink cowboy boots, Mario observed, knowing perfectly well as he moved towards the bench that it wouldn't be her but needing to prove it to himself nevertheless.

Oh God, it *was* her.

He gazed down at Amber, peacefully asleep with her head resting on one arm and her sequinned handbag clutched to her chest. What was she doing here? If she was waiting for bloody Quentin, he'd . . . well, he'd . . . was this really happening or was *he* still asleep in the departure lounge in Palma?

Reaching out, Mario touched her shoulder and gave it a tentative shake. When Amber's eyes opened he snatched his hand back as if she were a growling pitbull. Terrific, very manly. And what was he supposed to say, now that he'd gone and woken her up?

'Off on holiday?' Mario couldn't believe he'd just said that.

Amber looked at him. 'No.'

'Oh.'

'What's the time?'

He checked his watch. 'Half past midnight.'

'Of all the planes in all the world,' said Amber, 'you had to be on that one.'

Mario didn't allow himself to hope. 'It was delayed. We were supposed to be here nine hours ago.'

'That's typical of you,' said Amber.

Still not daring to hope but compelled to ask the question, Mario said, 'Have you been waiting here since three o'clock this afternoon?'

'No, I have *not*.' Amber pulled herself into a sitting position and took off her hat. 'I've been waiting here since *six* o'clock this morning.'

'Why?' Mario braced himself for bad news.

'Why? Because Lottie didn't know what time you were flying back, did she, so I had to make sure I got here early enough to meet every plane.' Exasperated, Amber said, 'Except I fell asleep instead, on a stupid metal *bench*. You could have walked straight past me without realising I was here. I'd have spent all that time waiting for nothing!'

Mario exhaled slowly. 'I don't think I could ever walk straight past you without realising you were there. It just wouldn't happen. And you do have to tell me what's going on, by the way. Because at the moment I'm at a bit of a loss. . .'

'You know exactly what's going on. I'll also have you know, it's all your interfering ex-wife's fault.' Amber paused. 'So, how was your holiday?'

'Terrible.'

She smiled. 'In that case I'm glad I didn't go with you.'

'If you'd gone with me it wouldn't have been terrible.' Reaching out, Mario pulled her to her feet. 'Where's Quentin?'

'That's all over. I told Quentin yesterday.'

'I bet he took it well,' said Mario. 'Like the decent chap he is.'

'He did.' Amber nodded. 'And he *is* a decent chap.'

'But?'

'He wasn't enough. Dammit, he wasn't *you*. Oh God,' Amber groaned, 'I can't help wondering if I'm going to regret this.'

He loved her so much. 'You won't. And that's a promise.'

She fixed him with a warning look. 'You'd better keep that promise. Because I'm telling you now, if you *ever* cheat on me, I swear I'll—'

'I never have. And I never will. And excuse me for mentioning it, but you were the one who played away, sneaking off on holiday with another man.'

'You're right. And I'm sorry, I was wrong to do that.' Amber shook her head. 'I swear on my life I'll never do anything like that again.'

Mario touched her face, momentarily unable to speak. If he was honest she'd been right to do it. Discovering the hard way how it felt to be cheated on and dumped had been the wake-up call of his life.

But he wasn't going to tell Amber that. He wasn't completely stupid.

'**O**w, bugger,' yelped Lottie as she lost her balance, toppled over sideways and at a stroke destroyed the festive tableau she'd spent the last twenty minutes painstakingly arranging.

The door opened and Tyler appeared. 'Are you all right?'

'Oh, wonderful! Really, couldn't be better.' Lottie gestured from the floor, surrounded by holly branches, swathes of variegated ivy and pine cones. 'I had the fireplace looking gorgeous, like something out of a *magazine*, and now it's all wrecked!'

'Here.' Reaching down, he helped her to her feet—OK, *foot*—and plonked—plonked!—her back into her wheelchair. Feeling like a stroppy toddler, Lottie pointed to the berries scattered over the carpet. 'And this holly's rubbish. All the berries just bounced off! How can I decorate a fireplace with naked holly? It's just going to look *stupid*.'

'Do you want me to go out and cut some more?'

'You won't know which trees to avoid. I don't want any more of this useless stuff.'

'Fine.' Tyler abruptly left the room. Cursing herself and her hormones, Lottie hurled a pine cone at the fireplace. It was the Sunday before Christmas and to say they weren't getting on well was an understatement. Wheelchair or no wheelchair, she really couldn't stay on any longer at Hestacombe House. It was time to go home.

The door swung open again and Tyler threw her black sweater and cream fake-fur gilet at her. 'Put these on. It's cold outside.'

'Is it?' Affecting surprise, Lottie gazed out of the drawing-room window at the garden glittering with frost. 'And there was me, thinking I might wear my bikini.'

'Any more of your backtalk and you will. Do you want more holly or not?'

Lottie fought her way into the black lambswool sweater, dragging it on over her cropped T-shirt. As her head popped out through the hole she said irritably, 'Well, what are you waiting for? Let's go.'

As the wheelchair jiggled over the path leading down to the lake, Lottie's breath formed opaque puffs that hung in the air before being whisked behind her. Tempted though she was to complain about the jiggling she didn't want to be turfed out of the chair and left on the stony ground to die of hypothermia.

'Not those. That's where the last lot came from.' Dismissing the inferior specimens on their left, she pointed instead to a holly tree closer to the water's edge. 'We'll try that one.'

Wordlessly Tyler steered her down to the beach. The swans glided across the water towards them, then figured out that they hadn't brought anything edible and promptly lost interest.

Rather like Tyler with me, thought Lottie as he reached up for the first branch. She watched him clip through the branch and give it a shake to check the berries were hanging on by more than just their fingernails before handing it to Lottie.

Lottie looked at the holly, glossy-leaved and still sparkling with frost. 'Actually, don't bother. I'd rather go home.'

He shook his head in disbelief. 'Don't be such a wimp, we'll be done in five minutes.'

'I mean there's no point in me decorating that room. I want to go back to my house.' There, she'd said it. At last.

Tyler surveyed her levelly. 'Why?'

'Because we've imposed on you long enough. It's almost Christmas. After putting up with Nat and Ruby for the last fortnight you must be desperate for some peace and quiet.'

'Is that the real reason?'

No, Lottie wanted to shout at him, of *course* it isn't. But I'm hardly going to tell you the *real* reason, am I?

Tyler's gaze was still upon her. To her absolute horror Lottie heard herself saying, 'Actually, I'm just a bit confused. The thing is, I don't know if you even remember this but back in the summer you seemed really keen on me and things between us were getting quite, well, you know. Until Nat and Ruby made things impossible and we agreed that we couldn't see each other any more.'

'Go on,' said Tyler.

Go *on*? Good grief, hadn't she already said enough? Oh no, and here *was* more, bubbling up and out of her mouth as uncontrollably as if someone had slipped her a truth drug.

'So that was fine, we were adults, we knew we had no other choice,' Lottie babbled on. 'Then I met someone else and not long after that Liana turned up, but deep down I was still crazy about you and call me stupid but I hoped that deep down you were still crazy about me.'

Tyler raised an enquiring eyebrow. 'And?'

'And?' Her voice spiralling, Lottie said in exasperation, 'But they're out of the picture now, both of them, and you even managed to change the way Nat and Ruby felt about you, which has to be some kind of miracle, but what it means is that there are now precisely *no* reasons why we . . . why we shouldn't . . . um . . .'

'Shouldn't what?'

He sounded mildly interested. This was awful, *worse* than awful. Flushed with embarrassment Lottie blurted out, 'Look, all I'm saying is that if you've gone off someone it's only polite to tell them, then they can stop wasting their time wondering if you still like them or not.'

Tyler nodded, absorbing this pronouncement. At last he said, 'You're right, that makes sense. OK, I'll do that.'

Lottie waited, her fingers gripping the wheelchair's armrests.

And waited.

Finally, light-headed with waiting—and forgetting to breathe—she managed to get out, 'You aren't saying it.'

'I know.' Tyler shrugged and at long last Lottie thought she detected a glimmer of a smile around his mouth. 'That's probably because I haven't stopped liking you.'

It was a jolly good job she was sitting down. 'So you still . . . ?'

'Oh, yes.' Tyler nodded again, this time with undisguised amusement. 'I definitely still . . .' He waited. 'Go on then, your turn. Do you still . . .'

'You bastard!' Lottie flung aside the branch of holly that had been lying across her lap. 'You know I do!'

'I thought you might. I hoped you did. But I didn't know for sure,' Tyler pointed out. 'You haven't been giving me any clues.'

'That's because you haven't said anything!' Out of her chair now, hopping furiously on her good leg, Lottie yelled, 'You didn't give *me* any clues. I thought you weren't interested in me any more, so why would I want to make a complete wally of myself?' As she said this she lost her balance in the sand, wavered wildly on one foot for a couple of seconds and almost went crashing to the ground. Again.

Tyler caught her in the nick of time. As, deep down, Lottie had kind of hoped he would.

'Heaven forbid,' he drawled, 'that you should ever make a complete wally of yourself.'

He smelt wonderful, just as she remembered. The heat from his body was drawing her towards him like a magnet but there were still questions to be asked.

'So were you *ever* planning to do anything?' Lottie's eyes blazed with a mixture of indignation and lust.

'No.' Tyler shook his head thoughtfully. 'Of course I would have said something eventually. I just didn't want to jump the gun.'

'Are you mad?' Lottie blurted out. 'I've been waiting so hard for you to jump the gun that I've been ready to *burst*.'

'Maybe, but this isn't only about you, is it?' He gave her that maddening look again.

'Isn't it?' Her stomach gave a lurch of alarm. 'So who else is it about then?' If he told her Liana was on her way back over here . . .

'There are other people to consider. Like . . . *two* fairly important people?'

Oh *phew*. 'Ruby and Nat? But they love you now!'

'They've loved me for nine days. Possibly nine and a half.' Tyler shrugged. 'Before that they hated me with a passion. Who's to say they won't change their minds again tomorrow?'

'They won't. You've won them round completely.' Joyfully Lottie exclaimed, 'We can be together!'

'I hope so. But I still think it's better to ask them how they'd feel about it, rather than just presenting them with a fait accompli.'

'That's so thoughtful. And you're right. We'll ask them as soon as they get back.' Nat and Ruby had been taken Christmas shopping in

Cheltenham by Mario and Amber. Checking her watch, Lottie said, 'They won't be home for a few hours yet.' She frowned. 'Gosh, I wonder what we could possibly do to pass the time?'

'Stop that. Not until we know.' Tyler removed her wandering hands from the front of his shirt before she had time to undo even one button.

Spoilsport.

Taking his phone out of his pocket Tyler said, 'Just give Mario a call.'

'Mario?'

'Say, have you asked them yet?'

'You mean you . . . ?'

'Just do it,' prompted Tyler.

Flabbergasted, Lottie keyed in Mario's number. When he answered, she said, 'Tyler's asked me to ask you if you've asked them yet.'

Moments later she said, 'OK, thanks,' and switched off the phone.

'Well?'

'He asked them. They said it's cool.'

A slow smile spread from Tyler's mouth to his eyes. 'Cool. Well, that's a relief. Cool is more than I dared hope for.'

'See? I knew they'd be OK about it.' Triumphantly Lottie wrapped her arms round his neck and kissed him. 'I'm always right.'

Tyler kissed her in return, until she was tingling all over. 'All that trouble, solved by one little word,' he drawled. Then, as Lottie launched herself away from him and began hopping backwards: 'What are you doing now?'

'You're taking me back to the house.' Lowering herself into the wheelchair Lottie said, 'It's way too cold out here for what I have in mind.'

'Really? Oh well, in that case.' Tyler swung the chair in a homewards direction. *'Cool.'*

Chatting to . . . Jill Mansell

As I boarded the ten o'clock First Great Western train to Bristol, I made my way to the 'quiet carriage' where mobile phones, iPods and MP3 players are discouraged and passengers can enjoy a peaceful journey or—as in my case—lose themselves in a good book. Before I knew it, we were pulling into Bristol Temple Meads and Jill met me in her elegant silver Mercedes and swept me off to a chic French bistro for lunch.

'Oh, I never sit in the quiet carriage,' Jill told me as we settled down at our table and studied the menu. 'For any author, the best part of travelling by train is listening in to other people's conversations. What you hear can be absolutely fascinating!'

Having chosen from the menu we chatted about Jill's latest best seller, *Making Your Mind Up*, and where the idea for the novel had come from. 'There is always one hook that gets me going and in this novel it all started with the character of Freddie. I thought to myself, What would you do if you were told that you only had six months to live? We are always saying, "Oh, next year we'll do this or one day we'll do that." In fact, I know it's silly but one of my biggest fears is of dying halfway through writing a book—I would so hate not to finish it first! Anyway, as well as having Freddie as the initial hook, I also wanted to explore a dilemma that is becoming more and more common—the growth in step-families and children not liking their parents' new partners.'

I asked Jill if she knew how the story was going to play out. 'Writing is like walking into a party full of strangers,' she replied. 'It takes the first couple of chapters to get to know your characters. And what is truly fascinating about people is how they change—they can start off appearing really nice, like Seb in the novel, and then you realise that they are not. (It's a bit like having your perceptions changed while watching *Big Brother*—which I love by the way!) I always know what's going to happen for roughly thirty pages or so but that's all.'

So does Jill have a strict writing régime? 'Oh, yes, if you call putting the telly on—explains my recent addiction to *Big Brother*—feet up on the coffee table and packet of fruit gums by my side a strict régime! I write longhand, using a fountain pen, into wide-lined A4 pads from WH Smith—I use about five in the course of book. I usually write around a thousand words a day. That's my comfort zone.'

As we ate lunch and chatted about how idyllic the make-believe Hestacombe Holiday cottages sounded, Jill suddenly leaned across the table and said in a conspiritorial whisper, 'Do you know, we discovered the best familiy holiday in the history of the world last year.' I, too, leaned forward eager to be let in on the secret. 'Cruising,' she continued. 'On a whim I booked a cruise on P&O's *Oriana* around the Mediterranean and we had the best time. The children were happy from the moment we stepped on board, and when they are happy so are we.'

So will a cruise ship be the setting for a future novel, I asked her? 'Maybe,' Jill replied, evasively. 'I don't know. I've been thinking about those older men who are hired by the cruise ships to dance with the widows. They have to be personable, well-groomed, chatty and great dancers. Who knows, maybe one will creep in.'

'Writing is like walking into a party full of strangers. It takes the first couple of chapters to get to know your characters.'

Jill also told me that just before Christmas last year, she was delighted to rediscover a piece of writing from when she was eleven. 'I was so thrilled to have found this because it was such a part of my past. It was all very serious and entitled 'Best Christmas Ever', and the first page listed my likes and dislikes. I liked Spam and chips and disliked cabbage and onions—no change on the dislikes. My daughter had never heard of Spam, so we rushed out and bought some—and it still tasted good. And my best Christmas present was a "very gay skirt that was red and orange with purple flowers". It sounded horrific!'

So if, aged eleven, her likes were Spam and chips, what does Jill like nowadays? 'That's easy, ' she replied. 'Anything that glitters. Let me show you what I got for Christmas,' She grabbed her bag and pulled out the most beautiful Swarovski crystal key ring. 'I love it and it makes me feel good every day.'

With glittery key ring in hand, we returned to Jill's car and she drove me back to the station. 'I must just pop into WH Smith after I drop you off,' she said as we weaved our way through the traffic. 'I need to buy more A4 pads of paper. I guess it's time to get back to the telly and the sofa, but maybe not the fruit gums after that lunch—I've got a book to write, you know.'

Jane Eastgate

Second Honeymoon

JOANNA TROLLOPE

Edie and Russell have been loving parents of Matt, Rosa and Ben for almost thirty years and now, at last, their youngest, Ben, is finally leaving home. Edie is distraught, even though Russell is relishing the thought of having his wife to himself. But Edie is blind to his love—all she can see is the gaping hole in her empty nest . . .

CHAPTER ONE

EDIE PUT HER HAND OUT, took a breath and slowly, slowly pushed open his bedroom door. The room inside looked as if he had never left it. The bed was unmade, the curtains half drawn, the carpet almost invisible under trails of clothing. There were single trainers on shelves, mugs and cereal bowls on the floor, scatterings of papers and books everywhere. On the walls the same posters hung haphazardly from nuggets of blue gum: a Shakespeare play from a long-ago school outing, Kate Moss in a mackintosh, the Stereophonics from a concert at Earls Court. It looked, at first glance, as it had looked for a large part of his twenty-two years. It looked as if he was coming back, any minute.

Edie stepped through the chaos on the floor and pulled the curtains fully apart. One side rushed headlong to the left and slid triumphantly off the pole to the floor. Edie looked up. The finial that stopped the end had probably been missing for months, years, and Ben's solution had been simply, pragmatically really, not to touch the curtain. Edie picked it up and held it hard against her, swallowing against crying.

'He hasn't gone to Mongolia,' Russell had almost shouted at her that morning. 'He hasn't *died*. He's gone to Walthamstow.'

Edie had gone on jabbing at a hermetically sealed packet of coffee with the wrong kind of knife and said nothing.

'End of a tube line,' Russell said unnecessarily. 'Walthamstow.'

Edie flung the coffee and the knife into the sink. She hated Russell when he was like this, when he knew perfectly well what was the matter and refused to admit it.

'Sorry,' Russell said.

Edie pulled the curtain up now and covered her face with it. It smelt of years of grimy London dust. She hadn't acknowledged Russell's 'Sorry'. She had remained silent, distanced by emotion, until she heard him go out of the room and down the hallway—fumble, fumble by the coat rack—and out through the front door, letting it crash behind him the way they all had—two parents, three children—for close on twenty years. Twenty years. Almost all Ben's lifetime—almost a third of hers. You come to a house, Edie thought, carrying almost more life, more people, than you can manage. And then, over time, almost everything you have carried in begins to leak out again.

She dropped the curtain back onto the floor. If she turned, slowly, and half closed her eyes, she could persuade herself that Ben had left his room in a mess as a signal to her that he hadn't really left it. That this notion of his to put all the essentials of his life into a duffel bag and carry it off to live with Naomi, in a spare room in her mother's flat in Walthamstow, was in truth no more than a notion. That he would begin to miss things—the cat, his pillow, his mother—and would see that life was not to be lived so satisfactorily anywhere other than his childhood home. But if she made herself open her eyes wide, really wide, and looked at the calibre of things he had left—the outgrown garments, the discarded books and discs and papers—she could see that what Ben had left behind was what he didn't want any more. He had left the past, leaving it in such a way as to emphasise its irrelevance to him. Edie bent down and began, without enthusiasm, to pick up the cereal bowls.

It wasn't as if Ben had ever, really, been away from home. His school days had melted comfortably into his college days and then into irregular, haphazard days of assistant to a self-employed photographer who specialised in portraits. All through these years Ben had come home, more nights than not, to sleep in the bedroom across the landing from his parents' bedroom, which had been allotted to him when he was two. The detritus of his life, from *Thomas the Tank Engine* to trailing computer cables, had spilled out of his room and across the landing, symbols of his changing taste, his changing world. The thought of the order—no, not order, the absence of chaos—that might follow his departure brought Edie close to panic. It was like . . . like having a light extinguished. It was far, far worse than when Matt or Rosa had gone.

She began to pile mugs and bowls on Ben's table. He had done homework at that table, made models, hacked with blades at the edges. She sat down by it, on the chair with the broken cane seat, filled in by a gaudy Indian cushion. She looked at the mess on the table. Ben was her youngest. When the others went, she had felt a pang, but there had always been Ben; there had always been the untidy, demanding, gratifying, living proof that she was doing what she was meant to do. And, if Ben wasn't there to confirm her perception of herself, what was she going to do about the future? What was she going to do about herself?

'It's awful,' her sister Vivien had said on the telephone. 'It's just awful. You spend all these years and years developing this great supporting muscle for your children and then they just whip round, don't they, and hack it through.' She'd paused, and then she'd said, in a cooler tone, 'Actually, it's not so bad for you because you've always got the theatre.'

'I haven't,' Edie said, 'I—'

'Well, I know you aren't working at this precise moment. But you always *could* be, couldn't you? You're always going for auditions.'

'That,' Edie said, her voice rising, 'has nothing to do with Ben going, nothing to do with *motherhood*.'

There was another pause and then Vivien said, in the slightly victim voice Edie had known since their childhoods, 'Eliot's gone too, Edie. And he's my only child. He's all I've got.'

Eliot had gone to Australia. He had found a job on a local radio station in Cairns, and within six months had a flat and a girlfriend there. Ben had gone five stops up the Victoria line to Walthamstow.

'OK,' Edie said to Vivien, conceding.

'I do know—'

'Yes.'

'Lovely,' Vivien said, 'for Russell. Having you back—'

Edie felt a flash of temper. Eliot's father, Max, had drifted in and out of his wife and son's life in a way that made sure that the only thing about him that was predictable was his unreliability. Vivien might be able to trump her over the pain caused by distances, but she wasn't going to trump her over the pain caused by husbands.

'Enough,' Edie said, and put the telephone down.

'Enough,' she said to herself now, her elbows on Ben's table.

Downstairs the front door crashed again. She heard Russell's feet on the tiles of the hall, heard him say something companionable to the cat.

'Edie? I've got the newspapers,' Russell called. 'An orgy of them—'

Edie looked up at Ben's bookshelves, at the space at the end where his teddy bear always sat. The bear had gone. She stood up, holding an awkward stack of crockery. 'Coming,' she said.

The garden was one of the reasons they had bought the house twenty years ago. It was only the width of the house, but it was seventy-five feet long, long enough for Matt, then eight, to kick a ball in. It also had a shed. Russell had loved the idea of a shed, the idea of paraffin heaters and listening to an old battery-operated radio. He saw seclusion in that shed, somewhere set apart from his family life and his working life because both were, by their very nature, all talk. He had a vision of being in the shed on winter weekend afternoons and looking back down the garden to the house, a dark shape with lit windows, and knowing that all that life and clamour was there for him to step back into, when he chose. And he had clung to it when the shed filled up with bikes and paint tins and garden chairs, leaving no space for him.

This Saturday afternoon, he told Edie, he was going to clear it out.

'Why?'

'Because it's full of useless junk.'

She was chopping things, making one of her rough-hewn salads. 'And when you have cleared out the shed, what will you do with it?'

'Use it.'

Edie threw a handful of tomato pieces into the salad bowl. 'What for?'

Russell considered saying 'for reading pornography in', but decided against it. 'The purpose will become plain as I clear it.'

Edie picked up a yellow pepper. She had gathered her hair on top of her head and secured it with a purple plastic comb. She looked, in some ways, about thirty. She also looked small and defiant.

'You were clearing Ben's room this morning,' Russell said gently.

'No,' Edie said.

He went over to the fridge and took out a bottle of Belgian beer. The boys would drink it straight out of the bottle. Russell went across the kitchen, behind Edie, to the cupboard where the glasses were kept.

He said, his back to her, 'What were you doing then?'

'Nothing,' Edie said. 'Thinking.'

Russell took a glass out of the cupboard. He said, his back still turned, 'They just do grow up. It's what happens.'

'Yes,' Edie said.

'It's what's *meant* to happen.'

'Yes.'

Russell turned. He put down the glass and the bottle and came to stand behind her. 'He's doing what he wants to do.'

Edie sliced through the pepper. 'I know.'

'You can't—'

'I know!' Edie shouted. She flung the knife across the table.

Russell moved to retrieve it. He held it out to her. 'Stop chucking things. It's so childish.'

Edie took the knife and laid it on the chopping board with elaborate care. Then she leaned on her hands and looked down into her salad.

'I love Ben as much as you do,' Russell said. 'But he's twenty-two. He's a man. I met you when I was twenty-two.'

'Twenty-three.'

'All right, then. Twenty-three. And you were twenty-one.'

'Just,' Edie said.

'I remember us thinking we were quite old enough to get married. We'd left home. We wanted to leave home. I left home at seventeen.'

Edie straightened up and folded her arms. 'Ben didn't. He liked it here, he loved it—'

'And now he loves Naomi.'

Edie gave a little snort.

Russell said, pouring his beer, 'This happens to everyone. Everyone with children. It started with Matt, remember. Matt left at twenty-two.'

Edie moved away from the table and leaned instead against the sink. 'You just don't think,' she said, 'that it's going to end.'

'God!' Russell said. 'End! Does parenthood ever, *ever* end?'

Edie turned round and looked at the table. 'If you want any lunch,' she said, 'you finish that. I'm going out.'

'Are you? Where are you going?'

'A film maybe. Sit in a café.' She began to walk towards the door to the hall. 'Better practise, hadn't I? For the next chapter?'

Outside the shed, Russell made a pile of things to keep, a pile of things to throw away, and a pile to ask Edie about. He had made a cheese-and-pickle sandwich from the last of the white sliced loaf and had eaten it sitting in a mouldy Lloyd Loom chair that had belonged to his mother, in the pale April sunshine.

Edie wasn't back. She had returned briefly to the kitchen, wearing a cast-off denim jacket of Rosa's, and kissed his cheek. He had wanted to say something, to hold her for a moment, but had decided against it. Instead, he let her bump her face against his, fleetingly, and watched her go. The cat watched her too, from a place on the crowded dresser where he was not supposed to sit. He waited half an hour after Russell went out to the garden and then he came out to see what was happening, stepping fastidiously over the damp grass. As soon as Russell left the Lloyd Loom chair, he leaped into it and sat there, watching.

He was really Ben's cat. Ben had been the only one of their children who had longed for an animal, who had gone badgering until, on his tenth birthday, Russell had gone to a pet shop in Finsbury Park and come home with a tabby kitten in a wire basket. Ben called the kitten

Arsenal, after his chosen football club, and remained indifferent to the implications of this being inevitably shortened to Arsie. Arsie was now twelve and as cool as a tulip.

'Look,' Russell said to Arsie, 'Rosa's tricycle. She loved that.'

Arsie looked unmoved. Rosa's tricycle, once metallic lilac with a white plastic basket on the front, was now mostly rust.

'Keep or chuck?' Russell said.

Arsie yawned.

'Chuck,' Russell said. 'Chuck, but inform Rosa.'

He crouched and inspected the tricycle. Rosa had stuck glitter stickers of cartoon animals and fairies everywhere. She had looked sweet on that tricycle, pedalling furiously, straight red hair flapping. Sometimes when he looked at her now, twenty-six years old and working for a public relations company, he caught a glimpse of the child on the tricycle, like a ghost in a mirror. She had been a turbulent little girl full of noise and purpose. The turbulence had translated itself into something closer to emotional volatility, a propensity to swerve crazily in and out of relationships. At least one had to be thankful that she did swerve out again, particularly in the case of the appalling Josh.

Russell straightened up and looked at the house. Rosa's window was on the top floor, on the left. Since Rosa had left home, they'd had the odd lodger in that room, and in Matt's, next to it: drama students Edie was teaching or impoverished actors she'd once been in repertory with who had small parts in plays in little North London theatres. They had provided, unconsciously, the perfect excuse to postpone any decision about moving to something smaller. The house might be shabby, in places very shabby, but it was not something Russell could imagine being without. It was, quite simply, a given in his life: the result of being left a small legacy in his twenties, when he and Edie were living in a dank flat, with two children and a baby, above an ironmonger's.

The house had been damp and neglected, with a hole in the roof you could see the stars through. But somehow, then, with Edie enjoying a steady spell of television work, and the agency getting going, the house had seemed to them needy rather than daunting. They'd had no kitchen for a year, no finished bathroom for two, no carpets for five. Matt wore gumboots all his childhood, from the moment he got out of bed. It was perhaps no surprise that he should turn out to be the most orthodox of their children, the one with an electronic diary and polished shoes. When he came home, he was inclined to point out that the crack in the sitting-room ceiling was lengthening, that the smell of damp in the downstairs lavatory was not just a smell.

'It's hard,' Russell said, 'for us old bohemians to get worked up about such things.'

'Then listen to me,' Matt said.

He said that often, now. He had started saying it after he left home, and returned, just for occasional meals, with a newly critical eye. 'Listen to me,' he'd say to Edie about a part she was reading for, to Russell about some new direction the agency might take, to Ben about his A-level choices.

'You're so adult,' Edie would say, looking at him fondly. 'I love it.'

She loved it, of course, because she didn't listen to him. She loved it the way she loved his regular haircuts and well-mannered clothes and competence with technology. It was amusing to her, and endearing, to see this well-put-together grown man in her kitchen, explaining to her how to send text messages on her mobile phone, and visualise him, simultaneously, once asleep in his cot or sitting, reading earnestly, on his potty. She could play games like that, Russell thought, because she still had Ben; the security of Ben gave her the licence not to take Matt seriously, not to see his maturity as anything other than sweet play-acting.

If Matt was irritated by her attitude, he gave no sign. He treated her as he had always treated both his parents, as very well-meaning people of whom he was fond and who he needed to take practical care of. He worked for a mobile-telephone company and shared a flat with his girlfriend, who had a job in the City. He was entitled, Russell thought, inspecting a stack of broken lampshades, to say, 'Listen to me.'

Russell did listen. He had listened while Matt had explained, at length, one evening in a bar in Covent Garden, that Russell should specialise. Matt described his father's agency, which represented actors who were interested in film and television work, as 'limping along'. Russell, nursing a glass of red wine, had been mildly affronted. After the next glass, he had felt less affronted. After the third glass, Matt's proposal that Russell should specialise in providing actors for advertising voice-over work seemed less unattractively practical than it had an hour before.

'I know it's not theatre,' Matt had said, 'but it's money.'

'It's *all* about money!' Edie had cried, two hours later, brushing her teeth. 'Isn't it? That's all it's about!'

'Possibly,' Russell said carefully, 'it has to be.'

'It's sordid. It's squalid. Where's the acting in bouncing on sofas?'

'Not bouncing on them. Talking about them.'

Edie spat into the basin. 'Well, if you can *bring* yourself—'

'I rather think I can.'

'Just don't ask *me*.'

Russell let a pause fall. He climbed into bed and picked up his book. 'No,' he said. 'No. I rather think I shan't.'

Since 1975, Russell Boyd Associates (there were none) had occupied three attic rooms behind Shaftesbury Avenue. For thirty years, Russell had worked in a room that had undoubtedly once been a maid's bedroom. It had a dormer window and sloping ceilings and was carpeted with the Turkey carpet that had once been in Russell's grandparents' home in Hull. Matt, encouraged by Russell's acceptance of his advice about the agency, tried to persuade him to modernise the office, to put down a wooden floor and install halogen lights on metal tracks.

'No,' Russell said. 'I like it and so do my clients.'

'But, Dad—' Matt had kicked at several straining cardboard folders piled against the bookshelves. 'It's awful. It's like your old shed.'

Russell looked now, at his shed. It was half empty, but what remained looked intractable. Arsie had left the chair and returned to the house and the sun had sunk behind the houses, leaving a raw dankness.

'Russell!' Edie called.

He turned his head. She was standing at the corner of the house, by the side door to the kitchen. She had Arsie in her arms.

'Tea!' Edie shouted.

'Look,' Edie said, 'I'm sorry. I was fed up with you because you wouldn't understand.'

'I do understand,' Russell said. 'It's the end of a particularly compelling phase of motherhood. And it's very hard to adjust to.'

'I don't want to adjust,' Edie said. She had made tea in the pot with cabbage roses on it. It was vulgar but it had intense associations for Edie, as everything in her life did, everything that reminded her of a place, a person, a happening. She poured tea into the huge cracked blue cups she had found in a junk shop while on tour in Scarborough.

'I want Ben back,' Edie said.

Russell poured milk into his tea.

'I want him back,' Edie said fiercely. 'I want him back to make me laugh and infuriate me and exploit me and make me feel *necessary*.'

Russell picked up his teacup and held it, cradling it in his palms. The aroma of Darjeeling tea rose up to him.

'Are you listening?' Edie said.

'Yes,' he said, 'but you forget I know.'

She leaned forward. 'But how do I make you *mind*?'

'Good question.'

'What?'

He put his cup down and said, not looking at her, 'How do I make *you* mind?'

She stared. 'What?' she said again.

'I've been out there,' Russell said, 'for about three hours. I've been sifting through all sorts of rubbish, things that mattered once and don't any more. And that's quite painful, knowing things are over for ever.'

'But—'

'Wait,' Russell said, 'just *wait*. Rosa's not going to ride that trike again, Matt's not going to hit with that bat, you're not going to read under that lampshade. That's not comfortable, that's not easy to know, to have to accept. But we have to, because we have no choice. And we also have something left.'

Edie took a swallow of tea and looked at him over her cup. 'Yes?'

'You talk about wanting Ben back. You talk about his energy and neediness and the way it makes you feel. Well, just think for a moment about how *I* feel. I didn't marry you in order to have Matt and Rosa and Ben, though I'm thankful we did. I married you because I wanted to be with you, because you somehow make things shine for me, even when you're horrible. You want Ben back. Well, you'll have to deal with that as best you can. And while you're dealing with it, I'll give you something else to think about, something that isn't going to go away. Edie—I want you back. I was here before the children and I'm here now.' He put his cup down with finality. 'And I'm not going away.'

CHAPTER TWO

WHEN IT CAME TO BUSINESS, Bill Moreton prided himself on his firing technique. His father, who had been a general surgeon, had followed the basic belief: 'Cut deeply, but only once', and Bill had adopted this mantra as his own. He had carried it, grandiosely, into the world of public relations where, in the process of building up a company, there had been a good deal of hiring and firing to do.

Because many of Bill's hiring choices were disastrous, he got in plenty of practice at subsequently firing them, which was exactly what he planned to do, this cool April day, to Rosa Boyd. He stood by the window of his office and rehearsed what he would say to Rosa. She was twenty-six, perfectly capable at her job, and a good-looking redhead if you liked your women on the big side and redheaded into the bargain. The reason for sacking Rosa was not the one Bill planned to give her, smilingly and briefly. He was going to tell her that she was not, he regretted, suited to public relations work because she lacked the patience to build up a relationship with a client that could take, oh, five or six years in some cases. What he was not going to tell her was that the company's figures, drawn up as they always were in anticipation of the end of a tax year, were alarmingly poor, and that he had decided—against his accountant's advice—to sack two members of staff.

One, Victor Basinger, was to take early retirement, but Bill knew that for all professional and practical reasons, the other should not be Rosa Boyd walking into his office to be sacked, but Heidi Kingsmill. The difficulty was that four years ago Bill had spent an energetic night with Heidi after an office Christmas party and, although the girl had not as yet exploited this fact, she had made it plain that, if pushed, she would.

Bill heard a sound behind him. Rosa Boyd was standing in his office doorway, her right hand resting on the doorknob. She wore jeans and an orange tweed jacket and boots with immensely high heels. Her hair was loose. She looked to Bill about eight foot tall and mildly alarming.

'Rosa!' Bill said. He smiled. 'Hello.'

Rosa said nothing.

Bill moved round his desk and patted the chair nearest to Rosa invitingly. 'Sit down. This won't take a minute.'

Rosa gave a small sigh, and relaxed onto one leg.

'Come in,' Bill said. 'Come in and shut the door. We don't want the office hearing, do we?'

'They know,' Rosa said.

Bill opened his mouth to speak, but Rosa said, before he could begin, 'They're taking bets. On how quickly you'll do it.'

Bill swallowed.

'I'm going to win,' Rosa said. 'I said it'd be under a minute.' She stepped in and pulled the door shut behind her with a slam.

Kate Ferguson lay on the bathroom floor waiting to be sick again. She had been prepared, she thought, for morning sickness in early pregnancy to afflict her in the mornings when Barney could bring her tea and a biscuit, but she was not at all prepared to feel sick all day, every day, too sick to go to work, too sick to be even remotely civil to people who wanted to congratulate her on being pregnant so soon after getting married.

'So lovely,' her mother's best friend had said, 'to see someone doing it *properly*. None of this heartless career-girl stuff, leaving having babies until you're practically old enough to be a granny.'

At this rate, Kate thought, moaning faintly against the floor tiles, she'd never be a granny because she'd never even be a mother if this is what it took to get there. It was such a terrible kind of nausea, so devoid of any possibility of relief. The baby, down somewhere in those tortured realms, felt like an enemy, a malevolent walnut-sized goblin. One minute, it seemed, she and Barney had been honeymooning in Malaysia and planning their excited newly married lives back in London, and the next she was lying on the bathroom floor, clammy and ashen.

The phone rang.

'Sod off!' Kate shouted.

The phone rang four times, and then stopped. Then it started again. It would be Rosa. At university, Kate and Rosa had started a four-ring pattern as a kind of signal to one another, first as a let-out for dull or dangerous dates and then as a demonstration of consciousness of the other. Kate began to pull herself across the bathroom floor and into the bedroom next door where her phone lay, muffled in the duvet.

'I want to die,' Kate said into it.

'Still? Poor babe.'

'Four weeks, nearly five. I hate this baby.'

'Try hating your hormones instead.'

'I can't picture them. I can't hate something I can't picture.'

'I'll give you something to picture,' Rosa said, 'and you can hate him all you like. Bill Moreton.'

Kate crawled up on to the bed and fell into the folds of the duvet. 'What's he done?'

'Sacked me,' Rosa said.

Kate groaned. 'What did you *do*? People don't get sacked for nothing.'

'In Bill Moreton's skin-saving world they do. He can't sack Heidi because he screwed her and she'd squeal. And the business isn't doing well enough to support us all.'

Kate rolled onto her side and crushed a pillow against her stomach. 'Rosa, you *needed* that job. What did you say, five thousand on your credit cards?'

'Nearer six.'

'You'd better come and live with us.'

'No.'

'Barney wouldn't mind—'

'He would. So would you. So would I. But thanks, Kate, all the same.'

'How soon,' Kate said, 'are you going?'

'I've gone. I cleared my desk, mostly into a black bag, and dumped it outside his office.'

'So you won't get any kind of reference—' Kate sighed heavily. 'I feel too awful to cheer you up.'

'I'm still in a rage,' Rosa said. 'I'm fine as long as I'm furious.'

'Aren't you worried?'

'Of course I'm worried,' Rosa said.

'What are you going to do?'

Rosa said slowly, pacing out the words, 'Haven't thought. Yet.'

'I wish—'

'You can't do anything. I had to tell you but I didn't tell you so's you'd feel you had to do anything.'

'I'll be more use when I can think about something other than dying.'

'You ought to be so happy—'

'Because I've got everything?' Kate said sharply.

'I wasn't going to say that.'

'But you thought it.'

Rosa said crossly, 'Of course I did. What do you expect?'

Kate closed her eyes. 'I meant it. I meant it about coming here.'

'I know. Thank you.'

Kate's stomach heaved and turned. She flung the phone into the dented pillows and scrambled off the bed. 'Bye!' she shouted after it and fled towards the bathroom.

Rosa bought a Mexican bean wrap from the sandwich bar and took it to a bench in Soho Square. She peeled back the plastic film from the wrap and took an awkward bite. Three red beans immediately fell wetly on to the knee of her jeans—clean that morning—and thence to the path where they lay, bright, exotic and faintly sinister. She laid the wrap on the seat beside her. In these circumstances, it didn't manage to taste exotic and foreign, only alien.

Rosa looked up at the steady grey sky and the spidery branches of the trees already lumpy with incipient leaves, and thought that one of the hardest aspects of what had just happened was that she had not reckoned on it. She had not supposed, for one moment, that five years after leaving university she would have failed to find absorbing employment, failed to sustain a romantic relationship, and failed to gain control over her life.

Education had, by contrast, been easy. Rosa had been good at education, good at friendships, comfortable with achievement. She had negotiated, from the age of eleven, a subversive but successful pathway between intelligence and rebelliousness; a pathway that her elder brother admired and her younger brother emulated. She had cultivated, all those long, busy, educational years, a subtle flamboyance, which she had believed would carry her through both dullness and difficulty. And, almost, it had, until falling for a man who preferred to believe her publicity rather than the more vulnerable reality that lay beneath it.

Everyone had taken pains to tell her how much they disliked Josh. Under the conventional but false banner of telling her that everything they were about to say was because they had her welfare at heart, family and friends told her that Josh was spoilt, unreliable, immature and selfish. In reply, she would simply say, 'I know.' She did know. She knew from the first few exciting but unnerving dates that Josh was neither able nor prepared to give her the steady glow of supportive love that women's magazines assured her was every girl's absolute right. But the relationship with Josh was not about anything steady or supportive. It was about being, in every sense, bowled over—bowled over by the electricity of his unpredictable company, bowled over by desire. Josh could have anything he wanted as long as he didn't go.

He didn't go for almost two years. He moved into Rosa's flat and spent hours playing poker on her computer or ringing long-distance on her telephone. He booked seats at ballets and theatres, nights in hotels, tables in restaurants without ever, mysteriously, managing to pay for them. He left roses on her pillow and messages on the bathroom mirror and tiny, beguiling presents in her shoes. And, when he finally left, she was convinced that not only had he left her with a frightening amount of debt, but also without any capacity to feel alive ever again.

'He wasn't *drama*,' Kate said to Rosa, 'he was *melodrama*.'

Rosa had looked at the list in Kate's hand. It was the beginning of her wedding-present list and it featured saucepans and bath mats and an espresso machine.

'Give me melodrama any day,' Rosa had said.

She wouldn't, she thought, sitting on her bench beside her unwanted lunch, say that now. Josh had been an addiction and, when he had gone, she missed the tension and the sense that her adrenalin was always racing. And then, hour by hour, day by day, the enthralling substance Josh had represented drained out of her veins and left her disorientated, lost, as if she had entirely abandoned the person she grew up with and was too altered now by experience to go back and retrieve it.

Rosa picked up the remains of her wrap, rose from the bench and carried the package over to the nearest litter bin. She dropped it in and then set off purposefully southwards, towards Shaftesbury Avenue.

Russell was on the telephone. An actor, who possessed a wonderfully flexible voice and no sense of obligation to any work he considered beneath him, however lucrative, was explaining at length why he had failed, for the second time, to turn up for a studio appointment to record the voice of a cartoon tiger representing an insurance company.

'Sorry,' Russell said at intervals. 'It's no good. It's no good my putting in effort if you won't match it.'

The door of Russell's office stood open. Beyond, in the small reception area, furnished with wicker sofas and copies of *Spotlight* and *The Stage*, Russell's assistant, Maeve, who had been with him almost all his working life, administered the agency with the assistance of a computer she referred to as the Prototype, on account of its age. Russell liked Maeve to hear most of his conversations. He liked her to be a witness to his reasonableness in the face of often great provocation.

'I'm sorry, Gregory,' Russell said, 'but I shall have to send them someone else. It's very nice of them, actually, even to agree to that.'

The doorbell to the street door rang, a peculiar vibrating growl.

'Oh!' Maeve said into the intercom with pleasure. 'Oh, it's you! Come on up!'

Russell put his hand over the mouthpiece of his telephone. His heart had lifted a little. 'Who, Maeve? Edie?'

Maeve's face appeared round the door. 'No,' she mouthed, 'Rosa.'

Russell took his hand away. 'You've blown it, Greg. Go away and think about it.' He took the telephone away from his ear, listened for a few more seconds, and then replaced it softly on his desk.

There were footsteps running up the last flight of stairs. He heard Maeve open the door.

'Well, there's a cheerful sight. What a wonderful colour, *nobody* but—'

'Nobody but me,' Rosa said. 'Anybody else would have had more sense and bought black.'

'I'm sick to death of black,' Maeve said. 'Leave it to the beetles, I say.'

Rosa appeared in the doorway of Russell's office. 'Dad?'

He got up and leaned across the desk to kiss her. 'Lovely surprise—'

'Well,' she said, 'passing—'

'At lunchtime.'

'Well . . . Actually I'm not hungry.'

'Even,' Russell said, 'if I'm paying?'

She glanced down. Her shoulders drooped a little. Then she straightened up, shook her hair back and gave him a familiarly full-on smile. 'That would be great. Because—well, because there's something I'd like to ask you.'

Russell looked at her over his reading spectacles. 'Is there?'

'Yes,' she said. 'Please.' And then she smiled again, 'Daddy.'

Rosa looked at her father's plate. Hers was empty, but his still bore half of his order of gnocchi. She raised her fork, questioningly. 'May I?'

Russell gave his plate a little nudge. 'Help yourself.'

Rosa speared two gnocchi and put them in her mouth. Then she said, round them, 'I mean, I'm not worried about finding another job. And I'm not at all concerned by what Bill Moreton thinks of me. I know I was doing a good job. I know it.'

'Hmm,' Russell said.

'It wasn't as if I was earning a fortune there anyway,' Rosa said, spearing more gnocchi.

'Have you ever worked out,' Russell said, 'what you *need* to earn?'

Rosa stopped chewing. She gave him a quick, direct look and dropped her gaze. 'No.'

'Don't you think—'

'Did you? Rosa demanded. 'Did you? At my age?'

Russell picked his plate up and exchanged it for Rosa's empty one. Rosa looked down. 'I couldn't eat all that—'

'Rosa,' Russell said, 'I've listened to you. I've listened to you very patiently and I quite agree with you that Bill Moreton was a second-rate boss who behaved accordingly. But you'd been in that job eight months. He didn't exactly owe you a pension and a gold watch.'

Rosa said nothing. It seemed to her she was behaving as she always vowed she would never behave again when with a parent. She could hear in her voice an undertone of whining and cajoling.

'It's a very nasty thing to have done to you,' Russell said, visualising Edie listening to him, 'especially when it so plainly wasn't justified. But it was just a job, wasn't it? Not a career.'

Rosa pushed her father's plate aside. 'It isn't that.'

Russell sighed. 'No.'

'You see,' Rosa said, 'I'm in debt. I owe nearly six thousand on my credit cards.'

'Ah.' Russell leaned back. It occurred to him to ask how the situation had arisen, but then it struck him forcibly that he did not, somehow, want to become involved. He loved Rosa dearly, but she was twenty-six. He said, as gently as he could, 'That will take a while to pay back.'

She nodded.

'Have you thought of that?' Russell said. 'Have you made any plans?'

She said, in a small voice, 'I'm beginning to.'

'Economies,' Russell said. He picked up his wineglass and put it down again. 'My mother loved economies. If she could make one haddock fillet feed four she was triumphant. Frugality was rather encouraged in the fifties. Postwar and all that. Now, it just looks as if you are crabbed of spirit and letting life pass you by.'

Rosa leaned forward. 'I think it was trying not to let it pass me by that got me into this mess.'

'Josh,' Russell said, without meaning to.

'Oh, Dad . . .'

'No,' he said, hastily. 'No. I shouldn't have mentioned him. We must focus on what is rather than what was.'

She gave a faint smile. 'I knew you'd help.'

'It depends—'

'On what?'

'On what form you see that help taking.'

Rosa said quickly, 'I don't want money. I want to straighten myself out. I want to find another job and change the way I do things.'

'Mmm.'

'Don't you think I sound like you'd like me to sound?'

'Oh, I do . . .'

'Well, then?'

'I'm just waiting,' Russell said. 'Patiently, fondly even, but wearily and warily, to see what it is you are working up to say.'

Rosa fiddled with some cutlery. 'I'm not very proud of myself. And I hate having to ask this . . . but can I come home?'

Russell closed his eyes for a fleeting second.

'I know it's not what you want,' Rosa said. 'I don't want it either, really, if you see what I mean, but it wouldn't be for long, probably only a few months, but if I'm not paying rent, the rent money can go towards the credit-card debt, and it would make such a difference.' She stopped. Then she said, much more slowly, 'Please, Dad.'

Russell looked at her. He said sadly, 'I'm so sorry, darling, but no.'

She stared at him. 'No!'

'I want to help you,' Russell said. 'I *will* help you. But you can't come back home to live.'

Rosa said, stunned, 'But it's my home!'

'Well, yes, in a way. It was your childhood home, your growing-up home. But you're grown up now. You need your own home.'

'Of course!' Rosa cried. 'In an ideal world, that's exactly what I'd have by now! But I can't, can I? I can't have what I ought to have because of what's happened!' She glared at him. 'I cannot believe you said no.'

Russell sighed. 'It isn't about you. It's about us, Mum and me. It's—well, it's *our* home.'

'Your *family* home.'

'Yes, when children are dependent—'

'Ben was allowed to stay, Ben was always—'

'Ben has gone,' Russell said.

'So there's room for me.'

'Rosa,' Russell said with sudden force, 'it's not about room, it's about distraction. It's about Mum and me having time to be married again, it's about us, having time and space for that.'

'But,' Rosa said, gesturing wildly, 'I'm not going to stop you! I'm not going to get in the way of your . . . rediscovering each other.'

Russell said carefully, 'You may not *mean* to.'

There was a pause.

Then Rosa said, in a quite different voice, 'I see.' She stood up clumsily, shaking the table, then gathered up her bag and scarf and telephone. 'Just forget I said anything, Dad. Just forget I even *asked*.' She twitched her bag onto her shoulder and glared at him. 'Luckily for me, I have *friends* who care.'

CHAPTER THREE

EDIE WATCHED THE CAT make a nest for himself in a basket of clean laundry. It wasn't ironed—Edie had never been able to see ironing as other than faintly neurotic—but it was clean, or had been.

'Arsie's missing you,' Edie said to Ben on the telephone.

'Yeah,' he said, 'poor old Arse. But I can't have him here.'

'No, I wasn't suggesting that.'

'Naomi's mum has allergies.'

'Does she?'

'And our room is only about big enough for the bed.'

'It doesn't,' Edie said lightly, 'sound very comfortable—'

'It's ace,' Ben said. 'It's fine. Brilliant. Look, I've got to go.'

'Why don't you come to supper one night? Bring Naomi, of course. And her mother, if you'd like to—'

'Mum,' Ben said, 'I'm late.' He'd taken the phone from his ear. 'Going. Take care, Mum. Gone!'

Edie stepped over the washing basket and began to sift restlessly through papers on the kitchen table. Russell had produced catalogues about garden furniture and city-weekend breaks in Europe. He'd also brought her a bunch of anemones, a novel that had won a literary prize, and a bottle of scented bath oil. It was touching, all this, Edie thought, but it was also mildly irritating. As conduct, it reminded her of a dog her sister, Vivien, had once had, a small spaniel-ish dog, which always wanted to sit on your knee and gaze into your face with an intensity that required you to give something in return. Not only did Edie not want, particularly, to be given flowers and bath oil and weekends in Ghent, but she also, most particularly, did not want the accompanying obligation.

'It isn't very grateful of you,' Vivi said, on the telephone. 'Poor Russell—'

'*Poor?*'

'Perhaps he's been waiting, all these years, to be other than on the edge of your peripheral vision.'

'He liked family life, you know. He liked the children. He adores Rosa.'

'Men love women,' Vivi said. 'Women love children. Children love hamsters.'

'Oh, I know. I *know*.'

'You just don't know how lucky you are.'

'Don't start—'

'I have to remind you sometimes.'

Edie leaned against the wall. 'Rosa's lost her job.'

'No! Poor girl.'

'She sounded completely matter-of-fact. Wouldn't let me sympathise, really. I said come back home—'

'I bet you did.'

'And she said no, no, she was fine, she'd got friends who were helping.' Edie paused. 'I do find that hard. Friends, not family.'

'Friends are the new family.'

'Sometimes I wonder why I bother to turn to you for consolation.'

'I know,' Vivi said. 'I won't do drama, will I? I won't do it because, compared to mine, your life isn't drama. Speaking of which . . . what *about* drama? What about work?'

Edie sighed. 'Nothing much. I must be turned down twenty times for every part I get. There's a casting for an Ibsen next week—'

'Yes?'

'Mrs Alving. In *Ghosts*. I won't get it. I can't *feel* about it at the moment. I'm all jangled up and raw.'

'And cross with Russell for being romantic.'

'Yes.'

Edie sat down at the kitchen table now and made space for her elbows among the papers. It was not like her, she told herself, to be so miserable and—Ben's favourite word when he was small—grumpy. He'd say stressy, now, Edie thought, if he was still seven, and Rosa was eleven and Matt was thirteen, and there were still school mornings, with their inevitable chaos of uneaten things and forgotten things and unbrushed things. She'd imagined those times were never-ending somehow, or that she would change, gradually, as they changed, so that she would be ready to face a new chapter, ready, even, to confront herself.

She brought her hands up to her face and held it. That was the problem, really, that was the element that was proving so difficult, this business of knowing how to arrange oneself. For almost thirty years she had known what she was for, what she was supposed to do. Sure, she'd been passionate about the theatre at school. But, if she was honest, it had all been a bit sketchy since she'd gained a place at RADA: stints in regional repertory companies, stand-in presenter on children's television, advertisements. Nothing—nothing to boast about.

'I'm a jobbing actress,' she'd said for years, holding a child, carrying groceries. 'I'm up for anything. As long as it'll fit round the children.'

Secure in the essentialness of motherhood, she'd even, she recalled, been able to lecture herself. There'll come a time, she'd told herself, when you'll have to identify yourself *without* your children. They will simply shed you, like a snakeskin. Well, the time had now come. And, like most anticipated things, the reality did not match the imagining. Motherhood had been such a solace, had acceptably papered over so many cracks, had given her, if she was honest, such a seemly excuse for not risking failure or disappointment or loss of confidence, that she could not think what she was going to do, without it.

She took her hands away from her face and laid them in front of her, palms down on the table. On top of the pile about two feet away lay the copy of Ibsen's plays that Russell had brought down from the bookcase on the first-floor landing when he heard about the casting for *Ghosts*. Ibsen had been obsessed by the past. He'd written once that 'we sail with a corpse in the cargo'. Ibsen was, Edie decided, the very last thing she needed at the moment.

Holding a telephone between his hunched shoulder and his ear, Matthew Boyd was writing down some information.

'Open plan. Interior walls of glass brick. View of Tate Modern and

Millennium Bridge. Four hundred thou—wow,' Matthew said. 'Four hundred thousand?'

'That was what Ruth told me,' the agent said. 'Admittedly, top whack. But she said she could consider that if the place was right.'

'She—'

'And the value of lofts in Bankside have tripled since the mid-nineties.'

Matthew drew an angry line under his jottings. He and Ruth had discussed Docklands and Hoxton and Clerkenwell, but not Bankside. Bankside was much more central and therefore much more expensive. The budget—putative, but shared, obviously—had been three hundred. Tops. Matthew added teeth to his line.

'I've made an appointment for Ruth to see it,' the agent said. 'She asked for Saturday morning at ten thirty, so this is a courtesy call. It's about three hundred square metres, by the way. Shall I tell Ruth or will you?'

Matthew wrote 'Sod off' above the teeth. 'I will,' he said, and rang off.

He dropped the phone on his desk and shoved his chair back so violently that it cannoned into Blaise's desk behind him.

Matthew stood up. He mouthed 'Sorry' in Blaise's direction as he was on the telephone. Then he bent over his desk and retrieved his phone. Ruth's was the first number in his speed-dial address book.

'Hello,' her voicemail said, cool and friendly. 'This is Ruth Munro's telephone. I'm away from my desk just now so please leave me a message.'

'Ring me,' Matthew said. He took a breath. 'Please, I mean.'

He dropped the phone in his pocket and turned to make coffee-drinking gestures at Blaise. Blaise nodded. Matthew went quickly across the office and made for the lifts. He made a face at himself in the brass panel that lined the wall between the lifts.

'Cross,' Ruth had said to him at the weekend, tapping away at her laptop and not looking up. 'You look so cross.'

He looked at himself now, stretched and blobbed by the soft reflections in the brass. Cross might be how he looked: frightened was how he felt. And frightened was how he had always hated feeling, ever since those first unnerving nights in that new ramshackle house when he was a child and they expected him to sleep, knowing that there were holes in the roof, real holes through which anything might swoop, anything clawed and fanged and malevolent. His gumboots, Matthew remembered, had been his salvation. Solid and reassuring and rubber, he had worn them in the uncarpeted house all day for years, and slept with them by his bed. When they began to cramp his toes, he would pester Edie for new ones, so great was the terror of being without a pair, without their simple reassurance. When he finally had to trade them in for trainers, he'd known he'd never have such a straightforward mechanism for consolation ever again. And he'd been right.

The lift doors slid open, revealing walls and floor made of stamped silvery metal. Matthew rode down to the ground floor and emerged into the immense glass foyer that in turn gave on to a vast pale outdoor concourse where architectural trees planted in concrete drums blew stiffly about in the wind from the river. He buttoned up his jacket and plunged out towards the coffee shop on a distant corner. A large latte would restore him, he was sure.

He carried his tall white mug to a table by the window. Across the square he could see a huge, clear sweep of sky full of racing clouds and the sharp white trails of aeroplanes. He had never liked weather much, had always seen its unpredictability as vaguely threatening, but it was a pleasure to look at from behind the safety of glass. He had once confessed to Ruth that he enjoyed the idea of the presence of chaos, somewhere out there, but he couldn't handle it if it came too close to him.

'Oh, I know!' she'd said, her eyes shining. 'We couldn't have a world with perfect control, but please may we be allowed to control our own bit of it, for ever and ever, Amen!'

After Edie, Matthew could not believe Ruth's sense of order: her make-up in Perspex boxes, her T-shirts in piles of three, her papers filed in translucent plastic folders. There were no leftovers in her fridge, no scattered newspapers on her sofa. Ruth had been a business consultant when he met her, and was now, at thirty-two, a junior head hunter for a firm that specialised in finance directors. When they met, she was earning a third again as much as he was; now, her income was closer to twice his. For the sake of his dignity—undefined as a danger area, but well understood by both of them—they had shared everything as an equal financial commitment on both sides: rent, bills, entertainment, travel. To create flexibility within this equable arrangement, a further understanding grew up that if Ruth contributed more money (a cashmere sweater for Matthew, Eurostar tickets to see an exhibition in Paris), Matthew would repay, without being asked, in kind (replant the window boxes, breakfast for Ruth in bed). It was a system, Matthew thought, that had worked very well for two and a half years, and that his parents would consider over-controlled to the point of inhumanity.

His parents' opinion on most things was, in fact, something Matthew never sought, despite loving them in a suspended, unexamined way. When he saw Ruth—these occasions were very seldom—seated at their kitchen table and forming such a contrast to the evolved disorder of her surroundings, he felt an unmistakable affection for the way he had been brought up, and a profound pride in the way he was living now. It was made easier, of course, by the fact that Edie and Ruth liked each other, that each fulfilled the expectations of how the other should be.

'Ghastly cat,' Edie would say, snatching Arsie off Ruth's cashmere.

'Bliss,' Ruth would say, sinking into one of the deep, battered armchairs in the sitting room, full of the kind of food she would never buy.

Periodically, Matthew would urge his parents to mend the house, reconsider their futures. Encouraged by the success of persuading his father to specialise more, he had hoped to nudge his mother towards more commitment to work and thereby detach her from the long, long nurturing of Ben. He was actually slightly congratulating himself on the success of initial conversations with Edie about how life might be after Ben, when Ben confounded them all by announcing he was off to live with some girl in her mother's flat in Walthamstow.

It had been impulsively done and had left all kinds of ragged ends behind, which Matthew was only just beginning to collect his thoughts about when Ruth announced, quite suddenly, that it was time they were thinking of buying somewhere to live.

'Actually,' she said, 'it's not just time. It's overdue. I should have bought five years ago.'

Matthew was in the middle of assembling a flatpack cabinet to house the television and DVD player. He said stupidly, 'You didn't know me five years ago.'

'I'm not talking relationships,' Ruth said. She was sorting gym kit. 'I'm talking property investment.'

Matthew looked down at the screws in his hand, hoping that there would be sixteen as promised and not fifteen as seemed likely. It would be so annoying to have to go shopping for one single screw.

'Matt? Did you hear me?'

'Yes. You need four screws a hinge and they have given me fifteen.'

Ruth put the gym kit down and came across to where Matthew was standing. She put her hand into his and scooped up the screws. 'Just concentrate on what I'm saying. It's time we bought a flat of our own.'

That had been a week ago. One week. In the course of that week they had talked endlessly about the subject and Ruth had given Matthew a number of things to read. One of these was a newspaper article that asserted that there were now over 300,000 professional young women working in the City with liquid assets of at least £200,000 each.

'I'm not there yet,' Ruth said, 'but I'm getting there. It's time to start buying property for the long term.'

Holding his latte mug in both hands and gazing over it now at the flying clouds, Matthew knew she was right. What Ruth was proposing was not only shrewd and sensible but also indicated, from her use of the word 'we' in so many of these conversations, that she saw their future as something that they would unquestionably do together. All that, her rightness, her evident commitment, made him long to be able to seize upon this great step she was proposing as the exciting next stage of their relationship. But he couldn't. He couldn't because—he shut his eyes and took a swallow of coffee—he couldn't afford it. Every penny he earned was already committed. He was not, baldly, in a position to finance any borrowing whatever, and such assets as he had were so small by comparison with Ruth's that they were hardly worth mentioning. What crowned it all was that Ruth had little or no idea of how stretched he was for the simple reason that he had preferred her not to know. And as a result, here she was proposing to embark on something she assumed, because she had no reason not to, that he could comfortably join her in.

Money should not be like this, Matthew told himself, swirling the tepid last inch of his coffee round the mug, money should not dictate or stifle or divide. He gave a huge sigh and thumped the coffee mug down. Money should simply not matter this much. But the trouble was, it did.

'**I** would have paid,' Rosa said. 'I wasn't suggesting I go home for free. I was going to offer to pay but he never gave me the chance.'

Ben, lighting a cigarette, said indistinctly, 'I give Naomi's mum fifty quid a week.'

'Do you?'

'She pays all the bills. Says she'd rather have it that way.'

Rosa examined her brother. He looked more sorted, somehow, even in the dim lighting of a pub. She said, 'She also plainly likes ironing—'

'Nope.' Ben drew on his cigarette. '*I* iron.'

Rosa gaped. 'Didn't know you knew how.'

He grinned, not looking at her. 'Lot of things you don't know.'

'Clearly.' Rosa picked up her drink. 'So you're now playing happy families with Naomi's mum.'

'Hardly ever see her. She's a caller at the bingo hall.'

'I thought she worked in a supermarket.'

'She does. And cleans offices.'

'Heavens. Poor woman.'

Ben glanced at her. 'No, she isn't. She says she likes being independent.'

Rosa flushed. 'Thanks a—'

'Don't patronise Naomi's mum, then.'

'I wasn't—'

'Your voice was,' Ben said. 'Your *tone*.'

'Sorry.'

'And I'm sorry about Dad. What's going on?'

'I think,' Rosa said, taking a swallow of vodka, 'that he doesn't want any competition for Mum's attention.'

Ben gave a snort.

'I only meant for a few months,' Rosa said. 'Till the summer. September at the latest. I'd pay rent. I'd feed the cat . . .'

Ben blew smoke out in a soft plume. 'Have you told Matt?'

'No point. He and Ruth are thinking of buying a trendy loft.'

'Room for you then.'

'No, *thank* you,' Rosa said. 'Ruth is great but I don't feel I could begin to lay the mess of my life out in front of her.'

'So,' Ben said, holding his beer bottle poised, 'Have you asked Mum?'

Rosa looked full at him, as was her wont when skimping on the truth.

'I can't. I can't be turned down by Dad and go straight to Mum.'

Ben grinned again. 'Why not? You always used to.' He tilted his beer bottle. 'Mum'd have you back.'

'How do you know?'

'Just do.'

'Ben,' Rosa said again, 'I can't.'

He shrugged.

Rosa said slowly, 'Kate said I could stay there. But they've only been married five months and Barney's lovely, really lovely, but he wants Kate to himself, he doesn't want—'

'Just like Dad,' Ben said. He looked at the clock over the bar. 'Gotta go, Rose. Meeting Naomi.' He bent sideways and retrieved from a canvas bag at his feet a black knitted hat, which he jammed down well over his hairline. He slid off his bar stool. 'Hope things work out, Rose.'

'Thanks.'

He winked. 'You'll find another job.'

'And a flat. And a man.'

Ben leaned forward and grazed her cheek with his unshaven one. Then he shouldered his bag and pushed his way through the happy-hour drinkers to the door.

Rosa looked down at her own drink. Before seven o'clock, if you paid for one, you got the next one free. Two vodkas might provide her with enough brief courage to ring Katie and ask if, after all, for just a short while and paying rent of course, she might sleep in the tiny room beside the front door that Barney was intending to decorate ready for the baby. She raised a hand and signalled, smiling, at the barman.

CHAPTER FOUR

VIVIEN MARSHALL WORKED part-time in a bookshop. She would have liked to have worked more, but if she did her husband Max, from whom she had been separated for four years, might notice and stop paying her the maintenance that he was perfectly entitled not to pay now that Eliot really had left home definitively, and gone to Australia. It wasn't the money in itself that Vivien wanted, useful though it was in maintaining the cottage in Richmond, and the car, but the contact it provided with Max. When he had suggested that they separate—she had known it was coming—she had agreed in order to prevent him reacting to any objection by insisting that they divorce.

Vivien did not want to divorce Max. She didn't even, maddening and undependable as he had always been, much want to be separated from him. Not only was he Eliot's father but he was also, for Vivien, an exciting presence whose absence had rather drained the colour out of things.

'You'd think,' she said to Alison who managed the bookshop, 'that you'd be thankful not to live on tenterhooks any more, whatever tenterhooks are. But actually, I rather miss them.'

Alison, who was not attracted to men of Max's type who wore leather and denim well into middle age, said she thought they had something to do with stretched damp cloth in the dyeing trade.

'What do?' Vivien said.

Alison sighed. Max might not, as a type, be to her taste but there were times when she felt a sympathy for him. Vivien was someone who couldn't help, it seemed, being a permanent small test of patience.

'Tenterhooks,' Alison said, and put her glasses on.

Vivien went back to dusting. When Alison had offered her the job, years ago when Eliot was still young enough to let her kiss him at the school gates, she had made it plain that bookselling was not an occupation involving delightful literary conversations with cultivated customers. 'It's more like always moving house. Endless heavy boxes and books parcelled up in shrink wrap. Non-stop tidying and cleaning.'

'I like housework,' Vivien had said.

She always had, if she thought about it. When she and Edie had shared a bedroom as children, her side of the room—fiercely marked out by a strip of pink bias binding drawing-pinned to the carpet—had been both tidy and clean. It was this fondness for keeping house that she supposed drew her towards Max, towards a man who, although outwardly organised, was inwardly chaotic. He gave her the excited feeling that she had kicked over the tidy traces of her upbringing and embarked on a heady and abandoned adventure. The trouble was that, in time, the tidiness reasserted itself and Max said he couldn't breathe.

Eliot, Vivien thought now, as she worked her way along the travel section with a new duster, was not like his father. Nor was he much like her. Eliot wanted life to be as simple as possible. His Australian girlfriend, as far as Vivien could detect from telephone conversations, made laconic seem an urgent word. They had a flat five minutes from the beach, they worked lightly, played water sports and drank beer. Eliot had emailed a photograph, showing them both on the beach, thin and brown, with similar bleached spiky hair. The girlfriend was called Ro.

'Short for Rosemary?' Vivien had asked.

'No,' Eliot said, after a pause. His voice already had a faint Australian edge to it, making every statement a question. 'Not short for anything.'

When he had rung off—'Gotta go, Mum. Take care'—Vivien had cried a little. Then she had got up from the kitchen table where she had been crying, blown her nose and assembled some clothes for dry-cleaning in a carrier bag. An hour later, she had managed to recount her conversation with Eliot to his father on the telephone without crying at all.

'That's good,' Max said. She could hear the faint tap of laptop keys as he spoke. 'Good for you, Vivi. You're getting used to him being grown-up.' He paused, then said, in the voice he had always used to indicate he knew he'd chosen the right sister, 'Not like Edie.'

Maybe Max was right. Maybe what made her cry after talking to Eliot was not that he was twenty-two and had chosen to live in Cairns, Queensland, Australia, but that he wasn't eight or ten any more, with a life that she had control over. Crying for Eliot was crying for a lost small boy, not crying for a lost role, like Edie.

Vivien pushed her duster to the back of the Prague guides. Edie was quite unhinged by the last of her children going and pretty well indifferent to poor old Russell's feelings. And their children, with the exception of Matt, were making a very amateurish business of leaving home. Poor Rosa: too proud to go home, too short of money to stay independent. And Ben living with a girl he'd met having his hair cut, one of the Saturday-morning juniors. She gave the final volumes of the travel section a little triumphant flourish of the duster. Poor Edie.

'For how long?' Barney Ferguson said. He was standing at the foot of the bed, wearing a bath towel wrapped round his hips. His hair was wet.

Kate lay against the pillows with the tea he'd brought her. She shut her eyes. 'A month?'

'A *month!*'

'Four weeks. Only.'

'Four weeks isn't only,' Barney said. 'That's a fifth of the time we've been married.'

Kate opened her eyes. 'Barn, I couldn't not ask her. She's my best friend and she's on her absolute uppers.'

'*I'm* your best friend.'

'My best woman friend.'

'Suppose she doesn't get a job—'

'She will. She's got to.'

'And supper, us having supper together—'

'She'll go out.'

'You said,' Barney pointed out, 'that she's got no money.'

Kate shut her eyes again. 'Please, Barn.'

He moved round the bed so that he could sit close to her on the edge. 'I just want you to myself.'

'I know.'

'And although I like Rosa, I *do*, I don't quite like her enough to want to live with her. And I wanted to paint that bedroom,' Barney said. 'Yellow, with elephants.'

'Why elephants?'

'I loved elephants, when I was little.'

Kate looked at him. 'Suppose this baby likes bears?'

'It can have bears.'

'Rosa can draw,' Kate said. 'Rosa could do bears, by way of rent.'

'You mean you haven't asked her for *any* rent?'

Kate said in a small voice, 'Just bills. Sorry.'

Barney stood up. 'I can't be cross with you. You look too pathetic. But I might be cross with Miss Rosa Boyd if she doesn't prove herself the *model* lodger.'

Kate gave him the half-smile he said had been the first thing he noticed about her apart from the backs of her knees. 'Promise I won't ask anyone else.'

'You bloody *will* promise.' He looked down at her in mock exasperation, then walked towards the bedroom door.

'Barney—'

He turned.

Kate smiled again. 'Thank you.'

Barney smiled back. Neither of his married sisters had produced any children yet, and his parents were treating him as a miracle of potency. He wagged a finger at Kate. 'Strictly on sufferance,' he said, still smiling.

The readings for *Ghosts* were held in an upstairs room above a pub on the Canonbury Road. The room was used for all kinds of purposes, including ballet classes, and along one wall ran a barre screwed into a series of huge dim mirrors. At one end, sharing a littered card table, the director and producer of the play—both, Edie thought, about half her age—were sitting on grey plastic chairs. There was also a thin girl in black sitting by an upright piano and another man, in a grey ski jacket, reading a newspaper.

Edie had decided that, as she was doing this reading to placate her agent, who had complained that Edie was not, repeat not, in a position to be choosy, she was *not* going to prepare meticulously. She had read the play once, quite fast, and had determinedly not decided to dress in any particular way, not to think herself into the mind of Mrs Alving.

She had also seen Russell look at her that morning, wondering.

'I'm not in the mood,' she'd said, pouring coffee. 'I can't apply myself.'

'Pity,' Russell said. 'It's a wonderful part.'

'This is a wonderful part,' the director said now. He had a narrow dark face and a goatee beard. 'Have you played Ibsen before?'

Edie shook her head.

The producer looked at her. 'What do you know about Ibsen?'

Edie looked back. 'He was Norwegian. And short. Very short.'

'I see.'

The director turned to the man reading the newspaper.

'Ivor will read Pastor Manders for you. Act One. The scene revealing her husband's conduct.'

'OK,' Edie said. She walked to a chair by one of the huge mirrors and dumped her bag on it, before rummaging in it for her book.

'From this copy,' the director said. 'If you would.'

Edie turned. He was holding out a sheaf of papers.

'We have slightly annotated the Peter Watts translation.' He glanced at the man with the newspaper. 'Ivor speaks Norwegian.'

Edie came slowly forward.

'We'll hear you read,' the producer said. 'But, personally, I think Mrs Alving should be taller.'

The man with the newspaper looked up for the first time.

He said, in accented English, 'Good face.'

'But height,' the producer said. 'So important for dignity. This is a woman who has *suffered*.'

'How do you know I haven't?' Edie took the sheaf of papers from the director's hand. 'Are you sure you want me to do this?'

He gave her a fleeting smile. 'Miss Allen, you *applied* for this casting.'

Edie swallowed. 'Sorry.' She had begun to feel faintly sick.

The man with the newspaper put it down and stood up. He was burly, even allowing for the ski jacket, and had light, blank blue eyes. He said to Edie, 'This will be the seventh time I have played Pastor Manders. Three times in Oslo, once in Edinburgh, once in Scarborough and once in London already.'

She gave him a nervous smile. 'Heavens. Are you Norwegian?'

'Half. My mother.'

The director leaned forward. 'We should start.'

Edie looked at the script in her hand. 'Where would you like—'

'I will start,' Ivor said, 'I will start with the line: "It almost makes my head reel."'

Edie looked at him. 'No script?'

He smiled. 'No need.'

Edie gave a little laugh. 'How very disconcerting—'

'Not at all. Quite the reverse. Reassuring for you. Like,' Ivor said, smiling, 'playing tennis with someone much better than you are.'

Edie swallowed. A rising tide of temper was beginning to eliminate the sensation of sickness. 'Of course.'

'We will begin. And I will indicate when we will stop.'

Edie glanced at the director. He was looking neither at her nor at his own copy of the script. She cleared her throat.

'Sorry,' he said, without moving. 'Sorry, Ivor. *I'll* tell you when to stop.' His gaze travelled across the room and came to rest on some object outside the window. The producer was looking at his fingernails.

'Fire away,' the director said.

Ruth Munro was, as was her wont, one of the last to leave her office. She felt that, not only did her conscientiousness set a good example, but it also gave her the chance to leave everything in the state she would like to find it in the following morning: as many emails from the US cleared as possible, work-to-do papers assembled in a pile weighted with a large, smooth grey-and-white pebble, picked up on a north Devon beach during the first weekend that she and Matthew Boyd had ever spent away together. Being alone in the room also gave her the chance to slow the pace, to be reflective. It also gave her time to stay in touch.

Ruth's closest friend, Laura, had gone to Leeds two years previously, to join a law firm. In those two years, Laura had become engaged to a fellow lawyer and had bought an apartment on Leeds's regenerated waterfront that had two bathrooms, a balcony and a basement laundry. It was Laura, now owner of a Tiffany engagement diamond, who had intimated to Ruth that if she did not buy a flat of her own soon she would be making a grave mistake.

Ruth had emailed Laura photographs of the loft on Bankside and Laura had been most approving. 'Go for it!' she'd written.

Ruth had waited three days while she adjusted her need to confide against her loyalty to Matthew, and then she'd written, 'I really want to. But there's Matt. I think he's worried about the money.'

'You mean he can't afford it?'

'Yes.'

'Can you?'

'Yes,' Ruth wrote.

'Well?'

Ruth looked up from the screen. If the truth were told, Matthew had not actually said he could not afford to share equally in the loft on Bankside: he had, instead, made it very plain that he would—could?—not talk about it. Ruth looked back at the screen.

'The thing is,' she wrote, 'that we have never had an I-have-this and you-have-that conversation. I suppose neither of us wanted to spell out the difference. And the difference hasn't been a factor, really, up to now. We've managed rather well.' She paused. Laura was bound to challenge that. 'Don't ask why we didn't sort it at the beginning. You know what beginnings are like. You don't care who earns what as long as you can be together.' She stopped and then she typed, 'I love Matt.'

She lifted her hands off the keyboard and put them in her lap. Laura would tell her that everybody loved Matt, that Matt was the kind of thoughtful, decent, straightforward man who it would be perverse not to love. She might also say—and she would be right—that Ruth and Matthew should have worked out this inequity early on in their relationship. That no amount of rapturous hand-holding on Devon beaches should have blinded Ruth to the fact that they had driven there in Ruth's car, Matthew not possessing one, and were staying in the kind of hotel he quite candidly would not have considered.

It wasn't, Ruth reflected, that he didn't pay his way because he did, with sometimes almost painful eagerness, but she couldn't help noticing that a tension about money had grown in him in the last year and, while she was sympathetic to that, she also felt that his concerns couldn't take precedence over her ambitions. If you made too many personal sacrifices, she and Laura had often agreed during late-night talking sessions with bottles of wine and Diana Krall on the stereo, you only ended up resenting the person you'd made the sacrifices for. You couldn't, as a woman, make yourself into someone lesser in order to accommodate a man's weaknesses. You couldn't agree not to want, not to strive for, a very desirable flat on Bankside because the man you were sharing your life with couldn't afford to match your input. She picked up a pen.

Does that mean, she wrote across her jotting pad, *that I don't love him enough?* She looked across her desk. There was a photograph of Matthew there, taken on holiday in the Maldives, a holiday he had suggested and had then—she could see it—had anxieties about paying for. He looked quite without anxiety in the photograph. He was wearing a white T-shirt and a wide smile and his hair was ruffled.

Ruth ripped the sheet off the jotting pad and tore it across. She glanced at her email to Laura. What possibilities it opened up for Laura to implore her—or instruct her—not to let herself down. She ran the cursor up the screen to cancel the message.

'Do you,' her computer asked politely, 'wish to save the changes to this message?'

'No,' Ruth clicked. She looked at Matthew, laughing on his tropical beach. 'Sorry,' she said.

She could see, from the pavement below their building, that Matthew was home before her. She could also see, from the way the light fell, which lamps he had switched on and, from that, what sort of ambience there would be when she reached the second floor and even what kind of atmosphere. Sometimes, she wished she didn't notice so much. Sometimes, she thought how peaceful it would be to be someone who didn't observe so minutely and deduce so analytically.

She put her key into the main door. The communal hallway contained only a small reproduction side table on which all the mail for the building was piled. Matthew would already have sifted through the pile for their own mail, but something in Ruth needed to recheck it, every time she came in. Her father had been the same, she told herself consolingly, perpetually reassuring himself that everything was in order, even down to counting the change from his trouser pockets every evening before piling the coins, in order of size, on the chest of drawers in her parents' bedroom.

Forcing herself past the side table without pausing, she ran up the two flights of stairs to their landing.

The front door was slightly open and there was the sound of music. She pushed the door wider open. 'Hi there!'

Matthew appeared from the bedroom, feet bare on the wooden floor, but still in the shirt and trousers of his business suit. He bent to kiss her.

'I like it,' she said, 'when you're back first.'

He straightened. 'I haven't done anything, though, except take my jacket off—'

'I didn't mean—'

'I know,' he said.

She went past him into the sitting room. 'Any mail?'

'Only dull things.'

She picked up the envelopes and glanced back at him. 'Good day?'

'So-so.'

She put the envelopes down. 'I thought I'd go to the gym. Want to come?'

'No, thanks.'

'Then I—'

'Ruth,' Matthew said.

She looked down at the envelopes. Notifications of payment by direct debit every one, evidence of system and organisation, evidence—

'Ruth,' Matthew said again. 'Sit down. Please.'

Ruth moved to the leather sofa—joint purchase, half-price in a January sale—and sat down, her knees together, her back straight.

Matthew padded past her and sat down at her side. He took her nearest hand. 'Look,' he said, 'this isn't very easy to say—'

'Does it have to be now?'

'Yes. There isn't a right time or, if there is, it mightn't occur for weeks and I have to say this thing, I have to tell you.'

She gripped his hand. 'What?'

He said, looking at the floor, 'I'm really sorry.'

'Matt—'

'I wish it wasn't like this. I wish I could match you in everything. You're quite right to want to buy the flat. You're quite right to want to climb the property ladder and I'm sure you're right about not leaving it any later. And it's a great flat.' He stopped and gently took his hand away. 'It's just,' he said, 'that I can't manage it. I've tried and tried to see how, but I can't afford it. I can't, actually, afford how we're living now and I haven't faced up to that. Until now. I'm having to, now, because I'm having to face the fact that I can't even think about buying the flat on Bankside with you.' He looked up from the floor and gave her a small smile. 'So if you want to go ahead, go ahead without me.'

CHAPTER FIVE

'AREN'T YOU GOING to get up?' Kate said. She was dressed in a velour track suit and had pulled her hair back tightly so that she looked about thirteen and far too young to be pregnant. 'It's twenty to eleven.'

'Yesterday,' Rosa said, 'I went to four crappy interviews and was turned down at every one. This afternoon I have three more. This morning I have decided not to punish myself any more than life seems to be doing anyway.'

Kate kicked at a pile of clothes and bags on the floor. 'You could clear all this up a bit.'

Rosa looked. 'Yes, I could.'

'You know,' Kate said, 'none of this is very easy for me. I want to help you, I want to make things nice for Barney, I want to stop feeling so awful and start feeling pleased about this baby, but it doesn't *help*, Rosa, if you lie in bed in all this mess, not even *trying*.'

There was a pause. Rosa twisted her hair into a rope and held it against the back of her head. 'How do you know I'm not trying?'

Kate kicked at the bags again. 'Look at this—'

'No cupboards,' Rosa said, 'no drawers. Floor last resort. Floor it is.'

'There's floor and floor. There's attempt-at-tidy floor or there's throw-everything-about-like-a-sulky-teenager floor.'

Rosa let her hair go. 'I can't believe we're having this conversation. This is like talking to my *mother*.'

'Then tidy *up*,' Kate said shrilly. 'Stop abusing my hospitality and make an *effort*.'

Rosa stood up. She looked at Kate. 'What would you like me to do?'

'I would like you,' Kate said, 'to clear up this room. I would like you not to put washing in the machine and then just leave it. I would like you not to finish the milk or the bananas and then not replace them.'

'Do you know,' Rosa said, 'you were never like this when we were students. You didn't, as I recall, give a stuff about washing or bananas.'

Kate sighed and rubbed her eyes. 'Being married changes things. It puts you in a different place, somewhere where it just suddenly seems childish to live in a student mess.'

'Childish.'

'Yes,' Kate said.

'I've had a flat, you know. I've bought milk and paid bills and taken washing out of machines. I've done all that.'

'Then why—'

'Because I've lost control of things,' Rosa said. 'It's all kind of got away for the moment. I'd love, frankly, to be back in charge of my own fridge.'

There was a small silence. Then Kate shuffled through the bags on the floor and put her arm round Rosa. 'Sorry.'

'Me too.'

'But you see—'

'Yes,' Rosa said, 'I see. Of course I see.'

'I can't share my life with you the way I once did—'

'I know.'

'But I want to be there for you, I want to—'

Rosa looked at her. 'You are helping. You've given me a roof and a bed and I'm grateful. I am also sorry about the bananas.' She bent and picked up a bra. 'I will sort this.'

Kate watched her as she pulled off her nightshirt. 'You're so lucky,' she said, 'to have *normal*-sized breasts still.'

There had been no word from the director of *Ghosts*. From past experience, Edie knew that this meant she hadn't got the part, but then, she told herself, she'd known that the moment she'd walked into the room for her casting and sensed the profound boredom her presence aroused.

'They are a good outfit, Edie,' her agent reminded her. 'They do pull off some marvellously fresh interpretations, but *every*one complains about the way they behave and I know really distinguished people, if you'll forgive the comparison, dear, who've been simply treated like dirt and it just isn't right that they can fill theatres the way they do after treating people like that, but the fact is they do and that's why I put you up in the first place because it would have been such a step up for you, but there we are. *Sorry*, dear, *sorry*. But we'll get you there, promise. You're just about right now for one of Shakespeare's mad old queens. Don't you think?'

Yes, Edie thought, lying on Ben's bed in the middle of a Thursday afternoon, still clasping the clean towels she'd been bringing upstairs to the airing cupboard when she had spied his bed through the open door of his room and been irresistibly drawn towards it. Yes, mad certainly, and old any minute and why not a queen since being anything more realistic seemed to be, at the moment, out of the question? Why not continue pretending that the world, as she knew it, hadn't fallen to pieces and left her washed up somewhere alien and empty with no notion of how to proceed?

She sat up, hugging the towels. Two towels, two adult-sized bath towels, which had washed over time from sage green to pale grey. Once there would have been five towels, plus swimming towels and—stop this, Edie said to herself, stop this *nonsense*, stop indulging yourself.

From downstairs, she heard the telephone ring. She sat where she was, her chin on the towels, listening to the cadences of Russell's polite, easy answering-machine message and then the same cadences saying something quite brief, like he'd be having a drink with someone after work or he'd be bringing something back for supper that had caught his fancy. He rang a lot now, little inconsequential messages about this or that, sometimes just to say he was thinking about her. Which was lovely of him, but which left her strangely, disconcertingly, guiltily unmoved.

She stood up. Vivien had said, in a rare moment of not needing to score a point, that Edie should just wait, that this was a kind of grief, and that griefs of all kinds were susceptible to time and that, even if time didn't heal them, it made them possible to accommodate to.

Edie moved slowly out of Ben's bedroom and across the landing to the airing cupboard. There was a trick to opening the door, a trick involving lifting the handle slightly as one pulled, while pulling slowly in order not to precipitate an avalanche of towels and duvet covers. Holding a bulging pile back with one hand, Edie half threw the clean towels up towards a space near the top of the cupboard, shut the door hastily, waited for ten seconds to make sure the catch would hold, and went downstairs. She glanced at the telephone. Sweet though it was, imaginative, loving, kind—Russell's message could wait.

Russell decided he would go home early. At four in the afternoon, the underground was strangely easy and accessible, and the people using it looked altogether less driven and self-absorbed. He even found a seat, and extracted the books section of the previous weekend's newspaper for a leisurely read about books he would never read himself, only to discover that he couldn't somehow concentrate. It wasn't leaving work early that was troubling—although he couldn't remember when he had last done that—it was Edie, really. She was, one way and another, worrying to Russell. It was natural, perhaps, to feel the final departure of your youngest child as keenly as she felt Ben's, but was it natural to go on feeling it so keenly, to sink so deeply into the effects of loss that you couldn't see the point of, or colour in, anything else?

She hadn't, it was perfectly obvious, made any effort for the Ibsen casting. She had only gone in the end because Russell and her agent had almost forced her to, and this in itself was worrying because, in the past, however busy, however preoccupied with family life, Edie had displayed an eagerness about every chance that came her way, a kind of optimistic determination that Russell had marvelled at, admired. She had even said every so often while yanking clothes out of the drier or dumping mountains of groceries on the kitchen table, 'Just *think* what it'll be like when I can think about lines and not lavatory paper!' And now that time had come, and she seemed utterly indifferent to it.

Perhaps, Russell thought, it was just a matter of time. Perhaps—more disconcertingly—it was a kind of depression. Perhaps—more disconcertingly still—Edie had been so changed by all those years of nurture that she couldn't now remember how it was to be just married, how it was to *want* to be still married. He shook his paper. So many books on the best-seller lists, on the review pages, were about love. Well, of course. In all its myriad forms. What else mattered, really? If it wasn't for love, indeed, why was he sitting on an afternoon train going home to someone whose unhappiness he would gladly have shouldered himself?

He let the front door fall shut behind him with a bang. The hall inside was very quiet and the cat, who had been washing in a small patch of sunlight on the stairs, stopped to look at him.

'Edie?'

She came slowly out of the kitchen holding a mug.

'Edie—'

'Sorry,' she said. 'Oh my God, sorry. I didn't listen to it.'

Russell put his bag down. 'Didn't listen to what?'

'Your message. I was fiddling about upstairs and I heard the telephone and I didn't do anything about it. And then I got deflected.'

Russell came closer and gave her a brief kiss on the cheek. 'I didn't leave you a message. I came home on impulse.'

Edie looked suspicious. 'What impulse?'

'Uneasiness,' Russell said. 'May I have some of that?'

'It's green tea,' Edie said. 'It is supposed to be invigorating.' She paused. 'What are you uneasy about?'

Russell went past her and crossed the kitchen towards the kettle. 'You know perfectly well.'

'I am waiting for it to pass,' Edie said. 'Like glandular fever.'

'Ben left a month ago.'

'What's a month?'

Russell ran water into the kettle. 'That's quite a long time.'

'What do you *want* of me?' Edie demanded.

Russell plugged the kettle into the wall and switched it on. 'When Ben left, I wanted you to look my way again. Now I would settle for you being able just to rouse yourself, climb out of this—this *inertia*.'

'Inertia,' Edie repeated calmly.

'Yes.'

'Like—like not jumping up and down, every time you come home—'

'No!' Russell shouted.

'Then—'

'Like,' he said more calmly, 'not even bothering to listen to your telephone messages.'

He went back past her out of the kitchen to the answering machine in the hall. Edie drifted to the window and thought, without any urgency, how dirty the glass was.

'It was Freddie Cass,' Russell said, from the doorway. His voice was excited. 'The director of *Ghosts*.'

Edie turned.

'He wants you to ring him. He wants you to ring him *now*.'

Ben had been on an assignment as assistant photographer taking pictures of a major newspaper editor at Canary Wharf. In the midst of the shoot he had remembered, in the slow, amazed way he often did remember things, that his brother Matthew also worked somewhere in Canary Wharf. He couldn't remember where or who for, but the idea of seeing Matthew suddenly seemed a most attractive alternative to returning to the studio on the Docklands Light Railway with his boss, who was currently giving him a hard time about every last little thing. Ben went out into the corridor outside the newspaper boardroom and scrolled to Matthew's number on his mobile.

'Wow,' Matthew said, 'Ben? Where are you?'

'Near your office.'

'What are you doing here?'

Ben leaned against the nearest wall. 'Working. Nearly done. You free?'

'What, now?'

'Half an hour or so—'

'Well, yes. Yes, I could be.'

'I need a beer,' Ben said. 'This afternoon has done my head in.'

'Fine. Fine. It—it would be good to see you.'

'Half an hour,' Ben said. 'OK?'

'Yes,' Matthew said. He sounded, abruptly, very tired. 'See you.'

'We can drink in here,' Matthew said.

Ben peered through the glass doors. 'Looks a bit posh—'

'It's all posh round here,' Matthew said. 'Artificial and posh.'

He pushed the door open, leaving it to swing in Ben's face. Ben followed him and seized his arm. 'What are you in such a strop about?'

Matthew sighed. He looked, Ben thought, not just tired but drained and without that air of confident togetherness that Ben had supposed, for the last five years or so, to be inbuilt. He watched Matthew order, and pay for, a couple of bottles of beer, and then he followed him to a table in a corner, under a plasma television screen. Matthew put the beer bottles on the table and glanced up at the screen. 'I watched the rugby World Cup on that.'

Ben grunted. He put his duffel bag down on the floor and eased himself into an Italian metal chair. 'How's things—'

Matthew went on looking at the screen. 'OK.'

Ben said, 'My afternoon was shite. My boss put me down the whole time over stuff he'd told me to do anyway.'

Matthew glanced away. 'But apart from this afternoon, everything's OK?'

'Yes. Aren't you going to sit down? I can't talk to you if you're standing.' Ben pulled off his knitted hat and ruffled his hair.

'Sorry,' Matthew said. He sat down slowly, on the chair next to Ben's. Then he said, 'Sorry to snap at you.'

Ben took a swallow of beer. 'It's all right.'

Matthew looked at him. 'Naomi OK?'

'Great. And the flat. It's cool. I really like it. Don't tell Mum,' Ben said, 'but I should have gone two years ago, three.'

Matthew picked up his beer. 'We all do that.'

'Do what?'

'Stay too long.'

Ben eyed him. 'Matt,' he said, 'what's happened?'

Matthew put the neck of the bottle in his mouth and took it out again. 'I'm not sure.'

'You and Ruth—'

'I think it's over,' Matthew said abruptly. 'It was so sudden. And I didn't see it coming.' He took a mouthful of beer and shut his eyes tightly, as if swallowing it was an effort. 'I should have.'

'Hey,' Ben said. He leaned towards his brother. 'Hey, Matt. Mate—'

'She wants to buy a flat,' Matthew said, 'and I can't afford to. I can't afford to because it's been costing me every penny I earn to live the way we do and I'm a stupid bloody idiot to have got in this mess. I am twenty-eight years old, Ben, and I'm back where I was at your age.'

Ben said slowly, 'It's hard to say to a woman, that you haven't got enough money. And if the woman has more than you do—'

'It isn't good,' Matthew said. 'You may not have failed, but it feels as if you have. So you don't say, and she makes assumptions. She's perfectly entitled to make assumptions, if you don't say.'

Ben drank some more beer. 'Don't you want to live in her flat?'

'Not under those circumstances. I'd feel like a lodger.'

'So—'

'So I've said to her that if she wants the flat she should go ahead and buy it, but that I can't come with her.'

'So you're making her choose—'

'No,' Matthew said, 'I'm setting her free to choose.'

Ben stared ahead. Then he said, 'I'm sorry.'

'Thanks.'

'Will you tell the parents?'

'I'll have to.' Matthew looked down. He said, almost bitterly, 'I may need a bit of help. For a while.'

Ben adjusted his gaze from the distance to his beer. This was the moment, if he was going to take it, to tell Matthew that Rosa had already asked for help from their father, and been, however reasonably, turned down. But it occurred to Ben that if he mentioned Rosa, it might just be one more depressing thing for Matthew to have to factor in, one more difficulty in an already difficult situation. He picked his bottle up again. 'Talk to Mum.'

Matthew turned to look at him. 'Really? I was going to talk to Dad.'

Ben shook his head. He put an arm briefly across Matthew's shoulders. 'No. Talk to Mum,' Ben said. 'Trust me.'

CHAPTER SIX

CLEANING, ROSA THOUGHT, hunting for rubber gloves under Kate's sink, wasn't something she had exactly been brought up to do. Edie had been very strict about helping, had made sure that everyone—with the frequent exception of Ben—realised that the task of keeping a house going was a communal responsibility. But she was not the kind of woman for whom crushed cushions and unscaled kettles represented the first signs of domestic anarchy; washing the kitchen floor was never, for her, going to take priority over helping Matthew make a model or dancing with Rosa in front of the landing mirror. It was only staying over in school-friends' houses that had revealed to Rosa that people—some people—bought vacuum cleaners for their efficiency and not solely because they had a jolly little face painted on the cylinder.

Kate and Barney had gone away for the weekend, and it was her intention, that Saturday, to create exactly that order in their flat. It was partly that she might find personal solace in burnishing surfaces and straightening rugs, but also because she might gain a form of unspoken forgiveness from Barney, in particular, and even—this was a long shot but desperate situations required desperate measures—prepare the way to asking if her month in the flat might be extended into two. She was keenly aware that she had not behaved well in the past fortnight, that she had conducted herself with the sort of sulky resentment associated with disaffected fourteen-year-olds.

If she was honest, she thought, spraying cleaning fluid lavishly across the kitchen surfaces and then scrubbing at a stain, she was envious of Kate and Barney wanting to be together and having the unspeakable luxury of a future to look forward to. At the same time, however, she knew that this kind of envy was a bitter, destructive thing. She straightened up. A pleasing sort of calm was beginning to overtake the kitchen. She wanted to make the flat look, by the time Barney and Kate returned, like a humble but unmistakable token of gratitude.

From the sitting room, her mobile rang. Rosa went slowly to answer it, pulling off the rubber gloves and saying to herself, under her breath, 'Make it a surprise, make it something nice, make it—'

'Darling?' Edie said.

'Mum, hi—'

'Are you all right? What are you doing?'

'Actually,' Rosa said, 'cleaning.'

'Cleaning? Why?'

'I want to. I like it. It's Saturday morning. Cleaning time.'

'Not in this house,' Edie said.

'I remember.'

'Rosa, what's happening? We haven't spoken for weeks—'

'Five days.'

'I want to know if you're OK. Have you found a job?'

'Yes. Not a good job. But a job. In a travel agency.'

'Rosa—'

'Don't start.'

'You're so bright and beautiful,' Edie said, 'I don't want you wasting yourself.'

'Nor do I.'

'Darling—'

'Mum,' Rosa said, interrupting. 'What's going on with you? I can tell there's something.'

'Well,' Edie said, 'I got the part.'

'Mum! The Ibsen?'

'Yes. Isn't it odd to get a part you don't want when you weren't trying!'

'I think it's wonderful,' Rosa said. Her throat hurt, as if she were about to cry. 'Congratulations! It's brilliant!'

'We'll see,' Edie said. 'Read-through on Tuesday. I get to meet my stage son. Have you heard from Matthew?'

'No—'

'What about this flat he and Ruth are buying?'

Rosa put a hand to her throat. 'It sounds very hip young professional.'

'Darling, I wish—'

'I don't want an urban loft, Mum. Or a job in the City.'

'Have you spoken to Ben?'

'I haven't spoken to anyone.'

'Rose, are you all right?'

Rosa shut her eyes. She mouthed, 'Don't keep asking' at the ceiling. Then she said loudly, 'Fine.'

'If you're not OK—'

'I am. Ring me and tell me how Tuesday goes.'

'Oh,' Edie said, 'OK.'

'How is Dad?'

'In his shed.'

'Give him my love,' Rosa said.

'Darling—'

'Back to Mr Sheen!' Rosa called. She held the phone away from her ear. Edie's voice came faintly from it, thin and small.

'Bye, Mum!'

She went slowly into the kitchen. Edie in her kitchen, herself in Kate's, Matt and Ruth no doubt buying Alessi-inspired kettles for theirs. She sighed. She had not given her mother what she wanted, on the telephone. She hadn't given it because she couldn't, for all the tired old reasons of loyalty and disloyalty that bedevil family life, the kind of reasons that made her mother and her mother's sister ring each other and bitch about each other daily in equal measure. She leaned against the sink. It struck her, with a small ray of dawning hopefulness, that this thought of her aunt coming into her head might not be totally arbitrary and that, beyond fathers and mothers in the leaky support system provided by families, there could sometimes also be aunts. Rosa stood straighter and laid the rubber gloves down on the now gleaming draining board. Then, thoughtfully, she went back to the sitting room, and her mobile phone.

'I'm playing Osvald,' the young man said.

Edie smiled at him. 'I guessed.'

He gave a small snort of laughter. 'Not difficult, with a cast of five.'

He had fine features and the slight build Edie had always somehow associated with First World War poets.

He said, 'Well, we're the same colouring, anyway. Mother and son.'

She gave him an appraising glance. 'I expect you got your height from your father—'

He grinned. 'Among other things.'

'I *know*,' Edie said. 'What a play.'

'Not much light relief—'

'That means rehearsals will be hilarious. They always are, if the play is dark.'

The young man said, 'My name's Lazlo.'

'I know. Very exotic.'

Lazlo made a little gesture. 'I've never played Ibsen before.'

'Nor me.'

'It was an awful casting—'

'Horrible.'

He smiled at her. 'But here we are, Mama.'

'I think,' Edie said, smiling back, 'you call me Mother dear. At least, in this version.'

He bowed a little. 'Mother dear.'

She looked across the room. A dark girl with her curls tied on top of her head with an orange scarf was standing in an extravagant dancer's pose, feet and hips sharply angled, talking to the director. 'What do you think of Regina?'

Lazlo turned his head. 'Scary.'

'You get to kiss her.'

'Double scary.'

'In two weeks' time,' Edie said, 'you won't be thinking that.'

He said, eagerly, 'I've only been out of drama school a year, you see.'

She smiled at him and took his hand. 'How lovely,' Edie said.

In the coffee shop after the read-through, Lazlo said he was starving. 'I was so nervous. I kept thinking, This isn't how I'm going to play it, this is *wrong*. I made him far more petulant than I want him to be. I don't want to sound so sorry for myself. Would you like a bagel?'

'I'll get you a bagel,' Edie said.

'No, really, I asked you to have a coffee with me.'

'And I am your mother,' Edie said. 'Don't forget that.'

He regarded her. He said soberly, 'I thought you were wonderful.'

Edie's chin went up a little. 'Don't forget I've been doing this since you were in your pram.'

'I don't think so.'

She took her wallet out of her bag. 'How old are you?'

'Twenty-four.'

She looked satisfied. 'I've been doing this since you were in your pram. What kind of bagel?'

'Toasted, please. Would two bagels be out of the question?'

'Certainly not. And cream cheese?'

'How did you know?'

'Mother stuff,' Edie said.

She threaded her way between the small metal tables to the counter. Behind it, a huge mirror reflected the room and she could see that Lazlo was watching her and that he looked exhilarated and exhausted. He was going, she thought, to be a good Osvald, just the right blend of intensity and youthful spirit, frightened enough to arouse sympathy, self-absorbed enough to be maddening.

She went back to their table and put the tray down.

'Can I ask you something?' Lazlo said.

'Yes.'

'I want you to be honest—'

'Oh, I am excellent at that,' Edie said, unloading the tray, putting the bagels down in front of him. 'I have a diploma in honest. Ask my family.'

He picked up a knife. 'Your family—'

'One husband. Three children, two of them older than you are.'

'I don't believe it—'

'True.' She turned and put the empty tray down on a nearby table. 'What do you want to ask?'

'Will I—' He stopped. 'Will I be any good?'

It was rather nice, Vivien thought, lying in the bath with a mug of tea balanced on the edge, to think of Rosa settling down in her spare room. The room had been made up, of course, as it always was, in obedience to the dictates of Vivien and Edie's childhoods, where whole areas of the house had been consecrated to this mythical creature called the visitor, who would expect exaggerated standards of perfection and formality were he or she ever to put in an appearance. Edie's reaction to this arrangement had been to make sure her family lived abundantly in every corner of her house; Vivien's, to emulate her mother. Rosa, in Vivien's spare room, would find two beds shrouded in candlewick covers, a wardrobe empty of everything except extra blankets and a clatter of hangers, as well as books, tissues and lamps with functioning bulbs.

When Rosa had telephoned and asked to come and see her, Vivien had said of course, come to supper. Then she had suggested coming on Sunday and added, 'Why don't you stay the night?'

Rosa had hesitated. 'Would that be all right?'

'Of course.'

Vivien didn't think Rosa looked very well. She had made an effort—clean hair, ironed shirt—but there was a kind of lustre missing. It became plain, as supper progressed, that Rosa's current state of distress had been advancing upon her for several years. First there was the affair with Josh, and then the ending of the affair and subsequent derailment of prudence and capability, and now unemployment and debt.

'Probably,' Rosa said, eating grapes. 'I shouldn't be telling you this. In a grown-up world, I should be sorting it. I shouldn't be wandering about like some hopeless animal that's escaped from its field and can't find the way back in.'

Vivien got up to make coffee. 'Nice image.' She reached up for the cafetière from a high shelf. 'Did you think of going back home?'

There was a pause and then Rosa said reluctantly, 'I tried.'

Vivien turned round. 'I can't believe your mother turned you down.'

'No. Dad did,' Rosa said. 'But nobody knows that except Ben. You're not to say.'

'Wouldn't dream of it.' Vivien spooned coffee into the cafetière. She said carefully, 'Your mother couldn't think why you chose to go and live with friends. Couldn't understand it. Why you didn't go home.'

'Well,' Rosa said, 'I can't, now. I can't go whining to Mum after Dad said what he did.'

'Which,' Vivien said, switching on the kettle, 'I can imagine. Men always want their wives to see them first. Except,' she added, 'mine.'

Rosa looked up. 'Perhaps that's why you still like him.'

Vivien came back to the table and sat down. 'More wine?'

'Yes, but no,' Rosa said. 'I'm selling bargain breaks to Lanzarote tomorrow.'

'Nothing wrong with that. I sell a lot of books I wouldn't read myself. 'You'll get another job. It's easier to find a job if you've already got one.'

Rosa rolled a bruised grape around the rim of her plate. 'It's not really the job that worries me so much. It's how I'm going to live so that I can start on this debt, how I—' She broke off and then said, in a slightly choked voice, 'Sorry.'

Vivien said. 'Come here. Come and live here for a while.'

Rosa stared at her. 'I couldn't—'

'Why not?'

'Well, you're my aunt.'

'Exactly.'

'And Mum—'

'Might be very pleased.'

'I don't think so,' Rosa said.

They looked at each other.

'Does it matter? Does it really matter? Just while you get yourself sorted and start paying off these cards and find another job?'

Rosa said slowly, 'It would be wonderful. I'd make an effort—'

Vivien got up to get the coffee. 'We both would.' She looked at Rosa over her shoulder. 'It might be quite fun.'

It might, she thought now, indeed be fun. It might also, dwelling upon the prospect, be both a relief and comfort to become in some way necessary again. Vivien picked up her tea. Rosa had kissed her warmly before she had disappeared into the spare room, with a kind of sudden fervour people feel when they have unexpectedly been thrown a lifeline.

'I only really came to talk,' Rosa said. 'I never thought—'

'Nor did I,' Vivien said. 'One seldom does.'

She smiled into her tea. There was no hurry, really, about telling Edie.

CHAPTER SEVEN

THE LOFT ON BANKSIDE was in a vast converted Victorian warehouse. Its brick walls, newly cleaned and pierced with modern windows in matt black frames, reared up from the newly cobbled alley that separated the building from a similar one ten feet away.

When Matthew had announced that there was no way he could share in the purchase of the flat, Ruth had become very still. She had looked at him for a long time, thoughtfully, and then she had said, 'Will you do one thing? Come and see the flat. Just see it. Please.'

Now, standing uneasily on the carefully patterned cobblestones, Matthew pushed open the heavy glass door of the warehouse and entered an immensely tall foyer, floored in granite with long windows running right up to the roof. There was an industrial steel staircase curving up behind a bank of lifts and besides that nothing but high, quiet acres of expensively gleaming space. He stepped forward into an open lift and pressed the button for the sixth floor.

When the lift doors slid open, there was a sudden flood of light.

'I saw you!' Ruth said. She was standing in an open doorway with apparently nothing behind her. 'I was watching from the balcony.'

He bent to kiss her cheek. She moved to meet his mouth and missed it. He looked past her.

'Wow.'

'Isn't it wonderful?'

He nodded. The room beyond the open door was pale and high, and at the end there was nothing through the huge windows but sky.

Ruth took his hand. 'You see? You see why I had to buy it?' She towed him through the door. Then she let go and spun down the length of the room. 'Isn't it great?'

'Yes.'

'Come and see the bathroom,' Ruth said. 'The shower is so cool. And in the kitchen, the microwave is built into the cooker unit.'

Matthew followed her across the wooden floor, through a doorway in a translucent wall of glass bricks. She was standing in a shower made of a cylinder of satin-finished metal, punctuated with little glass portholes.

'Did you ever see anything like it?'

'No,' Matthew said, 'I never did.'

Ruth stepped out of the shower. She said, more soberly, 'I wish it wasn't like this. I wish it wasn't you coming to stay in my flat. I wish it was ours.'

He leaned against the wall. The glass felt solid and cold through the sleeve of his jacket. 'I'm afraid I won't be coming.'

She said nothing, but walked past him very quickly and went back into the big room. He followed her. She was standing by the sliding doors to the balcony looking at her view of the river.

She said, 'Please don't talk like that.'

He stayed standing a little behind her. 'Ruth, I have to. If I come and stay here, it'll change the balance between us. It's changed already, of course, but it'd be worse. You can imagine how it would be. It'd be pitiful.'

She said fiercely, turning round, 'You couldn't be pitiful. I wouldn't *let* you.'

He tried to smile. 'You couldn't stop me. It would just happen.'

'Matt—'

'We've had a wonderful time,' he said, 'and it's got nothing to do with not loving you.'

She stepped forward and seized his arms. 'Suppose I don't buy it! I mind far more about you—'

He stepped back, gently extricating himself. 'It wouldn't work.'

She dropped her arms. 'I didn't mean this to—be like this.'

'I know you didn't.'

'Are—are my values all skewed?'

'Nope.' He looked around. 'It's a wonderful place. You'll be really happy here.' He leaned forward and laid the palm of his hand against her cheek. 'And you're doing the right thing.'

Then he took his hand away and walked back across the echoing floor to the landing and the lifts.

Edie took a garden chair into the angle of the house where, if you tucked yourself right into the corner, you could elude every breath of wind. She also carried a mug of coffee, her script and, somehow, two ginger biscuits, a pen and her telephone. Behind her, sensing a sedentary moment of which he might take advantage, padded Arsie.

The sun, shining out of a washed blue sky, was quite strong. It showed up unswept garden corners, and interesting patterns of blistered paintwork and lingering blackened leaves on the clematis above Edie's head. She thought, settling herself into the chair and arranging her mug and phone and biscuits on a couple of upturned flowerpots to hand, that this was the first time, the first moment, in the last five weeks, when she had felt the possibility of pleasure. She let Arsie spring into her lap, waited while he trampled himself down into position, and then rested her script on top of his purring tabby back.

'I can't believe this is work,' Lazlo had said to her at the first rehearsal.

She'd been looking at her lines. Without glancing at him, she said, 'By the end of this rehearsal, you'll know it is.'

By the end of the rehearsal, he'd been ashen. He'd been all over the place, not listening, in panic, to what the director was saying.

'Go away,' Freddie Cass said to him. 'Go away and learn those lines and come back to me *empty*. We're starting again.'

Ivor, the Norwegian, had taken him and Edie for a consoling drink. He put a hefty arm round Lazlo's shoulders. 'Drink that. Relax.'

Lazlo looked like a boy in a fairy tale, rescued by a genial giant. He drank his drink and shivered, and Edie and Ivor smiled at each other across his bent head and told him that everyone had first rehearsals like this, everyone made fools of themselves at one point or another.

Lazlo looked mournfully at Edie. 'You didn't,' he said.

'Not on this occasion.'

'Tell me,' Lazlo said miserably, 'about a time when you did.'

They'd ended up drinking two bottles of wine and putting their arms round each other and when Edie got home, Russell took one look at her and said, 'Shall I say I told you so?'

It was true that the play was drawing her in and therefore providing a distraction from her preoccupations, but that didn't mean, Edie decided, tilting her face to the sun and closing her eyes, that she didn't notice that none of the children were telephoning, nor that she didn't feel painfully aware that she knew very little about Matthew's new flat or Rosa's living arrangements, or Ben's girlfriend, or any of their working lives. She had promised herself that she wouldn't keep ringing them, but it didn't mean she didn't think and wonder and worry. And feel left out. Playing Mrs Alving was only a diversion.

Beside her, quivering on its upturned flowerpot, her phone began vibrating.

'It's me,' Vivien said.

'Damn.'

'Thank you so very much—'

'I was hoping you were Matthew. Or Ben.'

'At eleven thirty in the morning?'

'Why not?'

'People only ring their mothers in the early evening. It's a tradition.'

'Vivi,' Edie said. 'You sound very perky.'

'Well, the sun's out and my new little blue clematis is flowering and Eliot has passed his first diving exam.'

'How useful.'

'It is, if you're living in Australia, near interesting coral reefs.'

'Would you call it a career?'

'I rang,' Vivi said, 'to ask how you are. Actually.'

'And, actually, I'm very pleased to hear you. Nobody rings me now. Nobody. I've vanished. Was it Germaine Greer who said that women over fifty are invisible?'

'Probably. But I expect she was thinking of them as sex objects.'

Edie shifted in her chair and the script slid to the ground. Arsie didn't move. 'I only want to be a mother object. I'll think about sex again when I've sorted this stage. Actually, talking of mothers, I've got a sweet new stage son. He's twenty-four and pads round after me like a puppy.'

'Well,' Vivien said, 'there you are then. Sorted.'

'I want to know how my *real* children are.'

There was a tiny pause and then Vivien said, almost cautiously, 'I can tell you how one of them is, I think—'

'Can you?' Edie said sharply. She sat up, pulling her knees together. Arsie dug his claws in. 'Ow. What do you mean?'

'I saw Rosa—'

'Did you? Why did you see Rosa?'

Vivien said lightly, 'Oh, she came to supper. And stayed the night.'

Edie said, in a voice that entirely betrayed her feelings, 'Good!'

'I rather thought,' Vivien said unkindly, 'that she'd have told you.'

Edie leaned forward to detach Arsie's claws from the fabric of her trouser knees. She said, as normally as she could, 'How was she?'

'Well,' Vivien said, 'I thought she was putting on a bit of a brave face. I mean, this travel agency job is fine, but it isn't really stretching her, you know. She knows that, of course, but it's money, isn't it?'

'Yes—'

'The real trouble was living with Kate and Barney. They're too newly married, really, to cope with having anyone else there. I could tell she was having a bad time.'

'Was?'

'Oh, yes,' Vivien said, airily. 'We sorted the living thing at least.'

Edie closed her eyes.

'She's coming to live with me, for the moment,' Vivien said. 'That's why I'm ringing, really. I thought you should know.'

Edie opened her eyes again. She gripped the telephone. 'Let me get this straight, Vivi. Rosa is working in a travel agency, and living with Kate and Barney didn't work out, so she's asked to live with *you*?'

'No,' Vivien said, 'I asked her. I could see she was desperate.'

'Why,' Edie cried, wishing she could restrain herself, 'didn't she ask *me*? Why didn't she come *home*?'

'Ah. Now that I couldn't say. I couldn't tell you about that.'

'You're a smug, manipulative cow. I don't want to talk to you.'

'Oh, don't be so melodramatic and *silly*, Edie. I'm Rosa's aunt. I'm *family*. As long as Rosa is safe and comfortable, why does it matter whose roof she's under?'

Edie scooped her free hand under Arsie and lifted him off her lap.

Then she stood up. 'You know very well why it matters.'

'Only if you're possessive.'

'I'm not possessive!'

'Well,' Vivien said, 'you think of another word for it.'

Edie put a hand over her eyes. 'To cook up this plan behind my—'

'I'm *ringing* you.'

'Rosa didn't.'

'Well,' Vivien said triumphantly, 'can you wonder?'

Edie looked down at the ground. The sheets of her script were scattered about and the cat was sitting, washing, on some of them.

'I must go,' she said to her sister. 'Got to learn my lines.'

Maeve was sorting the invoices for Russell's quarterly VAT return.

The door to Russell's office stood open, as usual. Russell himself wasn't in his office, having gone to a meeting with a television production company that was in search of both actors and actors' voices. Maeve could visualise him at the meeting, slightly rumpled amid the black T-shirts and business suits, but not to be lightly dismissed on account of having known the business, and the people in it, since before some of his competitors were born. If Russell wasn't the kind of agent who commuted to Los Angeles and had a country house for weekends, it was because he didn't want to be.

'Not blazingly ambitious,' he'd said to Maeve when he first interviewed her all those years ago. 'Just want to have a nice time. It's what growing up in the North does to you—you're either driven by the work ethic of your childhood, or you decide to react against it. What you see, Miss O'Leary, is my small rebellion.'

Maeve got up from her desk and went into Russell's office to collect the small receipts that he threw into an old leather collar box on the cluttered shelves behind his desk. The collar box had belonged to his grandfather, whose initials, the same as Russell's, could still be seen, faintly stamped into the leather. Maeve took down the collar box and opened the lid. There wasn't much in it. Russell might like a nice life in some ways, but that didn't include taking many taxis.

From her own office, the street doorbell rang. Maeve put down the box, went back and pressed the audio button on the intercom.

'Russell Boyd Associates.'

'It's Edie,' Edie said.

'You come on up,' Maeve said. 'He's not here, but I'm expecting him.'

She pushed the door release, and a second later heard its muffled crash, closing behind Edie. She opened the office door and waited for

Edie's steps up the stairs, light and quick, to come closer. Edie was wearing jeans, and a green wool jacket, with her hair pushed into the kind of cap Maeve remembered people wearing in the sixties, a gamine kind of cap, with a big peak.

'I've to congratulate you,' Maeve said, as Edie reached the final landing, 'on getting that play.'

Edie gave her a pat on the arm. They had known one another for twenty-five years and had never kissed. A mutual sense of propriety had kept them friendly but formal.

'It's good,' Edie said. She was panting slightly. 'I'm enjoying it.' She looked into Russell's office. 'Where's he gone?'

'Meeting with Daydream Productions. Should be back any minute. Now, will you have a cup of coffee?'

Edie considered. 'I don't think so.'

'I make it all day,' Maeve said. 'It's never enough for these people just to come here and see Russell and go. They need nourishment and a sympathetic ear and I'm the provider of both.'

Edie walked over to the window of Russell's office. She said, almost idly, 'I suppose Rosa hasn't been in?'

'Not for a while,' Maeve said. 'Not for a month or so. Looking at you, I can't see where that height of hers comes from.'

Edie shrugged. 'They're all taller than me.'

'It's modern nourishment,' Maeve said. 'It's all this feeding.'

The street door crashed again.

'That'll be him,' Maeve said. 'Not another soul in this building slams the way he does.'

Edie took her cap off and put it on Russell's desk. Then she sat down in his swivel chair and leaned back.

'If you're taking him away,' Maeve said, 'I've some letters for him to sign before you do.'

Edie shook her head. 'I just want to ask him something.'

Russell's footsteps could be heard on the landing and then crossing Maeve's office. He appeared in the doorway. 'Well,' he said. He was smiling. 'How lovely.'

Edie regarded him.

Maeve said, 'And how did it go?'

Russell was looking at Edie. 'Good,' he said. 'Good. Several nibbles that might well amount to a bite or two.' He put the battered canvas bag in which he carried papers down on a chair and went round his desk, stooping to kiss Edie. 'Hello.'

Edie said, 'I could have rung but I was restless.'

'Good,' Russell said again. He perched himself on the edge of his desk. 'You wouldn't be here otherwise.'

Maeve moved towards her office. 'Will I shut the door?'

Russell half turned. 'Don't bother.'

'Please,' Edie said, past him.

He turned back. 'What's happened?'

Edie waited until Maeve had closed the connecting door. Then she said, 'Something a bit puzzling.' She put a half-closed hand up near her face, as if she was examining the cuticles. 'Vivi rang.'

'And?'

'She said Rosa was moving in with her.'

'So,' Russell said, a shade too cheerfully, 'isn't that a good thing?'

'Why didn't I hear it from Rosa? Why isn't Rosa ringing? Why don't I know what's happening to Rosa?'

'Well,' Russell said, 'I don't know what's happening to her either.'

Edie took her gaze off her cuticles and directed it at Russell. 'Don't you think we *should* know?'

'Darling, she's twenty-six—'

'I don't care if she's a hundred and six. She's not settled or happy and we are her parents and we should *know*.'

Russell stopped smiling. 'Yes.'

Edie leaned forward so that she could look penetratingly up at Russell. 'There was a hint in something Vivi said, just a hint, that something has been going on, to do with Rosa.'

'Ah.'

'And when I'd rung off and was pacing about learning my lines, it came to me that perhaps something had been going on to do with Rosa, to do with Matt too, for that matter, something that I didn't know about, but which you possibly did.'

Russell looked out of the window and waited.

'Well, I couldn't concentrate any more, so I got on the tube, and I came here. Russell?'

'Damn Vivi,' Russell said lightly.

Edie put a hand on his sleeve. 'What have you and Rosa been doing?'

Russell looked down at Edie's hand on his arm. He felt a sudden uncharacteristic loss of temper, and moved his arm so that Edie's hand fell from it. 'Nothing,' he said furiously. 'Nothing to do with you.'

'But—'

'Did you hear me?'

Edie stared at him. Then she said uncertainly, 'If you say so—'

'I do.'

'But is she OK?'

Russell turned away and bent over his desk, staring deliberately at the computer screen. 'When she isn't,' he said more calmly, 'I'll tell you.'

There were four messages on Rosa's mobile phone, one from her mother, one from her father, one from her aunt, and one from her older brother. Only the last one did she have any inclination to return. The others—well, how depressing was it, at her age, and stuffed into the sky-blue polyester blazer with yellow plastic sunburst buttons required by the travel company, to have a string of messages on your phone that are all, but *all*, from your family?

The messages were all, except for Matt's, of a kind that she didn't much want to hear. It was evident that her aunt had rung her mother to have a small but unmistakable gloat about Rosa's living arrangements, and, in the course of conversation, had hinted that something had occurred to prevent Rosa's turning at once to her parents in time of need. Her mother had then, it appeared, gone straight to find her father, and they had both subsequently left messages, her father's apologetic but brisk, her mother's imploring her to come home. Matthew's, by contrast, was completely unemotional. He just said he'd like to catch up sometime soon. He was plainly calling from the office because his call took ten seconds.

Rosa dropped her phone back in the bag at her feet. She was not going to deal with any of this just now. Despite the blue polyester blazer, today had been a reasonably good day. She had sold a weekend in Venice to a party of six, booked a stag group to Vilnius and reserved several family-holiday special offers in Croatia. If they all came good, it was the most commission she had made so far, which might translate into the first tiny repayment of debt, the first small step back to even a vestige of independence. If you coupled that with the prospect of Vivien's spare bedroom—a bit fussy, a bit overfurnished, but comfortable and convenient and almost free—it was not, Rosa considered, quite as black an outlook as it had been a month before.

She moved the mouse for her computer to access her emails. It was not permitted, in the travel company, to use the email service for personal messages, but who was going to check on her if she bent the rule just once? She typed in Matthew's work address.

'Tx for message,' Rosa wrote, one eye on the office manager eight feet away straightening the rack of brochures. 'Yes, would be good to meet. When? Where?' And then she added, pulling a booking form towards her in order to look like work, 'Need to talk. Parents!!!'

'Like the blazer,' Matthew said, nodding at the sunburst buttons.

'It would be kinder not to mention it.'

'I can't *not* mention it.'

'Yes, you can,' Rosa said. 'Unless you want to make even more of a point about contrasting my life with yours.'

There was a tiny pause and then Matthew said, indicating the menu, 'What d'you want to eat?'

'Are you paying?'

'Yes.'

'Well, I'll have the courgette-and-broad-bean thing with a grilled chicken breast.'

'Please.'

Rosa smiled at him. 'Please.'

Matthew turned and gestured for a waiter.

Rosa said, 'And possibly a glass of Sauvignon?'

Matthew glanced at her. 'All right.'

'Matt, one glass—'

He turned back. 'I don't begrudge you a glass, Rose. You can have a bottle if you want. It isn't that.'

'What isn't what?'

A waiter appeared, in a long black apron, holding a pad. He smiled at Rosa. She held up her menu, so that he could see, pointing at what she wanted. Then she looked up at him and smiled back.

'I'll have the kedgeree,' Matthew said, 'and a salad. And one glass of house Sauvignon.'

'Aren't you having any?'

'No.'

'Why not?'

'Because,' Matthew said, 'I really don't feel like it.'

'Why not?' Rosa said again. 'Tummy? Head?'

Matthew picked up the menus and handed them to the waiter.

'Heart,' he said shortly.

Rosa sat up. 'Matt. What's happened?'

'Well,' Matthew said, leaning his arms on the table, 'Ruth and I are—over.'

'Oh, no.'

'Yes.'

'Has she met someone else?'

'No.'

'Well, from the look of you, you haven't.'

'No.'

'Matt—'

'I'll tell you,' Matthew said, 'if you'll just shut up a minute.'

The waiter put a glass of wine down in front of Rosa.

She said, 'I can't believe it, I can't grasp—'

'Nor can I.'

'This flat—'

'That's it really,' Matthew said, 'the flat. The bottom line is that she can afford it and I can't. And she should be on the property ladder. It's the right decision for her, I've told her so. But I can't join her.'

Rosa said slowly, 'I thought you were earning a shed of money.'

Matthew made a face. 'Half what Ruth earns.'

'Heavens, I always thought—'

'I know. I didn't stop anyone thinking that. But the truth is, it's been a struggle to keep up and lately—well, lately I haven't been keeping up. And I certainly can't begin on fancy flat buying.'

Rosa took a mouthful of wine and then she said, 'Poor you.'

He shrugged.

'What—what if she doesn't buy the flat?'

'Too late,' Matthew said.

'You mean too late, she's bought it?'

He shook his head. 'No, too late to retrieve where we were. The flat was just the catalyst. It made us face the disparity.'

'Did she throw you out?'

'No!' he said angrily.

'Sorry—'

'I threw myself.'

'Oh, Matt,' Rosa said. She leaned forward. 'Do you still love her?'

The waiter appeared again, holding their plates of food. Matthew leaned back. He waited until the kedgeree was in front of him and then he said, 'Of course I do. You don't just switch that off in an instant.'

Rosa looked at her plate. She said hesitantly, 'I meant, do you still love her enough to try again?'

Matthew sighed. 'Not under present circumstances.'

'But Ruth will just go on being successful. Won't she?'

'Yes. And she ought to.'

'What, put work before relationships?'

'Well,' Matthew said, putting his fork into the rice and taking it out again, 'you've got to put something first, haven't you? Not everything can take priority.'

Rosa waited a moment. She cut a strip off her chicken. 'Matt, what about you? Couldn't you have compromised? A cheaper flat . . .'

'Ben said that.' Matthew sighed. 'But I couldn't afford even a cheaper flat. And she was—kind of stuck on this Bankside one. Elated.'

Rosa stopped cutting chicken and looked soberly across the table at her brother. 'What about you?'

Matt said, not looking up, 'I've still got a job. But it feels different now. It was just one part of life and now it's got to be almost all of it. I can't quite remember what it's *for*.' He took a tiny mouthful.

'Have you told Mum and Dad?'

'It's only just happened,' Matthew said. 'Ben knows, that's all.'

'Before me?'

'He just rang me,' Matthew said patiently. 'Just happened to be around.'

Rosa picked her wineglass up. 'Where are you sleeping?'

'On the sofa at our old flat.'

'Ruth in the bedroom, you on the sofa—'

'Yup.'

'You can't do that—'

'No. Not for long.'

Rosa said, as if an idea was slowly dawning, 'Maybe, if you got a flat, we could share.'

Matthew put his fork down. 'Sorry, Rose.'

'What?'

He looked at her. 'I just feel—a bit demoralised, I suppose. As if everything has come to a halt, as if I can't decide anything for a while. I never thought I'd say this, I mean, I left about seven years ago, for God's sake, but I think I might go home. Just for a while.'

CHAPTER EIGHT

'I WONDER,' FREDDIE CASS said to Edie at the end of rehearsal, 'if I could ask you something.'

Edie was putting on her jacket. 'Of course.'

Freddie put out an arm to hold a shoulder of the jacket. 'It's Regina.'

'Ah.'

Regina was being played by the defiant girl called Cheryl Smith who chain-smoked and stamped about rehearsals in slouched pirate boots.

'She's good,' Freddie said. 'She knows what she's doing. But Lazlo's frightened of her.'

Edie shrugged her jacket round her neck. 'She's in-your-face sort of sexy.'

'Exactly. That's what I wanted. Especially for Act Three. But there's no chemistry between the two of them because she's contemptuous and he's scared.' He smiled at Edie. 'You're mothering Lazlo so excellently.'

'Don't ask me to mother Cheryl—'

'Oh, no. Just have her to supper.'

Edie looked across the room. Cheryl, her legs arranged in their distinct dancer's pose, was smoking and talking to Ivor.

'With . . . with Lazlo?'

'That was my idea.'

'She'd never come if he came.'

Freddie switched his smile off. 'She'd come,' he said, 'if you told her your husband is an agent.'

Edie said indignantly, 'Look, sorry, but you're the director. This is *your* job!'

Freddie leaned forward and gripped her arm. 'Indeed I am. But in a production like this, dear, it's *our* job. I'll buy the wine.'

Later, on the bus going home, Edie found herself thinking about having Lazlo and Cheryl to supper and how their presence in the kitchen—both in their twenties, both in a precarious profession—might serve as a useful bait for tempting Rosa to come back, just for the evening, just for supper. And once she was there, it might be possible—or, at any rate, less impossible—to discover why she had chosen to seek help from her friends and her aunt rather than from her mother.

Vivien had emptied all the cupboards and drawers in her spare room, for Rosa. The drawers, Rosa noted with awe, were lined with sprigged paper. There were also two sizes of towel, a new cake of soap and a copy of *Glamour* magazine. It was kind, Rosa thought, bundling her sweaters on to the sprigged paper, it was really very kind, but in the context of complicated family loyalties it was also making a point. It would be perfectly acceptable to thank Vivien for making her so welcome, but it wouldn't be acceptable at all to applaud her for it. Applause would imply that a comparison with Edie had been made in which Vivien was the victor. Rosa sighed. She picked up an armful of shoes and boots and dumped them in the bottom of the wardrobe. They looked terrible, with the sad intimate terribleness that worn shoes always have. And in addition, if Vivien were to come into Rosa's room while she was at work—not a happy thought, but not one that could be discounted, either—she would expect to see Rosa's possessions in sufficient order to denote gratitude for housing them. Rosa bent down and began to sort her shoes into pairs.

Below her, in the hallway, Vivien's telephone started to ring. Vivien still had a landline with a cord; a cream plastic handset that sat on a little table with a shelf for directories and a pad and a pot of pens. Vivien drew mouths and eyes on the pad while she talked on the telephone, curvy mouths and thick-lashed eyes, swimming about the page.

'Hello?' Rosa heard Vivien say. Her voice was perfectly clear, even from a floor below and with Rosa's door closed.

'Oh,' Vivien said, her voice lifting a little. 'Oh! Max—'

Rosa got up from her knees and went quietly to the door, a red canvas basketball boot in one hand.

'Saturday,' Vivien said. 'Saturday. Let me see. I'll have to look.' Then she laughed. 'I know. So old-fashioned. But you know me. Can't even work the video machine. I'll never get beyond paper and pencil.'

There was a rustling of paper.

Then Vivien said, 'I'm working in the shop on Saturday. Yes, I do have to. Alison's going to some literary festival for the weekend. Max, I— Well, the evening would be lovely. Goodness. Are you asking me out to *dinner*? What's the etiquette for that, if we're separated?' She laughed again and then she said, in a fond tone Rosa recognised, 'You don't change. See you Saturday.'

There was the sound of the receiver being replaced, and then Vivien's heels went clicking down the wood floor of the hall with an unmistakable jauntiness. Rosa looked down at the boot in her hand. Josh had given her those. Or at least he'd been going to, right up to the moment of standing by the till in the shoe shop and Josh discovering, as he always discovered, that he had no means of paying for them except a crumpled five-pound note and a few coins. After she'd paid for them, he spent the five pounds on a single yellow rose for her, a rose so large and long-stemmed that people stared at her on the underground. A rose as showy as that must mean that something had happened, something romantic and definitive. Rosa dropped the boot on the carpet. All that had actually happened was that she had paid for yet another thing she didn't want.

Her phone, lying on one of the twin beds in a slew of socks and tights, began to ring. Rosa glanced at the screen and picked it up.

'Mum.'

'Darling,' Edie said, 'how are you getting on?'

Rosa looked round the room. It remained somehow very much Vivien's spare room. 'Fine.'

'I wondered,' Edie said, her voice nonchalant, 'if you'd help me out?'

'In what way?'

'I have to have two members of the cast to supper. To help them bond. You know. The director asked me.'

'I thought that's exactly what directors are supposed to do.'

'Not this one. Will you come? Will you come for supper and help make a crowd?'

Rosa frowned down at her socks. 'When?'

'Saturday. Are you busy on Saturday?'

'No,' Rosa said, shutting her eyes. 'No, I'm not busy.'

'Will you come? No strings. No thin end of wedging. Promise.'

Rosa opened her eyes again. She could always stay here, of course, sitting in front of Vivien's television while Vivien skipped out in a cloud of scent and anticipation. And how sad would *that* be?

'OK,' Rosa said.

Cheryl Smith arrived for supper wearing red satin jeans tucked into her pirate boots and a black off-the-shoulder sweater. She kissed Russell warmly, leaving a cherry-coloured streak on his cheek, and said he'd been wonderful to her friend, Mitch Morris (whom Russell couldn't remember ever having heard of), and maybe she could come and see him sometime?

He handed her a glass of red wine. 'Anyone with talent who is prepared to work and to pay me ten per cent of their earnings is very welcome to come and see me.'

She laughed and drank half her glass in a swallow. 'Great house,' she said, turning to Edie.

Edie was stirring coconut milk into a pan of curry. 'When we bought this house, houses were affordable. It wasn't surprising to have a house when you got married, it was normal.'

Cheryl arranged herself in her dancer's pose. 'I can't see me ever owning anything.'

Russell looked at her, strictly above the shoulders. 'What would you like to own?'

'Oh, a car. A Morgan.'

Edie picked up a flat plastic box of kaffir lime leaves. 'How many of these, do you think?'

Cheryl twirled her wine. 'I never cook. At drama school I lived on vodka and cheese sandwiches. Now it's red wine and pizza slices.'

'Disgusting,' Russell said, smiling.

Cheryl smiled back. She held her glass out to him.

Edie said, crumbling leaves, 'Your mother would be horrified.'

'My mother doesn't cook either. It was my father that cooked. No wonder he left. Five kids refusing to eat the same thing.' She looked at Edie for the first time properly. 'Wasn't Lazlo supposed to be coming?'

Russell gestured towards the window. 'He's in the garden. Talking to my daughter, Rosa.'

'Our daughter,' Edie said.

Cheryl moved over to the window and leaned to look out, stretching the red satin tight over her bottom as she did so.

'He's quite good,' she said.

Russell looked at Edie.

Edie said, without turning, 'Then why are you making it so hard for him?'

'Because he's only just out of drama school. It's no good them thinking it's easy.'

Russell hitched his leg across the corner of the table and regarded Cheryl's bottom. 'But possibly it isn't very helpful for them to think it's impossible and unpleasant either.'

Cheryl turned. She said, smiling, 'Unpleasant? Oo, what a word.'

'I would think,' Russell said, 'that you'd be rather good at unpleasant.'

Cheryl winked. 'Very good.'

'Can you do pleasant too?'

'Duller.'

'But better,' Edie said, coming across the kitchen with a spoon held out for Russell to taste, 'if trying to work with other people, which is, on the whole, what actors in a theatre *are* trying to do. Is that rather sweet?'

Russell took the spoon from Edie. 'I think,' he said, 'that if I were Freddie Cass I'd have told you I could find another Regina very easily.'

Cheryl laughed. 'Really?'

Russell handed the spoon back to Edie. 'No. It's the right sort of sweet.' He glanced at Cheryl. 'Really.'

'Cheryl's here,' Lazlo said miserably to Rosa.

Rosa was wearing a sweater of Russell's over her own clothes and had pulled the sleeves down well beyond her knuckles. 'Well, you knew she was coming—'

'Look what she's wearing.'

Rosa peered. 'I expect that's deliberate.'

'She said to me in rehearsal the other day, "I'm not kissing you until I absolutely have to."'

'That wasn't very nice.'

'I don't know,' Lazlo said, 'what I'd do without your mother.'

Rosa looked at him. He was taller than she was, but as thin as a lath, with one of those sensitive, handsome faces that looked somehow neither girl nor boy. Not her type at all.

'It's not just that she's so nice to me,' Lazlo said, 'it's that she knows what she's doing and that helps me surrender to the part. D'you know what I mean?'

'I'm not an actress.'

He glanced at her quickly. 'What do you do?'

Rosa looked away. 'I'm in the travel business.'

'You don't sound as if you like it very much.'

'I don't.'

'That's what's so extraordinary about acting. It isn't a choice.' He stopped and then he said, apologetically, 'But you know that. Because of your mother.'

Rosa looked towards the kitchen window again. Edie was gesturing at them to come in. Rosa sighed. 'She wasn't like that. She did jobs around us. We sort of knew she did it, but I suppose we didn't take it in.'

Lazlo stared at her. 'Don't you know how good she is?'

Rosa stared back. 'Oh, yes.'

'Well,' he said, 'it just sounded as if you weren't quite aware . . .'

'She's my mother,' Rosa said.

Lazlo said nothing.

Rosa began to move away from him across the damp grass towards the house. 'That didn't come out as I meant it to.'

'No.'

Rosa stopped. She said, without meaning to, 'I sound spoilt . . .'

There was a long pause, and then Lazlo said, from behind her, in the spring dusk, 'Actually, you do.'

Sitting on the underground on his way up into town, Matthew looked at the other people in the carriage. It was early evening, just after work, so the train was full, not just with tired men holding computer cases and newspapers, but tired women with computer cases too and handbags and supermarket shopping bags. Some of the women were young, and made Matthew remember, unhappily, the way Ruth had kept all the strands of their life together, persistently rounding up stray aspects in a manner that made him marvel.

Blaise, at the desk behind him at work, said that personally he had marvelled himself to a standstill about modern women. 'They're too much for me,' he'd said by way of commiseration over Matthew's break-up.

'Girls now, I mean. Now-girls.' He was giving up girls for a while, he said, and concentrating on getting his pilot's licence.

The train pulled into Moorgate Station and stopped. Edie had said to meet her after rehearsals. She had described where to find her, saying he would recognise the rehearsal hall in Clerkenwell because it had a yellow poster outside advertising 'Pilates in Pregnancy' classes. She'd said that they could go for a drink together, possibly even have supper. She'd sounded so pleased to hear him, so relieved and gratified that he'd rung, that he wondered what had happened to propel him into her personal spotlight. It was the place, after all, usually occupied by Ben.

The rehearsal hall was, Edie said, about ten minutes from the underground station, and he should aim for the spire of St James's Church. Matthew thought, gazing skywards from the Farringdon Road, that that was exactly the kind of directions his mother had always given, instructing you to look out for a memorable, preferably romantic landmark that was not actually visible until you were standing almost beside it. Perhaps, by the same token, Edie would have no trouble in seeing through the miserable thickets Matthew had got himself tangled up in, and out beyond to something altogether brighter and more hopeful.

She was waiting for him outside the hall, leaning against the Pilates poster with her arms folded and her sunglasses on.

He bent to kiss her cheek. 'Am I late?'

Edie put both arms round his neck and pulled him down towards her. 'No. We finished early. We did a lot of the joy of living today and it wore everyone out, being joyful.'

Matthew said, his face against his mother's, 'I didn't think Ibsen was joyful.'

'Norway wasn't. Norway was *dire*, in Ibsen's day. Work was a curse and a punishment for sin.' Edie let Matthew go and looked up at him. 'You don't look good at *all*.'

'No.'

'Matt?' she said. 'Matthew?' She took his hand. 'What's happened?'

He glanced down the street. 'Let's find a pub.'

'Are you ill?'

'No,' he said, 'nothing like that.' He moved back towards the pavement, pulling her. 'I'll tell you,' he said, feeling the loosening sensation of relief flowing into his chest, into his head. 'I'll tell you everything.'

Russell went to the preview of a new American play at the Royal Court Theatre, left at the interval and made his way home on a number 19 bus. He had asked Edie to come to the theatre with him, but she had a late rehearsal, she said, and some other commitment that she was vague about but not mysterious in a way that might cause Russell disquiet. There *had* been disquieting moments in the past, to be sure, moments when Edie seemed suddenly over-alert about an actor she was playing opposite or, once at least, a father on the parent–teacher association panel at one of the children's schools. And, if he was honest, Russell had had lunches, and some afternoons, and even a weekend once, when he had been reminded of how powerfully attractive a new personality, a new face and body, can be to even the most faithful of eyes.

It wasn't anxiety about what Edie might be doing that propelled Russell on to his bus before the second half of the play, but more a resurgence of the feeling that was becoming very familiar to him now, a feeling of just wanting Edie to be there, to be with him. He looked out of the bus window at the thronged mid-evening pavements and wondered how he would arrange himself, in his mind and in his feelings, when he reached home and found that Edie wasn't there.

But she was. She was sitting at the kitchen table reading the evening paper with her glasses on and a mug of tea. Beside the paper on the table, where he was not allowed, Arsie was posed like a cat on an Egyptian frieze, elongated and very, very still.

'Bad play?' Edie said, taking her glasses off.

'Wordy,' Russell said. He bent to kiss her. 'Wordy without grasping the subject. You indulge that cat.'

Edie looked at Arsie. He didn't trouble to look back. 'I know.'

'Good rehearsal?'

'Not bad. Lazlo isn't making Osvald bright enough yet.'

Russell went to the fridge and opened the door. 'What about supper?'

'I've had it,' Edie said, 'but there's plenty of ham.'

Russell bent to look into the fridge. He said nonchalantly from inside it, 'Supper *with* anyone?'

'Yes,' Edie said, 'Matthew.'

There was a silence.

'Matthew,' Russell said, without straightening.

'Yes.'

Russell stood up, holding a plate of ham. He put the plate on the table and went across the kitchen to the breadbin. 'How was he?'

'It was awful,' Edie said. 'He's in a terrible state.'

Russell turned round. 'Matthew? Has he lost his job?'

'He's lost Ruth.'

Russell came back to the table. 'Has she thrown him out?'

'No. It's sadder really. He's left her because she wants to buy a flat and he thinks she should and she's chosen this rather glamorous one, and he can't afford it and he hasn't been able to afford their lifestyle anyway, for ages, it turns out, and he doesn't want to hold her back, so he's gone.'

Russell sat down and stared at the ham. 'Matt has left Ruth because he can't afford to buy the flat she wants?'

'Basically, yes.'

He raised his eyes. 'Edie, what's the *matter* with them?'

'With Matt and Ruth?'

'Yes. No. With all of them. With all these children and all they're earning and still can't manage.'

'It isn't them,' Edie said, 'it's now. It's how things are. We got married young because people did and we didn't have any money or furniture because people didn't, but now they do and it's different.'

Russell sighed. 'Does he still love her?'

'I think so.'

'And does she love him?'

'Well, she texts him most days saying so, apparently.'

'I don't get it.'

'It doesn't matter whether you do or not,' Edie said. 'It's how it *is*.'

Russell folded his arms on the table and leaned on them. 'Poor Matt. So it's back to bachelor flats and nosing around clubs for women.'

'Certainly not,' Edie said.

Russell raised his head and looked at her. 'Oh, Edie . . .'

'I can't watch him flounder.'

'He's twenty-eight.'

'That's got nothing to do with anything. He's in trouble and miserable and lost and I can't bear to see it and I've told him he can come home.'

Russell sat back in his chair and crossed his arms on his chest. He said to the ceiling, 'I thought only the royal family continued to live with their parents when adult. Oh, and Italians.'

'His room is there,' Edie said, 'and empty. He'll give us rent.'

'That's not the point, really.'

'I know. You told Rosa.'

Russell shut his eyes.

'You told Rosa,' Edie said, 'that she couldn't come home because you wanted my undivided attention.'

'I didn't quite—'

'Well, that may be what you want, but it isn't what I want. I want my children to know they are wanted and supported.'

'It isn't good for them,' Russell said. 'It isn't good for them or for us. You just don't want to let go.'

Edie brought her fist down on the table. She said furiously, 'You can't let go of being a parent. Not ever. It's the one relationship you're stuck with, besides yourself. It's rubbish this idea that you undermine someone by helping them, that it's good for people to struggle—'

'It is.'

Edie stood up and began to move towards the door. 'God,' she said, 'it's like pushing a bloody elephant upstairs.'

'Where are you going?'

Edie turned in the doorway. 'To Matthew's room,' she said. 'To see what he needs. He's coming on Saturday.'

CHAPTER NINE

THE WEATHER IN CAIRNS, Eliot told his mother, was bloody great. Twenty-five degrees and not a cloud and Ro was going to be a Buddhist.

'A Buddhist?'

'Yeah,' Eliot said. 'She's going to meditation classes.'

'Well,' Vivien said, 'good for her. Are you going too?'

'Nah,' Eliot said, 'I'm helping a mate service his powerboat.'

'You sound so Australian, darling.'

'Yeah. Well.'

Vivien said, 'I'm having dinner with Dad on Saturday. Again.'

'Yeah.'

'Do you know why he's asked me a second time?'

There was a pause and then Eliot said, 'Why shouldn't he?'

'Well, we're separated—'

'So? Don't you want to see Dad?'

'Yes, darling, I do, but'—Vivien gripped the telephone—'but do you know if Dad has a girlfriend just now?'

There was another pause and then Eliot said, 'I've no idea. We don't talk about that, we talk about footie.'

'Of course.'

'Ma,' Eliot said, 'I have to go. I'm meeting someone.'

Vivien looked at her watch. 'How nice. Lovely to hear you, darling. Give my love to Ro.'

'Cheers,' Eliot said. 'Take care.'

Vivien put the telephone down. While talking to Eliot she had drawn a huge pair of parted Roy Lichtenstein lips, with teeth just glimpsed, and a high shine. It was the biggest mouth she'd drawn for ages, taking up half a page. She wondered briefly if it meant anything, and if so, what. Possibly something a bit excitable, louche even, the same sort of thing that had propelled her into buying some pink suede sandals, on impulse. They were rather high, higher than Vivien was used to, and would need a little practice. Before Saturday. Vivien put out a hand and tore the drawing of the big lips hastily off the pad.

Rosa had left a note propped up against the kettle that morning. She'd written that she was meeting a friend for a drink after work and she wasn't sure when she'd be back so not to bother about supper. Then she'd drawn a small sunflower with a smile and added, 'Hope you hadn't planned anything?' Well, Vivien had, of course, because she couldn't help planning. It was one of the elements that Max always wanted to loosen up in her, this propensity to live life in detail before she actually got to it.

She went out of the kitchen and up the stairs to her bedroom, decorated entirely in white during a moment of feeling I-am-a-strong-woman in the aftermath of Max's departure. The new suede sandals were sitting neatly at the end of the bed. Vivien sat down beside them, kicked off her shoes, and bent to buckle them on. Beside her bed, next to a china tray of all her manicure things, the telephone began to ring.

'Are you hoovering?' Edie asked.

'No. Naked, actually.' Vivien lay back on the bed, the telephone to her ear, and thrust one leg upwards to admire her pink sandal.

'You sound happy—'

'I've just spoken to Eliot.'

'Not that kind of happy,' Edie said. 'Who is he?'

Vivien hesitated a moment, then she said, 'Max.'

'No change there then.'

'We had a really good time on Saturday—'

'Did he kiss you?'

'Edie!'

'Did he?'

'No,' Vivien said. 'I haven't been kissed for years.'

'Nor have I.'

'Yes, you have. On stage.'

'That doesn't count and it isn't usually what you'd choose, anyway.'

'Russell kisses you—'

'Yes. But . . .'

'Did you ring,' Vivien said, lowering her leg and raising the other, 'to talk about kissing?'

'No,' Edie said. 'Matt's coming home.'

'What?'

'He's broken up with Ruth and he's miserable and he's coming home.'

Vivien let her leg fall. 'Poor boy. Was it about a flat? Rosa said—'

'I had to shout at Russell,' Edie said. 'He thinks you spoil children if you help them. Or at least, that's what he says he thinks. Do you think I should buy a double bed?'

'Don't you have one?'

'For Matthew!' Edie shouted. 'They all sleep in big beds now. Everyone. Nobody over ten has a single bed.'

'But if Matthew hasn't got Ruth,' Vivien said, 'who will he put in it?'

'Someone else, I hope. Someone who doesn't put her ambition first.'

'I thought you liked Ruth—'

'I did. I do. But I want to kill her for hurting Matthew.'

Vivien turned on her side. She could, from this angle, see herself in the full-length mirror on the back of the door to her bathroom. It wasn't a bad angle, in fact, nice curves of hip and shoulder, good ankles. She said, 'Shall I tell Rosa?'

'No, thank you,' Edie said. 'I'll tell Rosa. I'll ring her at work.'

'She's going out with someone after work—'

'Who?'

'I do not know,' Vivien said in a voice that implied the opposite.

'Vivi—'

'Rosa living here,' Vivien said, 'Matt back with you.' Vivien rearranged her legs at a better angle. 'Poor old Russell,' she said.

Rosa much regretted having asked Lazlo to have a drink with her. She knew she shouldn't have, for the simple reason that she didn't really want to, but there was something about supper the other night, and the Cheryl Smith person flirting with her father, that had compelled her to say, in Cheryl's hearing at the end of the evening, to Lazlo, 'What about a drink on Wednesday?'

He'd hesitated. 'Wednesday?'

'I'm afraid,' Rosa said, 'it's the only night I can manage.'

'You aren't rehearsing,' Cheryl said to Lazlo. 'Not Wednesday.' She glanced at Rosa. 'You could go wild on Wednesday.'

Lazlo nodded. 'Thank you. I'd like it.'

So here she was, in the refurbished bar of a central hotel, sitting on a black leather stool at a tall metal table, waiting for Lazlo. Edie had not heard them make the arrangements, and Rosa had said nothing on the subject. She hoped that Lazlo, despite his puppy-like devotion to Edie, hadn't said anything, either. She wanted to have one drink and leave. After he'd told her he thought she was spoilt, it was difficult to think of him without dislike, but also, rather disconcertingly, without feeling distinctly interested.

She saw Lazlo before he saw her. He was in black, with a brilliant turquoise-blue scarf looped round his neck and, for a moment, she thought that he looked almost attractive. She waved. It took him some time to see her and when he did, he only gave the smallest of smiles.

'I hope you haven't been waiting—'

She indicated her glass. 'I needed a drink.'

He dropped a black canvas rucksack under the metal table. 'Can I get you another?'

'Thanks,' Rosa said. 'Vodka and tonic.'

He nodded and went off to the bar. She wondered if he had enough money to pay for their drinks and then reflected, rather grimly, that she hardly had, either. But Lazlo would be on the minimum Equity wage.

When he came back with her vodka and a bottle of beer, she said, rather shortly, 'Sorry. I should have paid for those.'

'No, you shouldn't.'

'I asked you for a drink.'

He shrugged.

She added, 'And now you'll think I'm even more spoilt.'

He hitched himself on to the stool opposite her and picked up his beer bottle. He said quietly, 'It wasn't about that. I shouldn't have said it. It isn't the kind of thing you ought to say to anyone twenty minutes after meeting them.'

'OK,' Rosa said. She raised her glass. 'Cheers. So what did you mean?'

'Please forget it—'

'I meant not to mention it but now I have and I'd like an answer.'

He hunched forward over the table. He looked weirdly glamorous. Perhaps it was the exoticism of the scarf. It was made of the kind of rough silk that came from somewhere in the Far East. 'I suppose I just thought you—you gave the impression of taking things for granted. Your mother. Your parents. Having a home, somewhere to go to.'

Rosa looked directly at him. 'Haven't you?'

'Not really. Not like that. My father lives in Arizona. My mother married a Russian and they have two children and live in Paris. My sister is a medical student and she lives in hospital accommodation.'

'And where do you live?' Rosa said.

'In a room in Kilburn,' Lazlo said. 'In a house belonging to my sister's ex-boyfriend's grandmother. She charges me almost nothing because she likes having a man in the house. She's panicked about security.'

'Is it awful?'

Lazlo was silent.

'Depressing?' Rosa said.

'Well,' Lazlo said, 'I don't have hang-ups about old people, but this is pretty extreme. She won't ever open the windows.'

Rosa took a swallow of her drink. 'So when this play is on, you'll be travelling from Kilburn to Islington?'

'Lots of theatre people have to live in awkward places.'

'Theatre people,' Rosa said mockingly.

He flushed. 'I *am* one,' he said, 'I'm an actor. So is your mother. I don't know why you feel the need to sneer.'

'I'm not sneering—'

'Well, that's what it sounds like.'

'I am sorry,' Rosa said.

Lazlo said nothing.

'Please,' Rosa said, 'I am truly sorry.'

'I believe in acting,' Lazlo said seriously. 'In—in its radiant energy. In being possessed and passionate, yet still yourself after a performance. I like having chosen something so difficult it makes me display fortitude.'

'Well,' Rosa said, 'I certainly hadn't thought of any of that.'

'You didn't listen to your mother?'

'My mother never said anything like that in all her life.'

'She didn't need to,' Lazlo said vehemently. 'She didn't need to *say* it. If you'd ever taken her acting seriously, you'd have *seen* it.'

Rosa fidgeted with her glass. Rising up in her was a peculiar wish to show herself in a better light. She said slowly, 'Your room in Kilburn.'

'What about it?' He looked irritated.

'Have you told my mother,' Rosa said, 'about how you have to live?'

'**I** hope you'll be comfortable,' Russell said from the doorway.

Matthew was standing by the window of his old bedroom, looking down into the garden. He had his hands in his pockets and the set of his shoulders was not one that Russell could deduce anything from.

He looked at the walls. Edie had not removed a single childhood picture. 'Of course,' Russell said, 'you can change anything you want to. No need to live with Manchester United 1990.'

Matthew said, without turning, 'I don't mind.'

Russell said, 'I am so very sorry about what's happened.'

'Thanks. It's much harder than I thought it would be.' Matthew turned. He looked as if he hadn't slept for days. 'When you go back somewhere, it's not the same—'

'Or perhaps,' Russell said, 'you aren't.'

Matthew looked at the bed. 'I haven't slept in that for seven years.'

Russell moved into the room and put his hands on Matthew's shoulders. 'Poor Matthew. Poor old man.'

Matthew shook his head. 'It's not that I'm not grateful. I just feel such a bloody *failure*.' He looked round the room.

Russell said gently, 'You don't want to be here . . .'

'I thought I did.'

'Maybe it won't be for long. You have a job, after all.'

Matthew nodded. He pulled a face. 'Flat sharing—'

'Perhaps.'

'Hard,' Matthew said, 'to go back to.'

Russell took his hands away. He said, 'Sorry, old son, but we do have to talk about money.'

Matthew looked puzzled. 'Money?'

'Well,' Russell said, 'coming back home as a salaried twenty-eight-year-old isn't the same as living at home as a student.'

Matthew took a step backwards.

'I thought,' Russell said, 'that you and Mum had discussed it?'

'No.'

'Well—'

'I see,' Matthew said, 'of course I do. I was just a bit taken aback that you should mention it even before I'd opened a suitcase.'

Russell sighed. 'Like all awkward topics, I wanted to get it over with.'

'Couldn't you have waited,' Matthew said, slightly desperately, 'until we were having a beer or something?'

Russell sighed again. 'All right,' he said, 'let's postpone the topic until later. Stupid me. As usual.'

Matthew bent to retrieve a chequebook from his briefcase. 'No, Dad. The subject's broached now. Why don't I write you a cheque for the first month? What d'you want?' Matthew looked suddenly rather feverish. 'Two hundred pounds a month? Two hundred and fifty? Three hundred?'

'Don't be—'

'All in?' Matthew almost shouted. 'Two hundred and fifty all in and do my own ironing?'

Russell shut his eyes. 'Stop being so melodramatic and putting me in the wrong.'

'Melodramatic? Couldn't you have waited, knowing how I was feeling, *seeing* how I was feeling?'

Russell opened his eyes. 'Probably,' he said tiredly.

Matthew stooped to find a pen in his briefcase. 'How much do you want? You started this, and it's all gone wrong, so let's finish it and get it over with. How much?'

'You manage,' Russell said, 'to make a perfectly reasonable adult request sound very sordid.'

Matthew sat down on the edge of the bed and opened his chequebook and looked up at his father. 'Dad?'

Russell didn't look at him. 'Two fifty all in, and as you know no ironing is done in this house unless you do it yourself.'

Matthew wrote rapidly and then tore the cheque out of the book. He held it out. 'Here.'

'I didn't want it now. I just wanted to talk about it, raise the subject.' He folded the cheque into his hand. 'Thank you.'

Matthew said nothing. He stood up and watched his father slowly turn and walk out of the room.

'**I**t's Ruth, isn't it?' Kate Ferguson said.

Ruth turned round. She was holding a small melon she had just taken from a pyramid on a market stall.

'I'm Kate,' Kate said. 'You probably don't remember. I'm a friend of Rosa's, Matthew's sister. We met once, ages ago.'

'Oh,' Ruth said. 'Oh, yes. Kate. Sorry, I was sort of concentrating—'

'What are you doing here?' Kate asked. 'I thought you worked in the City?'

Ruth put the melon back in its place on the pyramid. 'I do. But I live here now.' She gestured out towards the edge of the market. She said, with a kind of pride, 'I've got a flat on Bankside.'

Kate hesitated. Something in Ruth's expression and tone was half expecting her to say, 'Wow. Lucky you.' But something else, at the same time, suggested that she knew it was too luxurious to hope for.

Kate put out a hand and briefly touched Ruth's sleeve. 'Actually,' she said, 'Rosa told me. Just a bit.'

Ruth said quickly, 'It's so brilliant here, all this air and views and location. And then, Borough Market on my doorstep—'

'I always shop here on Fridays,' Kate said. 'I leave work early and come here. Goodness knows what I'll do when I can't.'

'Can't?'

'After the baby.'

Ruth looked at the swell under Kate's jacket. 'Oh, congratulations.'

'It's a bit of a surprise,' Kate said. 'We've only been married a minute. I'm rather shell-shocked.' She looked at Ruth's black briefcase. 'Sorry—'

'Why sorry?'

'Not very tactful.'

Ruth said, 'Rosa told you about Matthew and me?'

'Yes.'

'We'll have to see how things work out—'

Kate nodded.

'It's just,' Ruth said in a rush, 'that however enlightened you are, you *both* are, you still seem to be swimming against the norm. If you're a woman earning more than a man.' She glanced at Kate. 'Sorry. I don't know why I said that.'

'It's on your mind,' Kate said, 'like being pregnant's on mine.'

'Will you go back to work?'

'Yes,' Kate said, and then, in a different tone, 'probably.'

'I hope it's easy,' Ruth said earnestly.

'So do I. I'm hopeless at being uncomfortable, never mind in pain—'

'No, I didn't mean that. I didn't mean having the baby. I meant afterwards. I meant I hope it's easy deciding what to do after the baby.'

Kate gave her a smile. 'Thank you.'

'I never knew,' Ruth said, 'that deciding was going to throw up such problems.' She put a hand out and picked up the melon again. 'Why is the only way you learn something the hard way?'

Edie was sitting sideways on a moulded plastic chair in the dimness at the edge of the hall. She had her arms along the back of the chair and had leaned forward to rest her chin on them. About ten feet away, on the small bare stage illuminated by clumsy lights, Pastor Manders and the carpenter, Engstrand, were rehearsing the opening of Act Three. In a minute, she would have to go and join them. In a minute, Mrs Alving would come in from the garden, dazed by calamity, and say, in a voice Edie hadn't quite decided upon yet, 'I can't get him away from the fire.'

The fire, Freddie Cass had explained to Lazlo, was metaphorical as well as actual. The fire that burned the orphanage built in his dead father's name was also the fire that was consuming all the lies that had been told to protect him. Edie could see that Lazlo loved this kind of direction, for he'd come to find Edie afterwards, eyes shining.

'I know what it's about now, it's not just something that's happening, it's something that had to happen, and you don't know it yet, as my mother, because you've always thought you could protect me, by telling lies, by keeping the truth from me.' He gave Edie a quick, fervent hug.

He was sitting on the floor at the side of the stage now, in jeans and a shrunken grey T-shirt, hugging his knees and watching the others. His arms, wound round his knees, looked to Edie like a boy's arms. Whether they were the result of Lazlo's genetic make-up, or of the haphazard way he lived, was uncertain, but they lent a pathos to him that had been uppermost in Edie's mind ever since Rosa had telephoned and said, at the end of a conversation, 'D'you know where Lazlo's living?'

'No,' Edie said, 'why should I? He's rather private about all of that.'

'He lives,' Rosa said, 'in a room in Kilburn in someone's granny's house and she won't open the windows because she's panicked about burglars.'

'Why is he living there?'

'It's all he can afford.'

'What about family?'

'All over the place,' Rosa said, 'and they don't care. He didn't tell me all of this, Mum. I had to get it out of him.'

'And why are you telling me?'

'Because,' Rosa said casually, 'it's the sort of thing you like to know.'

Edie sat up a little straighter and took her gaze off Lazlo's arms. Then she put it back again. She thought of Matthew—unhappy but somehow safe—back in his own bedroom. She thought of Rosa's empty bedroom next to it, and Ben's on the floor below.

Freddie Cass turned towards her from the stage. He didn't, as was his custom, raise his voice. 'Stage left, Edie, please,' he said.

The restaurant Max had chosen to take Vivien to, for dinner, was one she had never been to before. It had a conservatory at the back, which, Max said, was opened up in summer to the paved garden behind and they put up big white Italian umbrellas, and lamps in the trees.

Vivien, walking carefully to the table in her new sandals, decided not to ask how Max knew so much about this restaurant. In the four years they had lived apart, Vivien had been out with two men, neither of whom became more than perfunctory lovers, and Max had had, to her certain knowledge three, and to her sharp suspicion five girlfriends, all younger, and all sexually available and active. Max had never mentioned any of them by name, but Vivien knew that one was an air hostess whom Max had met on a flight back from Chicago and who had subsequently, and annoyingly, engineered a very cheap flight for Eliot to get to Australia. Maybe they'd all been to the restaurant with the conservatory, with Max.

Vivien sank into her chair and looked at Max across the candles.

'Lovely.'

He indicated the menu. 'Have what you want. Have lobster.'

She smiled at him. He wore a pale suit and a strong blue shirt and he looked, Vivien thought, very distinguished. 'I don't like lobster, Max.'

He smiled back. 'Nor you do.'

'What else don't I like?'

He closed his eyes. 'Let me think—'

'Green peppers,' Vivien said. 'Rhubarb. Coriander.'

He opened his eyes. 'Battenberg cake.'

'Battenberg *cake*? You don't even know what it is.'

'I do,' Max said. 'Pink and yellow squares. I bought you some once, on the way up to Scotland. You threw it out of the car window.'

Vivien smiled delightedly. 'You made that up.'

'Never. I remember it as if it was yesterday. I've ordered champagne.'

'Champagne!'

'Why not? We're celebrating, aren't we?'

She looked at him coquettishly. 'Are we? What are we celebrating?'

He winked. 'A little . . . rapprochement, Vivi.'

'*Oh*,' she said, 'is *that* what this is?'

A waiter put a metal champagne bucket on the table between them.

'When did you last drink champagne?'

'Can't remember.'

'Well, it's time you did. It's time you *lived* again a little, Vivi.'

The waiter poured champagne slowly into a tall, thin glass flute and set it ceremoniously in front of Vivien. 'I bet he gives you champagne,' Rosa had said, waving Vivi off. 'I bet you get the works tonight.'

Max raised his glass. 'To—' he said, and stopped.

Vivien waited.

'To Eliot,' Max said.

'Of course,' Vivien said, a fraction too eagerly. She raised her glass, too, and touched Max's with it. 'To Eliot.'

'What about this Ro?'

Vivien made a small face. 'I've never spoken to her.'

'Nor me.'

'She's learning to be a Buddhist.'

'A Buddhist?' Max said. 'Oh, please.'

'But she surfs and drinks beer.'

'All you could ask, really.'

'Now, Max—'

'We'll let it go, shall we,' Max said. 'For now?'

Vivien took a small sip of her champagne. 'And the diving?'

'My feeling is,' Max said, 'to let that go for now too. If he's still doing it, and only it, when he's thirty, we'll fly out and give him a rocket.'

'Aren't you going to see him before he's thirty?'

Max looked at her. 'Any time you're ready, we'll go out and see him.'

Vivien smiled at her champagne glass. 'Oh.'

'Say the word,' Max said.

Vivien leaned back in her chair. She said, looking away across the restaurant, 'What happened to the air hostess?'

'She went back to her airline.'

'And,' Vivien said, feeling a small and happy surge of confidence, 'you didn't replace her?'

'Oh, I tried,' Max said, 'I tried like anything.'

'Should I know about this?'

He put his head on one side. 'Only if you want to be very bored. As bored as I got. What are you going to eat?'

'Guess.'

He looked down at the menu. 'Avocado and red mullet.'

'There,' she said, 'you haven't forgotten.'

'No,' he said, 'I haven't.'

'And you'll have wild mushrooms and guinea fowl.'

'Or duck.'

'Oh, yes, duck. I haven't cooked a duck for four years.'

Max glanced at her over the menu. 'We should rectify that.'

'I cook girls' food now,' Vivien said. 'Rosa's on a diet.'

'I hope you aren't joining her.'

'Well, I thought of it—'

'Don't,' Max said, 'you don't need to. You're—' He stopped and grinned. Then he said, 'What was I going to say, Vivi?'

'I have no idea.'

'What did you *hope* I'd say?'

'Stop it,' Vivien said.

Max leaned forward. 'Actually, I *am* going to say something. I was going to say it later, but I think I'll say it now.' He put the menu down and leaned towards Vivien across the table. 'Things have changed, haven't they, Vivi? I've had a bit of freedom, you've had a bit of time to sort yourself out, Eliot's grown up and gone . . .' He paused and looked at her. 'I was just wondering, Vivi, if you'd let me try again?'

While she was in the shower, Ruth played Mozart. It was a recording of *Don Giovanni*, and she turned it up very loud, so that she could hear it above the water, and the music and the water could combine in a way that would be briefly overwhelming and stop her thinking. Her mother had once said to her that it didn't do to think too much, that you could think yourself out of being able to cope with ordinary life.

Her offer on the flat had been accepted. She had arranged a mortgage through the bank used by her company. And all the time she was involved in these transactions she had felt she was right in proceeding, and had not sensed any diminishment in her excitement. How could it be that one could feel such heartache and such hope at the same time?

Every time she thought of Matthew, which she did constantly, she was invaded by an aching distress. But at the same time, she was certain she couldn't slow her life to accommodate his. He had, in a way, taken quiet charge of their last meeting in the empty flat. He had told her that, even if she withdrew from buying it, the dynamic of their relationship had changed in a way that could not be changed back again.

Ruth turned off the shower and stepped out into the bathroom and a wall of singing. She'd keep it that loud, she thought, until somebody from a neighbouring flat complained. She picked up a towel and wound herself into it, like a sarong, then went barefoot across the smooth, pale wood floor of her sitting room to her desk. She bent over her computer. There was one new message on her email. She sat down in her bath towel and clicked her mouse.

The message was from Laura, to whom she had written four days ago, when, without Matt to talk to, she'd needed both a listening ear and a response. 'Dear Ruth,' it said. 'Just ring him!'

Ruth looked up at the ceiling high above her and closed her eyes.

Just ring him!

CHAPTER TEN

'ARE YOU SURE?' Lazlo said.

Edie pushed the sugar towards him across the café table. 'Oh, yes.'

'But it would be your son's room—'

'Or my daughter's. We've had lots of actors there, over the last few years, on and off—'

'Really?'

'Oh, yes.'

'What about,' Lazlo said, taking two packets of sugar, 'your husband? Have you told him that you were going to offer a room to me?'

Edie watched him tear the sugar packets across and pour the contents into the cushion of milky foam on the top of his coffee.

'Lazlo, dear, I don't need to ask Russell. He is used to actor lodgers.'

'I said tell—'

'I don't need to tell him either. He likes having the house full.'

Lazlo began to stir his coffee. 'I must say, it would be wonderful.'

'Good.'

He looked at her. 'I would try . . . not to be a nuisance.'

'If you were,' Edie said, 'I probably wouldn't notice. My children, with the possible exception of Matthew, are usually a nuisance.' She reached across the table and grasped his wrist. 'We'll like having you, Lazlo. Really.'

He shook his head and gave her a quick glance, and in the course of it, she saw he had tears in his eyes.

'Heavens, Lazlo,' Edie said, laughing. 'Heavens, it's only a *room*.'

The evening paper had two columns advertising rooms and flats to let. They varied in monthly price by several hundred pounds and also in tone of advertisement, some being baldly commercial and some more haphazard, personal offers of flat sharing. Ben was certain that Naomi, even if she could be persuaded to leave her mother's flat, would be adamant about not sharing any accommodation with anyone other than Ben. It had been an eye-opener for Ben, living with Naomi and her mother, to see the fierceness with which privacy and possessions were not just owned, but guarded.

'Feet off my coffee table,' Naomi's mother had said to him on his first evening. 'And the way I like my toilet seat is down.'

Ben had felt little resentment about this. Faced with a rigidly organised kitchen and an expectation of conformity, he had, rather to his surprise, felt more an awed respect. Naomi's mother spoke to him in the same way that she spoke to Naomi after all, and as Naomi plainly thought her mother's requirements were as natural as breathing, Ben was, at least for a while, prepared to pick up his bath towel and replace the ironing board on its specially designated hooks behind the kitchen door. Only once, in his first few weeks, did he say to Naomi, watching her while she made a neat sandwich, 'Has your Mum always been like this?'

Naomi shook her long blonde hair back over her shoulders and said evenly, 'It's how she likes it.'

Living the way you liked, even Ben could see, was what you were entitled to if you owned a house or paid the rent. Indeed, one of the reasons he had left home, besides the consuming desire to spend the nights in the same bed as Naomi, was a strong, if unarticulated, understanding that he wanted to live in a way that didn't coincide with the way his parents were living but, as it was their house, their entitlement in the matter came before his. Living with Naomi's mother was, especially at the beginning, no problem at all because of Naomi herself and because her mother was someone whose palpable industry and independence required—and got—Ben's deference. In addition, and to Ben's abiding and grateful amazement, she seemed to find his presence in her flat and her daughter's bed perfectly natural.

All this, for some time, made Ben amenable to making his large male presence in a small female flat as invisible as possible. Indeed, it was only gradually that he began to feel a sense of being both watched and stifled. Naomi's mother didn't operate by correcting her daughter or her daughter's boyfriend more than once. After that, she took matters into her own hands and effected the changes she wanted, in silence. That morning, the hunt for his boots had ended in discovering them in a plastic carrier bag hanging on a hook under his overcoat.

He'd said nothing to Naomi about her moving out with him. With the newly hatched confidence of having had his older brother recently take his advice, he had decided that the best course of action was to identify some flats, or even rooms in flats, and choose one or two to show her. If he just said to her, 'What about a place of our own?' she'd look at him as if he wasn't in his right mind and say, 'What for?' But if he had a key to a door, and opened it, and showed her the possibilities of a way of living that lay beyond it, she might be persuaded.

'I'll have tomato juice,' Kate said.

Rosa paused on her way to the bar. 'Are you sure? I'm paying—'

'I only half feel like "drink" drink,' Kate said, 'and I don't like the way people look at me when I drink it. Should you be paying?'

'Yes. I got a bonus this month,' Rosa said. 'Slovenia will be overflowing this summer, thanks to me. I can afford to buy you a tomato juice.'

'I don't want you—'

'I do,' Rosa said and went away to the bar.

Kate shrugged off her jacket and pushed her shoes off, under the table. She hadn't told Barney she was meeting Rosa for a drink because, for some reason, Barney had assumed that not having Rosa in their flat meant not having Rosa in their life, either. He maintained that this was not because he didn't like Rosa, but only that he didn't think Rosa was good for Kate: too demanding, he said, too exhausting, too needy.

Rosa came back and put two glasses on the table. Kate's tomato juice had a stick of celery planted in it and a wedge of lemon balanced on the rim. She took the celery out and said, licking tomato juice off her fingers, 'I saw Ruth.'

Rosa looked up from her drink. 'Why did you?'

'It was chance,' Kate said. 'We were both buying fruit in Borough Market. She looked awful. I think she feels everyone disapproves of her.'

'I do,' Rosa said.

Kate leaned back. 'Do you now? For hurting Matthew? Or for being very good at what she does and earning a lot of money?'

Rosa eyed her. 'For hurting Matthew, of course.'

'I don't believe you,' Kate said. 'I think you can't handle her being ambitious.'

'Well, *you* aren't ambitious—'

'Yes, I am,' Kate said. 'I didn't think about it before I got pregnant, but now I know that I don't just like my job, I want it.'

Rosa picked up her drink. 'I don't think I am.'

'And that's fine. What's not fine is thinking badly of poor Ruth because she is. She looked to me like she misses Matthew like anything.'

'Well, "poor Ruth" chose to go ahead with this flat.'

'And he chose—'

'He had to,' Rosa said. 'It was humiliation or get out.'

'But *she* wasn't doing the humiliating,' Kate said. 'Or do you think she should have taken a lesser job and earned less just to make him feel better? How humiliating is that? Don't load all the blame on Ruth just because she's doing what a man would be praised for doing.' She leaned forward again and said, 'What does your mother say?'

'She's thrilled Matt's gone home.'

'Is that all?'

Rosa sighed. 'Of course not. She likes Ruth but she doesn't understand why she's done what she's done. It was always family first with Mum.'

'That's generational.'

'Kate,' Rosa said, 'I thought we were going to have a quiet drink and be pleased to see each other, but all you do is want to argue.'

Kate took a swallow of tomato juice. 'You *need* arguing with. You need jolting and galvanising. You need to stop just drifting along.'

'Oh, shut up,' Rosa said.

'Rose, I'm your *friend*, I'm—'

'Sorted and organised and married and interestingly employed and pregnant and insufferable.'

Kate picked up the stick of celery and jabbed it at Rosa for emphasis. 'When did you last do anything decisive?'

Rosa said, without looking at her, 'Last week. I helped someone I don't really like to find somewhere to live.'

'Oh?'

'An actor. In Mum's company. He's going to rent my room.'

'What?'

'He's going to rent my bedroom. Mum offered it to him. So she's got two bedrooms full now and Dad is not happy.'

Kate stared at her. 'This is *bizarre*. And you living with your aunt—'

'Yes. So don't go on at me about drifting and being hopeless.'

Kate put the celery down and reached across to grasp Rosa's hand. 'Sorry. It's probably hormones,' she said. 'Everything I do at the moment seems to be hormones. I have this urge to get everything sorted.'

Rosa turned her hand over to give Kate's a squeeze, and then took it away. 'I hope it's catching.'

Kate grinned at her. 'What's it like, living with your aunt?'

'Very comfortable and very restricting. It's so funny, she's dating my uncle, who she's separated from. She keeps skipping out on Saturday nights, all kitten heels and chandelier earrings.'

'Does she come into your room and sit on your bed and tell you all about it?'

'No, thank you.'

Kate reached awkwardly behind her, for her jacket. 'I ought to go. Barney's cooking supper and he does quite like to be admired.'

Rosa leaned back, holding her glass. 'There you go,' she said with satisfaction. 'There's always a price to pay.'

The door to Ben's bedroom on the first-floor landing was open. Through it, on the bed, Russell could see a pile of cushions that looked familiar but out of context and a mauve felt elephant and a lampshade made of strings of pink glass beads. He moved closer. On the floor by Ben's bed was an old white rug, appliquéd with animals and flowers, which he recognised as the rug they had given Rosa when she was five.

Russell went out of Ben's room and up the stairs to the top floor. The door to Matthew's room was closed, but the one to Rosa's room, next door, was open. Through it, he could see that although the furniture in Rosa's room hadn't been moved, there was a plaid rug on the bed, new dark-blue shades on the lamps, and the chest of drawers was empty except for a mirror propped against the wall. Edie had taken all the girl she could find out of the room and replaced it with boy. And she had done this for the benefit of someone Russell hardly knew, who was not just homeless but penniless also, so Edie was only asking him to pay forty pounds a week, which had infuriated Matthew—who was their own son and paying almost twice that—as well it might.

Russell walked into Rosa's room and sat down on the edge of the bed. He put his elbows on his knees and leaned forward to stare at the carpet and a new, modern, striped cotton rug that had been laid on it. He had always, he told himself, liked the challenging quality in Edie's nature, he enjoyed the way she wouldn't take any form of rubbish lying down, the way she rose up to argue and rebel. But the more he thought about it, the more he felt that not only was Edie asserting a right to use her house as she pleased, but that she was also making it painfully plain that the last thing she wanted was to be left alone in it with him.

Russell shifted his feet. He couldn't remember when he had started looking forward to being alone with Edie, but it seemed to be a very long time ago. As each of his children left, he had felt an unmistakable pang, but at the same time as those doors were closing, he had had a happy, anticipatory feeling about another one opening; one that led back, or perhaps led on to the relationship that had started it all, the relationship with the short, excitable girl in a cherry-coloured beret who he'd first seen queuing for cinema tickets to see *High Society*.

And if that feeling wasn't reciprocated, if Edie could no longer quite stand the thought of being left alone with him, then at best he was very disappointed and at worst he was very hurt.

He got up, sighing, and went over to the window. The garden, from up here, looked pleasingly controlled and almost cared for. Neither he nor Edie had ever been enthusiastic gardeners but if he was honest, he'd actually indulged in a little fantasy or two about Edie and him being out in the garden together that summer, companionably trimming things or drinking wine under the torn garden umbrella. He shook his head. What had he been thinking of, sad old fool that he was?

He moved slowly back, past Rosa's bed all ready for Lazlo and out onto the landing. At the age of fifty-six, and faced with a situation in his personal life he could neither control nor adjust to, he would devote all the energies he had planned to use for a renewed life with Edie to his work.

When Max finally kissed Vivien, she had been ready for both him and it. The steady succession of dates and the new gravity of his goodbyes had made it absolutely plain to her that when he kissed her it would not be on impulse. And so, when he stopped the car outside her house, and switched off the ignition and turned towards her, she was very excited and quite prepared. The kiss itself was possibly one of the best he had ever given her, being both familiar because of the past and unfamiliar because it hadn't happened for well over four years. She received it with skill and enough response to engage him. Then she got out of the car.

He got out too. 'May I come in?'

Vivien looked up at her house. Rosa's bedroom window, above the front door, was still lit. 'No, Max.'

Max looked up too. 'Vivi—'

She reached out a hand and laid it flat on his chest. 'No, Max.'

He seized her hand in both his. 'But will you think about it?'

'Yes.'

'Promise, Vivi, promise. And I promise it'll be different.'

She disengaged her hand and took a step away. 'I said I'd think about it, Max,' she said, 'and I will. Thank you for a lovely evening,' and then she stepped away from him and crossed her little front garden to the door. When she turned to wave good night he was standing staring after her in a way she had never dared to hope he would again.

Inside the house, Rosa had left the hall light on and a note by the telephone: *Alison rang. Can you do Tues p.m., not Wed, this week?* and underneath: *Will take washing out of machine first thing, promise. X*

Vivien went past the telephone table and down the hall to the kitchen, which Rosa had left approximately tidy in the way Edie always left things tidy. Most nights, she would have spent ten minutes brushing up crumbs and putting stray mugs in the dishwasher, but tonight, in her mood of command and composure, she merely filled a glass with water, switched off the lights and made her way upstairs.

There was a line of light still, under Rosa's door. Vivien hesitated a moment and then knocked.

'Come!' Rosa called. She was sitting up in bed in a pink camisole, reading *Hello!* magazine. Her hair was fanned out over her shoulders.

'You do have lovely hair,' Vivien said.

Rosa smiled at her. 'And you plainly had a lovely evening.'

Vivien hitched her cream wrap over her shoulders and settled on the edge of Rosa's bed, cradling her glass of water.

'Fusion tonight. Sea bass and curried lentils.'

'And champagne?'

'Oh, yes,' Vivien said smiling, 'always champagne.'

Rosa put down the magazine. 'You're costing him a fortune.'

Vivien nodded. 'Oh, I should hope so—'

'Is this payback time now, then?'

'Oh, no,' Vivien said, 'it's just that a man like Max only understands value for money as exactly that.' She looked at the magazine. 'Have you had a nice evening?'

'No,' Rosa said, 'but that's not what I want to talk about. I want to hear about yours.'

Vivien took a savouring swallow of water. She said, artlessly, 'Well, it was just dinner, you know.'

'Just dinner,' Rosa said. 'So why come and tell me about it? You don't usually.'

Vivien looked away across the room as if she were either visualising or remembering something satisfying. 'I think,' she said, still gazing, 'that Max hasn't found the bachelor life all he thought it would be.'

Rosa said nothing.

'Max says that none of those girls of his was prepared to look after him in any way, but at the same time they wanted him to look after them; holidays and meals out and Centre Court tickets at Wimbledon. He said they made it sound like they were *entitled* to be treated like that.'

Rosa leaned back against her pillows. 'How *very* shocking.'

'Well,' Vivien said, 'it's not the way your mother and I were brought up. It wasn't take, take, take, with us. We were brought up to keep house and put food on the table.'

'I thought,' Rosa said slowly, 'that one of the troubles with Max was that he never came home to eat the food you'd put on the table.'

Vivien raised her eyes and looked seriously at Rosa. 'He's changed.'

'I saw him out of the window when he came to collect you, and he looked exactly the same.'

'He's changed,' Vivien said. '*Inside*. He knows how badly he behaved. He knows he exploited me. He knows that almost nobody would have put up with him the way I did.'

Rosa sat up suddenly. 'Oh, Vivi. Oh, Vivi, do be careful.'

Vivien smiled at her. 'He's learned so much in the last four years,' she said. 'He's been so unhappy and he's missed me and our life together so badly.' She let a small, eloquent pause elapse. 'That's why he wants to come and live with me, and try again.'

Lazlo was being very quiet. Lying on his bed against the wall between their bedrooms, Matthew wondered if he was sitting staring into space like a petrified rabbit or earnestly reading the Theban plays. He was a nice enough guy, even if slightly geeky, and obviously pathetically grateful to be in Rosa's room. His pathos made Matthew regret his outburst over money. He shouldn't have done it, he shouldn't have shouted at his father for asking for money or his mother for not asking Lazlo for more.

He shifted a little on his pillow. All those years of living a wall away from Rosa meant that every creak and thump from the other side was familiar. Rosa, of course, was something of a banger and crasher, flinging drawers shut and slamming doors. Lazlo on the other hand made no sound at all, as if elaborately tiptoeing about, closing cupboards with stealth, inching himself on to his bed with his breath held. Matthew lifted his fist and held it up in the dusky late-spring dark. If he swung it sideways, he could thump the wall and imagine Lazlo starting up, gasping, dropping his book. It would be a childish thing to do, of course it would, but perhaps childishness was what descended on you when you found yourself back in your boyhood bedroom after years—yes, years—of living independently.

He lowered his fist and laid his hand across his chest.

'Come back,' Ruth had said the other night. 'Please. Come back.'

She'd been in bed with him, or he with her, whichever, they'd been in her bed—their old joint bed—in her new bedroom, where he'd never intended to be, but where he somehow still was, holding her, with her head where his hand now was, and her saying, 'Please. Come back.'

He'd stroked her hair back from her face, saying nothing. After a while, she raised herself on one elbow and said, 'Don't you love me any more?' and he said, truthfully, 'Of course I do, but that doesn't solve everything,' and she said, 'It does, it *can*,' and he said, tiredly, 'We've been through this. We've been through all this, over and over.'

'But you came tonight,' Ruth said. 'You've made love to me.'

He couldn't say it didn't mean anything because that was neither true nor constructive. Of course going to bed with Ruth was significant, even important, but at the same time he hadn't meant it to happen, hadn't wanted it to happen, and now that it had, he was filled with a dreary desolation. He had only made things worse. He had only made Ruth hope again for something that couldn't happen.

He'd kissed the top of Ruth's head and squeezed her bare shoulders and then began to disengage himself as gently as he could. He'd waited for her to start crying but she hadn't, merely remaining where he'd left her, crumpled and silent, a picture of misery and reproach. Once dressed, he stood in the doorway of the bedroom and wrestled with what he might say. Sorry was pathetic, thank you for dinner was ludicrous, I love you was unkind and dangerous. In the end he simply said, 'Bye,' and went out of the flat and into the lift, and leaned against the wall of it with his eyes closed. How was it possible to get into a position where you kept somehow inflicting pain on someone you loved? When she had rung him and begged—awful, mortifying word, but accurate for how she'd sounded—him to come round for supper, it had seemed more difficult to refuse her than to agree.

From next door came the sound of Lazlo opening his window. Matthew turned on his side and punched his pillow up under his neck. If you couldn't just un-love someone, perhaps you could at least starve that love. He shut his eyes. No calls from now on. No emails. Nothing.

'We have six days,' Freddie Cass said, 'until press night. And I am far from happy with this scene.'

Edie did not look either at Lazlo or at Cheryl. Cheryl was probably, anyway, looking as if any imminent reprimand had nothing to do with her, and Lazlo would be expecting the worst.

'Don't strut, Cheryl,' Freddie Cass said. There was a pause. Then he said, 'Don't bleat, Lazlo.' And then, after another silence, 'Good, Edie.'

'I'm supposed to strut,' Cheryl said, boredly, 'in this scene.'

Freddie ignored her. He moved forward, towards the footlights, and touched Edie on the shoulder as he passed. 'As you were.'

Edie went past Lazlo, upstage to the spot where the door to the garden would be when the set was up. Lazlo caught her eye as she passed him and gave her the briefest of winks. She widened her eyes at him. He looked quite unlike his usual easily wounded self. Perhaps, she thought, picking up the shallow flower basket that Mrs Alving was to bring in from the garden, this new energy and confidence could even be attributable to the simple fact that she had offered breakfast to Lazlo that morning. She'd felt an extraordinary satisfaction, almost a relief, sitting opposite him with her coffee mug, and watching him eat two bowls of cereal and a banana and four slices of toast. It had been so pleasurable that she had turned to Russell, to smile that pleasure at him, and found that he was reading the paper like someone in a pantomime, with the paper held up high, a screen against the outside world.

She reached across and banged the paper with a teaspoon. 'Oy. Rude,' Edie said cheerfully. 'Meals are for conversation.'

Russell moved the paper sideways so that only Edie could see his face. 'Not breakfast.'

Lazlo put his second piece of toast down. 'Sorry,' he said contritely.

Edie smiled at him. 'Not you,' she said, 'him.'

Russell moved the paper back to its original position. 'If you ever marry,' he said, not addressing Lazlo by name, 'you'll discover that all roads of fault and blame lead to "him".'

Edie put her coffee mug down. She looked at Lazlo. 'More toast?'

'No, thank you,' Russell said.

'I wasn't addressing you. You have only had one slice of toast since the dawn of time. Lazlo, more toast?'

He looked longingly at the sliced loaf on the counter. 'Could I?'

Edie stood up. 'Of course you could.'

Russell shook the paper out and folded it with care. 'I'm off.'

Edie, putting bread into the toaster, turned to glance at the clock. 'You're early. You never get in before ten.'

Russell said nothing. He stood up and pushed the newspaper across the table to Lazlo. 'Have a good day.'

'Thank you.'

He looked briefly across the kitchen, at Edie's back. 'See you later.'

She turned and blew him a kiss. He went out of the room, and they could hear him treading heavily up the stairs to the bathroom.

'If it would be easier,' Lazlo said diffidently, 'I could always take breakfast up to my room.'

The toaster gave a small metallic clang and ejected two slices of toast onto the counter. Edie snatched them up and tossed them hastily onto Lazlo's plate. 'So overenthusiastic, that thing. And nonsense. About breakfast, I mean.'

'I don't want to upset anyone.'

Edie looked straight at him. 'You aren't. Russell is fine. Eat your toast.'

He began to butter it. She walked behind his chair, giving him a tiny pat on the shoulder as she did so, and went out of the room and up the stairs to the bathroom. Russell was bent over the basin, brushing his teeth. Edie leaned against the door jamb and crossed her arms.

'I suppose,' she said, 'I could do breakfast in relays. Matthew at seven, you at eight to fit in with your new work schedule, and Lazlo at nine.'

Russell stopped brushing, picked up a wet flannel from the edge of the bath and rubbed vigorously at his face with it. 'Very funny.'

'There's no need,' Edie said, 'to be so unwelcoming. So *rude*. That poor boy is about as intrusive as wallpaper.'

Russell tossed the flannel into the bath. 'It's not him,' he said, 'as well you know.'

'So,' Edie said, 'things don't go according to plan. What you picture as the future doesn't turn out to be the reality of the future. That's *life*.'

Russell turned from the basin and walked past her into their bedroom to find his jacket.

Edie detached herself from the bathroom doorway and went after him. 'Russell?'

'I am not complaining about life,' Russell said, hunting in his jacket pockets for something. 'I'm not objecting to the way things happen, the way things just turn out. What I find so difficult is when changes are made deliberately and obstructively.'

'You mean me asking Lazlo here.'

Russell found his transport pass and transferred it from one pocket to another. 'You could construe it like that.' He sighed. 'You seem to be finding every excuse not to be alone with me.'

Edie gave a small bark of incredulous laughter. 'Really? And who urged me to audition for the Ibsen?'

'That's different. It doesn't involve your personal emotions.'

Edie let a small silence fall, and then she said witheringly, 'How little you know. And you an actors' agent.'

Russell took a step towards her. He looked down at her. 'This is fruitless.' He put his hands on her shoulders. 'I had just hoped that we could move on from what we'd been doing for close on thirty years to something we've never had a chance to do.' He took his hands away. 'I suppose I was hoping to be married. Pure and simple. Just *married*.'

Edie reached out and straightened his jacket collar. 'Maybe we have different ideas about what being married means.'

'Not always—'

She looked up at him. 'But this is now,' she said. 'We're not dealing with always, we're dealing with now. Which means me going downstairs now, and seeing what else I can stuff into that boy.'

Russell made a huge effort. 'Well, he's certainly appreciative.'

'Yes,' Edie said with emphasis, 'he is,' and then she left the room and went down to the kitchen where she found Lazlo putting plates in the dishwasher and Arsie on the table regarding the butter.

Lazlo straightened up as she came in. He was smiling. 'That was so great,' he said. 'I never eat breakfast. I never thought about it.'

Now, looking at him across the stage, whether it was breakfast that was responsible or not, Edie could see that something had turned a corner in Lazlo. When he made his entrance, in five minutes or so, they would all know, Freddie Cass included, that the whole production had moved into another gear.

'**I**s this a bad moment?' Vivien said, into the telephone.

There was silence the other end.

Then Edie said, 'When have you ever considered such a thing?'

'Well, I thought you might have been rehearsing and be tired.'

'I have and I am.'

'Well,' Vivien said, 'maybe I could ring a bit later?'

'Where are you?'

'I'm at home,' Vivien said, 'in my hall, speaking on my landline telephone, sitting on the chair next to my telephone table.'

'You sound really peculiar.'

Vivien craned up so that she could see herself in the mirror on the opposite wall. She touched the back of her hair. 'I don't look it.'

'Oh, good. I look like the wrath of God. These last rehearsals are always completely exhausting. One minute you think you've got the play and the next minute you think you've lost it.'

'That,' Vivien said, 'was really why I was ringing. I was thinking of coming for the first night. I wondered if I could bring Max. I thought Max and I might come together, and maybe bring Rosa.'

There was another silence. 'You're joking.'

Vivien decided to keep her nerve. 'No, not at all. I'd like to come and so would he and we'd like to come together.'

'But why?' Edie demanded. 'Max doesn't know a play from a puppet show and this, Vivi, is *Ibsen*.'

Vivien leaned forward. 'This is different. Max and me. It's all going to be different.'

'Oh God,' Edie said in a resigned voice.

'I want to reintroduce Max to everyone. I want you to stop sniping at him and give him a chance. We're not divorced, you know. He's still my husband. You've known him for twenty-five years.'

'Exactly.'

'Edie,' Vivien said, 'Max has never talked to me the way he's talked recently. He wants to do things my way, he wants to join my life, if I'll let him, rather than try to make me join his, the way he used to.'

'So no more girls and flash cars?'

'No,' Vivien said.

Edie said, in an altered tone, 'D'you think anyone *can* change that much?'

'Oh, yes,' Vivien said, 'I've changed, after all. I'm much stronger than I used to be. I've told Max, Edie. I've told him he can only come back if there really is a change, if certain things just never happen again.'

'Come back?' Edie said, her voice sharpening. 'Is Max suggesting he should come back to the cottage?'

'I told you. I said he wanted to join my life, not the other way round.'

'So Max is moving back into your virgin bower?'

'My bedroom. Yes.'

'And what happens to Rosa, may I ask?'

Vivien began to draw a huge eye on her telephone pad, in profile, with absurdly lavish lashes.

'Actually, that's a bit difficult . . .'

'She can't stay there if Max is there!'

'No,' Vivien said, adding lower lashes to her eye, 'I'm going to ask her to find somewhere else. I'm cooking a special supper for her tonight and I'll tell her then. I'm sure she'll understand. I mean, she's seen it coming. She's been so sweet, waiting up for me and being so interested.'

'Oh, good,' Edie said faintly.

'She's doing so well,' Vivien said. 'She's working hard and—'

'That's enough,' Edie said. 'Rosa is *my* daughter.'

'I'll tell her very gently . . .'

'Frankly,' Edie said, 'you could do it on your knees, and in a whisper, and it still wouldn't alter the fact that you're telling her to go.'

Edie turned her head on the pillow and looked at Russell. He was on his side, face turned towards her, eyes closed. His hair, worn rather long as it always had been, and thank goodness it wasn't thinning, was ruffled. He was breathing neatly and evenly through his nose. His mouth was closed. The clock radio beside their bed showed 2.45 a.m., but even in the half-dark of summer city night-time, Edie could see that really Russell had worn very well, that he hadn't got wizened or paunchy, that he hadn't let himself go. He looked, lying there, like a real person to Edie, like someone you could trust because what you saw you got. He looked, as a man, as a human being, as far away from Vivien's Max as if he'd come from another planet.

He'd always, in fact, been amused by Max. When her brother-in-law had appeared once in a camel-hair overcoat, Russell had been much more good-natured about it than Edie had been. He let her make jokes about second-hand car dealers but he didn't join in. He'd been of the opinion that if this liaison made Vivien happy then that was all that was necessary to know. Sometimes this forbearance had driven Edie nuts.

She reached out a hand and touched one of his. 'Russ.'

He didn't open his eyes. 'Mmm,' he said.

'Are you awake?'

'Mmm.'

She took hold of the hand she had touched. 'Vivien rang today. She's started it all up again with Max.'

Russell opened his eyes. 'Has she?'

'Yes. Big time. Dates and flowers and promises it'll all be different.'

'Well, perhaps it will.'

'You know Max—'

Russell gave a small yawn. He squeezed Edie's hand and then

extracted his own and tucked it under his shoulder. He closed his eyes again. 'Maybe he's changed.'

'Well, I do hope so,' Edie said, 'because she's letting him move back in.'

Russell opened one eye. 'Good luck to her.'

Edie moved her face an inch or two closer to Russell's. 'He'll move back into her cottage. She says that's what she wants.'

'Yes.'

'Russell. *Listen*. Vivien's cottage is where Rosa is living. Rosa is living in Vivien's spare bedroom.'

Russell opened both eyes. 'Oh my God—'

'She's there now,' Edie said. 'She's had supper with Vivien because Vivien was cooking something special in a really weaselly Vivien-ish way before telling her she was throwing her out.'

Russell gave a groan and turned over on to his back.

'I just keep thinking about her,' Edie said. 'I keep picturing her lying in bed there, with Vivi all excited and starry-eyed through the wall, wondering what on earth she's going to do now, where she's going to go.'

Russell said nothing.

'Look,' Edie said, 'I know how you feel. I know it isn't what you want. But I can't bear thinking Rosa's got nowhere to go. I just can't *bear* it.' She paused, and then she said, 'I want to make a move before she feels she has to. I want to tell her she can come home.'

CHAPTER ELEVEN

'ONE SEAT IN THE BACK ROW, please,' Ruth said, 'and as far to one side as possible.'

The young man in the box office, who had clearly been surprised to find Ruth waiting when he opened up, said that there were better seats in the centre of the back, for the same price.

'I know,' Ruth said. She had put on a black bucket hat and sunglasses. 'I'm sure they're better, but the side is where I'd like to sit, please.'

The young man sighed, and slid the ticket towards her. Behind him, on the back wall of the little foyer, was a blown-up grainy poster photograph of Edie and Lazlo, in profile, facing each other.

She picked up the ticket. 'Thank you—'

The young man nodded. Behind her, other people were beginning to open the glass doors from the street; other people who might include Edie's family, and therefore Matthew, and although Ruth was there in order to catch sight of Matthew, she was not at all certain that she could handle his catching sight of her. She went quickly into the auditorium.

It was completely empty. Ruth crept round the back of the stalls and took her seat in the far corner. If Matthew came, he would come with his family, naturally, and they would also, naturally, have seats towards the front. It would not occur to him to look round the small auditorium and notice that there was a young woman giving out elaborate signals of wishing strenuously not to be noticed.

It was no good, she thought, bending her head over the programme, telling herself she shouldn't have come. It wasn't a question of should or shouldn't. It was more a question of desire urgent enough to amount to need. She was sure that just the sight of the back of Matthew's head for two hours, just the knowledge that they were breathing the same air, would replenish the fuel in her emotional tank enough to get her through another few days. Simply to see him might help reassure her that she had, in truth, done nothing wrong, that she was not the reason for his leaving, that she had not failed in some essential quality of womanliness, of femininity.

'I thought,' Laura had emailed from Leeds, 'that Matthew was always so supportive of your career.'

Ruth hadn't replied. Now she felt a prick of incipient tears. She swallowed. No self-pity, she told herself sternly. You've chosen to come here so you'll have to take the consequences. Whatever they are.

'In the seventeenth century,' Russell told Rosa, 'there weren't any theatrical foyers. In fact, I don't think there were any before Garrick. The audience came in off the street and made their way through narrow dark tunnels and then, wham, suddenly emerged into the candlelit glory of the auditorium. Can you imagine?'

Rosa wasn't listening. She was distracted by the fact that her uncle Max had turned up wearing a double-breasted blazer with white jeans, and also that Ben, having said he'd come, and that he'd bring Naomi, was still not there.

'I always liked this theatre,' Russell said.

He looked round. The auditorium was filling up and across the seats he could see several well-known newspaper theatre critics in their usual places, right on the edge, so that they could spring up the moment the curtain came down to file their copy. He waved in a general sort of way.

'There's Nathaniel. And Alistair. So nice of people to come. Halfway to Watford, after all—'

Rosa said suddenly, 'That must be Naomi.'

Russell turned. Ben, in his beanie hat and a denim jacket, was steering a slender girl with spectacular primrose hair through the door from the foyer. She was wearing a tiny dress with sequinned straps.

'Barbie,' Rosa said under her breath.

Russell pushed past her and made his way towards them. He put a hand on Ben's shoulder. 'Old man—'

Ben looked awkward. 'This is Naomi.'

Russell smiled. He took his hand off Ben's shoulder and held it out to Naomi. 'How nice to meet you.'

She transferred her doll-sized handbag from one hand to the other, and put the free hand into Russell's. 'Hi there.' She gave a tiny smile, revealing gappy white teeth. Her skin was flawless.

'It's nice of you to come,' Russell said. 'I'm afraid this isn't a very cheerful play.'

Naomi said, 'We go to musicals at Christmas. My mum likes Elaine Page.'

Rosa appeared at Russell's elbow. She loomed over Naomi.

'This is Rosa,' Ben said, slightly desperately.

Naomi looked her up and down. 'Pleased to meet you.'

'Me too,' Rosa said. She glanced at Ben. 'Glad you made it.'

He shrugged. 'Mum called me.'

'Mum did? *I* called you.'

Ben sighed. He rubbed his hand over his head. 'She rang to ask if I minded you having my room.'

Naomi was watching Rosa with brown eyes that were extremely sharp. 'Well, Ben doesn't need his bedroom now, does he? So you can have it.' She looked up at Ben. 'Can't she?'

'Sure,' Ben said.

Russell gestured for them to sit down. 'Five minutes to curtain-up.'

Rosa looked at Naomi. 'Won't you be cold?'

Ben put an arm round Naomi's smooth narrow shoulders. He said to Rosa, 'She can always have my jacket.'

Rosa said nothing. She watched them turn away from her, Russell shepherding Naomi down the aisle to her seat. She saw Matthew—suited, with a tie—half get up from his seat to greet Naomi, and then Max leap up and bend over her hand like some afternoon-television games-show host, and then she saw them all settle down into their seats, all in a row, couple by couple, and then Matthew, in a seat next to Russell, and then a space left for her, at the end. Her eyes moved back along the row and rested on Vivien.

'No hurry to go, darling,' Vivien had said, putting the largest prawn from the seafood risotto on Rosa's plate. 'Absolutely no hurry. Max can just wait till you're ready to leave.' She'd giggled. 'He can wait.'

Rosa began to walk slowly down the aisle towards her seat. There had been, really, nothing she could say but yes when Edie rang to tell her she'd heard about Vivien and Max and of course Rosa could come home, that day, if she needed to. But, if there had been nothing else to say, that didn't mean that she had said yes with any relief, any thankfulness. A few months ago, I wanted this, she thought, looking at her family. I wanted to go back home. And now I am, all I feel is a failure.

She eased herself into the end seat, next to her father. He was looking straight ahead, at the drawn curtains of the stage, and she could tell, from the look on his face, that he was thinking of nothing but Edie.

Vivien thought that if only Eliot could have been there too—with or without Ro, who was somehow very hard to visualise—she would have been completely happy. As it was, sitting in a darkening theatre with Max on one side of her—his pristine white knee lightly touching hers—and Ben on the other, and all the family beyond Ben, was a pretty good approximation to complete happiness. She was, she told herself, very pleased for Edie that she'd got this part, just as she was very pleased for Edie that she'd managed to fill the house again, and that all the broken bridges were mended. In fact, Vivien thought, it had all turned out really well and everybody had got what they wanted, except that she wished Eliot was not in Australia, but even that was more bearable now that Max had suggested that they fly out for Christmas.

'Our son,' Max had said, speaking of Eliot, the other day. 'Our son.'

Vivien smiled in the darkness. The curtains gave a quiver and parted, slightly unsteadily, to reveal a large garden room with a view of a gloomy fiord visible through the back window. In the doorway to a conservatory beyond stood a working man; opposite him, as if preventing him from coming any further, was a remarkable-looking girl in a maid's uniform.

'Good God,' Max said, in an audible whisper, 'that's never Edie?'

'"**A**h, but you see,"' Edie said, as Mrs Alving, '"here he has his mother. He's a dear good boy, and he still has a soft spot for his mother."'

Matthew shifted a little in his seat. Edie looked impressive really, in a black dress with great full skirts and her hair drawn back under a white lace cap with black ribbons. He'd seen her act before, of course, but not, as far as he could remember, in anything where she wasn't still recognisably his mother.

He could feel that Russell, on his left-hand side, was concentrating with the effort you use when you are willing someone to do well. That concentration, he thought, was typical of his father, typically generous, typically reasonable. Russell, after all, had had plenty to resent Edie for in the last few weeks, but for tonight had managed to put all grudges aside in order to focus on this production working, on Edie achieving something that had nothing to do with relationships or family.

He gave the briefest glance sideways, at his father. He was completely absorbed, his elbows propped on the seat arms, his hands loosely clasped below his chin. Abruptly on stage, Edie became extraordinarily illuminated. She flung out an arm, gesturing towards the open doorway.

'"Listen,"' she said, her voice full of sudden rapture, '"there's Osvald on the stairs! Now we'll think about nothing but him."'

And then Lazlo, in a long pale coat, a hat in one hand and a pipe in the other, stepped dreamily onto the stage and the whole theatre turned to look at him.

Up in the little balcony—only three rows deep and uncomfortably steeply raked—Kate and Barney Ferguson watched the Boyd family rise for the interval.

'I can't move,' Kate said. 'It was enough trouble getting me in here and I'm not trying to get out again until the end.'

'Oughtn't you to go and see them?'

Kate looked down into the stalls. 'Well, you could find Rosa and ask her to come and see *me*.'

Barney stood up. 'I'll just climb my way out and go and find her.'

'Past an ice cream, perhaps?'

'Not that kind of theatre.' Barney bent down and dropped a kiss on her head. 'I like,' he said, 'knowing exactly where you are,' and then he climbed over the seats behind him and made his way down to the foyer, which doubled as a bar during the interval.

Russell was standing at the bar lining up glasses.

Barney touched his arm. 'Evening, sir.'

Russell looked round. He was glowing. 'You must be the last young man on the planet with manners. Isn't she wonderful?'

'Brilliant,' Barney said.

'I mean,' Russell said, starting to riffle through his wallet for notes, 'I knew she could, I knew she had it in her, but she's bringing something else to this. I'm bowled over. And by the boy.'

'Not surprised.'

'Barney,' Rosa said, from behind them.

Barney turned. He said, 'She's wonderful.'

Rosa nodded. 'It's given me quite a turn.'

'Ignorant child,' Russell said affectionately. He turned back to the bar and began to gather up glasses.

Rosa said, 'Where's Kate?'

'Waiting for you. In what passes for the dress circle.'

'Lovely of you to come,' Russell said, over his shoulder. 'Lovely of everyone. Lovely evening. Lovely everything. Wine?'

Rosa took a glass from her father's grip and handed it to Barney. 'I'll go and find Kate.'

'She'd like that. She's wedged.'

Rosa slipped past him and vanished up the stairs. Barney took a sip of his wine. He raised his eyes and looked across the group. Rosa's brother Matthew—pretty successful, from the cut of his suit—was talking to the kind of girl Barney's father would have referred to as a popsie. Barney made his way over to them and stared openly at Naomi. She was like something out of a sweetshop.

Matthew stopped what he was saying and said to Naomi, 'This is Barney. He's married to my sister's best friend.'

'Pleased to meet you,' she said.

'Likewise—'

'Naomi,' Matthew said, 'is Ben's girlfriend.'

'Lucky Ben.'

Naomi didn't smile. She said instead, 'Your wife's pregnant, isn't she?'

'How did you know?'

'I listen,' Naomi said. 'I pay attention. I always did, even at school.'

'More than I ever did.' Barney switched his gaze from Naomi to Matthew and said, 'Your mother is amazing.'

Matthew nodded. He looked a little bright-eyed, as if he was feverish. He also looked a bit gaunt, older, somehow.

Barney smiled and said, 'I have to say, I wouldn't exactly have hurried here, without Kate, but I'm awfully glad I did.'

'It's brilliant,' Naomi said, 'brilliant.' She turned to Matthew. 'You must be so proud of her. If that was my mum up there, I'd be so proud.'

Matthew nodded. 'I just wish everyone could see her.'

'*Everyone*?'

'Well,' Matthew said, swirling the inch of wine left in his glass round and round, 'everyone I know.'

'I'd feel like that,' Naomi said. 'I'd make them all come. I made Ben come.'

Matthew looked sharply at her. 'Did you?'

'Course,' she said. 'Family is family, isn't it?'

'Yes,' Matthew said.

Barney looked at Naomi's shoulders, and the sequins lying over them, like little trails of stars. Then he thought of Kate sitting upstairs with her hands resting on the mound that was their baby. Amazing how different women could be, how different they could become, how—differently they could make you feel about them. He swallowed. 'Better get back.'

'OK,' Matthew said.

Barney glanced at Naomi. 'Nice to meet you.'

She nodded. 'All the best for the baby.'

'Yes,' Matthew said. 'Give my love to Kate. Good of you to come.'

Barney put his wineglass down on the nearest surface and made for the stairs. A young woman was standing a little way up them, staring down into the bar; she was dressed in black, with a hat and sunglasses.

'Penny for them,' Barney said cheerfully, as he went up past her, back to Kate.

'I think,' Edie said, 'I'll just stay downstairs for a bit. I couldn't sleep yet. I'll just stay here and revel.'

Russell, filling his nightly glass of water at the sink, turned the tap off and turned round. 'Would you like me to stay with you?'

She shook her head.

He came across the room to where she was leaning against the cooker, and bent a little, to look into her face. He put the hand not holding the tumbler under her chin. 'Look at me.'

Edie raised her chin an inch. 'You were absolutely wonderful and I am unspeakably proud of you.'

She looked at him, saying nothing.

'And I'm really sorry to have been such a grumpy sod about the children coming back and everything.'

'Forget it.'

'I loved watching their faces,' Russell said. He let go of Edie's chin and straightened up. 'I loved seeing all that amazement and awe. If they'd had thought-bubbles coming out of their thick heads, they'd have read: "This is Mum? My Mum?"'

Edie laughed. 'They're not thick.'

'Only when it comes to seeing you as other than the provider of home comforts. Dear old room service.'

'Not just them,' Edie said, 'guilty of that.'

'I know. I'm sorry. I'm truly sorry about—'

She put a hand up, across his mouth. 'Enough.'

He nodded and she took her hand away. 'I'll be twenty minutes. You go up.'

He leaned forward and kissed her. 'See you in twenty minutes, fantastic Mrs Alving.'

She smiled. 'You can't imagine how it feels.'

'No,' he said, 'I can't, quite. But I can see,' and then he turned and went humming out of the kitchen and Edie could hear him going up the stairs at a run, the way he had when they first had the house.

She looked at the clock on the wall above the dresser. Twenty past one. Arsie was curled up on the nearest kitchen chair. She stepped forward and scooped him up into her arms, then went over to unlock the kitchen door to the garden. Arsie stiffened slightly, alert to the awful possibility of spending the night outside, like any other cat.

'Don't worry,' Edie said, holding him. 'I'm only taking you out for company.'

The air outside was cool and sweet. She walked slowly down the damp dark grass, holding Arsie against her neck and shoulder. There was a wooden bench at the far end of the garden, beside Russell's shed. Edie sat down on it and settled Arsie, rather tensely, in her lap.

Down the far end of the garden, the black outline of the house stood sharply against the reddish sky. Every single window was lit, oblong after oblong of clean yellow light, with a shape moving here and there, Matt perhaps, Lazlo in Rosa's bedroom, Rosa in Ben's, Russell in the bathroom. To look at that, to look at what she was shortly going to return to, and to remember Freddie Cass's arm briefly round her shoulders a couple of hours ago and his unengaged voice saying clearly in her ear, 'Outstanding, Edie. Possibility of West End transfer not a fantasy,' gave her a feeling of such hope and such pleasure and such energy that she could only suppose it was triumph.

Vivien laid three heavy books of fabric samples out on her white bed. The woman who ran the local interior-design shop had said pointedly that, while it was difficult to advise precisely on the changes Vivien was after without seeing the room, she herself thought that a strong neutral colour, such as tobacco or anthracite, often helped to make an all-white room less, well, *bridal*. She suggested plain linen curtains and possibly a valance for the bed, with maybe a dark alpaca throw.

'It's not that I don't like it,' Max had said, lying against a pile of her white broderie anglaise pillows. 'It's just that I don't feel very comfortable in it. It's a beautiful room, doll. I mean it. It's just that it makes me feel a bit out of place.' He grinned at her. 'A bit hairy.'

Vivian was sitting at her dressing table, watching him in her mirror. She turned slowly on the dressing-table stool and crossed her legs. 'I'm not changing the bed.'

He winked. 'I'm not asking you to.'

She waved a hand towards the curtains. 'Maybe those . . .'

Max looked at the curtains. They were heavy white voile, looped up with white cords. They reminded him of the day his sister got confirmed. 'That'd help, doll.'

Vivien stood up. She was wearing satin backless mules he'd bought her and walking in them required concentration. She said, 'What do you suggest instead?'

Max looked at the curtains a bit longer, and then said, 'Velvet would be nice.'

'*Velvet*! You, Max, are stuck in the seventies.'

'I was young then—'

'I know.'

'And in some ways,' Max said, transferring his gaze from the curtains to Vivien's feet, 'I haven't grown up at all.' He grinned again and sat up a little straighter. 'Luckily for you.'

Now, looking at the blank squares of linen laid out on her bed, Vivien tried to recall the warm feeling of acquiescence that had induced her to think of changing her bedroom. Max hadn't actually called it 'our' bedroom but, with his clothes in the cupboards and his aftershave on her bathroom shelf, she knew she had conceded exclusive possession.

Vivien turned her back on the samples and went across the landing to her guest room. Max had given up—'I only want to be with you, Vivi'—his large flat in Barnes and, despite the fact that all his furniture and a lot of his possessions had gone into store, he had still managed to arrive at the cottage in Richmond with an astonishing number of things. Vivien's guest room had vanished, almost completely, under piles of boxes and bags, sliding heaps of clothes on hangers, small mountains of shoes and sports kit. Some of it, Vivien thought, was familiar, but much of it, most of it really, was not. She gave a little shiver of excitement. She had got Max back, certainly, and a lot of him was known of old. But there were other aspects that were changed, new almost. She glanced down at a pair of tan suede driving loafers with studded backs. Vivien had never seen them before. It was, she thought with a little internal skip of pleasure, like having a *lover* in the house.

It had not occurred to Rosa that, in a household of five people, she would ever find herself alone. Yet here she was, six days into being at home again, mooning round the kitchen by herself on a Tuesday evening, watched by Arsie from his position next to the fruit bowl, with a kind of knowing pity. Edie and Lazlo were at the theatre, Russell had gone to a reception somewhere, and Matthew was having dinner with a colleague from work. It wasn't simply that they were all out that was upsetting Rosa, but that no one had seemed to notice that she would be on her own. Of course, it wasn't reasonable to expect a family of working adults to behave like a family of school-aged children, but reasonableness, Rosa realised, was not top of her reaction list just now. She couldn't help resentfully noticing, either, that Edie rather clucked round the boys at breakfast. Did you have to be a boy, then, to get maternal attention? Rosa made an angry lunge for an apple from the fruit bowl.

What added to the sense of disorientation, she decided, was that the kitchen itself was so very much the same. She could remember that blue paint going up on the walls and Edie madly machining the striped curtains on the kitchen table. The dresser was so much a fixture it had almost grown into the wall behind it, the table and chairs she'd known all her life, also the yellow pottery sugar bowl, the mismatched mugs, the Spanish ceramic jar of wooden spoons. Oh, it was all so achingly, deeply familiar, but managed, simultaneously, to be disturbingly alien because the life lived in it had changed. Rosa had been away five years, and in five years this room, this house, this street had stopped, in essence, being her *home*, and turned itself into merely the place where she grew up.

She took her apple and dawdled across the hall to the sitting room. Unlike Vivien, Edie was impervious to crushed cushions, just as she was impervious to piles of old newspapers and magazines. The sitting room looked as if several people had simply walked out and left it at the end of a day. Rosa leaned in the doorway, chewing, and wondered whether anyone would notice if she shook up the sofa cushions and removed discarded papers. Was it, in any case, her sitting room any more? If this was now her parents' house, what level of domestic responsibility would constitute interference? Rosa threw her apple core accurately into the wicker waste-paper basket by the fireplace and took her shoulder away from the doorframe. She turned and began to trudge up the stairs. She had anticipated a small feeling of triumph in occupying Ben's bedroom—the bedroom of the cherished baby, after all, right opposite his parents and significantly larger than either her or Matthew's bedroom on the top floor. But the reality had been rather a disappointment. Ben's room might be larger, but the view wasn't as good as from higher up, and it wasn't as private. Also, the decor was dismal and the curtains ran off the rail with alacrity if drawn without the utmost delicacy.

She went on slowly up the stairs to the top floor. Matthew's bedroom door was closed. Rosa opened it a little and put her head inside. The room looked much as it had always looked, rather careless and impersonal. There was a towel thrown over a chair back and an American thriller by his bed. Rosa closed the door again. Poor Matthew. The room had reeked of stoicism, of someone bearing something painful and inevitable. It had seemed to Rosa more like a cell than a room.

Lazlo's door was half open. Rosa gave the door a push and looked in. Then she moved forward, stepping across a new rug on the floor, noticing a *Ghosts* poster on the wall. Lazlo, she decided, was very tidy. The track suit on his chair was folded, the boots on the floor in a pair, the rug on his bed straight. Rosa went over to the *Ghosts* poster pinned to the wall and examined it. The portrayal of Edie as Mrs Alving gave Rosa a queer little rush of possessiveness, a desire to say loudly to all those people who simply saw her as an actress giving a fine performance, 'Excuse me, but this is *my mother*.' She wasn't used to feeling like this, it wasn't what she expected to feel, it was, in fact, as unbidden a feeling as the one of pure admiration that had overcome her when she saw Lazlo on stage, when she saw the way he and Edie could make her, for a while, utterly believe in something that bore no relation to the people they were in real life. Looking at their two profiles now, pinned up on the wall by Lazlo's bed, Rosa felt herself consumed by a desire to be part of whatever it was they could make between them.

She turned sideways and looked down at the bed. Then she bent and put a hand on it. His bed. *Her* bed. She stood on one leg and then the other and pushed her shoes off. Then she sat down on the side of the bed, swung her legs up sideways and lowered her head onto the pillow.

'Goldilocks,' Rosa said, with a giggle, to the empty room.

Naomi said she didn't want a curry. It then transpired that she didn't want a pizza either, or pasta. Or Chinese. By then they were, for some reason, standing outside Walthamstow Town Hall, and Naomi was facing away from Ben, and staring at the fountain in front of it.

'What then,' Ben said. He had his hand in his pockets.

Naomi raised her eyes from the fountain and gazed instead at the door to the Assembly Hall. 'I'm not really hungry.'

Ben sighed. 'You mean you're pissed off with me.'

Naomi didn't move. 'Course I am. Upsetting my mum like that.'

Ben waited a moment, and then said, 'I didn't upset her. I didn't say anything to her. It was you that upset her.'

'I had to tell her you wanted me to move into a flat with you, didn't I?'

'But you hadn't said yes.'

'I had to tell her I was thinking about it. I had to.' She gave Ben a brief, withering glance. 'I tell her everything.'

Ben gave a gusty sigh. 'You'll have to move out one day. No one lives with their parents for ever. It isn't normal.'

'Are you,' Naomi said sharply, 'calling my mum and me not normal?'

'No, of course not, but you'll get married one day—'

'Not to *you*.' Naomi lifted one bare arm and inspected its immaculate surface. 'I can't leave her. Since Dad went off, it's just been me and her. We've done fine.'

'I know.'

'We've done fine having you there. She's made you welcome.'

Ben said, slightly shamefacedly, 'I know.'

'It's not like your family. I'm all she's got, Ben.'

Ben took off his beanie and scratched his head. 'Don't you want to live with me?'

She gave a tiny shrug. 'Don't know.'

He said, with some energy, 'I thought you liked me.'

Naomi put her arm down again and turned to face him. 'I do. But liking someone isn't the same as living with them. How do I know what it'll be like, living with you? I know what you're like in my place. I don't know what you'd be like in our own, without Mum there.'

He gave an exasperated little laugh. 'Well, how will you ever know if you won't even try?'

Naomi looked down at her white miniskirt, at the toes of her sharp white shoes. 'Why can't we go on as we are?'

Ben rolled his beanie into a tube and beat lightly against his chest with it. 'Because I'm getting a bit cramped in there. I need to live without parents. Without anyone's parents.'

Naomi suddenly looked acutely miserable. 'I can't imagine being without my mum.'

Ben said slowly, 'Could you imagine being without me?'

She stared at him. 'What d'you mean?'

'I mean,' he said, 'that if you can't leave your mum, and I can't stay at yours any more, would you choose your mum?'

'You're a bastard,' Naomi said. 'You're a typical man selfish bastard—'

He took a step forward and put his arms round her.

She put her own arms up and held him off. 'Get off me.'

'I didn't mean it,' Ben said. 'I shouldn't have said that. I shouldn't have asked you to choose. I'm sorry.'

She relaxed a fraction and tipped her smooth fair head against him.

'I'm sorry,' he said again. 'It's only because I want to be alone with you.'

Naomi snuffled faintly against his T-shirt.

'It's got nothing to do with not liking your mum—'

'OK.'

Ben bent his head so that he could see part of her profile.

He said, 'I expect I'm a bit jealous.'

'OK.'

'I'm sorry I started this.'

Naomi looked up. She said in a whisper, 'I don't know what I'll do about Mum.'

Ben looked at her mouth. He tightened his hold. 'Nothing for now.'

It had been a bad audience. From the moment she stepped on stage, Edie could tell that the audience was going to be unhelpful. By the end of the first act, she'd decided that it was not just unhelpful but obnoxious, laughing in all the wrong places, rustling and coughing. She'd wanted to lean over the footlights and suggest they all took themselves off to a nice easy musical instead.

'It's just as well,' she said to Lazlo on the journey home, 'that audiences don't know the power they have. I was rubbish tonight because *they* were rubbish.'

Lazlo didn't argue. He sat hunched on the night bus beside her, staring at the painted metal ceiling. When they reached the house, he didn't go upstairs, as he often did, but trailed into the kitchen behind her and leaned against the cupboards.

There was a note from Russell on the table: *Bed. Fuddled.*

Edie gave a little exclamation and dropped the note in the bin. She went over to the sink to fill the kettle. 'Tea?'

'Actually,' Lazlo said, 'I'm a bit hungry.'

There was a beat, and then Edie said, 'Bread in the bin, eggs in the fridge, fruit in the bowl.'

'Yes,' Lazlo said. 'Sorry.'

She turned to look at him over her shoulder. 'Well?'

He said sheepishly, 'I don't know how to turn the cooker on.'

'Goddammit,' Edie said, hunched theatrically over the kettle. She turned round. '*Can* you scramble eggs?'

'Sort of—'

She regarded him for a moment. Then she said, sighing, 'I suppose there's nobody to blame but myself.' She looked round the kitchen. 'Nobody's cleared up in here, I shouldn't think anybody's straightened the sitting room, I expect everybody has rolled upstairs and into bed—'

'Look,' Lazlo said, 'I'll just have bread and cheese.' He began to move towards the fridge. 'I'll make a sandwich and take it up to my room.'

Edie waited for her customary sandwich-making impulse to take over. It didn't. She shook her head. 'Sorry, Lazlo. I've been really wrong-footed this evening.'

He was laying slices of white bread out on the table. 'It doesn't matter. They were horrible.'

Edie moved two steps to give his shoulder a pat. 'I'm going to watch television. Add rubbish to rubbish. Will you turn the lights out?'

'Of course.'

'Sorry,' Edie said again. Lazlo began to slice cheese. 'Night, night.'

He didn't look up. 'Night.'

Lazlo turned out the kitchen lights and carried his plate of sandwiches and glass of milk across the hall. Edie had not closed the sitting-room door and he could hear the squawk of the television. Arsie was sitting on the stairs, waiting for Edie. He did not acknowledge Lazlo as he went past. The first-floor landing was in dimness. Russell and Edie's bedroom door closed, Rosa's slightly ajar, giving onto a deeper darkness. Lazlo didn't let his imagination stray for one second to the image of Rosa lying asleep eight feet away, her red hair tossed on the pillow.

Matthew had, as usual, considerately left the light on, on the top landing. Lazlo stopped at the foot of the stairs, put down his plate and glass and took his boots off, setting them to one side of the bottom step. Then he picked up his plate and glass again and went silently up the stairs in his socks. Matthew's door, also as usual, was closed. His was open. He bent, in the doorway, to set his glass down and free up one hand for the light switch and, as he stooped, he caught sight of something unusual about his bed. He put the sandwiches down too, and tip-toed a little closer. Rosa, fully dressed in jeans and a T-shirt, which had ridden up to expose a few inches of pale skin, was asleep on his bed.

Lazlo moved quietly over to the wooden chair in the corner where he had hung his bath towel, lifted the towel up and carried it across to drape carefully down Rosa's torso. She didn't stir. Then Lazlo stepped back across the carpet to where he had left his supper, and transferred it to a spot beside the small armchair. He returned to the door to close it until only a narrow line of light fell into the room, and then he sat down in the chair and began, as noiselessly as possible, to eat.

CHAPTER TWELVE

BARNEY'S PARENTS SENT so many lilies to the hospital after their grandson was born that Kate had to ask the nurse on duty to put them outside the door. 'I can't breathe, with them in here . . .'

The nurse, who came from Belfast, said she quite agreed and anyway they reminded her of funerals.

Kate leaned cautiously sideways and peered into the Perspex crib moored beside her bed. The baby, swaddled as neatly and tightly as a chrysalis, slept with newborn absorption.

'I'm pretty overexcited myself.'

The nurse paused, holding the lilies. 'You've every right to be. That's a lovely baby.'

'I'm in love,' Kate said, 'I know I am. I've never felt like this before.'

'Give me babies for love any time,' the nurse said. 'Babies don't let you down. *And* you know they're going to get smarter.'

'You are amazing,' Kate said to the baby. 'You are the most amazing baby there ever was.'

He slept on, wholly committed to his own fierce agenda of survival.

'Well,' the nurse said, 'I think you've a visitor.'

Kate turned awkwardly and looked over her shoulder. Rosa was standing in the doorway, holding a pineapple. She gestured at the vase of lilies in the nurse's hands. 'I thought you might have enough of those.'

Kate abruptly felt rather tearful. She put an unsteady hand out. 'Rosa.'

Rosa put the pineapple down on the end of Kate's bed. 'They're supposed to symbolise hospitality. I thought that might stretch to welcome.'

'Oh, Rosa,' Kate said, sniffing, 'he's so perfect . . .'

Rosa bent and kissed Kate. Then she moved round the bed and bent over the crib. 'Oh my God,' she said, 'he is *minute*.'

'No, he's not, he's huge. He was almost eight pounds.' Kate put a finger out and touched the damp dark spikes of the baby's hair. 'Isn't he wonderful?'

'Yes.'

'I can't believe it. When I'm not snivelling, I just hang over him and breathe him in.'

Rosa reached down to touch his little body. 'Does he cry?'

'Like anything,' Kate said proudly.

'And . . . um, feeding him?'

'Getting better. It's not very easy but I am so determined to do it.'

Rosa straightened up. 'This is all a bit life-changing, isn't it?'

'Telling me.'

'One minute you're a couple pleasing yourselves and the next minute everything's changed for ever.'

Kate was still gazing at the baby. 'I can't believe he wasn't ever not here.'

'Is Barney moonstruck?'

'Completely,' Kate said. 'Bought me an eternity ring—'

'Heavens,' Rosa said, 'how very . . . established.' She sat down on the edge of Kate's bed and looked at her. She said seriously, 'He's very lovely.'

Kate began to cry in earnest. She hunted about blindly for a tissue.

'Here,' Rosa said, holding one out.

'Sorry—'

'What d'you mean, *sorry*? I thought you were supposed to cry.'

Kate blew her nose. 'Talk to me. About the outside world. About something not to do with the baby, something that won't make me cry.'

Rosa looked back at the baby. 'I thought one of the best things about a baby was that you didn't have to think about the outside world.'

Kate blew again. She gave Rosa a nudge. 'Do as you're told.'

'Well,' Rosa said, 'Vivien and Max are playing *Blind Date* and I am—oh God, Kate, something so funny!'

Kate bent back towards the baby. 'What?'

'I went to sleep on Lazlo's bed.'

Kate's head whipped round. 'You *what*?'

'Well, the house was empty and it is my bedroom after all, and I just lay on my bed for a second and next thing I knew it was three in the morning and I was still there and he was asleep beside me on the floor.'

Kate sat bolt upright and winced. 'Ow. *Ow*! What did you *do*?'

'Got up,' Rosa said, 'really stealthily. He'd put a towel over me . . .'

'That was so sweet—'

'So I put it over him and tiptoed downstairs.'

'And next morning?'

Rosa looked away. 'I haven't seen him since.'

'Have you told your mother?'

Rosa turned her head back. 'No. I haven't told anyone.'

Kate screwed her tissue up and put it on her bedside locker. 'When you do see Lazlo again, what will you say?'

'Oh,' Rosa said. 'I'll say don't get any ideas. What else would I say?'

Lazlo was in the bathroom. He had been in the bathroom, Matthew calculated, for twenty-eight minutes. What any man could find to do in a bathroom for twenty-eight minutes was beyond Matthew, especially a man whose life seemed dedicated, in a manner that was unfairly but unquestionably irritating, to being no trouble to anyone. He raised his fist and thumped the panels. 'Hey there!'

There was a pause, and then a slight scuffle and then Lazlo opened the door. He was fully dressed and his eyes looked pink.

He said at once, 'Sorry.'

'You OK?'

Lazlo nodded. He stepped aside so that Matthew could go past him. He didn't even seem to be holding a towel.

Matthew wondered, fleetingly and awkwardly, if he'd been crying.

He said gruffly, 'Got to get to work.'

'Yes,' Lazlo said, 'of course.' He moved away from Matthew across the landing towards the stairs.

Matthew called after him. 'No big deal, you know!'

Lazlo turned briefly and gave a wan smile. Then he began to climb the stairs to the top floor. Matthew shut the bathroom door and locked it. Someone—Rosa probably—had left a towel on the floor and there were red hairs—Rosa definitely—plastered to the side of the basin. The shower curtain—was this the last bathroom in civilisation to have a horrible plastic shower curtain still?—clung to the tiled wall in clammy folds, and the plug to the basin, which Matthew had attached to its chain a dozen times since returning home, had become detached again.

Matthew took off his bathrobe and attempted to hang it behind the door. The hook on the door, never large enough, now bore his father's bathrobe, his mother's cotton kimono—that must be fifteen or twenty years old now—some oriental garment of Rosa's and a large towel mounded on top. The towel rail, never adequate for a family of five in the first place, was draped with a large, drying duvet cover.

Matthew let out an exasperated breath. 'Nowhere in this whole bloody house even to put down a *towel*.'

He dropped his robe and towel on the floor and yanked the shower curtain rattling along the length of the bath. He stepped in and leaned down. He turned the bath taps on and pressed the chrome button that would divert the water through the shower-head. The button sprang out again and ice-cold water deluged Matthew's feet. He swore and pressed again and ice-cold water cascaded onto his back.

Someone thumped on the door.

'Sod off!' Matthew shouted.

'I need a shower,' Edie called.

Matthew turned the taps off and climbed out of the bath. 'There's no hot water—'

'Nonsense.'

Matthew bent and retrieved his towel. He wound it round his waist and unlocked the door. Edie was standing outside in her nightgown and a long purple cardigan.

He said distinctly, 'There is no hot water. I can't have a shower, you can't have a shower. No one can, unless they want it stone cold.'

Edie pushed the sleeves of her cardigan up. 'Who's taken all the water?'

'I don't know,' Matthew said. 'Dad, Rosa, Lazlo—'

Edie peered past Matthew into the bathroom. 'Look at the state of it in there. It's like living in a student flat.'

'Doesn't matter. I'll get a shower at the gym.'

Edie stared at him. 'Are you intending to leave this bathroom looking like this?'

Matthew hesitated, then he said childishly, 'It's not my mess. I keep all my things in my bedroom.'

'But you *use* the bathroom.'

'Of course.'

'You all *use* the bathroom. But none of you seems prepared to pick up so much as a sock.'

Matthew wondered if Lazlo could hear them. 'I pick up my socks, Mum. I'm sure Lazlo picks up his.'

'Don't be so *idiotically* literal, Matthew,' Edie said crossly. She wrapped the edges of her cardigan tightly around her and took a step towards him. 'I am working, in case it's escaped your notice. I am working six nights and two afternoons a week. If this play transfers, I shall be working like that for months. I am also, for some reason, expected to shop and cook and clean for five adults, never mind the laundry. How dare you suggest that lending a hand isn't your responsibility?'

Matthew said, 'It isn't like it used to be. We're paying to live here.'

Edie said with incredulity, 'You mean that absolves you from being obliged to contribute *any*thing except money?'

'No.'

'What then?'

Matthew said desperately, 'Oh get a *cleaner*, then. Get someone to do the ironing. Get the hot water fixed. Stop—stop being such a *martyr*.'

Edie watched him for a moment, then she said sharply, 'Go to your gym, then.'

'It isn't easy,' Matthew said. 'None of this is. It isn't easy for anyone. We're all too old to live like this.'

'Only if you want it to be like a five-star hotel.'

Matthew looked back at the bathroom and felt a wave of rage and hopelessness flood through him. 'I wish,' he said bitterly.

Ruth chose a French sleepsuit for Kate's baby. She took a long time choosing it, mooning along a rack of tiny socks and garments labelled '0–3 mois' in a daze.

In addition to the sleepsuit, she bought Kate a bottle of bath oil and a candle in a glass tumbler. She had seen in a magazine at the hairdresser's a photograph of a mother and a baby in a candlelit bath together, both, naturally, extremely beautiful and deeply contented, and the image had struck Ruth as so completely desirable that it had made her want to cry. She had taken all the presents back to her flat and wrapped them in tissue and ribbons and then sat looking at the package and wondering if she was, in fact, overdoing it for someone she knew as little as she knew Kate. The answer was that yes, she probably was overdoing it. The package sat on the table by the window of her sitting room for almost a week before she had the courage to take it to the hospital and, when she did finally get there, she was told that Mrs Ferguson and the baby had gone home three days ago.

Ruth took the package back to her office and sat it on her desk where she could see it. It felt extremely important that she should get it to Kate, extremely important that she should see Kate, but she—she who was all boldness in her professional life—felt a disconcerting diffidence about telephoning. Supposing Kate was feeding the baby? Supposing Kate didn't recognise her voice? She looked at the baby package again, then she took a deep breath and dialled Kate's number.

It rang and rang and just as she was about to ring off Kate said breathlessly, 'Hello?'

'Kate?'

'Yes.'

'It's . . . Ruth.'

There was a fraction of a pause. Then Kate said, 'Oh, Ruth!'

Ruth swallowed. 'Were you feeding the baby?'

'I wouldn't answer the phone if I was doing that,' Kate said. 'When I'm feeding him, the world goes away. It has to.'

'I was wondering . . . could I . . . could I come and see him?'

'Oh,' Kate said, and then, in a different tone, 'Of course.'

'After work, perhaps?'

'Yes,' Kate said, 'yes. Come after work. What day is it?'

'Thursday.'

'Come on Monday,' Kate said. 'Barney's back early.' She paused and then said, 'It's nice of you to ring.'

'I wanted to,' Ruth said. She looked at the package again. 'I really did.'

Russell intercepted Rosa on the stairs, her arms full of the sheets she had just stripped from her bed.

'Rosa—'

'Yes.'

'I wonder,' Russell said, 'if you could take those to the launderette?'

Rosa stared at him. 'What?'

'Well,' Russell said, 'I think you heard me. In case you didn't, I asked you, sensibly and courteously, if—'

'Dad,' Rosa said, 'I'm going to put these in the machine myself, and then I'm going to take them out of the machine and put them in the dryer and when they are dry I'm going to take them upstairs again and put them back on my bed so that *no* one but me—I repeat, no one—will be inconvenienced by my washing my sheets.'

Russell sighed. 'It isn't that. It isn't your self-sufficiency. It's the number of loads going through the machine.'

'But it's Saturday.'

'Exactly. Two performances for your mother today and everybody's doing their washing and the kitchen is invisible under sheets and shirts.'

'So Mum has sent you—'

'No,' Russell said, 'I just watched her for ten minutes. And I thought she could do with a bit of a break on the laundry front at least.'

Rosa considered. 'So have you told Matthew and Lazlo to take their sheets to the launderette too?'

'Unfortunately,' Russell said, 'Matthew has already put his sheets in, on what I gather is an unacceptably long cycle, and gone out. I am on my way to ask Lazlo the same favour as I'm asking you.'

Rosa looked down at the sheets in her arms.

'I'll ask him,' she said nonchalantly.

Russell looked relieved. 'Thank you.'

'Dad?'

Russell, about to turn to descend the stairs, paused. 'Yes?'

'Why doesn't Mum send all our sheets to the laundry?'

Russell hesitated. Then he simply gave a shrug and started downwards.

Rosa dropped her sheets on the landing and looked upwards. There was no sound from the top floor. She glanced at her watch. Eleven fifteen.

If Lazlo wasn't up he should be: he had a matinée at two thirty. She went firmly up the stairs and banged on Lazlo's door.

There was a small silence and then he said, 'Yes?'

Rosa opened the door. 'Only me.'

Lazlo was sitting in the small armchair, wearing jeans and a black shirt, with a book open on his lap. On the floor beside him was a bowl with a spoon in it and an empty mug.

Rose gestured at the bowl. 'Breakfast?'

Lazlo unfolded himself and stood up. 'I brought it up here. I thought I'd get myself out of the way.'

Rosa came further into the room and sat on the bed. She stretched her arms behind her, and leaned on her hands. 'You're hardly in it.'

Lazlo looked away. He put the book he'd been reading down on the bedside table. Rosa noticed it was a Beckett play. He said, quite firmly, 'I don't know about that. I think it's all too much for your mother. I think it's too much for all of you. I think I'm literally the last straw.'

'No, you're not—'

'It's wearing your mother out,' Lazlo said. 'She should be keeping her energy for acting, not for worrying about whether she's remembered to buy more milk. And I shouldn't be in your room. It's *your* bedroom.'

Rosa looked at the ceiling. 'Oh,' she said, 'that.'

Lazlo said nothing.

She turned her head, very slowly, to look at him. 'I didn't come up here that night because I was missing my room. I came up here because it was trespassing. I came up for a bit of mischief.'

Lazlo gave a quick smile. 'Really?'

'Really. I was fed up with being alone in the house and I was just prowling about.' She sat up straighter and put her hands in her lap. 'You're not displacing me. Promise.'

He said awkwardly, 'It's not just that. It's . . . well, you're a family. I could easily find a room. I'm always finding rooms.'

Rosa stood up. 'Don't go,' she said. 'I like you being here. Don't go.'

From the landing below there was the sound of some disturbance and then Edie's voice came clearly up the stairwell. 'Who left these bloody sheets here? I nearly broke my neck. Rosa? Rosa!'

Rosa put her finger to her lips.

'You'd better go,' Lazlo whispered.

She shook her head.

'Rosa!' Edie yelled.

'I'm not going,' Rosa whispered, 'and nor are you,' and then she stepped right up to him and kissed him on the mouth.

'I don't know why she's coming,' Kate said irritably to Barney. 'Do stop asking. I could hardly tell her not to, could I?'

'I don't know her—'

'Well, I hardly do. But she sounded rather urgent, poor thing, and—'

'Why "poor thing"?'

'She *is* poor thing. Because of Matthew. I expect in her mind she somehow thinks coming to see us and the baby—'

'He's called George.'

'I'm not sure about that. I'm not sure about that at *all*. He's just "the baby" to me because there *is* no other baby as far as I'm concerned.'

Barney pointed to the front of her T-shirt. 'You're leaking.'

Kate looked down. 'Sometimes you are so like your father.'

'No, I'm not,' Barney said. 'My father would never have gone shopping for nipple pads and a breast pump like I did. I only said you were leaking in case you wanted to change before Ruth came.'

The doorbell rang. Kate began to dab at her chest with a tea towel.

'I'll go,' Barney said.

She heard him go down the wooden floor of their small hallway, and then the click of the door being opened.

'Hello!' she heard Barney say, sounding just like his father. 'You must be Ruth.'

They materialised together in the kitchen doorway, Ruth in a black trouser suit carrying a pale blue gift bag frothing with ribbons. She put the bag on the kitchen table.

'Hello, Kate.'

Kate put the tea towel down. 'Nice of you to come—'

'I just brought you and the baby something—'

'Thank you.'

Barney moved behind her and laid the flat of his hand against the fridge door. 'Drink?'

Ruth shook her head. Her hair, Kate observed, was flawlessly cut.

'Go on,' Kate said.

'No. Really no. Thank you. I'd just love a glimpse of the baby.'

'He's called George,' Barney said, taking a bottle of white wine out of the fridge. 'After my father and grandfather.'

Kate smiled at Ruth. 'He isn't,' she said, 'but that needn't trouble you. Come and see him.'

'George,' Barney said comfortably, pouring wine. 'George Barnabas Maxwell Ferguson.'

'All his family do that,' Kate said. 'They all have these great strings of names. Mental.'

Ruth shot a glance at Barney. He looked perfectly composed.

He said happily, picking up his wineglass, 'He's brilliant. You'll see.'

Kate led Ruth across the hallway back towards the front door. The little room beside it was in darkness except for a nightlight lamp shaped like a crouched rabbit. The room smelt of something sweet and new.

'Oh—' Ruth said.

Kate tiptoed across to a handsome cot that stood against the far wall. In it was a carrycot, and in the carrycot the baby slept on his side under a blue knitted blanket stitched with letters of the alphabet.

Ruth stooped forward. '*Oh*,' she said again.

'I know,' Kate said.

Ruth put her hands on to the rail of the cot and bent down towards the baby. 'He's perfect—'

'Yes,' Kate said, 'he is.' She looked at Ruth's tailored dark shoulders dipping into the cot.

'May I . . . may I kiss him?'

'Of course,' Kate said, surprised. 'Go ahead.'

Ruth's sleek dark head went down over the baby's for an instant, and then she raised it, but only a little. Kate looked at her hands on the cot rail. Even in the dimness of the room she could see that her knuckles were white with tension.

'Ruth, are you OK?'

'Yes,' Ruth said. Her voice sounded slightly strangled. 'Yes, I'm fine.'

She straightened up slowly, and then she put the back of one hand up against one cheekbone and then the other.

Kate peered. 'Ruth, you're not OK, you're crying . . .'

Ruth shook her head. 'I'm fine, really.'

Kate waited.

Ruth looked back into the cot. 'He's so lovely.'

'Ruth—'

Ruth turned and looked straight at Kate. A strand of hair had glued itself lightly to her cheek. She gave Kate a small and hopeless smile.

'I'm pregnant,' she said.

Because they cost him nothing and simultaneously made him feel he was achieving something, Lazlo had begun taking long walks in the afternoon, accompanied by Russell's copy of *The Blue Guide to London*. He had walked round Aberdeen Park and Highbury Fields, he had looked at churches and chapels and libraries and prisons, he had followed rivers and canals and handsome Georgian and Victorian terraces. And when he returned, after two or three hours of walking and thinking, he was struck both by how glad he was to be home and by how painfully impermanent that home inevitably was.

What was particularly disconcerting about this state of affairs was that his life was, really, going better than it ever had. He might still be on close to Equity minimum wage because *Ghosts* was hardly a lavish production, but he had had excellent notices, two better-known agents were offering their services, and he was, thanks to Edie and her family, living in the least hand-to-mouth circumstances he had known. Yet an anxiety possessed him about what would happen next. Living as he was, he could visualise the downward slide back to somewhere like Kilburn very easily, and that prospect could reduce him, to his shame, to clinging to the edge of the basin in Edie's bathroom, as he had the other morning, and panicking at the sight of his own frightened face in the mirror above it. What Matthew must have thought, Lazlo couldn't, and daren't, imagine. He was obviously the sort of guy who knew what to do with his inner demons.

Not knowing what to do with his own was one of the reasons, Lazlo was sure, that made him able to play Osvald. Maybe that was also what made him so certain that if he couldn't be an actor then he couldn't be anything. Freddie Cass had said to him that acting wasn't something you wanted to do, it was something you had to do. Lazlo had felt a relief and a gratitude at having his own need sanctioned, but it hadn't, oddly, assuaged the feeling of being an outsider; a person who could only fully engage with other people if he was pretending to be someone else.

Which is why it was so very astonishing to have been kissed by Rosa. At first, he had thought she was teasing him, that kissing him was just a little more of the mischief that had led her to lie on his bed and fall asleep there. But although she had been flirtatious before she kissed him, she was quite different when she stepped back again.

'Typical Rosa—'

'What?'

She'd looked away, pushing her hair back.

She muttered, 'Always blundering in where she's not wanted—'

He'd been in too much of a turmoil even to consider saying, 'You are wanted.' Anyway, what, in fact, did he feel about being kissed by her? What had he felt when he found her lying, quite unselfconsciously, on his bed? He couldn't believe how many walks were occupied in wondering about this; how many miles he seemed able to cover while asking himself if this girl, whom he'd rather dismissed as spoilt and careless and unappreciative, was, appealingly, something of a fellow wanderer.

He'd shaken his head at Rosa. He'd meant her to infer that kissing him wasn't a blunder. She'd put the back of her hand up against her mouth, and then taken it away and said, with a slightly uncertain smile, 'Better go and sort the sheet crisis.'

He'd nodded. He hadn't moved as she went over to the door and hesitated for a moment. He waited for her to turn so that he could at least smile at her, but she didn't.

Lazlo closed his eyes and slumped against the wall. Nil points, he told himself. Nil points to self.

'Look at this diary,' Maeve said.

Russell looked up. Maeve was standing in the doorway between their offices holding up the large cloth-bound book she preferred to use instead of anything more up-to-date.

'You are out,' Maeve said, in the tone of one reprimanding a student about an overdraft, 'every single night this week.'

'Yes.'

'And last week. And four nights next week.'

'Yes. So is Edie.'

Maeve slapped her hand against the diary. 'These are invitations you wouldn't have countenanced accepting six months ago.'

'Probably not.'

'Why,' Maeve said, 'don't you do something worth while, like going to a lecture? Why don't you broaden your horizons?'

Russell reached across his desk for the telephone. 'You mean well,' he said, 'but I have enough to bear without you adding to it.'

'I'm trying to alleviate it—'

Russell was pressing buttons.

'I'm trying,' Maeve said, 'to *help*.'

'Hello?' Russell said into the telephone. 'Hello? Russell Boyd here. I was hoping to speak to Gregory—'

Maeve backed out of Russell's office in time to hear the bell to the street door ring. She pressed the intercom, and on the tiny television screen that filmed whoever was standing outside she saw an unpromising-looking boy in a parka with a knitted hat. The hat leaned nearer the mouthpiece. 'It's Ben.'

'Is it? Take your hat off.'

Ben pulled off his beanie and pushed his face towards the camera. Maeve pressed the door-release buzzer to let him in. He came up the stairs at a slow and heavy trudge.

Maeve met him in the doorway. 'Sorry, dear. You looked like one of those posters for Brixton Academy.'

Ben grinned at her. 'Good.'

'I'm afraid your father's on the phone.'

Ben shrugged. 'I thought we might go out for a beer—'

'Well,' Maeve said, returning briskly behind her desk, 'all he ever does at the moment is go out for beers, so I don't see why one of them shouldn't be with you.'

'OK,' Ben said amiably. He wandered over to his father's office and gestured through the doorway. Russell waved and motioned to his son to sit down. Ben leaned against the door jamb and folded his arms.

Russell said, 'Well, let's be in touch at the end of the week,' and put the phone down. 'Well,' Russell said, loudly enough for Maeve to hear him quite clearly, 'what brings you here?'

It was early still, so the bar was only occupied by a few people left blurrily over from lunch. Russell put his glass and Ben's beer bottle down on a table below an engraved mirror. 'Is this an emergency?'

'Not really.'

'I mean, no phone call, no warning, you just turn up in the office.'

'I just thought I would,' Ben said. 'It just occurred to me. Going to the house would have been such a big deal.'

'Six stops down the line . . .'

Ben sighed. 'Not geography, Dad. Other stuff.'

Russell picked up his glass and took a swallow. 'I don't know why it is, but when any of you children come and seek me out I feel instantly defensive. Have you come to tell me that you and Naomi have broken up?'

'Only sort of—'

'What d'you mean, "sort of"?'

Ben turned his beer bottle round as if he needed to read the label on the back. 'It's just,' he said, 'that we need a bit of space.'

'You *have* broken up.'

'No,' Ben said patiently, 'we haven't. We're going to live together.'

'I thought you were living together.'

'We're going to live together,' Ben said, 'in our own place.'

'Good for you.'

'Yeah. Well.'

'So I suppose you need money for a deposit?'

Ben shook his head. 'We haven't found the place yet. We can't start looking until things are a bit calmer.'

Russell closed his eyes briefly. 'What things?'

Ben said carefully, 'Naomi and her mum have never been apart before. It might take her mum a bit of time to come round to the idea.'

Russell gave Ben a long look. 'Sometimes I get the feeling that I'm living in one of those unfunny family comedy series on television.'

'Why?'

'Because you're going to ask me something to which I'm going to say no and I can write the scenario for both speeches in advance—'

'Dad—'

Russell sighed. 'Ask me anyway.'

'It's hard for Naomi,' Ben said. 'Her dad walked out years ago and it's just been her and her mum.'

'Plus you.'

'She's cool with it,' Ben said. 'It's more me. I want to live like I want to live.' He took a mouthful of beer. 'So I thought I'd give her some space.'

'And come home.'

'Yes.'

'No,' Russell said loudly. 'It's appalling at home, already. There are too many people and too much laundry and too many what you would call "issues". Mum is exhausted. I am—well, never mind what I am. But there is no room for you to come home, Ben, there is no more *energy*.'

'I could,' Ben said calmly, 'sleep on the sofa.'

'No!' Russell said, almost shouting. 'No! The sofa is the last indoor space left.'

'OK, Dad.'

'What?'

'I said,' Ben said calmly, 'OK, Dad. It's OK. I won't come home. I thought it was worth asking. That's all. I'll sleep on Andy's floor.'

'You can't—'

'Why not?'

'Your mother will never forgive me.'

Ben said kindly, 'She won't know.'

Russell stared at him. 'Won't you go straight to her?'

'No. Why should I? It's not a big deal, Dad.'

'I thought it might be.'

'Nope.'

'But I wish you didn't have to sleep on Andy's floor.' Russell gave a faint groan. 'Ben, I'm so sorry. I'm really sorry. And I'm wrong, quite wrong. Mum will kill me. I'll kill myself. Have the sodding sofa. *Have* it.'

Ben stirred uneasily in his chair. 'It's OK, Dad, honest—'

'No!' Russell said almost shouting again. 'I can't turn you away to sleep on the floor, of course I can't. What am I thinking of?' He put a hand out and clasped Ben's arm. 'Come home, Ben. Have the sofa.'

Ben looked at his father's face. Then he smiled. 'Cool, Dad,' he said.

Rosa telephoned Kate to say that she'd been made employee of the month. She had been given a metal badge, like an elaborate medallion on a pin, to wear on her uniform jacket.

'Brilliant!' Kate said. She had the telephone held to one ear and the baby was asleep on her other shoulder. As long as he was on her shoulder, he slept deeply; the moment she transferred him, however gingerly, to the carrycot, he woke up and cried.

'Thank you,' Rosa said.

'Rosa,' Kate said, summoning all the generous energy she could manage, 'this is good! I mean this is progress, real progress. You'll be able to think about your own place again any minute.'

There was a beat and then Rosa said, 'Oh, I don't think so.'

'Why not? Debt?'

'Mmm.'

'D'you mean you're intending to stay at home until you've paid off everything?'

There was another brief pause and then Rosa said, 'Not—entirely just that,' and then she said quickly, 'How's the baby?'

'Asleep. As long as I hold him. It's amazing the things you can do with one hand.'

'Has he got a name yet?'

'No,' Kate said, 'he's called Baby. Barney calls him George.'

'I'll be round soon,' Rosa said, 'or he'll be old enough for school and I'll have missed him.'

'Rosa . . .'

'What?'

'Nothing,' Kate said.

'What nothing? Are you OK?'

'Yes,' Kate said, 'I'm fine. I'm going to ring off now because my arm is aching. Bye bye, star saleswoman.'

'Bye,' Rosa said.

Kate dropped the telephone on to the sofa and collapsed beside it, transferring the baby from her shoulder to her lap. He opened his eyes to check on his surroundings and then, satisfied, closed them again. It was so hard, so abidingly hard not to tell Rosa about Ruth's visit, but Ruth had made Kate promise to tell no one.

'I only told you because you've just had a baby,' Ruth said.

'But you must tell Matthew, if, that is, if it's—'

'Of course it's Matthew's,' Ruth said, 'of course it is. And I will tell him. I will. But nobody must know before he does. Nobody.'

'But,' Kate said pleadingly, 'this is so lonely for you.'

'Yes,' Ruth said.

She had left soon after. She had left before Kate could ask her what she planned to do after she had told Matthew, what she was going to do about her flat, her job, her future.

Very gradually, she eased the baby off her lap and onto the sofa. Then she lay down beside him and put her face as close to his as she could get it. 'You have no idea,' she said, her mouth almost touching his cheek, 'the difference you've made. You have no idea how hard you've made some things, how you've made me feel.'

The baby yawned in his sleep, unclenching one hand in the process.

'I said I'd go back to work,' Kate told him, 'I said I would. I want to. I don't want not to. But I can't. I can't do anything but be with you.'

She put a finger into the baby's hand. He grasped it, never opening his eyes. 'Just don't grow up,' Kate said. 'Just don't get any bigger and then we won't have to do any of it. Either of us.'

'Goodness,' Edie said, 'you still up?'

'Obviously,' Russell said.

She dropped her bag on the kitchen table and took off her jacket. She didn't look at Russell.

'Good tonight?'

'Yes,' she said.

He put his hand on the wine bottle in front of him. 'Drink?'

She nodded. She went over to the sink and ran water into a mug and drank it. Then she came back to the table and sat down, at the opposite end to Russell. He filled a wineglass for her and pushed it a foot along the table. 'Here.'

She didn't move. 'Thanks.'

'What,' Russell said, 'is the matter?'

Edie reached for the wineglass, failed to grasp it, and sat back. 'I'm just so tired.'

'Um.' Russell got up and moved Edie's glass so that she could reach it.

'Thank you.'

Russell looked round the kitchen. He said guardedly, 'I think you should go straight to bed now, and I'll do whatever needs to be done.'

Edie took a gulp of her wine. 'Are they all in?'

'I have no idea.'

'I can't go to bed unless they're all in.'

'Edie—'

'I can't,' Edie said idiotically. 'I never could and I never will be able to.'

Russell closed his eyes. He said under his breath, 'Mad and untrue.'

'What?'

'Nothing.'

'Don't *mutter* at me,' Edie said. 'Don't wait up for me just to *mutter*.'

Russell took a breath. 'What needs doing?'

Edie let out a little yelp of sarcastic laughter. 'It would be quicker to make a list of what doesn't need doing.'

'Look,' Russell said. 'This is worse than when they were at school. This is worse than when they were students. Just stop trying to do everything. Just *stop*. They'll all do more if they know what you want!'

Edie turned her face aside.

'I can't let them.'

'Why not?'

'Because they're poor and broken-hearted and in a mess of one kind or another and it's all my fault.'

'Rubbish,' Russell said vehemently. 'Absolute rubbish. You're behaving like this because you need to justify not wanting to let go.'

Edie put her face down sideways on the table. 'Give me strength.' She said, not moving from the table, 'Why on earth did you stay up if you only want to bawl me out?'

There was a silence. Russell cleared his throat. Edie stared at the cooker and thought how the tiles on the wall behind it needed cleaning.

Then Russell said, 'There's something I have to tell you.'

CHAPTER THIRTEEN

'SHE'S IN RECEPTION,' Blaise said to Matthew.

Matthew was looking determinedly at his screen. He didn't reply.

'She's been there since nine. She says you know she's here.'

'Yes.'

'Matt,' Blaise said, bending down to try and interpose his head between Matthew and the computer screen, 'you can't leave her sitting out there. You can't.'

Matthew said, 'The only way I've been coping with any of this is by not seeing her.' He transferred his gaze from the screen to Blaise. 'D'you know what will happen if I go out to her? She'll ask if we can go and talk and because it'll be a public place and I can't make a scene I'll say yes, and we'll go and have a coffee or something and then she'll start saying that it can work, that she'll do anything I want and I'll say it's too late, because it is, and then she'll cry and I'll feel a complete bastard and say I have to go and I'll get up and come back here and everything will be even worse, yet again, than if I hadn't gone in the first place.'

Blaise straightened up a little. Then he sat on the edge of Matthew's desk and stretched his legs out. 'She says she's just got one thing to tell you and it won't take long.'

'It doesn't matter *what* it is—'

Blaise flung his head up and looked at the ceiling. 'Matt, you don't have a choice. Whatever you feel about her, you were in a relationship and you do have to listen to her, one more time. It's humiliating for her, sitting out there, with people like me, who knew about the two of you, tramping through.'

'Don't *lecture* me,' Matthew hissed. 'Don't *preach* at me.'

Blaise shrugged. 'Leave you to it.' He went back to his desk.

Matthew shot his chair back in towards his desk, counted to fifty and then got up and walked, as nonchalantly as he could manage, across the office towards the reception area.

Ruth, wearing a business suit, was sitting in a black leather armchair, reading a copy of the *Financial Times*. Matthew paused. Ruth glanced up, on cue, and regarded him over her newspaper.

He walked across and stood in front of her. She was wearing a completely inscrutable expression. 'Well, here I am,' he said, lamely.

She folded the newspaper without any particular hurry, laid it on the glass-topped table beside her and stood up. Matthew suddenly felt a little shaky.

'This won't take long,' Ruth said, then she bent and picked up her handbag and her briefcase. She moved past him and began to walk towards the bank of lifts. He turned to follow her, and as he did so it came to him, from some weird reservoir of sheer instinct, exactly what it was that she was going to tell him.

Ben had left a bath towel draped over the back of an armchair. The rest of his possessions, including a duvet and a pillow, were piled behind the sofa, where Arsie had immediately found them and made a nest. It was a neat pile but it wasn't, however you looked at it, a small one. The mere knowledge that it was there made Edie feel rather tearful.

It was awful, really, that Ben should be reduced to sleeping on the sofa in the first place. But what was worse was that Edie's own feelings at

He shifted a little on his pillow. All those years of living a wall away from Rosa meant that every creak and thump from the other side was familiar. Rosa, of course, was something of a banger and crasher, flinging drawers shut and slamming doors. Lazlo on the other hand made no sound at all, as if elaborately tiptoeing about, closing cupboards with stealth, inching himself on to his bed with his breath held. Matthew lifted his fist and held it up in the dusky late-spring dark. If he swung it sideways, he could thump the wall and imagine Lazlo starting up, gasping, dropping his book. It would be a childish thing to do, of course it would, but perhaps childishness was what descended on you when you found yourself back in your boyhood bedroom after years—yes, years—of living independently.

He lowered his fist and laid his hand across his chest.

'Come back,' Ruth had said the other night. 'Please. Come back.'

She'd been in bed with him, or he with her, whichever, they'd been in her bed—their old joint bed—in her new bedroom, where he'd never intended to be, but where he somehow still was, holding her, with her head where his hand now was, and her saying, 'Please. Come back.'

He'd stroked her hair back from her face, saying nothing. After a while, she raised herself on one elbow and said, 'Don't you love me any more?' and he said, truthfully, 'Of course I do, but that doesn't solve everything,' and she said, 'It does, it *can*,' and he said, tiredly, 'We've been through this. We've been through all this, over and over.'

'But you came tonight,' Ruth said. 'You've made love to me.'

He couldn't say it didn't mean anything because that was neither true nor constructive. Of course going to bed with Ruth was significant, even important, but at the same time he hadn't meant it to happen, hadn't wanted it to happen, and now that it had, he was filled with a dreary desolation. He had only made things worse. He had only made Ruth hope again for something that couldn't happen.

He'd kissed the top of Ruth's head and squeezed her bare shoulders and then began to disengage himself as gently as he could. He'd waited for her to start crying but she hadn't, merely remaining where he'd left her, crumpled and silent, a picture of misery and reproach. Once dressed, he stood in the doorway of the bedroom and wrestled with what he might say. Sorry was pathetic, thank you for dinner was ludicrous, I love you was unkind and dangerous. In the end he simply said, 'Bye,' and went out of the flat and into the lift, and leaned against the wall of it with his eyes closed. How was it possible to get into a position where you kept somehow inflicting pain on someone you loved? When she had rung him and begged—awful, mortifying word, but accurate

o unlike the rapture she had
e furious with first. She had
before she was and then at
only been prevented from
forceful intervention.
d. 'Just because you've got
rd of a dressing room, paint-
over her jawline. She didn't
her and looking directly at
versations before a show.'
oment. This hardly suits me
xpression was one of weary
wonderfully kind and I am
ck down. 'Please don't.' She
't.'
can have their rooms back.
re. I wanted it to work. I
way sadly.
ed up her make-up again.
on't go just yet.'
ound somewhere.' Then he
oulder and said in Osvald
Mother, all this time!'
up to touch his briefly and
n't see him again until they
r dynamic seemed to have
more fragile and fevered.
ssessions, fragile was what
ncertain.
l laid on the empty restau
to learn to sleep through

everything I do because he's coming with me everywhere I go. For ever.'

'Even back to work?'

Kate closed her eyes briefly. 'Please don't talk about it.'

'And you intend him to be the first grown man called Baby?'

Kate picked up a menu and studied it. 'He's called Finlay.'

'But you aren't a Scot!'

'Barney's family are Scottish,' Kate said, 'and this baby is called Finlay.'

'And by Barney?'

'Barney calls him George. He tells everyone he's called George. He told Ruth—'

'Ruth?'

Kate took a sharp intake of breath. Then she said, 'What day is it?'

'What does that matter?'

'What day is it?'

'Thursday,' Rosa said. 'Kate—'

Kate said hurriedly, 'That's OK then. She'll have told him by now.'

Rosa twitched the menu out of Kate's hands. 'Tell me.'

Kate put her hands on the table. 'Ruth came to see us last week. To see the baby. Bringing one of those incredibly expensive baby suits—'

'Go *on*.'

'And she seemed rather agitated and wound up and she cried when she saw Finlay and I asked her what the matter was and—'

'She's pregnant,' Rosa said.

Kate regarded her. 'Yes.'

'Why didn't you *tell* me?'

'I couldn't. She made me promise. Until she told Matthew.'

'When was she telling Matthew?'

'Early this week.'

Rosa looked away. 'I haven't seen Matthew. We live in the same house and, apart from hearing him thumping about over my head, we might as well not be.' She stopped and then she said, in a different voice, 'Poor Matt. He's been so down—'

Kate leaned forward. 'What'll this do?'

Rosa swung her head back to look at Kate. 'I don't know.'

'You'd think,' Kate said, 'in this day and age, we could at least get contraception right, wouldn't you? First me, now Ruth . . .'

'Yes.' Rosa leaned sideways and looked down at the baby. 'Ruth of all people . . . I wonder if Mum knows?'

'What'll she say?'

Rosa put out a hand and laid it on the baby. 'Can't tell. She's all over the place at the moment. It's—well, it's a nightmare at home.' She straightened up, and then said, with a smile, 'But rather interesting, too.'

Kate waited.

Rosa went on smiling privately to herself.

Kate said crossly, 'Well, go on. Something happening? Between you and Lazlo?'

'Not exactly, but I'd quite like it to.'

'I'm surprised. I thought he was geeky.'

'He is rather. But—' She stopped. 'Kate, what about Matthew? Once I'd have rushed round to Dad's office and rung Mum and generally gone into overdrive. But I don't want to now. I don't remotely feel like it.'

'What do you feel then?'

'Sad,' Rosa said. She looked down at Finlay again. 'Yes. Sad. Sad that if it's a baby, it had to be this way.'

The afternoon in the bookshop seemed to Vivien to be taking an unusually long time. It was the end of summer after all, so customers weren't coming in for those optimistic stacks of paperbacks to take on holiday but, all the same, the few people who did come in seemed to be passing time rather than buying a book and Vivien watched them with irritation as they drifted about, fingering books they would never buy.

She had taken up her position next to the birthday cards. The card rack gave her a good view of the shop, which contained, at that moment, a young mother with a toddler in a buggy looking at board books, and a man in a faded gingham shirt browsing in biography.

It was not the sort of shirt, Vivien reflected, that Max would wear. If Max wore gingham at all, it would be very new and either navy blue or pale pink. Most of those shirts had been acquired in that peculiar space of time when she had been excluded from knowing any details of his personal life. And in those four years, Max had, sartorially speaking, started again. His wardrobe had changed and Vivien found it was very difficult to launder with equanimity garments that had plainly been to exotic places with women who were not her.

But then, Max was being very careful not to allude to his 'bachelor' days. He'd been to Jersey on business the week before, staying in a hotel he'd stayed at previously and, Vivien suspected, not alone, and had arrived home a night early, claiming that the whole place was depressing and all he wanted was to be home again.

'Bad memories?' Vivien said, putting a glass of whisky in front of him.

He blew her a kiss. 'Horrible,' he said.

The man in the gingham shirt approached the till with a large single-volume life of Napoleon. 'Please,' he said, over his shoulder.

Vivien slipped the card she was holding into a slot and hurried across. The man, staring dreamily into the space behind the till, was holding out his credit card. As she reached to take it, her mobile phone, in her handbag under the counter, began to ring.

'I'll ignore that,' she said brightly.

The man nodded. He watched her run his card briskly through the machine. Then he bent and signed his name with elaborate care. Vivien watched him leave the shop, and then she seized her bag and rummaged in it for her telephone.

The caller had been Eliot. What was Eliot doing, ringing at five thirty on an Australian morning? Vivien dialled his number rapidly.

'Hi, Ma,' Eliot said.

'Are you all right?'

There was a pause and then Eliot said, 'I'm great, Ma. Why?'

'It's five thirty in the morning where you are. Why are you awake at five thirty? Why are you calling me Ma?'

'It's a beaut morning,' Eliot said reasonably. 'We're going to the beach.'

'So you rang to tell me it's a lovely day?'

'No,' Eliot said, 'I rang because Dad rang me yesterday and I'd forget if I left it.'

The young mother pushed her buggy slowly past Vivien towards the door. 'What,' Vivien said more loudly when the shop was empty, 'what would you forget?'

'That it doesn't matter to Ro and me that you can't come for Christmas. We're going to Bali. We've got cheap flights. So it doesn't matter.'

Vivien perched on Alison's stool. 'You said Dad rang you?'

'Yeah. Dad said he thought you'd be a bit upset so I thought if I rang you and said we wouldn't be here anyway you'd feel better.'

'And Dad said we couldn't come for Christmas after all?'

'Yeah.'

'Did—did he say why?'

'You should know,' Eliot said. 'Work or something.'

'But as I didn't know . . .'

There was another silence and Vivien said, with an effort, 'How lovely. Going to Bali.'

'Yeah,' Eliot said, 'we'd like a break.' In the background, on a sunny blue morning in Cairns, a girl's voice said something Vivien couldn't hear. Eliot said, 'Mum? Gotta go.'

'Yes, darling.'

'You take care.'

'Yes,' Vivien said. 'Yes.'

The shop door opened and the man in the gingham shirt came in again holding the bag with the book in it.

'Thank you for ringing,' Vivien said. 'That was very—thoughtful.'

The man came slowly up to the counter and laid the bag on it. 'I'm afraid,' he said, staring past Vivien, 'I'm afraid I've changed my mind.'

Maeve paused in the doorway to Russell's office. She was carrying a takeaway beaker of coffee and a complicated document from their accountant, flagged with little yellow stickers. Russell was standing in his dormer window, hands in pockets, staring out.

'Room service,' Maeve said. She put the coffee down on his desk.

Russell sighed. Then he turned round completely and lowered himself into his desk chair as if he was convalescent.

Maeve laid the folder from the accountant down in front of him. 'Three signatures. I've marked where.'

Russell glanced at her, then he slowly reached to pick up his pen.

'After all these years,' Maeve said, 'do I still have to tell you that you should never sign anything you haven't read and understood?'

Russell put his pen down.

'The fight's gone out of you,' Maeve said. 'Hasn't it?'

He said, staring at the document in front of him, 'I'm just tired.'

'You've been tired for weeks,' Maeve said. 'You've been out all hours at things a tinker wouldn't trouble himself with, and your house isn't your own, and nor is your wife and you can't get up the energy to lick a stamp. Your present circumstances are not conducive to your health and well-being. What are you trying to prove?'

There was a pause and then Russell said, 'I was trying to fill a gap.'

'Well,' Maeve said, 'there you have it.'

'And the gap is still there.'

'Tell her.'

'I can't,' Russell said.

'Why not?'

He looked up at her, his face slightly sideways. 'Because she's got a gap of her own. One she'd never thought she'd have.'

'Oh,' Maeve said, 'those children—'

'No,' Russell said. He picked his pen up again and pulled the folder towards him. 'No, not the children. Work.'

'I was going to tell you, doll,' Max said. 'Cross my heart.'

Vivien sighed. Max had been an hour later home than he had promised and she had spent that hour vowing that she would not, the moment he walked through the door, confront him about not going to Australia. And then she had heard the front door slam and Max's quick steps coming down the hall and the minute they were in the kitchen she'd spun round from the cooker and said, 'Eliot rang today.'

Max had taken a pace backwards. He'd always done that, when attacked, as if physically retreating before gunfire, and it annoyed her quite as much as it always had done.

He then put his hands up, as if surrendering. 'How was he?'

'Don't,' Vivien said. She was holding a spoon coated with sauce.

'Don't what, honey?'

'Don't,' Vivien shouted, 'pretend you don't know!' She turned back to the cooker. 'Ringing Eliot about something that concerns *me* isn't just something that slips your mind.'

Behind her back, Max closed his eyes for a moment. Then he opened them and said, 'The thing is, Vivi, I didn't know how to tell you.'

Vivien didn't turn. 'Tell me what?'

'That—oh hell, this is so embarrassing. It's money, doll. I'm really sorry, but I'm afraid this isn't the year for going to Australia. I'm so ashamed. I'm so ashamed to tell you that there just isn't the money.'

Vivien tasted her sauce and reached for the salt.

Max came and stood beside her and seized her outstretched arm. 'I'm so sorry, Vivi. I shouldn't have got your hopes up.'

Vivien removed her arm from Max's grasp. 'You're not running the flat. Your expenses have halved. What d'you mean, there isn't the money?'

Max drooped. 'Sorry, sweetheart. Honour bright, it's not there.'

Vivien said unsteadily, 'You promised me.' She put the saucepan to the side of the cooker and turned out the gas.

'Look here,' Max said, 'we'll go in the spring.'

Vivien looked at him. 'Where's the money gone?'

He spread his hands. 'Maybe it wasn't there, doll, maybe I didn't want you to think I couldn't give you everything you wanted.' He tried a smile. 'Maybe I was just being a bit over-optimistic. You know me.'

'Yes,' Vivien said. She took a step nearer and when her face was only a foot from his, she said loudly, 'Liar!'

'Now wait a second, Vivi—'

'Liar!' she said. 'Liar! Just like you always were!'

'Please, doll—'

'Promises!' Vivien shouted. 'Promises, to get what you wanted! There never was the money to go and see Eliot, was there? Or if there was, you've spent it, haven't you? You've gone into some stupid venture—'

'No!'

'Then you're paying off debts. Aren't you? Who is she? Who's the tart you're paying to keep quiet?'

Max reached out and gripped her upper arms. 'Vivien, darling, don't. Please don't do this! This is just like the bad old days—'

'Yes!'

'There's nothing to get steamed up about,' Max said. 'Nothing.'

'Then why did you ring Eliot first?'

'Well, I—'

'You rang him first,' Vivien said, 'so that I couldn't talk you out of it. I bet you bought his flights to Bali, I bet you did that because you don't want to spend all that money going to Australia with me!'

'Nonsense—'

Vivien wrenched herself free. 'I sound like I used to,' she screamed, 'because you sound like you used to. Exactly like!'

'I didn't buy those flights to Bali—'

Vivien glared at him. 'Liar!'

'Don't keep calling me that.'

She spun round and stormed across the kitchen. In the doorway, she paused, her hand on the knob, and then she said furiously, 'I wouldn't have to, if you weren't!' and crashed the door shut behind her.

Matthew's computer case lay in the hall. As far as Rosa could tell, he was the only one at home. The kitchen and sitting room were disordered but empty, and the doors to both first-floor bedrooms were open. Rosa looked upwards for a minute, and then made her way back downstairs to the kitchen.

It didn't look as if anyone had had supper. It didn't look, in fact, as if anyone had done anything in the kitchen that day except have breakfast in a scattered sort of way and then leave in a hurry.

Rosa ran water into the kettle and switched it on. Then she assembled a cafetière and two mugs and a packet of digestive biscuits on a tray. She added Edie's dusty bottle of cooking brandy and two pink Moroccan tea glasses. When the kettle boiled, she made coffee in the cafetière, took a plastic bottle of milk out of the fridge and carried the tray out of the kitchen and up the stairs.

There was silence on the top landing and no line of light under Matthew's door. Rosa stooped and set the tray down. Then she tapped.

'Matt?'

Silence.

Rosa turned the handle very slowly and opened the door. Matthew hadn't pulled the curtains and the queer glow from the night-city sky illuminated the room enough for Rosa to see that he was sitting, fully dressed, in a small armchair. 'Matt,' Rosa said, 'are you OK?'

He turned his head. In the dimness she couldn't make out if his eyes were shining or tearful.

'Yes,' he said. '*Yes*.'

'**W**hy the silence?' Laura emailed from Leeds. 'What's happening? Is it something I said?'

'No,' Ruth typed rapidly. 'Nothing to do with you, don't worry.'

She took her hands off the keyboard and laid them in her lap. It was that time of the day in the office when most people had gone home, taking the possibility of interruption and urgency with them. She could, she thought, answer all the emails from America, or she could, if she chose, leave responding until the morning when the Americans would still be asleep, and concentrate instead on the fact that the last thing Matthew had said to her when they parted was, 'I'll ring you.'

He hadn't, but she wasn't anxious that he wouldn't. She had, in almost a single second, shed the anxiety that had been such a burden for so long the moment she had realised he was crying. She'd been so tense about telling him about the baby, so braced for rejection that, when the words were out and he said nothing, it took her some little time to realise that he was crying. She'd put a tentative hand out towards him but he'd shaken his head and grabbed handfuls of tiny napkins out of the holder on the café table and scrubbed at his face with them.

Ruth said, immediately regretting it, 'You're not angry?'

He moved his head again. 'Of course not—'

'I thought,' she said, 'that you might think you'd been very unlucky.'

'No. No—'

She gave a little laugh. 'I did wonder if I'd been unlucky.'

He stopped mopping his face. 'Don't you want a baby?'

She stared down at the tabletop. 'I don't know. I think I want—your baby. But it wasn't what I planned.'

He said, a little more sharply, 'Aren't you pleased?'

She hesitated.

He said, insistently, 'Aren't you pleased, that you *can* be pregnant?'

'Yes, I suppose—'

'I think,' Matthew said, leaning forward, sniffing, 'I think it's wonderful to get pregnant. I think it's amazing to make a baby.'

She said, 'It wasn't very wonderful alone in the bathroom looking at that little blue line. And it isn't very wonderful not knowing what will happen. Not—knowing how you feel.'

Matthew pointed to his face. 'Look at me. It's just knocked me out. This news.'

'Yes.'

He looked at her. Then he said, 'It's wonderful, you—you're wonderful,' and he picked up her nearest hand and kissed it and returned it to her as if he was afraid of becoming responsible for it.

When she and Matthew first met, Ruth reflected now, staring unseeingly at her half-finished email to Laura, Matthew had often told her she was wonderful. Her hair was wonderful, and her body, and her laugh and her driving and her taste in music. She was wonderful to him for what she was, for the package of a person that seemed to him desirable enough to warrant persistent and energetic pursuit. But, sitting at that café table with him and listening to him tell her she was wonderful, it had come to her, with a kind of glow, that she seemed wonderful to him at last for something she had done, rather than something she was. She couldn't remember if he had ever looked at her professional efforts and accomplishments with the respect and approval he seemed all too ready to accord to her now.

She couldn't, of course, blame Matthew for withholding admiration in the past. When she had fallen in love with him, and the discrepancy in their earnings inevitably dictated the mechanisms of their life together, she had almost unconsciously played down her achievements, withdrawn all visible evidence of her paying power behind a barrier of standing orders and direct debits. It was only when this curiously primitive need to own her own flat expanded to become something she could not give up that she confronted him—no, both of them—with the bald fact that she did not want him to hold her back.

And the consequence of that determination to buy the flat was that she had been made to feel—or, she thought truthfully, just found herself feeling—that in behaving in a way that was not automatically deferential she had surrendered the chief defining quality of femininity, that of being the giver. Essential womanliness, that warmth and tenderness and loyalty that makes girls conventionally desirable, was, apparently, something that Ruth had turned her back on. She had acted with all the decisive independence that would have been so much applauded in a man, and felt her very sexuality had been assailed in consequence.

And now, look at her. *Look* at her. Deflected into carelessness about contraception by the urgency of her own need not to seem some unattractive freak, she was pregnant. She was in, by mistake, the most supremely female condition she possibly could be. And the news had touched Matthew emotionally in a way she would never have predicted, a way she was not even sure she felt herself. And that reaction meant that he would now do what she had longed for him to do: ring her.

When he did, he would want to make plans and, as yet, she wasn't sure what she wanted, how she saw the way ahead. What was so extraordinary, especially given the fact that babies had not even featured near the bottom of her agenda up to now, was that the painful loneliness she had felt since she and Matthew parted seemed to have subsided. She laid a hand across her flat stomach. Perhaps she now, oddly enough, held all the cards. She put both her hands on the keyboard.

'I am,' she wrote formally to Laura, 'very well indeed.'

Vivien was lying on her bed when the telephone rang. She was lying there because she had planned to lie there anyway, to rest before Max took her to have dinner with a new client whom he said he wanted her to impress. So, when he rang and said that he was mortified but the client wanted to have dinner alone with Max because it was strictly business he wanted to discuss, Vivien had decided to go to bed anyway even if for different reasons.

'I don't know what to say, doll,' Max had said. 'But this one could be quite a big one, and you know how things are with me just now. A big one could make all the difference.'

Vivien, sitting by her telephone in the hall, said nothing. She felt herself invaded, drawn back by the Vivien of the past, the Vivien who had stopped shrieking at Max and had taken to stonewalling him with silence.

'Vivi?' Max said. 'Darling?'

'Bye,' Vivien said. 'Hope it works,' and then she put the telephone down and went upstairs to her bedroom and kicked her shoes off. She settled herself on the bed with angry little twitches, and looked at the dress hanging on the cornice of her wardrobe. It was layered chiffon, printed in grey and white. She had been going to wear it that evening.

The telephone on her bedside table began to ring. She looked at it thoughtfully. She let it ring six times and then picked up the receiver.

'Vivi?' Edie said.

Vivien shut her eyes tightly for a second. 'Why aren't you at the theatre? Don't you have matinées on Saturday afternoons?'

Edie said deliberately, spacing the words out, 'I have a headache.'

Vivien made a sympathetic noise. 'But you never have headaches.'

'I have one now.'

'You should take HRT. You should just admit your age and—'

'I'm just tired,' Edie said loudly. 'I didn't ring up to be lectured!'

There was a pause and then Vivien said, 'Why did you ring up then?'

'I was lying on my bed,' Edie said, 'and I wanted to talk to someone.'

'So I'll do.'

'Yes,' Edie said, 'you'll do. How are you?'

'Fine.'

'Ironing Max's Jermyn Street shirts and concocting a seduction supper and planning your trip to Australia—'

'We aren't going to Australia.'

'Vivi! Why *not?*'

'Max says,' Vivien said staring towards the window, 'he can't afford it.'

'Excuse me . . . but he sold his flat!'

'I know.'

'And it was a *big* flat—'

'I know, Edie. I know, don't go on about it, don't—it's just a trip.' She looked up again at the chiffon dress. 'Nothing else to worry about.'

'You sure?'

'Oh, yes. He's very contrite. You can tell a really sorry man, can't you?'

From downstairs came the two-beat tone of the doorbell.

'Damn,' Vivien said, sitting up. 'Someone at the door.'

'Ring me back, if you need to. I'm here till six—'

'I thought you had a headache?'

'It's going,' Edie said, 'it's really going. Vivi, what can I do—'

Vivien stood up and pushed her feet into her shoes. 'Nothing,' she said. 'Thanks, but nothing. Nothing needs doing. It's all fine.'

Outside the front door, a man from the local florist's was waiting. He grinned at Vivien over a bouquet of red roses wrapped in cellophane. 'Afternoon!' he said. 'The lucky lady, I presume?'

Rosa had ordered a salad. It came with a ring of bread balls circling the rim of the dish, and Rosa had picked these off and piled them neatly on her side plate and pushed the plate away from her.

Lazlo paused in cutting up his pizza and eyed them. 'Aren't you going to eat those?'

Rosa shook her head. Her hair was loose on her shoulders. She glanced, smiling, at his pizza. 'Isn't that enough?'

He looked mournfully at his plate. 'It's never enough.'

She pushed the bread balls towards him. 'Feel free.'

He said, in a rush, helping himself, 'You were in the theatre this afternoon, weren't you?'

There was a tiny beat and then Rosa said, 'Yes. I was.'

Without looking at her, he said, 'To see if I could cope without your mother there?'

She selected an olive from her salad and looked at it. Then she put it back. 'I didn't think of that.'

'Didn't you?'

'No,' she said, glancing at him, 'I didn't. And you could.'

He directed a small smile towards his plate. 'Yes,' he said, 'I could, couldn't I? I did wonder a bit. I hoped—' He paused.

'You hoped you could swim without your armbands.'

'Yes,' he said. He looked straight at her. 'I did. Is that—' He stopped.

'No,' Rosa said. 'No. She'd want that, too. She'd want that for you.'

Lazlo cleared his throat. 'The thing is,' he said, 'I've—well, I've got another part.'

'Oh!'

'In television,' he said. 'A six-parter. I've got quite a big role.'

Rosa leaned forward. 'This is wonderful. Mum will be thrilled.'

He gave a little intake of breath. 'Are you sure?'

'Sure, sure.'

'It's just,' he said, 'I owe her so much. Helping me, sheltering me . . .'

'She was there when you needed her. And vice versa.'

Lazlo put a mouthful of pizza into his mouth and chewed. 'Why did you come this afternoon?'

'Oh,' she said, 'to look at you. Without any distractions.'

'I'm not very good at this,' Lazlo said, 'but—but what did you see?'

She leaned back and folded her arms. Her hair was very preoccupying. 'Enough. I saw enough to give me courage.'

Lazlo put down his knife and fork. He had the anxious, excited sensation he'd had several times recently, that some outside force was going to come bowling into his life and make changes for him. The kind of changes he knew he didn't have much capacity for making on his own.

Rosa said, leaning back, watching him, 'You're moving out.'

Lazlo nodded. 'I must. I feel awful, Ben sleeping on the sofa . . .' He looked at his plate. 'I've started looking for a flat. The money will be better in television.'

'I'll come with you,' Rosa said.

He felt his face flame up. 'Come *with* me! I—I don't *know* you . . .'

Rosa unfolded her arms and leaned forward. She put her elbows on the table and propped her chin on her hands. 'Yes, you do. You're just so much in the habit of thinking of yourself as an outsider that you don't believe you know anyone.'

He raised his eyes. 'You are suggesting we live together?'

'Yes. Live together,' Rosa said, 'as in *live* together. Not sleep together.' She paused and then she said lightly, 'Necessarily.'

'I wasn't expecting this,' Lazlo said. 'I couldn't even have *imagined* this. Why are you offering to share a flat with me?'

Rosa said seriously, 'Because I must move out and on too. Because I need the motivation to get a better job. Because I can't afford to live on my own yet. Because I like you.'

He felt his skin scorch again. 'I don't quite know what I—'

'Don't bother,' Rosa said. 'Don't try and say anything. Or feel it, for that matter. Just think about what I've said.'

Russell was half turned away from Edie in bed, half asleep, when she clutched him. 'Russell—'

Her fingers were digging into his shoulder, into his upper arm. His mind came dragging back from the soft dark place it was falling into. 'Edie? Edie, what is it?'

He twisted himself back towards her and she shoved her face against him. She said, almost into his skin, 'We're not going in.'

He extracted his arms from the folds of the duvet and put them awkwardly round her. 'Edie, love, you knew that—'

'We're not going in,' Edie said again in a harsh, tearful whisper. 'The play's not transferring. It's all over.'

Russell adjusted his hold. He said gently, 'You knew that. You knew Freddie wasn't really trying to find a theatre, you knew that was all talk.'

'I've only just *realised* it,' Edie said. 'I don't want this play to be over.'

'There'll be other parts—'

'No, there won't. This was freak luck. Freddie's taking Lazlo with him to do this Italian detective thing and he never mentioned it to me.'

'Perhaps there's no part in this cast for you—'

'I thought,' Edie said, 'I'd be in the West End. I thought—'

Russell said, 'And I thought you were so tired and fed up you just wanted it all to stop.'

Edie said nothing. She moved so that her cheek lay against his chest.

He waited a few moments and then he said, 'You've loved this run, haven't you? You've loved being on stage.'

Edie nodded. She said in a whisper, 'I'm so afraid of it stopping.'

'It's not the last.' He felt her face move as if she was looking up at him.

'Do you really think I'm any good?'

'Yes,' Russell said, 'and so do other people.'

'I don't think,' Edie said, laying her cheek back against him, 'I don't think I could bear it if I couldn't work again.'

Russell let a small silence fall, and then he said comfortably, 'And I'm sure you won't have to bear anything of the kind.' He moved slightly, to free up an arm, and then he yawned into the dimness above Edie's head. From somewhere above them, the floorboards creaked.

Edie stiffened. She said, in quite a different voice, 'There's something going on between Rosa and Lazlo.'

'Is there?' He felt another yawn beginning. 'Does it matter?'

Edie said vigorously, 'I don't like it, Russell. Not here in my house. I mean, if you take people in, take people back, it's only fair, isn't it, to expect a little—' She stopped and then said sadly, 'I don't mean that.'

'I thought you didn't. I hoped you didn't.'

She said, in a dejected voice, 'But it all feels so fragile.'

'What does?'

'What they're doing, both of them without a planned future.'

'Don't you think,' Russell said sleepily, 'that we looked just as fragile in our day? That dismal flat, all those babies, me earning three thousand a year if I was lucky?'

'Maybe.'

'I think we did. In fact I'm sure we did. I expect our parents—mine certainly—had a version of exactly this conversation.'

'Russell?'

'Yes.'

'I just wanted,' Edie said, 'to keep everything safe. I just wanted to make everything all right for all of them.'

'I know.'

'And I can't.'

Russell gave Edie a brief kiss. 'I know,' he said again.

CHAPTER FOURTEEN

THE TROUBLE WAS, Ben reflected, that he hadn't thought things through. He had supposed that he would go back to a few weeks of his old life—unexciting but familiar and easy—and then he would take up, in an unspecified but attractive way, his new life with Naomi. It had not crossed his mind that Naomi meant exactly what she said when she told him she needed space to think, and that included hardly being in touch with him at all beyond a few text messages. And it had certainly never struck him that ambling back home would prove to be anything but easy.

He had thought, for the first few nights, that it didn't feel right because he was sleeping on the sofa. But, as the days wore on, he suspected that, even if Rosa were to surrender his bedroom, it wouldn't now be the bedroom he had left only a few months before, and therefore the strangeness of the sofa didn't belong to the actual sofa: it belonged to the situation.

The situation was, as far as Ben could see, that his childhood home had changed. You could know a thing, it seemed, you could feel a thing to be deeply, powerfully familiar, but at the same time you were keenly aware that this known and familiar thing was no longer in the least relevant to the place you were now at, never mind the place where you were going. When Ben put the key in the lock of the front door of the house, he knew precisely how to do it, but that was no comfort or pleasure because he didn't, fundamentally, want to be doing it any more.

The same was true of his family. Given everyone's work schedules, no one saw very much of anyone else, but all the same, the household had no coherence about it any more. It was only after a few weeks, lying wakeful one night on the sofa, that it struck Ben that what was the matter with him was not really the sofa, or the accessibility of his family, but that he was missing Naomi.

Once he had considered this, he realised that he had never actually missed anyone before. And, once this revelation had broken over him, he could see that it was neither the house nor the family that had changed, it was him. Naomi's mother, for all her rules and regulations, had unconsciously allowed him to take the first tentative steps towards independence.

The feeling of missing Naomi was, once acknowledged, extremely acute. It rendered him eager to mend fences with Naomi and to set about achieving what he now urgently wanted: a place of their own.

The difficulty was, how. Naomi's texts had not suggested, in any way, that she was missing him as he was missing her. But Ben's heart, buoyed up with his new self-knowledge, did not feel faint. He would shower and shave, he decided, put on clean clothes, buy flowers for both Naomi and her mother—a significantly larger bunch for her mother—and take the tube, that very day, to Walthamstow.

The water in the shower changed abruptly from tepid to gaspingly cold. Edie, her eyes tightly shut against the shampoo cascading down her face, gave a scream. Then she gave another, a scream of rage this time, rather than shock. They had all had showers, of course, and left her to do battle with the aftermath of their leaving.

She stumbled out of the shower, found a damp towel and wrapped it round her. Next, she ran a basin of cold water and dipped her hair into it and rinsed her eyes. Then she straightened up a little and peered at herself in the mirror. Her hair hung in wet dark snakes. Her eyes looked as if they'd been buried. She reached out and pulled another dank towel off the pile on the chair and wound it round her head.

From downstairs, the doorbell rang.

'Go away!' Edie shouted.

It rang again, politely but firmly. Edie dropped the towel she had tucked round her armpits and clawed her way into Russell's ancient bathrobe that was hanging on the back of the door. Then she went cautiously out onto the landing and pressed her forehead against the glass to see down into the street.

On the step directly below her a young woman was standing. She wore a dark suit and was carrying a briefcase and there were sunglasses perched on top of her head. Edie looked at the briefcase. It was Ruth's briefcase. Edie unscrewed the security bolt on the window and put her head out.

Ruth glanced up. 'Edie,' she said uncertainly.

Edie put her hand up to her blue turban. 'Just washing my hair—'

'I'm sorry,' Ruth said, 'not to tell you I was coming, but Matt said you'd be in, and I—'

'*Matt* did?'

'Yes,' Ruth said. 'Matt suggested I just come. When I said I wanted to.'

'Wait,' Edie said. She slammed the window shut and tore off her turban. Then she ran downstairs. Arsie was sitting in the hall. Edie picked him up and held him against her while she opened the door.

Ruth said at once, 'I'm so sorry—'

'Don't be,' Edie said. She stepped back. 'I'm very glad to see you.'

'Are you? I thought you thought—'

A drip from Edie's hair slid onto Arsie's shoulder and he sprang from her arms. 'I *did* think. But a lot's happened and I—well, my thinking has shifted a bit. You look very smart.'

Ruth made a little self-deprecating gesture.

'You'll have to forgive me,' Edie said. 'I was in a temper as well as in the shower. Coffee?'

'Could I have tea?'

Edie looked at her. 'I didn't think you drank tea.'

'I . . . didn't.'

'Come into the kitchen. There's too much to apologise for in there so I won't even start.'

Ruth said from the kitchen doorway, 'It's nice to be back—'

'Is it? Have you been very unhappy?'

'Yes.'

Edie picked up the kettle. She said from the sink, her back turned towards Ruth, 'So has Matthew.'

'I know.'

'Ruth,' Edie said, 'couldn't you have made a compromise? Couldn't you just have made it possible for him to contribute *something*?'

Ruth went slowly across the room to the table and leaned against it. Then she put down her briefcase and took her sunglasses off her head.

'I came,' she said, 'to tell you that I'm pregnant.'

Edie froze for a moment. Then she turned off the tap and set the kettle down in the sink. 'Pregnant? I thought,' she said with emphasis, 'that you and Matthew hadn't seen each other since you parted.'

'He came for dinner,' Ruth said. 'He came to my flat. I asked him to. I was missing him so much.'

Edie put her hands up to the collar of Russell's bathrobe and held it against her neck. Then she turned round. 'Does Matthew know?'

'Of course.'

'And . . . forgive me . . . but are you going to keep it?'

There was a small pause and then Ruth said, with barely suppressed fury, 'Yes.'

Edie shut her eyes. 'But if you and Matthew aren't—'

'We are,' Ruth said. 'That's why I've come. I've come to tell you what we're planning.'

Edie put a hand out for a chair and lowered herself into it. 'But why come and tell me? Why not both of you? Why not tell Russell and me together? Why like this, out of the blue?'

'Because I wanted to,' Ruth said. 'Because you needed to know. Because I think you were angry with me. I'd hurt your son. I'd achieved more than he had. In your view, I'd rubbed his nose in it.'

Edie put her elbows on the table and her face in her hands. She said, muffled by her hands, 'You'll learn.'

'Oh,' Ruth said, 'I felt awful myself, awful at what I'd done and furious at being made to feel awful.'

Edie took her hands away from her face. 'You'd better sit down.'

'I'm fine—'

'Sit down,' Edie said. 'Sit down and I'll make you some tea.'

She got up and retrieved the kettle from the sink. 'Do your parents know?'

'Not yet. I'll tell them next,' Ruth said. 'I'll tell them at the weekend. I wanted to see you first. I wanted to do something for Matthew.'

Edie spun round. 'Matthew's not afraid of *me!*'

'It wasn't about that,' Ruth said, 'it's about saving him having to explain himself again. It's about me explaining to you how hard it is for women my age to deal with motherhood and work when both are so demanding and important, and how wonderful it would be if you could be on my side.' She paused, then added, 'Irrespective of Matthew.'

Edie said nothing. She went back to her chair and sat down in it and pulled the belt of the bathrobe tighter. Then she looked at Ruth across the table, at her polished hair and her sharply cut suit. She stared at Ruth as if she was seeing her properly for the first time.

'Oh my God,' Edie said. 'A *baby*.'

Russell looked at the glasses of wine Rosa had already carried to the table from the bar.

'No wish to be churlish,' he said, 'but this makes me suspicious—'

'You like red wine.'

'I do indeed. But usually I have to buy the red wine I like. In the case of my children, I invariably buy the red wine.'

'Well,' Rosa said, 'things are changing. I'm being promoted.'

Russell picked up his glass. 'I thought it was a crap job.'

'I've been asked,' Rosa said, 'to run the branch in Holborn. I get a thirty per cent rise in salary and my uniform will no longer have sunburst buttons.'

Russell eyed her. 'So I congratulate you. But why couldn't you tell me this at home?'

'Home's difficult,' Rosa said. 'I probably help to make it difficult but it's not, well, it's not really working, is it, us all living together?'

Russell said, still looking away, 'I never thought it would.'

'Well, you were right. You're right about lots of things.'

He said tiredly, 'Don't try to placate me, Rosa. I'm beyond all that.'

'I mean it. And I don't mind going to Holborn and I don't mind working in a travel agency.'

'Ah,' Russell said. He turned to look at her. 'Why don't you?'

'Because,' Rosa said, spreading her fingers flat on the table and regarding them, 'another avenue has opened up.'

Russell took a swallow. 'Lazlo?'

'Yes. I didn't know you knew.'

'I didn't *know*,' Russell said, 'but I guessed. It would be hard to live in the same house and not guess.'

Rosa smiled down at her hands. 'It's very early days. And he's terribly shy. I'm not sure he's ever had a real girlfriend before.'

'He's a nice boy,' Russell said. 'An honest boy.'

'So you don't mind if Lazlo and I move out to live together?'

Russell leaned forward. 'No, Rosa, I don't. I'm very pleased for you.'

She eyed him. 'Will Mum be?'

'I should think so.'

'Will you tell her?'

Russell shook his head. 'No. You must tell her. Lazlo must tell her.'

Rosa made a little gesture. 'It's just that I know how tired she is, I know how disappointed she is about the play not transferring, and I don't want to add to everything, add to the feeling of losing things.' She paused and then she said in a rush, 'I mean I'm worried she'll really feel it, with Matt going and now us—'

'Matt?' Russell said sharply.

Rosa put her hand over her mouth. 'Oh my God.'

'Rosa'—Russell leaned across the table and grasped Rosa's wrist—'What about Matthew?'

Vivien sat in her hall beside her telephone table. On it lay a list of all the people she was going to telephone, one after another, in a calm and orderly fashion, and when the list was completed she was going to go upstairs with a new roll of heavy-duty dustbin bags and begin, without hysteria, to fill them with Max's possessions.

She had been extraordinarily composed when she discovered, by asking Max outright about the amount of money he had received for the flat in Barnes, that he had never actually sold it. She had been rather less composed when it became evident that, not only was the flat not sold, but it wasn't even on the market since it was still inhabited by Max's last girlfriend, who was both refusing to leave and refusing to pay the bills. And she had, to her subsequent regret, lost all control when Max fell on his knees on her bedroom floor and told her that only she could save him from the rapacious harpy who was bleeding him dry.

She had, of course, cried all night after that episode. She had expected to. What she hadn't expected was to feel such relief the next day, knowing that she was at last emerging from something that had beguiled her for too long in a profoundly unsettling way. When Max had stared into his coffee the next morning and said, 'I need you, doll. I love you. Please, please forgive me,' she'd been able to say, to her amazement, 'Of course I forgive you, but I don't want you any more.'

Sitting now on her telephone chair, she carefully tested her feelings again. Did she still love Max? Did she even still want or need him? No, quite decidedly. Could she face the thought of all the days and months and years ahead without him? Yes, not quite so decidedly, but that was more, she thought, the prospect of no man at all rather than no Max.

She looked again at her telephone list. She intended to ring her solicitor and her bank manager, and Alison at the bookshop to tell her that something had come up that would prevent her coming into the shop, but that she would be in as usual on Wednesday. But perhaps it would be better to ring Edie first, to ask her advice about how she should tell Eliot. It was only when she thought of Eliot that she felt unsteady.

She picked up the receiver and dialled Edie's number. It would be an hour or two before Edie needed to go to the theatre.

'Hello?' Edie said.

'It's me—'

'Vivi,' Edie said, 'you are just brilliant at picking the very moment when I really can't—'

'No,' Vivien shouted. 'No!'

'What?'

'Listen to me!' Vivien shouted. 'Listen to me!' And burst into tears.

Now that he had switched off even the television, the house was eerily quiet. Even the perpetual hum of London seemed to have withdrawn itself to a distance. The only sound, really, was Arsie who, having leaped on him the moment he lay down on the sofa, was now extended up his chest with languorous purpose and purring loudly.

Beside them, on a padded stool, lay the evening newspaper, an empty wineglass and the plate that had borne Russell's unsatisfactory supper. He had cleared up the kitchen in a perfunctory way against Edie's return, made himself an unsuccessful omelette over too high a flame, finished the last third of a bottle of red wine, done the crossword in the paper and was now prone on the sofa wondering why an empty house should feel so peculiarly unrelaxing.

'Is it just waiting for them all to come in?' he said to Arsie.

Arsie yawned. The inside of his mouth was as immaculate as the rest of him. He stretched one paw upwards and laid it, claws only just sheathed, on the skin of Russell's neck, just above his shirt collar.

'Don't,' Russell said. 'Please take pity on how weary I am. Please don't behave like all the others.'

Arsie unfolded his second paw and stretched it up to join the first one. Then he slowly curled his claws over the edge of Russell's shirt and into his skin.

'Get off!' Russell yelled, flinging himself upright.

Arsie flew in a neat semicircle and landed lightly on the rug. He composed himself at once, with his back to Russell, and began to wash.

'I'm sorry,' Russell said, 'but that was the limit. You had been warned.'

He swung his legs off the sofa. In an hour, Edie would be home and, however tempting it was to think of going to bed, it was a temptation he must resist. He got stiffly to his feet and picked up the plate and glass. Part of the hour might be beguiled by making some strong coffee.

'Aren't you in bed?' Edie said from the doorway.

Russell swam dizzily to consciousness. 'No, I—'

'Isn't Ben in?'

'No.'

'Lazlo's having supper with Rosa, Matt's out somewhere with Ruth and I thought at least Ben—'

Russell struggled out of his armchair. 'I think some of his stuff's gone.'

Edie looked sharply at the sofa. 'Has it?'

Russell went across to the doorway and bent to kiss her. 'Would you like a drink?'

She thought for a moment. 'Not much.'

'Why don't you,' Russell said, 'why don't you just be accommodating for once and have a drink while we talk?'

Edie hesitated. 'Talk?'

'Yes,' Russell said. He moved past her and went across the hall to the kitchen. 'Coffee? Wine? Whisky?'

Edie went slowly after him. 'Wine, perhaps.'

He glanced at her, then jerked his head towards one of the chairs by the table. 'Sit down. White? Red?'

'Anything,' Edie said, 'anything. I feel too stunned after this week to make decisions that size.' She pulled her arms out of her jacket and let it slump on the chair behind her. 'Matt, Rosa, Lazlo, Ruth, Vivi—' She paused and then she said, 'Poor Vivi.'

Russell put a glass of white wine on the table in front of her. She looked at it without enthusiasm.

'I thought you couldn't stand Max.'

'I can't. It's not Max, it's the situation, Vivien's situation. Divorce and everything. She's going to have to sell the house.'

There was a pause and then Russell, standing at the other side of the table with the wine bottle in his hand, said with emphasis, 'Yes. May I say something?'

'Go on.'

'Well,' he said, 'if the children are all branching out like this, it would—it would be nice to help them, wouldn't it?'

Edie's gaze didn't waver from his face. He put the bottle down on the table and leaned on his hands. He said, in a different tone, 'I know how hard this might be for you even to contemplate, heaven knows, it isn't very easy for me, but I've been thinking in order to give the children a bit of help and rearrange our own lives, I think we ought, really, if you think about it, to—to sell up too. We ought to sell this house.'

Edie went on looking at him. There was a silence that seemed to go on for a disconcerting length of time, and then she said, 'I know.'

The estate agent had said that, on the plus side, it was very rare for a house of this size and quality, and still unconverted, to come up in this particular area. However, he said—and he was quite difficult to take seriously, Edie thought, because of looking rather younger than Matthew—the minus side, which was quite a significant minus, was that the house was so very unconverted that most buyers would find it difficult to visualise it in an improved and modernised state.

They had both looked at him when he finished speaking.

'So,' Russell had said. 'The house is in too bad a state to sell?'

'No, no, it's a very desirable house in a good area. It's just that'—he glanced round the kitchen—'it's just that, the way it is now, the way—'

Edie had leaned forward and said, 'You think we should tidy it up?'

The agent had stared at her with something approaching violent relief. 'Yes.'

'Well, that's easy.'

'No,' he said, suddenly desperate again. 'No. Not tidy up. *Empty*. Just—almost empty it.' He waved his arms. 'This room—' He gestured out of the window. 'That shed . . .'

'Empty it?'

'Yes.'

And so, Edie was in Ben's bedroom on a Saturday afternoon, with a roll of black bags and a bucket of water in which floated a new green pot scourer. If she looked out of the window, she could see the piles of objects that were growing in the garden as Russell emptied the shed.

Edie moved Ben's bed away from the wall and found several socks nesting furrily against the skirting board. She picked them up gingerly. Ben was buying new socks now, and bedlinen and a screwdriver for this little flat he'd found in Walthamstow, two streets away from the flat Naomi shared with her mother and then he was going to lay siege to Naomi.

'What do you mean, "lay siege"?'

'I'm going to make it really nice and then I'm going to wait.'

'Wait? For what?'

He'd been filling his rucksack with possessions from behind the sofa.

'Wait for her to see.'

'Will she?'

Ben spread out a faded black T-shirt with a skull printed on the front and then he tossed it on the floor. 'Oh, yes,' he said.

'D'you mean,' Edie said, 'that you'll cook supper and light candles and buy *flowers*?'

Ben inspected another black T-shirt. 'Might do.'

'And if it doesn't work?'

'Then,' Ben said, chucking the second T-shirt after the first, 'I'll still end up with my own gaff and I'll think again.'

Edie began on a couple of gum patches left by his Kate Moss poster with her scourer. Ben wouldn't let her see this flat of his any more than Rosa and Lazlo would let her see the one they'd found in Barons Court.

'Barons Court!' Edie had said. 'But that's the other side of London!'

'It's a nice flat,' Lazlo said seriously. He looked at Rosa. 'Piccadilly Line.'

Rosa looked at Edie. 'Good for work.'

'Why can't I see it?'

'You can,' Rosa said, 'in time. When we've—done something about the bathroom.'

She looked at Lazlo. He said, 'And the kitchen.'

They both giggled.

Edie said, 'I really don't see why you have to be so secretive.'

'Not secretive, Mum. Just private.'

'They're paying two hundred pounds a week,' Edie said to Russell, 'and Ben's paying a hundred and twenty-five. How will they *manage*?'

'We don't ask them,' Russell said, 'and we don't worry. Certainly not until this fails to sell.' He put a hand on the nearest wall. 'Which it won't because I am going to paint the front door.'

'I really think,' Matthew had said, surveying the house from the street, 'that you should at least paint the front door.'

'It's always been that colour.'

'It isn't the colour,' Matthew said patiently, 'it's the chips.'

Matthew, Edie thought, aiming her scouring pad towards the bucket, and missing, was different. He was, in one way, back to the Matthew he had been when he first met Ruth, the Matthew who had kindly, if patronisingly, told his parents how much better their lives might be if only they followed his advice. But there were new elements now, as well, elements that were softer and more sympathetic, elements induced, it seemed, by his knowledge that he was going to be a father. He had, for example, gone, almost at once, to live with Ruth in the flat that had been such a bone of contention between them.

'I want to look after her. I want to make sure she eats the right things and gets enough rest. I'm going to the doctor with her and for every ultrasound.' He was proposing not only to devote himself to his girlfriend's pregnancy but also to put his own career on hold when Ruth's maternity leave was over in order to care for their child. He said it was what he wanted.

'Is it . . . is it what Ruth wants?'

'Of course.'

'But I thought you couldn't bear the flat—'

'What I couldn't bear,' Matthew said, 'was the situation. But now everything's changed. Everything.'

Edie looked at him. 'Yes,' she said faintly.

She sat down now, on the edge of Ben's bed, and then she lay back and contemplated the ceiling. When she and Vivien were growing up, she had always prided herself on being like their father, a restless man who found any kind of routine not so much anathema as impossible. Vivien, of course, was like their mother, the kind of person who sees change as some malevolent plot deliberately devised to distress her.

Yet it was Vivien who, in between looking for flats in Fulham for herself—'Who's to stop me living exactly where I want?'—was urging Edie to think of where she and Russell might live after the house was sold. 'Why don't you think about Clerkenwell? Or Little Venice? Why don't you have an adventure?' It was Vivien who had said to Edie, crying down the telephone one night after Edie had returned from her last but one night in *Ghosts*, 'Going on is hard, but going back would be a whole lot worse.'

Going back. Edie focused on a long, wavering crack in the plaster above her head. To think how she had longed to go back, how fiercely she had told herself that all she wanted, all she was truly able to do, lay in what she had already done, in the way she had lived her life since they had moved into the house. But if she was truthful with herself now and somebody—some fairy godmother—offered her the chance to go back, what she would have to say was that she would indeed like to go back, but only as far as the first night of the production of *Ghosts*, when she had known that she had done something exceptionally well, and been applauded for it.

'How odd,' she'd say to the fairy godmother, 'to have one hunger almost replaced by one so very different.'

'Not replaced,' the fairy godmother would reply, adjusting her gauzy skirts, 'merely added to. Nothing, you see, stands still.'

Russell had said that. He'd been shuffling through some property brochures that Vivien had sent and he said, 'I never thought I could leave this house, but now I wonder if I could stay. Nothing stands still, does it? It's not change that's so painful, it's just getting used to it.'

Edie sat up slowly. It actually wasn't getting used to change that hurt, it was getting used to the truth. Once you'd started doing without the illusions, you got braver, you could allow yourself to make claims. And the claim I want to make, Edie thought, getting to her feet and moving towards the window again, is to work. I want to act again, I want to be on a stage or in front of a camera.

She looked down the garden. Russell was standing outside the shed holding Rosa's old fairy cycle. She leaned her forehead against the glass of the window and stared at him. He looked purposeful and determined and, at the same time, as if this task was far from easy. He looked like someone who was doing something he didn't want to do in order to be able to move on to something better. He looked like the kind of person Edie was going to have to be when she asked him for work to tide her over until . . . until something better came up.

'I'll do anything,' she planned to say to him, 'and I'll do it properly,' and he would give her a long look back and say, 'Yes, you will.'

She took her face away from the window and bent to pick up the bucket. She would go downstairs now, and make a mug of tea and carry the tea down the garden to Russell, and she would ask him, *humbly*, there and then, if he could help her. She looked back from the doorway, at Ben's room. It was his bedroom but it was also the past and there was, suddenly, excitingly, frighteningly, no time like the present. Not, that is, if you wanted a future. Edie closed the door behind her, and trod carefully down the stairs.

'"Perhaps,"' Lazlo constantly said to her as Osvald Alving, '"Perhaps there'll be lots of things for me to be glad about—and to live for . . ."'

Arsie was waiting at the foot of the stairs. He looked up as Edie passed him and made a small, interrogative remark.

Edie paused and bent to touch the top of his head with her free hand.

'"Yes,"' she said, as Mrs Alving had always said. '"I'm sure there will."'

Just before publication of *Second Honeymoon*, I went along to the offices of Joanna Trollope's London publisher, Bloomsbury, to ask Joanna a few questions.

Have you, like Edie in* Second Honeymoon*, suffered from empty nest syndrome?

Joanna: Oh, yes. The theme of the empty nest had been on my mind since my own children left home. Which, of course, is a very long time ago—they're in their thirties now. I remember thinking that this was the most enormous event, and I was disconcerted by the strength of my own reaction. It really hit me when my eldest daughter got married. It was her wedding that suddenly made me realise that, for me, that stage of motherhood was over. And I just remember, the week after her wedding, this extraordinary feeling of deprivation and loss, and feelings of 'What am I for?' and 'Have I vanished?' And the realisation that a completely different phase of motherhood had now started. I think that I enjoy the kind of motherhood I have now more than almost any stage I've had before. Particularly if you have daughters, the relationship you have with them when they become mothers is quite extraordinary.

What do you find the hardest part of writing?

Joanna: Oh, all of it. All of it and it doesn't get any easier. And in a rather grim, puritanical way, I don't feel it ought to get easier. I feel that there is something quite decent about it being difficult. It is terrifying starting—and it is terrifying starting every day. Harold Pinter said something once about sitting down in front of his typewriter and being overcome with the urge to go out and buy a forty-watt light bulb! Anything rather than face the blank page. I've often thought about this because musicians seem to long to get back to the instrument, and painters to the canvas, and sculptors to the marble. And it is only writers who have this terror of being shut up with themselves, I suppose it is because you are facing yourself in a very naked way and you have only yourself to rely on. There is no external discipline, there is only the discipline that you create.

Just recently you have participated in the 'Quick Reads' campaign, aimed at adults with reading difficulties, which is to be launched on World Book Day in March. How difficult was writing* The Book Boy *for this project?

Joanna: It was fascinating, once I got the hang of writing in this way. It's really just a question of reining back the craft bit, not the skill of it, but the mechanics. You shorten sentences, you shorten paragraphs, you include a lot of dialogue, you would say 'sad' not 'miserable'. The Quick Reads campaign is about those who have limited reading ability. From the start I decided that the best way not to patronise was to write in my ordinary voice but with a slightly simpler vocabulary. I also wanted to grasp the nettle, go straight to the heart of the matter and write about the topic. So *The Book Boy* is about a thirty-eight-year-old mother of two with a secret—she cannot read. Her teenage children are embarrassed by her and her husband is a bully. So it's also a subject that I love: a woman reinventing herself, discovering herself, empowering herself.

Have you been pleased with the televised adaptations of your books?

Joanna: All TV can do is capture the spirit of a book because the medium is so utterly different. I think the BBC made an appalling job of *The Choir* and a perfectly wonderful job of *Other People's Children*. What I have absolutely loved is that my novel, *Marrying the Mistress*, has been adapted for the stage and is in the middle of a country-wide tour in repertory theatres.

For many years, you have had homes in the Cotswolds and in London. Is it true that you are finally moving out of the Cotswolds?

Joanna: I'm renting a flat in Oxford at the moment, but I think I'm slowly inching towards London. I have always lived in two places because I had dogs but just recently the last of my black Labradors, Max, went to paradise, bless his heart. He died with such dignity and peace. And that's rather loosened my ties with the country. I suddenly realised that I was keeping the cottage going for Max and that's why I think that I will probably make London my main base. I have so many friends and family in the country that I'm sure I will become a regular weekend house-guest.

What would you say is your main indulgence?

Joanna: Goodness. Um. Well, I suppose it's freedom to choose. Just now, for me, It's the single life. Only having myself to answer too. It's quite liberating.

Jane Eastgate

Be Careful What You Wish For

Alexandra Potter

I wish . . .

I could get a seat on the tube . . .

I could eat an entire tub of

Häagen-Dazs without getting fat . . .

I could meet a man who loved

washing up and monogamy . . .

Little, everyday wishes—but just

what might happen if they all

suddenly started to come true?

Chapter One

WHAT DO YOU WISH FOR? World peace? A cure for AIDS? Gisele's bottom?

Wincing with pain from my new diamanté thong sandals that have rubbed two blisters the size of jellyfish on my big toes, I press the button for the pedestrian crossing and wait on the kerbside. I mean, whatever it is, we all wish for something, don't we? Every single one of us. Unwrapping the yoghurt-coated flapjack that's my breakfast I stare down at my throbbing feet. And I'm no different from anyone else. Except whereas everyone else is busy changing the world and looking fabulous in a G-string bikini, I'm standing here looking at my blisters—and do you know what I'm wishing for?

'Ouch.'

As if on cue, a blister pops and fluid trickles between my toes.

Flip-flops.

It's July and the UK's in the grip of a heatwave. For most of the sunshine-starved population this means a blissful merry-go-round of picnics in the park and deck chairs in the back garden. For us Londoners it's hell. Stuffy offices, stinking traffic fumes and tube trains without air-conditioning make life miserable. Tempers are fraying. Noses are peeling. And my feet are killing me. Cursing silently, I unearth a grotty piece of tissue and squat down on the pavement.

Chic, very chic, I muse, stuffing the raggedy tissue between my toes. Sometimes I wonder why I even bother buying *Instyle* every month when I can put together such a stylish look myself.

Feeling a shove in my back I notice the lights have changed. I begin hobbling across the road, engulfed by a crowd of commuters, everyone pushing, rushing, jostling, bumping. A briefcase bashes me in the calf and I yelp. Not for the first time do I find myself wishing I lived by the sea. Instead of in the polluted inner-city hellhole I've called home for the last six years.

Managing to make it to the pavement before the little green man disappears, I limp along Marylebone Road. To tell the truth, sometimes I feel as if I spend my whole life wishing for things. Not the close-your-eyes-and-make-a-wish-type wishes that involve throwing coins into fountains, watching for shooting stars or rubbing Aladdin's lamp. I'm talking about all the ordinary, inadvertent and, quite frankly, *boring* wishes I make a dozen times a day without thinking about them. For me, wishes have nothing to do with magic: they're just a part of everyday life.

Like I wish I hadn't just eaten that great big flapjack.

OK, so I bought it from a health-food store, but who am I trying to kid? I squint at the nutritional information on the wrapper. Oh my God, *healthy*? This stuff should carry a health *warning*. Have you any idea how many grams of fat there are in a flapjack?

Scrunching up the wrapper I stuff it hastily into my bag, which as usual is full of all the crap I carry around with me: leaky Biros, a lip gloss that's lost its top and a couple of those little tickets from the electronic weighing machines at Boots.

Which reminds me of another one of my wishes. When I popped into Boots at lunch time I couldn't resist stepping on to the scales and wishing the little digital display was going to say I was a couple of pounds under nine stone—and not, as it turned out, a couple of pounds over.

Well, all right—make that five pounds. Sucking in my stomach, I continue hurrying along the main road. In fact, now I'm thinking about it, I make so many wishes I'm not even sure I can remember them all. Take the last twenty-four hours, for example. If I had to write them all down I'd end up with a whole wish list . . .

I Wish

- *I'd stayed in last night instead of going to a karaoke evening with my best friend Jess.*
- *I hadn't started doing tequila slammers.*
- *The ground had opened up and swallowed me when I'd started yodelling Barbra Streisand's 'Woman In Love'.*
- *That when I got home at 2 a.m. I hadn't texted the-bastard-ex-boyfriend.*

I'm mortified at the memory. Sending a text message is one thing. But remembering what I put is quite another.

- *I hadn't squeezed that spot on my chin in the loos at work. But I did and now it's brought along a couple of friends for moral support.*
- *Someone had warned me that on my thirtieth birthday I wouldn't automatically be given an amazing career along with all the other presents to unwrap. (You mean that's not how it works?)*
- *There was always an empty seat on the tube. No queue at Starbucks. And a parking space for my car outside my flat.*
- *I'd win the lottery.*

Admittedly a tricky one, having never actually bought a ticket.

- *There was no such thing as a 'bad-hair day'.*
- *I could actually manage to drink eight glasses of water a day.*

Eight whole glasses! I mean, it's just so boring.

- *I could meet a man whose hobbies include washing-up, monogamy and foreplay.*

Instead of making a mess, cheating and tweaking my left nipple back and forwards as if it's the dial on their car stereo. Not that I'm referring to Daniel, my ex, or anything.

- *There were no calories in Häagen-Dazs double chocolate chip.*
- *I hadn't believed the sales assistant when she said it was easy to do a St Tropez tan at home and that the secret was bodypolishing.*

I glance down at my legs. Think orange stripes. Like a deck chair.

- *Dad wasn't married to the bitch from hell.*

Whose real name is Rosemary, and whom I refer to as proof that wicked stepmothers aren't just the stuff of fairy tales.

- *My Visa card hadn't been refused at the check-out at Sainsbury's.*

Embarrassing enough without being ushered into a little room by a sour-faced supervisor who'd called my bank, picked up a pair of scissors and cut my flexible friend in half 'on orders from your bank manager'.

Phew-wheeh. I hear a wolf whistle and zone back in. Only to see a gang of workmen staring at my chest. Which brings me swiftly to the next wish on my list:

- *That I was wearing a bra.*

OK, just ignore them, Heather. Just a few more steps and you'll have got past them . . . Easy-peasy. See, workmen aren't so bad.

'Oy, show us your tits.'

- *I wish all workmen had small penises.*

Blushing hotly, I hurry past, pretending to look at my watch to avoid their gaze. Which is when I see what time it is. Oh shit.

- *And I wish I wasn't late to meet Brian at the registry office at ten.*

Because it's already twenty past. And he's going to kill me.

On the front steps of Marylebone registry office, a slim, attractive, grey-haired man in a charcoal flannel suit, who could pass for his mid-fifties but is a decade older, checks his watch, looks up and down the road, then sighs and digs out his mobile from his breast pocket.

That's Brian, and although he can't see me hurrying towards him because of all the pavement traffic, I can see him. He flips open the mouthpiece, taps in a number, then presses the phone to his ear.

A hundred yards away, I hear a familiar tune. Sticking my hand into my bag I wiggle my fingers around until finally I locate my Nokia. I wave frantically at Brian but he's got his back to me and all I can see is the hunch of his shoulders as he lights a cigarette.

'Heather. It's me, Brian. I'm outside the registry office and I'm getting a little nervous. Where the bleedin' 'ell are you?'

'Right here,' I gasp, sneaking up behind.

It's an attempt to defuse the situation with humour. Instead it nearly causes a heart attack. Brian swings round clutching his chest, then glares at me accusingly. 'You're late,' he snaps into his mobile. Then, realising what he's doing, he curses and flips the mouthpiece shut.

'I know and I'm so sorry,' I apologise. 'My alarm didn't go off and the tube took for ever and I'd bought these stupid new sandals—'

'Well, at least you're here now,' he interrupts. 'But we'd better hurry.'

'Where is everyone?' I rush after him up the front steps.

'Inside. Waiting for us.' He pulls open the front door and holds it for me. 'I've been here ages. I came outside to look for you.'

'I'm really sorry,' I apologise again and duck my head under his arm. I'm a lot taller than Brian, especially in my new sandals, and I have to stoop as I step into the cool darkness of the lobby, where I pause to check my reflection in the gilt-edged mirror.

I'm your typical redhead, pale skin and freckles, lots of wavy scarlet hair, and painful childhood memories of being called something unrepeatable that involves pubic hair and rhyming slang. Honestly, I'm surprised I'm not in therapy for the rest of my life. Not just at the hairdresser's having blonde highlights put in every six weeks to turn me into a strawberry blonde. Usually I blow-dry it straight, but today it's gone all puffy in the heat. I try to smooth it down. Which is when I notice Brian. In the mirror I can see him standing behind me, staring at the floor. 'What happened to your feet?' he demands.

Remembering, I look down. 'Fashion,' I quip, bending down and trying to hide the toilet paper that's sticking out from between my toes.

Usually he'd laugh, make some wisecrack, or quiz me about my latest shopping spree. Unlike most men of his age Brian makes sure he keeps abreast of new trends and is fastidious about fashion. But this time he huffs dismissively. 'Shall we?' He glares at me with flashing grey eyes. Despite his mood he's incredibly handsome for an older man.

Together we cross the marble lobby, our footsteps unnervingly loud. Ahead of us is an impressive set of mahogany doors. Muttering something about how the next wedding party is due to arrive at any minute, Brian reaches for the brass door handle.

I place a hand on his arm. 'Hang on a sec.' Tugging a packet of tissues out of my bag, I tear open the Cellophane and hold out a tissue. 'I know how you cry at weddings.'

He frowns, not giving an inch. I wave the little white triangle like a flag. It's too much. He surrenders and the tension drains from his face. 'I'm sorry. I was beginning to think you weren't going to turn up.' Accepting my peace offering he tucks it deftly up his sleeve.

'What? Jilt you at the registry office?' I whisper.

The corners of his mouth twitch. 'Mmm, something like that.'

We share a smile. He throws back his shoulders. 'Ready?'

I pull at the hem of my skirt and tuck a stray curl behind my ear. 'Ready.' I nod, feeling a jangle of nerves. I brace myself.

'OK. This is it.' Brian takes a deep breath. '*Showtime*.'

A vista of multicoloured hats greets us as we enter. The room is absolutely jammed. The guests are sitting shoulder to padded shoulder, fidgeting uncomfortably in the stifling heat and trading family gossip.

No one notices as Brian and I enter from the back, except the registrar who hurries towards us. 'Oh my word, thank goodness,' he whispers. 'I was beginning to think we were going to have a riot on our hands.'

'Don't worry, the cavalry's here now.' Brian tugs a little black object out of his pocket, and points it in different directions.

The registrar stares at him quizzically. 'What's that?'

'A light meter,' I reply, and spot the pile of cases in the corner. Unzipping a black holdall, I pull out a tripod and begin to assemble it. 'We need to check the readings for the exposure.'

The registrar nods. 'Oh, I see.'

'As the official wedding photographer it's my job to make sure the happy couple get the photos they've always dreamed of,' interjects Brian, reaching for his camera. 'Because memories fade . . .'

On hearing my cue I join in: '. . . but a photograph lasts a lifetime,' we chime together.

'That's the motto of Together Forever,' Brian continues, unable to keep the pride out of his voice. He passes me the lens cap and points the camera at the registrar. 'I thought of it myself.'

'You did?' The registrar looks dubious. 'I thought . . .'

The shutter releases with a loud click, which brings us to the attention of the wedding party, who turn round in their chairs in excited anticipation. A hush falls as all eyes turn towards us. But I know they're not looking *at* us—we're just the wedding photographers—they're too busy looking *beyond* us, at the doors that are swinging open as someone presses 'play' on the tape recorder. The sound of a sax fills the air and Whitney Houston blasts into 'I Will Always Love You'. As the registrar scuttles back up the aisle, Brian and I take our positions. Here we go.

I wait expectantly. This is the moment when the bride makes her grand entrance and you get to see the dress. It's my favourite bit.

There's a loud sob from the mother of the bride. Oohing and aahing from the elderly relatives. And a gasp from me.

Only this time it's not because of my blisters.

Before me, in a bright pink dress that looks like something worn by a Spanish flamenco dancer, is a bride who's old enough to be my mother. Actually, no, I'm mistaken. *My grandmother*.

'You look gorgeous, sweetheart,' gushes Brian, rattling off frame after frame. What can I say? This man is a pro.

'The dress is stunning . . . Now, big smile for the camera . . .'

Passing him a new roll of film I watch him in admiration. Brian's been doing this for so long he's caught full-blown wedding fever. It doesn't matter whether they're big or small, traditional or themed, he adores every last one of them. He was married once, way back in his early twenties, to some model called Phoebe, but they divorced amicably after a couple of years (I'm not sure if that was before or after he admitted he was gay) and since then he's had a string of failed affairs.

Not that this has stopped him being a true romantic. If anything, it's made him even *more* romantic. He gets all misty-eyed at the first sight of a white Rolls. Can't listen to the Bridal March without dabbing his eyes with his sleeve, and borrowing tissues from the mother of the bride to blow his nose all the way through the vows. Honestly, he's a complete mess. By 'till death us do part' he has to go outside for some fresh air.

Which leaves me in charge. Officially I'm supposed to be his assistant, but I usually end up taking most of the pictures. Despite the unwritten rule in society that decrees women have to goo-goo over new-born babies, puppies, cuddly toys and—the *pièce de résistance*—weddings, they just don't have that effect on me. It doesn't mean I'm against marriage. On the contrary, I love the idea of falling madly in love and living happily ever after. But just recently I've begun to wonder if 'ever after' really exists. I mean, maybe it should be more a case of 'happy until I get bored'. Or, in the case of me and my ex, 'happy till he starts shagging someone else.' Not that I'm bitter or anything.

Violent nose-blowing zones me back in and I see Brian sniffing into his handkerchief. His eyes are all red and puffy and he's trying to focus on the bride and groom who are saying their vows. Patting him reassuringly on the back, I pass him a dry tissue and ease the camera out of his hands. I look down the lens and zoom in on the happy couple.

'Priscilla Klein, I want you to know that even though I've been married eight times before, this marriage to you will last for ever . . .'

'David Wolstenhume, I promise I will always love and honour you, even if you do have to go back inside . . .'

Which brings me on to my next wish.

- *That when I get married it isn't in a pink flamenco dress. To a man who's about to go to prison.*

The flash pops as I take their picture. See? There I go again . . .

When it's all over we pack up the cameras and Brian offers me a lift to the tube. The traffic is backed up all the way along Marylebone Road and we end up stuck in it. Brian's driving the Mini van, which has Together Forever painted down the side in swirly weddingy writing. He hasn't always been a wedding photographer. He used to be one of the big paparazzi photographers, travelling the world, snapping celebrities at flashy film premières, but the death of Princess Diana changed everything. Brian's a big royalist. When Diana died he was devastated. As a paparazzo he felt he was partly to blame so he jacked it all in, hung up his zoom lenses and his stepladders, and set up Together Forever.

Which was where I came in.

I'd just finished a photography course at college and I replied to his ad for an assistant. It wasn't exactly what I'd had in mind—at the time I was wearing head-to-toe black and taking moody shots of graffiti-covered walls—but I figured it would only be temporary. Just long enough to get some experience and build up a portfolio before I turned freelance. Six years later I'm still here. Not that I haven't applied for other jobs, but it's all about networking and contacts and getting your big break. I'm still waiting for mine.

'So what did you think of the wedding?' Brian is asking.

'It was interesting, though I wasn't sure about the dress . . .' I venture cautiously.

'I think she forgot her castanets.'

I giggle, which sets off his smoker's laugh.

'Now, come on, we're being rotten.' He tries to compose himself. 'It wasn't that bad.'

'Yes, it was.' I smile, which lets him off the hook: the floodgates open.

'What about when the best man lost the rings? He looked gutted.'

'And broke out in that nervous rash.'

'And started scratching all over.'

'I saw him with his hands down his pants. I swear to God. I've got it on film!'

Brian and I both crack up. The absurdity of our job provides us with the best in comic entertainment.

'So, what time's our job tomorrow?' I wipe my streaming eyes. 'I promise I won't be late for this one.'

'Don't worry about it. I'm giving you the day off.'

'A day off?' I repeat incredulously. 'On a Saturday?' For people in the wedding business, weekends are always manic. I can't remember the last time I had a whole weekend to myself. How fantastic. I can sleep late. I can laze around in the back garden reading trash mags. I can even spend the entire weekend in bed . . . *By myself*.

Abruptly, my day off loses its appeal. Weekends are for couples. It's like the city suddenly turns into Noah's ark—people walking two by two. Usually my best friend Jess and I hang out together. Most of our old gang have long since paired off, and as we're single we figure it's safety in numbers. But she's an air stewardess and this weekend she's on a back-to-back to Delhi. 'Are you sure? Saturdays are always our busiest days,' I start backtracking.

'Were,' corrects Brian. 'Things have been slow for a while.'

True. I'd noticed that things had eased off over the past few months, but I hadn't given it much thought.

'The business is doing OK, isn't it?'

There's an ominous pause. 'Well, that's what I was going to talk to you about . . .' Sighing, Brian turns to me and I get a horrible sinking feeling. Something is definitely up. 'Now I don't want you to panic . . .' I panic. '. . . because you're a wonderful assistant and a talented photographer . . .'

Oh God, I'm being fired. '. . . and I've enjoyed working with you.'

Enjoyed? As in past tense? My stomach dives towards my blistered toes. Until now I've never entertained the thought of losing my job. I've been too busy wishing something better would come along. Now, faced with unemployment, I see all the great things about it. Going to work in floaty dresses, eating smoked-salmon canapés for lunch, having a boss like Brian . . . 'Please don't fire me,' I blurt.

'*Fire you?*' he gasps, his voice high with astonishment. 'Lord, no! Why would I fire the best assistant I've ever had?'

'I thought . . .' I begin in confusion.

'But I might have to let you go.'

My heart sinks. Brian's doing that thing boyfriends do when they break up with you and try to make you feel better by saying it's not you, it's them. The outcome is exactly the same: you're still being dumped.

'What I'm trying to say is that I've been looking at the books. The business isn't doing very well. It might be wise to start looking for another job.' He glances at me, trying to gauge my reaction.

'It's that bad?' I say quietly.

'Worse. The bank's calling in my loan.'

'Things might pick up.' I attempt to inject a note of optimism. I'd no idea the business was so close to bankruptcy and I feel terrible—not for me, for Brian. I might lose my job, but he stands to lose everything.

'They might,' he agrees, forcing a smile. 'Maybe by some miracle we'll get a big wedding to pay off all our debts, hey?'

'Yeah, maybe.' I smile back determinedly. Mentally I dig out my list and scribble down another wish:

• *That miracles really could happen.*

Eventually the traffic moves again and soon I'm standing on the pavement outside Baker Street station. 'Well, I can't let my assistant go home barefoot, can I?' Brian is saying, a grin on his face.

'You could have paid for a cab for me,' I grumble as he pulls away from the kerb, gazing at my feet. Where once there'd been a pair of stylish diamanté sandals, there are now Brian's golf shoes. Caked with mud. In a size eleven.

As I walk onto the tube platform the heat hits me. Excusing my way through the jostling scrum of pungent body odour, I edge towards the yellow danger line. Which reminds me of the ticket I got last week for parking on a double yellow line. Which I must remember to pay. I tug a pen from my bag. My memory's like a sieve so I'm always making lists. My fridge is covered with dozens of multicoloured Post-it Notes. The only problem is, I forget to look at them.

Scribbling 'PARKING TICKET' on my hand, I hear the train approaching. It's packed, as usual. My spirits sink. Like every other night of my commuting life, I wish there was an empty seat.

The doors slide open and, propelled forwards by the momentum of the crowd behind me, I pop, like a cork out of a bottle, into the carriage. Trying not to focus on the condensation trickling off the windows and down the other passengers' faces, I cling on to one of the overhead handrails as we move out of the station, manoeuvring myself sideways so my nose isn't squashed into someone's armpit. God, I wish I could sit down. I gaze enviously at those lucky enough to have a seat, and freeze on a man with a distinctively strong jaw, a cleft in the chin and a thatch of black hair, underneath which lurks a familiar pair of hazel-brown eyes. Oh my God, what's *he* doing here?

My stomach does a little flip. It's my neighbour. My exceedingly *handsome* neighbour. I've lived across the street from him for the past year but I still don't know his name. That's London, though.

I do, however, know everything *about* my neighbour, who from this moment onwards shall be referred to as 'him'. I know that he drives a Range Rover, shops at Waitrose and Joseph and orders takeout from the Vietnamese restaurant on the corner at least once a week. I also know he's a keen tennis player and has recently bought himself a white sofa.

Not that I'm *stalking* him or anything. I just happen to notice him occasionally. As he turns the page of his book I squint at the front cover to see the title. Would you believe it? It's *Life of Pi*. My own unread copy is currently doubling as a coaster on my bedside table.

For a brief moment I picture myself sitting on my front steps, bathed in the evening sunlight that photographers love to call 'the magic hour' as it makes everyone look fabulous, engrossed in a chapter, my hair tumbling seductively over my face, when I hear, 'Hey, what do you think of the book?' I look up to see my neighbour and before you know it we're chatting about characters and plot and the clever use of dialogue . . .

A sudden influx of new passengers pushes me further up the carriage, throwing me back to reality. In which my neighbour has never noticed me. To him I'm invisible. But perhaps that's not a bad thing, since I look ridiculous every time I see him. Hastily I try to hide my golf-shod feet behind someone's briefcase.

Take last week, for example. After jogging round the park I'd been catching my breath by the entrance, legs all wobbly, hair pasted with sweat to my forehead, when who should appear jauntily round the corner all freshly shaved and *perfect*? Him, of course. And there was the time when I'd popped outside to put out the recycling in my bobbly old dressing gown and a self-heating face mask—the one that turns bright blue when it's ready—and he'd just so *happened* to be at his window. Right at the very second my dressing gown unravelled and he was treated to an impromptu full-frontal.

'Him' suddenly glances up, in the way people do when they feel someone's eyes upon them, and stares right at me. *Staring right at him*. Oh Christ, how embarrassing. Spotting an abandoned copy of *Loot*, a free-ads paper selling everything from secondhand cars to soul mates, I grab it as if it were a life raft and bury my burning cheeks behind a page of flatshares. Pen in hand, I go through them as if I'm really interested.

Just in case he's watching. 'Clapham Common: Cat-loving lesbian household seeks like-minded sister'; 'Earl's Court: Space in three-bed flat—share with eight Aussies'. And then my heart sinks. There it is. Right near the bottom. Just a single line: 'Little Venice: Single room in flatshare, £150 a week, bills included.' I stare at it, absent-mindedly doodling a love heart round it as I think about 'him'. It has to be the most uninspiring, boring advert ever. Which was what I'd intended when I'd placed it three weeks ago.

I don't want to have to let my spare room. I don't want some stranger living in my flat, sharing my sofa, *my loo seat*. But I don't have much choice. When Daniel moved out he took his Bang & Olufsen TV, half of our photograph collection and his share of the flat's deposit. Leaving me with no TV, no pictures of me with dodgy blonde highlights when I was twenty-seven and huge mortgage payments. For the last nine months I've been living off my savings and now I'm stony broke. The last two months I defaulted on the mortgage and the bank are threatening me with repossession, so it's either find a flatmate or . . . Or what? I gaze out of the window, wishing I could see an answer to all my problems.

I'd always been under the impression that by the time I hit thirty my life would be more sorted. I'd have some money in the bank, a high-flying career as a photographer, and at least one pair of designer shoes. But last year it happened—the big three-O—and I realised that while most of my friends are climbing up the ladders of life, being promoted, getting married, having their hair done at Nicky Clarke, *I* just keep sliding down the snakes. I'm up to my overdraft limit—*whoosh*, slide down a snake. My beloved MG Midget is in the garage after a run-in with a BMW—*whoosh*, slide down another snake. As for my high-flying career as a photographer—*whoooossssh*, there I go again.

For a while back there I thought I might have had it sussed. Meeting Daniel, falling in love, buying a flat and moving in together gave me a sense of achievement. Direction. Maturity. Suddenly I had a mortgage, life insurance, *a partner*. Even though most of the time I felt as if I was playing at being a grown-up, everyone treated me with new respect. My wicked stepmother sent me recipe books, a mug tree and lots of Tupperware for a mysterious 'bottom drawer'. Even the doctor at my local family-planning clinic gave me an approving smile as she wrote out my prescription for the pill.

So what if the career piece of the jigsaw was missing? All the bits for my love life were there and fitted together perfectly. Surely the rest would fall into place? Well, no, it didn't. Instead it had all fallen apart rather dramatically when I'd borrowed Daniel's Saab and discovered condoms in the glove compartment. I know—it's such a cliché. I'd always assumed things like that only happened to characters in soaps or guests on *Jerry Springer*, but there I'd been, sitting at the lights, singing along to The White Stripes, rummaging in the glove compartment for a rogue packet of cigarettes. Publicly I'd given up months ago, but secretly I'd had a few drags now and again. But instead of a packet of Marlboro Lights, I'd discovered a box of Durex.

My mind froze in shock. Not only had I just found condoms in my boyfriend's car, but a bumper pack of twelve . . . I'd tipped it upside-down and the condoms spilt into my lap. Correction: *condom*. There was just one left. And it was ribbed.

I remember a bizarre urge to laugh. It was just so ludicrous. Daniel? Having sex with someone else? Followed by an equally intense burst of anger. *The bastard. The two-timing bastard. How could he?* Finished off with a pathetic desire to break down in tears.

I'd confronted Daniel as soon as I got back to the flat. He'd come up with every excuse he could think of until finally he'd confessed that he'd been sleeping with someone else—but he wasn't in love with her, it was just sex. *Just sex*.

The way he had said it had been so flippant, as if it was inconsequential, *unimportant*. Yet those two little words had impacted on my world as if they'd been an iron ball swinging from a bulldozer. Forget breaking my heart, he pretty much demolished it.

Of course I got over it. People always do. And now I'm fine. I've got my photography, my friends and Billy Smith, my cat, if I get a bit lonely. That's not to say I wouldn't like the odd *date* now and again, but it's not as if I fall asleep every night wishing I could meet the perfect man who's going to fall madly, truly and deeply in love with me. Well, perhaps not *every* night. Blushing guiltily I glance at my neighbour. He's gone. Which is when I realise that the train has stopped and we're at a station. My station.

Beep-beep-beep-beep-beep-beep.

Oh, shit. The doors are making the high-pitched noise that means they're about to close. Frantically I begin excusing my way through the packed carriages, accidentally dropping the copy of *Loot*, which falls, scattering green newspaper pages all over the floor of the carriage. Oh, double shit. I scramble for them.

Beep-beep-beep-beep-beep-beep-beeeeeeeeeeeep.

The doors are sliding shut as I abandon the remaining dropped pages and lunge for them. Luckily I make it onto the platform in one piece, only to be greeted at the exit by dark, angry storm clouds. I wish I had an umbrella. Heavy raindrops pummel the pavement, and everyone's getting soaked. Myself included.

I try holding what's left of *Loot* over my head as I run along the high street, but within seconds it's all soggy. The rain's bouncing up my legs and drenching my dress, making it cling to my chest as if I'm in a wet T-shirt competition—bad enough if I was in some drunken, foam-filled club in Lanzarote, but much, much worse in my local high street. Someone I know might see me—and my nipples, which are now protruding through my dress like cocktail cherries.

Just as I have that humiliating thought I spot my neighbour, completely dry under his sturdy golfing umbrella. He's a few metres ahead, waiting outside Oddbins. How does he always manage to look so damn gorgeous? In a moment of madness I consider saying hi, only he doesn't see me as he's turning to a pretty brunette who's appeared at the shop doorway hugging a bottle of wine. She ducks under his umbrella, links his arm and they set off down the street together.

Deflated, I can't help wishing that it was me who was tucked under the umbrella with him, all dry and happy with a spring in my step.

'Heather.' A loud yell makes me spin round. 'Lucky heather.' I see a straggle of Irish gypsies by the cash machine.

'You've got a pretty face, love.' A gypsy breaks away from the others to barge in front of me. I try to dodge her, but she blocks my way. 'Here, take some lucky heather. Use it wisely and it will bring you your heart's desire. Good fortune will come your way . . .' She thrusts a tired sprig tied with a fraying pink ribbon into my face. 'Never underestimate the power of the lucky heather.'

'No, thanks,' I say firmly.

'Just two quid, my darlin'.'

'No, honestly.' I try to avoid her gaze, but the gypsy grabs my hand. She waggles the heather. 'Keep it with you. Trust me, the heather will work its magic. Your luck will change. All your wishes will come true.'

Yeah, right. Do I look like a complete sucker?

But from the glint in her piercing green eyes I know she won't take no for an answer and I'm getting even more soaked standing here, so I give in and stuff a couple of pound coins into her sandpapery palm. And then she disappears into the rain-soaked crowds, leaving me clutching a sprig of heather. *Lucky heather*. The irony isn't lost on me. I peer at the spindly, feathery twigs. *This* is supposed to have magical powers? I shove it into my bag—I'll chuck it away when I get home. After I've taken off these wet clothes, cracked open a bottle and climbed into a steaming hot bath.

Dextrously turning off the tap with my big toe, I lie back on the pillow of scented bubbles. Bliss. Sheer, unadulterated bliss. Sipping my wine I inhale the delicious aroma of vanilla and cinnamon, then balance my glass on the side of the bath, and grab the loofah and a bar of soap. Raising one pink shiny thigh, I lather it and rhythmically brush backwards and forwards. Up and down. Side to side. Sloughing off dead skin, pounding cellulite, kneading dimples.

Discarding the loofah I reach for the razor and inspect the blade. It's stuffed full of bristles from the last time I used it. And it's the last one. Damn. I wish I had a new packet. I give the blade a quick rinse under the tap and get to work, cutting through the lather with well-practised strokes. Shin, calf, ankle, knee. Ouch. I watch a spot of blood appear like a red bubble on my leg.

'Shit.' Grabbing the flannel I fold it into a makeshift bandage and am just pressing it to my knee when the phone rings. Probably Jess, I decide, then remember she's in Delhi. And it's not my father as I spoke to him earlier today. He'd just read an article about how they've started teaching yoga to cats in Hollywood, and was wondering if Billy Smith might fancy some classes for his birthday. I smile. My father's an artist and a little eccentric, but I wouldn't change him for the world.

I decide against answering it. It's probably my stepmother calling to annoy me about something anyway. Although there is a slim possibility that it's Daniel, calling in reply to my drunken text.

As the thought occurs to me I'm unsure whether that's a good thing or a bad thing, considering the text: 'I miss you. Fancy sex with an ex?' That was the tequila talking, not me: I don't miss him, I *hate* him.

After what feels like forever the phone stops ringing and I hear the answering machine click on. I wait to hear my stepmother's affected voice. Ashamed of her working-class Manchester roots, Rosemary adopts an accent not dissimilar to the Queen's.

'Hey there . . .'

Hang on a minute, since when was my stepmother a man? Oh, my God, it's not Daniel, is it? But then I register that this man has an American accent and I feel a flash of foolishness—and something that feels like disappointment.

'I'm calling about the ad you placed in . . . er . . . hang on . . .' There's the sound of rustling pages. '*Loot*,' we say in the same beat.

Shit. I vault out of the bath and dash naked into the hallway, dripping soapy water onto the floor. Keep talking, I pray, lunging for the receiver with slippery fingers.

'Don't hang up,' I pant, tearing the phone from its cradle—then remember I'm a prospective landlady, and I should sound like one. 'I mean, good evening,' I say, adopting my best telephone voice.

'Oh, hi, yeah. I was . . . er . . . calling about the ad.'

'And you are?' I demand, and then cringe. I'm trying to rent my room. I need to sound friendly, laid-back, *cool*. 'Sorry, you caught me in the bath—' I break off. 'I mean, hi, I'm Heather.'

'Oh, hi,' he says. 'I'm Gabe.'

Hmm. What an unusual name. Momentarily I wonder what Gabe looks like. Being American, he's probably tall, broad, with really good teeth—unless, with *my* luck, he's short, fat and balding. And what if he is? This is a prospective lodger, not a date.

'Erm . . . so I was wondering . . . about the room?'

The room. I snap back.

'Is it still available?'

'Well, there has been a lot of interest,' I lie, standing next to the window. It faces directly on to my gorgeous neighbour's and, unable to resist, I lift the edge of the blind and peek round the side to see if I can catch a glimpse of him.

'Oh, well, in that case, don't worry about it. I was only looking for something short-term.'

'Short-term?' My ears prick up.

'Yeah, I'm here in London for three weeks, maybe a month.'

I like the sound of a month. It's nice and temporary. It's four weeks, which, at a hundred and fifty pounds a week, is . . . I do some mental arithmetic . . . Enough to pay the mortgage.

'But I haven't made a decision yet so I'm still interviewing people,' I add, accidentally jerking the blind. It shoots up, leaving my window bare and exposed, not to mention myself. At the exact moment that my neighbour is drawing his curtains. '*Agggh!*' I shriek.

There's silence at the other end of the line. Then: 'Er . . . are you OK?'

Having jumped away from the window, 'Yes, I'm fine,' I reply.

'Are you sure?'

'Absolutely,' I reply peering round the corner like a sniper. I glance back across the street. 'Him' is still at the window. No doubt frozen with shock. I throw myself to the ground in an army dive. '*Agggh.*'

'Perhaps this isn't a good time . . .'

'No, now's a good time,' I pant, inching forward on my elbows. 'In fact . . .' Reaching the coat rack I stand up, grabbing a jacket from a hook. I wrap it round myself. 'Why don't you come along and take a look at the room, see if you like it? See if you like me.' I laugh nervously.

'When? What about tomorrow?'

'Tomorrow?' I squeak.

'Sorry, I forgot, it's Saturday night. You've probably made plans.'

'Um . . . well, actually . . .' My voice trails off as I remember the truth. I have no plans. I'm single. I'm staying in alone. On a Saturday night. For God's sake, don't be such an idiot, Heather, think of your credit-card bills. Think of the fact that you've been advertising your room for weeks and this is the first reply you've had. 'Tomorrow's fine,' I say quickly.

'Awesome.' There's a pause. 'I'll need your address.'

'Oh, yes, my address . . . of course.' I proceed to gabble it so quickly that he has to ask me to repeat it twice.

'Thanks. I'll see you tomorrow. Around seven?'

'Great, see you then.'

I replace the handset and lean against the wall. Reeling at the unexpected speed of events, I take a couple of deep breaths. Although it's a balmy seventy degrees in the hallway, I shiver. Sticking my hands in my pockets, my fingers brush against something. Soft yet scratchy. Puzzled, I pull it out. It's that stupid lucky heather. How did that get there?

Walking to the bin I keep near the front door, I'm about to toss it in when I notice a small package on my doormat. One of those freebies you get in the post: a packet of razor blades. Well, would you believe it?

Chuffed, I hurry back into the bathroom and reach for my razor to swap the blade for a new one. Which is when I see that I'm still holding the sprig of heather. For some reason, I can't get rid of it. Maybe it really is magical. *Magical?* I smile ironically. Heather Hamilton, what on earth's got into you? Of course it's not magical, it's just a plant. I gaze at the delicate white sprigs. Superstitious nonsense or not, it's actually rather pretty. Filling the top of a deodorant can with water I place the lucky heather in its makeshift vase and pop it on the windowsill. For now, anyway.

Chapter Two

ALONG THE BANKS of the River Avon a group of art students are huddled round wooden easels. This class is part of a summer-school programme run by Bath's art college, and the students are being taught by Lionel, a robust, bearded man in his early sixties, who looks as if he's travelled there in a time machine from the French impressionist era. Wearing a paint-splattered smock, a neckerchief and a beret angled sideways over thick, black curls worthy of a man half his age, he's striding round the class bellowing enthusiasm and advice. 'Fabulous use of the magenta, Sandy.'

A large-chested woman beams and continues daubing vigorously.

'Lionel!'

My voice catches my father by surprise and he swings round, smock billowing round him like a parachute. Waving at him from the wooden stile where I've been perched for the last five minutes, watching him proudly, I feel my heart tug. I'm very much my father's daughter and I miss him. A wide smile stretches across my face.

'Heather, darling!' Lionel bellows, abandoning his students and striding over to greet me. 'What a wonderful surprise!' Throwing his arms round my shoulders he pulls me into a bear hug. 'Why didn't you let me know you were coming? Or did you, and I've forgotten?'

'I'm sorry, it was a last-minute decision. Brian gave me the day off and I just got my car back from the garage so I thought I'd come and see you.'

Well, it's partly true. Yes, it wasn't until I'd woken up this morning that I decided I needed to escape London for the day. But not calling beforehand was deliberate. I hadn't wanted to let Rosemary know I was coming. If I had, she would have made some excuse about them having a prior engagement, or told me she had one of her migraines, or suggested that another weekend might be better. This way, she can't spoil things—but then again she did that when she married Dad.

'Marvellous, marvellous,' beams Lionel, releasing me from his embrace. Digging out his fob-watch from the pocket of his voluminous corduroys, he flicks open the brass cover. 'Well, that's about it for today, everyone,' he declares. 'It's twelve thirty on the nose. Time for a spot of lunch.'

Lunch is back at the house, an imposing Regency building high on a hill in the centre of Bath. Built from honey-coloured stone, by anyone's standards it's a truly beautiful house.

I, however, hate it. It belongs to Rosemary and, like its owner, it's cold and unwelcoming. Before she and Dad were married, he was living in our cosy cottage in Cornwall, with its uneven walls, tiny porthole windows and thatched roof. Now it's used only for holidays and family get-togethers—Rosemary complained it was too small for her furniture.

What she'd meant was that the house reminded her of my mother.

Lionel bought it when Mum was first diagnosed. Hoping that the warmer climate and sea air might do her good, he sold our house in Yorkshire and moved the whole family hundreds of miles south to Port Isaac. Ed and I were still children, and had hated being uprooted, leaving our friends. Our mother, however, fell in love with the place and her happiness was infectious, changing our minds but never her diagnosis. She died less than three years later.

'So, how long are you staying?'

We're all sitting round the kitchen table. There's my dad, me and my stepmother, who'd greeted my appearance with the customary tight lipped kiss on the cheek, then complained that they probably wouldn't have enough food. 'I wasn't expecting guests.'

I turn to my father, who's cutting himself a large slice of Brie. 'Just for the day,' I say. 'I've got to be back in London by tonight.'

'Tonight?' Disappointment clouds his face. 'Aha, I get it!' His face springs back up again and Lionel pounds his fist on the table. 'You've got a date. When do we get to meet your new fella, then?'

'*Lionel*,' I gasp, suddenly feeling about thirteen again. Back then he would pick me up from the youth club and quiz me about boys as we walked back to our tiny cottage. It was just after Mum had died, and suddenly he was taking me through puberty, first boyfriends, sex education. It had been a learning process for both of us.

Somehow we got through it. As he told me when, in tears, I'd barricaded myself into the bathroom with my first trainer bra, if we could get through losing a wife and a mother, we could get through anything.

Including this lunch.

'I've been too busy working to have a boyfriend.'

'Your boss keeping your nose to the grindstone, hey?' mumbles Lionel through a bite of Brie.

'Something like that,' I say vaguely, deciding not to mention the possibility of losing my job. I don't want to worry him—or give Rosemary some more ammunition against me. If I hear one more time about Annabel, her daughter who's only a year older than me but is happily married to Miles, 'a high-flier' in the City, and has two adorable children, a loft conversion and a French-speaking nanny, I'll . . . Well, I don't know what I'll do but I'm sure I'll do something.

'Oh, I love weddings!' I'm distracted from my thoughts by Rosemary clasping her hands. 'I do envy you, your job must be so romantic.'

Taken aback by this uncharacteristic compliment, I'm unsure what to say. Rosemary and I don't *do* compliments: our conversation consists of a form of jousting, each trying to knock the other off balance. It's exhausting. 'Er . . . well, not really,' I begin hesitantly. 'When you've done as many weddings as I have, one is very much like another.'

'Not when it's your own,' she says pointedly, looking at Lionel.

I squirm. It really annoys me when Rosemary gets all soppy around

Lionel. 'No, maybe not,' I agree reluctantly. To agree with Rosemary is usually tantamount to defeat, but this time I change my mind. Maybe I've been wrong about her all this time. Maybe, like Lionel says, she really does want to be friends.

'Never mind, dear.' Reaching over for the wine, she pats my arm. 'It'll be your turn one day.'

'Actually I'm single out of choice, not necessity,' I point out casually. 'Plenty of men ask me out on dates.'

'I'm sure they do, a pretty girl like you,' agrees Rosemary, to my surprise. So, she really is trying to be nice. 'Though it was different in my day. If you weren't married by the time you were thirty, you were considered an old maid.' Ouch. See what happens when I let my guard down?

After lunch, we go outside and have Pimm's on the lawn and a game of chess. A keen player, Lionel has built a giant chessboard on the patio, and when Rosemary goes inside to lie down he and I pace round the board, carrying the four-foot-high polystyrene pieces onto different-coloured squares. As father and daughter we're the best of friends; as chess opponents we're sworn enemies.

'Checkmate,' I announce triumphantly, setting down my bishop.

'Good Lord, how did you manage that?'

'I had a good teacher,' I reply.

'Aah, you're too kind,' Lionel mutters, patting my shoulder affectionately. 'I was a terrible player until I met your mother. Did I ever tell you about the first time we played chess?'

'You were both eighteen and in your first year at Cambridge.' I know this story off by heart.

'That's right,' nods Lionel, reminiscing. 'A tutor had organised a chess tournament with one of the ladies' colleges. It took place in the banqueting hall and I remember walking in and looking for my opponent. And then I saw her, sitting under a shaft of sunlight, waiting for me . . .'

'A dazzling redhead who played chess like a Russian.'

'She had me within six moves. Six moves was all it took.' Lionel shakes his head as if he still can't believe it, even after all these years.

We fall silent, drinking in the memory like vintage wine.

'I still miss her,' I say eventually.

'I know, darling.'

'I wish she was here with us right now.'

'Now, that would make me a bigamist.'

I smile wryly at his feeble joke. I know he's trying to make me feel better, but it still hurts. 'I just wish things were different.'

Puffing at his pipe, Lionel fixes me with his pale grey eyes. 'You mustn't wish your life away, Heather.'

His face is serious but it doesn't stop me quipping, 'Why not?'

'Because life's far too short to waste a single drop of it. Your mother taught me that.' He pauses to watch a bird hovering by the fountain. 'You know I once read somewhere that yesterday is history, tomorrow is a mystery, but today is a gift. That's why we call it the present.'

Absorbing the words I'm struck by their profundity. I wonder which philosopher came up with that. Presumably some Buddhist monk. 'Who said that?' I ask, reverentially.

The bird darts away and my dad turns back to me. 'I think it was Joan Collins,' he confesses.

The drive back to London always takes for ever. For some strange reason, the M4 is always 'currently undergoing roadworks', which means hours in traffic jams or crawling at 30 m.p.h. through elaborate patterns of orange cones. Yet you never see any evidence of any 'works' taking place. It's one of life's mysteries. Like crop circles, I muse, accelerating onto the motorway from the slip road and wishing there was no such thing as roadworks or traffic. Just imagine, if it was clear like this all the way I'd be home in no time.

As I speed up I increase the volume to drown the sound of the wind. In preparation for the inevitable delays I've made myself some new cassettes. I've also packed supplies in the form of a bumper bag of Liquorice Allsorts. Well, if I'm going to be stranded on the M4 I might as well have *The Best of Duran Duran* and my favourite pink and yellow ones with liquorice in the middle to keep me company.

But twenty minutes into the journey, I'm feeling a little disconcerted. I can't put my finger on it but I feel as if something's missing. Music? Nope: Simon Le Bon's belting out 'Rio' at full volume. Food? Nope. I pick a bit of liquorice out of my back molar. Then I get it. Orange cones. There aren't any. And neither are there any traffic jams. Smiling in happy disbelief, I press my flip-flop against the accelerator. At this rate I'll be home in less than two hours.

Correction: one hour and forty-two minutes exactly. I know because I check my watch as I turn into my street. I slow down and idle along the tree-lined pavement, looking for a parking space. I don't hold out much hope. In all the years I've lived at my flat I've never parked outside it. 'I wish there was a space,' I murmur, but it's bumper-to-bumper all the way down my street. I'll have to circle the block and . . . ohmygod! I nearly drive straight into a Range Rover. Parked facing the wrong way, it's indicating right and, as it swings in front of me, I slam on the brakes.

I come to an abrupt halt, my head flung back like that of a crash-test dummy, and look up at the windscreen of the Range Rover. 'Sorry,' I mouth silently at the driver.

It's him. My neighbour. He nods a curt response, swerves round me and roars off down the street.

Typical! I've done it again. I've bumped into him like a complete idiot. Depressed, I slump over my steering wheel and rest my forehead on the shiny MG badge—then spring up again. Hang on a minute. If he's gone, that means . . .

There, where the Range Rover was just parked, *right opposite my flat*, I see a modern-day miracle. A parking space.

It's six o'clock. The stranger with the American accent's due to turn up in an hour. And I'm wondering what on earth I'm going to say, what I'm going to ask him, what rules I'm going to lay down. And, most importantly of all: *what the hell am I going to wear?*

I'm no closer to answering this question thirty minutes later when every inch of my bedroom floor is covered with clothes. Usually in a moment of crisis I'd ring Jess for advice, but she's in India. I glance at my digital alarm clock: 18:50. Oh, bugger bollocks. I've got to make a decision. OK. Grab a few items from the bed and start to get dressed.

19:05. *He's late.* I puff nervously at a cigarette, then catch myself. *Jesus.* I think back to the list of house rules I came up with when I put the ad in the paper. Number one: no smoking indoors.

I haul open a window, then waft my arms around manically, trying to get rid of the smoke. Before realising that I'm still holding the cigarette, which probably isn't helping. I stub it out in a coffee cup on the mantelpiece. Oh, shit. Number two: no using the crockery as an ashtray.

19:18. *Where the hell is he?* Having downed two gin and tonics, now I'm getting antsy. 'Don't tell me I'm being stood up,' I huff, as I stomp into the bathroom for a pee.

Flushing, I stand up and give the bathroom an extra squirt of air-freshener, then replace the cap. Which is when I catch sight of the lucky heather, still in its makeshift vase on the windowsill. Irritated by my sentimentality in keeping it, I give the plastic top a quick rinse and put it back on the deodorant. The lucky heather goes into the bin.

Having emptied the bathroom bin in preparation for the American, I head for the silver one in the kitchen. But I only get halfway down the hallway when I decide to make a quick detour via the front room. The plan being I'll take a last peek through the window and then, if there's no sign of him I'll abandon the whole thing and defrost a pizza, I decide, as I lean across the back of the sofa. The plan not being to have my face squashed up against the glass like Garfield on a car window when someone knocks on the front door.

A blond stranger is on the doorstep, wearing a motorcycle jacket and carrying a helmet. He's checking his reflection in the brass door knocker—brushing his shaggy fringe out of his eyes, pushing his tortoiseshell glasses up his nose, turning his head from one side to the other . . .

The stranger is suddenly looking right at me, his large blue eyes filled with curiosity. It throws me off balance and, giving a muffled squeak, I promptly fall down the back of the sofa.

'I'm Gabe.'

The first thing I notice are his freckles. He's got even more than me.

'Hi, I'm Heather.' Rubbing my elbow, I show him into the flat. 'I was, er . . . just doing a spot of housework . . . cleaning the windows.' I laugh awkwardly. There follows a toe-curling silence.

'So, can I see the room?'

'Of course,' I say hastily, and lead him down the hallway. 'This is it.' Pushing open the door I stand back. 'Not very big, I'm afraid, but it's got everything. Bed, cupboard, chest of drawers, portable TV . . .'

As I speak Gabe walks into the small, L-shaped room and regards the pale yellow walls, the polished mahogany wardrobe, the sheepskin rug. I've even put a couple of books on the empty shelves: the *Hip Hotel* guides, something by Salman Rushdie and Nick Hornby's *About a Boy*. Books say a lot about a person so I ignored my stack of chick-lit and *Harry Potter* in favour of something more literary to make a good first impression. I rub my bruised elbow. Well, that was the idea.

Earlier, I opened the sash window wide to give a full view of the back garden, and now he walks over to it. With his back to me, he leans against the sill, but doesn't speak. Obviously not much of a talker, I decide, tracing the silhouette of his shoulders. He's tall—over six foot—and much broader than I'd first thought. My eyes travel down the back of his jacket, lingering over the baggy arse of his combat trousers—well, I'm only human—to the tattered hems. Nope, definitely not my type. Too grungy. Too quiet as well.

'I'll take it.'

'Oh . . .' I'm not prepared for this. I'd expected lots of questions, rehearsed lots of answers, but now, faced with a *fait accompli*, I'm suddenly unsure. Do I really want this stranger living in my flat? I mean, I hardly know you, pipes up a little voice inside me.

'OK, so what do you want to know about me?'

As Gabe turns I realise I spoke aloud. I blush. 'Sorry, I'm not used to this,' I confess. 'I've never let a room before and it just feels weird.'

'Sure, I understand.' He sits on the windowsill, and pushes his hair out of his face. 'Fire away. Ask me anything you like.'

'Really?' Well, in that case . . . I disappear out of the room for a few moments, and when I return with a notebook Gabe's still on the windowsill. Only he's got company in the shape of a large ginger tomcat curled up on his knee, head tucked in one end, tail the other, purring loudly.

'Oh, you've met Billy Smith,' I say, surprised to see my cat snuggled up in his crotch. The same cat that hisses and digs his claws into anyone he doesn't know who tries so much as to stroke him. 'He normally doesn't like strangers.' Traitor, I hiss silently. Who buys you Fancy Feast?

'Animals usually like me.' Gabe tickles Billy Smith between the ears. He's rewarded by an even louder purr.

I can't believe it! Even my bloody cat's cheating on me.

'It's people I have a bit of a problem with.' His face is serious, but I recognise the joke and smile. Despite my reservations I am warming to him. Plopping down on the bed, I turn over the first page of my note book. 'I jotted down a few things I wanted to ask you, in case I forgot,' I begin. Actually that's a lie. 'Jot' gives the impression that I casually scribbled down a few reminders, when in fact I made one of my lists.

'Fire away,' he says again.

I clear my throat. 'Erm . . . do you smoke?'

'I'm trying to take it up.' He grins.

I'm not sure if he's making fun of me, but I make a note anyway. 'Well, there's no smoking indoors. By all means smoke in the garden but not using crockery, plant pots or my flowerbeds as an ashtray.'

'Sure.'

'Drugs?'

'Only prescription,' he answers solemnly.

I make a scribble. 'No leaving tea bags in the sink.'

'I drink coffee.'

'Oh, OK . . . Great.' I smile. *Tightly*. This isn't going to plan. If I'm honest I'd been secretly hoping my rules would deter him from wanting the room. He seems very pleasant and everything—if you'd bumped into him in a bar. But outside my bathroom. In his underpants?

Panic grabs me. This is never going to work. I can't have a stranger parading around my home in his Y-fronts.

'Moving on to the kitchen.' I stand up hastily. 'No leaving the dishes. I don't have a dishwasher so you'll have to wash up after every meal.'

Gabe gives me a mock-salute.

'As for the fridge, you can have the top shelf and if you want to put meat in there make sure it's covered. I'm a vegetarian.'

I march into the bathroom. 'I only have one bathroom so we'll have to share.' I push open the door and, as he peers inside, I start rattling through Daniel's habits which drove me mad. That should do the trick. American or British, men are men, and one thing I've learned is that they hate nothing more than a nag. So I nag: 'No taking your socks off and leaving them in little balls on the floor, no shaving and leaving your bristles all over the basin, no using all my shampoo . . . Oh, and no leaving the loo seat up.'

'The loo?'

'You know—the bog.'

No recognition.

'The toilet?' I try.

'Oh . . . right, yeah, of course.' He nods solemnly and rubs the end of his nose. It's a large nose and has a lump in the middle. It looks as if it's been broken. I wonder how he did it, I think, as he gazes at me with those big blue eyes. 'Rule number ten?'

'Ten?'

'I've been counting.'

'Oh, right . . . yes.' My eyes dart back to the jotter on my lap. 'The TV.' I stride past him into the living room. 'I have satellite but no hogging the sports channel and watching football every night.'

'In America we call it soccer.'

'I call it boring,' I reply tartly.

'Not a big sports fan, huh?' Gabe raises his eyebrows.

'Nope.' I shake my head firmly. Right. That must have done it. I've called football boring. He'll be out of that door in less than five seconds.

'Don't worry. I'm not a fan of watching sports either.' He runs his fingers along Billy Smith's spine. 'I prefer doing them.'

Hang on a minute. He's not moving.

'Back home I'm a big surfer,' he continues, 'but I guess I won't be doing much of that in England.'

'Actually, they have great surfing in Cornwall where I grew up,' I hear myself say eagerly. 'Every year they have this big competition in Newquay and surfers come from all over the world.

'Wow, that sounds awesome. I'd love to take a trip down there.'

'It's really beautiful, you'd love it,' I say enthusiastically. Abruptly I'm hit with a wave of nostalgia. It's ages since I've been. 'You should definitely go.' I'm talking to myself as much as to him. Perhaps we can go together, share the petrol money. I watch him tickle Billy Smith's ears, like a pro. Perhaps having a flatmate won't be as bad as I've imagined.

There's a pause, which Gabe breaks first. 'So, do I pass?'

I consult my notebook. Admittedly he's ticked most of the boxes. But . . . I'm still not sure. He seems nice but maybe I should wait.

'You've dropped something.' Gabe picks it up from the carpet and holds it out to me. 'Looks like some kind of buttonhole.'

I look down at the ribbon-tied sprig between his fingers. It's the lucky heather. Suddenly I have the strangest feeling. Funny how it keeps turning up. Maybe it really is lucky.

I take it from him. 'So, when do you want to move in?'

Remember the Boomtown Rats? I don't, really, I was too young, but I remember Ed, my brother, playing their seven-inch single and I have to agree with Sir Bob on one thing: I don't like Mondays much either. But this Monday morning is different. I'm in an extraordinarily good mood and the reason I've got a great big smile on my face is because . . .

'You've been shagging.'

As I push open the frosted-glass door that leads into the small office upstairs I'm accosted by a familiar East End accent.

'What?' I scoop up the pile of mail from the mat.

Brian is sitting with his feet up on the desk, munching a croissant and eyeing me. 'That smile. I'd know it anywhere. It's a shag smile.'

Rolling my eyes, I tug off my denim jacket and walk over to the mahogany coat stand overflowing with old coats and jackets.

'So, come on, who's the lucky devil?'

Damn! I wish there was a free peg to hang my coat on.

'There is no lucky devil,' I retort, then fall silent. There is an empty peg. I stare at it in disbelief. How weird. Before slipping my jacket onto it I turn back to Brian.

'You have the whole weekend off and you waltz in here with a grin the size of a ventriloquist's dummy. Put your hand on your heart and tell me you haven't met a bloke.'

'OK, so I met a man . . .' I confess. 'But he's my new flatmate.'

Brian is crestfallen. 'You mean there's no gossip?'

'Nope. I'm single, remember? I spend most of my evenings doing my hand-washing and getting into bed with a good book.'

'You and me both.' He shrugs gloomily. 'You're looking at a man who hasn't had a whiff of action since the last millennium. No, I'm serious,' he protests, before I've had a chance to disagree.

Not that I'm going to. Ever since I've known Brian he's only ever had three topics of conversation. Sex (lack of). West End musicals/Michael Crawford (a genius). And the fact that he hasn't been in a relationship for seven years. Three things I can't help feeling are directly related.

'Actually, if you really want to know why I'm so happy it's because this morning I got a seat on the tube.'

'A seat on the tube?' echoes Brian, visibly disappointed. 'That's it?'

There's no point in explaining. I know Brian is never going to understand the huge relevance of what happened to me this morning after I'd gone down the steps onto the platform and waited for the next approaching train, wishing as always for an empty seat.

At first I hadn't been able to see a thing for jostling commuters filling the carriage, but then slowly, imperceptibly, people had shifted to the sides until there, directly opposite, was—believe it or not—an empty seat.

'That's it?' repeats Brian. 'That's the reason for your good mood?'

'Yep, that's it.' Well, OK, that's not *exactly* it. I suppose it's also got *something* to do with there being no queue in Starbucks, no traffic on my way back from Bath, a parking space. And then, of course, there's Gabe, my new flatmate who just so happens to be moving in today.

My stomach flutters. Not that I'm excited or anything. 'Hmm . . . hmm . . . hmm . . . hmmmm,' I suddenly realise I'm humming the Boomtown Rats. Only I'm sorry, Sir Bob, I'm afraid I've changed my mind. *I love Mondays*.

By late afternoon the phone hasn't rung once and Brian's early joviality has turned sour. After looking at the diary, which is practically empty, I don't blame him. Taking his advice, I spend my lunch-hour updating my CV. I've just made a start on developing the last wedding in the darkroom when I hear knocking.

It's Jess. Air stewardess, fellow Zara-shopper and general all-round best friend. She's wearing her uniform. 'Guess what!'

'Aren't you supposed to be in Delhi?' I usher her inside the tiny red-lit room. There's no need for hi-how-are-you between Jess and me. It's like we've been having one never-ending conversation since we met. Which I suppose we have, really.

'I was. We just flew back.' She plonks herself onto a stool and turns to me excitedly. 'I've got a date!' she announces.

'With Simon?' Simon is the architect Jess met on the Internet and had dinner with last week. Jess loves the Internet: when she's not flying all over the world, she's bidding for handbags on eBay and looking for love on findahusband.com, or whatever the dating site is called.

'No. His name's Greg. He's a banker. Thirty-five. Hobbies include mountain-biking and eating sushi. Not at the same time.' She chuckles at her joke—although I fear it may have been his. 'I met him on the Internet while I was in Delhi—not that he lives in Delhi, of course. He lives here in London. Because of the time difference we've spent the last few days emailing . . .'

'But I thought you were really into Simon?' I bleat.

'He never called,' she says, wrinkling her nose. '*C'est la vie*.'

'I take it you're not heartbroken.'

'Honey, I'm thirty-six. I don't have time to be heartbroken.' She kicks off her shoes and rubs the heels of her stockinged feet. 'Time is men.'

Jess is supremely practical. For her, finding the right man is like finding a secondhand car. Year of make? Nice body? Number of previous owners? Reliable? I used to think her attitude to love was *too* practical—after all, it's the heart you're dealing with, not a two-litre engine—but after my disaster with Daniel I'm beginning to think she might have the right idea.

'And so far there's been no red flags,' she boasts proudly. 'No ex-wife, no fear of commitment, no deeply held religious beliefs . . .'

I take a moment to wonder if this is the time to point out that she said that about Simon. And Dennis. And Reuben.

'I think this could be it.'

On second thoughts, perhaps not.

'When are you meeting him?'

'Saturday. He's taking me somewhere special.'

'Where?'

'I don't know. He said it was to be a surprise.'

'A surprise?' I enthuse. 'Wow, how exciting.'

I'm lying. If there's one thing I hate it's surprises. I like to know what to expect so that I can be prepared. Take surprise birthday parties, for example. I can't think of anything worse than arriving home from work and someone jumping out from behind the sofa yelling, 'Surprise!' I mean, can you imagine? There you are, about to make yourself look fabulous and spend the evening at a swanky restaurant, and suddenly you've got to be thrilled that fifty of your nearest and dearest are crammed in your living room spilling vodka and cranberry on your new cream carpet. Meanwhile, you're standing there with ratty hair and a spot that's crying out for cover-up, wishing you could hide in the bathroom with your hair serum and Estée Lauder Double Wear foundation.

'I just hope it's not London Zoo.' Jess's voice breaks into my thoughts.

'London Zoo?'

'Phil Toddington took me there on our first date. *Our only date*.'

'Was it that bad?'

She rolls her eyes. 'Heather, I was at the penguin enclosure for three hours. In the middle of February. In a pair of snakeskin slingbacks and my backless dress from Karen Millen. I nearly froze to death.'

'Mmm, very romantic.' I giggle, and despite herself she joins in.

'Oh, bloody hell, Heather, it was awful,' she says, 'I remember thinking, This is it. This is my love life. Can it get any worse?'

Well, you could have fallen in love with him, bought a place together, then discovered he'd been shagging a girl at work for the past six months, I muse, as an image of Daniel pops into my head.

'He could have taken you to a comedy club,' I say instead.

Immediately we stop laughing and exchange a look.

Stand-up comedy is our pet hate. That was how we met. Imprisoned in the Laugh Factory in Covent Garden by my then-boyfriend, I'd been bored to tears and gazing round the audience when I'd seen an attractive black girl, chin cupped in her hands, mouth wide open in a yawn. I don't know which of us was more miserable, me or her, but we'd caught each other's eye and had both burst out laughing.

'So, how do you fancy a trip to Zara after work? Help me buy something to wear for my date?'

''Fraid I'm busy. My new flatmate's moving in,' I explain.

'Ooh, tell me more.'

'He saw the room on Saturday and was going to move in yesterday but he had to spend the day with his uncle or something.'

'It's a he?' She raises her eyebrows with interest. 'So what he's like?' she asks, trying to be nonchalant. And failing.

'He's American.'

'Oooh, really?' Her eyes open wide. 'Let me guess. He's an actor.'

'Actually, I don't know,' I confess. 'I guess I'll find out tonight.'

'Is that really safe, Heather?' warns Jess. 'He could be a crazed serial killer. Do you need me as a chaperone?'

What she really means is he could be a *single* crazed serial killer. 'I doubt it, he seems really nice,' I say, having seen right through her concerned-friend act. 'He's a bit of a hippie.'

'That's what they said about Charles Manson. I think I should come over, safety in numbers and all that.'

I give in. 'OK, OK. My place. Eight o'clock.'

Her face splits into a huge grin and she gives me a hug.

'**A**ny more wine?' Sucking in her stomach, Jess reaches for the bottle of white she brought over. She's wearing her new black satin Alexander McQueen bustier she bought on eBay, hipster jeans and a pair of vertiginous pink stilettos, otherwise known as her 'fuck-me' shoes. 'It's

Gabriel, isn't it? Like the angel.' She pouts, lips slick with lip gloss.

'Friends usually call me Gabe.'

'As in, rhymes with "babe"?' she teases. 'Any more wine, *Gabe*?'

The three of us are outside in the garden. The air is scented with a cocktail of jasmine, lavender and sausages from my next-door neighbour's barbecue, and Norah Jones is playing on the portable stereo. I've even lit tea lights and placed them round the shrubbery.

I glance round my garden now and feel a glow of pleasure. In retrospect I don't know why I was so nervous: everything's turned out just as I wished it would. Well, not everything. As my eyes rest on Jess, who's wiggling round like a Playboy bunny, I feel a lump of irritation in my throat.

He'd turned up with his 'things'—a motorbike helmet and one teensy-weensy rucksack that would barely accommodate my toiletries—a couple of hours ago. When he'd dumped it on his bed he'd asked 'mind if I have a smoke outside?' padding into the back garden.

'Er, no . . . please, make yourself at home,' I'd called after him. Somewhat redundantly: he had already stretched out on a sun-lounger.

Well, I couldn't just leave him there, could I? As his landlady, wasn't I supposed to be making him feel at ease? I say *supposed*, because for some reason my ability to make small-talk deserted me. I'd groped, like a man in a blindfold, for something to say. 'Wonderful weather we're having'; 'Oh, I saw the funniest thing on *Ali G* the other night . . . erm, but I've forgotten what it was' until Jess had tottered into the garden, pulled two bottles of Pinot Grigio, a corkscrew and a Norah Jones CD out of her fake Louis Vuitton bag, and taken control of the conversation in full air stewardess mode.

'So, what brings you to London?' she's now asking flirtily. 'Business or pleasure?'

'A bit of both, actually,' he answers, in such a way that either he hasn't noticed Jess is flirting, or if he has he's politely ignoring her. 'But before I bore you with the details you'll have to excuse me a moment.' He turns to me and asks shyly, 'Heather, remind me where your bathroom is?'

'Second on the left,' chimes Jess, before I can answer.

As soon as he has disappeared, I turn on Jess. 'What are you doing?'

'Breaking the ice,' she says simply, all wide-eyed and innocent.

It doesn't fool me for a minute. 'Breaking the ice is asking someone about the weather,' I hiss furiously.

She looks at me sheepishly. 'OK, so I admit I've been a bit flirty.'

'A *bit*?'

'Oh, c'mon, hon, I just thought in case Greg doesn't work out. You know, it's always a good idea to have Plan B.'

'My flatmate's Plan B?' I say indignantly, feeling suddenly protective of Gabe—and something that is weirdly like possessiveness.

'Well, why not? You don't fancy him, do you, Heather?'

'No, of course I don't,' I protest hotly. 'It's just . . .' I trail off sighing.

She squeezes my hand. 'I know. I'm sorry. Maybe I have come on a bit strong.'

'A *bit* strong?' I grin ruefully. 'I'm surprised you didn't bring your scented candles and aromatherapy oil.'

'Who says I didn't?' She laughs and I can't help giggling.

'What's so funny?' Gabe reappears as Jess is topping up our glasses.

'Not Big Dave Desmond, that's for sure,' says Jess, referring to the stand-up comedian who was on stage when we first met.

Gabe is evidently confused, but she doesn't bother to explain. Instead: 'Where in America are you from?' she asks.

OK, so the fuck-me shoes are a bit much but I'm glad Jess is here. And, I have to admit, she and Gabe seem to be getting on pretty well.

'Los Angeles.'

'Oooh,' gasps Jess. 'I've flown there a few times. I lurve LA.'

'It has its good points. I live in Venice, a few blocks from the ocean.'

'Venice?' I repeat. 'What a coincidence.'

'Yeah, I know. Weird, huh? Venice, California, to Little Venice in London.' Sipping his wine, he fixes me with those large blue eyes.

'I guess you could call it home from home,' pipes up Jess, giggling.

'Or lucky,' smiles Gabe.

'Yeah, lucky Heather.' Jess winks at me.

Now, it's not the first time I've been called that—in fact, I must have heard it a million times—but as soon as Jess says it I hear the gypsy outside the station: 'Trust me, the heather will work its magic. Your luck will change. All your wishes will come true . . .'

Slipping my hand into the back pocket of my jeans my fingers brush against a wad of notes. It's Gabe's rent. A whopping six hundred pounds. I'll be able to pay the mortgage this month, maybe even make the minimum payment on my Visa bill. I feel a surge of happy relief—it's like a wish come true.

Barely has the thought popped into my head when a gust of wind appears from nowhere, rustling through the trees and causing the flames of the tea lights to flicker and dance like tiny jewels sparkling in a sea of inky darkness. The cascade of metal discs on the wind chime begin jingling, and the garden seems almost enchanted. A shiver scurries up my spine and goosebumps prickle on my arms. What the . . .?

'More wine, Heather?'

I snap back to see Jess staring at me. Spooked, I fidget in my seat. 'Oh, erm, yeah, great,' I say. When I hold out my glass my hands are all trembly. 'Fill her up,' I joke and plonk it on the table.

So she does. And as I watch her I realise the wind has dropped as quickly as it blew up. That the flames of the tea lights are now as motionless as the stars in the sky and the wind chime is silent. Everything is as it was before. My goosebumps have disappeared too. I feel warm. And a little ridiculous. What's got into me? Gypsies? Magic? Enchanted gardens? Honestly, Heather, you're letting your imagination run away with you. Grabbing my wine glass I take a glug. Any minute now I'll start believing wishes really can come true.

'**D**o you ever go to Muscle Beach?' Twenty minutes and another bottle later, Jess is still chatting animatedly about Venice Beach.

'Oh, all the time.' Gabe pretends to flex his biceps. 'Do you think a body like this comes naturally?'

I catch him grinning at me and I can't help grinning back, but Jess isn't listening. She's too busy reminiscing. 'Oh, Heather, you'd love it. It's this outdoor gym by the sea and you can watch all these big, bronzed body builders pumping iron . . .'

As she gushes on about coconut-oiled men posing with six-packs and dumbbells I haven't the heart to tell her I can't think of anything worse. So instead I do what I usually do when I don't know what to say: I say something stupid. 'Is it true everyone in LA has fake boobs?'

But Gabe doesn't look offended, more amused. 'No, I wouldn't say everyone.' He peers at his chest. 'Mine are real.'

'Really? Let me check.' Jess giggles and, without missing a beat, lunges for his right pec. 'Mmm, nice and firm,' she slurs approvingly.

Oh, shit. My body stiffens. Jess, I realise with horror, is pissed. In less than a few minutes she's leapfrogged from tipsy to hammered, bypassing the middle bit. 'So, are you an actor?' I ask, trying to cause a diversion.

'Me? An actor?' Gabe gives a pretend shudder. 'No way.'

My eyes flick from Gabe to Jess and back to Gabe. As far as I can tell he doesn't seem to have noticed Jess edging towards him, but I have. I feel a spasm of fear. She's drunk. And single. It's a lethal combination.

'But my girlfriend is, and she says it's pretty tough.'

Enveloped in a blurry haze of alcohol, Jess might not be able to drive, operate heavy machinery or undo her own bra strap, but she can still recognise words like—'*Girlfriend?*' she repeats.

'Yeah, she's back in LA. She just got a small part in a movie.'

'*A movie?*' Jess sits bolt upright on her sun-lounger.

'Mmm, it's a big break for her,' enthuses Gabe. 'Mia's really talented.'

'Wow, how exciting,' I gush. 'I'm really impressed.' And I am. An actress in Hollywood? It's a lot more glamorous than being a wedding photographer, isn't it? Reminded of my current career status, I feel a painful stab of thwarted ambition.

'I think I'll catch a cab.' Jess is standing. 'It was lovely meeting you.' She holds out a hand to Gabe.

'Oh, er, yeah. You too.' He's nodding, a little ruffled by her sudden departure through the patio doors. As am I.

'Are you sure you don't want me to phone for a minicab?' I call, hurrying after her. I hear the door slam and glance out of the window just in time to see her jump into a black cab.

'Your friend left early.'

Back in the garden I see that Gabe is gathering up the glasses. 'Erm, yeah.' I nod. 'She's tired. She has to get up early for work.' Feeling awkward now that it's just the two of us, I fake a yawn. 'Talking of which, I think I'm going to go to bed too.'

We go inside and hover in the kitchen.

'Night, then. You can use the bathroom first, if you like,' I offer.

'No, it's OK, you go ahead. Ladies before gentlemen,' he replies, politely.

'No, please, you're the guest.'

'Honestly, it's cool.'

Backwards and forwards it goes, like ping-pong, until finally I win and he disappears inside the bathroom with a sponge bag no bigger than a pencil case. I go into my bedroom and start to undress, pulling off my T-shirt and jeans and tugging on my old tartan pyjamas, the ones whose elastic has perished at the waistband so my arse is all baggy and it looks as if I'm wearing a nappy. *Wearing. A. Nappy*.

On catching sight of myself in the wardrobe mirror, I freeze. Oh, my God. It's like seeing myself for the first time. Think Gandhi.

Think new flatmate.

Stripping them off and chucking them onto the floor, I yank open my drawers and reach for my Snoopy nightie—then recoil. I can't wear a Snoopy nightie. Why have I never noticed that I have appalling nightwear? What on earth did I wear when I lived with Daniel?

Nothing, I remember, thinking back to my old life when I went to bed wearing eyeliner and Thierry Mugler's Angel. That was before I turned into the single, celibate, thirtynothing cliché who sleeps with her cat.

Shuddering, I grab hold of myself. There's the nightgown that Rosemary bought me two Christmases ago, still in its Marks & Spencer carrier bag. I hold it against my naked body. It's floor-length, decorated with rosebuds and frilly. Very, very frilly.

But I'm desperate. Next door I can hear teeth being brushed, the loo flushing, the basin draining. Any minute now it will be my turn. I'm going to have to try to make it from my bedroom to the bathroom without being seen. I strain for the noise of the lock. Nothing. A cough. Silence. Then I hear it. The sound of the key turning, the soft click of the door . . .

I press my cheek against the doorframe to peer through the crack between the wall and the door. Like a learner driver I look left, right and left again. All clear. With a flush of relief, I ease open the door and tiptoe bravely into the hall. Tiptoe, tiptoe, tiptoe. Nearly there, nearly there—

'Argggh!' I shriek.

'Wow, sorry, did I frighten you?'

Gabe is still in the bathroom. I mean, he's just standing there. On my shagpile mat. In the middle of my goddamn bathroom.

'Oh my God, yes—I mean, no—no, it's OK.' Clutching my embroidered lacy chest, I try to catch my breath. Which is when it dawns on me that (a) he's naked but for a pair of white, rather snug boxer shorts (not that I mean to look, I just can't help it), and (b) I look like someone's granny in a full-length nightgown that comes up to my neck.

'By the way, you never did say why you're visiting,' I blurt, in an attempt at casual chitchat. It's not easy when he's standing there, all naked flesh and tufts of chest hair and snug white pouch.

Oh, my God, I've done it again. Eyes straight ahead, Heather.

'Didn't I tell you?' He squeezes out a facecloth that I hadn't noticed he was holding. Just as I hadn't noticed that the bathroom is spotless. No loo seat left up, no soggy towel on the floor, no bristles on the soap. 'I'm putting on a show at the Edinburgh Festival.'

'Oh, really?' I say vaguely, throwing him my best smile of approval. I catch sight of our toothbrushes standing side by side in a mug with a tube of Colgate Extra and notice its top is firmly screwed on. I get the warm glow of satisfaction that comes with knowing I've made a right decision. We're going to get on great. 'What kind of show?'

Picking up his clothes he walks out of the bathroom. Then he goes and spoils it all by telling me something I *really* don't want to hear.

'**H**e's a stand-up comic.' The next morning, as soon as Gabe leaves the flat, I phone Jess to tell her my terrible news.

There's muffled laughter. 'Knock knock,' she teases weakly.

'Oh, please, don't.' I plonk myself down at the kitchen table and begin munching on a mouthful of All-Bran. 'It's not funny,' I say.

'They never are.' She laughs throatily. 'That's the problem.'

'So, is he still your Plan B?' I ask, still munching.

'No. He's too American. I'm looking for a serious boyfriend. I don't want a long-distance relationship. And then there's the culture clash.'

I love Jess. Ever the romantic.

'What are you going to do?' she asks.

'About what?' Curiously I eye a little leather notebook lying on the table among the mess. It looks like the one I've seen Gabe scribbling in.

'Gabe being a stand-up comedian,' she says.

I'm beginning to think Jess is enjoying this. 'Isn't there a saying about how you've got to laugh or you'll cry?' I say absently, stretching out my arm and flicking open the notebook. Well, one little peek won't hurt.

On the first page, are the words: '*My Top Ten Mother-in-Law Jokes*'. I snatch my hand back. Actually, on second thoughts . . .

As it turns out I'm spared any mother-in-law jokes over the next day or so as I barely see my new flatmate. In fact, it's almost as if he never moved in. Almost, but not quite.

Little things begin to appear. A collection of spices in the kitchen, a carton of soya milk in the fridge, a new loofah the size of a French baguette in the shower. But there's something else—a feeling.

For weeks I'd been dreading the thought of having a stranger in my flat, hated the idea of a man who wasn't Daniel soaking in my bath, but all my fears were unfounded. It's fine having another person around. In fact, it's more than that: it's *nice*. And not just because I no longer lie awake at night any more worrying about flat-repossession. It's as if Gabe's presence has exorcised the ghosts of the past. Despite the shock discovery that I'm sharing my home with a stand-up comedian, I feel happier. More positive. *Thinner*.

It's Wednesday evening after work and I've popped into Boots to buy some cotton-wool balls when I noticed the electronic weighing machine. Impulsively I decide to weigh myself. Which is why I'm now staring at the digital display in astonishment. I've lost five pounds? For the past couple of months I've been trying vaguely to shift the weight I put on at Christmas. I've been jogging—twice—and I've been sacrificing my breakfast *pain au chocolat* for All-Bran, which tastes like cardboard. Suddenly those few pounds have gone. It's amazing. *Weird.*

Puzzled, I prod my stomach. I don't feel any thinner. But I have been under a lot of financial pressure recently. Isn't that when you lose weight? Yep, that must be it. I knew there'd be a sensible explanation. I mean, it's not as if weight can disappear magically overnight, is it? Beaming at the sales assistant, I pull my purse out of my pocket. The lucky heather drops out. How did *that* get there? I'm sure I left it at home. Stuffing the heather back into my pocket I count out my change. Whatever the explanation for my weight loss, I get my wish: no more All-Bran.

Leaving Boots in a cheerful mood, I cross the main road and walk quickly through Notting Hill. I'm meeting my brother Ed at the Wolsey Castle, a gastro-type pub just round the corner, and as usual I'm late. I speed up. Ed's a real stickler for timekeeping and I don't want one of his lectures before I've even had the chance to order a gin and tonic. Though to be honest, I'm anticipating a lecture. He said he wanted to 'talk about something', which, translated into Ed-speak, means *give me a talking to*, his favourite starting point being, 'Why haven't you got a pension plan yet?' which probably gives you some idea about Ed.

But when I turn the corner into a street lined with shops and restaurants, I catch sight of something that stops me dead in my tracks. Pink, satin and with an adorable peep-toe: they are the most gorgeous pair of shoes I've ever seen, just waiting for me to walk past.

I step back to see the name of the store—Sigerson Morrison. I adore this shop: it's always chock full of the most exquisite shoes—which are completely out of your price range, Heather, pipes up a stern little voice inside me. I lean closer. Which is when I see the sign. '75% OFF'.

My stomach somersaults. Shoes are my weakness. I look at the time on my mobile. I'm already late. Oh, what the hell? I'll only be five minutes.

Inside, it's bedlam. A scrum of women are snatching, grabbing, pushing, shoving. Squashing myself between the racks of shoes, I begin the hunt for those gorgeous pink satin stilettos in my size. When I finally reach the shelf marked 'Size 5', though, I see it's empty but for a lime-green Mary-Jane that won't go with anything. I feel a kick of disappointment. Especially since, over to my left, the shelf marked 'Size 7' contains a dozen pairs of the pink satin peep-toes. I pick one up, wondering if I could make it fit with an inner sole, or maybe a couple . . .

'Can I help you, madam?' An assistant has swooped down on me.

'Erm, no,' I reply, and glance down to see that not only am I cradling the shoe in the crook of my arm, but I'm *stroking* it. 'I was just looking.'

'Fabulous, aren't they?' she says conspiratorially, in a hushed voice. 'Would you like me to bring you the other one?'

I smile regretfully. 'I'm afraid you don't have my size. I'm a size five.' I turn to walk out of the shop. Oh, well, it's only a pair of shoes, Heather. Reaching the door I try ignoring the window display, but at the last moment I can't help giving it one last glance and sighing wistfully.

I wish they had a pair in my size.

'Excuse me, madam.' I spin round. It's the same assistant, her face flushed with excitement. 'You're in luck. I found the very last pair. They'd been put in the wrong box.' She produces the shoes and gasps triumphantly, 'Size five!'

'Oh, wow . . .' I splutter. I can't believe it.

But even on sale you still can't afford them, whispers that voice.

I feel a crush of disappointment. It's true. My credit card's been cut up and I've only got twenty-five pounds in cash. Damnit, I wish they were cheaper. I'm about to give them back when I become aware of her talking in the background.

'. . . but I'm afraid there's a tiny mark on the heel, nothing anyone would notice. Of course we'll discount them further . . . Another fifty per cent off from the sale price.'

Hang on a minute. 'You mean they're only . . .'

'Twenty-four ninety-nine,' she announces breathlessly.

A few minutes later I'm standing at the cash register, watching as she wraps them in tissue paper, a huge smile plastered over my face. I'm not superstitious, but I'm beginning to think that heather really is lucky.

Chapter Three

'WHOOOOOAAAAAAAAHHHHHHHHH.' Pushing open the door of the Wolsey Castle I'm greeted by a roar of testosterone. I head through the fog of cigarette smoke towards the bar. The place is jam-packed with men, eyes glued to the TV. Of course. I might have guessed. *Football*.

'Thought as much.' I turn to see Ed looming down on me, all six foot five of him. Having come straight from work he's in his uniform of grey suit with white shirt and brown brogues. Actually, he wears that at weekends too. 'Shopping again?' He studies me disapprovingly. That's the problem with my brother. He likes to spoil your fun.

'Lovely to see you too.' I give him a hug.

'And you.' He kisses me on both cheeks. 'So, what did you buy?'

I swear, he's like a dog with a bone. 'Oh, this?' I say lightly, looking at the bag as if I've only just noticed it's there. Think, Heather. I rack my brains for a feasible excuse. It's either that or a lecture on saving for the future. 'It's a present,' I gasp, and I feel a rush of triumph.

'For whom?'

'Erm . . . Rosemary.'

'Really?' Ed is suitably impressed. 'That's rather nice of you, little sis.'

I smile uncomfortably. 'Well, it's only a little something,' I say, knowing full well I'm digging a hole for myself.

'I'm glad you two are finally getting on better,' he continues, gazing at me with brotherly approval. Ed has a completely different relationship with Rosemary from the one she and I share. Partly because he's a successful orthodontist with his own business in Harley Street, which endears him to Rosemary's snobbery, and partly because he's always so busy with work that he rarely travels to Bath, so he never has to spend any time with her.

'I know Lionel will be pleased,' says Ed, and I feel a stab of guilt. The last thing I want to do is hurt my father.

'Yeah, I went up to Bath last weekend. He was on fine form.'

'I don't suppose he's started his diet yet, has he?'

'What do you think?' I'm glad that I'm not the only one on the receiving end of Ed's sermons. Lionel is always being nagged about losing weight but, of course, he never listens.

Frowning, Ed shakes his head. 'He needs to consider cutting back on his saturated fat and going on a healthy-eating plan. I'm serious, sis. His cholesterol must be through the roof.'

'So, how's Lou?' I change the subject to his wife. Lou is six months pregnant and really cool. On the outside she's a nursery-school teacher who wears bubble-gum pink Birkenstocks, but on the inside she's a reformed Goth who still has her nose pierced. How my brother managed to persuade this bright, funny woman to marry him I have no idea.

'Well, the sickness is finally over, thank goodness, but now Boris is kicking her black and blue,' he says gloomily.

'You mean you know it's going to be a boy?' I say excitedly. Then add, 'And you're going to call him *Boris*?'

'Don't be ridiculous. Of course not,' he snaps. 'We want the baby's sex to be a surprise, but Lou insists on calling it Boris,' he explains, then sighs. 'Apparently all expectant mothers give their unborn babies a nickname, which, quite frankly, is as bad as people naming their car . . .'

Honestly, I love my brother, but sometimes I want to shoot him: he's so bloody grumpy. I know that secretly he's thrilled about the baby, but he'll never admit it. He just loves to moan.

'Drink?' I say brightly, hoping to cheer him up.

'Huh, if you're lucky,' he grumbles, handing me a tenner. 'I've been trying to catch the barman's attention for the last twenty minutes.'

Despairing of him, I turn to the bar—I see what he means. It's at least five men deep, it's going to take for ever. Glumly I join the back of the queue. After a moment a man behind me taps me on the shoulder. 'Are you being served?' he asks hopefully, waggling his empty glass at me.

'I wish,' I sigh, shaking my head.

And then the oddest thing happens. In the middle of ringing up a round of drinks the barman turns and stares right at me. Not at the half-dozen men jostling in front of me, but *right at me*. 'Sorry to keep you waiting, what would you like?' he says.

'Erm . . .' I smile uncertainly. 'Two G and Ts with ice and lemon. Please,' I add. I can't believe my luck.

'Coming right up,' winks the barman.

A few minutes later I return to Ed. 'Crikey, that was quick,' he comments, taking his glass without removing his eyes from the football match.

'You'll never guess what happened,' I hiss. 'I was served before anyone else. It was really strange.'

'What do you mean, strange?' Scowling as the crowd shuffles to accommodate a new influx of people, he clutches his drink to his chest to avoid spilling it. 'Bloody hell, it's bedlam in here.'

'I know. I wish there was somewhere to sit down.'

No sooner have the words left my mouth than the couple next to me start to put on their coats. *No, surely not*. 'We're going—would you like these seats?' The man has turned to me. Not to Ed, but to me.

Suddenly I'm all light-headed.

'Er, yes, thanks.' I smile gratefully and glance at Ed, who's astounded.

He claims one of the empty stools hurriedly then hitches up his suit trousers to get comfortable. 'What a stroke of luck.'

Wordlessly I slide myself on to the seat. My mind is whirling. All those niggly doubts about superstition and luck magnify as one episode after another unravels like frames on a reel of film thrown out of sequence, the empty seat on the train, no queue at Starbucks, the packet of razor blades, the parking space, Gabe replying to my small ad. Driving back from Bath and there being no traffic, hanging my coat on an empty peg at work, finding my perfect pair of shoes *in my size*. Getting served at the bar, being able to sit down . . . I can't stop myself blurting, 'Actually, no, it's not.' My heart is thumping. 'It's more than luck.'

Ed stares at me in confusion. 'I'm sorry, Heather, you've lost me,' he says eventually. 'What on earth are you talking about?'

I hesitate. I'm not really sure *what* I'm talking about. He's going to think I'm an idiot. But he thinks I'm an idiot anyway. 'Well, you see, the thing is . . .' I take a deep breath. Oh, sod it! Just say it, Heather. 'Everything I wish for seems to come true,' I say loudly.

But not loudly enough: my words are swallowed in another roar from the crowd. 'Damn! That was close,' gasps Ed. 'We nearly scored.'

'Ed, did you hear what I just said?'

'Sorry, sis. You were saying something about wishful thinking . . .'

I can tell he's only humouring me, but I persevere. It's a relief to tell someone. 'No, it's not wishful thinking. It's more than that. Over the last few days every little thing I wish for seems to happen.'

'Well, you know what they say, don't you?' Ed looks at me solemnly. 'Be careful what you wish for.'

'*Careful?*' I repeat in astonishment. The most amazing, fantastic, wonderful thing is happening and my brother is telling me to be careful?

'Well, consider the implications. We think we know what we want, but we can never really know until we've got it. And sometimes when we have, we discover we never really wanted it in the first place—but then it's too late.' He raises a smile. 'Like, for example, I remember once wishing for some time off work. And then I went down with flu and had to spend my week off in bed. Not much of a wish, eh?'

'Ed, I'm being serious.'

'Are you feeling all right?'

'Yes, I'm fine. And, no, it's not the flu,' I add impatiently.

'OK, I'm sorry, but come on, how can you expect me to be serious? I mean, *really*,' he scoffs. 'Wishes coming true?'

Right, that does it. 'OK, dare me to wish for something,' I retort tartly.

'You're being ridiculous,' sighs Ed. He lets out a taunting little laugh.

I'm infuriated. 'OK. Well, if it's so funny, play along with me then,' I demand. 'Or are you scared you'll be proved wrong?'

Now, one thing I know about my brother is how competitive he is. Years of playing Monopoly with him have taught me how much he loves to win; as much as he loves to be always right. But then again, so do I.

'Well, if you insist . . .' he says immediately. Exactly as I'd thought. He thinks, then clicks his fingers. '*The match,*' he says triumphantly.

'What about it?' I ask.

'Well, at the moment the score's one–all, and there's less than five minutes to go . . .' He motions towards the TV screen. 'We need to score another goal against France to win the championship.'

'So?' I prompt.

'So if all your wishes come true, why don't you wish England scores before the final whistle?' he continues.

'Because I don't really care,' I say.

'Would you care if I said I won't mention to Rosemary that you've bought her a present . . .' He looks at me and I realise I've been busted. 'And you get to keep it yourself?'

'That's blackmail.'

'And this is madness,' he says wearily.

'OK, OK.' I turn to face the screen and concentrate as a French player begins to charge towards the goal. I hold my breath, straining to see what's happening, suddenly aware of the tense atmosphere around me.

Come on, England, come on, you can do it.

I catch myself as I hear a voice inside my head. Hang on a minute, is this me? Watching a football match? In a pub? And enjoying it? I'm white-knuckling my glass—the tension is unbelievable. I can barely watch. France are going to score another goal; England are going to lose.

'For Godsakes, come on, England, come on,' I hear Ed say.

Even though it seems hopeless, he's willing them to win. And suddenly I'm wishing the same thing. 'Come on, England!' I yell. '*Win!*'

And then, out of the blue, England intercepts and scores.

The bar erupts with shrieking, whooping, yelling, whistling. But I can't hear it. It's as if I'm watching a movie with the sound turned down. An unexpected blast of wind bangs the door open, and when I turn to Ed he's staring at me, jaw dropped in shock.

'Bloody hell, Heather,' he stammers, when he finds his voice.

I feel a flurry of exhilaration, excitement . . . *possibility*.

'Excuse me, do you sell lottery tickets?' I smile broadly at Mrs Patel, who is standing behind the counter of my local corner shop.

'Yes, of course,' she says. 'By the window.'

'Thanks.' Tucked away in the corner I find a red plastic lectern that I've never noticed before and eagerly help myself to a ticket. Right. 'Choose six numbers and mark with a line.' Hmm, well: my age, my address . . . this is rather fun. Number of years I've worked at Together Forever, my mum's birthday . . . I grind to a halt. I need two more. I concentrate on the numbers, hoping one will jump out at me yelling 'Pick me! I'm a winner!' *A winner*. Oh, wow, can you imagine it?

Automatically I make one of my wish lists:

(1) *A house in Holland Park. One of those ones with large white pillars.*
(2) *An Italian hideaway somewhere in the Tuscan hills.*
(3) *A Matisse. He's Lionel's favourite painter. Any picture will do.*
(4) *Premier-league season tickets for Ed.*
(5) *A pension plan to beat all pension plans.*

(6) *A boob reduction for Jess.*
(7) *Highlights at Nicky Clarke, by Nicky Clarke.*
(8) *Shoes. Lots and lots and lots of shoes.*
(9) *A silver Aston Martin Vanquish like the one Bond drives.*
(10) *Or maybe one of those new Mini convertibles so that when I'm in Italy buying all those shoes I can zip around the tiny alleyways.*

By myself. Abruptly I feel a familiar pang of loneliness.

'Ahem.' Someone clears their throat and over my shoulder I see a queue of people waiting.

'C'mon, get a bloody move on,' I hear someone grumble.

Chastised, I choose the last two numbers at random, grab my ticket and beat a retreat to the counter.

Mrs Patel is waiting for me. 'So, you're feeling lucky, eh?'

I hesitate. Now I'm standing here at 8.30 a.m., in the cold light of the shop it does all seem rather far-fetched. Last night I'd been sure that it wasn't all coincidence. The only reason England won was because . . . what, Heather? Because you wished they would score?

All of a sudden I realise how ridiculous I'm being.

The machine whirs and spits out the printed ticket.

'Maybe,' I reply, taking the ticket.

I leave the shop in a state of nervous anticipation. Outside, the morning rush-hour is in full swing. I keep walking, a million questions running around in my mind. On the one hand the logical, sane me knows there has to be a rational explanation. Yet on the other, the part of me that avoids walking under ladders can't help getting carried away.

Leaving the traffic behind I head along beside the canal. This is one of my favourite places in the city. It's picture-postcard pretty and I never tire of looking at all the brightly painted narrow boats. Sod the boats, what about the wishes? interrupts a voice in my head.

Startled, I ignore it and gaze instead at the hanging baskets spilling down the sides of the boats in an explosion of colour. Look, they're beautiful. And isn't it ingenious how the owners of that barge over there have used old Wellington boots as plant pots? Squinting in the sunshine, I shade my eyes with my hand. Gosh, I wish I had my sunglasses. Silent, subconscious wishes that are part of everyday life.

I push my hands into my pockets—and stop. My fingers brush against something smooth like plastic. It can't be . . . I'm positive I left them at home. With a flutter in my stomach I tug out my sunglasses. What would happen if those subconscious wishes suddenly started coming true?

With trembling fingers I put my sunglasses on, trying to calm myself, but it's no good. This is ridiculous. If everything you wished for actually happened? Oh, for God's sake, shut up, why don't you?

I spot a little café and abandon my tour of the canal. With my recent weight loss I can treat myself to a *pain au chocolat*. Then I notice a house covered with scaffolding and a skip outside. My heart sinks. Builders. I hate builders. They look up as I approach, I've been spotted.

I lower my head, but I feel indignant. I wish they'd mind their own business and leave us women in peace. Walking towards them I wait for the inevitable 'Cheer up, love, it'll never happen.'

And you know what? It doesn't. Nobody's even looking in my direction. I keep walking. Waiting. Still nothing. I slow down and strut—yes, strut—past a barechested builder mixing cement without bothering to tug down the hem of my miniskirt. Not even a sideways glance.

Which is when I notice the front pages of the newspapers they're reading. In large black capitals the headlines read: 'Shrinking manhood: new sex survey shows builders have smallest penises.' I clap a hand over my mouth to stifle a giggle. Then I hear that voice again in my head: What if all your wishes were granted?

Only this time I don't ignore it. Finally I'm convinced. As weird, inconceivable and mind-boggling as it might be. That it's got to be magic. And then—I don't know what comes over me but before I know it I'm putting my fingers into my mouth and letting out a long, liberating wolf whistle. I watch with satisfaction as a couple of bricklayers blush beetroot with embarrassment. It's absolutely fantastic.

And it gets better.

It's like the floodgates have opened, and I spend the rest of the week in a whirl of pleasant surprises. Pots of wrinkle cream that actually seem to be working. Earrings I thought I'd lost suddenly appear from out of the back of the sofa. One by one, the dozens of inconsequential wishes I make every day, without thinking, begin to come true. At first it's just the little things. My fake tan doesn't go streaky round my ankles. They don't sell out of my favourite sandwich at Marks & Spencer. But it doesn't stop there. In fact, this is when the fun really starts. Instead of *accidentally* wishing for things, I test it out by *deliberately* wishing for things.

Take ice-cream, for example.

My whole life I've never been able to eat just one or two spoonfuls. I always polish off the lot, then wish I hadn't because I feel sick and have to undo the top button on my jeans. But when I tried out my theory by scoffing a whole pint of Häagen-Dazs Belgian chocolate, I didn't feel even a teensy bit nauseous. Furthermore, my jeans weren't tight!

But even more astonishing is that when I went to buy a fresh tub, I didn't feel like ice cream. Now I know that I can eat it guilt-free, the fun's gone out of it. I ended up buying some bananas instead.

Then it was the weather. Whenever I blow-dry my hair it always rains. Without fail. But not this week: this week it's been warm and dry and my hair hasn't gone frizzy once. It's looked fabulous every day.

But best of all has to be the traffic lights. From Little Venice to Hampstead to Elephant and Castle, I haven't had a red light. Driving around London has been so much fun. Well, apart from the fine I got for speeding along the Embankment, but it's only three points on my licence and a sixty-pound fine . . .

'. . . **A**nd I've saved myself some money already because—would you believe it?—a traffic warden let me off a parking ticket!' I exclaim.

Jess is staring at her reflection in the mirror, pulling a face. It's Friday evening after work and we're both squashed into a changing cubicle at Zara looking for an outfit for her first date with Greg tomorrow night. It's a quest that's beginning to take on *Lord of the Rings* proportions.

She pushes up her ample chest with her hands and frowns. 'Wouldn't it look better if I had smaller boobs?'

'You're not listening, are you?' I say sulkily. I've just spent the last hour telling Jess everything and she's not impressed.

'Yes, I am,' she protests, tugging a dress off over her shoulders. 'Something about not getting a parking ticket . . .'

'But that's just it! I *didn't* get a parking ticket,' I continue indignantly. 'When I saw him the warden was punching all my details into one of those little computers and I was thinking, Oh God, another fifty quid, I can't afford it, and wishing he'd let me off. And guess what? He did!' I smile triumphantly. 'Don't you think that's amazing?'

'A football match, some builders, a set of green lights and a parking ticket is hardly exciting, is it?' Jess says, ticking them off on her fingers. 'What about the big stuff we all wish for? You know. Success. Happiness. *Lurve*.' Hands on her hips she gazes at me and I know what's coming. 'You've got to go out there again some time, you know.'

I change the subject. 'What about this black off-the-shoulder T-shirt, and those three-quarter jeans?' I suggest, picking up two items and waggling them at her.

'Don't you think they're a bit, well, boring?'

I dangle the fashionista's carrot. 'I saw Sienna Miller in something similar.' I cross my fingers behind my back.

'Really?' She snatches the items from me and pulls on the jeans. She wriggles into the top and adjusts it off the shoulder. Jess is all boobs and butt and it looks amazing. 'You're a genius, Heather!' She throws her arms round me. 'This is perfect. But as I was saying . . .'

Damn. I'd thought I'd got away with it.

'You've got to forget about Daniel.'

'I have forgotten,' I reply defensively.

'Well, then, what are you waiting for?'

'The perfect man,' I quip, hoping that'll shut her up.

Jess laughs ruefully. 'I hate to be the one to break the news, honey, but he doesn't exist.'

I follow her to the cash register. 'I think you're wrong,' I say. 'I think the perfect man does exist. He's just different for different people. I mean, look at Camilla Parker Bowles—sorry, Windsor. Her idea of the perfect man is Prince Charles.'

Jess winces. 'Oooh . . . and with those ears,' she whispers.

'Exactly. It's like the woman who's married to Robin Williams. I think he's the most unfunny man alive, but she must think he's perfect.'

Signing the credit card slip, Jess takes her new purchase and stuffs her receipt in her bag. 'So, c'mon, then,' she says. 'If the perfect man is different for different people, what's yours like?'

I play along, because of course I've got a list of what the ideal man would be like. 'Monogamous, of course. He hates sport, but loves Dido . . .' I can feel myself warming up. 'He doesn't just chuck his clothes on the floor, or leave the cheese unwrapped in the fridge so it goes all cracked and hard . . .' Actually, this is rather fun. 'He's not scared of commitment . . . or asking for directions if he's lost . . .' Everything I've ever wished for in a man comes rushing back. 'He likes holding hands and candlelit dinners. He's not just interested in getting into my knickers, he buys me flowers . . .' I stop to think. Is that everything? 'Oh, and he has to fall madly in love with me, of course.'

'**A** couple of hunters are out in the woods when one falls to the ground. He doesn't seem to be breathing and, in mad panic, the other guy whips out his cellphone and calls the emergency services . . .'

Standing in front of the full-length mirror on the back of his wardrobe door, wearing a Ramones T-shirt under a black suit jacket, Gabe pauses to study his reflection and runs through a variety of expressions: pensive; shocked; upset. Sighing, his shoulders slump forward. 'Jeez, what kind of look does this joke need?' Angst-ridden, he scratches the bristles on his chin, then suddenly breaks into a huge smile. 'Jesus, that's it. *That's the look!*'

His grip tightens on the hairbrush he's holding as a microphone, he splays his legs in a sort of Elvis pose and continues: 'He gasps to the operator: "My friend is dead! What do I do?" Calmly the operator replies, "Just take it easy. I can help. First, let's make sure he's dead."' Gabe's mouth twitches. He's trying not to laugh. He reprimands himself: 'Gabriel Hoffman, you've gotta be angry, tortured, deadly funny. C'mon, concentrate!' He clears his throat. 'There's silence. Then a shot is heard, and the hunter's voice comes back on the line.' After a comic pause, Gabe goes for the punch line: '"OK, he's definitely dead. Now what?"'

Oh, my God, he's *terrible*. Standing in the hallway, watching Gabe rehearse in his bedroom through a gap in the door, I clamp my hands over my mouth to suppress a groan. He's going to bomb at the Edinburgh Festival. He's going to die on stage, in front of thousands of people. I mean, all that scowling and trying to be the angry, uptight comedian, it's just not Gabe. He's sweet and kind *and from California*. He drinks soya milk and does yoga. He's not angry, he's totally chilled out. And that outfit! A Ramones T-shirt under a suit? It's such a cliché. What's happened to his kooky shirts and flip-flops?

My heart goes out to him. I should try to stop him.

A floorboard creaks, and I snap to. Oh shit, he's going to come out of his bedroom and catch me here. *Spying*. You're not spying, Heather, you just got home from shopping with Jess and happened to be walking past, I think frantically, as I dive into the bathroom. I lock the door and turn on the taps. There must be something I can do to help. OK, so I hate stand-up comedy, but I don't hate Gabe. He's a really nice bloke.

'Heather?' There's a polite knock on the door and Gabe's voice. 'Are you in there?'

'Erm, yes . . .' I reply, startled. 'Sorry, are you waiting?'

'No, it's fine, take your time. But when you're finished come outside to the back yard. I've gotta surprise,' he adds.

Oh, bloody hell. What was I saying about hating surprises? I emerge tentatively from the bathroom and pad barefoot down the hallway, when I'm distracted by a funny smell. It's almost as if something's burning. As the idea strikes I hurry across the kitchen and glance through the patio doors at the back garden. It's full of smoke. Something *is* burning.

Panic sets in. My house is on fire! Did I remember to pay the household insurance? Frantically I start looking around the kitchen. I need something like—something like that jug. A large glass jug of lilies sits on the table. I grab it, dump the flowers in the sink and dash outside. Grey smoke is billowing from behind the shed. Vaulting over a flowerbed, I spin round the side of the shed, my fingers slipping on the wet glass as I swing it back with all my might. Only there aren't any flames.

Just Gabe.

'Tad-daaahhh.' He throws his arms wide and grins as he sees me, but it's too late: like a pendulum, the vase has swung. Which means it has to swing back. Suddenly everything is happening at once. But it's as if someone has slowed the time right down and I'm watching it on film. The water swooshing out of the vase, soaring through the air like a huge wave, every droplet magnified as Gabe's face comes into shot and begins its journey through a remarkable range of emotions—from happiness, to confusion, to open-mouthed shock as the water hits him square in the face. *Boom*. We're back in normal time and Gabe, totally drenched, is standing there dripping, blinking, gasping. 'Jeez, Heather, what's going on?'

'Oh. Shit,' I mutter, as I watch him wiping his wet hair and face with his apron. *Apron?* At the same moment I notice he's holding tongs in one hand, a packet of veggie sausages in the other and standing in front of a shiny metal object that looks suspiciously like . . .

'*A barbecue?*' I blurt.

'It's a housewarming present—well, for my housewarming. I thought you might like it. But if I'd known I was gonna get that reaction I might have stuck with a scented candle.'

'I'm *soooo* sorry.' I try to apologise as he dabs at himself with a tea towel. 'I thought something was burning.'

'It was the veggie sausages.' With his frilly shirt sticking to his chest in a sodden lump, he gestures towards the barbecue, which is defiantly emitting a faint spiral of smoke. 'I bought them especially, with you not eating meat and all.' He pauses. 'Maybe this was a bad idea.'

'No! No!' I protest. 'It was a *great* idea—I mean, it *is* a great idea.' Enthusiastically I grab a fork and lean over him to pluck a charred object from the grill. I force myself to take a bite. 'Mmmmmm.'

Gabe watches me with what I could swear is a glimmer of amusement. 'I wasn't sure how long to cook them.'

'Mmmmm. Mmmm,' I continue as I begin to chew. Ouch. Pain shoots through a back molar as I bite down hard on a tough bit.

'Good?'

'Delicious,' I reply, covering my mouth. With great difficulty I swallow. Thank God for that. I breathe a sigh of relief. It's short-lived.

'Cool. Have another.' With the tongs Gabe pops a few more onto a plate and holds it out to me. 'There's plenty.'

'Erm, no . . . Actually, that's fine for now.'

But he's insistent. 'Hey, c'mon, it's my treat.'

Treat? This is torture. 'Erm, great, thanks,' I stammer.

At which point Gabe bursts out laughing. I'm astonished. Until I twig. This is his idea of a joke and I fell right for it.

'Your face,' he doubles up, 'when you ate that sausage.'

'You bastard,' I mutter, mouth twitching.

'Hey, do you blame me? You threw a great big jug of foul-smelling water at me.'

At the memory I start giggling. 'You should've seen *your* face.'

He stops laughing. 'Well, I guess that just about makes us even.'

Fortunately there are some veggie burgers lurking in the freezer and we put them on the grill, along with some corn-on-the-cob. After we've sorted out the food and he has changed into a T-shirt (I thought the pistachio-green shirt with the ruffle down the middle was bad, but his orange Mr T T-shirt, which I now notice has Velcro hair, is much worse), Gabe pulls out two ice-cold Sols from the fridge and offers me one. '. . . And I've been doing my stand-up around LA, open mikes, that kinda thing, but going to the Edinburgh Festival has always been a dream so I decided I was gonna go for it. I booked a venue, printed up some fliers and I'm taking my show up there for a whole week.'

I'm sipping my beer as I listen to Gabe, who's now manning the grill, flipping burgers like a pro. 'So you just quit your job?' I ask, from the comfort of the sun-lounger. Wow, this is the life, lying here not lifting a finger. Now I know what it must have felt like to be Daniel.

'No, a friend and I have a clothes store on Abbot Kinney—it's a street in Venice that's got some real cool shops and cafés,' he explains. 'Oh, and a great Mexican that does the most awesome chilli *rellenos*.' His eyes light up and he pauses, obviously reliving a chilli *relleno* moment.

'I take it you like your food?' I smile.

He's shamefaced now. 'It's a Jewish thing.'

'You're Jewish?'

He turns sideways to show me his profile and runs his finger down his nose. 'Can't you tell by the schnoz?'

'Hey, at least you have an excuse.' I turn sideways and do the same with mine.

'You have a great nose,' protests Gabe. 'It's like a toucan's beak.'

'I'll take that as a compliment.' I pull a face. 'But, anyway, about your job . . .' Swiftly I move the conversation away from my nose. That's something I've learned as I've grown older: don't talk to men about the bits of your body you're unhappy with.

'Oh, yeah, well, let's put it this way, my partner owes me a favour so he's taken the reins for a while. It's only going to be for a few weeks.'

'And what about your girlfriend, Mia—doesn't she mind?'

Gabe blushes. 'Nah—too many nights spent watching me on the open mike. She probably wanted to get rid of me.' He's smiling as he says it, as only a person confident that that's not the case can.

'So, what's your story?' He flips a burger and looks at me.

'My story?'

'Yeah, you know, relationship, job, family . . .'

'Oh, *that*. I've been single since last year when I discovered my boyfriend, whom I lived with at the time, was cheating on me.'

Gabe throws me a sympathetic look but I move on swiftly. 'I've been working as a wedding photographer for the past six years but now I'm about to lose my job.'

'Aha, I wondered what the pile of résumés was doing on the table.'

'Yeah, well, I didn't exactly dream of being a wedding photographer, so let's just say I haven't had my big break as yet.'

'What about your folks?'

'I've got one older brother, Ed, and he's married to Lou—they're about to have a baby—and then there's my father, Lionel, who's an artist and married to my wicked stepmother Rosemary.'

'And your mom?'

'She died when I was twelve.'

There's a pause. 'Hey, I'm sorry.'

'Me too,' I say quietly, feeling my throat tighten as it always does when I think about Mum. Even now, nearly twenty years later. I hoist myself up from the sun-lounger to walk over to the barbecue. 'Mmm, that smells good. I'm starving.'

'The corn's going to be another fifteen minutes.'

'In that case I've got time to pop to the corner shop for a bottle of wine. Red or white?'

'You choose.'

I go to leave, then stop and turn. I look at my new flatmate and feel an unexpected fondness for him. Somehow I feel as if I've known him a long time. 'Gabe, I love the barbecue. It was really sweet of you.'

'Hey, don't mention it.'

'And about earlier, with the water . . .'

'Is that how you English say thank you?'

'No. This is how we say thank you.'

Impulsively I lean over and kiss his whiskery cheek. And before either of us has time to think about what just happened, I hurry inside.

Barbra Streisand is wailing from the tape deck as I enter the corner shop. Mrs Patel squints at me over the top of her glasses. I smile, give a little nod, then head to the back of the shop where she keeps the wine. When I first moved into the neighbourhood, I remember thinking it was going to be a limited selection—a dusty bottle of Liebfraumilch or an overpriced Chianti in a straw basket. But I was wrong. Mrs Patel is something of a *sommelier*.

Now, in the depths of the shop, I ponder over a bottle of Sauvignon Blanc. It's always my preferred choice, but perhaps this time I should get something different. I swing back to the reds. No, too heavy, and red wine stains my teeth. I just can't decide. And then I have an idea.

Closing my eyes I begin muttering: 'Eeny, meeny, miny,' I let my finger choose a wine, 'mo.' But instead of prodding a hard, cold surface, I feel something soft, warm . . . alive? My eyes snap open. My finger is embedded in someone's shoulder. A man's shoulder. *My neighbour's shoulder*.

Cue stomach dropping as if I'm in an aeroplane and we've just plummeted three hundred feet. I catch my breath just long enough to stammer. 'Oh . . . sorry . . .'

This really is terrible. Why do I always have to look like such an idiot around him? No wonder he ignores me. I turn away.

'Choosing wine is never easy, is it? You spend ages reading all the labels, and when you get it home it hardly ever tastes like you expect.'

Er, hello? Is he talking to me? My eyes travel up from his feet, past the cleft in his chin to his mouth. It's smiling at me. One of those kind, benevolent smiles you give to old people when their memory is befuddled. It's the type of smile Meryl Streep always does so well.

My heart sinks. He probably doesn't recognise me.

'We've never been introduced. I'm James. We live opposite each other.' He holds out his hand.

'Oh, yeah . . . Hi, I'm Heather.' I try smiling back, but mine's all wobbly and nervous, like a kid on a bicycle without stabilisers.

'I had a wonderful white from here a few days ago. It's here.' He drops my hand and reaches for a bottle. I watch him lustfully. He's probably come here to choose some wine for him and his girlfriend to share, I muse, thinking of the pretty brunette I saw him with last week. Gosh, she's so lucky. I wish he was my boyfriend.

Suddenly aware that I'm gawping at him open-mouthed, I snatch the bottle from his hands. 'Erm, great . . . thanks for the recommendation,' I say quickly, and turn to go before I make an even bigger fool of myself.

'On the other hand there's also a great Chablis . . .'

I look over my shoulder to see him holding an amber-coloured bottle. 'Maybe I can tempt you?' He smiles at me again, but this time it's not the befuddled-old-people smile, it's more like a . . . 'Listen, I'm sorry, I'm not doing this very well, am I?' *Rueful smile?* Standing there with a bottle of wine in each hand, he shrugs. 'You probably think I'm some kind of idiot going on about wine the whole time . . .' *Embarrassed smile?* '. . . when really I've been wanting to ask you . . .' *Nervous smile?* '. . . if you'd like to go out for a drink some time.' *Chatting me up smile?*

I'm in shock. After two and a half years of never even speaking to each other, my gorgeous, handsome neighbour, who just so happens to be the living embodiment of Mr Perfect, has asked me out on a date.

'Well?'

I zone back in: he's waiting for my answer. But isn't it obvious? Why on earth wouldn't I want to go out for a drink with him? Give me one good reason. *The brunette*. I knew it was too good to be true—the two-timing slimeball. 'I have no respect for men who cheat on their girlfriends.'

'Excuse me?'

'My last boyfriend was unfaithful,' I explain.

'Oh, er . . . really? I'm sorry to hear that.' There's a pause as he stares at me quizzically. 'I'm sorry, but am I missing something?'

Respect, honesty, integrity, I feel like saying, as I'm reminded of Daniel. But instead I smile tightly and say casually. 'I'm sorry, what did you say your girlfriend's name was?'

'My girlfriend?'

'The pretty brunette.'

'Oh! For a moment there I wondered what on earth was going on. I thought maybe you had me confused with someone else.' He smiles, then says, 'That's Bella, my little sister.'

I don't know whether to jump for joy or howl with embarrassment.

'Did you want her to come for a drink as well?' His mouth twitches.

I stifle a nervous giggle. 'No, just you is fine.'

'Great,' he replies, looking relieved. It's then that it strikes me: *he's nervous*. 'When are you free this week? Tomorrow?'

'Perfect,' I reply, grabbing his suggestion with both hands. Sod playing it cool. I'd rather be drinking martinis with James.

'Great,' he says again. He grins, finally relieving himself of the bottles. 'Of course, there's always another choice. Champagne. If you've got something to celebrate.'

By the time I reach my flat, say goodbye to James, who's accompanied me to the doorstep and kissed my cheek, I'm walking on air. James has asked me out. James is taking me out for dinner—on the way back from the corner shop, it progressed from a drink to dinner. James is picking me up tomorrow at eight. I, Heather Hamilton, have a date.

Delighted, I kick off my flip-flops and pad down the hallway into the kitchen. 'Hey, Gabe, you'll never guess what . . .' I hurry through the patio doors and into the garden. He's not there.

'Gabe?' I glance at the barbecue, which looks as if it's gone out. The grill's bare and most of the coals have turned to powdery grey ash. Already? I check the time on my watch . . . Crikey, I've been gone for ages! I go back inside and knock softly on the door of his room. 'Gabe? Are you there?'

'Hey.' He's holding a book entitled *How To Be Hilarious*. 'I was thinking of sending out a search party.'

'Hi . . . Look, I'm sorry,' I apologise. Then I can't help blurting, 'I've just been asked out on date. It's someone I've had a bit of a crush on. I bought champagne instead of wine. Would you like a glass?'

'Thanks, but not for me. It's been a long day.'

'Oh, OK . . . Look, about the barbecue.'

'Hey, forget about it.' He smiles. 'Night, Heather.'

'Right. You too, Gabe.' Giving him a little wave good night with the champagne bottle, I head back into the kitchen to put it into the fridge. My thoughts turn back to James and I'm so absorbed that when, a few moments later, I hear Gabe's door click softly behind me, it occurs to me only vaguely that he must have remained standing there after I left him. But I'm too caught up by the evening's events to take much notice.

Chapter Four

OUTSIDE THE IVY-CLAD WALLS of Kew Gardens, a dozen or so wedding guests are congregating. They look to be mostly in their early twenties, wearing an assortment of mismatched suits and Friday-night dresses that are too short and revealing. And for one particular blonde way too tight, I note, and try not to stare at her Visible Panty Line as I weave my way through the guests looking for someone suitable to cadge a cigarette from. ''Scuse me, I don't suppose you've got a spare cigarette . . .' With every last drop of my female charm, I smile at a lanky twentysomething who's still sporting the remnants of teenage acne.

Clearly unused to female attention, he seems startled. 'Oh, er, yeah,' he stammers. 'So, um, are you part of the bride's party?' he asks self-consciously, as he pulls out a packet of Silk Cut Ultra Low.

'Oh, no. I'm here to do the photographs.'

'You're a photographer? Hey, cool,' says his friend, to whom I haven't paid much attention as he's been on his mobile with his back to me. He's incredibly handsome. And knows it. 'Maybe you could take my picture some time. I'm the lead singer in a band.'

I'm about to tell him that I'm only the assistant when the boy with the cigarettes says, 'Don't listen to Jack, he's always like this.' Then he holds out his lighter. 'I'm Francis, by the way.'

I smile appreciatively. Why is it that when men are in pairs there's always the sweet, kind one who's every girl's best friend, and the handsome bastard who gets all the girls?

'Hey, listen to you, Pizza Face,' snorts Jack. Two spots of colour burn in Francis's cheeks, but Jack is grinning confidently, safe in his good looks. God, what a bully. I wish someone would put him in his place.

I turn to Francis. 'Thanks.' I smile. 'Nice meeting you.'

'And you.' He smiles gratefully. Unlike Jack, who mutters something unrepeatable about me having no sense of humour and turns to the blonde girl with the VPL.

I begin to make my way back through the crowd to the Together Forever van. I hardly ever smoke, especially not on the job, but today I'm anxious. I take a puff of my cigarette. Very anxious.

I knew something wasn't right as soon as Brian picked me up this morning. There was something on his mind, that was for sure, but I didn't like to ask what—I'm too much of a coward.

But, then, just as we were pulling into the car park, his phone rang. He mumbled something about it being an important call and gestured for me to give him some privacy. He's still pacing the car park, mobile phone wedged to his ear, face solemn. The warm breeze blows over snippets of conversation. 'Uh-huh . . . Yes . . . I completely understand . . .'

My stomach tightens. It sounds like bad news.

'So what kind of numbers are we talking? Hm . . . Hm . . . Oh really? As much as that?'

Oh, God. It's someone from the bank calling about the loan. I wish I could conjure a great big fat wedding out of thin air.

'Heather, I need to talk to you.' Brian's hurrying towards me, coattails flapping. 'I've got some wonderful news,' he whoops, a delighted smile breaking across his face. 'I think you should sit down.'

'But I thought it was about the loan?' I gesture to his mobile phone.

'Not exactly.' He's jigging up and down on his heels. He's so twitchy he can't keep still. 'But we're talking about a lot of money here.'

'But how can that be good news?'

'It's not good news. It's *wonderful* news, Heather.'

I snap: 'Brian, will you please stop talking in riddles and explain why owing a lot of money is wonderful?'

'Who said anything about owing money?'

'You did. Last week. The conversation in the van about having to let me go.'

'Now, now. A lot can happen in a week. In a week a business can go from owing a lot of money to making a lot of money. Especially if it gets a client who just happens to be the Duke of Hurley, whose daughter just happens to be getting married—'

'You mean Lady Charlotte?' I interrupt.

'Uh-huh.'

'The blonde socialite who's always in all the magazines? There was a picture of her this week at some party with Paris Hilton. I swear, they're almost identical.' I shake my head.

'Lady Charlotte has much thicker ankles,' confides Brian. 'Word among a few of my old *paparazzi* pals is she's got legs like a man.'

'Really?' I whisper. 'But surely she can't be getting married. Isn't she only about twenty-one or something?'

'She can be sixteen for all I care, just as long as she's legal.'

Suddenly the penny drops. 'What? You mean . . . we're going to cover her wedding?'

'Yep, you and me, kiddo. In three weeks!'

'Isn't that a bit short notice?' I'm so astonished it's all I can say.

'Apparently it's all very last-minute and hush-hush because they don't want the press to find out. That was the Duchess on the phone just then. Said she remembered me from the sixties.'

'Oh, Brian, it's fantastic news!' Overcome with relief I throw my arms round him.

'It's more than that—it's a bloody miracle!' he gushes, and as I hug him tight I feel a ripple of excitement. I wished for a miracle, didn't I?

A commotion interrupts my thoughts. 'Oh, look, is that the bride arriving?' I glance towards the driveway where people are circling.

Brian stands on tiptoe to see over the heads. 'No, some idiot's just had a drink thrown in his face.' He laughs derisively.

I peer over his shoulder: it's Jack, the wannabe rock star. Only he doesn't look like one now. His face is dripping and his white shirt is soaked. I feel a glow of satisfaction. What was that about wishing someone would put him in his place?

'You two-timing creep!' I recognise the blonde girl with the VPL. 'Who do you think you are? Some kind of stud? I wouldn't mind, but for all the big talk, you've got a willy the size of a—'

'Cocktail sausage?' James guesses. He's listening to my story from the other side of the restaurant table. Oh bloody hell, Heather.

And our first date had started so perfectly. James picked me up at exactly eight and we drove in a cab to this gorgeous little Italian restaurant in Soho. The maître d' showed us to our candlelit table, a waiter poured me a glass of perfectly chilled champagne and James told me how lovely I was looking. Then came the pause. And I did what I always do when I get nervous: I filled the silence. Even worse, I filled it with the first thing that came into my head, which just so happened to be my anecdote about Jack the wannabe rock star. And his penis.

I look at James across the candlelit table and want to crawl underneath it. 'Erm . . . I can't actually remember . . .' I say evasively. I take a large gulp of champagne. Come on, Heather, think of something to say—*think*. Suddenly it comes to me in a blinding flash of light: 'I'm reading this wonderful book.'

He looks at me with interest. 'You are?'

'Yes. It's amazing.' I look him in the eye as I play my ace. 'It's called *Life of Pi*.' I try not to smile triumphantly, but it's hard.

'Oh, yeah, it's had some great reviews.' Then—to my disbelief—his nose wrinkles. 'But I couldn't get past the first couple of chapters. I'm obviously a bit of a philistine.' He reaches across the table and strokes my hand. 'So, tell me, why are you loving it so much?'

Oh, my God, me and my big mouth. 'Well it's the perfect size for propping underneath my coffee table,' I quip, 'to correct the wobble.' I laugh nervously.

James doesn't. Laugh, that is. In fact, there's not a flicker of a smile. 'Oh, right.' He seems puzzled. Then there's another pause. Fortunately a waiter fills it by arriving to take our order and reeling off a list of specials. There's chicken, beef, rabbit, pastas, risottos.

'Mmm, it all sounds good,' murmurs James. 'What do you feel like, darling?'

Darling? He says it casually, so naturally, so affectionately, it's as if he's unaware he's even said it. Except he did say it. All my earlier embarrassment vanishes. I can't believe it. A term of endearment. Women can wait years for this level of intimacy from a man, and yet here's James, calling me 'darling' on our first date. 'It all sounds great,' I reply, as if nothing out of the ordinary has happened, 'But I'm actually a vegetarian—'

'Are you serious?' interrupts James, all wide-eyed. And I'm just wondering what I've said now when he clinks his champagne glass against mine. 'I'm a vegetarian too.'

'What a coincidence.' Wow, he really is my perfect man, I tell myself.

'So tell me, are you a mohair-sweater-wearing-lentils-and-nut-roast-vegetarian? Or the microwaveable-macaroni-cheese type?'

'Oh, definitely the second.' I smile. 'I hate nuts—I'm allergic to them.'

'No way! So am I!'

'Really?'

'No, not really.' Smiling, he shakes his head. 'But I can be if you want.'

'No, it's OK.' I laugh. 'You seem fine the way you are.'

Reaching across the table he brushes my fingers, which are entwined round my wine glass, with his thumb. 'Really?' he asks quietly.

I look down at his hand, that's now covering my own, and feel a delicious tingle run all the way up from my groin. 'Really.'

The waiter coughs to attract our attention. 'Have you decided?'

James, turning to the waiter with his lovely, lazy grin, asks, 'Would it be possible to make two macaroni cheese?'

The evening gets better and better. After dinner we drink lattes, then grab a cab back to our flats. En route, James entertains me with stories—about how his sister regularly beats him at Scrabble; he can cook a mean mushroom risotto; he's been plucking up courage to ask me out for months. 'There was never a right time. We kept bumping into each other but I was scared of looking like an idiot . . . Whenever we saw each other you ignored me—I got the impression you weren't interested . . .'

Close your mouth, Heather.

'. . . but yesterday I just thought, What the hell. Ask her out.'

I don't believe I'm hearing this. It must be a dream and I'm going to wake up, like Bobby Ewing in the shower.

'Sorry, am I freaking you out telling you all this?'

'No, no . . .' *Yes. Yes.*

By now the cab has dropped us off at the top of our street and we're walking along the pavement together. 'I've never been into playing games,' James confesses quietly. 'I'm not interested in all those rules about waiting three days before calling. If you like someone, why can't you call straight away? Why can't you be honest and say how you feel?'

I am just at the point of thinking that all this seems too good to be true when he does something completely unexpected. He holds my hand. In public. Without being asked. Now, this might not sound like much to most people, but to me it's a minor miracle.

'Well, here we are.' I stop outside my flat reluctantly. It's in darkness. Gabe must still be out, I think, as James wraps his arms round my waist and pulls me towards him, saying, 'I've had a wonderful evening.'

'Me too,' I murmur, gazing into his dark eyes.

'And I was wondering . . . Can I see you again?'

Having been debating how far I should go (kissing is fine for the first date, but if he wants to stay the night I have to be firm and say no) I hadn't anticipated this question. 'Oh . . . of course,' I reply, feeling a surge of delight—but disappointed that this is where our date ends.

'What about the cinema tomorrow night?' he suggests.

I consider pretending I've got to check my diary first, not because I might be doing something (I know I'm not) but out of habit. And then I remember: James doesn't play games so I don't have to either. 'Sure.'

'How about I pick you up around seven? We can go for a drink beforehand.'

'Great.'

Smiling sexily, he leans closer. 'Good night, Heather.'

So this is it. *The kiss*. I feel a delicious fizz of anticipation. Closing my eyes, I lift my face towards his expectantly.

I feel his lips brush my cheek. My eyes snap open. *Is that it?* I give it a few moments, half expecting a follow-up, but when there's no sequel I say briskly, 'Right. Good night, James.'

He waits dutifully until I find my keys and let myself in, then walks across the street to his own flat. In my hallway I watch his retreating figure, thinking how James is everything I've always wished for in a man—handsome, kind and a real gentleman. And I'm not disappointed that he didn't want to come in for coffee. Or try to kiss me.

No, I'm not disappointed at all.

'**W**ow, this place is so quaint.'

It's Sunday morning and Gabe and I are having breakfast at a busy pavement café in Hampstead. I laugh, 'You sound like such a tourist.'

'That's because I am a tourist,' he smiles, picks up the sports section of the newspaper and disappears behind it.

It has to be one of the most amazing things about life that within a week you can go from not knowing a person even exists to sharing your home, the TV remote and the Sunday papers with them. It's amazing for anyone, but for me especially, as I'm very protective of my Sunday-morning ritual: reading the *Style* magazine over a plate of fluffy yellow scrambled eggs—alone.

But on this particular Sunday morning I bumped into Gabe in the kitchen, pacing around in his Tibetan slipper-socks somewhat at a loss. And felt guilty. There he was, a stranger in a foreign country, and I hadn't once offered to show him the neighbourhood. So, I made the ultimate sacrifice and invited him for breakfast.

Finishing my scrambled eggs I watch Gabe as he studies the sport. Eventually he puts down the paper. 'So,' he says, 'you haven't mentioned how your date went last night.'

I blush, I don't know why.

'That good, huh?' He laughs.

'Yeah, I guess you could say that. Anyway, how did you know my date was last night?' I ask casually.

'I'm psychic.'

'*You are?*' I ask, then realise that he's trying to be funny.

'No, not really. I was in my room and heard him come pick you up. Eight o'clock on the dot.'

I smile bashfully. 'Well, it's rude to keep a lady waiting.'

'That's what Mia's always telling me, but I'm always late.'

At the mention of his girlfriend, I smile sympathetically. 'You must really miss her.'

'Yeah.'

He doesn't elaborate so, of course, I blunder on: 'How's her movie going?' I ask, which is really code for 'What's going on with you two?'

'OK.' He shrugs, and then adds, 'At least, I think so.'

Like I thought. Something's definitely up.

'I haven't spoken to her in a while. It's difficult for her to call from the set. And the time difference doesn't help.'

He's obviously making excuses for her, I decide, feeling suddenly protective of him. 'Long-distance relationships, hey?' I say.

He nods, then changes the subject. 'So, you like this new guy? What did you say his name was?'

'I didn't.' I smile. 'It's James. And, yeah, I like him. The funny thing is, apparently he's been wanting to ask me out for ages but thought I wasn't interested.'

'When are you seeing him again?'

'Tonight,' I reply casually, taking a sip of my latte.

'Wow,' Gabe drawls. 'Has he got the hots for you, girlfriend.'

'Oh, I don't know about that . . .' I say modestly, but Gabe stops me.

'Heather, listen to me.' He eyes me seriously. 'You've liked this guy for ages, and after what you told me he said last night it's pretty obvious he's liked *you* for ages—so where's the problem?'

'OK, OK, you're right. There isn't a problem . . . *that's the problem*.'

Gabe looks at me with amusement, 'Are you sure you're not Jewish?'

I have to say, that when Gabe isn't in stand-up comedy mode, he can be rather funny and I'm swatting him playfully with the *Style* section when someone bangs into the back of my chair, knocking my coffee, which slops into my lap. 'Hey! Can't you watch where you're going?' I yelp as I jump back in my seat.

'Sorreee!' There's a chorus of yelling from a crowd of boys as they rush past down the high street.

'You OK?' Gabe asks, passing me a napkin.

'Fine.' I begin to blot my lap.

Gabe digs out the magazine and flicks straight to the back. The actions of a seasoned horoscope reader. 'Shall I read you your horoscope?' he asks brightly.

'Oh, go on, then,' I say. 'I'm Pisces.'

'"With all your planets aligning this is an important time for Pisceans in the areas of your career, family and love. Major changes will be happening. You're on a winning streak, so watch out for a sudden windfall."' He looks up. 'Wow! Sounds like you're going to win the lottery.'

'Me? I never win anything,' I laugh, then suddenly remember my lottery ticket. My heart starts to beat very, very quickly. 'Quick, Gabe, pass me the papers. I want to see something.'

I fumble with the different sections until I find the one I need, and start flicking through it. No, not there . . . Then I see them: last night's lottery numbers. *They look familiar*.

I take a moment to remember to breathe. 30 my age; 14, my address; 6, number of years I've been working at Together Forever. Cautiously I edge my eyes along the page: 27, Mum's birthday was 27 April . . . I try to remember the last two numbers I chose hastily at random. I'm pretty sure one was 13 . . . Bloody hell! Sure enough, it's there. My stomach flips. Now for the last one. It's 41—did I pick 41?

'Heather?'

I jump. I'd forgotten about Gabe.

'Are you sure you're OK?'

'Fine . . .' *Oh my God, I think I've won the lottery*.

'You don't look too good. You've gone pale.'

'Honestly, it's nothing.' *I'm going to be a millionaire*.

'Maybe we should go home. I'll get the check.' He beckons the waiter.

'Wait a mo. I just want to check my lottery ticket.' I reach feverishly for my bag.

Er, hang on a minute. I run my hand along the back of my chair, feeling for the leather strap. A tiny flame of panic ignites in me and I glance over my shoulder to where I'd slung my bag earlier. It's not there.

'It's been stolen,' I whisper. I jump up in horror, eyes darting under the table, around the side of the chair, along the pavement.

'Hey, what's up?'

'My bag!' I wail desperately. Then I remember the gang of boys banging into my chair. Jesus, Heather, it's the oldest trick in the book. 'Those kids must have stolen it,' I jabber wildly.

'Oh, Jeez.' Gabe stands up and begins to look with me. 'Was everything in it?'

I feel tears prickling. 'My phone, house keys, wallet . . .'

'Did you have a lot of cash?'

'Not much, maybe a tenner,' I murmur. 'But that's not important.'

'Hey, I know, it's the sentimental stuff.'

'No, it's not that . . .' I begin, then stop. I can't tell him. He'll think he's sharing a flat with a complete idiot.

'Is it the shock?' Gabe squeezes my hand.

I nod mutely. Shocked? I'm bloody mortified. One minute, there I was in my Holland Park pad, with my Italian villa and my new Aston Martin, and now—*poof*—it's all gone. Along with my wallet, keys, mobile, Filofax—which has my address in it, which means I'll have to change the locks . . .

'I know it sucks,' Gabe is saying, 'but there's not much we can do here. We should head back to the flat, report it stolen to the cops.'

'Actually, I might as well go straight to the police station,' I say, 'but you don't have to come with me.'

'Hey, of course I will.'

'No, honestly, it's fine.' I say firmly. 'I'll have to fill in a report—might as well get the boring paperwork over with now.' Great. Just how I wanted to spend my Sunday afternoon.

'Oh, OK . . .' There's a pause, and then he adds shyly, 'Look, I don't know if you're interested, but I'm meeting my uncle later at some comedy club he knows about. It's open mike tonight and I could use a little practice . . . you're more than welcome to join us.'

I'm flattered by his invitation, but the words 'open mike' are enough to bring me out in hives. Thankfully, however, I already have an excuse. 'Thanks, but I'm seeing James,' I remind him.

'Oh, yeah, I forgot—*duh* . . .' For a second I swear I see a flash of disappointment in his eyes, but now he's smiling and saying, 'Well, I guess I'll see you later.' Gabe moves towards me and, presuming he's going to kiss my cheek I move my face to one side. Only it goes wrong and, bumping noses, our lips collide. We jump back as if we've been stung.

'Oops! Sorry about that.' I laugh uncomfortably.

'Don't worry, it's the big schnoz.' Gabe grins, but I'm sure he's as embarrassed as I am.

'Well, 'bye then,' I say briskly. Left behind on the pavement, I watch him striding out towards the Heath, mingling among the dozens of people heading for a lazy afternoon lying on the grass. Feeling a stab of envy, I curse the thieves who stole my bag. And then, completely out of the blue, I remember something Ed said that night in the pub: *Be careful what you wish for*. His words make me strangely uneasy. Did wishing I could win the lottery somehow cause my bag to be stolen? Was it because the ticket was in my wallet? Or because my wish was about simply *winning* the lottery, not about *keeping* it?

As the thought strikes I feel a spark of panic. Of responsibility. Fear. But then I catch myself. Honestly, Heather, since when did you ever listen to anything your brother said? And feeling foolish for even considering his words, I march off resignedly.

'So, what did you think of the film?'

It's later that evening and James and I have just been on our second date—to the cinema—and are driving back in his Range Rover.

'I really enjoyed it,' he replies, 'I thought Renée was really funny, and that bit with the adorable little girl . . .' He laughs faintly. 'Hilarious.'

I feel like the cat that's got the cream. Not only is this man drop-dead gorgeous he also loves romantic comedies. *And he's not gay.*

'What about you, darling?' James is saying, as he indicates left, then drives down our street. 'What do you think?'

That we're outside your flat and I'm wondering if you're going to invite me in for coffee, I think lustfully. But instead I reply, 'It was great.'

He swings into a parking space, switches off the engine and turns to me. He says, 'I'm afraid I've got a confession.'

'Oh?'

'Uh-huh.' He's holding my gaze. 'I don't have any coffee.'

'Oh.' The man has reduced me to monosyllables.

'So I don't have any excuse to invite you up.'

I feel crushing disappointment. Followed by tingles all through my body as he strokes the side of my face. Before I know what's happening, he's kissing me . . . 'Do I need one?'

He pulls away and my breath catches in the back of my throat. Struggling to find my voice, I smile shyly. 'No.'

He unlocks the door to his flat, takes my coat politely and offers me a nightcap. 'Cheers.' He passes me a glass of champagne and clinks his glass against mine.

Surprisingly, his flat isn't anything like I imagined. Instead of being modern, it's traditional, with old-style standard lamps, floor-to-ceiling book shelves and a gilt-edged mirror hanging over the fireplace. It's also immaculate. I feel secretly pleased. I've always wished I could meet a man who's neat and tidy. And, hey presto, here he is.

I watch James walk over to his CDs. 'What do you feel like listening to?' he asks, running his finger along the spines—in alphabetical order I notice, unlike mine, which are piled in a messy jumble on the shelves, minus their cases.

'Oh . . . well, why don't you choose something?' I say brightly.

'OK, let's see . . .' He begins to throw out names: 'Billie Holiday, Bob Dylan, David Bowie, Coldplay, Sting, Madonna . . .' As he reels off one name after another he could almost be reading out my own CD collection '. . . Roxy Music, *The Best of Spandau Ballet* . . .'

I feel a buzz of happiness. I've always wished I could meet a man who shared my taste in music.

'What about Dido?'

'Perfect.' I beam.

James looks relieved. He's adorable when his face is all scrunched up with worry, and I resist the urge to go over and kiss him. It's not easy.

He slides open the CD drive, opens the case and frowns. 'Damn. After all that there's a different CD in here.'

His expression is so hangdog I start to laugh. 'Oh, don't worry, that happens to me all the time.'

'Well, it doesn't happen to me,' he grumbles.

'Perhaps you put it back in the wrong case by accident,' I suggest.

'But that's impossible,' he protests. 'I'd never do that.'

My smile fades. Surely one CD in the wrong case isn't going to throw him into a bad mood? 'Why don't we listen to that CD anyway?' I say. I'm fast regretting wishing he could be neat and tidy.

He glares accusingly at the silver disk in his hand as he puts it into the player. 'This should be interesting . . .'

From concealed speakers swell the opening chords of a guitar, and a woman's voice, soft and sexy. She's singing in French. 'Who's this?'

James's face is flooded with recognition. 'Emmanuelle. She's an old friend of mine—she used to play in clubs in Paris.'

'You lived in Paris?'

'For a couple of years after university. A long time ago.' Slipping his fingers through mine, he leads me over to the large suede sofa.

'Wow, how exciting,' I blurt, more out of nerves than anything else as now we're sitting on the sofa and he's slipping his arm around my shoulders and pulling me towards him. Then he kisses me full on the lips. *Wow*. It's been so long since I've been kissed by someone I've forgotten how thrilling it is. For the next few moments I don't ever want this to stop.

Only my bladder's got other ideas. It twinges. I try to ignore it and not to think about the litre of Diet Pepsi I drank in the cinema. Instead I cross my legs and concentrate on James's tongue, his hands . . . But it's no good. My bladder feels as if it's about to burst. 'Where's your bathroom?' I ask, pulling away reluctantly.

'On the right, through the bedroom—it's *en suite*.'

I make a mad dash for the bedroom. Like the rest of his flat, it's immaculate. No overflowing drawers, no clothes or shoes strewn on the floor, which is sort of how I left my own. Feeling a tingle of excitement as I imagine us in his bed later, I hurry through to the bathroom and flick on the light. Aaaah, the relief.

I walk back into the living room with an empty bladder and a pair of lips all pink and glossy and ready to be kissed. The sofa is empty.

Oh.

Standing alone in the room I feel a twang of disappointment, then notice a light in the small office at the end of the hallway. I wander in and find James bent over his laptop. He looks up. 'Just dealing with a few emails. I've got a client in Sydney, a very impatient client,' he adds, interlacing his fingers with mine and pulling me towards him. 'Darling, would you mind if we leave tonight to be continued? Australia's nine hours ahead. I'm afraid I really need to work on this now.'

Ha, ha, very funny. I search his eyes for a dart of humour, but all I see is his laptop screen reflected back at me. Which is when I know he's not joking. I'm disappointed and frustrated all at once. 'Yeah . . . of course,' I say. 'That's fine. Actually, I could do with an early night anyway,' I lie, pretending to yawn.

He smiles. 'So, are you free tomorrow night?'

'Sorry, I'm busy.' I'm about to explain that Lionel and I are going to see a new art exhibition in Kensington then decide not to. Childish, I know, but I can't help feeling a little indignant that James is sending me home and not even *trying* to persuade me to stay. Honestly, sometimes you can be too much of a perfect gentleman.

'What about the night after?'

'I have to work.'

He raises his eyebrows with interest.

'A mock-Tudor wedding at Hampton Court,' I elaborate, stiffly.

'Oh, right,' he nods seriously, his mouth twitching with amusement. 'Well, unfortunately I have to go to Zürich on Wednesday for a couple of days.' He's looking at me as if he's weighing up what my reaction will be when he says, 'What about Friday?'

'Maybe.' I attempt to appear elusive.

'In that case, *maybe* I'd like to cook you dinner.'

I look into his dark irises and remember the months I've spent wishing he would notice me. Now here he is wanting to cook me a romantic candlelit dinner. Honestly, Heather, you really are an ungrateful old cow. 'That would be lovely,' I murmur, tilting my face to kiss him.

I mean, for goodness sake, what more could I possibly wish for?

Arriving at the Serpentine Gallery in Hyde Park the following evening, I discover a hive of activity. A crowd has spilled outside on to the grass, filling the balmy evening with a cacophony of chatter and laughter.

I'm early, thanks to the lucky heather, which I tucked into my new purse before I left the house: a bus appeared immediately, all the lights were green and I was whisked here in no time.

'Good Lord, I never thought I'd see the day.'

Lionel is bearing down on me, a smile plastered across his bearded face. Heads turn at the sound of his thunderous baritone and I brace myself. 'Hi, Lionel.'

'My daughter? *On time?*' He throws his arms round me in the customary bear hug and succeeds in spilling my drink all over my shoes.

'When have I ever kept you waiting?' I protest. I link my arm through his and steer him to the drinks. 'Let's have a martini, and these smoked salmon thingies look yummy.'

'Mmm, yes, darling,' he says, through a mouthful of crumbs. 'Rather smashing. I think I'll have a couple more.' He beams appreciatively at the waitress as he piles a few into a napkin. She giggles and a mild flirtation ensues, even though she's only in her early twenties.

I watch with amused affection. It never ceases to amaze me how people love Lionel. For me it's understandable—he's my father—but he has this magical effect on everyone he meets.

'I thought we were here for the exhibition, not the food,' I point out.

'So we are, so we are. Righty-ho, then . . .' He steals another mini-quiche from the tray, pops it into his mouth and throws a huge arm round my shoulders. 'Let's go look at some art.'

For the next half an hour or so we walk round the different 'installations' while Lionel tries valiantly to explain to me the symbolism of a washing-machine that's been taken apart and strewn all over a roll of dirty shagpile carpet.

I don't get it. I'm a complete heathen when it comes to that sort of thing. 'So, how are things?' he says, noticing my glazed expression and abandoning his explanation of how the washing-machine is a metaphor for global warming spinning out of control.

'Pretty good, actually.' I'm happy that, for once, I mean it, and am not simply saying it to ease his fatherly concern. 'We're booked to do a huge society wedding in a few weeks. I'm renting out my spare room to an American for a few weeks to help with the bills . . .' I look sideways at his face. 'And I've met someone.'

Without flinching Lionel continues to gaze at the installation. 'Would that someone be a fellow?'

'His name's James,' I say, trying to sound normal and act as if it's no big deal, while I'm struggling to stop the smile that's threatening to take over my face, which is what happens every time I think of him. Which is every few seconds. 'He seems really nice.'

'*Nice?*' repeats Lionel. 'Nice is such a wishy-washy adjective. If it were a colour it would be a pastel.'

'OK, in that case . . .' I'd planned to play down my feelings for James, but now I change my mind. 'What about "wonderful"?'

'Oh, my goodness . . .' A wide smile breaks across his face. 'Heather darling, that's marvellous news. Tell me all about him.'

Without further prompting, I describe how James and I met and how he used to work in the City but left five years ago to establish a property business with clients as far afield as Australia. I also tell him James is handsome, funny and incredibly well-mannered and that he's going to cook me dinner later this week. I don't tell him that I keep wondering why James didn't ask me to stay over last night. How the kiss on the sofa was lovely but left me wanting more, and that although I've spent months wishing I could meet a man who was interested in my brain, not just my body, I'm now having doubts.

'Hmmm, he seems like a great chap,' says Lionel, as I draw breath, and we move in front of a sculpture of a naked torso made of knitting needles. 'However, one thing concerns me. Sex.'

I blush hotly. '*Lionel*,' I groan.

He ignores me. 'You haven't mentioned it,' he persists, without the teeniest smidgen of embarrassment. 'Is everything all right?'

'Yes, it's fine. He's being the perfect gentleman,' I say briskly. 'Which, after Daniel . . .' I allow my voice to trail off pointedly.

'Ah, yes, of course.' Lionel is nodding understandingly. 'You don't want another cad, do you?'

'Two-timing bastard is how I usually refer to him.'

Lionel lets out a roar of approval. 'And so you should. In my day if you were found cheating on a girl the father would have gone after you with a shotgun.' He shakes his head. 'But it was all very different then. There was an unspoken code of behaviour we had to follow. When I met your mother, I had to ask her father's permission to court her.'

'Were you nervous?'

'Dreadfully. I shook like a lily.'

'You must have been in love.' I laugh.

'From the moment I saw her,' he says quietly, squeezing my arm.

We fall silent and move to the last exhibit, but I don't really see it. I'm still thinking about my parents, trying to picture them in their early twenties when they first met. Lionel's right: it *was* different back then, but there's something about my relationship with James that feels like theirs. It's almost as if he's courting me. We've still only kissed. Today it seems unusually chaste, but back then it was obviously normal to take things slowly. And so much more romantic, I decide. Mum and Dad would have fallen in love long before they fell into bed.

Reassured by this thought, I turn to Lionel and, unable to resist, ask, 'Tell me, how long did you and Mum wait? You know, before . . .'

'Wait?' He looks at me in astonishment, then guffaws. 'Oh, my word, no. Your mother and I were at it like rabbits on our first date.'

Bzzzzzzzzz. Forty-five minutes later I'm standing on James's doorstep, finger on the doorbell, stiletto heel tapping agitatedly. I've had enough. Or, to be more precise, I haven't had any. You know there's something horribly wrong when you're having less sex than your parents.

Bzzzzzzz.

'Hello?' Finally I hear James's voice on the intercom. He sounds sleepy. I look at my watch: it's late. 'Who is it?' He yawns.

'It's me, Heather,' I say. So what if he's sleepy? I've made a decision. Sod waiting. Sod getting to know each other. And sod him respecting me in the morning.

There's a pause, before: 'Is everything OK?'

'Yeah, fine,' I fib. Well, you can hardly call abandoning your father at an exhibition, jumping into a cab and turning up at your boyfriend's house in a sexual frenzy fine, can you? 'Can I come up?' I demand forthrightly. And a bit drunkenly. Those martinis were strong.

'Of course.' There's the sound of the door being released. I push it open and dive for the stairs, taking two at a time. Turning the bend I see James waiting in his doorway. 'Heather, what's wrong? You seem—'

I silence him by sticking my tongue down his throat.

'**A**nd then he said, "Jessica, you make me want to be a better man."'

The next morning I'm in a yoga class with Jess. After a seemingly never-ending round of sun salutations I'm resting in what the instructor describes as 'child's pose'. In other words, I'm face down on a mat. I take a deep breath. 'Isn't that a line from a movie?' I hear myself ask.

When Jess called earlier, reminding me that I've been promising for weeks to go with her to Bikram yoga—'it's amazing, they heat up the room to about ninety degrees so you can reach these really deep poses'—I felt my chakras tie themselves up in a knot. Exercising? In ninety-degree heat? For two hours? 'Sorry, but I've got a mock-Tudor wedding at Hampton Court that starts at three,' I replied, relieved that I was booked to take photographs of a bride and groom dressed up like Henry VIII and Anne Boleyn. Which shows how much I hate yoga.

But Jess wasn't taking no for an answer and so, reluctantly, I met her before work for an early class. Only when I arrived I discovered she had an ulterior motive for seeing me, which had nothing to with Bikram yoga and everything to do with Greg.

'Heather, do you always have to be so cynical?' she grumbles. For the last forty-five minutes she's been all dreamy-eyed in her blow-by-blow account of Greg, but now she's scowling at me from her mat.

'I'm not being cynical,' I protest hotly. 'I was just saying—' *Damn, what was the title of that movie?* It's niggling me now.

'Well, don't,' she interrupts crossly. 'OK, I admit in the past I've kissed a lot of men I thought were princes who turned into frogs, but Greg's different. He seems really genuine and honest. *And* he's got a perfect record when it come to relationships. Never been married, several girlfriends but no one special . . .' she's counting off the points on her fingers '. . . wants to settle down and have children.'

'Jack Nicholson,' I blurt triumphantly. '*As Good As It Gets*.'

'What?'

'That's the line from the movie. Jack Nicholson says it to Helen Hunt.'

Jess glowers. Oh, shit, why did I just say that?

'*. . . and so, bringing ourselves up to a standing position, let's take some deep breaths . . .*'

'It's a great movie,' I add feebly. 'And Greg sounds great too.'

'He is,' she says curtly, inhaling deeply.

I make one last attempt at the peace process. 'I've had sex.'

It's like an Exocet missile, obliterating all her earlier thoughts of being offended. '*Sex?* With whom?'

'My gorgeous neighbour.'

Jess's eyes grow saucer-wide. 'You're serious?'

'Deadly.'

'I can't believe it.'

'*. . . and now move slowly into Warrior One . . .*'

We move into position—Jess with the graceful ease of someone who did childhood gymnastics, I with the crunching of knees that makes both me and the woman next to me wince.

'I want dates, times, places, size,' she demands.

I smile coyly. 'His name's James and we've already been on two dates. He's great.' I get a flashback of last night, all tangled up in James's sheets. His naked body. Him kissing every single bit of me, starting at my toes and working his way up to . . .

'*. . . it's important to keep yourself focused . . .*'

The memory throws me off-balance and I wobble over. 'Amazing, actually,' I whisper, trying to steady myself.

'That's fantastic.' Jess grins with delight, then gets down to business. 'What age bracket is he in?'

Trust Jess. She's not interested in how James makes my stomach flip over or his lazy smile. She's interested in make, model and income.

'He's thirty-six,' I say, trying to focus on my yoga pose.

'Excellent.' She nods knowledgeably. 'The twenty-six to thirty-five bracket are too immature, but the thirty-six to forty guys are ripe for commitment.'

'*And . . . Swan dive . . .*'

Smoothly touching her toes Jess moves swiftly on: 'Does he have a clean relationship record?'

'Clean?' I repeat dubiously, swan-diving for my toes but unable to get any further than my knees. I strain as hard as I can.

'You know—ever been married?'

'Nope.' Ouch. The backs of my knees are killing me.

Obviously this is a good answer: she looks pleased. 'Lived with someone?'

'Jess,' I plead, 'I like him, he likes me. It's that simple.'

'It's never that simple,' she warns solemnly.

'Sense of humour?'

'*. . . and let's see if we can hold this position for three minutes . . .*'

I glare at the instructor. Three minutes? Is he mad? 'Uh . . . well . . . he can be a bit serious sometimes . . .' I need to lie down.

'Serious is good. You don't want a joker.'

'Annoying habits?'

'Nugghhh.' I groan, wishing this class was over.

'*And now it's time to relax. Lie down on your mats and close your eyes . . .*'

With relief I do as I'm told. This is great. I'm getting used to all my little wishes coming true.

'Bank balance?' Jess's voice snaps me back.

I groan, 'Oh, God! I don't know and I don't care.'

'There's nothing romantic about being poor,' she warns. 'So that only leaves one thing. Sex.'

'Let's just say you can definitely put a tick in that box.'

'What about foreplay?'

I really want to ignore her but when she leans closer and asks, 'Less than ten minutes?' I can't help shaking my head.

'More than ten minutes?'

I nod more than a little proudly.

'More than twenty?'

I nod again, reliving last night for the umpteenth time. As a lover James was so—how shall I put it?—*unselfish*.

'Thirty?'

'A whole half-hour,' I confess. 'All to myself.'

'Wow! So your wish really did come true.'

'My wish?' I repeat, trying to sound casual as a now familiar tingling erupts in my toes and whooshes up through my fingertips.

'Yeah. Don't you remember wishing for a perfect man?'

Chapter Five

FAST FORWARD to Friday morning, 8 a.m., and I'm standing on the doorstep staring down in amazement at the huge Cellophane bundle in my arms. A dozen perfect red roses gaze up at me lovingly. I quickly read the message. 'Just because you're beautiful—James.' Wow, how romantic. I often see the little Interflora vans zipping around and wish they'd stop at my address with a delivery. But they never do.

Never *did*.

Since Wednesday morning that little van has stopped outside my flat, not once, not twice, but three times! I still can't believe it. Some people might think it's a bit over the top, but isn't it what every girl dreams of? When Daniel and I were together I was always wishing he could be more thoughtful, but James couldn't be *more* thoughtful: he's always calling and text-messaging me . . . which admittedly might feel a bit suffocating if it was anyone else, but with James it's different.

Hugging my bouquet to my chest, I turn to go back inside. I try to manoeuvre into the hallway but the roses and I get squashed between the door frame and the wall. I tug at the Cellophane and accidentally break a couple of stalks. *Damn.* Dismayed, I poke my fingers through the wrapping, trying to straighten them. A thorn pricks my finger, which starts bleeding. Ouch. I glare accusingly at the roses. In fact, to be honest, I'm not really into cut flowers at all. They remind me of hospitals, of being a child and visiting Mum when she was ill.

But I don't want to sound ungrateful. It's the thought that counts, isn't it? And the roses are beautiful, apart from the broken ones, but I'll throw those away. No one's going to count them, are they?

As I walk down the hallway I push my nose into the petals, breathing in their perfume. Mmm, they have such a strong scent. I take a deep breath. Mmm . . . Oh . . . I feel a tickle in my nostrils—hang on, it's my hay fever—all these flowers have brought on an attack. Throwing back my head I let out a violent sneeze.

I walk into the kitchen and see Gabe hunched over the toaster with a chopstick, poking around for something that's got stuck.

'Lost something?'

'Another darn Pop-Tart,' he mutters, pushing his glasses up his nose. His face lights up when he sees me. 'Secret admirer?'

Realising the bouquet, not me, is the reason for his smile, I feel curiously deflated. 'Actually he's not so secret.'

'Wow, that guy's got a real habit.' Gabe scratches his head. 'He needs Red Roses Anonymous.'

'You're not funny.' I fish for my nasal spray in the pockets of my dressing gown, then inhale deeply. With all these flowers I've spent a fortune in Boots this week—eyedrops, sprays, two boxes of antihistamine pills.

'I'm not funny?' Gabe is looking at me with genuine concern.

Of course I can't go around telling stand-up comedians they're not funny—even if it does happen to be true. 'I was joking, silly,' I lie hastily. 'You're hilarious.' I rest the bouquet on the draining board and start opening cupboard doors to find something to put the roses in.

'Are you looking for a vaize?' he says, after a moment.

'A what?' I ask, crouching to bury my head among the saucepans.

'A vaize,' he repeats, only louder.

I reappear empty-handed from the cupboard. 'What's a vaize?'

'You know, they're made of glass or ceramic. They're for flowers?'

'Oh, you mean a *vase*.'

'No, I mean a *vaize*.'

'But in England it's pronounced vase.'

'Well, in America it's a vaize.'

'But you're in England,' I insist and hurriedly change the subject. 'Can I ask you a favour? As you're much taller than me, will you look on top of that cupboard?' I gesture above the oven. '*For a vaize*,' I add pointedly.

A wicked grin threatens to spread across his cheeks. 'Sure,' he says, standing on tiptoe. But that's not enough with my eleven-foot-high Victorian ceilings so he climbs onto the counter. After a few minutes' rummaging, he says, 'What about this?' He's holding a spaghetti jar.

'Nope.' I shake my head. 'Too skinny.'

He puts it back and grabs the next object: the glass jug from the coffee percolator I never use. 'Or this?'

I look up, almost cricking my neck. 'Nah. Too small.' Shrugging, he roots around until finally he finds 'This?'

'Oh, wow! I've been looking for that everywhere.' He's holding out the orange plastic watering-can I bought months ago. 'But no,' I add, taking it from him, 'it'll clash with the red of the roses. Anyway, it's too big.'

'Jeez, who are you? Goldilocks?' he grumbles.

I watch him grope around on top of the cupboard until my neck aches and I look down. And come face-to-face with his hairy calf muscles splayed on the counter. I'd never noticed them before but Gabe has really nice calves. From a distance they seem really tanned, but if I peer closer—I move my face so that my nose is just inches away—I can see that they're covered with millions of tiny freckles that have sort of joined up to give the impression of a tan.

'*Awesome*.' Brandishing a filthy object, Gabe is looking down over his shoulder at me. 'Guess what I . . .' Which is when I realise my head is stuck between his legs and jump back. '. . . found.'

Oh, shite. Trying to appear innocent, I reach up to take it from him. It's an ugly ceramic vase Rosemary once gave me. 'Great, thanks,' I gush enthusiastically, hot with embarrassment. I dunk it in the washing-up bowl and try to look all busy, busy, busy.

OK, now what?

After I've chucked away the broken roses, stuck the rest on the windowsill and made myself another cup of instant coffee, I wonder what to do with the rest of my day off. Normally I like to lie in till noon, but I'm already up and wide awake, courtesy of my new alarm: the man from Interflora. I glance at the fridge door, which is wallpapered with Post-it notes, bills that need paying, and a pair of tickets for *The Rocky Horror Show* on Monday night. I'd forgotten about that. Jess arranged it with a bunch of her gay steward friends and I've got a ticket for James. Though

I'm not sure if suspenders are his thing, I muse, grabbing a pen and a notepad and sitting down at the kitchen table.

OK. I need to write a list. I flick open the pad to find a dozen lists I've already made and forgotten about. OK, I need to write a *new* list.

Friday—My List of Things to Do

(1) Ring James.

Well, that's easy. I dial his number but he's not there so I leave a message thanking him for the roses and telling him how lovely they are.

(2) Hand-washing.

One of the downsides of having sex. Before James, I wore comfy old knickers that I could throw in the washing machine, but now it's all about scraps of frilly lingerie that don't fulfil any of the roles of underwear (support, comfort, protection) but act simply as decoration. Expensive, uncomfortable decoration that's a complete faff to wash.

(3) Get a high-flying job as a photographer.

Initially I think of skipping this one and going straight to 'Buy a new shower curtain' as I fancy a trip to IKEA, but I can't ignore it. It's made the top five on my list for the past six years, and while everything else gets crossed off eventually, it stays there. *Taunting me*. Which is why, many hours later, I'm sitting at my computer Googling 'photography jobs'.

'Hey, how's it going?'

Gabe has stuck his head round my bedroom door with two steaming mugs of peppermint tea and a bag of Liquorice Allsorts.

'Wonderful,' I say dolefully, as I take a mug. 'The only thing I've found is an ad for a staff photographer on *Farm Machinery Monthly*. "Exciting opportunity for an experienced photographer. Knowledge of tractors and silage equipment an advantage. Must like cattle and being outdoors in all weather conditions . . ."'

Gabe throws me a puzzled look and offers me a Liquorice Allsort.

'I'm trying to find a job,' I explain, nibbling off the yellow fondant.

Propping his bum on the edge of my unmade bed, Gabe chews slowly as he strokes Billy Smith. 'But I thought you said your job was safe now you've got this fancy royal wedding.'

'It's not a royal wedding. It's the daughter of the Duke and Duchess of Hurley,' I explain. 'Which means she isn't a princess, just a lady.'

'Not necessarily,' he quips.

'I know it's all rubbish,' I admit, smiling weakly, 'but it's good for business. They're paying my boss a fortune, and one of the big celebrity magazines has offered to buy our pictures, which means we'll be credited as photographers.' I pause.

'But?' Gabe has sensed I'm unhappy about something.

'But when I dreamed of having my photographs published, it wasn't in a magazine with Jade from *Big Brother*,' I confess.

'Who's Jade from *Big Brother*?'

'Exactly.'

Unfazed, he waggles the bag of Allsorts at me. 'You've got me addicted to these things,' he confesses. 'Especially the blue and pink jelly ones.'

'Yuk. They're my least favourite.'

'Jeez, I can't get enough of them. It's the coconut ones I hate.'

As he speaks, I pluck one out. 'Mmm, my favourite,'

'I guess that makes us the perfect people to share these, then?'

Chewing, I nod happily. 'I guess so.'

We smile at each other for a moment, my bad mood forgotten. That's the annoying thing about Gabe: he'll never let me wallow in a bit of self-pity. He's always so positive.

'So what's this dream of yours, then?' he says. 'Where do you want to get your photographs published?'

I blush. It's been my dream ever since I was a teenager, but I feel awkward about admitting it to someone. 'The *Sunday Herald*'s magazine,' I blurt shyly. 'I want my photographs to be on the front cover,' I continue, my mind flicking back to Sunday mornings in Cornwall, Lionel hogging the arts section, Ed the business pages and me leafing through the magazine.

'So why don't you go and work for them?' Gabe says it as if it's the most obvious thing in the world.

'Have you any idea how hard it is to get a job there? Every photographer in the world wants to work for them. I've been trying for years.'

'So why don't you give it another try?' persists Gabe. 'Maybe this time will be different. Maybe you'll get lucky.'

It's as though someone's flicked on a light inside me. Of course. This time *is* different. This time why don't I try *wishing* for a job?

As soon as the thought pops into my head, I notice the lucky heather lying next to my computer. How strange, I'm sure it wasn't there before. But then I forget about it as I'm hit with a surge of excitement. Why on earth didn't I think of it before? If I can wish for little things like parking spaces and they can come true, why don't I try wishing for something important that I've dreamed about since I was a little girl?

'OK. What shall I put?' I open a Word document. 'Dear Sir/Madam . . .'

Gabe grins at my new-found enthusiasm. 'Say you're a wonderful photographer and they'd be crazy not to hire you immediately.'

'I can't put *that*.'

'Hey, there's no room for modesty in this business.' He wafts his hand for me to continue typing. 'I'll dictate . . .' And he does exactly that, until I finish up with a letter whose tone, I argue, sounds as if I'm 'blowing my own trumpet', but which Gabe insists is 'just selling yourself'.

We're in the middle of bickering about it when the doorbell rings.

'Expecting anyone?' Gabe peers towards the front door.

'No, I don't think so,' I say, getting up.

But Gabe stops me. 'No, print off the letter and sign it. I'll get it.'

I'm watching it spool out of the printer when I hear, 'Heather?'

James is standing in my bedroom doorway, dark eyebrows knitted.

'James? What are you doing here?' I begin, then suddenly remember. *Our romantic dinner*. How could I forget?

'I waited for you. I was getting worried.' He's sounding all wounded.

Mortified, I jump up. 'I'm sorry, please, make yourself at home. I'll just go and freshen up.' Trying not to make eye contact as I'm not wearing a scrap of make-up, I gesture round my room, which seen through James's immaculately tidy eyes, looks—I realise, with horror—like a pigsty.

'Erm . . .' He smiles uncertainly, but doesn't move—apart from his eyes, which dart about and finally come to rest on his feet. And yesterday's G-string, discarded on the floor. Triggering two thoughts: (a) Damn, I've already done my hand-washing; and (b) *I want to die*.

I look at James. All shaved and polished and smelling divine in a pale blue shirt and jeans. While I'm a complete mess in my fleecy tartan pyjamas. I just don't measure up. This man has no faults. I, on the other hand, have a long list:

- *I don't floss.*
- *My sofa's covered in cat hair.*
- *I have no pension plan and zero savings.*
- *I have an unhealthy obsession with gossip magazines.*
- *I slurp my tea. And leave rings all over my coffee table as I don't own any coasters.*
- *I am a terrible drunk. And I'm even worse at karaoke.*
- *My fridge hasn't been defrosted for over a year.*
- *My culinary expertise consists of sliding M&S meals out of their cardboard packets and popping them into the microwave.*
- *Mould is growing out of a mug next to my bed that resembles a Portobello mushroom.*
- *I can't park. There—I've said it. May feminism strike me down.*
- *And last but not least my most shameful confession of all: I have been known to pick my nose. And eat it.*

'Actually, maybe I should get back, check on the food.'

I tune back in to see James backing out of the door. And then, just as I'm thinking how completely I've blown it, he steps on Billy Smith's tail. There's an ear-splitting screech. My cat rears up, his jaws wide, and sinks his claws into James's leg. James lets out a howl and hops around in the hallway while I flap around him asking if he's OK. Then Gabe appears with a tube of antiseptic and checks to see if he's bleeding. It's like something from a comedy sketch, only it's not remotely funny.

Thankfully, on closer inspection it turns out to be just a scratch. James, however, is a bit embarrassed because of the fuss he made but, like Gabe says, it was probably shock rather than the pain that made him yell. 'Anyway, I'm just relieved you're OK,' I say, pouring him a glass of wine as we cluster in my living room.

James takes a sip. 'Luckily, yes. But those claws were pretty sharp. Haven't you thought of getting him declawed?'

I freeze mid-mouthful. '*De-clawed?* But that's so cruel,' I protest.

'You've got to be cruel to be kind,' he says simply.

'Kind to whom?' I ask.

'Well, your furniture for a start,' he says, gesturing towards my sofa, whose legs have been shredded over the years into tiny ribbons.

Staring helplessly at my sofa, I can feel my fantasy of James and me living together happily ever after fading fast. 'Oh, I don't care, it's old.'

'I can see.' He laughs as he sits down and brushes off the cat hairs.

'I take it you're not a cat person,' comments Gabe, squatting and rubbing his fingers together. Immediately Billy Smith pads over to him.

'Oh, no, I love animals,' disagrees James. He smiles flirtily at me. 'Your cat's probably just jealous of another male vying for your attention.'

Unexpectedly embarrassed by the compliment in front of Gabe, I smile back awkwardly. This is the first time Gabe and James have met and things feel cool between them. But maybe I'm imagining it.

'And I don't blame him,' adds James, reaching out a hand and pulling me onto his knee. I feel a flicker of something from James that might be mistaken for possessiveness. Not that I'd ever mistake it, of course.

'Hey, I'm gonna go out. Do you want me to post that letter for you?' Gabe stands up, eyebrows raised questioningly.

'Oh, yeah . . . It's in my bedroom, I'll just fetch it.' I jump up from James's lap, pad into my room and grab the letter. 'Thanks.'

'No problem. Well, have a great evening, you guys.' Gabe pulls open the front door. 'Nice to meet you, James.'

'And you, Dave.'

'It's Gabe,' I correct him.

'Sorry, Gabe,' apologises James, curling his arm round my waist as Gabe disappears. I eye him suspiciously. Did he do that on purpose?

'Aren't you going to change?' James glances down and I remember I'm still in my pyjamas. 'Oh, yeah . . .' Honestly, I don't know what's wrong with me. My mind's all over the place. 'I won't be a minute,' I add hastily.

I arrive at James's flat to find it candlelit, the dining table set for two, and an ice bucket with champagne already chilling. It's so romantic it's almost textbook in its perfection. I feel a little overwhelmed.

'A toast,' says James, passing me a flute of champagne.

I look at James. I know I should be feeling all—well—romantic. 'To us,' he says, his voice heavy with implication.

But instead I feel faintly ridiculous. 'To us,' I whisper. Out of nowhere I have an urge to giggle.

'So,' James is saying, touching my cheek, 'did you like the roses?' He begins to nuzzle my neck.

'They were beautiful,' I whisper, standing still, the urge to giggle vanishing. Oooh. As his mouth circles the soft flesh under my chin. I close my eyes and tilt my head back with pleasure.

'Because I couldn't help noticing . . . they only sent nine roses.'

I snap my eyes wide open.

'Didn't you notice?' he says, looking at me now with concern.

I can't believe it. *He noticed*. 'Erm . . . no, I don't think so,' I say.

'Yes, there were definitely only nine,' says James, kissing my neck again, only now it's irritating rather than sexy. 'I counted them while you were changing. I'll call the florist tomorrow.'

'No, don't. Honestly, it's fine, it doesn't matter.' Pulling away I reach for the champagne bottle to top up my drink, only I do it too quickly and the bubbles overflow down the side of the glass.

'But I asked for a dozen red roses,' he continues, quickly grabbing a napkin and pressing it around the side of my glass to blot up the excess.

'Don't worry, I have plenty.' I squeeze his arm.

'I know, but that's not the point,' he says, dropping to the floor and feverishly dabbing at the rug, although I'm sure I didn't spill that much. It was only a dribble. 'You can't send nine,' he mutters.

'Why not?' I tease, half joking, half serious. Taking another elaborately folded napkin from the dining table I go to help him but he shoos me away, telling me I'm the guest. A vague feeling of unease descends on me, and before I know it I say, 'Who made the rule that it has to be a dozen roses? What's wrong with nine?'

'Because you just can't,' he says, perplexed, as if I'm challenging a universal truth, like saying the earth's flat. 'That's not how it works.'

How what works? *Romance?* As I gaze down at him squatting on the floor I suddenly feel my whole belief system being shaken. I've spent my whole life dating unromantic men when I wanted to be sent flowers and treated to candlelit dinners and now—I glance at the candles on the table, the champagne chilling—instead of being romantic, all the rules and this formality feel a bit contrived.

'Hey, let's forget about it, shall we?' I smile lightly, taking the napkin from his hand and replacing it with his refilled champagne glass. 'Don't let it spoil tonight.'

'You're right. I'm sorry, darling.' He stands up and strokes the hair off my forehead. 'I just wanted everything to be perfect for you.'

'Everything is perfect,' I say reassuringly, putting my arms round him. He looks so crestfallen I try to cheer him up. 'Hey, I'm going to go down to Cornwall tomorrow. It's my family's annual get-together and, well, I was wondering if you'd like to come with me. We own a little cottage in Port Isaac, it's nothing fancy but really pretty. It's called Bluffer's Cove as it's set right on top of a hill.'

James's face immediately brightens. 'That sounds great! I can't wait. I'd love to meet your parents,' he says, kissing the tip of my nose.

'You would?' Wow, this is amazing.

'Of course. And mine are dying to meet you. Maybe we can drive to Kent and visit them next weekend?'

I hesitate. Gosh this is all very serious. *And very soon*, pipes up a warning voice. 'Yeah.' I'm suddenly nervous. 'That sounds great!'

The rest of the evening slips past in a hazy blur, James is a terrific cook, and we eat oysters, pumpkin risotto and the most delicious passion-fruit sorbet all washed down with three different types of wine. In fact, by the time we've finished and he asks me to dance I'm a little drunk.

I giggle tipsily. 'But we need some music.'

Picking up the remote he points it towards the stereo. 'Your wish is my command,' he murmurs. There's a faint whir as the disk inside begins to spin and pulling me to my feet he wraps his arm tightly around my waist. Now *this* is what I call romantic.

A song begins and I close my eyes. I recognise the opening chords. I stiffen. No. It can't be. But it is. Wet Wet Wet. This has to be a joke.

'I love the lyrics, don't you?'

Is he insane? I open my eyes to see James gazing at me earnestly. 'Mmm . . .' I nod. Honestly, what can I say? That they're corny?

'I thought you'd love it, that perhaps this could be our song.'

Oh. My. God. I can feel the earlier mood of seduction fast disappearing. Much longer and it will be totally ruined. As we continue slow-dancing round the living room I wait hopefully for James to make the next move. Dinner, champagne, music . . . Surely by the rules of romance the next on the list should be the bedroom? I wait until I can't stand any more Marti Pellow and decide to make the first move by steering James into the bedroom and unbuttoning his shirt.

Thankfully he gets the hint and we take it in turns to remove each other's clothes until I'm lying naked on his super-king bed and James is . . . Where is James?

Standing at the foot of the bed. With a hard-on. *Folding our clothes*.

I stare at him indignantly. I'm lying here. Naked. Ripe. And up for it. And my boyfriend is putting his socks into little balls. Honestly. Neat and tidy is one thing—but this?

'There, all done.' He strides over to the bed, slides his naked body next to mine. 'Now, where were we?'

I'm tempted to sulk—after all, it's not exactly flattering to come second place to someone's underpants—but it's hard to stay mad while James is kissing those deliciously erogenous zones behind my ears. Mmm, this is amazing—I wish it would go on for ever. I swear I've died and gone to foreplay heaven.

Feeling him hard against my thigh, I reach down but he pushes me away and circumnavigates my bellybutton with tiny kisses.

I smile at his teasing and wait. After a moment, I let my hand wander back. 'What's the rush?' he whispers, pushing it away again, only this time with a lot more determination.

Oh, OK. Feeling a little redundant, I lie there as he continues to run his hands over my body and kiss my nipples. Wow, this is incredible . . . It's phenomenal . . . It's . . . I stifle a yawn . . . *A bit boring*.

No sooner has the thought appeared than I'm shocked. I never thought it was possible to have too much foreplay. But you can, I realise. I take matters into my own hands: 'Erm, do we have any condoms?' I mumble. Not exactly subtle, I know, but hey, what's a girl to do?

But instead of taking the hint, James merely murmurs, 'Sssh,' and begins doing this funny thing with his eyelashes against my nipples.

Over his shoulder I catch sight of the digital alarm clock, the time illuminated in the dark. It's nearly two in the morning. *We've been in the bedroom for over an hour. So now can we have sex, please?* begs a silent voice inside me as I press myself closer to him. I try wriggling my hips. Usually this works a treat, but James merely hugs me and for a while we just lie there like that. Hugging.

I try looking on the bright side. It's so rare to find a man who likes cuddling: normally they get a hard-on and it's just wham, bam, thank you, ma'am. But not James. James lurves to hug. Last time we slept together he spooned me all night long. Admittedly it was a bit hard to sleep as I like sleeping face down, and the next day I was so knackered I kept nodding off at work, but it was very romantic.

'Heather?' In the far distance I can vaguely hear James's voice, 'Are you asleep?' I shake my head dreamily. Then it goes quiet and just as I'm drifting off I hear his voice again: 'I love you.'

I turn my head sharply to him. I feel a twinge of panic. Just a twinge, nothing major, and I'm sure that's a completely normal reaction as I'm not used to men telling me they love me first. I tend to go for emotional cripples who have difficulty expressing their feelings.

Yes, that must be it. That's why I feel a little freaked. And a bit claustrophobic—but I'm sure that's because, with the heat of the duvet and James, it's actually getting a bit difficult to breathe. I push the goose down away from me to get a little air. Ah, that's better. I stop wriggling and smile flirtily at James, only he doesn't smile back.

And then I realise: he's waiting for an answer.

Oh, fuck. Here's me wanting a bit of good old-fashioned nooky, and here's James wanting to declare his undying love. By rights, I should be delighted. Only the funny thing is, I'm not. Instead I feel cornered, confused and overwhelmed. I really, really like James. Honestly I do. *But?*

But you don't love him, Heather.

Like eyes in a haunted-house painting I peer sideways and see him gazing lovingly at me from across the pillow. I feel myself melt. Oh, for Godsakes, Heather, just look at him. He's perfect. You must love him. I mean, what's not to love? And so I say it. 'Me too,' I whisper.

He breaks into a grin and grabs hold of me and—

Well, put it this way. I get my wish.

'**W**hereabouts are you?'

Ed's voice nags at me from my mobile, which I've wedged under my chin, 'Ummm, not far . . .' I reply evasively.

Sitting bleary-eyed on my bed I continue stuffing things randomly into a leather holdall. It's Saturday and James and I were supposed to be leaving bright and early this morning to drive down to Cornwall for my family get-together, the plan being we'd arrive—oooh. I peer at my watch. Ten minutes ago.

My hangover thumps dully, and cradling my throbbing head in my hands, I take a few deep breaths. I say *supposed* because we slept past the alarm and now it's already lunch time.

'What's the nearest town?' Ed is demanding impatiently.

'Erm . . . Brighton.' It's the first place that pops into my head.

'*Brighton?* But that's miles out of your way!' Ed's bleating. 'What have you been doing all this time?'

Shagging, I'm tempted to say, but instead I spot my hair dryer under the wardrobe and drop the phone, grunting, 'Hang on, I need to change gear.' Lying flat on my stomach I reach under the wardrobe and resurface to hear him complaining at the other end of the line: '. . . you're talking and driving at the same time? Surely you know it's illegal . . .'

As he launches into one of his lectures I have a quick root through the tangled mess that is my underwear drawer, then give up. Sod it. I pull out the drawer and tip the whole lot into the holdall.

'. . . the police are really cracking down on offenders . . .' In the background I can hear Ed getting himself all worked up.

'OK, OK, Ed, calm down,' I say picking up the phone. 'You don't have to worry. I'm not really driving.'

'Is this your idea of a joke?' he gasps. 'Are you on a train?'

Oh dear, I should never have started with these stupid fibs. Fibbing only gets you into trouble, Heather, warns a voice in my head. I get a flashback of last night. In bed with James. Telling him I loved him. Regret grips me like a vice. Oh God, I wish I hadn't said that. But I did, and I can't wish for something to *un*happen—*can I*?

'No, I haven't left yet,' I confess.

It takes a moment to sink in. And then: 'I can't believe it,' he thunders. 'You haven't left yet? But it's nearly two in the afternoon! You know you're going to hit appalling traffic now, don't you? And you'll miss dinner. Rosemary's going to be very upset.'

Oh, I very much doubt it, I think grimly, imagining her delight when she discovers I'm not going to be there to spoil her hostess-with-the-mostest routine. 'I'll buy her some flowers on the way,' I say, to appease him. Now, what about another pair of jeans? I grab another pair from the pile. Just in case.

'Just in case' is the curse of packing. It's the reason why I always end up going away with far too much stuff that I don't wear.

'. . . and I hope you're going to hire a car and not take your own. It's completely unreliable, Heather . . .'

'Actually, I'm going in my boyfriend's car,' I interrupt, before I can stop myself. Gosh, how weird. It's the first time I've referred to James as my boyfriend and it feels a bit strange. 'And it's a very reliable Range Rover.'

I wait for his reaction, but there's complete silence at the other end of the line. 'Ed, are you still there?'

I can hear a muffled whispering at the other end of the line. I can see him breaking the news to my family, who are gathered around, waiting to hear what crazy mess Heather has got herself into now.

'Ahem, yes, we're all here,' he says hurriedly.

'Well, I'm afraid I'm not,' I say breezily. 'Which is why I can't stand here chatting to you all day, now can I, Ed? Otherwise I'll never get there.' And grinning smugly because, for once, I've actually managed to get in the last word with my brother, I hang up.

Ten minutes later I'm not feeling so cocky. 'You can't come?' I wail, as James tells me he's discovered he has to fly to Paris for crisis talks with some client. Oh God, my brother's going to be insufferable. And as for Rosemary . . . I say goodbye to James and reach resignedly for the keys to the MG, which are lying on the windowsill, next to the sprig of heather.

My gaze falls upon it, and I pause for a moment, my spirits lifting. It's quite incredible how long it's lasted. It might just be down to me looking after it—it's in an egg cup now, which I refill with fresh water—but since every spider plant I touch turns brown and crispy it's evident that a stronger force is at work here than my not-so-green fingers. Some might call it luck. *But I like to call it magic.*

No sooner do I think this than the weirdest thing happens. I've been standing in a little spot of sunlight on the kitchen lino, enjoying its gentle warmth, when it suddenly intensifies into a searing heat and floods through me. And I get the strangest feeling. It's almost as if . . . I'm being watched. Automatically I glance up at the window, fully expecting it to be empty. But there, peering through the slats in the blind, a pair of emerald eyes glitter hypnotically. I feel a jolt of shock. No—it can't be. *It's the old gypsy woman.*

'Heather?'

My heart nearly jumps out of my chest. With a sharp intake of breath I twirl round to see Gabe in the doorway. He's wearing another of his strange wardrobe manifestations—a bright orange boiler suit and flip-flops. 'Oh . . . hi.' My mind is falling around all over itself. Was that . . .? Could it have been . . .? I glance back nervously at the window and catch a streak of ginger as Billy Smith jumps from the ledge. Or was it just a trick of the light?

'Going away for the weekend?' Gabe is saying.

'To Cornwall, to see my family,' I murmur, feeling dizzy. I sit down at the kitchen table, resting my hands on its scratched wooden surface. It feels warm and solid beneath my fingers. 'James was supposed to be coming with me,' I say. 'But he had a meeting.'

'Oh.' Gabe studies me for a moment. 'Are you OK with that?'

I'd thought I wasn't but now it's occurring to me that, actually, I'm fine with it. I'm relieved that James and I are going to have a break from each other. Last night was lovely, but it's left me uneasy.

'Yeah, it's just a long drive. And with the traffic . . .' I add. 'I'll just have to make sure I take lots of chocolate to keep me company.'

'You could always take me. I don't have any plans for this weekend and you were saying the surf's pretty good down there . . .' He trails off and waits for my reaction.

Gabe? Spend the weekend with my family in Cornwall? I'm sure they won't mind, but what about James? Well, what about him? Gabe and I are platonic, and he'll love it there. He'll be able to surf, eat Cornish cream teas and be a complete tourist. I mean, if he thinks Hampstead's quaint, he'll go nuts over Port Isaac.

But what about you, Heather? *What do you want?*

I pause to think about it. Not because I need to, but because I think I ought to. I know the answer, though—I'd known it before I went through all this in my head. I want him to come with me.

'The surf's great.' I smile shyly.

'Awesome!' he whoops. 'Now can I make a suggestion? Forget sitting in traffic. We're gonna take the bike.'

We're going to crash! We're going to end up in some horrible, gruesome wreckage! Racing down the M4, I squeeze my eyes shut inside my full-face helmet and tighten my already vice-like grip round Gabe's waist. I'm travelling at nearly a hundred m.p.h. with no seat-belt, balancing on a skinny little leather seat and *trying to stay alive*.

It's early evening by the time we reach the turning for Port Isaac. I slide open my visor and take a deep lungful of Cornish air. Mmmm, delicious. It smells of salt, surf and wood smoke and, as always, I'm hit by nostalgia. This is the smell of my childhood. Of days spent on the beach collecting sea shells. Of walks along the cliff top, holding hands with my parents, who swung me high into the air as I squealed with laughter.

The exhaust is reverberating loudly now as we weave along the narrow lanes, past the patchwork of fields dotted with grazing sheep. Gradually the green meadows give way to rows of stone cottages, and as we whiz past them up the hill I feel a tingle of anticipation, because in just a second I know we're going to get our first glimpse of the sea. I hug Gabe tightly. I'm bursting to point over his shoulder and yell at him to watch out for it. But I don't want to spoil the surprise.

And now we're flying over the brow of the hill and it's there. A silvery blue streak clinging to the horizon.

'Wooo-hooo,' howls Gabe into the wind.

The sea stretches out in front of us, like the cinema screen before a movie. Wider and wider, until it's filling the entire horizon, the frothy peaks of the waves turning pink, red and orange in the setting sun.

Gabe pulls over to the side of the road and turns off the engine. 'Wow.'

I watch him walk to the cliff edge and stare out at the horizon. I climb stiffly off the bike and go to join him. I follow his eyes, watching the sun sink into the sea, and for a moment we stay like that. Side by side. Silhouetted against the sky, changing from orange, to red, to purple.

Then, out of the corner of my eye, I see him turn to me. I hold my breath tight inside me. Is he going to do what I think he's going to do? The air between us seems charged. I lift my face towards his and shyly meet his eyes. *Is he going to do what I want him to do?*

'Shall we go?'

His voice brings me crashing to earth. 'Erm . . . yeah . . .' I fluster. It was all that damn sunset's fault. I got carried away. Deserted cliff top, beautiful scenery, attractive man by my side—*who isn't your boyfriend.*

'By the way, I must warn you about my stepmother,' I say.

'Why? Does she bite?'

Despite myself, I giggle.

Gabe watches me thoughtfully. 'Do you know? That's the first time I've ever seen you laugh at one of my jokes,' he says.

Abruptly, I stop. 'I laugh at you all the time,' I protest defensively.

'At me, but not my jokes,' he says, pretending to be offended.

At least, I think he's pretending but I can't be certain. I feel myself sliding into an awkward situation. I can't admit to hating stand-up comedy, and I'm certainly not going to confess about the time I heard him practising and thought he was terrible. The wind whips at my coat, and all at once I notice how dark and cold it's become. I glance at my watch. 'It's getting late, we should go.' This is true, but it's also an excellent way to create a diversion. I link my arm through his to walk back to the bike. So what if I misread the signs? I didn't want him to kiss me anyway.

As it turns out Gabe is an instant hit with my family, including Rosemary who, from the moment he walks into the kitchen and shakes her rubber-gloved hand—'Stepmother? No way! You look like sisters'—is eating out of his hand. Blushing like a teenager she pours him sherry in one of her best Waterford crystal glasses and never once tells him to take his shoes off, while I'm left to pour my own sherry and not allowed off the doormat until I've removed my boots. Honestly, everyone makes such a fuss of him that I almost feel miffed.

'So, what happened to the muzzle?' I whisper as we're squashing ourselves round the dining-table.

'She seems pretty cool . . .' shrugs Gabe, shuffling past Ed's wife Lou, who's listening politely to Rosemary's daughter Annabel and her husband Miles explaining how they've decided to go for laminate flooring '. . . although she did give me some of that funny brown stuff to drink.'

'Sherry,' I inform him, then notice he's about to walk straight into an exposed beam and yell, 'Watch out!'

But it's too late. He bangs his head hard and grimaces. 'Ouch, that hurt!' Pulling up a chair, he tries cramming his long legs under the table. He's still wearing his orange boiler suit but my family are pretending not to notice. 'The people who built this place must have been tiny.'

'Indeed,' nods Ed, gravely. 'Their poor diet stunted their growth.'

'Wow that's terrible.' Concern flashes across Gabe's face. 'You knew them?'

A bellow of raucous laughter erupts from Lionel as he sweeps into the room with two dusty bottles of Cabernet Sauvignon. 'Dear boy, this cottage was built in 1642. It's over three hundred and fifty years old.'

There's a pause. Just as I'm worrying that Gabe is offended by my father's brusqueness, he replies good-naturedly, 'Hey, what can I say? I'm American and the oldest thing we have is Joan Rivers.' Which, as Gabe's jokes go, isn't bad at all. But there's confusion around the table.

'Joan who?' asks Annabel, politely.

'She's kind of a comedian,' explains Gabe, 'and she's gotta be nearly a hundred but the woman's had so much surgery . . .'

I look at the blank faces around the table. Unlike me, my family are not on first-name terms with celebrities.

'Oh, I know! Her face makes her look like she's in a wind tunnel. There was an "At Home" spread about her in one of my magazines.'

I look at Rosemary with surprise, and a certain grudging respect.

'In the *Lady*?' asks Annabel, frowning.

Last year Annabel bought Rosemary a year's subscription to the *Lady* for Christmas, and whenever I go to Bath copies are always spread out like a fan on the glass coffee table. Rosemary hides her secret stash of *OK!* and *Hello!* in the pantry. Now, caught out, she stutters incomprehensibly, her middle-class cover threatening to crack under Annabel's glare.

Around the table we're preparing ourselves for one of their arguments to erupt when Lou deftly changes the conversation. 'So, Gabriel, what brings you to England?' she asks, throwing him a friendly smile.

'The Edinburgh Festival,' he says. 'I'm going up there in a couple of weeks to put on a show.'

A couple of weeks? The time has passed so quickly. He'll be gone in no time. I snatch a sideways glance at him, feeling vaguely troubled.

'Oh, bravo, a theatre man!' Lionel bellows, from across the table.

'No, actually, comedy's my thing,' corrects Gabe. 'Stand-up.'

'So how did you two meet?' asks Rosemary.

'Through an ad,' says Gabe. 'Heather was advertising for a roommate, and I needed a place for a few weeks.'

'So you're not Heather's new boyfriend?' demands Ed.

'Nope, that's not me,' says Gabe, good-naturedly.

'So, where is your new boyfriend, Heather?' Rosemary says 'new boyfriend' as if she's putting inverted commas round the words and it's only now I realise the table has suddenly gone quiet.

'You mean James?' I wonder why I feel as if I'm facing a jury. 'He had to work,' I explain. 'It was really important.'

'Well, it would have to be,' Rosemary murmurs, 'for him to let you down at the last minute.' She says this in such a way that I might think she was being genuinely sympathetic—if I didn't know her better.

'Yes, but did she tell you about the bouquets?' interrupts Gabe, squeezing my hand supportively under the table.

'*Bouquets?*' repeats Lou, dark eyes sparkling. 'Ooh Heather, how romantic. The most I ever get is a bunch of daffs.'

'Yep, he sent three separate bouquets—a dozen red roses in each,' continues Gabe, laying it on thick. 'The guy's crazy about her.'

'And who can blame him?' booms Lionel, with fatherly pride. 'Wouldn't you say, Rosemary?'

Rosemary has fallen unusually quiet. Silenced, no doubt, by the astonishing fact that I actually have a man sending me flowers. 'Yes, absolutely,' she says tightly. 'More Brussels, anyone?'

After dinner everyone heads off to bed, until it's just me and the boys in the front room, eating second helpings of apple crumble and custard and talking about—yes, you've guessed it—football.

'Are you a soccer fan?' Gabe is asking, prodding doubtfully at his custard. I made it earlier to show I'm not completely crap in the kitchen.

'Absolutely,' says Ed proudly.

'Yes,' says Miles, slapping Ed's arm. 'An amazing win we had the other week. A real stroke of luck. The papers described it as a miracle.'

Ed and I exchange a look. 'Uhm . . . yes, so they did,' he says. It's been some time since that strange night at the pub, and although Ed and I have spoken on the phone, he hasn't referred to it. Ed's way of dealing with anything he doesn't understand is simply to ignore it.

'I heard England won a big game,' says Gabe. 'Awesome.'

'Well, we've got some really good players, so I'm hoping for big things from them . . .' grins Ed, delighted. 'With any luck I'm pretty much going to be glued to the box these days.'

'I bet the missus isn't too happy about that,' grins Miles.

Ed smiles uncomfortably and I get the feeling that Miles might have touched on a sore subject there. Oh dear, I hope I haven't caused any trouble with that silly wish of mine.

'Erm, Heather?' Gabe is looking at me with a nervous expression. 'About this custard stuff you all love . . .'

I glance at his bowl. His spoon is standing upright.

'I don't suppose you'd have any ice cream,' he asks apologetically.

'There might be some Häagen-Dazs left from when I was last here,' I whisper, not wanting Miles and Ed to hear me and want some too. 'I'll go and look in the freezer.' Then I lean close to his ear: 'Meet me upstairs in the bedroom in five minutes.'

As soon as I've said it I realise how it sounds. 'So we don't have to share the ice cream,' I explain hastily, indicating Ed and Miles who are also prodding warily at their custard.

But if Gabe notices my embarrassment, he doesn't show it. 'Which is our bedroom?' he asks.

'Up the stairs, first door on the right,'

'Cool.'

'I don't think you'll be saying that when you see the flowery wallpaper.' I smile ruefully and leave on my quest for double chocolate chip.

'**D**o you want to go on top or underneath?' One tub of ice cream later, Gabe is looking at me with one eyebrow raised.

'Hmmm.' I pretend to think about it for a moment. 'I always like to go on top,' I confess, sticking the spoon back in the tub of Häagen-Dazs and passing it to him.

He scrapes the bottom of the tub. 'Well, that's lucky. I prefer underneath.'

For the last five minutes Gabe and I have been standing at the doorway of my old bedroom, eating ice cream and staring at the wooden bunk beds we're going to sleep in tonight. Fortunately, however, Gabe isn't unnerved by it and instead finds it amusing. Hence our *double-entendre*-laden conversation. Which is fun.

That's not fun, Heather. That's flirting.

Oh, my God, so it is. What am I doing? I have a boyfriend. And Gabe has a girlfriend, I remind myself.

Gabe puts down the empty tub. 'So, what now? Bed?'

It's an innocent enough question, but now I'm feeling so self-conscious that everything seems laden with innuendo. 'Yes, definitely. We'll need to get up early if you want to surf.'

'Well, if you want to use the bathroom first . . .'

'No,' I say briskly. 'I'll go after you. It's at the end of the corridor.'

He bends down and rummages in his rucksack for his toothbrush. I can see him pushing up his glasses, which keep sliding down his nose, and try not to think how sweet he looks when he does it.

'Back in five.' He pulls out a toothbrush and some toothpaste, turns to leave, then pops his head round the door. 'In case I forget, I wanted to say your family are awesome. I had a great time tonight.'

'Me too.'

'But there's something I should've told you before . . .'

I stiffen. Crikey, what on earth's he going to say?

Taking a deep breath he makes his confession: 'I snore.'

The next morning dawns another beautiful August day. It's early and most of the village is still dozing. Down by the harbour, the wooden fishing boats huddle quietly together, and around the cove, at the bottom of the steep grassy cliffs, the horseshoe-shaped beach lies empty.

It's the same all along the rocky coastline to Newquay. The day-trippers haven't yet arrived, and for miles there's just the frothy white waves rolling in and out like big wet butter curls and the distant squawking of a flock of seagulls circling overhead.

But not everyone is asleep. Further out from the shore, where the light is dancing on the waves like liquid diamonds, a dozen or so shapes bob up and down on the water: surfers waiting, watching for their next wave. Most are local men who rise at dawn every day—summer or winter—and rush down to the beach for a precious few hours.

And then there is Gabe. Straddling the board he rented early this morning, he concentrates on the horizon, waiting for a set to come in. Throwing his body flat on the board he begins paddling furiously. His hands are like mini-propellers, cutting through the water. Like a hunter chasing its prey, he focuses on the wave in the distance, moving closer and closer until, nimbly lifting his muscular body high into the air, Gabe plants his feet firmly on the board, his arms stretching outwards like a tightrope walker's as he catches the cusp. He keeps his balance seemingly effortlessly, zigzagging backwards and forwards, faster and faster, swooping and dipping as the wave arches its back beneath him, trying to throw him off like a wild horse.

Click. As the shutter of my camera releases I feel an immediate glow of satisfaction. For the last hour or so I've been waiting for that exact shot. Sitting on this hill running alongside the beach, I've been watching Gabe through the lens of my Nikon, trying to capture in one image the true emotion of surfing.

I'd forgotten how difficult, time-consuming and thrilling photography can be. When I first left college I was always taking photographs but in recent years I've stopped doing my own stuff. I tell myself it's because I'm busy taking photographs for a living but if I'm honest it's because it hurts too much: it's a painful reminder of all the hopes and dreams I had, and how I haven't achieved any of them.

Yet. I feel a tingle of excitement as I think about my letter to the *Sunday Herald*. Maybe I'll get a reply this week.

I feel a rush of positivity—the same positivity that prompted me to bring my camera with me to Cornwall and woke me up early this morning full of anticipation for the photos I would take.

I focus once more. Gabe is still riding the wave and I zoom in closer to catch the concentration on his face. I even catch a flash of his eyes, half hidden beneath the shaggy eyebrows. They seem to stare straight at me and then—Crash. He's in the water.

Startled, I glance up from my camera and look out to sea. I scan backwards and forwards across the waves, but there's no sign of him.

'Gabe!' I yell. I know he's a good swimmer, but the currents are pretty strong around here . . . I click on the lens cap, take the camera from round my neck and hold it as I make my way down the hillside.

It seems to take for ever, but eventually I reach the car park at the bottom and look again at the beach. There's still no sign of him.

Now I'm fretting. Something's wrong. Tugging off my socks and trainers I discard them by the bike and jump over the wall. My bare feet land on the soft, damp sand and I run into the sea. Breathlessly I scan the water. I can see lots of other surfers but no Gabe.

Panic takes a stranglehold. What if he's hit his head and is badly hurt or—I've got to do something—alert the lifeguard or ring 999 or . . . A sob escapes. I so wish he was here.

'*Boo!*'

I almost jump out of my skin and swing round, clutching my chest.

Gabe is standing behind me, holding his board with a grin spread across his face.

I feel a burst of heady relief—followed swiftly by fury. 'You nearly frightened me to death,' I yell.

'Hey, c'mon, it was a joke.'

'A joke?' I shriek. 'I thought you'd drowned!'

'I wiped out and when I came to the surface I was on the other side of the cove.'

'But I was looking for you and shouting—' I break off, furious that tears are pricking my eyes.

'You know you're cute when you're angry.'

I throw him an evil glare. 'You are *so* not funny.'

'Of course I'm funny. It's my business to be funny.' He laughs with mock-indignation. 'I'm a stand-up comedian, remember?'

Now this is the point where I probably ought to keep my mouth shut . . . 'Well, that's another thing.' *Except I don't.* 'I hate stand-up comedy.'

For a moment there's silence and then, 'You hate stand-up?' Gabe is staring at me in astonishment. 'And you don't think I'm funny?'

I consider bluffing, but realise it's no use and shake my head meekly.

'*At all?*'

I move my head just a twitch, hardly daring to look him in the eye, but when I do I see his solemn blue eyes filled with hurt. I wince. Me and my bloody big mouth. What did I have to go and say that for?

And then when I'm in the middle of beating myself up, Gabe throws back his head and roars with laughter. Literally *roars*. Confused, I watch him until he grabs my hands and snorts, 'I might not be funny but, goddamn it, you are, Heather Hamilton.'

I'm bewildered and humiliated. 'I thought you were dead,' I protest.

'I know and I'm sorry. I shouldn't laugh.'

We start to make our way up the beach in silence, until Gabe turns to me, eyebrows raised. 'So, c'mon, the suspense is killing me, why don't you think I'm funny?'

I squirm. 'I saw you rehearsing and I just don't think you should pretend to be someone you're not,' I blurt finally.

'What do you mean?' Gabe seems more than a little offended.

'You know, being *angst*-ridden, chain-smoking, all that anger and negativity.' In for a penny, in for a pound.

'Comedians are *supposed* to be angry and negative,' points out Gabe.

'But you're not,' I say simply. 'You're easy-going and laid-back, and most of the time you're pretty happy. You're American—what do you expect? You're from the world that has a nice day.'

'But it's part of the act,' he protests, pushing back his wet hair.

'But that's just it. It's an act. Why can't you be yourself?'

'I've spent thousands asking my shrink the same question,' he wisecracks. There's a pause. 'Oh, I dunno.' Suddenly serious, Gabe glances at me sideways, and I see that he's using flippancy to cover something that's a big deal for him. 'I guess I don't think I'm funny as plain old me.'

'But you're much funnier when you're being plain old you. Forget the jokes and talk about you.'

'But is anyone going to want to hear about me?'

'Try it and see.'

At the bike, Gabe digs out a towel and sits on the wall to dry his hair. 'For someone who hates stand-up, you've got a lot of opinions on it.'

I shrug. 'I'm sorry, I've got a big mouth. Next time tell me to shut up.'

He laughs. 'So, what now?'

'How about I give you a guided tour of the village before lunch?'

'Great. You mean I get to be a real American tourist?'

'You *are* a real American tourist,' I remind him teasingly.

'This is my old school.'

'Wow, it's so cute,' marvels Gabe, peering at the small stone building tucked away at the end of the street. 'Like a little doll's house.'

We continue up the steep hill and pass the post office, ablaze with hanging baskets. 'And this is where I had my first kiss,' I announce, gesturing to a spreading oak tree, tucked away at the edge of a field. 'His name was Seb Roberts and I was thirteen.'

'What an awesome place for a first kiss. Mine was in the den at home and my mom caught me. There I was with my hands up Hopey Smith's T-shirt, feeling up her trainer bra. Boy, was I embarrassed.'

I laugh, then feel a twinge of sadness. 'I remember wanting to run home and tell Mum all about Seb, but she'd died the year before . . .'

Gabe squeezes my hand. 'Hey, I'm sorry, I didn't think.'

'It's fine, honestly,' I reassure him. 'It's just the little things that make you remember. I had my father instead. Growing up I confided everything in him, I still do. That's why we're so close.'

We've started walking down the hill. I stop in front of the Badger's Arms. 'Have you worked up an appetite yet with all this sightseeing? What about a ploughman's?'

'What the hell's that?'

'Aha.' Pushing open the door to the pub I hold it open for him to pass. 'That's for me to know and you to find out.'

After placing our order, we carry two pints of cider into the garden where we find my family clustered round a wooden table eating lunch.

'We were wondering where you two had got to,' booms Lionel.

'We got up early so Gabe could surf.' I plonk down my cider.

'How does it match up to California?' asks Ed.

'Yeah, it was awesome.'

'Come on, budge up, everyone,' instructs Lionel. Everyone shuffles up obligingly and a gap opens next to Rosemary. I glance at it with dismay. Fortunately Gabe slides along the bench first.

'You know, we've got to stop meeting like this,' he quips light-heartedly and Rosemary blushes like a schoolgirl.

'Two Cheddar-cheese ploughmans,' hollers a voice. We wave her over and she puts them down before us.

Gabe stares at his, bemused. 'What's this?' he asks, spearing a pickled onion with his fork.

'Try it. You'll love it.'

Bravely he takes a bite and the whole table falls quiet. There's the sound of crunching and then, 'Eugggh, you eat these for pleasure?'

Everyone laughs. Honestly, his expression is priceless. In fact, I'm laughing so much I reach for a napkin to wipe my eyes when I hear a voice: 'Heather?' And get the shock of my life.

'James?'

'I can't believe you didn't tell me you were coming.' Holding my hair back against the wind, I turn to James. We've left everyone at the pub and are walking hand in hand along the rocky cliff top.

'I wanted it to be a surprise. I managed to fly back early. I had your address so I drove straight to the cottage. When you weren't there I guessed you might be at the pub. I felt terrible cancelling at the last minute.'

'It's OK. Don't worry about it. I got a lift with Gabe.'

'I noticed,' he says evenly, and I can tell from his expression that he's not exactly happy I rode pillion on my flatmate's motorbike. 'But don't worry, you'll be in the Range Rover on the way home.'

I feel a twinge of disappointment. The bike might have been terrifying, but it was also an incredible thrill.

'And I brought along some brochures on Tuscan villas you might want to look at on the ride back. I remember you saying you've always wished you could own one, and I know it's not the same but I thought maybe we could rent one this summer. I've provisionally booked one in Florence that I think you'll love.'

Despite his good intentions, I can't help feeling annoyed. Suddenly my fantasy of lazing around a villa in Tuscany doesn't belong to me any more: it belongs to James and his brochures. 'Are you sure you're OK to drive back tonight?' I ask, changing the subject. 'It's just that I've got this meeting tomorrow morning with Lady Charlotte so I have to go home.'

'Hey, it's fine. I've got work too. I just wanted to meet your family.'

'But I feel terrible you had to drive all this way.'

'A promise is a promise,' he says quietly. 'And I missed you.'

Only now, hearing those words, does it occur to me that, actually, I haven't missed him at all.

'You're leaving already?' It's late afternoon and Lionel is hugging me goodbye on the little patch of front lawn. 'Can't you stay a bit longer? It's quiz night this evening at the Forrester's. What do you say we go down and clean the place up, hey?' he says hopefully. Squeezing him tight, I smile apologetically.

'Sounds great but I've got to get back to London. *Work*,' I add, pulling a face.

'It was lovely to meet you, Mr Hamilton.' James holds out his hand formally.

Lionel ignores him. 'I've got a lovely ripe Brie and a bottle of Shiraz I've been saving,' he continues, pretending he hasn't heard what I said. 'We can have it later to celebrate our win.'

'*Lionel*,' Rosemary reprimands him, 'didn't you hear what Heather said? People don't just stop getting married because you've got a lovely Brie.' She smiles at James. 'So lovely to meet you at last, James. We were beginning to wonder if you were a figment of Heather's imagination.'

I roll my eyes but James smiles, then says he'll wait for me in the car.

'Actually, no one's getting married tomorrow. It's in a couple of weeks,' I say proudly, to Rosemary. I know it's supposed to be a secret, but I can't resist: 'The daughter of the Duke and Duchess of Hurley.'

'You mean Lady Charlotte?' asks Rosemary, visibly impressed. 'She was in *OK!* last week doing a fashion shoot.'

'Don't you mean the *Lady*?' asks Annabel, crossly.

'Oh, yes, of course, dear,' says Rosemary, meekly.

'Well, it's been a pleasure, you guys.'

In his leathers, Gabe is giving everyone bear hugs, even Ed. 'I'll see you back at the apartment,' he says, when he gets to me.

'Flat,' I correct him, giving him a hug.

'Apartment,' he repeats stubbornly.

He strides off towards his bike, and I turn to Lionel. 'James is waiting. I'd better go.' I wrap my arms round him again and kiss his cheek.

James pulls up next to us in the Range Rover and I climb into the passenger seat and slide down the window, while my father, who swore to Ed and me when mum died that he would never say goodbye to us, waves me off as he always does. 'See you later, alligator,' he says softly.

'In a while, crocodile,' I reply as always.

Chapter Six

'ABSOLUTELY NO SHOTS of your cankles . . . I mean ankles?' I repeat.

It's early the next morning and I'm in the office on the telephone to Lady Charlotte, who rang the moment I walked through the door.

I open the diary and turn to the date of her wedding. Already it's filled with dozens of notes. Resignedly I grab a pen. Although it's amazing for business that we're doing her wedding, the woman is an unbelievable nightmare. Even more unbelievable is that someone wants to marry her. Although he's probably one of those chinless Hooray Henry types she's always being photographed with, I tell myself consolingly. 'Don't worry, your ankles will be . . . er . . . strictly off limits,' I say, as she continues ranting in my ear. 'Oh, OK. Instead, you want lots of . . .' Surely she didn't just say what I thought she just said. *Did she?*

Brian appears and hangs over my shoulder to see what I've just written. 'Tits?' he says loudly.

'Mummy and Daddy have just spent a fortune on my breast augmentation—it's their wedding present to us. As I said to my fiancé, Daniel, which would you prefer? Dreary old china or perfect titties?'

'Daniel?' I repeat, before I can stop myself. After all this time that name still gives me a twinge.

'Yes, Daniel Dabrowski. He's a sculptor.'

It's as if someone's kicked me hard in the stomach.

'He's from Russia,' she continues.

'Actually he's Polish,' I say before I can stop myself. It's too much of a coincidence. There can't be two Daniel Dabrowskis who are sculptors.

'What?'

The indignation in her voice is like a slap in the face, and I pull myself together. I *can't* endanger this wedding. 'I saw an exhibition of his,' I fib, voice wavering, 'and there was some information about him.'

How can I tell her that he's my ex-boyfriend and I know every last thing about him? Or I did, I think, as his fiancée snappily informs me that her manicurist has arrived and rudely hangs up. Because now, I realise, I know nothing about him. Daniel? Getting married? To a twenty-one-year-old heiress?

'What is this? A wedding or a glamour shoot?' grumbles Brian, reappearing with two steaming mugs of instant coffee and a couple of muffins. 'Heather? Are you OK? You've gone white.'

'Me, yeah, I'm fine.' I force myself to tune back in, but it's a struggle.

'I was saying, what will she think of next time?'

'You mean there's going to be a next time?' For a split second I consider explaining to Brian that I can't do this, but then I see the post lying on the side. Bills, bills and more bills. I can't tell Brian.

'Of course,' Brian is saying. 'And I'd say, in less than an hour.'

'Well, this time it's your turn to answer the phone. I'm going into the darkroom. There's a dozen rolls of film that still need developing.' I head into the back. I need time and space to collect my thoughts.

'I might have to pop out. I need to sort out my costume for tonight.'

Of course. Tonight's *The Rocky Horror Show*. I'd forgotten. Unlike Brian, who's been looking forward to it for months.

'Well, in that case I'll leave the answering machine on,' I threaten. 'That way you can call her when you get back.'

'Oh, didn't I tell you? I gave her your mobile number, just in case.'

He ducks as I throw a muffin at him, but I've got a pretty good aim. It hits the back of his head as he dives, laughing, out of the door.

Several minutes later I'm in the darkroom, tugging the cord that switches on the special developing light. I flop onto a stool to absorb the shock of discovering that Daniel is soon to marry Lady Charlotte.

After a moment, I pull myself together. OK, so he's getting married. So bloody what? I stand up and turn my attention to the mess that is our darkroom filing system. From now on I'm going to block Daniel out of my mind. Now where did I put those films?

After a good fifteen minutes I unearth them. I lean over to flick on the CD player and hear the jingling ring of my mobile.

My heart sinks. Lady Charlotte? *Already?*

'Hello?' I grab a piece of paper, then rummage around for a pen.

'Hi, is it possible to speak to Heather Hamilton?'

I'm surprised to hear a male voice, oldish-sounding. Probably the butler. 'Speaking,' I grunt, tugging out a drawer.

'Oh, hello, Ms Hamilton, this is—'

'Sorry, can you hang on a minute.' I press my shoulder against the drawer, reach deep inside, right up to my armpit, and grope around. God, you'd think there'd be a Biro in here somewhere!

'If this isn't a good time . . .' In the background I can hear the voice on the phone still talking. Damnit. I give up. I'll have to use my eyeliner.

'No, now's fine,' I say resignedly, pulling out my kohl pencil. 'OK, so what are Charlotte's latest demands . . . I mean, thoughts?'

'Charlotte?' repeats the voice at the other end of the line.

'Sorry, *Lady* Charlotte,' I correct myself quickly.

'Look, I think there's been some mistake,' says the voice. Now I detect the faint drawl of an American accent. 'This is about a job vacancy, at the *Sunday Herald*.'

It's a moment before the words register.

'Did you just say the *Sunday Herald*?' I whisper.

'That's right.'

My chest tightens a notch. 'And you are?'

'Victor Maxfield, the editor.'

Oh my Lord, it is. I'm speaking to the editor of the *Sunday Herald*. Right now. Crumpling onto a stool I inhale deeply. 'Gosh, I wasn't expecting this. You see, I thought you were somebody else.'

'So it seems,' says the voice, and although I can't see Victor Maxfield, I could swear he's smiling now. 'But I wanted to call as I'm going to be out of the office from Wednesday. It's my annual fishing trip up to Scotland. Have you ever been to Scotland, Miss Hamilton?'

'No, never . . .' I stammer.

'Well, you should, my dear. Scotland beats everything, what with the mountains and the moors and, of course, your namesake.'

'Sorry?'

'Heather!' he exclaims. 'The moors are covered with it.'

His deep voice resonates in my ear and I feel a tingle all over. Heather. Lucky heather. All at once I get a dizzy sensation, as if I've been spun round quickly and made to open my eyes, and the room is swaying and blurring in the crimson light. It could be just nervousness, surprise or faintness, but it feels like something more. As if all my dreams are running up through my toes to my fingertips, and down the phone line. All the way to Victor Maxfield, the man with the power to make them come true.

'So, are you free tomorrow morning for an interview around nine? I know it's a bit short notice, but no time like the present, hey?'

'Yes, of course. Tomorrow sounds great.'

And then he hangs up. An interview. At the *Sunday Herald*. It's just like Gabe said. It's just what I wished for.

'Heather?'

A firm rap at the door startles me, and I jump. It's Brian, back already. 'Hey, Brian, guess what? . . .' I open the door.

'Ta-dah.'

My mouth opens and closes. *It's Cher*. Standing in the doorway is a vision in suspenders, fishnet stockings and a long curly black wig. 'I'm a *trrrransexual* from Transylvania,' pouts Brian, kicking his leg menacingly.

I stare at him wordlessly. Brian has exceedingly good legs.

Dropping the act, he smiles sheepishly. 'Sorry, I was getting a bit carried away there. What were you saying?'

'Oh, nothing,' I say casually. Now no longer seems the right time to tell him about the interview. 'I'll tell you later.'

As I walk through the grey concrete jungle of Hammersmith with Brian, I keep my head down and my eyes focused on the chewing-gum spotted pavement. Anything to avoid the gawps. You'd think no one had ever seen a sixtysomething man in suspenders, a PVC basque and four-inch stilettos before. It's just after seven and Brian and I are making our way to the nearby Apollo Theatre to see *The Rocky Horror Show*.

I catch my reflection in the window of Starbucks. I'm wearing a pleated pink skirt, American tan tights and a pair of lace-up shoes. The outfit was Jess's idea. She's one of those huge fans who've seen the show about a hundred times and know all the steps to the Time Warp. She organised the whole thing, ringing the tickets hotline months ago and lending me her spare costume. I stare doubtfully at my frumpy reflection. Think Doris Day in Hush Puppies.

By the time we reach the theatre it's nudging dusk. Crowds of outrageously dressed people are milling around outside, comparing costumes. Everyone—I repeat, *everyone*—is wearing fishnets.

Brian leads the way and I follow him into the foyer. 'Jess!' I yell, spotting her surrounded by a group of handsome men with buffed arms. Obviously the air stewards. 'You look fantastic,' I gasp.

'You think so?' she says, and does a little twirl. She's wearing the obligatory basque, fishnets and stilettos. 'So do you.' Her brow furrows. 'Hey, are you OK?'

Trust Jess. Only a best friend would notice I've got something on my mind. 'I just found out Daniel's getting married,' I say matter-of-factly. 'To Lady Charlotte.'

Jess's jaw drops.'Bloody hell, Heather. How are you feeling?'

I shrug. 'You know.' She nods understandingly. 'But what's worse . . .'

'*There's worse?*' For Jess, this is an impossibility. To her, marriage is a race and you have to beat your ex to the finishing line. The other way round is the ultimate shame.

'Brian and I are the official wedding photographers.'

In a rare occurrence, Jess is rendered speechless. Then she finds her voice: 'Well, you're far nicer than her anyway. She's got cankles. And as for that two-timing toad Daniel, you've met someone much nicer now.

You said yourself, James is an absolutely perfect boyfriend.'

'You're right. I'm fine, honestly . . .'

'Oy, slut.'

'Did you hear what he just called me?' I gasp, affronted.

'Get used to it, honey,' giggles one of Jess's stewards, who introduces himself as Neil and offers me honey-roasted peanuts. 'It's all part of the show. Whenever you see Brad on stage you shout, "Arsehole", and for Janet you shout, "Slut".' He winks at Brian, who blushes.

I pout good-naturedly, but Jess ignores me and grabs the elbow of a big man who's got his back to me. 'I want you to meet someone,' she says, unable to keep the pride out of her voice. 'Heather, this is Greg.'

'A pleasure,' he says, and smiles. And it's the smile I notice: it stretches out a pale silvery scar that seems vaguely familiar.

'You too,' I smile back, trying to place him. Not easy when a man's wearing false eyelashes and women's lingerie. 'Have we met before?'

'Oh, no,' he says. 'I'd definitely remember you.' And he looks at me in a way that, if he wasn't with my best friend Jess, I'd think was flirting.

'So, where's your man?' asks Jess.

'Oh, Gabe mentioned something about going to his uncle's for dinner.' It's still niggling at me: where have I seen Greg before?

'I meant James,' she says pointedly.

'Oh, right, of course.' Why did I think she was talking about Gabe? 'He should be here in a minute—he's probably stuck in traffic.'

'Hey, the show's about to start. We should go in,' interrupts a steward.

Everyone starts filtering off, leaving me in a rapidly emptying foyer waiting for James. It's getting really late. Where can he be?

'Excuse me, miss,' I feel a tap on my shoulder and turn round to see a uniformed attendant. 'You'll have to take your seat now.'

'Oh, sorry.' I give the door a last hopeful glance, then reluctantly hand him my ticket. I pause as I go into the theatre. 'If a tall, dark-haired man should arrive . . .' I hold out James's ticket.

'Of course.' He tucks it into his breast pocket.

The squeaking of the orchestra tuning up signals that the show's about to start, and I quickly try finding my seat in the packed theatre. There's a couple of empty seats right at the end of the row. Gosh, I wonder who's got those. I wish it was me.

Hang on a minute . . . That is me! For once I'll be able to see everything rather than the back of someone's head. Cheered, I sit down next to Brian. Only it's not Brian, I realise, as I turn to whisper in his ear. Brian has switched to sit next to Neil, leaving me beside a stranger. Which is fine, of course. I'm a big girl. It's just that James's empty seat is on the other side of me. Staring at its big, velvet emptiness I feel a bit sorry for myself. But then the curtains pull back and *The Rocky Horror Show* begins.

For the next hour I'm transported into an outrageously camp world of transsexuals from the planet Transvestite. The rest of the audience seems to know the entire script off by heart: most of the time I'm at a loss as to what's going on and try to pick things up as the show progresses.

Which isn't easy, especially when someone passes me a newspaper for no apparent reason. What am I supposed to do with it? Not read it, that's for sure, I tell myself, looking at it distractedly. Suddenly I get that weird sensation again, vibrating up through my fingertips, which are smudged with ink from fingering the headline: 'LOTTERY JACKPOT STILL UNCLAIMED. WINNING TICKET FROM WEST LONDON.'

Oh, my goodness! It must be my stolen ticket!

I stare hard at the headline, my mind whirling, but now I'm being dragged to my feet to do the Time Warp and I don't have time to think about anything but having stupid, ridiculous, outrageous fun.

'**S**o, what did you think?'

The show's over and we're inching our way towards the exit. I grin at Jess. 'It was great, really great,' I say.

'Even better than *Phantom*,' gushes Neil, and I see Brian glow with shiny-cheeked happiness.

'Is anyone hungry? I know a place that does the best chicken tikka,' says one of the stewards.

'Nah, not for me, mate,' mutters Greg. 'I've got to head back to Kent. Early start,' he explains, and throws an arm round a visibly dismayed Jess.

As we spill out into the cool evening darkness of the street I contemplate them together for a moment, a vague unease clinging to me. I try to put my finger on it, but I can't. Maybe it's nothing.

'Heather? Is that you?' I see a man walking towards me, dressed in black trousers, a checked jacket and a pair of thick-rimmed glasses.

'James?' I ask doubtfully.

'Yep, it's me,' he says, with a self-conscious smile. 'Sorry I was late. The show had already started. I had a drink at the pub.' He gestures across the road. 'Though in this outfit I got some funny looks.'

My mouth twitches into a smile. 'You didn't have to wait for me.'

'I know.' He pauses. Maybe I'm imagining it, but I can feel awkwardness between us. 'Do you want a lift home? My car's parked just over there.'

'Sure. That would be great, thanks.' Whispering to Brian that I'm leaving I hurry back to James before Jess sees him. I know she's dying to meet him and if she spots him, that will be it: interrogation time.

'So, how was the show?' asks James, as we walk towards the car.

'Great,' I say. 'But completely crazy.' I can't help noticing he's not holding my hand. Something's definitely up.

We reach the car, James beeps the alarm and we climb inside. James pulls into the traffic. And then neither of us speaks for ages. It's one of *those* silences. I feel as if it's suffocating me.

'I waited for you because I needed to talk to you.' James rakes his fingernails through his hair. 'You're not in love with me, are you?'

Out of the blue, his words disarm me. My knee-jerk reaction is to deny it, to persuade him otherwise. But what's the point? Why try to convince him *when you can't convince yourself*? 'No, I'm not,' I confess. 'I love everything about you, but I'm not in love with you.' As the words tumble out I feel an unexpected release. 'I'm sorry.'

'It's OK. I already knew,' replies James, and throws me a small smile as if to show that he's not angry with me. 'That night when I told you I loved you, I hoped you'd tell me you loved me . . . but you didn't.'

'I didn't? But I thought . . .' I break off. I'm sure I told him I loved him.

'You said, "Me too,"' says James, quietly. He pulls up at the traffic lights. 'And we both know that's not the same as saying, "I love you."'

He's right. I didn't fool anyone. Not myself. And certainly not James. 'I'm sorry, I don't know what's wrong with me.'

'There's nothing wrong with you, Heather. But it might have helped if you weren't in love with another man.'

Incredulity stabs me. 'You mean my ex? No, you've got it all wrong.'

'I'm not talking about your ex. I'm talking about your flatmate.'

'You think I'm in love with *Gabe*?' For the briefest, most fleeting moment I dare to wonder if he's right. 'That's ridiculous,' I say indignantly.

'I saw you together in Cornwall,' he counters. 'You might not be able to see it, Heather, but I can.'

I look across at James. He's still being lovely even though we're breaking up. The man has no faults. And then it dawns on me. 'You really are the perfect man, James,' I say quietly. 'You're just too perfect for me.'

He looks bewildered.

'It's true. We never row, you like the same music, you love romantic comedies, you're a vegetarian, you know how to find the G-spot without having to ask for directions . . . And you even dressed as Brad for my Janet without me telling you.' I slump in my seat. 'Trust you. I mean you're so damn perfect I feel like a complete mess.'

'Yes, well, your bedroom was a bit—' He grimaces.

I blush with embarrassment as we turn into our street. He pulls up outside my flat, but keeps the engine running. 'Well, I guess this is it,' he says after a moment.

'I guess so,' I agree. This is so amicable it's ridiculous. I kiss his cheek. "Bye, James.'

"Bye, Heather,' he says pleasantly. 'Look after yourself. And no more flashing at me through the blinds or I'll have to ring the police,' he calls after me.

I twirl round. 'You *saw* me?'

'Not just me. I was having a dinner party,' he says, lips twitching. 'Great tits.' He winks and buzzes up his window.

Next morning I wake with a start. I have my interview today. The sound of the radio is wafting down the hallway, intermingled with a sickly artificial smell I've grown to recognise these past weeks: Pop-Tarts.

'Morning,' I say automatically, padding into the kitchen knowing I'm going to find Gabe curled over the toaster with a chopstick. He's so engrossed in singing along to the radio that he doesn't hear me and I'm treated to an impromptu display of ball-scratching. Up and down, up and down goes his hand, his bony foot with the funny-shaped hammer toe tap-tapping along to Pearl Jam, the back of his hair all knotted up to resemble a sort of sandy Brillo pad.

Transfixed in the doorway I hear James, like a voice-over in my head: '. . . but it might have helped if you weren't in love with another man.'

Honestly. What was James thinking? Me? In love with *that*?

In the middle of yawning like a hippopotamus, Gabe turns and sees me. 'Oh, wow, Heather.' Like a thief who's been caught with his hands, quite literally, on the Crown Jewels, he yanks one free of his boxer shorts and pushes his glasses up his nose. 'I didn't see you there.'

'Uh-huh. So I gather.' I smile sweetly, flicking on the kettle.

'So, how was last night?' asks Gabe, trying to be nonchalant.

'You mean *The Rocky Horror Show*?' I say, trying to undo the milk carton. 'Or the part where James dumped me?'

'Shit,' he says. 'I mean, I'm sorry. That sucks.'

'It's OK,' I shrug. 'It was very amicable.'

I catch Gabe's eye and he looks down at his feet uncomfortably, as if he's afraid I'm going to start talking about feelings. I'm delighted by such good old-fashioned male avoidance. After my relationship with James I'm relieved *not* to have to talk about my feelings.

Fortunately we're distracted by the cat flap and Billy Smith. He miaows loudly. 'Someone's hungry for his breakfast.' I stroke his soft fur.

'I'm not surprised. He was pretty busy last night. Man, that kitty gets all the booty calls.'

'Booty calls?'

'You know, those phone calls late at night from some old boyfriend or a girl you had a fling with, calling you up and inviting you over for sex.'

'No, I don't know.' I pretend to be shocked. And try not to think about that 2 a.m. text message I sent to Daniel.

'Well, Billy Smith sure does.' Gabe is laughing now. 'I woke in the night to find a couple of stray cats sneaking through that kitty flap.' I laugh too—it's impossible not to—and grab a tin of Fancy Feast to scoop it into a bowl. 'Are you sure you're OK?' Gabe is watching me thoughtfully.

'I'm fine. Just a bit nervous.' I'm thinking of my imminent interview.

'Hey, don't worry. You're gonna be fine. You've got Billy Smith and me . . .' He looks at me so intently that I feel a bit weird.

'No, I'm not nervous about being single,' I correct hurriedly.

Instantly his face colours. 'Oh, I misunderstood, I thought—'

'I'm nervous about my job interview at the *Sunday Herald*,' I add shyly.

'Whoo-hoo!' He throws his arms round me. 'That's awesome.' I'm scooped into the air and twirled round, laughing with embarrassment. 'I know you'll get the job.'

I sink into a chair and take a sip of tea. My legs feel a bit wobbly and it's not from being twirled round. 'You think so?' I say. 'Thanks for the vote of confidence, but—'

'But nothing. Jeez, Heather.' Gabe sighs in frustration. 'You're so goddamn pessimistic. This interview is amazing—can't you be excited?'

'I *am* excited,' I protest hotly, and then, narrowing my eyes, I drawl, 'It's awesome.' It's a dreadful impression of him but he chortles.

'Much better. Believe me, you're gonna get this job. They'd be crazy not to give it to you. When they see how awesome and talented and cute . . .' Blushing, I roll my eyes at the outpouring of compliments. God, what is he like? '. . . your room-mate is.'

'Oy!' I snatch up the teaspoon, which still has a wet tea bag stuck to it, and flick it at him. 'Bull's-eye,' I cry as it hits him, splat, in the chest.

And then, unexpectedly, my stomach flutters.

What the . . .? Looking into his big blue eyes I don't know what comes over me. Suddenly he's not my flatmate in his underpants, he's this flirty, half-naked American who's actually quite sexy . . . *Heather*

Hamilton, what's got into you? I snap out of my daze. Christ. I don't fancy Gabe. And, anyway, he goes out with Mia, his model-Hollywood-actress girlfriend. He's hardly going to be attracted to me with my terry-towelling bathrobe and eyebrows that need plucking, is he?

Then noticing the time on the microwave, I catch myself. 'Shit, it's getting late. I'd better jump in the shower.'

Half an hour later, I'm in my bedroom. Showered, blow-dried and deodorised, I open the wardrobe door. I start rifling through the hangers. Now, where was that pink mohair skirt and lacy top?

Two squirts of perfume later I'm all set. Grabbing my black leather portfolio I start a hunt for my keys and mobile. Where are they? I'm going to be late. Damnit. I wish I could find them.

Hang on, what's this?

I spot my sparkly key ring under a tea towel. Fantastic. Now what about my . . . I do a double-take: there, in the fruit bowl, is my mobile phone. Wow, thank goodness for the lucky heather. What would I do without it? I spot it on the windowsill. I pluck it from its vase and hold it tight. Almost instantly I feel myself grow calmer. Gabe's right. I'm going to wow Victor Maxfield and he's going to *beg* me to work for them. My childhood dream is so close I can almost touch it.

Behind his desk, Victor Maxfield is telling me what makes the *Sunday Herald* the best-selling weekend newspaper in the UK. I'm so nervous I feel as if I'm going to throw up.

'. . . But enough about me and the paper. We're here to talk about you. So tell me, what made you want to be a photographer, Heather?'

I shouldn't have worn this stupid mohair skirt and the lacy granny blouse. Everyone's in jeans and T-shirts, all cool and funky, like real journalists and photographers. Not impostors like me.

'Heather?'

With a start I snap back from Planet Failure, and see that Victor Maxfield is waiting for what the interview-technique books call 'input'. 'I think . . . I'm sorry, what was that again?'

'I was wondering what sparked your interest in photography,' says Victor Maxfield, patiently, but I know his easy manner camouflages a steely demeanour.

I sit up straight in my chair and glance at him from under my eye lashes. Victor Maxfield is an imposing figure, but it's the eyes I notice most. They match the faded blue of his Ralph Lauren shirt, and briefly I'm reminded of Gabe's and how, when I looked into them this morning, they were filled with his belief that I can do this.

'I was eight,' I begin quietly, 'and my family and I were moving from Yorkshire to Cornwall.' It all comes flooding back as if it were yesterday. 'We were saying goodbye to all our friends and neighbours. I remember seeing all these faces and expressions and wanting to capture them for ever. There was Mrs Bird who lived next door and never put her teeth in and little Andrea swinging on the gatepost. Buster the Alsatian was barking and wagging his tail. I didn't want to forget any of them.'

Snapshots of their faces come alive in my mind, and I'm right back in Yorkshire again. 'I asked my father if I could borrow his camera,' I continue. 'He'd never let me use it before. But today was special, so he showed me where to look, what to press and how to focus.

'It was incredible, all this life, all these memories, all this emotion, and as I clicked away it was as if I was soaking it all up. I knew I'd be able to keep it for ever.' My voice falters when my mind flicks to Mum—as it so often does. 'I don't like saying goodbye and I knew this way I wasn't really saying goodbye because I was taking those people with me.'

I look at Victor Maxfield, who's been listening quietly all the time. 'I still have them today, Andrea, Mrs Bird and Buster.'

'Can I see them?' asks Victor Maxfield.

'I'm afraid they're a little blurred,' I laugh.

He laughs too and I'm buoyed up. 'But I do have lots of other pictures,' I say eagerly, pulling out my portfolio from under my chair, 'if you'd like to have a look.'

'Please.' He pats his desk.

For the next thirty minutes Victor Maxfield studies my photographs, nods admiringly and asks dozens of questions. As I talk about my photography, my nerves disappear. My voice becomes steady and confident, I stop fiddling with my clothes and use my hands to gesticulate depth and perspective. Engrossed in describing the different inspiration for each subject, I sneak sideways looks at Victor Maxfield and, although I barely dare to believe it, he seems impressed. When he comes upon one image he falls quiet and I watch him studying it. 'Who's this?' he asks.

He's holding a black-and-white photograph of my mother. She has her face tilted to the sunshine and a faint smile playing on her lips. She has a luminous quality. So luminous, in fact, that you might not notice she has no eyebrows, or that no tendrils of hair are escaping from beneath her head scarf. She died just a few weeks after it was taken.

'My inspiration,' I say quietly.

'She's a beautiful woman.' Victor Maxfield talks in the present tense.

'I know,' I agree. Because in this photograph she is alive.

There's a pause as we gaze at the picture. 'Well, I've very much enjoyed your portfolio,' Victor Maxfield is saying. 'Do you have an extra five minutes? I'd like you to meet our picture editor, Yvonne.'

'Of course.' Like he has to ask.

Yvonne turns out to be scary but friendly. She shows me briskly round the picture desk, introduces me to her assistant, shakes my hand, shows me to the lift and disappears 'for a fag'.

I think about her the whole tube journey to work. Well, not Yvonne specifically, but in context with the *Sunday Herald* and my interview. Excitement bubbles. If I get the job my whole life will change.

When I arrive at work I'm surprised to discover that the building is still locked up. Where's Brian? I check my watch—it's nearly eleven. Puzzled, I let myself in with my keys, turn off the alarm and wander into the little kitchen to make myself some coffee. I'm spooning Nescafé into my mug when I hear the electronic jingle of the door. That must be Brian. 'So, what time do you call this?' I shout.

'I beg your pardon?'

I put my head round the door and the grin freezes on my face. It's not Brian. Instead, it's a reed-thin blonde. With a suspiciously large cleavage. She stalks towards me. 'I'm looking for Brian Williams,' she demands, in a high-pitched whinny.

My stomach drops. I don't need any introductions to know who this is—Lady Charlotte. 'I'm afraid he's not here yet,' I reply. 'Can I help?'

'Perhaps.' She sniffs. 'I've come about my wedding.'

'You must be excited,' I enthuse.

'Very,' she says, in a voice that couldn't have sounded less excited. 'But, quite frankly, I'll be glad when it's all over. Organising a wedding for five hundred people is so completely stressful. What with Harrods saying they won't have time to gold-leaf the cake and my makeup artist breaking her wrist . . .' She rolls her eyes dramatically. 'My doctor's warned me I've got to be careful otherwise I'll find myself in hospital with exhaustion. But I told him, "No, Doctor. This is my wedding day and if I have to apply my own eyeliner, then I'll jolly well do it."'

'Good for you,' I say encouragingly. Er, hello? Is this woman for real? I'm almost tempted to ask her if she'll have the strength to apply her own mascara too, but I'm interrupted by the jingle of the door.

'Good morning!' Brian bounds into the office with more energy than I've seen in him for ages and smiles broadly at us both. 'Isn't it a glorious day?' Behind him, out of the window, the skies are still overcast and threatening rain.

'Erm . . .' I smile back, then brightly, 'Have you met Lady Charlotte?'

'Delighted,' she mutters, offering a limp hand.

Brian is unfazed. 'Lady Charlotte! What a surprise. I've been so much looking forward to meeting you.' Clasping his hands in delight, he beams at her like a politician. Actually, he's not unfazed, he's unhinged, I decide. Then I spot a crimson splodge on his neck.

Like a line of dominoes, everything falls into place. Last night. *The Rocky Horror Show*. Neil, the good-looking air steward. This morning. Late for work. Ridiculously good mood. *Love bite*.

I catch his eye over Lady Charlotte's shoulder, smile knowingly and give him the thumbs-up. He reddens and focuses his attention. 'Well, we need to get this matter sorted immediately. Ideally, we should go to the florist and take some Polaroids . . .'

'Oh, could you? Could you really?' pleads Lady Charlotte, her voice husky with hopeful gratitude.

Hopeful gratitude? Lady Charlotte? I'm amazed: Brian works his magic like a sorcerer.

'But that would mean me cancelling appointments, which would incur considerable costs.'

'Whatever. I've got access to Daddy's Coutts account. I'll write you a cheque right now.' She scrabbles for a pen.

'No, I'm afraid I can't accept that. It could reach into thousands.'

I gaze at him in awe. This man is a genius.

'Will this cover it?' begs Lady Charlotte, brandishing a cheque.

Brian looks at it, then hesitates for dramatic effect. He sucks his teeth and asks, 'Heather, do you think you'll be able to clear the diary?'

Honestly, the man should get an Academy Award. I play along: I adopt a solemn expression and open the diary. Blank pages stare back at me. 'It won't be easy, but I'll do my best,' I say gravely.

'Oh, marvellous!' Whooping with relief, Lady Charlotte clasps her hands together. 'How can I ever repay you?'

'Please, don't mention it,' protests Brian. Beaming, he tucks the cheque into his breast pocket and ushers Lady Charlotte out.

Half an hour later, one of our customers calls about extra prints of their wedding, which took place a few months ago.

Yes, of course, we have them on file, I assure them. I go into the little back room where I survey the overflowing cabinets, shelves cluttered with different folders and jumbled boxes of film. *This* is Brian's idea of a filing system. Sighing, I flick on the CD player and get stuck in. Oh, this is the one where the bride wore black; and this was on the London Eye . . . but that's not the couple I'm looking for. I rummage through a tray of contact sheets with no luck.

I flop dispiritedly onto a stool and chew my fingernails until my eye falls on a packet marked 'June 2005'. Pulling out a wad of photographs I angle them to the light. My heart skips a beat. No, surely not, it can't be . . . I stare at the photograph in horror, not sure what to do. And then realise there's only one thing I *can* do. I pick up the telephone and dial.

'**H**e's married?'

Sitting in a hotel bar near Heathrow airport, I look at Jess in her uniform. She's got a cigarette in one hand and in the other a black-and-white photograph of a smiling bride and groom: Mr and Mrs Gregory de Souza. Otherwise known as—

'*Greg?*' repeats Jess. 'Greg is married?'

It's nearly 7 p.m. After discovering the photograph this morning, I called her saying I needed to see her, but she was with Greg, having breakfast in some little café, and said she was flying out to Cape Town this evening on a two-week trip. Couldn't it wait till she got back?

No, it couldn't. But I so wanted it to. I wanted never to have found that photograph, recognised the pale silvery scar and realised that was why Greg's smile had been so familiar. And I wanted never to have to tell her that the man she'd been busy falling in love with is married and that I had photographed his white wedding. But I had to.

'Bastard.' Slumping forward over the bar Jess puts her head into her hands. 'I can't believe it. I've been sleeping with someone's husband.'

I stir the ice in my gin wordlessly. I can't think of a thing to say.

'But I don't sleep with married men, that's my one rule, Heather, my one rule.' A tear dribbles down her cheek.

'Oh, Jess, come here.' Putting my arm round her shoulders, I pull her close. As I listen to her muffled sobs it occurs to me that I haven't shed one tear over my break-up with James.

'I feel like such a fool,' she says eventually, sniffing into my lace blouse. 'I thought I'd got it right this time. I was so careful. I made sure he ticked all the right boxes.'

'That's no guarantee,' I say quietly, thinking of James.

'I know that now.' Jess surfaces and takes a slug of red wine. Then, her jaw set, she faces me. 'I'm not like you, Heather. I'm not looking for butterflies in my stomach. I don't want them. They're dangerous. I want security, commitment, financial stability. I don't want some lousy guy to hurt me, like Daniel did you. You were heartbroken.'

'It doesn't mean I don't want to fall in love again,' I say evenly.

'*Why?*' Jess gasps.

'Because it's the most amazing feeling in the world. You'll risk everything for it. Nothing comes close.'

'But you're so vulnerable.'

'True,' I agree. 'It's as scary as hell.'

'I guess I'm not brave enough. What's wrong with me, Heather? Everyone else manages to hold down a successful relationship. I mean, look at you and James . . .'

'We broke up.'

'You've broken up with James?'

'He broke up with me,' I correct her.

Her amazement morphs into pity. 'Crikey, Heather,' she whispers. 'I'm so sorry. Here's me going on about stupid Greg and all the time—'

'No, honestly, I'm OK,' I say firmly.

'You are?' she says doubtfully. '*Seriously?*'

'Seriously. No butterflies,' I add in explanation.

'Are they really as good as you say they are?'

'Better.' I smile.

'Maybe I'll try it some time,' she says, after a pause.

She says it with such hope that I can't help smiling. 'I'll drink to that,' I agree and lifting my glass I clink it against hers. 'To butterflies.'

The next day at lunch time I'm with Brian in the little pavement café on the corner when I discover Jess and I aren't the only ones with butterflies in mind. But while we're chasing them, Brian has definitely caught them.

'I think I'm in love,' he confesses.

'Love?' I echo, as my stomach rumbles.

'I wasn't going to say anything because of you and your fella,' he says, a reference to my break-up with James, the details of which I had told him earlier, 'but I just had to talk to someone. I haven't felt like this for years,' he adds quietly.

'But that's great.' I grab our sandwiches. 'I take it this is Neil we're talking about.'

'How do you know?' he asks, surprised.

We cross the street and walk towards the office.

'A wild guess. Or maybe it could have something to do with swapping seats at *The Rocky Horror Show*, then coming in late the next day, the love bite . . .' He blushes. 'He seemed really nice,' I reassure him.

'Oh, he is,' agrees Brian. 'But there's a bit of an age gap.'

'How old is he?' I ask, slipping on my sunglasses.

'Thirty-two,' admits Brian. 'Half my age.'

'Oooh, a toyboy.'

'That's what I'm worried about. People will laugh.'

'No, they won't. You're very handsome for an older man. And your legs are amazing in fishnets.' I nudge him affectionately as I take the first bite of my sandwich.

For a moment everything is quiet, but for the sound of our footsteps. Then I hear a muffled jingle. With my free hand I dig out my mobile.

'Hello, is that Heather? This is Yvonne from the *Sunday Herald*. Victor left for his annual fishing trip this morning but he asked me to call you . . .' she continues, obviously so busy she doesn't notice I haven't yet said a word '. . . as he was very impressed by your interview.'

She pauses momentarily, and I know this is my cue to say something but I'm still chewing frantically. I swallow hard.

'He'd like to offer you the job of staff photographer.'

And nearly choke.

'He would?' I gasp between coughs.

Brian holds out his bottle of Evian and I take a grateful glug. 'Thank you,' I say.

'Don't mention it,' stereo Yvonne and Brian.

'You'll be receiving a formal letter of confirmation in the post from our human-resources department,' she goes on. 'You know, the usual thing. Employment contract—holiday entitlement, salary.' Then, 'Did you discuss salary?' she demands.

'I'm not sure . . .' I look uncomfortably at Brian, who's striding alongside me, monitoring shop windows. Suddenly I feel horribly deceitful.

'It says here thirty-five thousand.'

My stomach flips. That's loads more than I'm earning now.

'With a review after six months.'

'Hmm.' I make a noise as if I'm giving this serious thought, but mentally I'm already spinning round with shopping bags.

'There's just one thing.'

Yvonne's voice stops me in mid-spin. 'Yes?' I say.

'Victor wants you to start on Monday. Will that be OK?'

I feel my delight wither. *Monday?* I can't give Brian such short notice. Although business *is* slow . . . Then I remember. *Lady Charlotte's wedding*. It's the weekend after next. That's it. I have to say no. 'Well, you see—' I begin, but Yvonne interrupts.

'Good. I didn't think it would be a problem. See you on Monday—shall we say around ten?' and before I can interrupt she's hung up.

'Good news?' Brian raises his eyebrows.

Oh, bloody hell, how am I going to tell him? We're outside the office now, and as I follow him inside it hits me. Wanting a high-flying career and getting one, I now know, are two completely different things.

'I've got a new job. It's with the *Sunday Herald*. They want me to start on Monday,' I blurt.

Brian's face drops with shock. Blink, and I'd have missed it: he recovers immediately. 'Heather, that's fantastic. Well done.'

'But what about Lady Charlotte's wedding?' I urge.

'What about it?' He pulls a face. 'I can find someone to give me a hand. Take the rest of the week off. Have a few days' holiday. Believe me, you'll be thankful for it once you start working for a newspaper. Bloody hell, girl, sod Bridezilla. This is your wish come true.'

He's right. But if this is something I've wished for my whole life, why do I feel so bloody miserable?

At six o'clock Brian and I say our final goodbyes, both of us hiding behind brave faces as we crack feeble jokes and promise to keep in touch. Then it's time for me to go home.

Struggling out of the tube station, the bags containing everything I've accumulated these past six years clanking against my shins, I begin traipsing down the high street towards my flat. I've heard about people going into shock after an accident or other traumatic experience, but after they've been offered their dream job? I'm pondering this when I notice I've reached the corner of my street and catch sight of a slouching figure in the window of Mrs Patel's. *It's me*.

I stop dead in the middle of the pavement. Honestly, Heather, what's wrong with you? Take that sorry expression off your face. Anyone would think you'd just *lost* your job. You should be celebrating. Just think. No more sniggering at parties when someone asks you what you do. No more comparing yourself to all your peers and feeling like a big, fat failure. You've done it! You're a success!

When I arrive at the flat, I dump my bags in the kitchen and start dialling. For the next half an hour I yabber away excitedly about my new job to Lionel, Jess's voicemail, and Lou, as I discover Ed's in Las Vegas at an orthodontists' convention, which 'is the best place for him as all we do when he's at home is row about football,' she huffs angrily. Then, once I've rung everyone, I stare blankly round the kitchen. Now what? I glance at the clock on the microwave: 19:03. Hmm, I wonder where Gabe is. I can't call him as he doesn't have a mobile, but I can't wait to share my news. I tug open the fridge and peer inside. The bottle of champagne I bought when Gabe first moved in is still chilling, just waiting for a special occasion. And now I've got one. Excitedly I clasp my fingers round its gold tinfoil neck and set it down carefully on the table.

My mouth waters. No, Heather, I tell myself sternly. You have to wait for Gabe.

Perhaps one little glass won't hurt.

Three glasses later, I'm tipsy. I pirouette round the kitchen in my satin stilettos, I feel exhilarated. Alive. So happy I'm going to burst.

I really wish I had a cigarette.

Then I remember. Gabe smokes.

Joyfully, I head for his room. I'm sure he won't mind, smoker in need and all that. I go to push open the door when I see the little green light on the answering machine blinking to tell me I've got a message. I forgot to check it when I came in.

Three messages. I press PLAY and wait expectantly. It beeps. '*Hello, don't hang up. This is IPC Finance . . .*' I hit delete impatiently and the machine beeps to signal the next. '*Hey, honey, it's me and I'm lying by the pool . . .*' Jess! I can hear her puffing away at a cigarette, which reminds me of my craving. I push open Gabe's door. She's chattering away in the background as I scan the room. Aha. Triumphantly I pounce on twenty Marlboros and pull out a cigarette.

Beeeeep. The answering machine cuts her off in mid-sentence. Trust Jess, I don't think she's ever left a succinct message. Unlike the owner of the next voice, which sounds short and efficient, as if they're in a hurry.

'*Hi, Gabe . . . It's your uncle . . .*' Huh, so this is the uncle he's always talking about. He's got an American accent, but it's much milder than Gabe's. In fact, it's really funny but he sounds just like . . .

'. . . *Victor*,' says the voice on the telephone.

Maxfield, finishes the voice inside my head.

I freeze. Victor Maxfield is Gabe's uncle? For an instant I'm numb. Then, like a ten-tonne truck, it hits me. *That's why I got the job.*

The message keeps playing, but I'm no longer listening. That's how come I got the interview. That's why after six years of getting absolutely nowhere . . .

'Hey, where are you?'

I'm not sure how long I've been sitting on the rug, deafened by the sounds of my dreams crashing around me, when I hear the voice. Dazed, I look up and focus on the figure in front of me. It's Gabe.

'*You bastard.*'

Gabe pales. 'What's going on?' he whispers, his eyes searching mine.

'You know exactly what's going on,' I sneer, hauling myself off the carpet. Everything is piecing together like some hideous, hideous jigsaw puzzle: Gabe dictating my application, his unerring optimism, Victor Maxfield's enthusiasm . . . 'God, I'm such an idiot.'

'Hey c'mon, calm down . . .' he begins placatingly.

'Calm down?' I know I'm shouting, but I can't stop. The alcohol is pumping through my veins, mixed with adrenaline and fury. 'How dare you tell me to calm down, after everything you've done?'

'Done? What have I done?' he stares at me in bewilderment.

'Victor Maxfield,' I say simply.

I see his back stiffen. Then he looks at me brazenly. 'What about him?' He shrugs, but there's no mistaking the guilt in his eyes.

'Don't lie to me,' I snap.

'When have I ever lied?'

'He's your uncle, Gabe,' My words strike him like an archer's arrow, and I see the flash of understanding in his eyes. 'I heard his message on the machine. The game's up,' I quip cuttingly.

'It was never a game—' he protests, steadfastness crumbling.

'Oh, yeah?' I interrupt. 'Pretending to come up with the idea, faking surprise when I got an interview. You should be the actor, not Mia.'

He tries to smile. 'Look, I can see why you'd be a little annoyed but you're making too big a deal out of this.

'Stop patronising me! It is a big deal to me.'

'It doesn't have to be,' he tries again quietly.

'Says who? *You*? What do you think gives you the right to play God with my life? Don't you understand? This was my big dream.'

'And I *know* that,' protests Gabe, suddenly vehement. 'That's *why* I did it. I knew it was what you'd always wanted.'

'But not like this,' I wail. 'Don't you understand? I wanted to get it on my own merit. I wanted Victor Maxfield to give me this job because he thinks I'm a great photographer—'

'But you *are* a great photographer! You've got real talent, Heather. You've shown me your stuff and you just needed a break . . . like we all need breaks,' he falters. 'And that day when you said it was your childhood dream to work at the *Sunday Herald*, and my uncle's the editor, it was such a coincidence. I mean, what are the chances of that happening?' For a moment his eyes seem filled with wonderment. 'It was like fate.'

'Fate?' My voice comes out all high-pitched. 'It's not fate. *It's cheating*. You even dictated that stupid letter,' I continue. 'Was this one of your jokes?' Even as I'm saying it I know I'm being cruel but I don't care. 'Because if it is it's not funny.'

Gabe's expression hardens and I feel a sudden shift.

'Well, it wouldn't be, would it?' Bitterness is audible in his voice. 'Because I'm not funny, am I? What was it you said on the beach? My jokes are crap. I'm a crap comedian.'

I flinch. Did I really say that? 'No I didn't say it like that—'

He cuts me off. 'Yes, you did. So now who's the liar, Heather?'

I'm shocked into silence. All the colour has drained from Gabe's face but for two red blotches high on his cheeks. 'And, yes, you're right, I'm going to go up to Edinburgh and probably die a fucking death up there.'

Like a river that's burst its banks, the argument has changed direction. *How did we get here?* Heart thumping, I feel dizzy and sick.

'You're not the only one with dreams, Heather,' he says.

'I know that,' I whisper. Oh, God, this is awful.

'I should go.' Gabe's face is grim. His eyes are filled with hurt. 'I'll pack my stuff.'

I hesitate for a second. I know that if I apologise right now I can probably persuade him to stay, that if he leaves I'm going to regret it for ever, that if I don't say something within the next breath Gabe is going to walk out of my life and I'll never see him again.

But I'm just too pissed off, too proud, too angry and too goddamn hurt to care. 'Good,' I say flatly.

For a second I think I see a flash of disappointment, then it vanishes. 'Fine.' He nods. 'I'll leave first thing in the morning.' 'You're right . . .' Now instead of sadness in his face there's something horribly like contempt. 'I made a big mistake.' And I know he's not referring to the interview.

I swallow hard, pride sticking in my throat. I am not going to let him see I'm upset. 'Yeah, me too,' I reply defiantly and walk out of the door.

A shaft of sunlight pokes its way through a gap in the blinds, stabbing my eyelids with urgent brightness. I let out a piteous moan. I haven't had a hangover like this for years. What was I drinking?

Champagne. Oh, fuck. *Gabe*.

Last night comes back to me. I sit upright, then lurch unsteadily out of bed and pad into the hallway, head thumping.

'*What was it you said on the beach? My jokes are crap. I'm a crap comedian* . . . His bedroom door is ajar and I push it open with trepidation.

My worst fears are confirmed. His room is bare. The bedclothes are piled neatly on the mattress, and perching on the edge I hug my knees to my chest. God, I miss him already. The flat seems so empty without him, *without his energy* that, like a new lens on a camera, made me look at my life in a different, brighter way.

Billy Smith pads in. I reach out to stroke him but he darts away, knocking over the wastepaper basket as he jumps on to the window-ledge. He can't leave fast enough. But I have the same effect on everyone, don't I?

Dismayed, I crouch down to pick up the rubbish that's spilled on to the carpet. Cigarette packets, Coke cans, an old copy of *Loot* . . .

My stomach flips.

It's the issue from a few weeks ago, the one with my ad for the flat-share—but that's not what makes me freeze. It's the small black Biro heart that's been drawn round it. *By me.*

I'd forgotten all about it, but now I remember that evening dashing off the train, dropping *Loot* in the rush and scrabbling to pick up all the pages. Gabe must have found the ones I'd left behind, noticed the love heart round my ad and called on the off-chance that the ad was mine. Coincidence after coincidence after coincidence. Or is it?

Suddenly I have a flashback: being squashed up on the tube, feeling sad and broke and lonely, staring out into the darkness of the tunnel, wishing I could find an answer to all my problems.

Followed by another: running home in the thunderstorm and meeting the gypsy with the lucky heather who promised me my luck would change and all my wishes would come true.

And then—*poof*—Gabe shows up on my doorstep like my fairy godmother with his magic wand, keeping the credit card companies at bay with his rent, inspiring me to start taking photographs again, being related to the editor of the *Sunday Herald*.

A shudder runs up my spine and I pull my dressing gown round me. Is that why I got that job? Not because of Gabe *but because I wished it*? Gabe might have pulled the strings, but he pulled them because *I* wished for that job. If I hadn't, none of this would have happened.

I'm reminded of Ed's warning, 'Be careful what you wish for.' And for once—just this once—I'm realising my big brother was right. Be careful what you wish for—*because it might just come true*.

And it has all come true, hasn't it? But whereas a few weeks ago being offered my dream job would have made me the happiest girl in the world, now I don't want it. It doesn't mean anything. I didn't get the job because of my talent, so I don't deserve it. It's an empty triumph that has cost me my friendship with Gabe. The realisation is like a kick in my stomach. What have you done, Heather?

All the wishes from the past weeks rush back to me. I've been on an amazing fun-filled shopping spree, indulging my every whim, never stopping to think of the consequences. Now it's time to face up to them.

Filled with apprehension, I work my way through the list.

I wished . . .

• *For the perfect man.*

I wished for him when I was with Jess in the changing room at Zara, and then—abracadabra—there James was, waiting for me in the wine section of Mrs Patel's. Only I didn't love him.

• *For a miracle to get Together Forever out of debt.*

And, boy, did we get one. A huge society wedding that will put the business firmly back in the black. Only it's my ex-boyfriend's.

• *To win the lottery.*

It hurts even to think about this one. One minute there I was, spending my millions, living in a mansion, driving around in an Aston Martin, and the next it had all been snatched away and I had to spend the afternoon in a police station, instead of with Gabe on Hampstead Heath.

• *England would win against France.*

Yes, their spectacular final goal made sporting history, but it's also thrown my brother's marriage into jeopardy. Instead of focusing on Lou and the baby he spends all his time watching football on Sky.

• *For no traffic on the roads.*

It was fantastic until I got a speeding ticket, three points on my licence and a sixty-pound fine—which I keep forgetting to pay.

None of my wishes has made me happy.

It's all such a mess. I want everything to be how it was before, but how?

Then it comes to me in a flash. The lucky heather.

Before, it seemed like a blessing, but now it's like a curse. If I can find it and throw it away, everything will be OK.

I jump to my feet. The last time I had it was at my interview—I put it in my pocket for good luck. I rush into the hallway, unearth my cream jacket and thrust my hand into the pocket.

But it's not there. I check the other side. Empty. I feel a pang of alarm. I can't have lost it. I look on the floor in case it's fallen out somewhere—and then notice something lying on the mat. A letter.

Distractedly I pick it up.

The Sunday Herald
45 Kings Way
London W1 50Y

Dear Miss Hamilton,

Further to our recent interview, I have great pleasure in offering you the position of staff photographer with the Sunday Herald. *Salary will start at £35,000 with a review after six months. Monica Hodgekins in Human Resources will be in touch to confirm your start date and provide details of our private health plan and pension scheme. If you have any queries in the meantime please contact her on ext. 435.*

Yours sincerely,

Victor Maxfield

I take a moment to absorb each word, to savour every syllable. Except I feel only bitterness and regret.

And so I do one of the hardest things I've ever done. I write a letter turning down Victor Maxfield's offer. In it I explain why: about Gabe, how I can't take a job I don't deserve, and how I still respect him as an editor. Then I slide it into an envelope, and seal it and my fate. Now I can forget all about it. I can forget about Gabe.

I pull on an old tracksuit and trudge to the postbox on the corner. For once I don't have to wish for a stamp: I have one in my purse. I stick it on to the letter and shove it through the slot. There. It's over.

The burble of my mobile interrupts my mood. I glance at the display: it's my father. A warm glow engulfs me.

'Hi there,' I say, feeling a rush of love for him.

'Heather, it's Rosemary. Something's happened.'

An icy hand grasps my heart. 'What is it?'

'Your father's had a heart attack.'

And the bottom falls out of my world.

Chapter Seven

TO MOST PEOPLE the thought of losing a parent is inconceivable—you can't imagine it, you don't want to imagine it. But when it's happened to you, it's all too real. My mother, a vibrant redhead with a laugh that made you feel as if you'd been dipped in melted happiness, isn't here to laugh any more. And now the prospect that Lionel might—

Fear stops the word forming in my mind. I cling to the steering wheel of my MG and force myself to stay focused on the car ahead.

I'm on the M4 on my way to Cornwall. I'm not sure how long I've been driving. Two, maybe three hours. Everything's a blur—vague memories of going back to the flat, asking a neighbour to feed Billy Smith, throwing some stuff into a bag. I think Lou must have called me as I know Ed's on a flight back from the States, but I don't remember speaking to her. In fact, I don't remember much at all about the last few hours, except Rosemary urging, 'Get here soon, Heather, you must get here soon,' her voice filled with foreboding.

Pressing the accelerator pedal to the floor, I stare fixedly ahead, concentrating on making it to the hospital in time.

In time. In time for what?

Until now I've been too afraid to acknowledge the unspoken fear, but huddled in my car on the stretch of grey motorway, I face up to it. I'm trying to make it to the hospital in time to say goodbye.

It's late afternoon when I reach Newquay and see the signs for St Luke's Royal Infirmary. But it's not until my first glimpse of the hospital that I recognise it: this was where Mum had her chemo.

I find what seems like the last space and, ignoring the 'Pay & Display' signs, I run across the hot Tarmac towards the automatic doors—then falter. Visitors are arriving with the obligatory grapes, and I move sideways so that they can enter. I need to go in too, but it's as if I'm twelve, visiting Mum—so scared that I've started wetting the bed again.

'Y'OK, love?' One of the visitors, is looking at me with concern.

'Er, yeah, I'm fine—thank you. I just needed a bit of fresh air.'

'It'll be all right,' she murmurs, giving my arm a supportive pat. I watch as she disappears through the doors and draw strength from this stranger's gesture. Dad made a promise never to say goodbye and neither will I. Gathering my courage, I go inside.

The hospital is a labyrinth of wards and corridors, but finally I'm directed to the intensive-care unit and find Rosemary sitting on a plastic seat in the corridor. She's staring straight ahead, jaw tight, face devoid of emotion. She turns as she hears my footsteps. 'Heather, you're here—finally.' Everything she says sounds like an accusation. She stands up, then hesitates. Eventually she kisses my cheek awkwardly.

'Where's my dad?' I don't want to call him Lionel. He's my dad. My flesh and blood. Mine, not yours, I think, staring defiantly at Rosemary.

'He's in intensive care. Your father's had a massive coronary.'

My throat tightens, and suddenly all the love I have for him mutates into anger for her. 'How?' I gasp accusingly. 'How did this happen? You live with him, you're supposed to look after him!' Even as I'm saying it, I know I'm being a bitch. It's not her fault—it's not anyone's fault.

But Rosemary doesn't react. 'Heather, you're upset,' she says stiffly. 'I did everything I could. As soon as it happened I called for an ambulance. He arrested twice on the way here. They had to rush him straight into theatre . . .' She leaves the sentence hanging.

And then neither of us speaks.

The terrible thing that should have brought us closer together is pushing us further apart. Instead of comforting each other, we sit silently side by side, two people, one fear and a million insurmountable miles between them.

A few moments later the clanging of the fire doors causes me to turn my head sharply. An older man in a green surgeon's gown and cap is walking towards us. 'Mrs Hamilton?' He looks at us both.

So, this is it. Fear crushes the breath out of my body. 'I'm Miss Hamilton, his daughter,' I manage.

He holds out his hand. 'I'm Mr Bradley. I performed your father's angioplasty.'

I brace myself.

'The operation went well . . .'

Like a drowning man, I come up gasping for air. Relief is flooding me.

'We had to perform an angioplasty to remove the blockage in the coronary artery. At the moment he's heavily sedated and in recovery . . .'

As he's speaking I'm standing statue-still, anaesthetised by the shock of everything that's been happening. Unlike Rosemary who breaks down and sobs almost hysterically. 'Oh, thank you, Doctor . . .'

The surgeon glances at me. I know he's expecting me to comfort her, but I don't move—I can't. I've never seen Rosemary betray emotion before and stare at her blankly. There's an awkward pause.

'Now I know this has been a tremendous shock . . .' The surgeon puts his arm round Rosemary's shoulders, easing her gently into her chair. He beckons a passing nurse. '. . . but you must try to be strong. I'm afraid your husband isn't out of danger yet. The first forty-eight hours after a heart attack are critical and he will need you to be there for him.'

As the nurse arrives, he gestures for her to take over and I watch her crouch to offer Rosemary tissues and words of compassion.

'Miss Hamilton?' The doctor's grey eyes are searching my face, and I think he's judging me. But then he smiles kindly. 'Would you like to see your father?' and I realise the only person judging me is myself.

The room is quiet, but for the faint beeping of the heart monitor. I creep up quietly and gaze down at his ashen face. My legs buckle.

This isn't my dad. My dad is a giant of a man who greets me with a bear hug so strong he almost cracks my ribs. Who loves food, art and life with a burning passion. Who, from the moment I was born, has wrapped me in a blanket of unconditional love that makes me feel safe.

In his place is a pale, shrunken figure, vulnerable, *fragile*. 'I'm here, Dad,' I whisper, slipping my fingers round his hand and holding it.

And as I do, my whole world melts away. All those stupid lists of things I need to do. All those trivial worries about cellulite and what to wear, or finding Mr Right. None of it matters any more.

Squeezing hard, I stare at his face. I've been so stupid and selfish, wasting all this time wishing for things I didn't have, all this . . . *stuff*. Stuff that I don't want, need or care about now that I have it. I took everything for granted—I didn't appreciate what I had. And now I'm in danger of losing it all.

Until now, wishing for things has been just a part of everyday life. But I was wrong. Wishes are sacred. They're about magic. It's just as the old gypsy woman said when she gave me the lucky heather: *Use it wisely and it will bring you your heart's desire*.

Great fat tears spill down my cheeks, blurring my eyes. Now I know what the old gypsy woman was trying to tell me. But I haven't been wise at all: I've been careless, irresponsible and so bloody foolish.

Well, I'm not going to be any more.

And it's here, in a tiny room in intensive care, that I make my final wish—and it's the only wish that's ever mattered.

I wish for my father to live.

I'm not sure how long I stand here holding my father's hand, but the next thing I know the doctor arrives and, gently unlacing my fingers, tells me to go home, to get some sleep: my father needs to rest.

I shake my head firmly. 'I'm not going home. I'm not leaving him.'

'Your stepmother said exactly the same thing,' he says.

'She did?' I feel a jolt of surprise. I had assumed Rosemary would want to spend the night at home. She likes her comforts.

'Lionel's a very lucky man to have both of you, and you're lucky to have each other. Family is very important at a time like this.'

I've never considered Rosemary part of my family: she's a usurper, an outsider, someone who doesn't belong. And for the first time it occurs to me that she might have felt like that too. 'Thanks, Doctor.'

'Shall I get us some coffee?'

Rosemary looks up from the scuffed linoleum floor as she hears my voice. Her eyes are red from crying. We look at each other and it's as if a few bricks in that invisible wall between us dissolve. Not many, just enough for us to see each other for the first time.

She smiles tentatively. 'That would be lovely. Do you need money?' She reaches for her handbag but I stop her.

'My wallet's in here somewhere.' I rummage through all the rubbish in my bag and locate it, only to discover that the coin compartment is empty. 'Can you change a tenner?' I pull one out and waggle it hopefully.

'Take my purse,' says Rosemary. 'There's change in the side pocket.'

'Are you sure? Maybe I could ask someone else . . .'

'I might be a pensioner, but I can still afford to buy you a cup of coffee,' she says.

I give in, take her purse and walk down the corridor in search of a vending machine. After a few minutes I discover one in a waiting room filled with tired, frightened-looking people, some huddling close to each other in tiny groups, others, like the old man in the corner, sitting alone staring blankly at nothing. I notice his fingers. Bent out of shape with arthritis, they're twisting his gold wedding band round and round and round.

I look away. It dawns on me just how lucky I am that I'm not alone, that I've got Rosemary, that we've got each other.

I begin feeding ten-pence pieces into the slot. There's a whirr and a plastic cup appears and begins to fill with powder and water. I retrieve it, then scrabble around for more change for the second cup. I'm tilting the purse to get at the coins when something falls out onto the floor.

I pick it up. It's a photograph of Rosemary and Lionel, but they both look younger. Absently I flick it over. On the back there's an inscription:

For my wonderful wife on our wedding day,
Thank you for making me happy again.
All my love
Lionel

Of course. This is a photograph of their wedding ten years ago, on a cruise ship, just the two of them. Ed and I couldn't go. Didn't want to, I correct myself. I've never even asked to see their wedding album.

I feel a stab of guilt. All this time I've been resenting Rosemary but now, seeing this inscription, I realise I'm indebted to her. Somehow, over the years, I've blocked out the memories of how devastated Dad was when Mum died, how for years afterwards there was always a lost, haunted look in his eyes, and how when he met Rosemary it went away.

I slip the photograph back into the purse and feed more money into the vending machine. The plastic cup fills quickly and I grab it along with my own. There's something I need to do. It's long overdue.

'I'm sorry.'

'I beg your pardon?' Rosemary's brow furrows.

'I want to apologise for the way I've behaved over all these years, for resenting you for taking Mum's place, for wishing you weren't part of our lives . . .' There. I've finally admitted it. 'I'm so sorry, Rosemary. I've been such an idiot.' I swallow hard. She's going to hate me now, and I don't blame her.

There's a pause while she absorbs what I've said. 'Thank you, Heather,' she says quietly. 'You have no idea how much that means to me.'

Her graciousness catches me by surprise.

'But I need to apologise to you too.' She's gazing at her coffee, deep in thought. 'I'm guilty too. I've been jealous of the close relationship you have with Lionel. I don't have that with my children. Annabel and . . . Well, let's just say we don't understand each other like you two do.'

We both smile, despite ourselves.

'And I'm jealous that you remind him of Julia . . .'

'Mum?' I whisper quietly.

'I know it's wicked of me,' she confesses, 'to be envious of my husband's daughter because she looks like her mother, to feel threatened because she's a constant reminder of his first wife . . .' Her eyes fill and she looks up at me, her face white and pinched. 'I'm a bad person.'

I've never thought of it from her perspective, but now suddenly I'm seeing just how difficult it's been for her. Instinctively I reach out and squeeze her hand. 'You're a good person, Rosemary, a really good one,' I say reassuringly. And I'm not just saying it. I mean it.

'Am I?' A tear rolls down the side of her nose.

'Well, either that or we're both horrible.' I shrug, and a smile breaks through her tears.

'I never tried to replace Julia,' she says quietly. 'I never could and I never wanted to. Just like Lionel could never replace Lawrence, my first husband.' She looks at me, and for the first time I see real fear. 'I couldn't bear to lose someone so dear to me again. I love your father so much, Heather. I don't know what I'd do without him.' Her voice trembles and bowing her head she breaks down and sobs.

And now it's up to me to be strong, I tell myself.

I hold Rosemary close—because that's what dad would want and I want it too. I glance at the clock on the wall. It's going to be a long night.

I wake up with a start. Where am I? I sit bolt upright. Then it punches me like a fist in the stomach. *Dad*.

Rosemary is asleep, curled up across three plastic chairs. I stagger to my feet. What time is it? The clock on the wall reads just after six. I've been dozing for hours.

As I hurry down the corridor towards intensive care, I don't see anyone. Even the nurses who were sitting outside on Reception have gone. With no one around to stop me, I push open the door.

Inside, the room's dimly lit and silent but for the sound of the heart monitor beeping rhythmically. A wave of relief sweeps over me.

He's still alive.

Breathing deeply, I approach the bed quietly so as not to wake him. I reach out to stroke his hand, then snatch mine away.

It's not my father. My stomach freefalls.

'Excuse me, but you can't be in here.'

I whirl round to see two nurses. 'Where's my dad?' I cry desperately. 'What's happened to him? What have you done with him?' They're trying to comfort me but I can't hear what they're saying. I can't hear anything but the howl inside my head. 'He's dead, isn't he? He's dead . . .'

They lead me, stumbling, out of the room.

'Miss Hamilton, it's Mr Bradley . . . Miss Hamilton, you have to listen to me . . .' A man in a white coat looms over me but I can't focus. Darkness is closing in from around the edges.

'We needed the bed for an emergency in the middle of the night. Your father has been moved to the coronary unit. He's doing fine. He's awake and asking for you . . .'

And then everything goes black.

'**D**id I give you two a bit of a shock?'

It's later. Rosemary and I are sitting at either side of Lionel's bed.

'I think it was Heather who gave us a shock.' Rosemary smiles. My cheeks redden. How embarrassing—fainting at Mr Bradley's feet.

Then I look at my father. Never forget, Heather. You came this close—*this close*—to losing him.

Apparently Lionel can't remember anything after the first heart attack and it's been something of a shock for him to discover that not only is he in hospital, but that he's undergone heart surgery. Much less dramatic, but momentous in its own way, is the change in the relationship between Rosemary and me. 'Just look, here I am with the two beautiful women in my life.' He smiles approvingly. 'I'll have to do this again.'

'Oh, no, you won't,' scolds Rosemary. 'And to make sure, Ed is going to be staying with us. I just had a message. He's arriving this afternoon.'

'With a nutritionist friend from LA,' I add.

Lionel manages a grimace.

'You heard what the doctor said. It's very important you stick to this diet. No cheese, no wine . . .'

'No fun,' he whimpers.

'Lionel, you're not going to make me a widow for the second time,' warns Rosemary, in a voice that makes even me a little scared.

'Me? Disobey doctor's orders? I wouldn't dream of it.' He puckers his lips for a kiss.

'You've had a heart attack, you need to rest.'

'I want a kiss, my dear, not a sexual marathon.'

Rosemary blushes, and I stand up. 'I'll leave you two lovebirds to it.' Once I would have felt resentful, but now I feel a warm sense of contentment, and pressing my lips lightly to my father's whiskery cheek, I whisper. 'See you later, alligator.'

And, smiling, he whispers right back, 'In a while, crocodile.'

I spend the next few days at the cottage. Ed duly arrives with his nutritionist friend, a woman named Miranda whom he met at university and who now runs successful practices in London and Los Angeles. She's here for a whirlwind twenty-four hours, meeting Lionel and his doctors, drawing up detailed diet plans and nutritious low-fat recipes.

Lionel was discharged at the weekend. I can call him Lionel again now, as he's definitely back to being Lionel, loud-voiced and larger than life—though soon to be sixty pounds lighter, if Miranda has anything to do with it. And I think he will be. He's had a shock. When Rosemary orders him to eat up his grilled chicken breast, he gets on with it like an obedient child, without so much as a whinge for a glass of Pinot Noir.

I'm more than happy. And it's on afternoons sitting outside on the lawn with Lionel, Ed and Rosemary, laughing at some crappy joke or other, I think of how I got my wish—and with it, much more than I could have ever imagined. We've just finished another healthy picnic lunch when Lionel brings up the subject of Gabe. Honestly, I swear my father's a bloody mind-reader.

'Er, he's moved out,' I say, as casually as I can, but it's as if I've been stung. 'He's gone up to the Edinburgh Festival,' I add.

Lionel beams. 'Are you going to go up and see his show?'

'No.'

'Oh, right.' He raises his eyebrows.

There's a pause and I can feel looks flying round. 'What?' I demand.

'Nothing, sis,' says Ed evenly and smirks into his mobile. Since his return from America he's been constantly on the phone to Lou. Lionel's brush with death has made him realise what's important in life.

'Oh, we don't want to talk about some boring old festival, do we?' pooh-poohs Rosemary. 'Tell us all about that high-society wedding.'

I smile gratefully at her attempt to rescue me, but I've been trying not to think about Lady Charlotte's wedding. 'It's this weekend at Shillingham Abbey.' My mind throws up an image of Daniel, all done up in his top hat and tails. I block it out.

'Oooh, just think of all the celebrities who'll be there . . .' Rosemary's eyes betray an excited gleam.

'So, when will you be heading back for it?' Lionel looks at me expectantly over his glass of Evian.

Oh, shite. How do I tell them I'm unemployed? I try to think of how to explain things, then, realising I can't, say simply, 'I'm not.'

'You're not?' gasps Rosemary.

I shake my head and glance at Lionel, who's studying me carefully.

'I'm going to be all right,' he says quietly. 'I don't need three nurses. I have Rosemary and your brother.'

'Why don't you call Brian?' suggests Rosemary.

I feel stuck. I'm not worried about leaving Lionel. The doctors are delighted with the progress he's making. But can I just call Brian and ask for my old job back?

'You can borrow my mobile,' pipes up Ed.

I'm suspicious. Since when has he ever offered to lend me his mobile?

Then I catch sight of Lionel who's got that guilty schoolboy look, and get a sneaky feeling that this has been planned. 'Is this a plot to get rid of me?' I take the phone from Ed.

'No, of course not, darling,' says Lionel. 'It's just that Ed mentioned your finances . . . and I know Rosemary was really looking forward to seeing your photographs of all those famous people . . .'

With all eyes on me I take Ed's mobile. I feel nervous. Despite what Brian said, I still feel terrible about letting him down at such short notice, and I want to make it up to him. But can I really face being the wedding photographer's assistant at Daniel's wedding? Taking close-ups of a man who broke my heart into a million pieces saying 'I do'?

Yes, you can, Heather, I tell myself firmly.

And all of a sudden I make a decision. So what if I'm dreading seeing Daniel? I punch in the number. Brian and the business are more important and I'm going to put them first.

'Hello, Together Forever.' It's Brian. He sounds stressed.

'I don't suppose you still need an assistant do you?'

'*Heather?*' His surprise is audible. Then he laughs quietly. 'You're going to need a fancy hat.'

As it turns out I need a lot more than a hat.

'Lights?'

'Check.'

'Tripods.'

'Check.'

'Two Hasselblads, a Nikon, the reflector, sixty rolls of film and three lenses.'

'Check, check, check, check . . . um . . . check.'

It's the morning of Lady Charlotte's wedding, and we're at Shillingham Abbey in Oxfordshire. The abbey is part of the ancestral home of the Duke and Duchess, and it's nestled in the type of picturesque village you'd expect on a postcard.

'Is that everything?' Brian is asking, looking up from the array of camera equipment laid out on the gravel driveway.

Pausing from unloading cases out of the back of the Together Forever van, I think hard. Then remember. I reach into the depths, rummage around and produce a large tub of Vaseline. 'For the lens,' I remind him.

'Oh, of course.' He rolls his eyes skyward.

Since my initial phone call a few days ago, Brian and I have spoken quite a lot and he knows all about Lionel's heart attack, Gabe's uncle being Victor Maxfield, and my decision not to take the job at the *Sunday Herald*. True to character, he's been a rock, listening supportively and immediately offering me my old job back. 'Which, of course, goes without saying, but there's no rush, take your time,' he's saying now, as he paces round the exterior of the abbey, taking readings from his light meter.

'Thanks, Brian, I really appreciate it.' Perched on a case, I smile gratefully. I haven't yet made any firm decisions on what I'm going to do about my career. Although I love working with Brian, we both know that after six years it's time for me to move on. To where, I have no idea.

'Oh, it's no problem, no problem.' He takes out a tissue and dabs the perspiration from his face. 'To be quite frank, Heather, after this dratted wedding we're both going to need a rest. Pity that poor groom, that's all I can say,' he mutters to himself.

'Well, that's another thing,' I say hesitantly. 'The groom's my ex.'

Brian stares at me, not understanding.

'Remember Daniel?' I say quietly, and feel a familiar knot in my stomach. Oh God, this is what I've been afraid of.

'Gordon Bennett, how could I forget? He broke your heart. You've known all along and you still offered to be my assistant today.' He gazes at me, his eyes filling up. 'Heather, that's the kindest thing anyone's ever done for me.' He hurries over to give me a hug.

'Don't mention it.' I smile, and then, gesturing at the equipment, say briskly, 'Come on, we've got a wedding to photograph.'

We spend the next ten minutes setting up: lights, reflector, a tripod at both ends of the aisle. In fact, it's only when Brian pops out to get more extension leads from the van—which means he's gone for a quick smoke—that I take a moment to look at my surroundings.

The abbey is breathtaking. Its sheer size inspires a kind of stunned awe. This is where Daniel, the man with whom I shared three years of my life, will get married today. Only not to me.

I feel a deep ache and the stirring of a wishful thought. I banish it quickly. Oh no you don't . . .

Interrupted by the creak of the door I turn round. *It's Daniel.*

He's thinner than I remember and a little older round the eyes, but he still makes my stomach flip. And now he's only a few feet from me and my heart's thumping so loudly I'm sure he can hear it.

'Hello, Daniel,' I say evenly, summoning every scrap of composure.

He takes off his top hat and smiles crookedly, 'Fancy seeing you here,' he retorts, but beneath his confident veneer he seems uncharacteristically self-conscious. 'You look great,' he blurts out.

I feel a ridiculous jolt of pleasure. 'Thanks,' I say nonchalantly.

'And different. Did you do something to your hair?'

'No.' I shrug, but inside I feel like yelling, Of course I did something to my hair! I did something to *every single part of my body*. I got up at 6 a.m. this morning and spent three whole hours getting ready. I even bought a new cream trouser suit for the occasion.

'So, was this your idea?' Cutting through the pleasantries, I ask him the question that's been bugging me for weeks. 'Brian and I photographing your wedding.'

'You're the best wedding photographer I know,' he answers jokingly.

'I'm the only wedding photographer you know,' I point out drily.

Immediately his face falls and he stares contritely at his feet. 'I dunno what I was thinking,' he says quietly. 'I thought it would be great for business . . .' He looks up at me from underneath his brows, and for a moment I'm sure I see more than just a flicker of regret. 'It's good to see you, Heather.' He sighs heavily. 'I've missed you.'

I stare at him in stunned silence. For months after we first broke up I fantasised about this happening. But now, listening to him actually saying the words, I realise I had confused nostalgia with reality. And the reality is I don't care any more. I don't care if Daniel has missed me, and I don't care that he's marrying someone else.

The only person I care about is Gabe.

Finally I admit it and, as I do, all the feelings I've kept hidden burst through my consciousness to the surface. The gratitude I felt when Gabe defended me to Rosemary at the dinner table, the terror when I thought something had happened to him surfing, the wretchedness after we rowed and he moved out. And all the hundreds of fleeting moments when I thought something was going on between us, but dismissed it. All those tiny fragments are piecing together now and suddenly I feel as if I'm looking at a loved-up jigsaw. Oh, God.

'I'm really sorry about everything. I was an idiot . . .' I zone back in to realise Daniel's still talking to me. 'Are you still angry with me?' he asks.

I stare at him calmly. In the beginning anger was the only thing that kept me going but now I can't find any left. It's trickled away without me noticing. 'No.' I shake my head. 'I'm not angry.'

'I got your text.'

'Oh, that!' I blush with embarrassment. 'I was drunk.'

'You were?' I'm surprised to see he seems disappointed.

'I can't remember what I put. Was it anything bad?'

He looks at me for a moment, then shakes his head. 'No, nothing embarrassing.'

There's a pause. 'I should go. I've got to get everything ready,' I say.

'Actually, there's been a change . . .'

I look at him sharply.

'Charlotte's had second thoughts about the ceremony.' He's rubbing his jaw agitatedly. This is the first time I've ever seen Daniel nervous. 'She doesn't want anything conventional,' he's saying, 'so we've decided on handfasting in the woods across the river. It's a pagan ceremony.'

I look at him blankly. '*A pagan ceremony?*' I repeat, staring at him. '*You?*'

He stiffens. 'Why shouldn't I have a pagan ceremony?'

'Daniel, you *hate* anything alternative.'

He stares at me for a moment as if prepared to argue, before letting his shoulders slump wearily in surrender. 'You're right. I hate it.'

And with those words I see him in a new light. This is a man I was in awe of. And yet he seems so pathetic so, dare I say it, *henpecked*.

'Charlotte's very particular about what she wants.'

'And what Charlotte wants, Charlotte must have,' I answer brightly, trying to keep the sarcasm out of my voice. And failing.

He heaves a huge sigh. 'Something like that.'

I open my mouth to say something, but—'*Dan-eee-al! Dan-eee-al!*' Like the siren of a police car, a voice echoes through the abbey.

Startled, we turn to see a flurry of white silk taffeta hurtling down the aisle. *Lady Charlotte*.

'Shit,' groans Daniel. 'What's wrong, Bunnykins?' he coos.

Bunnykins? From a man who didn't believe in Public Displays of Affection?

'Elton John's got laryngitis and won't be able to sing at the reception, the delivery of Cristal hasn't arrived, and I don't think I like my new titties any more.' Lady Charlotte appears not to have noticed I'm here.

'Darling, should you be here? I thought it was bad luck for me to see the bride before the wedding.'

'Oh, fuck superstition, Danny! This is a crisis!' With a tantrum-style howl she scuttles into the vestry.

A stunned silence settles. 'I should go after her,' Daniel says.

I nod, and for a moment we just stand there, the two of us, until I kiss his cheek. 'Goodbye, Daniel,' I whisper.

'Goodbye, Heather.' He smiles, but I can't help feeling I can see real regret in his face, and as I watch his coattails disappearing into the vestry, I feel unexpectedly sorry for him. Yes, he broke my heart. But a lifetime with Lady Charlotte is punishment enough for anyone.

Outside the abbey I find Brian leaning against the Together Forever van, smoking and waiting for me. 'How was it?' he asks gently.

'Good.' I nod. 'I had closure,' I say decisively.

'I'm so glad.' He laughs happily and reaches for his top hat. 'Shall we?' he says, with mock formality, holding out his arm.

'But what about all the stuff in the abbey that I need to move? I've left all the lights, reflectors and tripods—'

'The bride's changed her mind,' he says, stopping me in my tracks.

'Yeah, I know, it's going to be a pagan ceremony outside—'

'No, she's changed it about the style of photography. Apparently she saw some of the stuff I did in the sixties. Now she wants edgy, *paparazzi*-style photographs.' His face is buzzing with delight.

'You mean . . .' We share a euphoric smile. Translated, this means forget putting Vaseline on the lens and trying to get everyone together for the group photographs. Now all we need is one digital camera to fire off lots of spur-of-the-moment, out-of-focus black-and-white shots.

'And we still go home early with a big fat cheque,' he whoops, impetuously seizing me round the waist. 'OK. This is it. *Showtime*.'

As Brian and I make our way across the manicured lawns we observe the chaos that's ensuing. Bewildered crowds of people are being herded into the vast white marquee that was originally erected for the reception, and handed opera glasses so that they can watch the pagan ceremony in a small clearing across the river in neighbouring woodland. It's just immediate family in the circle of purification.

As we enter the clearing a woman in flowing purple robes, carrying a wand, wafts towards us. I'm not joking. It has a silver star on the end.

'I'm the celebrant.' She appears to be in her seventies, with silvery-white hair down to her waist.

'Gordon Bennett,' mutters Brian.

'Oh, um, hi. Pleased to meet you,' I say, and shake her hand.

A large bell on a long silver chain hangs round her neck. 'It's to ring out the old and ring in the new,' she says solemnly, having noticed me staring at it. Then she fixes me with startlingly blue eyes, and adds, 'In the circle of purification there is no place for superstition or tawdry charms, Heather.'

She knows my name? Any amusement I might have felt at her attire vanishes. 'How—' I begin.

'Now, if you'd all please form a circle,' she interrupts me.

Superstition and tawdry charms? Was she referring to the lucky heather? Out of habit I stick my hand into my pocket, although I know there's nothing in there, and feel my fingers go through the lining. There's a hole! I feel a rush of indignation. This jacket cost nearly three hundred pounds! Followed by a thump of alarm as I feel something soft and scratchy. *It's the lucky heather*.

I feel a tingle in my fingertips, like a current of electricity. It's turned up again. I wrap my fingers round it tightly, determined not to lose it again. I've got to get rid of it properly, once and for all.

'That means all of you.'

'But what about the photographs?' I whisper to Brian.

'Photographs break the sanctity of the circle,' the celebrant says. 'Now, if everyone will stand shoulder to shoulder in the circle we can begin.' Obediently I stand next to Brian as the celebrant picks up a broom and begins to sweep the clearing in an anti-clockwise direction.

'Sweep, sweep, sweep this place
By Power of Air, I cleanse this space.'

There are sniggers from the guests, and expressions of bewilderment, and scepticism on their faces. 'What's she doing?' asks someone.

'Casting a purification circle,' answers a middle-aged woman.

'Blessings and merry meet. We are here today to join Daniel and Charlotte together . . .'

The next few minutes are taken up by Daniel and Charlotte saying their vows. As I watch Daniel kissing his bride I feel . . . nothing. Well, actually, that's not true. I do feel something, but it's for Gabe. I can't stop thinking about him throughout the ceremony.

'Now, if everyone can hold their neighbour's hand tightly, we shall all close our eyes and focus on the circle . . . on its special power . . .'

Surely she's not serious? I glance around. Everyone looks horribly self-conscious, but gradually, one by one, people reach tentatively for their neighbour's fingers and close their eyes. Reluctantly retrieving my fingers from the lucky heather in my pocket, I clasp Brian's hand.

Then something weird happens.

It's like an energy. A force. A hot blast of euphoria surging through my body. Yet at the same time I feel the peace and calm of a lullaby. An eerie stillness descends. And for what feels like both a moment and an eternity, nothing and no one makes even the slightest movement or sound. Until the voice of the celebrant strikes up again:

'The web of life is an endless circle never to die, only to change form
What was begun is now complete
Welcome home these energies borne
The circle is open, never broken
So Mote It Be!'

From out of nowhere a breeze whips up, and as everyone breaks apart I open my eyes to see a dove circling overhead. Gosh, I feel as if I'm coming out of a trance.

I glance at other people, see their embarrassed smiles, as if they're not sure what happened, and know instinctively something's changed. Not around me, but inside me. I feel different. Lighter. Freer.

Immediately I put my hand back into my pocket. I'm going to get rid of the heather by throwing it into the river . . . Except—my pocket's empty. Where's the heather? Puzzled, I turn out my pockets. It must be somewhere. Out of the corner of my eye I catch sight of the celebrant. She's smiling at me. '*In the circle of purification there is no place for superstition or tawdry charms, Heather.*' It can't have just disappeared. *Can it?*

'Lost something?' Brian is dabbing his red eyes with a handkerchief.

'Er, no . . . nothing,' I say. I glance back at the celebrant but she's not looking my way at all. Maybe I imagined it.

'What did you think of the ceremony?'

'I'm not sure . . . What about you?'

'Load of old hocus-pocus,' he says derisively, blowing his nose. 'But this pagan wedding malarkey is going to be great for pictures,' he adds.

'**I** have to say, I didn't know you were such a good dancer,' I tease later, when we're loading all the equipment into the van.

'I wasn't dancing, I was being kidnapped,' grumbles Brian. He slams the doors. 'Right, that's everything. Now, can we change the subject?'

'To what?'

'To you. It's the American, isn't it? He's the reason you've had that look on your face all day.'

'I don't have a look,' I say hotly, digging my mobile phone out of my little clutch bag and turning it on to check my messages. Out of the corner of my eye I can see Brian staring at me. 'Honestly, you get a boyfriend and suddenly you're the expert on relationships,' I mutter. Finally the little Vodafone symbol appears and I dial 121.

'I don't need to be an expert on relationships to know when someone's in love,' he replies.

Is it that obvious?

'You have one new message.'

I jump as a loud, no-nonsense voice barks down the phone. It sounds like—'*Victor Maxfield here. I've just returned from my fishing trip and found your letter of refusal on my desk. My dear, don't you know the first rule of journalism is to make sure you're aware of the facts? Yes, my nephew Gabriel did put in a good word for you, and, yes, on his recommendation I gave you an interview. But that wasn't why you got the job. You got it because you're a bloody talented photographer.*'

Gabe isn't why I got that job? I'm a Bloody Talented Photographer? My stomach rushes upwards as if I'm on a swing, then plummets down again. And I've been a Bloody Stupid Idiot.

'*Gabriel might be my favourite nephew but the* Sunday Herald *is an award-winning newspaper and I'm not about to give you a job because the idiot's in love with you.*'

What? Gabe? In love with me?

'*So stop all this nonsense immediately. We're running a piece on the Edinburgh Festival and we need a photographer up there. There's a plane leaving at five from Heathrow. When you call me back, I want you to be on it.*'

I stare at my Nokia in disbelief. I've suddenly got a job at the *Sunday Herald* after all, and with it my first assignment—the Edinburgh Festival. *Which is where Gabe is*.

I walk round the van, tug open the passenger door and climb in. I take a deep breath. 'Brian, I need a favour. Can you give me a lift?'

We race towards Heathrow. My flight's in less than an hour.

After I've told Brian about my message from Victor Maxfield I discover he's actually a frustrated rally-car driver and rises to the challenge with aplomb. We cause quite a stir. People gawp in astonishment as the Together Forever Mini van whizzes past in a blur. I spend most of the journey glancing frantically from the busy roads to my watch. My heart leaps into my mouth every time we hit a red light, or have to brake at a zebra crossing. What's with all this traffic? And red lights?

But then, after what feels like for ever, I see a sprawl of grey terminal buildings. Heathrow Airport.

'Thanks, Brian,' I gasp, throwing open the door.

'Here, you nearly forgot something.' Brian is holding out one of his cameras. It's digital. 'You'll be needing this. And this.' He tugs out a black nylon laptop case. 'This way you can email your shots to your picture editor. Just in case you find you want to stay a bit longer in Edinburgh . . .'

As I walk into Departures the first thing I notice is the queue. Fuck. I'm going to miss the flight. Victor Maxfield will think I'm crap, I'll be fired and spend the rest of my life taking pictures of brides with leg-o'-mutton sleeves . . .

I struggle to calm myself. Slowly we drift forward inch by inch. Until finally—

'Next.'

I fling myself at the check-in desk. 'Phew! at last!' I gasp. 'I was worried I was going to miss my flight.'

The stewardess keeps typing into her computer, her fingernails clickety-clicking on her keyboard.

'I'm booked on the five o'clock to Edinburgh,' I gabble.

Nothing.

Has she heard me? 'I think it goes quite soon,' I add, louder this time.

There's a pause, and then, 'Name?' she monotones.

Finally.

'Heather Hamilton,' I gasp. 'Miss.'

'Uh-huh,' she mutters and continues tapping leisurely at her keyboard. Now, I know they must deal with this kind of thing every day, but can't we at least have *some* sense of urgency?

Apparently not.

She pauses to sigh. 'Oh dear, you might have missed your flight.'

'But that's what I've been trying—' I explode. Calm down, Heather.

'But if you hurry you might make it.' She passes me a boarding card. 'You're in seventy-five F, a window seat.'

'Oh, no, I can't have a window seat,' I say quickly. 'You see, I'm a nervous flyer and I like to be on the aisle because if there's an emergency and we need to jump out with our life jackets I can get to the exits quicker . . .'

Fellow travellers throw each other nervous looks and move away from me.

'It's the last seat,' says the stewardess. 'It leaves from gate forty-two. You have five minutes.' She throws me a sour look.

Running in heels is murder. My ankles are wobbling all over the place as I rush through Security and dash on to the moving walkway. '*Ow*,' I yell, as my ankle twists under me. I grab the handrail and look down. Shit! My heel has snapped off.

'Bloody hell!'

I look up to see an air stewardess heading in the opposite direction. 'Jess!' I gasp, as she glides past. 'What are you doing here?'

'What am *I* doing here? I'm a bloody air stewardess, what do you think I'm doing here? More to the point, what are *you* doing here?'

'I'm flying to Edinburgh . . .' I nearly trip over a businessman's briefcase and apologise profusely. '. . . on a shoot for the *Sunday Herald*. It's a long story,' I explain, remembering how I emailed her last week about my row with Gabe and his sudden departure.

'Isn't Gabe at the Edinburgh Festival?' She arches her eyebrows.

'Sorry, Jess, I've got to rush. I'm going to miss my plane.' Cutting her off quickly I hobble off along the concourse. 'I'll call you.'

'You go, girl,' she yells after me. 'Oh and, Heather!' She shouts something I don't quite catch, but it sounded an awful lot like 'Go catch some butterflies.'

Staggering onto the aircraft I limp down the aisle to my seat. Seventy-five F . . . Damn, it must be here somewhere . . .

And then I see it.

At the very back, shoved up right next to the toilets. Two seats. One is occupied by a man with a beer belly so ginormous it's divided into two—one half being on one side of the arm rest, and the other half bursting underneath, over and around it on the next seat.

My seat.

I squeeze past my neighbour, sit down and fasten my seat belt. I close my eyes. Still, it's only a short flight. With any luck I can sleep all the way.

'Well, well, well, isn't this cosy?'

Oh, no. Please, no. I've been accosted by a thick Scottish accent. I open my eyes to see my neighbour beaming down at me. 'Hello there. I'm Bruce and you are . . .?'

For the next fifteen minutes everything goes relatively smoothly. Well, apart from the constant sound of the loo flushing next to me, and Bruce falling asleep and slobbering over my shoulder.

'Coffee or tea?' a stewardess trills.

'Coffee, please.'

She passes me a little white plastic cup on a tray and pours the thick black liquid, expertly not spilling a drop.

Out of nowhere the aeroplane gives a little judder.

What the . . .? I shoot a glance at the stewardess. Her face remains impassive as she sways on her navy court shoes and continues to pour. Reassured, I take the cup from her.

Aggggh.

Without warning the plane is plummeting and I feel as if we're dropping out of the sky. Terrifying doesn't even come close. I hear children crying, my heart is pounding and a finger's prodding . . .

A what?

I look up to see Bruce is prodding me with his chubby finger. 'Och, lassie, it's OK. Just a bit of clear-air turbulence, everything's aal reet. Well, apart from your troosers,' he adds, gesturing to my lap.

I look down to see a large brown patch spreading across my crotch then transfer my gaze to my empty coffee cup, which I'm still gripping. Great. Just great. Can things get any worse?

Apparently they can. After we've landed I get trapped behind Bruce and am the last person to disembark. Which means I'm the last person through the Arrivals hall, and the last person to join the enormous queue for the taxis. And now it's raining.

Where did all the beautiful weather go? It hasn't rained for ages, not since . . . I rack my brains. Since that night I got drenched and met the old gypsy woman who gave me the lucky heather.

A weird feeling stirs. Wait a minute. It's not just the sunshine that's disappeared, what about all the green lights and empty roads? And what happened to never having to wait in a queue? Getting the best seat? The only cab? How come they've all vanished and been replaced with . . . With how things used to be, I realise. Because this is what it was like before—*before all my wishes came true.*

Surely . . . it can't . . . *can it*? I rewind back to the wedding, holding hands in the circle, the strange sensation, the lucky heather vanishing . . . As realisation dawns, I feel a tingle of joy spread over me.

'Oh, my gosh, look at this queue for a taxi,' I gasp, with a grin that stretches from ear to ear. '*It's huge*.'

A couple in front of me turn to me suspiciously.

'And it's raining,' I whoop. 'Yippee!' Throwing back my head I let the rain splash onto my face as I twirl round and round, getting completely and utterly drenched. I've never been happier.

A couple of hours later I'm sitting cross-legged on my bed in my hotel room. In one hand I have my trousers, and in the other the hotel's hair dryer. I've just spent twenty minutes getting out the coffee stains, and now it's just a case of drying them off and I'll be good to go.

I made the taxi stop at M&S on the way over and bought a rather natty pair of pumps, an umbrella and a three-pack of black low-rise g-strings. I should've bought flesh-coloured as I'm wearing cream trousers, but flesh-coloured underwear is so unattractive and, well, you never know . . .

You never know what, Heather? demands a voice sternly.

Honestly, I don't have time for all this nonsense. I can't sit here day dreaming about Gabe and me and . . . Oh, shit, I'm doing it again. Whatever my feelings, Gabe is just a friend, *was* just a friend, and if I happen to bump into him at the festival then, hopefully, he'll accept my grovelling apology and we can be friends again. But that's all. Just friends. He has a girlfriend already, remember? After what Daniel did to me, I do not go anywhere near men who are prepared to cheat on their girlfriends. Not even if they do have kind, freckly faces and hang towels neatly in the bathroom, I tell myself firmly.

Twenty minutes later I've finished getting ready and, after a quick phone call with the journalist who's writing the article, I hang up and reach for Brian's camera. OK. This is it. *Showtime*.

Any nerves I have disappear the moment I step out into the street. Everywhere I look street performers are mingling with crowds of tourists and people handing out fliers, and over the next few hours I take picture after picture after picture, until by nine o'clock my new shoes are hurting and I flop onto a bench to decide what to do next.

I've been given fistfuls of fliers so I leaf through them. By now I've resigned myself to the awful fact that I'm going to have to see one of the comedy shows, but the question is, which one?

Gabe's, I think, before I can stop myself.

Heather Hamilton, you're not here to think about Gabe. You're here on a professional assignment. Turning my attention back to the fliers, I try looking for something that sounds vaguely appealing, which is a bit like asking a vegetarian to choose something from the chilled-meats section at Tesco's, but I persist.

Oh for godsakes, Who am I kidding? I want to see Gabe. I have to see Gabe. I'm in love with Gabe. It's no use trying to deny it. From the very first moment I set eyes on him on my doorstep, with all those freckles and those big baggy blue eyes, I just knew.

Scrunching up all the fliers I walk over to one of the bins. It's already overflowing with multi-coloured paper and I'm resignedly stuffing mine on top when one catches my attention. A soggy pink and yellow leaflet, with a silhouette of a man's profile that looks just like . . .

ANGEL GABRIEL, SENT FROM HOLLYWOOD TO MAKE YOU LOOK ON THE BRIGHT SIDE OF LIFE. TONIGHT AT THE TAVERN, 9 P.M., TICKETS £7.50. COME AND BE SAVED.

Right on cue I hear the town-hall clock strike nine.

I run all the way there.

Fortunately the Tavern is located in a backstreet five minutes away, and when I arrive I discover Gabe's show hasn't started. Due to earlier technical problems everything is running late.

The Tavern is a tiny bar with a makeshift stage where a comedian is finishing his act, and although I don't know much about stand-up comedy, even I can tell he's dying. '. . . and then this pigeon landed right on my shoulder . . .' I watch him flounder on until my eyes drift through the fog of smoke towards some familiar-looking pink and yellow posters. Sure enough, there's the same headshot of Gabe in silhouette that was on the leaflet, and the words 'ANGEL GABRIEL' stencilled above.

Seeing them now, I feel a burst of pride. He's done all this. Printed leaflets, made posters, organised a show, come all the way from LA to Edinburgh to perform. Impressed, I glance around me. There must be twenty or so people in here, a respectable number for such a small space. And they've all paid to watch Gabe, I note, with satisfaction, as the pigeon-obsessed comic disappears off-stage to feeble applause and none of the audience disappears with him.

That means next up must be Gabe.

I scan the room for a place to stand. On the way over I decided I'd wait until after the show to approach him, but I need somewhere with a view to take photographs where he won't see me. He's probably really nervous, I tell myself. And even if he's not, I'm really nervous.

A darkened recess at the other side of the bar looks perfect and I edge towards it past a group of girls smoking cigarettes and talking loudly.

'Is this next bloke supposed to be any good?'

'Dunno. Who cares? The tickets were free.'

'You mean you didn't pay for them?

'Nah. Some American guy was giving them away earlier.'

There's a sickening lurch in my stomach. She means Gabe. And if he's giving away free tickets his show must be doing badly. My worst fears are confirmed—and then the lights dim.

A compère arrives on stage. 'Let's hear it for your very own Angel Gabriel . . .'

I should've stopped him. I should've done something.

As Gabe strides on to the stage I forget to breathe. He looks even more adorable than I remember. I was expecting him to be wearing that awful suit he thinks makes him look cool and edgy, but he's in his jeans and a sweatshirt. I feel immediately protective. And utterly besotted.

'Hi there, great to be here, it's my first time in Edinburgh. Anyone here from Edinburgh?'

There's a bored silence. My worst fears begin to get worse.

'I'm from California, but I've been living in London for the past few weeks. London's great. Big Ben, Leicester Square, though I have to admit I was a bit disappointed by Piccadilly Circus. There wasn't a clown or a performing seal in sight . . .' He smiles—and I must admit, combined with his drawl and languorous delivery, it's vaguely comical. But vaguely comical is not enough to give the kiss of life to this audience, who have been left for dead by Mr Pigeon. He's going to die on stage. Right here, in front of me.

'But seriously, this is my first time in the UK and I've noticed a few things that are different from back home . . .'

As I watch him on stage, lit by that harsh spotlight, I want to rush up there and save him. But I can't. No one is laughing. Seemingly bewildered by the lack of bitterness and exocet-missile delivery of most stand-up comics, they're looking at each other unsurely. The atmosphere's one of dismissal. They're not prepared to give him a chance. Shit! Maybe Gabe was right—maybe audiences expect their comedians to be angry and *angst*-ridden.

'Like, for example . . .'

I can tell he's nervous. There's an excruciating pause as he swallows hard. Oh God, I can't watch this.

Ducking, I squeeze past the bar, and dash into the ladies' loos. The door swings closed behind me, blocking out his voice until it's just a murmur. Turning on the taps I splash my face with cold water. I feel so bad for him. All that time and work and effort to be here—and for what? To be ignored? I feel a knee-jerk of indignation. Because, despite everything, I believe Gabe is naturally funny. And I hate to think of him up there on stage, with no one laughing . . .

Right on cue I hear a roar of laughter.

What? It can't be! *Can it?* Tentatively pulling open the door, I peer through the fog of smoke. I can't believe my eyes. I'm not mistaken. People are smiling, and quite a few are actually laughing.

'I was on one of those double-decker buses recently . . .'

I join the audience, and as he continues talking, I can feel the room warming to him. People stop talking and really listen.

'. . . and there was this little girl crying. I thought, What can I do? I felt terrible . . .' With perfect comic timing he pauses to pull a face that has the audience in stitches. 'Then I remembered I had a piece of candy in my backpack . . .' There's a beat. '. . . and so I took it out and popped it into my mouth. It was amazing. I felt so much better.'

The audience cracks up.

My eyes flit round them, mouths open wide, faces creased, eyes shining. And now Gabe has their full attention—mine too.

With new-found respect I watch him as he delivers his comical observations with a deadpan delivery and an angelic smile that reels you right in. He's so much better than I ever expected. The angry wisecracking comic has gone. Instead he's himself. I feel a tingle of pride. Maybe he took my advice just a little bit.

And then, before I know it, the show begins to moves to its climax like a snowball gathering momentum. The laughs are bigger and bigger.

'. . . but I can't leave tonight without talking about a special ginger-haired someone I've got to know over the past few weeks . . .' *What was that?* He's talking about me! Heart hammering, I wait on tenterhooks. '. . . a tomcat called Billy Smith . . .'

Disappointment throbs and I feel faintly ridiculous for even thinking he was talking about me. After all, why should he?

Because the idiot's in love with you.

I hear Victor Maxfield's voice again, loud in my head. But I dismiss it. For all I know he's probably confused me with someone else.

'I always used to wonder where that saying "you dirty tomcat" came from but now I know.'

I recover quickly.

'There's me and my room-mate every night in our pyjamas, drinking peppermint tea, watching *Sex and the City* on DVD—my room-mate has the entire series in a boxed set, sort of like an encyclopedia of men . . .'

Blushing, I glance round the room. I see men nudging their girlfriends, who are giggling with embarrassed recognition.

'I know we stand-ups lead a pretty wild life. Sometimes we cracked and hit the Liquorice Allsorts!' There's a wave of laughter.

'But Billy Smith?' On stage, Gabe raises his eyebrows. 'That cat is an *animal*. You wouldn't believe the traffic that went through that kitty flap. I swear, he was getting booty calls every night.' Suddenly I remember our conversation in the kitchen. Gabe is a genius. 'You know what a booty call is, right?'

Gabe smiles conspiratorially into the audience. There's a few sniggers, some puzzled looks, and a lot of people whispering explanations. Until, as people start to get it, there's a swell of rowdy guffaws.

He grins. 'Hmm, thought so.'

People are crying with laughter now as Gabe just keeps coming with his most wide-eyed innocent delivery.

'. . . Strays, tabbies, a couple of Persian blues . . . they were in and out all night long . . .' He pauses and looks out into the audience. Then he sees me. And as his eyes meet and hold mine, my breath stops at the back of my throat. And in that moment everything around me seems to disappear, the lights, the chatter, and there's just me and Gabe. Back in my kitchen in London with Billy Smith and his ridiculous booty calls.

His face crumples into astonishment. 'You're laughing,' he mouths silently.

'I know,' I mouth back, a smile on my face as a giggle rises inside me. Would you believe it? For the first time in my life *I'm actually laughing* in a stand-up comedy club. And as Gabe goes for the punch line I lift my camera, take a photograph and capture the moment for ever.

The next morning, thousands of *Sunday Herald* readers open their newspapers to see the black-and-white image of Gabe on stage at the Tavern. Underneath is the heading 'Comedians Taking the Festival by Storm' and an article about the top ten newcomers and their acts, of which Gabe is one. Turns out the journalist was in the audience too, and was so impressed that she rewrote her article to include him.

I was pretty busy myself. After Gabe came off-stage there was a lot of apologising and explaining to do on both sides and we stayed up for hours, talking about everything. There were a few revelations. His confession that he'd broken up with Mia being the one that caught my attention particularly. But there were others. How when he'd left the flat early that morning he'd circled the block three times before he could find the strength to drive away. How, after much soul-searching, he'd decided to follow my advice and change his act. It all came pouring out.

And then it was my turn. I told him about Lionel's heart attack, making up with Rosemary, Victor Maxfield's message. I told him everything. Well, not *everything*. I didn't mention the bit about his uncle calling him an idiot and saying he was in love with me.

But I didn't need to as he told me himself.

Just before we kissed.

'**S**o what do you think?'

Snuggled up in a tangle of feather duvet, I look at Gabe across the pillows. It's the morning after the night before and we're in my hotel room indulging in breakfast in bed and the Sunday papers.

'Hmmm, let me see . . . "sheepish, almost whimsical humour" . . . "one of the funniest comedians to hit Edinburgh".'

I swat him with my half-eaten croissant. 'I'm talking about the photograph.'

'Oh, I see, the photograph,' he repeats. 'Och, he's a bonny wee lad,' he declares, in his best attempt at a Scottish accent. I shoot him a look. 'And the photograph's not too shabby either.' He wraps his arm round me. 'You're very talented, Miss Hamilton.' He kisses me. 'You know, I've been wanting to do this from the first moment I saw you.'

'Hey, you had a girlfriend then,' I reprimand him sternly.

'Well, actually . . .' He rubs his nose self-consciously. 'When I told you we'd broken up I never said when.'

I look at him, puzzled.

'It was actually months ago, before I came to London.'

'So why on earth did you say you had a girlfriend when Jess . . .' It dawns on me. That first night. In my back garden. When she tried to seduce him. 'You were her Plan B.' I giggle.

'Plan B?' He looks wounded, then collapses into laughter. 'I must remember that.' He chuckles as he grabs his dog-eared notebook. As I watch him scribble it down earnestly, love swells inside of me.

'Hey, I've got this great joke for you,' he says. 'Have you heard the one about the comedian who fell in love with a redhead called Heather?'

'No, what happened?'

'He couldn't get out again.'

Now that has to be the best punch line I've ever heard.

Epilogue

'THAT'LL BE THREE DOLLARS and seventy-five cents.'

I place the magazine on the counter and pull out a five-dollar bill. The shopkeeper takes it from me, and as I wait for my change I pick it up and scan through the glossy pages. Then I see it. A black-and-white photograph of a woman peeling off her wet suit, illustrating an article about surfing. My eyes flick to the credit, written underneath in small block capitals: HEATHER HAMILTON. I feel a burst of pride. *Scene* is one of

America's best-selling magazines and it's my first shoot for them. And, though I say it myself, my photo looks pretty good . . .

'Miss?' The man behind the counter is holding out my change.

'Oh, thanks.' I blush, and stuffing the change into my pocket, I close the magazine and walk outside into the scorching heat.

It's late afternoon but the sunshine is still dazzling. I slip on my sun glasses and look across at the expanse of blue sky, yellow sand and glittery ocean. *Venice Beach, California*. I breathe in the scent of salt, coffee and suntan lotion. It's everything I dreamed it would be like and more. Filled with cyclists, girls in bikinis, dudes carrying surfboards, a roller-blading sitar player . . . I turn to my bike and push off from the kerb. I pedal lazily, allowing myself to daydream, my mind spooling backwards with every revolution of the wheels.

Back to Edinburgh and that morning six months ago when I woke up in my frilly pink hotel room next to Gabe . . .

As Brian had predicted I stayed until the festival ended. Gabe's show was a sell-out. In fact, he was such a hit that a much larger venue offered him a spot. As his audiences grew, so did the buzz. Before he knew it, all the judges of the comedy awards were coming to see him and he was being nominated for the prestigious Perrier Award.

When he won, I wasn't surprised. Gabe, however, was astonished, as was the whole comedy circuit who'd never even heard of him, but since then he's gone on to even bigger and better things. He's currently in talks about his own TV series, as well as performing a sell-out show in one of the biggest comedy clubs in LA.

As for me, Victor Maxfield loved my photographs from the festival and it was the first of many assignments. Over the next couple of months I had the most amazing time, photographing all kinds of people, places and events. Then I quit my job. Again.

I turn into the network of canals. Beams of sunlight are bouncing off the water, and I push my sunglasses further up my nose as my mind returns to the moment I made the decision to leave the *Sunday Herald*. Only this time it wasn't because of a stupid misunderstanding, it was because of butterflies. All I have to do is look at Gabe and I feel them fluttering inside me. And what better reason could I find for moving to LA than for us to start a new life together?

Not that it hasn't been without its scary moments. Letting my flat, applying for a visa, turning freelance, saying my goodbyes and promising to email. And then, of course, there was Lionel.

As much as I love my new life here with Gabe, I hate being so far away from my father. Sometimes I almost feel like wishing . . .

But obviously I *don't*, I remind myself. The lucky heather taught me a lesson and I'm a changed person. Take the other day, for example. Gabe and I were on the beach when I saw this girl wiggle past in a bikini: even Cameron Diaz would have died for her bottom, and just as I was about to wish it was mine—I stopped myself. Which wasn't easy. But I'm so glad I did because five minutes later Gabe told me I had the most perfect bottom he'd ever seen. Which proves you really do have to be careful what you wish for.

Although now, with hindsight, I'm not so sure any more if the lucky heather really *was* lucky. Maybe I *did* just let my imagination run away with itself. Maybe it really was all just a string of coincidences . . .

In the weeks following its disappearance a few things happened that made me think it might have been. The scales in Boots suddenly sported an out-of-order sign, and a sales assistant told me it had been giving the incorrect weight. *By five pounds*.

And then a dog-walker found my wallet tossed into a ditch on Hampstead Heath and handed it in. As expected, all the cash and cards were missing but the lottery ticket was tucked safely into the inside pocket. As for the million-dollar question, did I win? Yes, I did. Well, *sort* of. I got four numbers and won a tenner, which OK, didn't buy me an Aston Martin Vanquish, but it did pay for a cab home from the movies. And, as slushy as this might sound, snuggled up on the back seat with Gabe I felt as if I *had* won the lottery.

I don't think I'll ever know the truth about the heather. Part of me wants to believe it was magic, but, of course, the rational, reasonable, *sane* side of me knows that's impossible. Things like that happen in fairy tales, not in real life. *Don't they?*

Finally reaching a large wooden house painted baby blue, I wheel my bike up the path and lean it against the steps, where a large ginger cat is lazing contentedly on the porch. 'Hey, Billy Smith,' I whisper, tickling him behind the ears. He gives a rasping purr and I smile to myself. I'm not the only one to be enjoying the Californian lifestyle.

I push open the screen door and walk inside. The house is still and quiet. I pad through the living room and pause next to a photograph I took of Gabe. He's standing in front of the Laugh Factory on Sunset Boulevard, and on the sign above him 'ANGEL GABRIEL LIVE' is spelled out in big black letters, alongside 'SOLD OUT'.

Proudly I rub my thumb across the wooden frame. I'll never be a fan of stand-up comedy, but I'm learning to *appreciate* it. A bit like beer, I muse. Thinking how a chilled one might be rather nice right now. I go on into the kitchen.

'*SURPRISE!*'

I freeze in the doorway. Ahead, the patio doors have all been flung open and I'm looking out into my little garden. Strung with tiny fairy lights, and a huge party banner that reads, 'HAPPY BIRTHDAY,' it's crammed with people, whooping and screaming, yelling and shrieking.

Oh, my God. *It's a surprise birthday party.*

My first impulse is to run. I hate surprises. I'm not prepared. I look like shit. I need a shower. And at least half an hour to do my hair and make-up. But, like a rabbit caught in headlights, I'm too stunned to react.

Then I see them, and now a whoosh of sheer joy is rushing up inside me like a firework.

'Lionel! I can't believe it . . . And Rosemary! Wow! Jess! Oh, and this is your new boyfriend Dominic? Hi, nice to meet you, Dominic! Ed and Lou and—oh, my gosh—is this Ruby? She's so beautiful—Hey, Ruby, I'm your auntie Heather! Brian! It's so great to see you . . . Oh, and Neil, lovely to see you too!'

Breathless with excitement I hug them all, laughing as Brian snaps away, taking dozens of pictures. Crikey! I take it all back. I love surprises. Bloody love them.

Then I see Gabe. He's carrying a birthday cake. As he walks towards me everyone starts singing 'Happy Birthday'. Oh, my gosh, I'm going to cry. I'm so lucky. 'Happy birthday, gorgeous,' he whispers.

I laugh and as everyone gathers round me I go to blow out my candles. When he stops me. 'Hey! Don't forget to make a wish,' he laughs.

Goosebumps prickle. I feel a familiar tingle in my fingers and toes. *No, Heather. Remember, you promised.* I look back at the shimmering candle flames, take a deep breath and close my eyes.

But then again . . .

What's one little wish?

Alexandra Potter

PROFILE

Home: Los Angeles.
Former jobs: Freelance magazine feature writer for *Company*, *She*, *Red*, *More! Heat*. Sub-editor at *Vogue UK* and *Vogue Australia* in Sydney. And finally, a teddy-stuffer for three weeks when I was nineteen and at university.
Addictions: Crisps. Preferably Walkers Salt & Vinegar but they are hard to find out here. Trashy magazines.
Guilty pleasure: Taking long baths in the afternoon when I should be writing.
Fridge essentials: Organic milk, wild rocket, a good-sized chunk of crumbly Parmesan and a chilled bottle of Sancerre.
Writing necessities: My Mac iBook. A good supportive chair. The Internet. Coffee. And a lot of determination!

What would your top five wishes be?
Alexandra: Well, it would of course have to include the big stuff—such as world peace, a cure for AIDS—but these apart, I'd have to wish . . .

1. For my family and friends to be happy and healthy
2. To live happily ever after
3. To get to number one on *The Times* best-seller list
4. To go on a safari
5. To be able to become invisible . . . (imagine the places you could go!)

And then there's all the little things I wish for such as . . .

1. Wishing I could actually make that 8.30 Pilates class at my gym (instead of waking up, turning off my alarm, and pulling the duvet back over my head)
2. Wishing I could say no to that second shortbread finger . . .
3. Wishing I hadn't had that second glass of wine last night
4. Wishing I'd written more yesterday
5. Wishing I hadn't just 'popped into Zara' and several hours later popped out with far too many clothes . . .

The list is endless!!!

What do you enjoy most about living in L.A.?
Alexandra: Apart from the obvious one of sunshine all year round, I have to say it's the positive attitude. In the UK we tend to make fun of the Americans' 'have a nice day' attitude to life, but it's actually genuine and makes for a very happy, optimistic environment to live and work in.
What do you most miss most about England?
Alexandra: Marks & Spencer's! No, seriously, my parents and my friends. I

cope by sending huge quantities of emails and spending hours on the phone, but it's still not the same. Thankfully I'm taking the whole month of July off this year to travel back to England to see everyone. I can hardly wait.

Apart from that, I'd have to say the British sense of humour. There's nothing like it on earth . . .

Tell me a little about your day-to-day life. Do you have a writing régime?

Alexandra: Yes, very much so. I tend to wake up around 7.30 and spend the next couple of hours replying to emails, doing paperwork and drinking coffee. Then I either write from home, or cycle to a little café round the corner, which is filled with writers all working on various projects. Writing can be a very solitary profession, so it's nice to be around other people. Also, a lot of my inspiration comes from observing people, and so it's good to get out of my bedroom!

People think that writers only write when they are hit by inspiration, but the reality is very different. I've found that the most important thing is to write regularly, even if you feel as if you have nothing to say. Once you are sitting down in front of the keyboard, ideas begin to come to you. I've always believed it's getting your bottom on the chair that gets a book finished, and it's true. So if anyone out there is thinking of a writing a novel, don't wait for inspiration to strike—get your bottom on a chair and start writing!

Jane Eastgate

PICTURE CREDITS: COVER: © Taxi. Jill Mansell photograph and page 182 © Jill Mansell. Joanna Trollope photograph and page 332 © Véronique Rolland. Alexandra Potter photograph and page 479 © Alexandra Potter. MAKING YOUR MIND UP: pages 6 & 7: © Annie Boberg @ Organisation. SECOND HONEYMOON: pages 184 & 185: © Photodisc Red. BE CAREFUL WHAT YOU WISH FOR: pages 334 & 335: © Dorling Kindersley.

Printed and bound by GGP Media GmbH, Pössneck, Germany

601-035-1